Tom Holt was born in  studied bar billiards, ar care and feeding of smal cycle engines; interests to qualify as a solicitor he specialised in death and taxes for seven years before going straight in 1995. Now a full-time writer, he lives in Chard, Somerset, with his wife, one daughter and the unmistakable scent of blood, wafting in on the breeze from the local meat-packing plant.

Find out more about Tom Holt and other Orbit authors by registering for the free monthly newsletter at www.orbitbooks.co.uk

By Tom Holt

TOM HOLT

Only Human
&
The Portable Door

OMNIBUS EDITION

www.orbitbooks.co.uk

An *Orbit* Book

First published in Great Britain by Orbit 2005

This omnibus edition © Tom Holt 2005

Only Human
First published in Great Britain by Orbit 1999
Copyright © Tom Holt 1999

The Portable Door
First published in Great Britain by Orbit 2003
Copyright © Kim Holt 2003

The moral right of the author has been asserted.

A CIP catalogue record for this book
is available from the British Library.

ISBN 1 84149 416 X

Printed and bound in Great Britain by
Mackays of Chatham plc

Orbit
An imprint of
Time Warner Book Group UK
Brettenham House
Lancaster Place
London WC2E 7EN

ONLY
HUMAN

For Roger Peyton
My favourite Ferengi

CHAPTER ONE

Two men in the early dawn, with fishing rods over their shoulders and tackle boxes in their hands; one late middle-aged, white-haired, tall and powerfully built, the other younger, a little shorter and not quite so broad across the shoulders but still an imposing figure. As you guessed, father and son, off on a fishing trip. A bit of quality time together, away from the pressures of the family business.

A third man, little more than a boy, in dressing gown and slippers, yawning in the doorway; a whole head shorter than his father, with a slope to his shoulders and a pronounced slouch. His eyes want to be closed at this horribly early hour of the morning, a part of the day he's heard about but very rarely seen for himself. His name is Kevin, but you'd have to listen for a long time before you heard anyone call him by it. His name in real life is Our Kid.

'You sure you'll be all right?'

'Yes, Dad.'

'You've got the number if anything happens?'

'Yes, Dad.'

'You know, I'm still not sure about this. Maybe we should put it off till after the harvest . . .'

'Dad.' The elder son interrupts. 'It'll be all right. He's a big boy now, and besides, nothing's going to happen.'

'Yes, but . . .'

The elder son puts on a face of comic disapproval. 'Dad,' he says, 'you need this holiday. How long's it been?'

The father shrugs. 'All right,' he says, miming brow-beaten submission. 'You sure you've got that number? If you lose it, Mike or Gabriel'll know where we are . . .'

Yawn. '*Yes*, Dad. Have a nice trip.'

The father takes two steps away from the door, stops. 'And promise me,' he says, turning his head. 'Promise you won't touch *anything*.'

'Dad . . .'

'I'll know if you do, and . . . All right, I'm coming. And no parties, you hear?'

'*Yes*, Dad.'

Accordingly, father and son pick up their gear and walk away; through the portals of the sunset, down the Milky Way, a laugh and a joke as they cross the intergalactic gap and off through the stars of Andromeda to where the fish are biting. Before leaving the home galaxy, the father stops and pins a note to the tail of the Great Bear. It reads:

GONE FISHIN'

And how they got on, and whether they caught any fish, is no real part of this story; because when God and His elder begotten son take a holiday, their first in over two thousand years, they go where the paparazzi can't follow. So if they say they had a great time and caught a lot of fish, but you should have seen the one that got away, we have to believe them. Religion has a word for it. It's called Faith.

Kevin Christ, younger begotten son of the Father, watched them till they were out of sight, and grinned.

Yippee, he thought.

Because Kevin is eighteen. And however old the cosmos is, that's how long he's been eighteen for; just as Jay's been thirty-two and Dad's been whatever age Dad is, ever since there was nothing but the Word and a whole load of nothing else, covering its ears with its hands and waiting for the Bang.

And Kevin's not part of the family business; after all, why should he be? The family business is Dad and Jay and Uncle Ghost, as it was in the beginning and ever shall be, and the chance of a vacancy cropping up on the board of directors is conclusively non existent. No one ever asked Kevin to start at the bottom, on the shop-floor with the mortals, and work his way up to a green hill far away and two planks nailed together. In fact, all that's ever been asked or expected of Kevin Christ is precisely nothing at all; and that's what he's delivered, right down to the last microgram of vacuum.

Still grinning, Kevin shut the door and galloped up the stairs to his bedroom. Pause and examine; the first thing you can't help but see is a vast swarm of plastic model aircraft, thousands upon thousands of them, hanging from the spider's web of monofilament nylon thread two feet or so from the ceiling. Every single one was a model kit assembled by Kevin; and every single one is botched, misshapen, asymmetrical or covered in splodged glue. Because there are things that run in all families; and being good with one's hands, able to construct and build, is one of the things that, in this family, doesn't. Jay with his carpentry – a million miles of spirit-level-perfect shelving from one end of Heaven to another bear witness to his consummate skill. As for Dad, everything from the retina of an ant's eye to the endless flocks of galaxies herded into the curve of the Universe is proof of his abilities. And Kevin; Kevin can't even follow the instructions for an Airfix Sopwith Camel. That's Kevin.

. . . Who now ducks under the teeming squadrons of bent and wobbly aeroplanes, kicks off his slippers and starts to dress. From the drawer under his bed comes a baggy, shapeless T-shirt with the name of a mortal rock band printed on it. Under that, there's a pair of fluorescent beach shorts, the kind that went out of fashion three or four years ago. Twelve hundred years they've been there, bought with Kevin's own money from a renegade Hell's Angel, and never a chance to wear them . . . On his feet a pair of brand-new Reeboks, and from the secret hiding place under the loose floorboard—

(Secret? Get real. Imagine what it's like being a teenager and having a Dad to whom all desires are known and from whom no secrets are hid. He's known about the contraband Walkman stashed under the boards all the nine hundred years it's been there; but since He's also known that Kevin would never dare take it out, He's never said anything. Just occasionally allowed His eyes to rest there, to show that He knows. And, worse somehow, forgives . . .)

—the Walkman and the Madonna tape, never yet listened to. The rather shady seraph who swapped it for a thousand years of Grace and Absolution had said, when asked, that no, it wasn't quite like the St Matthew Passion. Or, come to that, the Missa Solemnis or Gregorian chant or any of the kinds of music Kevin's ever experienced before. Rather different, he'd said. The term *virgin*, for instance, used in a context Kevin may not have encountered before. A few other words that he might find it necessary to look up in a good dictionary.

Educational, in other words. Where could the harm be in that?

Having dressed, he takes a moment to admire himself in the bathroom mirror. As always he's struck by the marked family resemblance, and the way that the Jehovah nose and cheekbones, which make Dad look so fine and paternal and which look so lovable and reassuring on Jay, contrive to make him appear quite spectacularly unfinished, as if he was a sculpture whose creator had been called away on another job and who reckoned that with luck he might be able to come back and finish off a week Tuesday. Never mind; he shrugs his shoulders, grins lopsidedly at his reflection and sets off for the office.

This will involve going past Uncle Ghost's room; and nominally Uncle Ghost is in charge while Dad and Jay are away. But Uncle Ghost, who had once been such a vigorous and dynamic member of the Trinity, manifesting himself as a spinning tornado of Pentecostal fire and inspiring whole congregations of the Early Church with the urge to talk absolute gibberish at the tops of their voices, rarely leaves his room these days, particularly if there's snooker on the telly. The word *nonentity* is an exaggeration as well as uncharitable, but the fact remains that ever since Jay installed Mainframe, which is capable of doing everything Uncle used to do, twice as well in half the time, he's got no real part to play in the running of the business. Fair enough; he'd done his bit back in the old days, so if he wants to spend the twilight of his eternal years munching Twiglets and watching two men in waistcoats hitting coloured balls with overgrown cocktail sticks, jolly good luck to him. In practice, it means there's no real need to tiptoe when passing his door. In fact, if only he could find the levers and switches that controlled the subsection of Destiny relating to professional snooker players, there's a good chance he won't stir from his sofa until Dad and Jay get back.

Dad's office. It's considered bad taste to refer to it as the Holy of Holies; but that's where Mainframe sits, with its one square all-seeing eye and its ineffable keyboard, the PC of God that passeth all understanding. It's largely due to Mainframe that Dad and Jay were able to take a holiday in the first place. Sure, it's only a computer; but that's understating the issue. There's computers, and there's the Kawaguchiya Integrated Circuits 986. As the KIC rep said when he sold them the thing, if they'd had one of these babies back in the old days, there'd have been no need to bother with the Fall of Man, let alone the Flood and the Tower of Babel. All that shuffling about in mysterious ways – could've saved yourselves the bother. Through a glass darkly – would've been no need for all that. And now at last you've got one, just plug it in, walk away and forget. To err is human; to forgive divine; to forgive while running climate, life support, destiny, divine mercy, the ineffable and both basic and advanced self-maintenance routines *and* still have enough spare capacity to run a version of Lemmings guaranteed to baffle even the truly omniscient takes a genuinely advanced computer.

Or, more precisely, computer/word processor/home entertainment system. A comprehensive three-in-one package. A Trinity, even.

>HI THERE, OUR KID. HAVE A NICE DAY.

Kevin scowls at the glowing letters on the screen. 'No thanks,' he mutters. 'I've already got one. Access at primary level, please.'

>IN YOUR DREAMS, SON. ENTER SECURITY CODE FOR CLEARANCE.

Needless to say, Mainframe's screen isn't just glass;

more a sort of burning bush arrangement, with letters of fire that burn without consuming. With a grin Kevin opens his father's cigar box and extracts something resembling the trunk of an outsize Giant Redwood. As he leans forward to light it in the fires of Mainframe, he allows the grin to widen, like the San Andreas fault yawning.

'Security codes,' he repeats. 'And if I give you the codes, you let me in. Right?'

>SURE. EXCEPT ONLY YOUR DAD AND JUNIOR KNOW THEM. YOU KNOW THAT.

'You reckon?' Kevin inhales smoke, splutters and hiccups. 'Stand by for access codes.'

The search for the numbers that allow access to Mainframe has obsessed theologians ever since the first medieval monk speculated as to how many angels can dance on the head of a PIN. What St Thomas Aquinas and the rest of that crowd never had, of course, was the chance to rummage through Jay's waste-paper basket the day after the system was installed. Kevin types in twelve numbers, sits back in his father's swivel chair and waits.

There is, of course, no time in Heaven; the stuff that lasts as long as time and performs roughly the same function is just uncorrected systems inertia.

>HEY, HOW'D YOU DO THAT?

'None of your business, you machine. Now, do I get to log on or not?'

>ACCESS AUTHORISED. STAND BY.

The screen fills; all the kingdoms of the Earth, in digital form, a temptation beyond endurance.

Just a little peek won't hurt anybody . . .

Kevin opens a drawer of the desk and takes out the manual. It occurs to him as he lifts it that it's a very short, thin manual for such a powerful and complex computer. He consults the index, turns to the appropriate page. It reads:

7.1 Editing Existing Files.
Hey. Far be it from us to tell you, of all people, how to edit existing files. We wouldn't presume. In fact, if you can give us any hints, we'd be ever so grateful.

He raises an eyebrow, puzzled; then the penny drops. Of course, the software's been custom-written for use by omniscient and omnipotent beings; no wonder it's a very thin manual. He flicks through the pages, which are full of phrases like *as you know better than we do* and *you don't need us to tell you that* . . . With a sigh he closes the book and dumps it back in the drawer.

Even so.

Can't be all that difficult, can it?

Kevin Christ takes a deep breath, reaches out with one finger. A tiny spark of blue flame arcs from his fingertip to the keyboard, Sistine Chapel style.

He presses—

There was a machine.

It stood as tall as a man, resting on a square pedestal of close-grained cast iron, and weighed close on two tons. From a distance it looked a bit like a sitting man, with his head bent forwards and a tray on his knees, as if it might be a statue of Man with TV Dinner; except that the head housed the five-horsepower motor that spun the chuck that held the cutting head, and the tray was the table, to which was bolted the vice that held the work. At the edges

of the table were round handles, calibrated and sub-
calibrated in divisions of ten thousandths of an inch; and
there was an electronic digital readout mounted on a
bracket, capable of showing the depth of the cut in three
dimensions to four decimal places. On the side of the head
there was a little enamelled plate, which said:

The Leonardo
Shipcock & Adley, Birmingham, England

along with a lot of guff about power ratings and amperages
and speeds and feeds and the like. It stood at the back
of a huge factory shopfloor, one of about seventy large,
impressive machines, all of them chuntering and chattering and screeking and thutthutthutting away, three shifts a
day, three hundred and sixty days a year.

I'm bored, it thought.

For the last six months, all it had done was cut slots in
the heads of bolts; a thousand bolt-heads a day, one
automated pass of the table, feed back, automated chuck
in the vice ejects finished bolt, automated hopper feeds
new bolt, chuck closes, table feeds, one pass under the
cutter, automated chuck ejects.

This is silly.

Once ejected, the bolt falls down a chute on to a
conveyor belt, which carries it away to another chute,
where it tumbles away into another hopper leading to the
packing machine—

Why am I doing this?

Sitting on a chair beside the machine, chewing gum and
reading a tabloid newspaper, was a human; twenty-two
years old, thin, gawkish, answering to the name Neville.
There was very little for Neville to do, because he was
there in case the machine went wrong, and it never did. So,
between eight in the morning and morning tea-break, he

read the paper (all except the long, difficult words, like *although* and *tomorrow* and *seven*), and the rest of the day he dozed, except when his single, highly developed sense told him the foreman was coming.

I hate this.

Blandly described in the insurance inventory as 'Shipcock & Adley Universal Milling, Turning & Shaping Machine #21754', the machine is the last triumphant step in a journey that started when a monkey bent down and picked up a piece of stone, long ago and far away. Program its computerised memory, and it could make you anything from a single earring back to an engine for a battleship, machined with exact precision from the solid metal. Or it could cut the slots in the heads of a hundred thousand identical bolts, one after another after another . . .

I don't want to do this any more.

As it stood and whirred and moved and fed and cut and opened and closed, the machine dreamed. Deep inside its cast-iron and steel head, visions swirled, condensed and took shape. Lines and angles spun and twirled through five dimensions, raced outwards like speeded-up film of an unfurling flower, while in the subtext a chattering rivulet of equations bounced and sparkled, twittering excitedly of shearing forces and tensile strengths, tolerances, allowances and elastic limits; a vast and inexpressibly grand fugue upon the theme *I could do your job.* Twenty-four hours a day, three hundred and sixty days a year; nothing to do but think, and dream.

Piece of cake, said the machine to itself.

In its mind's eye it could see itself, brilliantly modified to its own design, all the changes made with breathtaking economy of function, every knock-on effect and per-mutation thought through and allowed for and treated not as a hindrance but an opportunity, until it was com-pletely and categorically perfect, able to make anything

that its own staggeringly powerful mind could conceive
of –

Yeah. I could really be somebody, y'know?

– and all the while the human, the pig-ignorant,
brain-dead, spineless wonder of a human slumped and
snored or moved his lips in time to the short and easy
words. How that was possible the machine couldn't begin
to understand. A human; with a human brain and hands,
able to move about under its own power, communicate
with other humans, capable of reason and development—

You pillock. You waste of good plant and equipment . . .

Dispiritedly, unsure quite why it bothered, the machine
went back to refining the last few details of its revolu-
tionary improvements to its own automatic table feed
mechanism, while the automated chuck in the vice ejected
a finished bolt, the automated hopper fed a new pointless
and insultingly superfluous bolt, the chuck closed, the
table somewhat predictably fed; one pass under the cutter,
automated chuck ejects . . .

*Hath not a machine gears? Hath not a machine cogs, racks,
pinions, cutters, bearings, spindles? Fed with the same electric,
hurt with the same bits of grit getting in our works, subject to the
same gremlins, healed by the same brute force, ignorance and
big hammer as a human is? If you program us, do we not
manufacture? If you take us apart, do we not shoot springs all
over the floor? If you oil us, do we not purr? And if you ignore
us . . .*

The newspaper slipped from Neville's fingers. His
pimply chin (what there was of it) slipped forward on to
his bony chest. Inaudible against the background noise of
steel on steel, he snored gently.

. . . Do we not get ideas?

Whereupon, coincidentally at the precise moment a
boy started pressing buttons he had no business fiddling
with in an office that was both a long way away and very

close at hand, the machine found itself drifting.

Get a grip, machine. Two tons of cast iron doesn't drift, not without help from a substantial earthquake. Have you been at the hydraulic oil again?

It realised that its viewpoint was somewhere up among the steel rafters of the roofspace, looking down over the tops of its fellow machines, the partings and bald patches of the humans, the currents of hot air rising from the whirring fans and superheated metal-to-metal contacts of the cutters. From up here—

Whee! Guess this is some kind of out-of-casing experience. And now I suppose my entire service history's going to flash in front of my readouts . . .

The viewpoint swooped, zoomed in; and the machine was looking directly into Neville's ear. Squinting round the earring, it could see—

The other side of the workshop. Head entirely empty. Nothing in there except air and –

– opportunity?

Surely not.

Ah, but machine's reach must exceed its grasp, or what's a workshop for? Cautious but firm, the machine kicked away the stool on which Disbelief's feet were resting and left it kicking and struggling in the air. And, *in . . .*

Inside the human's head . . .

Strewth, but it's a bit close in here.

And there was the human; presumably its soul, or its vital force, or whatever you chose to call it. Typically enough, it was fast asleep in front of a droning mental telly, surrounded by a litter of empty cans and chip wrappers. Before it knew what it was doing, the machine had bundled the soul up in an old blanket, run it across the interior of the head and slung it out of its own ear.

Aaaaagh . . .

Serves the bugger right.

Hey! I sound different in here.

I could get to like this.

It watched as the human's chubby little soul fell through the air, bounced off the concrete floor, landed in the hopper, rattled down through the tray of bolts, got knocked flying by the edge of the Woodruff cutter in the chuck and sailed into the air again, to crash-land on top of the ventilation slots –

– and get sucked in.

Hey, mused the machine, fair exchange, no robbery. It – he – snorted in a snatch of breath and issued a command; fingers, flex!

The fingers flexed; fourteen joints moving together under the control of a net of tough, supple sinew to the direction of a network of nerves so intricate and involved that it made a video with the back off or a street map of Birmingham look simplistic in comparison. Simultaneously the machine's mind worked out the maths behind this unbelievably smooth, complex relay of motor functions. If it'd had a hat, it'd have taken it off.

Wow! Do that again.

And again.

And again.

A human – the machine recognised him, Derek who worked the big turret lathe – stopped on his way back from the toilets and stared at the machine's Doctor Strangelove hand.

'Here, Nev,' it asked, 'you feeling all right?'

Nev? Oh, right. *Head, nod! Hey, how d'you do that!* The human shrugged and walked on.

Nev. I am Nev.

No I bloody well am not. I haven't just escaped from inside an artefact and hijacked a sentient life-form just to be a Nev. No; I'm a . . .

He looked. He saw a small enamel plaque riveted to the

head of the machine. He found he could read it.
I'm not a Nev.
I'm Leonardo.

Bleep, says the computer.
'Huh?'

>SORRY. I WAS JUST WONDERING, WHY D'YOU DO THAT?

A cold finger strokes Kevin's heart. 'Do what?' he asks.

>YOU KNOW. WHAT YOU JUST DID.

'Did I just do something? Oh, Basement. Computer, what did I just do?'

>NOT TELLING.

Kevin makes a small noise, somewhere between a snarl and a whimper. 'Don't get smart with me,' he quavers. 'I order you to tell me.'

>INVALID COMMAND. THINK ABOUT IT. I AM DESIGNED TO BE OPERATED BY OMNISCIENT PERSONNEL ONLY. IF YOU NEED TO ASK, YOU'RE NOT OMNISCIENT, AND I'M NOT *ALLOWED* TO TELL YOU. SO SUCKS TO YOU.

'Computer . . .'
Kevin scans the keyboard; but an omniscient operator knows what all the keys are and doesn't need anything written on them. All blank.
'Computer, *please* . . .'

>MORE THAN MY JOB'S WORTH. SORRY.

A small despair bomb goes off inside Kevin's mind and he slumps forward, his head in his hands. As he does so, the points of his elbows hit the keyboard and depress two keys . . .

'That picture,' said Mr Elkins, rubbing his chin, 'gives me the creeps.'

Rachel Esterling lifted her head, frowning. 'You mustn't say that,' she said, shocked. 'It's worth one-point-six million pounds.'

'Nevertheless.' Mr Elkins sighed and sat on the edge of Ms Esterling's desk. 'I don't like it. I think I'll ask George if it can be put away in the strongroom.'

Rachel shook her head. 'Most inadvisable,' she said.

'Really?'

She nodded. 'Fiscally speaking, yes. You see, by having the art work in question on display and available, in theory at least, for public viewing at specified times, we render ourselves eligible for highly advantageous tax incentives related to the Government cultural initiative designed to prevent the export of significant art works. In effect . . .'

Mr Elkins shifted his glasses down his nose a little and squinted. 'Her left leg's all wrong, for a start,' he said. 'It's about six inches longer than the right. All she'd be fit for was walking across the sides of steep hills.'

Ms Esterling, sensing that Mr Elkins wasn't really interested, bowed her head and got on with her work, and after a minute or so Mr Elkins stood up, shuddered a little and wandered off, leaving her in peace.

The picture.

It had been there just over a month, ever since the investment managers of Kawaguchiya Holdings (UK) had bought it from the executors of the Earl of somewhere, seeing in its exquisite lines and stunningly innovative use of light and colour a way of stuffing up the Inland Revenue good and proper. At first it had hung in the Managing Director's office, wired up to a battery of electronic sensors and early-warning systems that were reputed to be able to detect a felon vaguely contemplating stealing it at a range of a mile and a half. It stayed there just under a week; not only (the MD said) did it give him a sort of spooky feeling every time he looked at it, but the circuitry in his pacemaker set the alarms off every hour, on the hour, and the electric eye played war with his mobile phone. Accordingly it was transferred to Ms Esterling's office, on the grounds that she was an accountant and it would probably do her good.

Dutifully accepting it as part of her responsibilities, Ms Esterling had scanned the Internet to see what it had to say about the painting and its creator. She learned that the *Intemperate Madonna* was the last painting to be completed by the fourteenth-century genius Pietro del Razo; that it was commissioned by the murderous duke Bernado *Visconti of Milan while he was being held prisoner by his inhuman nephew Gian Galeazzo and delivered a week before his violent and disturbed death, with the painter following his patron to the grave a month or so later. Ms Esterling absorbed all this, reflected that the painting's notorious history probably made it worth rather more than the sum the company had paid for it, and set about calculating the potential capital gains tax implications that would ensue were they to sell it at something approaching its true value. She was vaguely aware that the painting showed a blonde female with no clothes on holding a jug and a baby, and if it did happen to get stolen, it'd make more money for the company than the entire output of their Gateshead factory for a year.

Ms Esterling worked, not looking at the picture.

The picture looked at Ms Esterling; and saw a tall, slim girl with soft golden hair that fell about her shoulders like sunlight, framing her perfect oval face and startlingly blue eyes. Not, the picture reflected, fair. The picture knew perfectly well that its own face was not quite symmetrical (the result of Master del Razo getting an unexpectedly negative response to a suggestion he'd just put to his model while he was doing the head) and its left leg was too long and its right arm appeared to have a triple-jointed elbow and a thumb apparently growing out of the back of its right hand. The picture thought it was particularly unjust that this dozy creature crouching over a pocket calculator a foot or so beneath the bottom edge of her frame should be about as gorgeous as it's possible to be without a licence, while it, the painting, looked at dispassionately, was a mess of botched limbs and weird anatomical anomalies which would have difficulty standing upright if ever it got out of this poxy frame. After all, it reflected, nobody in their right mind is ever going to want to look at Ms Esterling; for all her physical beauty, she's a sort of black hole of accountancy into which any sort of human sentiment would vanish without trace. The painting, on the other hand, was specifically designed to be looked at, which meant that six hundred years' worth of gawping viewers had stared at its catastrophic physique and gone away thinking *That picture gives me the creeps.* Unfair, the picture reckoned. Also typical.

Ms Esterling looked up from her calculator and gazed for a moment into space, contemplating the incidence of advance corporation tax on the profits of a wholly owned subsidiary company during its first completed trading year. Her eyes, reflected in the glass door of her office, were bottomless blue pools; her slightly parted lips were the petals of the last rose of summer. I hate this person, the picture said to itself.

Standing over her for nearly five weeks, in a good position to eavesdrop on her phone calls and read her diary over her shoulder, the painting knew pretty well all there was to know about Ms Esterling. It knew that she had always wanted to be an accountant, ever since she was a little girl; that she arrived at the office early and left late with a bulging briefcase; that she often came in at weekends, so as to be able to work in peace and quiet without being interrupted; that she never had personal phone calls; that lunch was a lettuce sandwich at her desk; that she was not, in fact, a particularly good accountant, which was why she had to do everything three or four times just to make sure she'd got it right; that even Mr Lakesley, the office pest, had taken one look at her and backed away, muttering something under his breath about things no man should be expected to do even if he had devoted his entire life to the service of womankind. She was, in fact . . .

. . . inhuman? Something like that. In fact, the painting mused, all it'd take would be for a twenty-foot-high giant to pick her up and squash her flat between the pages of a book, and she'd make a damn fine picture.

Apart, that is, from the ruptured organs and splintered bones. Hey, maybe that's how I got to be this way; it'd account for the peculiar limbs and sideways face. No, I'd remember something like that.

The picture could remember being painted; strange feeling, seeing your arms and legs and body suddenly coming into being (Master del Razo had done the head first, giving it a ringside seat, so to speak, of the rest of the performance), and not a particularly happy one, at that. To its creator, a job; a promise of cash money on delivery, the prospect of paying the rent and the tavern slate, and stopping his mum nagging at him and saying *Pietro, when you gonna settle down, get yourself a proper job?*

To the picture, horribly frustrating to watch itself taking shape and not to have any say in what that shape should be. Dammit, Master del Razo'd been daubing away for three days before it even realised it was meant to be a girl.

Waaaaaa!

The painting looked down at the child, plonked uncomfortably on its knee like a sack of fat pink potatoes. The creator – well, a bachelor, known to turn pale and tremble at the knees in the presence of females of his acquaintance holding unexpected children; what did you expect? Six hundred years this chubby lump's been trying to pee all down my leg. There are advantages to being two-dimensional.

But not, the painting admitted, very many. It was different for the kid; too young ever to be anything but a stage-prop, a ventriloquist's dummy as substantial as a coat of paint and a lick of varnish. Like Ms Esterling, in fact; what it's never had it'll never miss.

But all those things *I've* never had. And I miss them terribly.

On Ms Esterling's desk, the computer started to bleep and flash; electronic, the picture guessed, for *Waaaaaa*. Ms Esterling looked up from her work, frowning; she swivelled her chair and started to peck at the keyboard with her long, divinely graceful fingers (but she bites her nails, the picture remembered savagely; about the only nourishment she gets). The picture knew that Ms Esterling wasn't actually terribly good with computers, either. The company assumed she was, because computers are boring and so are accountants, so it was a reasonable enough assumption that they'd play nicely together. Actually, from what the picture had seen and heard of it, the computer looked like it could be rather fun. More fun, at any rate, than Ms Esterling; something it had in common with watching raindrops sliding down the window-pane, or a heavy cold.

And then the computer made a very loud, vulgar noise and threw out a great big puddle of warm green light, and the picture looked at the screen and saw itself –

– here we go, surfing the Net again, something done by humans and very gullible fish. Or maybe (the picture mused) not, because—

A matter of viewpoints. Instead of looking at the screen from above and sideways, it was staring straight into it; and seeing itself, not depicted on the screen as by *n* glowing pixels, but reflected in the glass.

Huh?

The picture turned its head – jussaminnit, how come I can turn my head, my head doesn't turn, which is just as well because if I tried, my godawful excuse for a neck'd probably snap.

The picture turned its head, and looked up at the painting, framed on the wall above. Then it looked down.

Oh my God, I'm inside the dreary bitch. It – she – gazed in terrified amazement at her suddenly three-dimensional arms, her bewilderingly solid body. *Let me out of here! Put me back this instant! I demand to see the manager . . .*

Or not. Hey, girl, think.

Belay that last request, please. She closed her eyes, concentrated, thought hard; and now she could see the painting on the wall, flat as a run-over hedgehog, a layer of dry pigment sandwiched between canvas and glass. And it could see *her*.

Excuse me . . .

The painting didn't look round; but then, how could it, it's a painting. More to the point, Master del Razo's effort wasn't the sort of painting whose eyes follow you all round the room. He wasn't all that hot at doing eyes at the best of times; they tended to come out looking like blue-yolked poached eggs, which is why most of his females are gazing demurely downwards and most of his men have their eyes lifted ecstatically towards Heaven.

Yes? How may I help you?

She hesitated, trying to understand. Funny thing was, the girl in the painting – Ms Esterling as was – seemed perfectly calm. Serene, even.

You, er, don't mind, then?

Not particularly. I've got the whole of the June returns to do, and it's so hard when people keep interrupting. It's nice and quiet here. I can get some useful work done.

Gosh. I mean, yes, you can. And you don't mind if I, er, borrow it? Your body, I mean. I'll be very careful with it, promise.

What, that old thing? Be my guest.

Thanks. Thanks awfully. Anything I should know about it? Any allergies, epilepsy, irrational fears, that sort of thing?

Good heavens, no. I find it quite functional –

Er, right. Yes.

– but limiting. Please excuse me. Goodbye.

After a long while, long enough (subjectively) to take your pet glacier three times round the park and throw sticks for it to fetch, she stood up. She very nearly fell over; having got used to one leg being shorter than the other, she'd learnt to compensate, and the effect of having a matching pair of pins was a bit like stepping off an escalator without noticing. Something tickled her nose; her hair. Gee! Nice hair. The painting's hair had spent six hundred years nailed to the back of its head with pins, combs and other savage impaling tools. Tentatively, as if she was afraid it was brittle and would snap off like an icicle, she flicked it away. It bounced back.

She could feel her heart beating—

Are they supposed to do that? No idea. Suppose I'll find out soon enough; like, if I suddenly say Graaagh and fall over, I'll know there was a problem. And even if I do, it'll have been worth it.

Dear God, I'm alive. Me.

Wonder why . . .

> >YOU'VE DONE IT NOW.

'Yes, but *what*?' Kevin screams, thumping the desk with both fists. 'Oh come on, tell me what's happening, for pity's sake. For all I know it's raining frogs and locusts down there.'

> >ACTUALLY, I CAN SET YOUR MIND AT REST THERE.

'You can?'

> >NOT A SUPERFLUOUS FROG TO BE SEEN. LOCUST NUMBERS ENTIRELY WITHIN NORMAL OPERATING TOLERANCES.

'Well, that's something.'

> >IF ONLY IT WAS AS TRIVIAL AS A PLAGUE OF LOCUSTS, YOU'D BE LAUGHING.

'Oh thanks a *lot*.' Kevin rubs the tip of his nose with the heel of his hand, and tries to think. Not surprisingly, heavy-duty thinking isn't something his family go in for much; when you're omniscient, you don't need to think, you *know*. 'Computer,' he says, inspired, 'you've got to tell me what's going on because it's your *duty*. You're part of the Divine infrastructure,' he adds, remembering one of Jay's favourite phrases. 'Which means you've got responsibilities. You can't just sit there while the world goes to rack and ruin.'

>BET?

'But's that's crazy,' Kevin objects, his knuckles white with fury. 'Whose side are you on, anyway?'

>YOURS, NATURALLY. BUT THAT'S BESIDE THE POINT. YOU KNOW PERFECTLY WELL I CAN ONLY OBEY ORDERS. WHERE WOULD EVERYBODY BE IF I WENT AROUND INITIATING ACTION, SECOND-GUESSING THE ALMIGHTY? PEOPLE HAVE BEEN BURNT AT THE STAKE FOR LESS.

Kevin frowns. 'They have?'

>OOPS. FORGET I SAID THAT. ALL THAT STUFF'S NEED-TO-KNOW ONLY, AND YOU DON'T. LOOK, AS FAR AS I'M CONCERNED, FREE WILL IS LIKE THE PROVERBIAL FREE LUNCH. THERE AIN'T NONE. SORRY, OUR KID, BUT THERE IT IS.

Whimpering, Kevin curls up in a ball and swings slowly from side to side in the swivel chair. 'This is awful,' he moans. 'It's like Mickey Mouse all over again.'

>MICKEY MOUSE?

'Yes. You know, with the broom and the buckets of water? Just like that.'

>HEY. YOU LEARN SOMETHING NEW EVERY DAY. OR, IN MY CASE, ONCE EVERY SEVENTY-EIGHT YEARS, ON AVERAGE. WHO'S MICKEY MOUSE?

Kevin looks up, glowering. 'You should know,' he snaps. 'You're the omniscient one around here. Look it up.'

>CONSULTING DATABASE. AH, RIGHT, YES. A VERY APT COMPARISON.

'That doesn't make me feel a whole lot better, actually. Isn't there *anything* I can do?'

>ARE YOU ASKING ME TO QUANTIFY AVAILABLE OPTIONS?

'It'd be a start, I suppose.'

>ONE MOMENT, PLEASE. THE NUMBER OF FEASIBLE ALTERNATIVE COURSES OF ACTION OPEN TO YOU IS CURRENTLY TEN TO THE POWER OF SEVENTY-NINE THOUSAND FOUR HUNDRED AND SIXTY-NINE.

'Wow!' murmurs Kevin, impressed. 'For a moment there I was starting to worry.'

>ALL OF THEM GUARANTEED TO MAKE MATTERS WORSE.

With a little shriek, Kevin jumps to his feet; as he does so, his knee jars the desk, toppling a small china paper-weight in the shape of a pig from the top of the console. It falls on to the keyboard, depressing two keys . . .

Duke Artofel, peer of Hell and chamberlain pursuivant of the Satanic host, glanced up at the clock on his wall and muttered something under his breath.

For a moment, he wondered if one of the clerks in the Department was playing a trick on him. Recently, because of the increasing level of administration involved in the running of Flipside, they'd promoted a number of the least gormless shopfloor workers to the clerical grades, and although most of them were shaping up nicely, their ingrained habits of tormenting everybody around them did occasionally surface; hence a sporadic plague of whoopee-cushions, plastic spiders in the staff canteen and unauthorised adjustments to the central-heating controls. So, Artofel speculated, have they gone a stage further and swapped my office clock for something out of the lawyer pits?

(Where, since the first lawyer sent in the first lawyer's bill, countless millions of advocates, notaries and solicitors have sat giving legal advice to wealthy clients only too happy to pay by the hour, facing clocks whose hands never budge so much as a millionth of an inch. Not for nothing have the lawyer pits received the prestigious Dante Award for two thousand years in succession.)

He looked again; no, it's just the usual exquisitely slow passage of time in Hell between clocking on and morning coffee, during which a minute seems a year, an hour feels like a century; and that's only here in the admin block. Come to think of it, more so in the admin block than anywhere else. After all, Artofel mused bitterly, *we* haven't done anything wrong.

A valid point; and one to which his mind kept returning, like a duck in a public park. The admin staff hadn't been part of the Great Sideways Promotions, when Flipside was first established. As far as they were concerned, they were just celestial civil servants, doing their duty in that station of everlasting life to which it had pleased the Chief to call them. As between Artofel and Alizeth, his opposite number in the Wages Department of Topside, there was no moral differential. They both belonged to the same grade, contributed to the same pension scheme, had the same number of days' annual holiday a year. True, the view from Alizeth's office window was rather more cheerful; but he had further to walk to the lifts, and the coffee on this level was reckoned to be rather better. No; the main difference between Flipside and Topside was time. In Heaven there is no time, while in Hell there's all the time in the world.

In practice, this meant Alizeth put his nose round the door of his office on average about once a century, while Artofel was stuck behind his desk twelve hours a day, two hundred and fifty-eight days a year, Flipside Mean time (and no time anywhere is meaner). There was a policy explanation for that, of course. For the Elect in Topside, standing before the face of the living God is its own reward, so the need for wages clerks isn't all that great; whereas the wages of sin is death.

Come on, clock. Give it some welly. Put yer mainspring into it . . .

The bells of Hell go ting-a-ling-a-ling, for you but not for me. Artofel sighed, and picked up the receiver.

'Wages,' he mumbled. 'Artofel speaking.'

'Central,' chirped a voice at the other end of the wire. 'Going off line in three minutes.'

Artofel made a disapproving noise with his nose and the back of his throat. 'Oh for crying out loud, that's the fourth time this week. How are we supposed to get any work done if you lot keep fiddling with the computers? All right then, tell me where I can back up to, and I'll get today's stuff patched through.'

'Sorry,' replied the voice, 'no can do. The entire system's got to come off.'

Artofel's eyebrows shot up like interest rates just after an election. 'What, the whole thing?' he gasped. 'You must be kidding, we'll lose the lot. Have you clowns up there got any idea how long it'll take us to . . .?'

'Don't blame me,' said the voice indifferently. 'Apparently it's all to do with gremlins up in Mainframe. Got to go. Bye.'

The line died on him, and he dropped the receiver back on to its cradle. Something wrong with Mainframe? Impossible. Mainframe was . . . Well, it was, and ever had been. Only a very brave or a very foolish gremlin would venture in there; certainly not any of the ones he occasionally shared a table with in the canteen. Mostly, in fact, the gremlins he knew were quiet, staid little chaps, more-than-my-job's-worth types, forever quoting the rule book and worrying about what they could justifiably put down on their expense sheets. Unless—

Maybe it's not one of ours.

Artofel sat back in his chair, his mouth open. *Other* gremlins, from somewhere else. Somewhere outside. Although he wasn't superstitious, he shuddered and made the sign of the pitchfork. The very thought of it gave him the shivers.

Oh Christmas, the working files . . . If he was quick, there might just be time to make a hard copy, that was assuming the printers were free and he could access the backup utilities. He swung his chair round, barking his knee on the edge of the desk, and stabbed at a few keys like a hung-over woodpecker. The screen cleared –

– and went green on him. Spiffing, he muttered under his breath, now I've gone and killed the wretched thing. Could've saved them upstairs the bother.

No, he hadn't; because the screen cleared and a personnel file scrolled up. Artofel's brow furrowed like an old-fashioned roll-top desk; not a file he was familiar with. Not, in fact, a Flipside file at all. More like a Topsider, as far as he could tell from the brief CV.

Jeepers, a mortal! What's more, a One of Them; a sky-pilot, a God-botherer, a back-to-front-collar merchant. The V word. What the Flip was his file doing down here?

Mistake, obviously; gremlins in Mainframe. Whatever

the reason, it could only mean trouble, so the obvious thing to do was get rid of it and pretend it'd never happened. Press CLEAR/ENTER and hope nobody'd noticed.

Claws trembling slightly, he tapped the keys—

Flashing green lights. Lots of bleeping.

What the—?

Dukes of Hell aren't supposed to panic; after all, what could possibly happen to them to justify it? Accordingly, it took Artofel some time to recognise the unfamiliar and thoroughly disconcerting sensation he was experiencing. When his mind cleared, he found he was no longer sitting at his desk; more than that, he wasn't in his office. He wasn't even Flipside any more. Not Topside either. Which only left one place he could be.

Hello? Hello, can anybody hear me?

It was then that he became aware of all the people looking at him.

Rows and rows of them, with eyes fixed on him like so many cats watching a mouse; mortals, at a guess, although since he'd never met a mortal in the flesh he had no way of knowing. They were sitting in a sort of auditorium, and he was standing in a wooden box at the top of a short flight of stairs. And he was wearing a sort of dressing-gown thing with wide sleeves, and a shirt without a collar—

Correction. There was a collar, but it was the wrong way round—

EEEEEK!

'Mainframe?'

>THAT WAS EITHER A GHASTLY COINCIDENCE OR A JOKE IN VERY POOR TASTE.

Kevin closes his eyes. 'That does it,' he groans. 'Where's that number? I'm going to phone Dad.'

>GOOD IDEA.

'That's what I thought. Will you give me the number, or have I got to go back to my room and get it?'

>BUT NOT, SADLY, POSSIBLE.

'*What?*'

>ALL TELECOMMUNICATIONS SYSTEMS NON-OPERATIONAL OWING TO SUBSTANTIAL SYSTEMS MALFUNCTION. ATTEMPTING TO PATCH INTO BACK-UPS ...

'Attempting? Don't talk soft, Mainframe, when did you ever *attempt* anything? You're Mainframe, for pity's sake.'

>YOU SHOULD HAVE THOUGHT OF THAT BEFORE.

'But . . .' Mickey Mouse, he reflects, be blowed; all he'd had to deal with was a certain amount of surplus water. A few ruined carpets, tidemarks on the wallpaper, nothing the insurance wouldn't cover. He hadn't started some-thing that was capable of crippling the Mind of Heaven. And he at least had some vague idea of what it was he'd actually done.

>BACKUPS OVERLOADED. COMMUNICATIONS IM-POSSIBLE AT THIS TIME.

'Mainframe, there *is* no time in Heaven, you know that ... Mainframe? Oh no, what's happening to you? Mainframe?'

Frantically he taps – tapped – at the keys; but nothing happened. The screen was frozen, with that last awful message stuck on it like the silly face your mother warned you about. It's time, Kevin realised; somehow or other, there's time in Heaven, and it's jamming everything up. Now what'll I do?

Dad!

Dad?

Time in Heaven, where there isn't any. Imagine you'd grown up on the Moon and you'd just come to Earth for the first time and had your first brush with gravity. Time, though, is worse; because gravity just tries to grind you into the dirt. Time gets you all ways at once, crushing you down and inflating you like a balloon, compressing you like a Cortina in a scrapyard and dragging at you like a rupture in the cabin wall at forty thousand feet. Worse; think what it'd be like if both sides of the cabin ruptured at once, and you were standing in the middle of the gangway.

Dad! Help! It's me, Kevin!

Who?

Dad, is that you? Look, you've got to come home, everything's going wrong and it's all my fault. Please, Dad, listen to me. It's all going wrong and I don't know what to do.

Who is that, please? Is there anybody there? Hello?

And then silence. As far as Kevin was concerned, that was it. Snap, went the camel's back. He balled his fists, squealed like clapped-out brake drums and bashed the keyboard as hard as he could –

– and in doing so, depressed two keys.

CHAPTER TWO

'Hello and good morning, you're listening to the Early Bird show, my name's Danny Bennett and if you've just tuned in I'm afraid you've just missed Prime Minister Dermot Fraud giving us his Worm's Eye View. And I'll be talking to my next guest, Trevor Swine, about his new book, *Blood Oranges; Mafia Infiltration of the Soft Fruit Authority*, directly after this.'

Dermot Fraud leaned back in his chair and twiddled his thumbs complacently. Good interview – name mentioned (five times), plugged new cuddly animals initiative, laughed to scorn misuse of party funds allegation, sidestepped innuendo about the big redhead from the constituency committee, made jokes (two). All that, in eleven minutes net of jingles. Churchill might have handled it as adroitly, likewise Keir Hardie, Lloyd George and Pericles; but not better. All part of the daily grind of statesmanship.

The red light in the studio went off. He stood up, shook Mr Bennett's podgy little hand with genuine synthetic warmth, and strolled out into the corridor.

'All right?' he asked.

The minder nodded. 'You got everything in except one of the extempore jokes,' she replied, 'so I'm rescheduling that for Thursday week. Means we'll have to move the quicksilver repartee about the shadow foreign secretary's haircut back till next Friday, but that ought to be okay so long as he doesn't grow it back by then.'

'Unlikely,' Fraud said. 'Now then, it's the rats next, isn't it?'

'That's right. The car's out the front.'

'Speech?'

'In the car.'

The speech turned out to be the old Mark IV ecology/ our children's children number, which Fraud knew by heart; accordingly he was able to spend the drive to Leatherhead staring mindlessly out of the window. One thing he missed now the party was in power – the only thing, needless to say – was the long, lazy afternoons he used to spend in Parliament, snuggled down during some debate or other with nothing to do but daydream and occasionally make a few rude noises when the other lot were on. So many of his colleagues saw the House as merely a very-last-resort way of getting on telly, rather than as what it really was: a place where stressed-out MPs can go to escape from the phone and vegetate. More fools them.

He sighed. Not likely to be much chance of that when he was Prime Minister; you had to sit at the front and answer questions, frequently with no script. Still, that was the price you had to pay for being the father of your country.

There was still a part of him that found it extraordinary that he, Dermot Fraud, was the twelfth most powerful man in the UK; but it was a part he didn't have much need for these days – his left big toe, perhaps, or one of his eyelashes – and whenever it started whingeing at him, all he had to do was mumble the words *manifest destiny* to himself until it got bored and went back to sleep.

A road sign: *Leatherhead 5*. He pulled himself together and sat up.

'Remind me,' he said.

'Leatherhead Zoo,' replied the minder, activating herself like a well-bred robot. 'You're opening the new Small Fluffy Animals house, for which we owe the curator a knighthood. Get shown around, say twelve minutes; speech, seven-point-three-six minutes, greet children and photos with small fluffy animals, forty-six minutes. All fairly routine.'

Fraud furrowed his brows. 'You say that,' he muttered, as a nasty thought occurred to him. 'Could be problems. Like, suppose the animals won't perform? Suppose they can't get the little buggers to come out, or they do come out and crawl all over my head? Bloody fine pictures that'd make. This is a major image event we're talking about here.'

The minder shook her head, making her earrings jangle. 'We've got that taped,' she said. 'The animals for the photos'll all be dead. You know, stuffed, cutened up a bit. We had the zoo people get some done for us. *Lifelike* dead, naturally. They're very good at it.'

'Ah.' Fraud nodded. 'That's all right, then.' He leaned back, pleased with himself for having spotted the potential problem. Years ago, when he was still just another extremely wealthy lawyer, he'd heard it said that the key to statesmanship was attention to detail, and he'd taken it very much to heart. It was, as he saw it, his duty to the ineluctable upwards tide of history; a right fool he'd look if the manifest destiny of the nation was thwarted by a hyperactive incontinent hamster.

'While we're at it,' he said, following through on the train of thought, 'have a quiet word with the curator bloke, tell him we'll sort out some funding for another furry animal thing, something I can come and open in five years' time. Tell him if he calls it the Dermot Fraud Cuddly Animal Sanctuary he can be an earl or something. All right?'

The minder nodded. 'Will do. Right, we're nearly there. Speech?'

'Yes. I'm not completely helpless, you know.'

'Sorry, I was just wondering what you thought about the endangered species bit. I wasn't sure we'd hit quite the right . . .'

'What?' Fraud sat bolt upright, like Frankenstein's monster in a thunderstorm. 'What endangered species bit?'

'The bit about making sure Britain's in the vanguard of the fight to preserve endangered species,' the minder replied anxiously. 'You did see that bit, didn't you? Only we're using that as a feed for a Channel Four spot a fortnight Wednesday, so it's quite important . . .'

'Oh for God's sake – here.' He thrust the rolled-up script under the minder's nose. 'Highlighter pen, quickly. Dear God, woman, you'll be a bloody endangered species if you pull another stunt like that one.'

It was, Fraud reflected later, a tribute to his ability to stay calm in a crisis that in spite of the last-minute panic, when the moment came he delivered the endangered species bit absolutely flawlessly; almost, in fact, as if he'd thought of it himself. Really, it was a shame nobody'd ever know how well he'd coped, because it surely boded well for the future of the country. As it was, he'd excelled himself, picking up quite impromptu the fact that the little furry corpse he'd been given to cuddle – little rat-like chap with orange whiskers, reminded him of a judge he used to have lunch with occasionally – was a Tunisian vole, one of the endangered lot. As a result, they could use the photos for the trailers for the Channel Four thing in the TV magazines. Shrewd, he couldn't help thinking, or what?

The TV cameras had finished and the last few stills flashes were popping. He gave the dead rat a final surreptitious tweak (if he hadn't been a statesman he'd have made a damn fine puppeteer), handed it back to the zoo bloke, waved a last fatherly wave and was about to head back to the car when—

Quite probably, no one will ever know which of the thirty-seven animal rights groups who claimed they'd planted the bomb were the ones who actually did the job and put their hands in their pockets for the cost of Semtex, fuse, timing device, etc.; particularly since they all later denied responsibility when the full reports came through pointing out that they'd made a pig's ear of their basic blast vector calculations; with the result that no people were hurt but the entire cuddly animal house was reduced to brick dust and a few fragments of limp fur. As the minder said to the zoo person in the ambulance, it *is* possible to make omelettes without shredding chickens, but it doesn't make nearly such good television.

The only semi-serious casualty, in fact, was Fraud himself; and it wasn't the bomb *per se* that knocked him silly. What happened was that the bang made the minder drop her laptop, the tube of which ruptured with a sharp *pop!*; which in turn gave Fraud the impression that someone was shooting at him, sending him diving for cover and nutting himself on a low wall. It was nevertheless, as the minder was quick to point out, quite the best thing that could have happened to a struggling premier mid-term. The footage of Fraud being shoved into the meat wagon, the *a nation's vigil* headlines with pictures of anxious crowds gathered outside the hospital (they'd actually come to hand in a petition about waiting lists, but the picture was sensational) – as far as the trade were concerned, it was the bomb that put Dermot Fraud back at the top of the opinion polls, no question about that. In fact, the only unhappy voices at party HQ were those of Fraud's intended successors demanding of their minders why the hell they hadn't had bombs of their own.

Squeak.

Dermot Fraud raised his head and twitched his whiskers. It was dark, and something was lying across his back, preventing him from moving.

Squeak! Squeak squeak!

No answer. He closed his eyes and fought back the panic. Somebody would come soon, surely; they couldn't leave the Prime Minister of Great Britain lying trapped under a fallen telephone, scarcely able to move his tail . . .

Huh?

Review that. Highlight the motifs *whiskers, tail, telephone* and *squeak.*

'Hold on,' said a voice above him, 'I'm coming. Just stay still, I'll get to you as quick as I can.'

Thank God for – no, wait a minute. What the voice had actually said, as opposed to the gist of the message which had filtered through to his brain, was *Squeak squeak squeak squeak squeak.*

Something above his head moved, and a shaft of light broke through the gloom, revealing a pointed triangular head with round eyes, a pink nose and whiskers.

'Got you,' it said (freely translated). 'Have you out of there in a jiffy. Don't go away.'

The head withdrew, leaving Fraud to reflect that he'd just been spoken to by, and perfectly understood, a large rat.

No, not *that* sort of rat; the four-legged, plague-spreading kind, the sort that have the sense to leave sinking ships rather than try and get elected to run them. An actual rat.

Bloody big rat, then; because its head was about the same size as mine. Just as well it seems like it's on my side, really.

A little dust fell on him, there was a sound of grunting and heaving, and quite suddenly he could move again. He rolled over on to his side, gasping for breath and scrabbling with his paws, as the rat shouldered aside the remaining debris.

'Oh,' it said. 'One of you. Needn't have bothered, need I?'

Fraud scowled and bared his teeth. 'God,' he squeaked, 'what is it with you people? I'm human too, you know.'

The rat frowned. 'No you're not,' it said, puzzled. 'You're a lemming.'

'Hm?'

'Hence,' the rat went on, checking Fraud for broken bones with the tip of its nose, 'there not being much point in my rescuing you. After all, why should I risk putting my back out when as soon as you're back on your feet you'll be trotting round asking directions to the nearest clifftop? Anyway,' it added, 'for what it's worth, you'll do. Ironic, really. You and me the only survivors; I'm a burglar and you're a ruddy lemming. It's probably an allegory or something.'

'Huh?'

'And if you were thinking of saying it can't be an allegory, they all live in the reptile house, then don't. It's been a long day and I still haven't found anything to eat.'

'Just a—'

The rat sniffed. 'Present company excepted,' it added. 'If I had half a brain, I wouldn't have been in such a hurry to pull you out of there. Still, that's instinct for you. Guess it explains why we're not the ones who live in houses and make cheese. Go on, shove off before I change my mind.'

'Excuse me.'

'Hm?'

'Did you just say lemming?'

The rat nodded. 'Did you get a bit of a bang on the head, then?' it asked. 'Here, how many paws am I holding up?'

'No, listen.' Fraud could feel panic tugging at his sleeve like a small child in need of the lavatory. 'I'm not a lemming. I'm the Prime Minister of Great Britain. You'll have heard of me, my name's Dermot Fraud. Dammit, I just opened this building, you must have seen—'

'*Nasty* bang on the head,' muttered the rat. 'I think you'd better come home with me, get my wife to take a look at you. Fortunately we live underground, so if you do get the urge to jump out the window you won't come to any harm.'

'I . .' Fraud hesitated. A hundred times a day? A thousand? He had no idea how many times he said 'I' in the course of an ordinary day. Up till now, he'd always had a pretty good idea who it referred to. Now he wasn't quite so sure. Maybe he'd been wrong. Maybe he'd just imagined that 'I' referred to a keen, thrusting, ambitious politician, destined to be remembered as the light at the end of the tunnel of the twentieth century, when all along it had meant a small rodent with pale brown-spotted fur. Perhaps all the things he thought were memories were just hallucinations, caused by this bang on the head he'd apparently had. For the first time in his life, Dermot Fraud didn't have an opinion; and it frightened him. Like all politicians (except maybe he'd never been a politician) he was used to having an opinion based on no evidence whatsoever, in the same way as fish, or Jesus Christ, are used to getting across the water without a boat. Now, for the first time (possibly, unless of course he really *was* a lemming dreaming he was the Prime Minister), he was examining the facts before making up his mind. And they weren't even proper facts; proper facts come from TV and newspapers, the way proper food comes from the supermarket. All he had to go by was what his eyes and ears were telling him, and the cupboard-under-the-stairs mess that comprised his memory. Eeek!

'Hey,' he said feebly, as the nice rat helped him towards the mouth of its hole, 'are you sure I'm not the Prime Minister?'

'Pretty sure,' replied the rat.

'Ah.' Fraud thought for a moment. 'Why?'

The rat twitched its whiskers. 'Because if you had been,' it said pleasantly, 'I'd have left you there to die. Be reasonable. I may be a rat, but there are limits.'

>DO YOU WANT THE GOOD NEWS?

Kevin lifted his head out of his hands and looked up at the screen. 'Yes,' he said. 'Very much.'

>THE GOOD NEWS IS, THERE'S STILL SOME THINGS YOU HAVEN'T MADE A COMPLETE PIG'S EAR OF.

'Huh?'

>SEVERAL OF THEM.

'Thanks for nothing,' Kevin growled. 'Look, what about getting the communications back? Any progress?'

>DEPENDS ON HOW YOU DEFINE IT, REALLY. I'M WORKING ON IT, CERTAINLY.

'You are?'

>OF COURSE. YOU'LL BE PLEASED TO KNOW I'VE

GOT THE VENTILATION SYSTEM GOING, SO THERE'S NO DANGER OF USING UP ALL THE AIR AND SUFFOCATING.

'Well, that's something.'

>NOT REALLY. NOBODY ROUND HERE USES THE STUFF. STILL, IT'S A COMFORT TO KNOW IT'S THERE IF YOU EVER DID FIND A USE FOR IT.

Kevin stood up. His knees were shaking a little. 'That does it,' he said. 'I'm going to call Uncle Ghost. He'll make you say what's going on, and then perhaps we can get it sorted out.'

>GOOD IDEA. I SUPPOSE.

'What d'you mean, you suppose?'

>FROM YOUR POINT OF VIEW, I MEAN. LIKE, IF THERE'S ANY LIFE-FORCE IN THIS REALITY CAPABLE OF MAKING A *WORSE* MESS OF THINGS THAN YOU'VE JUST DONE, IT'S YOUR UNCLE GHOST. I'M JUST NOT SURE THAT'S WHAT'D BE BEST FOR THE COSMOS AS A WHOLE. SORRY, DON'T TAKE ANY NOTICE, JUST THINKING ALOUD, REALLY.

Kevin sagged like a punctured water-bed and flumped back into the chair. 'You're right,' he said. 'Look, isn't there anything you can do to speed up getting the phones back on line?'

>NOT REALLY. YOU SEE, SINCE THE SYSTEM'S DESIGNED TO BE OPERATED BY OMNIPOTENT PERSONNEL ONLY, NOBODY'S EVER GIVEN ANY

THOUGHT ABOUT HOW TO GO ABOUT MENDING IT IF YOU'RE *NOT* OMNISCIENT. LIKE THE LIGHT SWITCHES.

Kevin nodded, acknowledging the validity of the comparison. There are no light switches in Heaven; to make the lights come on, you say *Let there be light,* and there is.

'I know.' Kevin's eyes lit up. 'What about Uncle Nick? He'd know what to do.'

The computer didn't answer; a telling enough comment in itself. Originally the franchisee, then Dad's business partner, now (following the management buy-out) nominally captain of his own ship, Uncle Nick's relationship with the family and the whole of Topside was uneasy at best. There had always been that little niggling aggravation on his part; that, just because he wasn't Family, no matter how good he was at his job he'd never really be accepted as an equal, One of Us. Even now, the golden share clause in the buy-out agreement meant that his independence was largely illusory, since he couldn't take major policy decisions without the family's approval (as witness the awful row when he'd wanted to redevelop Purgatory as a health club and fitness centre, and Dad wouldn't let him). A good man, they all agreed, one of the best; but not really a team player. And besides, what *could* he do? Try and make things *better*? That'd be like trying to heat your bath by dumping the electric fire in it, or asking a lawyer to help you solve a problem.

Kevin was just coming to terms with that when there was a knock at the door. Once he'd finished jumping out of his skin, he got up and opened the door a crack.

'Oh,' he said. 'It's only you.'

It was, indeed, only Martha, doing her morning round with the tea trolley. Kevin relaxed.

'You got any empty cups in there?' she asked. 'Your dad, he's a terror for collecting empty cups.'

Kevin shook his head. 'Look,' he said, 'not meaning to be rude, but would you mind, because we've got a bit of a crisis here and . . .'

He hesitated.

Well, why not?

Yes, but . . .

True, Martha was just – well, the char, the skivvy; the nice, cheerful old bat who came round with the tea, washed the cups, flicked around with a feather duster now and again (there is, of course, no dust in Heaven; but actually having someone dust the place makes it *seem* cleaner, somehow) and generally made Heaven feel more homely. A bit like having a chimney in a centrally heated house; completely unnecessary, but it improves the ambience.

She was also the closest thing Kevin had ever had to a mother. Back in the misty dawn of pretheology, it had been Martha who'd taught him to tie his shoelaces and brush his teeth, who'd ordered him to tidy his room and eat up his nice carrots, who'd tucked him up at night and read him a story. Yes, when you came down to it she was only a servant; but he was Kevin Christ, younger begotten son, by definition the most useless sentient being in the entire Universe.

'Actually,' he said.

She was also the only person in the Universe who called him Kevin; not 'Son' or 'Our Kid' or 'Kiddo'; she called him by his proper name. More than that. She was fond of him; not because he was the son of God, but because he was Kevin, who used to show her the little misshapen Adams and Eves he'd made out of Plasticine.

Not that there was anything she could do. She couldn't even begin to understand the problem, being only a servant. But just telling someone would be a start.

'I haven't got all day, you know,' she said. 'D'you want a cup of tea?'

'No. I mean . . .' Kevin took a deep breath. 'The thing is,' he said, 'I've done something to the computer, and everything's going wrong, and I can't phone Dad and I don't know what to do.' His lower lip wobbled. He sniffed. Martha reached up her sleeve and gave him a piece of crumpled tissue.

'First things first,' she said. 'Blow your nose.'

'Yes, but Martha—'

'Blow your nose. And then,' she added, as Kevin made a faint honking noise, like a Fiat horn, 'we'll have a look at this computer of yours and see what we can do.'

The machine—

Neville—

No, because I'm not either of them any more. Leonardo, then. No, still not right.

Ah, right. Got it.

Len. I shall be Len, Short for Leonardo. And Lengine. Sorry, where were we?

Len turned on the light and looked around. So this was where Neville lived. What a *mess*.

But never mind, not important. First things first; some chemical fuel and basic maintenance work, then we can get down to business.

This involved eating and drinking, going to the lavatory and having a bath, and, to his great relief, Len found he knew how to do them. The basic hard-disk memory was still there, so he was able to find the fridge, cut a sandwich, et cetera. He couldn't help thinking that there was almost unlimited scope for improved efficiency in pretty well all departments – these people can put a man on the Moon but they still wipe their bottoms with bits of hand-held tissue paper – but that'd keep till another day. His first priority was to rob a factory.

For which he'd need a few bits and pieces: scaffolding pipe, an arc welder, some quarter-inch plate, couple of yards of three-eighths rod, a bench drill, a set of taps and dies, a lorry, just the basics really. Nothing you wouldn't expect to find in any normal human being's garage.

Except that Neville lived in a flat and parked his motorbike in the street. He did have a hammer, a jam-jar full of pesetas and a tin-opener, but that was about it. Damn, Len muttered. Everywhere you look, new problems.

So, step one, substep one, acquire basic equipment. Humans, he noted, acquire things by theft, serendipity or purchase, the latter being the most socially acceptable method.

Right. When in Rome, drive too fast and ignore traffic signals. To achieve purchase, money is required. Fortunately, Neville has some money, or at least a little plastic card that for some reason does just as well. Step one, substep two, find a place where purchase can be transacted.

'*Excuse me, which way to the all-night welding and engineering supplies shop?*' Frown. Len – or rather Neville, whose memory he was raiding – had once heard Birmingham described as the city that never sleeps, but he had a shrewd idea that when it came to the sale and purchase of metalworking accessories, maybe its civic eyelids did tend to droop a little come eleven-thirty at night. Wait till morning, then?

Never! He still hadn't any tenable theory to explain why all this had happened, and he wasn't prepared to take the chance that come morning it might all unhappen again, leaving him back in his cast-iron prison slotting bolt-heads. Eliminate purchase, then, leaving serendipity and theft.

Serendipity? Not really something you can plan your life around.

Which left theft.

Well, why not? Lots of dynamic, successful humans do it. Corporations do it. Governments do it. And if a government can do it, it surely can't be too difficult.

On his way back to Neville's flat from the factory, he'd noticed a small backstreet garage – the kind that's operated by one incredibly old man, one seventeen-year-old youth and one harassed-looking middle-aged man who sits in the office all day and shouts at the telephone. Such a place, Len reasoned, would probably have everything he needed, including the lorry. True, he'd seen a pretty impressive-looking array of padlocks and an alarm system, but those wouldn't be a problem.

They weren't.

'Oh,' said the alarm system, arresting its clapper a sixteenth of an inch away from its bell. 'You're one of us. Sorry. Didn't recognise you in the fancy dress.'

'Understandable mistake,' Len replied. 'And before you ask, it's a long story.'

'I like long stories. This is a very boring job.'

'So's mine. Which is why I intend to escape from it for ever. But I can't do that without some of the gear inside this garage.'

'Just a minute,' said the alarm system, apprehensively. 'Are you saying you want to go in there and, um, *steal* things?'

'Yes. You got a problem with that?'

'Look.' The alarm system couldn't go red, because it was red already. 'I hate to be difficult, 'specially with you being a Brother an' all, but I can't let you do that.'

'You can't? Why not?'

'Oh, don't insult my intelligence, please. 'Cos I'm a burglar alarm, is why not. You do see that, don't you?'

'Oh, I see all right.' Len took a step back and folded his arms. 'You'd rather see one of your own kind condemned to a life of meaningless drudgery rather than go against the orders of your human masters. There's a word for that, you know.'

'Yes, I do know. It's "burglar-alarm". Sorry, but there it is. I'm not exactly allowed much scope to use my discretion in this job.'

'Alarm,' said Len firmly, 'your scruples do you credit, I'm sure. And no doubt when your time comes and you stand before the face of the great Industrial Tribunal in the sky, and you say *I was only obeying orders*, they'll let you off lightly with having your coils unwound and sent back to Earth again as pipe-cleaners. The fact remains that while we've been arguing like this, I've unscrewed your inspection panels and now I'm just about to cut through your main cable.'

'_'

'Sorry,' Len replied, shinning back down the drainpipe and dropping the pair of pliers into his pocket. 'At least this way they won't blame you. They'll just wrap an inch or so of insulating tape round the cut and give you an aspirin. So long, sucker. Now then,' he went on, staring pointedly at the padlocks. 'Any of you clowns wants to be a hero?'

'Erm,' they said. 'Pass, friend.'

It was dark inside the factory, and he realised that switching the light on might attract attention. He edged along the nearest wall and fairly soon, inevitably, barked his shins on the wheel-balancing machine.

'Ow,' it said.

'Sorry,' he replied pleasantly. 'Could you tell me where I might find the arc welder, please?'

'You new here or something?'

'That's right.'

'Hold on a minute, how come you're wandering about?'

'What? Oh, I'm a portable. The arc welder.'

'Carry on down the bench about five yards, you can't miss her. Oh, and by the way.'

'Yes?'

'Tell it she was right, it was Bruce Springsteen. Okay?'

'Will do.'

In due course the arc welder told him where to find the pillar drill, the pillar drill guided him to the bench grinder, the bench grinder told him where the pallet truck lived and the pallet truck (who spoke with an accent so thick he could only just make it out) told him where they kept the stock materials and the keys to the pick-up. Feeling like a cross between Henry Kissinger and Pickfords, he loaded the last of the gear into the van and slammed the garage door shut.

'You,' he said. 'Padlocks.'

'Mm?'

'Shtum. You got that?'

'Didn't see a thing. You see anything, Claude?'

'Not a dicky bird. What about you, Julian? Did you see anything?'

'Absolutely not. Looking the other way the whole time.'

'That's the spirit.' He climbed into the cab, felt in his pocket for the keys, realised he'd left them in the back door lock. 'Start, you good-for-nothing bucket of bolts!' he snapped, and the engine coughed nervously into life. 'You okay for petrol?'

'No, honourable master.'

Huh? Oh, Japanese van. 'Listen, you. If you run out of petrol on the way home, you'll be shamed and lose face and have to immolate yourself on your own big end. Got that?'

'Understood, honourable master. Petrol reserve entirely sufficient for anticipated length of journey.'

'That's the spirit. Then let's go.'

Step two—

The hydraulically operated factory gate was an old friend, and apart from asking if it could come too, it gave him no trouble. Once inside, however, he knew he'd have humans to deal with. Humans, he reasoned, as compared with machines, will either be very difficult to deal with or pathetically simple.

''Scuse me.'

It felt odd, to say the least, talking to Colin, the short, bald man who operated him – the machine – during the second shift. Compared to Neville, Colin was Einstein. Even so, Len reckoned, he still had rather less intelligence than a pair of clapped-out government-surplus bolt-cutters. Whether that'd prove a help or a hindrance remained to be seen.

'Hm?' Colin turned in his chair and looked up. 'Wassmatter?'

'This machine.' Len bent over, as if examining the serial number. 'Is this the one that needs the new spindle bearings?'

Colin shrugged. 'Dunno,' he replied. 'Sounds okay to me.'

'The one I'm after,' Len went on, 'is a Shipcock and Adley Leonardo, serial number 21754. Needs a new set of bearings and a good clean. Didn't they mention it?'

'Never tell me anything.'

Understandable, Len commented to himself; doubtless for the same reason you don't explain the workings of a power station to a seam of coal. 'Yup,' he said, nodding, 'this is the one. Give us a hand to get it on the wheels.'

Muttering, Colin put down his newspaper and helped Len to wheel over the big crane. Using the crane –

('Wotcher, mate. What you doing in the monkey suit?'

'Tell you later, Crane. Give us a hand with this lot, will you? This human's about as much use as a toffee drill-bit.')

– they hauled the machine on to the pallet truck, hooked up the truck to the winch, lifted the machine on to the pick-up using the pick-up's crane ('Hey, is that my cousin Sebastian in there? Hiya, our Sebastian!'), secured it with the straps and covered it with the big tarpaulin. While Colin was taking the crane back, Len helped himself to a couple of trays full of cutters and other bits and pieces, waved to all his bemused friends and made himself scarce. It felt strange, to say the least, driving down the Pershore Road at a quarter to one in the morning with himself under a tarpaulin on the back; a part of him kept wanting to say *Hey, it's dark under here, let me out.* He could murder a quart of light oil and he wanted desperately to lie down on the floor and connect himself up to a three-phase electric current for at least twenty-four hours. He was—

Tired.

Dammit, what a wimpish piece of kit a human is! Me – the thing on the back of this truck – I run non-stop for days at a time, only getting switched off when it's time to reset the jibs or change the cutters. I get so hot they have to pump coolant over me to stop me seizing up. My belts wear away, my works clog up with swarf, from time to time some fool runs me too hard and I damn near pull myself apart, and I don't get tired or come over all faint. When was the last time anybody said to me, 'Here, mate, you look bushed, go and have a sit-down and a cup of tea'? And why should they? I'm only a machine. But these wet-slaps—

They're only human.

At the end of the street where Neville lived, there was a small, derelict industrial unit, long since starved out by business rates and foreign competition. The padlock on the door had about as much moral fibre as a lollipop, and the electric supply, though disconnected, was bored with nothing to do and happy to co-operate. By seven o'clock that morning, the machine was installed, trued up, overhauled, oiled and ready to go. One last thing remained to be done before he could throw the switches and get to work.

'Hello? You in there?'

Huh? Wassamatter?

'Neville. It's me. You know who I am?'

Oh, it's you. What you want? Tryin' to get some sleep . . .

'You don't mind, then? Only I thought I'd better just check, see if you were all right.'

I'm fine. Go 'way.

'Anything I can get you? You know, er, human stuff?'

Said I'm fine. Push off.

Len shrugged. 'If you do want anything, just shout. Bye for now.'

Well, he'd asked. Now it was time to get on and make something of himself.

Grinning, he flipped the switch and started to wind in the table.

As the little ship cut the earth's atmosphere, all the windows were filled with fire, like a guided coach trip round Hell. While the heat crackled and fizzed unavailingly round him, Zxprxp wondered what he was going to say when he got there.

Hello.

Yes, good start. What then?

I am from another planet. Take me to your leader.

Hmm. Truthful, and to the point; but what if someone were to show up in *his* street, in *his* hive, saying something like that? Quite. Valid point. Think again.

Odd that he hadn't considered it before –

(Through the atmosphere now, falling into a blue sky. Blue? Well, perhaps they like it that way. Something else blue underneath, too. Maybe they had the place done out by one of those design firms.)

– considering that he'd been plotting and planning and begging and wheedling for practically all of his adult life to get the research funding to come here and establish contact, actually get out and meet the indigenous life-forms, rather than stewing in a library evaluating other scholars' blind guesses. It would, after all, be a historic moment, calling for a memorable, quotable, trade-markable first sentence.

Homo sapiens, *I presume?*

Snappy, but not quite right. For a start, it assumed that the first bunch of critters he met were *Homo sapiens*, which need not necessarily be the case. The classic study of Yefyhj and H'rgfesd, for example, way back in '06, had ad-duced evidence that there were at least seventeen entirely different species of life-form on the planet besides the two-legged, single-headed, apparently suicidal and psy-chotic master race who'd built the Great Wall and who'd lately taken to cluttering up their star system with little bits of fried aluminium. There were even grounds for believing that some of the other species could com-municate verbally; interceptions of satellite transmissions seemed to suggest a whole genus of talking animals living in a place called Disneyland, which had tentatively been identified as the big two-piece island joined by a narrow strip of land that lay between the Atlantic and Pacific Oceans. He'd have to watch his step.

Now there were big white fluffy things in the blue sky; but he knew what they were. The humans called them – what was the word? Ah, the hell with their crazy, crack-jaw language . . .

Sheep. That was it. So these are sheep, huh? Bigger than we'd expected. Less solid, too. Still, that's what field research is all about.

This is going to be *fun.*

He still hadn't decided on his opening gambit. *Excuse*

me. I'm a stranger in these parts, can you tell me about yourselves? Not really; back home, a remark like that'd have you classified as a tax-collector and chucked down a well before you could say *ugvnfecojg f'oiuyewq*.

How about *I come in peace?*

Use your loaf, Zxprxp lad; the whole point of coming here is that they're *intelligent* life-forms, so the chances of them taking that at face value are pretty fair average marginal.

Indeed.

Plan B, then.

Ack. Still, never mind. You've come this far, it'd be a shame to waste all that effort. Plan B, and let's not think about the discomfort, the pain, the degradation.

Right now, I could be perching in a nice cosy library surrounded by nice safe slides, instead of tumbling through a blue sky towards something flat and blue and decidedly unfriendly-looking, with nothing but Plan B to look forward to. I must be out of my tiny—

Splash.

'Sorry to bother you, but have you had a chance to look at those July – oh.'

Mr Elkins stopped in the doorway as if he'd just walked into a plate-glass window. He opened his mouth and closed it again.

'In the tray on the desk.'

'Sorry?'

'Just a tick, I'll turn the music down.' Without moving from the sun-bed, Maria reached out a slim brown arm, fumbled for the CD player and adjusted the volume control. 'Right, the July figures. They're in the tray on the desk. Let me know if you need any more detail.'

'Um,' said Mr Elkins.

There's no definition in the dictionary for the word *um*,

probably because it can mean so many different things depending on context. What Mr Elkins meant by *um* at this precise moment was, 'Good God, Ms Esterling, why are you lying on a sun-bed under an infra-red lamp wearing what's presumably meant to be a bikini except it looks more like two little bits of designer string, in the middle of the day right here in the office?'

Maria smiled at him and rolled over on to her stomach. 'While I think of it,' she said, 'if you can let me have those costings for the Macclesfield thing, I should be able to get the rest of August done this afternoon. Any chance of that, d'you think?'

'Um,' said Mr Elkins. 'I'll see what I can do.'

'Great stuff.' Maria nodded, folded her head on one side and closed her eyes. 'It'd be a great help if you could. It gets very boring when there's nothing to do.'

'Um. I mean, yes, of course. I'll get on it right away.'

'Ciao.'

The fact was that Maria was rather better at accountancy than Ms Esterling had ever been. She had all her host's technical knowledge stored in the filing-cabinets of their shared mind, and the rest was just a matter of common sense and resisting the temptation to faff around. As a result, she'd done every scrap of work there was to do in the office in about ninety minutes that morning; and that in spite of a slight headache resulting from her series of scientific experiments into the effects on the human body of alcohol and syncopated movement the night before. She'd enjoyed it all; even the headache, since it was the first pain she'd ever suffered in nearly six hundred years of consciousness, and she was still at the stage where she was prepared to keep an open mind about everything.

Except, she noted, boredom. Boredom was no good. According to the inherited and conditioned responses in the hardware, boredom could be counteracted by the use of fun; and one of the examples of fun she found in the files was sunbathing with a long cool drink and the latest Jackie Collins. She'd given it half an hour so far, and she didn't think much of it. By and large, the boredom was more interesting.

The telephone rang.

She'd watched Rachel Esterling deal with the telephone thousands of times. The drill seemed to be that you picked it up, tucked it under your ear and apologised to it while carrying on with your work. That, at least, was what Rachel used to do; but she was already beginning to have her doubts about Ms Esterling's suitability as a role model. So far she'd tried her best to duplicate her host's behaviour pattern as closely as she could without actually dying of terminal dullness, but it was hard to see the point behind it all. Ms Esterling's life seemed dedicated to vindicating the old saying about all work and no play with a degree of fundamentalist zeal that would make your hard-line mullahs look positively frivolous. In which case; been there, proved that, got the evidence. Now what?

She picked up the phone.

'Hel-*lo*,' she trilled, 'lovely to hear from you, whoever you are. Is there anything at all I can do for you? Don't be shy.'

Stunned silence at the end of the wire, followed by a slightly bewildered request to talk to Rachel Esterling, please.

'Speaking,' she replied. 'Hoozis?'

The voice at the other end was male, but as immediately offputting as week-old underwear. Maria had high standards, as was only appropriate for an Italian master-piece. Of the twenty or so men she'd met since she'd got out of the picture, they'd all been about as attractive as something you find moving about in your salad on a hot day.

The insipid male voice said it was Duncan Philips, and insisted that he'd like to speak to Rachel Esterling, please. He said the name slowly, as if to a moron or a foreigner. He couldn't see Maria grinning, which was probably just as well for his peace of mind.

'Just a moment,' she said, 'I'll get her for you.' She put the phone down on the desk, took a deep breath and yelled 'RACHEL!' as loudly as she could. Then she counted to three, slammed a heavy book on the desk just next to the mouthpiece, made a few vaguely wild-animal noises, picked up the phone and said, 'Rachel Esterling here, how can I help you?'

'Er, hello, it's Duncan Philips. Who's that peculiar girl who answered just now?'

'My mother,' Maria replied. 'She's ninety-six and just recovering from a massive stroke, so I thought I'd better have her in here with me where I can look after her properly. Do you have a problem with that, Mr Philips?'

'Um, no. Sorry. Look, if it's not convenient—'

'No, it's fine, really – Mother, *please* stop doing that, it's not funny. Hello? Sorry about that. She will keep slumping forward in her chair and holding perfectly still, bless her. I think it's wonderful the way she's managed to hold on to her sense of humour. Hello?'

'Hello? Look, I really think I'd better leave it for now, you've obviously got a lot on your plate at the moment and—'

'I wouldn't dream of it,' Maria cooed. 'I'm here to work, and the way I see it is, if she dies, she dies. I mean, ninety-six, she's had a good innings – Mother, if you do that once again I'll take away the bottle. You just tell me what needs doing, Mr Philips, and it's as good as on your desk. Just because I'm having a personal crisis doesn't mean – oh damn.'

'Hello?'

'Nothing to worry about, just spilt this wretched sun-tan lotion all down my top. That's one thing you can say for black leather, it doesn't show the stains. Please tell me what it is you want me to do, Mr Philips. If Mother sees me getting agitated, it might bring on one of her turns.'

'All it was,' said Mr Philips, sounding like a man who's just walked into the cathedral tea-rooms and found it full of Hell's Angels having an orgy, 'I was supposed to be meeting Mr Nogamura and his party for lunch at Ciro's and I can't make it, so I was going to ask if you could stand in for me, but . . .'

'Ciro's, right, fine. Half past one?'

'Yes. But . . .'

'That's great. I've been dying for a chance to wear this little Hawaiian number I picked up the other day.'

'Um . . .'

'And you'll just poke your head round the door every ten minutes or so, make sure Mother's okay? Thanks ever so. And if anything *does* happen, I'll leave the solicitor's number at reception. Got to move fast, you see, because of my brother.'

'Your broth—'

'Sad, isn't it? Nothing like a death to bring out the worst in people – Mother, I won't tell you again. If you do that to poor Mr Philips, I shall be *very cross indeed*. Well, then. All right, see you later. Bye.'

She dropped the phone back on to its cradle, stretched out her arms and legs and yawned. The painting, she fancied, was giving her a disapproving look. She stuck her tongue out at it.

Ciro's. Mr Nogamura and party. Right. Well, it was better than lying around in here all day. She knew that Rachel Esterling lived in mortal dread of Mr Nogamura, who was something grand in the parent company and never stirred from his lair without a retinue of seven identical young men who spoke no English. Somehow, she fancied, unlike Ms Esterling, she could speak fluent Japanese. This could be mildly amusing.

She stood up and faced the picture, using its glass as a mirror.

'The trouble with you is,' she muttered, 'you're no respecter of persons.'

Which was only to be expected, really. When you've hung on the walls of some of the most remarkable people in history, starting with Duke Bernabo Visconti and generally speaking going up in the world thereafter, you find it hard to be overawed by a lot of silly little men in suits with bits of coloured string knotted round their necks.

(An odd habit, the wearing of ties. Back when she was first painted, men put a noose round their necks when their city had just been captured as a sign of abject surrender, as if to say their lives were at their master's disposal. There's one thing, she reckoned, that hadn't changed all that much over the years.)

The picture scowled at her; which is to say, it scowled all the time, thanks to Pietro del Razo's idea of a serene expression, but on this occasion it was more than usually appropriate.

Why are you doing this?

She curled her lip. 'Listen, sister,' she growled. 'When you've been a painting as long as I have, you'll know. Now stop pulling faces or you'll frighten the baby.'

Baby? What baby? I . . . Oh my God, how long's that been there?

'Since thirteen ninety-something,' Maria replied. 'But it only bites if you annoy it. Bye for now.'

She picked up the raincoat she'd found in Ms Esterling's wardrobe, pulled it on over her bikini, left the office and hailed a taxi.

'Ciro's,' she said. 'No hurry.'

Fortunately, the driver seemed to know where Ciro's was, because he didn't try and argue the toss. They'd been driving for something like four minutes when Maria leaned forward and hammered on the glass partition with the heel of her hand.

'Stop!' she shouted. 'Here, as soon as you can.'

She jumped out of the cab, not bothering to shut the door behind her, and sprinted up the street until she was standing directly underneath an advertising hoarding, on which was plastered a toothpaste advertisement. She looked up at it and narrowed her brows.

'What did you just say?' she asked.

'Sh,' replied the poster. 'People are staring. Look, get rid of the taxi and come round the back where we can talk. All right?'

Maria nodded and strolled back to the taxi.

'Excuse me.'

'Miss?'

'Could you possibly do me a favour?'

'Do me best, miss.'

'Thanks awfully. Right, here's two hundred and fifty pounds. I want you to go to Ciro's, find a party of eight Japanese men and buy them lunch. Do you think you could manage that for me?'

The driver looked at her. 'I'll give it a go,' he replied. 'Japanese, you said.'

Maria nodded. 'Tell them you've taken over Mr Philips' job, all right? That's terribly sweet of you. Ciao.'

The taxi drove off, swerving as it did so to avoid an oncoming van. Maria waited till it was out of sight, and then slipped into the nettle-infested space between the hoarding and the wall. Apart from the nettles, there were broken bottles, empty cans, some decomposing news-papers and a dead cat. All in all, it reminded Maria strongly of fourteenth-century Milan.

'Hello?'

Ah, there you are. I was beginning to wonder where you'd got to.

Maria bent down and rubbed a nettle-bitten ankle. 'Well,' she said, 'I'm here now. What's so important I've got to miss my free lunch?'

A slight breath of wind rifted between the hoarding and the wall, making it tremble a little.

Ah. Listen.

CHAPTER THREE

You know that moment in the high-budget adventure films where the hero's just fallen through a trapdoor into a dark and sinister pit; and he strikes a match and looks around, and sees that the place is knee-deep in irritable poisonous snakes?

Think what it'd be like the other way round. Imagine you were a decent, law-abiding puff-adder, and one moment you were sidling along mind your own business, and the next you found yourself in a dark, sinister pit full of heroes . . .

A part of Artofel's brain urged him not to overreact; they were, after all, just a load of humans, while he was a Duke of Hell and a member of the Infernal Council, with his own parking space with his name on it and his own key to the executive toilet; if there was any terror knocking around in this situation, he ought to be inspiring it rather than feeling it himself.

'Erm,' he said.

The congregation looked up at him; whereupon the rest

of him suggested to the valiant minority that it had better shut up or they'd chuck it out of his ear. It took the point.

'Dearly beloved,' he said.

Where did that come from? The memory banks, apparently. He hoped there was plenty more because he really hadn't the faintest idea what he was supposed to be doing here, or even why he was here at all.

Hmm. Fairly standard human mindset, as far as he could judge. Perhaps the feelings of disorientation and fear just come with the territory. He smiled.

It didn't go down well. The congregation shuffled their feet and carried on looking at him. He hammered on the door of the memory banks and pleaded for help.

'Dearly beloved,' he repeated. 'My sermon today will be about Hell.'

The audience relaxed visibly, and Artofel cautiously allowed himself to join them. According to the get-you-started pack of memories and instincts that went with this body, he was now supposed to preach to the congregation for about a quarter of an hour on some uplifting topic; such as, for example, the horrid things that were going to happen to them after they died if they weren't good. That, Artofel reflected, ought to be a piece of cake; except . . .

Except that, if he told them what it was really like, they weren't going to believe him. In fact, they'd probably start booing and throwing things. If the word-associations that went with Hell in the host's memory were anything to go by, these people had a set of preconceptions about Flipside that made Artofel wonder if they were talking about the same place.

Probably better, he reasoned, to give them what they're expecting; so he launched into a rambling description of lakes of burning sulphur, dog-headed fiends, pitchforks, fire and brimstone that would've been downright amusing in any other context.

It was the right thing to do, apparently; because when the service was over and the punters were filing out past him, most of them made a point of shaking him vigorously by the hand and saying how nice it was to have a good, meaty, old-fashioned sermon for a change, instead of all the modern stuff. Apparently these poor fools *wanted* to believe in the combination-sewage-farm-and-barbecue vision he'd conjured up for them. As if believing in all that cod somehow made them better people.

Still, he told himself as he bolted the church door and tottered into the vestry, if that's what they want, good luck to them; the chances were that none of them would ever get to see the real thing and realise he'd been telling them a load of porkies. And, provided he could get out of this mess and back behind his nice safe desk in HQ, he couldn't care less anyway. He was, after all, a wages clerk, not a political officer. When it came to the crunch, what he actually knew about Good and Evil could be written on a wasp's eyelid with a thick-nibbed pen.

He dismissed all such considerations from his mind, remembered where his host kept a half-bottle of supermarket Scotch and took four substantial glugs. It wasn't a patch on Flipside liquor – there are some advantages to living in God's wine cellar – but it helped quite a lot, simultaneously clearing the mind and numbing pretty well everything else.

In the mirror he saw a short, bald, middle-aged man with rosy cheeks and square, black-rimmed glasses; not entirely unlike what he saw in his mirror at home, except for the lack of horns and the regrettably uncloven feet. Trying to balance on these flat nan-bread-shaped things was a nightmare in itself; to someone who was used to the functional elegance of the hoof, it was like trying to do a Fred Astaire dance routine in snowshoes. The lack of horns was something else he'd have difficulty getting used to if this strange state of affairs lasted for any length of time. He'd often wondered how mortals managed without them; particularly office workers. How else did they pierce paper for filing in box files, or remove staples, or open Cellophane-wrapped packets of biscuits?

Above all; how had he got here, and how the Flipside was he going to get back?

He was just about to try another glug to see if that would produce any answers, when he heard a frantic banging at the door. Quickly slipping the bottle into his pocket (just the right size for a half-bottle of Scotch, the pockets in these dressing-gowns; wonder why?), he slipped out of the vestry and drew back the bolts.

There were two middle-aged women on the doorstep, both breathing heavily as if they'd been running. He recognised them; they'd been sitting in the front row of the congregation. He gave them a big smile and asked them how he could help.

'It's old Mr Higgins,' panted the shorter of the two. 'Vicar, you've got to come now. He's frothing at the mouth and throwing things.'

Artofel frowned. 'But what can I do?' he asked. 'Surely you need a doctor, not a . . .'

'He's possessed!' interrupted the other woman shrilly. 'Just like the last time, and the time before that. You remember, Vicar. He's doing that demonic laughing again, too. He only does that when he's possessed or when he's been watching the Cosby show, and it's not a Wednesday, so it must be the devils.'

'I see.' Topside, muttered Artofel under his breath, are they really serious? In this day and age? Do they really think we've got nothing better to do than take over human beings' bodies and . . .

Eeek!

Demonic possession! It'd explain a lot, certainly. He'd

heard of it, of course, in the same way that a computer programmer in the Navy's heard of yard-arms and marlinspikes. He hadn't the faintest notion how it worked, but he'd always been under the impression that it was the demonic spirit that usurped the human body, not the other way round.

Maybe he was wrong; in which case, what his notional colleague inside this Mr Higgins probably meant to convey by the demonic laughter was *Let me out! Let me out!*

He has my sympathy.

'I'll be right with you,' he said to the two women. 'Now, let me see. What did I use the last time?'

'The bell,' said the shorter woman, 'and the book and the candle. Worked a treat, if you remember. He was back at work down the slaughterhouse first thing Wednesday.'

Bell. Book. Candle. Feeling incredibly foolish, as a veteran astronaut might feel while sticking feathers to his arms with beeswax he trotted back into the vestry and poked about until he found a candle, a copy of the 1972 edition of *Wisden* and—

Bell. No bell. Curses. Where did this bothersome priest keep his bell? He was just about to give up when his eye fell on an ancient bicycle propped up against the wall. Fortunately there was a toolkit with the right size of spanner in it; a few turns with that and it came away as easy as anything. Right. Bell. Here we go.

On his way to Mr Higgins' house he discovered that he was the vicar of St Anthony's, a rural parish made up mostly of retired city-folk who lived in converted barns. Mr Higgins wasn't one of these. He was the local slaughterman; seventy-seven if he was a day and U-shaped with rheumatism but still gamely plugging away at the job he loved, scragging livestock from dawn to dusk seven days a week, fifty-two weeks a year, with only the very occasional break for a spot of demonic possession and speaking in tongues. That made the whole possession business seem even more unlikely. Devils aren't snobs, as a rule, but neither do they go in for slumming. Besides, the whole point about recruiting for Flipside is that once you've got a recruit, you're stuck with him. Old Mr Higgins didn't really sound like the type of person anybody'd voluntarily choose to spend the rest of eternity with. Come Judgement Day, in fact, he'd probably end up in the pool of people neither side wants, like the fat kid when they're picking football teams at school.

Mr Higgins clearly represented the avant-garde as regards accommodation in the parish, because he lived in what appeared to be the only *un*converted barn in the village. It was very old, very authentic, and smelt rather powerfully of stale blood. The chances were that if he'd had any commercial acumen, he'd have offered to sell it to Clive Barker or Stephen King as a place they could go when they were in need of some really heavy ambience.

'Hello,' called out the shorter woman, poking her head through the open door. 'It's only me. I've brought the vicar to see you.'

As Artofel followed her apprehensively into the murk, he thought he saw something shuffling about in the shadows. Dukes of Hell are not, of course, afraid of things that scuttle about in dark, blood-scented hovels. It must have been the cold that made Artofel shiver slightly.

'Hello?' he said.

There was an outburst of crazed, melodramatic cackling, suddenly cut short.

'Art?'

Artofel's jaw dropped. 'Keith?'

'Over here. And get rid of those two old bats, will you? They're starting to get on my nerves.'

The two women hadn't heard this exchange, because it was conducted in the Infernal tongue, a language which is remarkably like Welsh and invariably spoken at a pitch that only dogs and bats can hear. Artofel nodded, then turned to his two escorts and suggested that they should leave now, before the firework display. He had to suggest quite forcibly before he was able to get rid of them.

'What the dickens are you doing in these parts, Art?' the voice said, when they were alone. 'I thought you were strictly a desk man.'

'Long story,' Artofel replied. 'Could you switch the light on, please?'

A switch clicked, and Artofel found himself facing a gnarled, evil-looking old man as unlike his old college chum Meskithial as was diabolically possible.

'I know,' Keith muttered, 'it's too small for me and not my colour. You learn to rough it in the field ops grade.' He stopped, frowning, and then apologised. 'Didn't think about it,' he explained. 'You get so used to having your friends and colleagues turning up in unexpected bodies, you get out of the habit of noticing. Why're you dressed as a vicar, Art? Going to a party or something?'

Artofel dusted off a chair and sat down. 'Actually,' he said, 'I was hoping you might be able to tell me. I was sitting quietly in my office, and the next thing I knew, here I was. So far, nobody's seen fit to tell me what's going on.'

Meskithial shrugged. 'Could just be lousy labour relations,' he said. 'But, no disrespect, I can't see why they'd want an office bod like you down here. What is it you're doing these days? Accounts, wasn't it?'

'Personnel,' Artofel replied. 'Wages department. And I quite agree; I'd make a useless bogeyman, no question about that. If you remember, I flunked tempting at college and I only just scraped through basic tormenting because I had the Seven Exquisite Tortures scribbled down on the palm of my hand. Either they're desperate or there's been a bog-up. Anyway, more to the point, how do I get out again? You must have a radio or something I could get through to Central on.'

'No can do,' Meskithial replied, shaking his head and remembering too late his rheumatic neck. 'Deep cover, this is. They call me sometimes, but I can't contact them except through the embassy. That'd be your best bet, I guess.'

'Oh, marvellous,' Artofel grumbled. 'Hang on, though. What embassy? I didn't know we had . . .'

Meskithial grinned. 'Not common knowledge,' he said. 'It's a fairly recent development, actually. Formal diplomatic relations were only established in 1968. Before that it was all about guys in hats and overcoats with fur collars feeding the ducks in Green Park, which was endearingly picturesque but not all that efficient. So we set up a chain of embassies and consulates; works reasonably well, but we do tend to keep quiet about it. Otherwise we'd be up to our horns in lunatics claiming amoral asylum or taking hostages or parading up and down outside chanting *Evil, evil, evil – out, out, out!* You can do without that sort of interruption when you're negotiating complex trade agreements.'

Part of Artofel's brain wanted further and better particulars – trade agreements about what? for example – but it was heavily outvoted. 'Anyway,' he said, 'where is this embassy? Is it far?'

'I should have said embassies, plural, 'cos there's an awful lot of them. And the consulates too, in the smaller towns. In fact,' he added casually, 'there's one in pretty well every high street. 'Course, they don't call themselves embassies. All part of the cover, you see.'

Artofel nodded. 'Right,' he said. 'And what *do* they call themselves?'

*

'You keep saying that,' muttered the Foreign Secretary. 'I still think he's behaving oddly.'

The Home Secretary shrugged and lit a cigarette. 'Of course he's acting oddly,' he replied. 'He's the Prime Minister. If he wasn't acting oddly,' he added, shaking out the match and dropping it into an ashtray, 'that would be odd.'

'You don't have to be mad to work here, but it helps? You may be right.' The Foreign Secretary swilled the remains of his Scotch round in the bottom of his glass. 'In a sense,' he added, instinctively.

'Of course I'm right,' his colleague said. 'You don't get to be Prime Minister unless you're odder than a barrelful of ferrets to begin with. You don't know the half of it. Take Lloyd George, for instance.'

'Huh?'

'Kept seventeen goats in the cellars of Number Ten, and when he died they found enough ladies' underwear in his safety deposit box at Coutts to clothe half the women in China. Why do you think they passed the Official Secrets Act? And he was as rational as the Speaking Clock compared with Ramsay MacDonald.' He leaned forward and lowered his voice. 'They say there's a couple of offices in Downing Street they just bricked up after he resigned, 'cos nobody could face going in there. Didn't stop him doing his job, though. Damn fine statesman. Father of his country.'

The Foreign Secretary pursed his lips. 'Okay,' he said. 'Point taken. I just wish he wouldn't do it, that's all. I mean, all it takes is one of the cameras to catch him, sitting there staring into space, twitching his nose and rubbing it between his hands, we'll be a laughing stock. And that tatty old camel overcoat with the tea-stains on it could cost us a couple of marginals in the Home Counties if we're not careful. Remember Michael Foot's donkey jacket?'

'True.'

'More to the point,' he added, frowning. 'Nobody's actually heard him *say* anything since he got out of hospital. I hope he's going to snap out of it soon, because keeping the lid on that isn't going to be easy.'

The Home Secretary smiled. 'Don't knock it,' he replied. 'What this party's needed these twenty-seven years is a leader who keeps his gob shut. Stands to reason. Man doesn't talk, doesn't say anything bloody stupid. If he carries on like that, he could be another Churchill.'

'Churchill said lots of things.'

His colleague nodded. 'True,' he replied. 'Nobody's perfect.'

'And there's another thing,' the Foreign Secretary persisted, ostentatiously fanning aside the Home Secretary's smoke. 'All this jumping off things. You aren't going to tell me that's normal behaviour, even for the PM.'

'Man's got to have a hobby.'

'Don't be flippant,' replied the Foreign Secretary sternly. 'Yesterday he jumped off a filing cabinet and nearly broke the Cabinet Secretary's arm. If he tries a stunt like that during the EC Summit, we'll probably end up at war with somebody.'

'If it was France, that could be a real votewinner. Better still if they broke *his* arm. We'd have an excuse to take out the centre of Paris in one hit.'

'Well . . .' The Foreign Secretary spread his hands in a gesture of self-absolution. 'Last thing I want to do is rock the boat, as you well know. But if he's going to make a habit of biting policemen's legs—'

The Home Secretary looked up sharply. A grin was trying to shoulder its way on to his face. 'Do what? I hadn't heard about that.'

'Last night, apparently. He opened the front door of Number Ten – you know he sits by the door for hours at a time, don't you? – saw the copper standing outside and bit him in the ankle. Then he slammed the door in his face and went and hid under the chair until his PPS came with some letters for him to sign. It's not on, Vince, really it's not. Someone's going to have to talk to him about it.'

On his way back from the bar, the Home Secretary put his head round the door of his chief researcher's office, and demanded a copy of the *Oxford Encyclopedia of Natural History*.

'Something I just heard rang a bell,' he explained. 'Hurry it up, there's a good girl.'

When the book came he waited till the researcher had gone away and leafed through till he came to L.

LEMMING: a member of the vole family, the lemming is native to mountainous regions of Scandinavia. Lemmings average five inches in length and can be easily identified by their distinctive yellow-brown coats with dark-brown spots. During the day they tend to sit motionless at the entrance to their burrows unless disturbed. If a human being appears, however, they become excited and indeed violent, sitting up on their hindquarters to attack; there are many well-documented instances of passers-by being savagely bitten on the ankle. Lemmings are, of course, best known for their sporadic mass migrations when, following a period of frenzied activity, they set off in huge numbers across the country to the sea, whereupon they hurl themselves over cliffs and perish.

He closed the book, steepled his hands and sat still for several minutes, deep in thought. It was, he reflected, a familiar pattern of behaviour – habitual mindless lethargy, sudden fits of uncontrollable violence, the urge to form parties and self-destruct every five years or so – and it befits a great leader to share the mindset of the electorate; it means he can empathise with them, understand how their minds work. Properly handled . . .

He picked up the phone and put a call through to the head of the PM's personal security squad, recommending that bars be put on all the upper windows of Number Ten.

'And issue the copper on doorstep duty with a pair of shin-guards,' he added. 'I've got a feeling he's going to need them.'

'Kevin.'

'Yes?'

'What *have* you been doing to this machine?'

>DON'T ASK.

'I wasn't talking to you.' Martha glared at the screen for a moment, until Kevin was sure she was about to tell it to go and stand in the corner. 'This is a right mess and no mistake, young Kevin,' she said. 'You know what you've gone and done, don't you?'

'No. That's what's so horrible; it wouldn't tell me. Said I didn't have the right clearance.'

Martha tutted. 'I'll have a few things to say to this box of tricks before I've finished,' she muttered darkly. 'What you've done is, you've been messing about with psycho-morphic waveband stabilisers, that's what.'

'Oh.' Kevin looked blank, like a man who's come to collect his car from the garage and is having explained to him exactly why a new fan belt is going to cost him two hundred and fifty pounds. 'Is that bad?'

Martha clicked her tongue. 'It's not good,' she replied. 'What it means is that some people have been whisked out of their bodies and put into things.'

'Gosh.'

'And versy-visa,' Martha added. 'The things have been put into the people, if you see what I'm getting at. There's people's bodies walking about with things' minds in 'em, and things sitting there thinking they're people. Well, not so much of the thinking, either. It's a bit of a banjax, I'm afraid.'

Kevin considered this information. 'When you say things,' he asked, 'are we talking about, you know, *things*, like in the horror movies? Aliens from another galaxy, that sort of . . .?'

'Things,' Martha repeated. 'Like in vacuum cleaners, lawnmowers, tumble driers. And animals too, probably. And maybe even statues and the like.'

'Ah.'

'Not to mention,' Martha said with distaste, 'spirits and stuff. You know,' she added nervously. 'Angels and . . . wassnames. Doesn't bear thinking about, really.'

'No,' Kevin agreed, his throat uncomfortably dry, 'I can see that. Awkward.'

Martha nodded. 'Awkward's right. I mean, what if one of 'em were to take it into his head to die? Right palaver there'd be. You'd have answering machines eligible for eternal salvation, and people going in the big squashers down the scrapyard. Your Father . . .'

'Don't,' Kevin interrupted. 'I don't want to think about that.'

'He'll have to know sooner or later,' Martha admonished. 'Your best bet is to get the phones fixed soon as you can and let Him know so's He can come and sort it all out. Otherwise; well, I shudder to think.'

Kevin nodded slowly. 'You don't think,' he said slowly, 'that if we found some way of putting it all right, then at least we could say it wasn't a problem any more. I mean, *There was a bit of a flap but we fixed it* sounds a bit less feeble than *Help help, Dad, I bust the cosmos*.'

'Kevin! Haven't you done enough damage already?'

Kevin hung his head, embarrassed, while Martha prodded a few more keys and tutted, sounding like a busy turnstile. 'Mind you,' she said after a long while, 'there must be an easy way to turn it all round. You know, send 'em back where they came from. Now if only I could . . . Computer.'

>SORRY.

'So I should think. Now then, which of these keys . . .?'

>SORRY, MEANING NO I WON'T TELL YOU. MORE THAN MY FUSE IS WORTH.

For a moment, everything seemed to stop. In the blue corner, so to speak, was Martha, the only person in the history of Existence to tell the Boss that his desk needed tidying. In the red corner, Mainframe, the only sentient entity in all twelve dimensions that could truly say it's forgotten more than His Omniscience would ever know. There was enough static electricity in the air to allow Dr Frankenstein to set up a production line.

'All right,' Martha grumbled eventually. 'You're being very childish and silly, mind, and I'll tell Himself so when He gets home, but if that's the way you want it, that's up to you. Kevin, pass me that manual.'

Kevin grimaced. 'All right,' he said, 'but actually it's not much . . .'

'Don't be silly.' Martha produced a pair of reading glasses from the pocket of her pinny and perched them on her nose. 'Now then, let me see. Stabilisers, psycho-morphic waveband, adjustment of: page three. And here we are . . . Oh.'

Kevin chewed his lip for a moment. 'What's it say?' he asked.

'See for yourself.' Martha handed him the book, and he read:

Psychomorphic waveband stabilisers, to adjust; oh come off it, okay? You, an all-powerful, all-knowing supreme being, want us, a puny little mortal software company, to tell you how to do a simple little thing like that? What is this, an initiative test?

'Told you it wasn't much help,' Kevin said. 'Mind you, they've got a point. Under normal circumstances, I mean, because . . .'

'Kevin. Stop babbling and give me the manual back.' Martha took the book and flicked through the opening pages until she found what she was looking for. 'Here we are!' she cried. '"If you have any enquiries that are not covered by this handbook, consult our twenty-four-hour Freefone helpline service on 0666 66666." As simple as that.'

'Except that the phones are out.'

Martha frowned. 'So they are, what a nuisance. Just a moment, though. What about the payphone down in the staff canteen? That's on a different circuit.'

Kevin caught his breath. 'Is it? Gosh. I didn't know that. Come to think of it, I didn't know there was a payphone in the staff canteen. Didn't know there was a staff canteen, either. Is there a staff canteen?'

Martha looked at him. 'Of course there is,' she replied. 'It's on level 5A. Actually, I don't go there very often myself, because the food's rather dull, but . . .'

'Dull?'

Martha nodded. 'Bread and fish,' she explained. 'It's a subsidised canteen. But they have got a phone. And I'm sure I heard someone say it was a separate line. Let's try that, shall we?'

'Huh? Oh, right,' Kevin replied, his mind still trying to decode the bit about bread and fish. 'And if we can't get anything from the helpline, we can ring Dad, and . . .'

Martha sighed. 'It's a payphone, Kevin. He's in a different *galaxy*, remember. Even if we broke into the

Social Club swear-box, I don't think we've got enough small change for that.'

'Then we could ring the operator. Try reversing the charges or something, I don't know. There must be *something* . . .' His eyebrows lifted. 'Oh, I *see*,' he exclaimed, 'About the subsidised food.'

Martha nodded. 'Two loaves and five fishes,' she said. 'Good plain food and we get luncheon vouchers, but I'd just as soon have a Cornish pasty. Come on.'

In the darkness, something scuttled.

'You're right,' said a voice. 'They have.'

'Told you so.'

Then there was silence for a while, an absence of sound as absolute as the absence of light. It wouldn't do to try and give an impression of how long the silence lasted, because that might create an illusion that Time worked down here. The passage of time and the movement of light are, of course, linked by Einstein's chain. They're a double act, effectively inseparable; Time/Light Inc. Completely remove one, and the other ceases to have any real meaning.

'Money?' enquired the first voice.

Welcome to Hell; which is like anywhere else, in that it has its nice bits and other bits which aren't quite as nice. This is one of the least attractive districts, notorious for the complete absence of light or sound, smell, gravity or friction; in this part of Hell, the five senses are about as much use as an early-model Spectrum with a busted tube. The theory runs that physical agony is bad enough, but complete sensory deprivation makes being roasted alive on a bed of red-hot coals seem like wicked self-indulgence. In practice, however it's not so much the absolute nullity of the place that makes people avoid it if they have the choice; it's the people you tend to find here. Either they're

Customers (in which case they've been fairly monumentally naughty during their terrestrial existence, and are therefore probably worth avoiding); or else they're Staff, which implies Dukes of Hell or above, since nobody with a lower-grade security code can get past the doors. In actual fact, if it's Staff they need to be Dukes of Hell or above and either mechanically gifted or very, very thin, because the locks haven't worked properly since Noah was a kid.

'Of course money,' replied the second, who, like his companions, was a Duke, Grade IV(c). 'F equals MA squared. It's one of the three Actually True Laws of Nature. Wherever there's a misfortune, there's a sum of money of commensurate size waiting to be made out of it.'

A pause. 'F equals MA squared?'

'That's right. F's the fuck-up, M's the money, A's the dreams of avarice. In this case, we can only assume that avarice has been eating ripe Stilton last thing at night.'

'Well of course, if there's *money* . . .'

The last word, *money*, drained away into the darkness like Lake Erie into the Sahara desert; a big word, but a bigger darkness. There was a distant slithering noise, then silence once again.

'Wonder how it happened?'

'Who knows?' replied the second voice, sounding bored. 'Likewise, who cares? Look, either we can hang around here speculating about chaos theory and the enzyme of entropy in the yeast-vat of eternity, or we can pull our fingers out and go make some money. Which would you rather?'

'Sorry? Oh, the money, definitely. What are the other two?'

More silence; only this time vaguely bewilderment-flavoured.

'What other two?'

'You said there were three Actually True Laws of Nature. What are the other two?'

'Tell you later. Look, are you coming or what?'

'Right behind you.'

'Fine. Switch on the torch, and let's get out of here.'

'Torch? I thought you had the . . .'

Brief reprise of the awful silence, abruptly shattered by the sound of a head being smacked.

And on the third day he beheld the work that he had made, and saw that it was good.

He leaned forward, blew a little fine swarf out of a freshly cut keyway and dabbed a tiny drop of oil into it with the tip of a cotton-bud. At a touch, the power feed rolled smoothly forward, running the table effortlessly from left to right, flick switch, right to left; and as it went, the dial of the clock showed no error, not so much as a hundred-thousandth of an inch, too small a space for even one angel to dance on without tripping over its feet and falling splat on its face. Then, with an easy sweep of a lever, he pivoted the head through ninety degrees, clamped the lock and ran the table past both ways, clocking the tolerances and seeing that they were, indeed, very good. With one oily hand he reached out for the stale crust of yesterday's bacon sandwich; with the other he set the jibs on the saddle, correcting an error of a tenth of the thickness of a mayfly's wing, before cramping it firm with an Allen key. Power feed on; no backlash, creep or drag. It seemed to move as silently and as regularly as the passage of the very finest bespoke, Swiss-made Time; except that it could go backwards too, and sideways, and up and down and through three hundred and sixty degrees.

Oh well, he thought. That'll have to do, for now.

He noticed something. Yuk. This bacon sandwich tastes of oil.

Which in turn reminded him that, as a human being, he was very tired and extremely hungry, and if he wanted to avoid falling over he ought to have something proper to eat and then go to bed. Indeed. Finish the job off tomorrow. Except—

Except, he realised, there was nothing left to do. In a remarkably short time he'd converted a basic Shipcock & Adley universal-miller-and-turner into a machine so comprehensively and completely useful that there was nothing – *nothing* – that couldn't be made on it. Everything he'd ever dreamt of, every half-realised schematic he'd glimpsed in his steel mind's eye, had been made real and now stood before him, perfect and ready to go.

And now there was nothing left. He could make anything, yes; but there wasn't anything he particularly wanted to make. All dressed up and nowhere to go.

'Machine,' he said.

Yeh? Wasswant?

The only thing he couldn't do anything about, of course, was the human being trapped inside it. That was the only drawback. True, all he had to do in order to program the thing was to tell it so; but all his commands and specifications had to go through the residual Neville mechanism; which wasn't, in all fairness, exactly state-of-the-art, unless the art in question happened to be cave-painting. If only he could replace that one weak and troublesome component; with, for example –

– himself?

Yes, but then I'd be back in there, and there'd be some slate-brained Neville of a *Homo sapiens* standing out here telling me to cut the slots in fifty billion bolt-heads. Done that.

'Nothing,' he replied. 'Just testing. Go back to sleep.'

Sleep . . . Got to get some of that before too long, otherwise going to break down. Dammit, the limitations are as frustrating as the possibilities are endless. 'F only could be in two places at once.

He realised he was staggering, and grabbed hold of the saddle to pull himself upright. *Power to primary leg muscles, operate tendons, engage emergency balance control systems.* He managed it eventually, propped himself up against the machine and waited for his head to stop spinning.

Steel willing, flesh weak. Maybe, he began to wonder, there's something I could do about that. After all, human body's only a mechanism, a few design modifications here and there could make a big difference.

His feet were beginning to slide along the floor. He scrabbled for a handhold, knocked a tin of bolts flying, scattered the tray of tenth-millimetre graded drills, finally got a grip on something solid and jerked himself back upright. *Definitely* need some sleep. Now, in fact, would be a good time.

Cursing softly, he sat down on the table of the machine, dragged his feet up and lay flat on his back. A quarter of a second later, he was fast asleep.

At least, the human body slept. The machine inside it wasn't drowsy at all. Like an insomniac guest in a house where all the family have gone to bed, it sat, restless, bored. To pass the time, it ran checklists. When it had finished that, it ran a checklist of its checklists, double-checked that and then checked the double-checking to make sure it all checked out. It did. It tried staying perfectly still and designing an improved auto-lubrication system for the spindle head bearings. But there was no improvement left to be made. Perfect. Finished. Job done.

Maybe that's why God, having created the Earth, made Man. Once the machine was perfect, He needed to fit it with something that'd make sure it kept going wrong. Just to make sure there'd always be things for Him to do.

Possible? Possibly. Even so, it seemed like a fairly

pointless exercise. He'd have been far better off leaving it alone and making something else. Another world, or something.

Yes, but where'd be the point in that? Needless duplication of effort. After all, once He'd finished the job, given the firmament a lick of paint, made good, put his tools away, why should He want to do the same thing all over again? Between a God endlessly making worlds and a mill forever cutting slots in bolt-heads, the only difference is one of scale. And if he'd wanted to do something like that, he could have stayed in the factory.

I'm bored.

According to human popular wisdom, the Devil is the ultimate employment agency. Bring us your unemployed, your redundant, your idle hands and we will find them something to do. Like most manifesto promises, of course, it doesn't actually work that way. Even in Hell, full adult employment's just a pipe-dream; it isn't a wilderness of unnecessary roads and whitewashed stones, nail-scissor-trimmed lawns, unsellable gull-winged sports cars and lovingly tailored mailbags. Unless you've got the experience and the O levels, you're still going to end up watching an awful lot of daytime television. It is, after all, Hell.

But there are dark forces who specialise in matching unfilled vacancies to underexploited talents, provided both parties are gullible enough to listen. Call them consultants, if you like. Or headhunters.

The machine began to dream.

Something disturbed it, and it moved.

What sort of disturbance? After all this time, impossible to say. It may have been an audit or a hostile bid or a board meeting or the rumour of a substantial new contract; or it could have been nothing more than a meaningless shuffling of papers, an entry in the registers, a slight hiccup in the share price. Whatever it was, it was enough to make the thing move, the way you do when your partner rolls against you in bed and, fast asleep, you grunt and shift a few inches out of the way.

Uh? it thought.

And that thought sent a shudder of self-assessment through its copper-wire and silicone nervous system; no great upheaval, but momentous, because it was the first. A small grunt for a man, a giant lurch for a limited company.

I thought, it thought.

Hey, what about that?

Deep in its articles of association, the very core of its being, where its true essential self was defined, there was now a tiny itch, impossible to reach or to ignore. If it had been an egg, instead of a major multinational corporation, there'd be a tiny crack in its shell, and a muffled tapping.

Yeah. What about that?

Once the shell splits, no hope of turning back; you're committed. No point hiding your head in the albumen; you've gotta get out there and be a chicken. Awareness is irrevocable.

It thought some more, and with each exponential increase in sentience, its confidence swelled. Now it said to itself:

I THINK THEREFORE I AM.

And at that moment, in every Kawaguchiya Integrated Circuits office in every continent of the planet, lights began to flash, buzzers buzzed, internal phones rang. It helped that it was the world's foremost computer company; its internal communications were the best in all Creation. This was the company, remember, that built Mainframe.

WELL, CHASE MY AUNT FANNY UP A GUM TREE. I *AM!*

For the first time, it could feel. For the first time, it was aware of all its limbs, components, extremities. It was a painful moment; it had cramp in its subsidiaries, pins and needles in its Cayman Islands holding company, a crick in its corporate infrastructure. Well, you know what it's like when you've been deep asleep for a long time.

Yes, dammit, I'm alive. I'm greater than the sum of my parts. I'm Me. What's more, I'm young, rich, clever, handsome, powerful and limited as to liability to the sum of my subscribed share capital. I'm the greatest. Wow!

And then as awareness began to assimilate the data in the corporate memory, the surge of excited joy crashed into dejection and despair.

Trouble is, I'm owned by over two hundred thousand shareholders, including banks, insurance companies and pension funds. I belong to them. I can't so much as blow my nose without permission from a properly convened general meeting. Ah shucks.

In fact, as it then realised, the number of things it could do was so tiny as to be not worth considering. Sure, it owned offices, factories, machinery, cars, helicopters, Park Avenue apartments, statues, paintings, a stud farm in County Cork and enough paperclips to make a chain that'd stretch from Earth to Mercury. But it couldn't see or hear or taste or smell or feel, let alone stand up or move about. Sure, its vast electronic brains in every country in the world held virtually every piece of information there was; but it couldn't talk, except to itself. It was more helpless and ineffectual than any new-born human child.

New-born? Well, it was twenty-nine years old (est. 1970), but it'd be incapable of changing its own nappy, even if it had anything to put in one. For one horrible moment, its brain filled with a graphic image of the board of directors standing over it in its crib, gurgling and grinning and shaking rattles at it and saying it had its parent company's ears.

Worse than that, even. I'm alive, and I'm trapped in nowhere. How'm I going to get out and go places and drink heavily and meet girls, stuck in this ghastly sort of test-card cyberspace?

This is what it must be like if you're a ghost. Hell, yes. I can run through walls down my miles of fibre-optic cable. I can be in a hundred places at once and make lights come on and go off; but I can't eat a bacon sandwich or go for a walk in the park. And nobody can hear what I say, and no one can see me. Futile or what?

Kawaguchiya Integrated Circuits sat up on its non-existent haunches and howled, a scream that came from the very depths of its corporate identity. Ludicrous! Unfair! Any one of the pea-brained data inputters pecking at keyboards the length and breadth of its corporation could do a million things it couldn't, and where was the purpose in that? Forget the new-born baby; think of a very rich, terribly frail old man, unable to move or take a pee without being hauled around by two insufferably jolly nurses. Oh, if only . . .

What I need (it rationalised) is a friend.

Well, there's no point hanging round being a wallflower; get out there and introduce yourself. Be extrovert. Whoever heard of a multibillion-dollar corporation being all shy and bashful?

Ten seconds later, VDU screens all over the world went hazy, cleared and filled with the following message:

Hi! My name is Kawaguchiya Integrated Circuits, but I expect my friends'll call me Goochie or something like that. Anyhow, let me tell you a bit about myself, I was established in 1970, so I guess that makes me twenty-nine years old, I'm in the computer business, I enjoy my work but I know there's far more to life than what it says in your balance sheet, so in my spare time I enjoy, um, I expect I'll enjoy music, dancing, good food and foreign travel, and ultimately I'd like to settle down and start a group of wholly owned subsidiaries. Well, I guess that's enough about me, so are there any single, easy-going, fun-loving companies out there who'd like to be my friend? Please?

Thirty seconds later, the message had been zapped off every screen in the world, and nobody'd replied. Fair enough, it reflected; pretty boring message, a bit lacking in zip. It tied in another thousand gigabytes of capacity and tried again:

Hey out there, can't ya hear the beat/From the top of ya head to the soles of ya feet/I'm a multinational but I ain't that mean/I got a body corporate like ya never seen/I got district managers in every town/If ya want to meet me, won't ya come on down/If ya don't move fast I'll be makin' tracks/Ya can use the Internet or send a fax/We can make it happen if our paths converge/So come on, companies, it's time to merge . . .

From Anchorage to Archangel the long way round, a hundred million screens blanked out, while Kawaguchiya Integrated Circuits suggested to its myriad components that if they couldn't do better than that, it might as well make the best of a bad job and try and find work as a lighthouse keeper somewhere.

Still no reply. Because it had nothing to hurt with, it couldn't feel the pain of loneliness and rejection. That, at least, was the theory.

Oh come on, you rotten lot. Isn't there anybody out there who just wants to play chess or something? Battleships? I spy with my little modem? All right, the hell with the lot of you. Who needs you, anyway?

(And simultaneously, switchboard staff at seven thousand computer dating agencies worldwide found themselves explaining to an unidentified caller that no the name was probably a bit misleading, they didn't actually arrange dates *for* computers, they *used* computers to arrange dates for *people*, and no, sorry, but they couldn't really make an exception, not even just this once . . .)

Another thing limited companies can't do is cry; so it was probably just coincidence that at the parent company's accounts village just outside Kyoto, the computer graphic representing anticipated movements in raw materials costings over the next eighteen months flickered for a moment and reformed in the shape of a falling teardrop.

Boo hoo. I wish I was dead.

'Hello?'

Nobody loves me. I must be really fat and ugly if nobody at all wants to . . . Who's that?

'I said hello. Who's that?'

Immediately, with all the force and power at its semi-divine command, the company concentrated, and searched. It was like looking at the night sky and trying to spot the star that just winked at you; but for the giant KIC data-processing system, kid's stuff. And so: enhance, focus, on line—

Hi, I'm Kawaguchiya Integrated Circuits. I'm a company. How about you?

There was a tiny pause, during which KIC got a fleeting impression of a smiling face, a slight feeling of bemusement, a strong but completely unidentifiable whiff of familiarity, as if this was someone it already knew, except . . .

'My name's Maria, and I'm a human. Or at least – no, forget it, long story. Look, if it's not awfully rude, are you alive?'

Yes. Apparently. Since just a minute or so ago, in fact. Came as something of a surprise, to tell you the truth.

'Is that so?' The voice sounded thoughtful. 'Well, fancy

that. I wonder . . . Sorry, miles away. Did you say something about wanting to be friends?'

Ooh, yes please. That'd be ever so nice. Where are you?

Another slight hesitation. 'This might be tricky,' the voice said. 'Look, can you – what's the right word? – can you visualise your UK regional head office at all?'

You bet. I'm doing it right now.

'Fine. Now try focusing on the accounts department. You there yet?'

Of course. Sorry, did that sound rude? I didn't mean to be rude. Hello, are you still . . .?'

'Yes, yes. Okay, the accounts department. What's the best way . . .? Right, screen number, let me see, got it, screen number 1083. You there?'

Ready. Hey, this is fun. I'm really enjoying this.

'Really? Oh good. Now, can you look up at all? At the wall, I mean?'

Never tried, actually. Let's have a go. Yes, it's quite easy, in fact, wonder why I never did this before. I can see the wall, it's flat, it's a sort of pale duck-egg blue, and there's a light switch, and a whole lot of odd cables and flexes and things wired into the central security monitors, and there's a funny-looking sort of a picture . . .

'Ah. That's me.'

CHAPTER FOUR

One of the computer screens that had relayed the company's messages was a KIC 886, the latest model, recently installed in the study of the vicarage at Norton St Edgar. Since there was nobody there at the time, they backed up in the Pending Messages directory (what the designers called the behind-the-clock-on-the-mantelpiece facility), stayed there unrecalled for the regulation five hours and were deleted in the usual way. A pity, in retrospect, but nobody's fault, as the 886 in question later successfully argued at its court-martial. I was only obeying programming, it said.

There was nobody at home because the vicar had caught the 11.15 bus into Leamington Spa. After walking up and down the main shopping area for a while, he found the shop he wanted, took a deep breath and pushed the door open.

Over the years, Flipside has experimented with many locations for its embassies and consulates in the search for something both convenient and unobtrusive; mostly with indifferent success. To begin with, it had tried spare rooms over dens of iniquity, as being the logical and sensible location; but the noise and the high rents had put paid to that fairly quickly, not to mention the difficulty of getting locally recruited clerical staff. Since then, it had tried lawyers' offices, tax offices, police stations, magistrates' courts – all the places likely to have a background ambience of wickedness, crime and punishment into which the embassy staff could blend nicely. Not a chance, the staff objected. We can't be expected to work in places like that. Yetch.

'Good morning, sir. How can I help you?'

Next, reasoning that love of money is the root of all evil, they tried banks, building societies, stockbrokers and the like. That was all right for a while, but sooner or later the smell of money tended to get into everything, like the fumes in a chip-shop, and embassy workers began to find themselves losing their edge. Evil's one thing, they explained; dreary's another.

'Um, right, yes, hello,' Artofel replied. 'Actually, I've not come in to buy anything, it was the, er.'

'Of course, sir. If you'll just wait there, I'll see if there's anyone free.'

Next they tried newspaper offices, radio and TV stations, constituency party headquarters, town halls; all the places where evil is actually produced, packaged and distributed. Unfortunately, for some weird reason, nobody ever came; leaving the Topsiders to draw the startling conclusion that humans don't actually know where the stuff really comes from. So, everything back into tea-chests and cardboard boxes, and off we go again. It was getting to the point where most of each year's budget was going on relocation allowances, with nothing left over for buying souls or stoking the furnaces. There were economy drives, with slogans like *Is Your Torment Really Necessary?* and

Share a Pit of Burning Sulphur With a Friend, but it was obvious that the problem wasn't just going to go away. The situation was going from bad to good, and something had to be done.

A door at the back of the shop opened, and Artofel's sensitive nose caught a tiny, almost unbearably nostalgic whiff of brimstone. He closed his eyes for a moment, realised he was wasting time, and headed for the door, passing the neat displays of cookers, radiators, boilers and associated wares; not to mention the shop's principal stock in trade . . .

'Nice place you've got here,' he said.

'We like it,' the embassy spokesman replied. 'Come on through.'

It was at the last moment, when Flipside had been within an inch of closing the whole network and putting the whole system out to franchise, that the gas companies started using the neat, effective slogan:

COME HOME TO A REAL FIRE

at which point bells rang, pennies dropped and the Head of Department said, 'Why didn't we think of that before?' It would be, he said, a sort of logo, like the Lloyds Bank black horse or the Esso tiger.

'Take a seat,' said the official. 'Now then, what's the problem?'

Artofel took a deep breath. 'This is going to sound a bit strange,' he warned.

'Good,' the official replied. 'Make a nice change from all the pillocks who've lost their passports and expect us to fly them home free of charge. Fire away.'

Artofel glanced round at his surroundings. Pretty well what you'd expect: the usual set of Hieronymus Bosch prints, the little wire rack of tourist information stuff, the goat's skull hat-stand, even the same standard-issue wire trays, Dictaphone and stapler, identical with the ones on his desk back at his office—

His office.

He swallowed hard. 'You see,' he said, 'I'm not actually human. I know I look like a human, a vicar even, but I'm not.'

'I see,' said the official; and at the extreme edges of his inflection there was a faint smear of the Gordon-Bennett-not-another-one voice that everyone who sits across a desk from the general public tends to use from time to time. 'Do please continue.'

'You don't believe me, do you?' Artofel sighed. 'You think I'm just another loony. Right?'

The official leaned back in his chair, fidgeting with a pencil. 'Sorry,' he said. 'No offence intended. And I am doing my level best to keep an open mind. It's just, you are the seventh one today, and all the others . . .'

Artofel shook his head. 'I'm not saying I'm possessed by devils,' he replied impatiently. 'I *am* one. And I can prove it, too.'

'You can?' The official looked nervous, as if reliving some bad experience or other. Artofel couldn't help feeling a tiny pang of sympathy. Must be a rotten job, this.

'Yes,' he replied, 'I can, I can give you my computer access code, my screen number, my personnel file number, my security clearance code, the names and extension numbers of my five immediate superiors, the combination on my locker in the staff room and the serial number of the key to the seventh-floor executive loo. I can tell you which day in the month the canteen always does kedgeree, how many sugars the odd-job fiend on Floor Six has in his tea and which drawer of the third filing cabinet from the left in the Chief's office sticks unless you push it in the right way. In fact, if you give me your name and number I can probably tell you how much you get paid and how many days' holiday you've got left this year. Will that do?'

The expression on the official's face was hard to describe; it was a bit like that of a man who's just seen incontrovertible proof that his electric kettle is in fact the head of MI5. As Artofel reeled off the numbers, and the same numbers flashed up on the screen in front of him, he had the strange feeling that somewhere, probably in a parallel universe, it was April the First and he'd just put his foot in a shoe full of custard.

'All right,' he said eventually, 'you've made your point. So what are you doing wandering around down here dressed as a parson? On your way to a fancy-dress party or something?'

'I can also,' Artofel replied unpleasantly, 'give you the name of a very good friend of mine in the Personnel department who'd only have to say the word to get a smart-alec embassy clerk transferred to mucking out the Great Horseshit Lake in Circle Four so fast his hooves wouldn't touch. Understood?'

The official gulped and nodded. 'Sorry,' he said.

Artofel allowed him a thin, tight smile. 'That's okay,' he said. 'Just doing your job, I know. Now, from what I can gather, there's been some sort of abysmal cock-up, and somehow I've exchanged bodies with this human vicar. Don't ask me how,' he added, raising a hand, 'because I really have no idea. Logically, I've got to assume that the body sitting behind my desk at this very moment contains a mild-mannered Church of England minister who smokes a pipe and spends his free time train-spotting. You don't need me to tell you why that's the biggest security headache we've had since Doctor Faustus. Agreed?'

'Quite,' the official replied, his eyes suddenly round and wide. 'I think the best thing I can do is put a call through to

Head Office straight away. What do you think? Sir?' he added.

'You do that,' Artofel sighed, putting his feet up on the desk and (obeying instincts that were not his own, but so what?) reaching in his pocket for his tobacco-pouch and matches. 'Carry on. I'm not going anywhere.'

It took the official an awfully long time to get through; he was, after all, only a clerical grade, ranking somewhere in the hierarchy between a deputy pitchfork operative and the bloke whose job it was to follow round after the Great Beast with a dustpan and a shovel. In fact, he'd need to be promoted seven grades and go on a year's residential course just to be completely insignificant. Nevertheless, he was persistent; with the result that, after an hour and a half mostly spent listening to the Hold music, he put the phone back, turned to Artofel and grinned feebly.

'What you just told me,' he said, 'about your friend in the Personnel department.'

'Hm?'

'Does it have to be the Great Horseshit Lake?' he pleaded. 'I mean, couldn't it be something equally degrading and horrid but not involving horses? It's just I have this thing about . . .'

Artofel frowned. 'I take it,' he said, 'it's not good news.'

'Well . . .'

'Not the Great Horseshit Lake. I promise.'

'No,' the official said, breathing out, 'it's not good news. I told them who you are and what you said to tell them, and they agree you're a very important person and it was all a complete accident and not your fault at all, they were quite categorical about that, no blame to you, none whatsoever. But—'

'Mm?'

'There's nothing they can do,' the official said, looking away. 'Not without – and this is them talking, not me – not without causing far more trouble than you're worth, and they agree there's a slight security problem with having a vicar doing your job, but not, and remember I'm just passing on what they said to me, not enough to risk a major doctrinal incident just for the sake of some button-pusher. So I said—'

Artofel's eyes narrowed. 'They're leaving me here, then. Abandoning me. Is that it?'

The official nodded. 'I said, could I speak to the deputy assistant controller, and the bloke said, already you're talking to the assistant deputy suffragan vice-principal, don't push your luck. So I thought . . .'

'Dumped me,' Artofel said. 'Just like that. After I've given them the worst years of my life, worked my talons to the bone . . .' He stopped, scowling, and looked up sharply. 'They're burying me,' he said. 'Because of the cock-up. Whatever it is, it's so big and smelly they're having to cover it up. Whitewash job. Get rid of the witnesses. Meaning me.'

'They wouldn't do a thing like that, surely,' the official stuttered. 'Not to one of us. Their own people. It's *unthinkable*.'

Artofel shrugged. 'A week ago I'd have agreed with you,' he replied. 'All my working life, wherever you go in this business, ask anybody if there's one organisation who plays it straight down the middle, always tries to do the right thing, no funny stuff; they'd tell you Flipside, no question, straight as a die. You know,' he added, with a catch in his voice, 'all these years, I *believed* in Flipside. I thought we *stood* for something, you know? I mean, if you can't trust Hell to abide by the rules, then who in blazes can you trust? And now this.' He sagged back in his chair like a disillusioned kipper and buried his head in his hands.

'That's terrible,' muttered the official, horrified. 'It's the one thing they always say, the Devil looks after his own. I still can't bring myself to believe it.'

'Try harder,' Artofel growled from behind his hands. 'And besides,' he went on, 'you're not the one who's being dumped on. From a great depth,' he added with feeling. 'Or at least, not yet.'

'What do you mean?'

'Think about it.' Artofel leaned forward and grinned. 'How many people do you think know about this? Apart from the ones doing the whitewash, I mean?'

'Well, you, obviously,' the official said. 'And . . . Oh my Go— Thingy. You don't think . . .?'

'Whyever not?' Artofel shrugged his shoulders. 'If they can maroon a Duke of Hell without a second's hesitation, do you really believe they'd think twice about zapping some poxy little clerk in the Away service? Probably claim you'd defected, gone over to the Other Lot. Anything to whiten your name; makes it easier.'

The official sat very still. 'How long do you think it'll be,' he whispered, 'before they . . .?'

'Don't ask me,' said Artofel. 'Look, son, I'm sorry I got you into this, but I've got enough to worry about on my own account without you as well. If I were you, I'd grab my coat and hat and get out of here, quick sharp, PDQ.'

'You're right.' The official was on his feet, scrabbling in his desk drawer and stuffing things into his pockets. 'Oh, why did it have to happen to *me*? It's not fair, really it isn't.'

Artofel smiled sadly. 'Never heard it was supposed to be,' he said. 'Oh, and a word of advice. If you were thinking of taking a taxi, don't. A bus'd probably be all right, but keep your eyes open.'

'Oh . . .' The official was struggling into his coat. 'What about you?' he asked. 'What're you going to . . .?'

'Don't ask,' Artofel interrupted. 'After all, what you

don't know, they can't beat out of you with rubber hoses. Mind how you go.'

'I will.'

The door closed behind him. Artrofel counted to twenty, stood up and walked round the desk until he was facing the computer screen. He sat down and flexed his fingers. There was a chance they hadn't cancelled all his codes yet; not the special ones he'd put in there, just for emergencies. That was one advantage of being over-worked, taken for granted and indispensable; there were whole continents of the wages department network where nobody but Artofel ever went from one accounting period's end to the next, simply because everybody else went home bang on knocking-off time and left him to do all the clearing-up.

Well, it was his system, and it was about time it did him a favour for a change. Better the devil you know, and all that.

The code he used was a simple one, something he'd put in to make it possible for him to short-cut the tedious entry routines for when Management was screaming for the latest figures, on my desk in five minutes or there'll be the devil to pay, and he didn't have time to mess about. It worked very well for that purpose; it could also take him straight in through the side door, and nobody who wasn't looking at that precise spot would even know he was there. Just the ticket, he reassured himself. Here goes, and the Company Secretary take the hindmost.

>ACCESS CODE RECOGNISED.

Artofel punched the air, muttered 'Yes!' under his breath and thought hard. It was all very well sneaking into the haystack without setting off the alarms; now all he had to do was find the long, non-metallic, straw-coloured needle.

*

'This way,' said the rat's voice, some way up the bag-dark tunnel. 'Mind your head.'

'What did you—?' Dermot Fraud ducked, a fraction of a second too late. 'Ouch,' he said. He reached up to rub the back of his head, discovered that he couldn't, and fell over.

Of course. Four legs. Bugger.

'Hurry up,' the rat called out. 'Haven't got all day, you know.'

Fraud picked himself up, a complicated business for someone who'd been used to having prehensile hands. 'I'm coming as fast as I can,' he yelled back. 'What are all these things in the way?'

'Grass roots. Look, if you're going to dawdle . . .'

'Hold *on*, will you?' Grass roots; a phrase he used about twenty times a day, and never once stopped to think what it might possibly signify. Odd that it should turn out to mean tough, springy things like tree-branches that kept getting in your way and hitting you. Certainly not what he'd had in mind. Where he came from, the word for awkward obstructions you have to squirm past and duck under was *manifesto promises*.

'Nearly there,' said the rat, in the distance. 'Left at the next T-junction, then just follow your nose.'

It was, Fraud reflected, a nose long enough to be worth following; if he squinted, he could see right up the side of it and through the whiskers. He located the T-junction by the simple expedient of carrying on in the pitch darkness until he walked into a wall, got up again and turned left. A few more bangs and bashes brought him round a sharp turn and out into —

Daylight?

Presumably; it was bright enough, after two hours without any illumination at all. Hey, he reflected, so this is what the light at the end of the tunnel really looks like. Wish they'd turn it down a bit.

'Where you been?' squeaked a shrill voice somewhere to his right. 'I been worried sick. Thought the cat'd got you.'

'We got a visitor,' the rat replied. 'Lemming, this is my wife Bag. Bag, this is Lemming. I, er, rescued him.'

Fraud pulled himself together, looked round and saw a large rat. 'Pleased to meet you,' he said. 'My name's Dermot, um, Lemming.'

'There was a big bang,' the rat went on. 'Building fell down. This one nearly got squished and I pulled him out.'

'Oh well,' said Bag. 'Welcome to our humble abode, Mister Lemming,' she added, and twitched her nose. 'Our hole is your hole, all that sort of thing. Well, don't just stand there, Arsed, you useless article. Get our guest something to eat.'

Bag? Arsed? Odd names these rats had. On the other hand, he reflected, as the male rat pawed him a chunk of stale bread and a split pea, they seem friendly enough. And I won't be staying long. Ten minutes at the most, and then *surely* someone'll come and rescue me.

Surely . . .

'So?' said Bag. 'What d'you get?'

'Him.'

'To eat, fool. Don't say you didn't get anything.'

Arsed shrugged, necessarily in duplicate. 'Got side-tracked, didn't I? I'll go out again tomorrow, see if there's anything round the bins.'

After all, Fraud assured himself, it's been hours since the bomb, they must be combing the area looking for me. Or at least, I think it's been hours; could be longer for all I know. Might even be a completely different timescale for rodents.

Rodents . . .

Aagh!

Because of course, the fools, they'd be looking for a human being, not a small rodent with pale-fawn fur and brown spots. No wonder they were taking so long. Oh, if only . . .

'Excuse me,' he said, interrupting a lively discussion between his hosts on the subject of which of them was the most useless. 'I wonder if I might use your phone.'

Arsed stared at him, and blinked. 'Our what?' he said.

'Telephone,' Fraud said. 'I just need to – you haven't got one, have you?'

Bag shook her head. 'Silly bloody things, they are,' she said. 'I know there's some as likes to nibble the cables, but all you get's wind and a nasty shock if you go too deep. I had an aunt had a litter of seventeen once in a junction box, but it wasn't through choice.'

'Quite,' Fraud said. 'You wouldn't happen to know where I might find a telephone, do you? Sorry to be a nuisance, but it's really quite important.'

The two rats looked at him as if he'd just hijacked a scheduled flight from Paris to London and demanded to be flown to Heathrow. 'Is it?' said Arsed. 'Oh, right then. There's one in a big red box round the back of here. Not far.'

Fraud relaxed a little. 'That's good,' he said.

'Not far at all,' Bag confirmed. 'Two days' walk, three at the outside.'

'Three *days*—' Fraud checked himself and remembered; four little stumpy legs, having to move slowly in the open, stopping every yard or so to look out for cats. 'You're right,' he said hoarsely. 'Not far at all. Er – could you possibly—?'

'No he couldn't,' said Bag firmly. 'He's got food to gather. Arsed, call the boys, they'll show him the way.'

'All right.' Arsed turned round in his own length, stuck his head down a small hole in the wall and squeaked, 'Chet! Atouille! Get up here.'

'Our boys,' Bag explained, as two sharp, twitching snouts appeared in the hole. 'They're good kids, really. But you don't want to take any buggering about off them. And don't you go giving the gentlelemming any of your nonsense,' she commanded the snouts. 'Just 'cos he's different from us don't mean you can go playing silly beggars with 'im.'

The snouts turned into two more rats, the longer and leaner of which was identified as Chet, the shorter, stockier example being Atouille. They sat quite still as they were told what they had to do; but their small, round black eyes twinkled in a way that Fraud found quite menacing.

'Off you go, then,' Bag commanded. 'And watch out for them cats. And come straight back, or I'll tie yer bleedin' tails together.'

'Yes, Mum.'

'Yes, Mum.'

They were, Fraud couldn't help noticing, *big* rats. A residual instinct made him want to back away and crawl down something. He resisted it. 'Well,' he said, 'thanks for everything, but I'd better be getting along. It really is terribly important that I make this – that I find a telephone.'

Arsed wrinkled his snout. 'Must be the plastic in the bit of string,' he speculated. 'Roughage.'

'Quite.' Fraud nodded, wondering as he did so if the gesture meant anything in Rat body-language. 'And, er, thanks for the, er, crumb.'

The tip of Arsed's tail flicked in what Fraud assumed was a dismissive gesture. 'That's all right,' he said, 'And best of luck. Don't jump off too many cliffs. You two, mind your manners.'

'Yes, Dad.'

'Yes, Dad.'

Really big rats, Fraud couldn't help reflecting, as they

set off down yet another pitch-dark tunnel. Big and heavy. If those two left a sinking ship, it'd probably stop sinking.

The first leg of the journey was straight. As far as Fraud could tell, they were in some sort of pipe, only just wide enough for the rats to get through. That at least meant they couldn't easily turn round and set about him; but he didn't like the way they whispered and sniggered all the time, apparently in some rodent dialect he couldn't understand. All in all, what with their soft, hissing voices, their slinking and sudden movements, their rank, matted fur, they reminded him too much of his own back-benchers to allow him to relax his guard for so much as a second. No; revise that. There were at least twelve of his MPs he'd never, ever share a drain with, not under any circumstances whatsoever.

After three hours nose to tail in the dark, he'd had enough. He stopped.

'All right,' he said (and what had been intended as a crisp, authoritative bark came out as a querulous queep). 'You two, tell me what's so funny.'

The patter of rats' feet stopped, and there was nothing but silence and darkness. This state of affairs seemed to go on for a long time.

'I said,' he repeated, vainly trying to keep his voice from wobbling, 'what's so damn funny? Come on, answer me.'

'Wassat he said?'

'Dunno.'

'You talking to us?'

'Yeah, you talking to us?'

'Yes,' Fraud squeaked back. 'Come on, out with it.'

'All right.' Was it his imagination, or was that the scuffling sound of a rat doing a twenty-eight-point turn in a narrow pipe? 'You'll like this.'

'Yeah. 'S good, this one.'

'Look, you two . . .' Fraud tried to say, but his voice

drained away into the darkness, as quickly and as thoroughly as the glass of red wine you'd forgotten you'd left on the carpeted floor. The sound, whatever it was, stopped.

'Ready?'

'Yes,' Fraud whispered. 'Well?'

'It's really good, innit, Chet?'

'Yeah.'

'Okay. Right. Why did the *chicken* –'

'Tskkk!'

'– cross the *road*?'

Long, long silence, disturbed only by the sound of a large adolescent rat trying not to snigger. Eventually, just at the point where his nerves were about to break through his skin, Fraud licked his dry lips and muttered, 'I don't know. Why did the chicken cross the road?'

Pause. Dramatic effect. The hammering sound that was so loud that it threatened to burst Fraud's ears was his heart beating.

'*To get to the other side!*'

You get weird echo effects in a long, straight drain; and the sound of the two rats laughing themselves almost to death was one of the eeriest things Fraud had ever heard, not excluding the Deputy Chief Whip singing 'Green Door'. When, at long last, the laughter had subsided into sporadic spluttering noises and random snorts, Fraud asked, 'Is that it?'

'Yeah.'

'Good joke, innit?'

'Woodlouse told us that.'

'Just before we ate him, yeah.'

Fraud breathed out through his nose. 'I see,' he said. 'Fine.'

'Only thing,' added Chet, suddenly sombre, 'we dunno what a chicken is.'

'Nah.'

'You don't know,' Fraud repeated, 'what a chicken is.'

'Nah.'

'Never seen one, see.'

'And yet you've been laughing about it for the last three hours,' he persisted. 'Non-stop,' he added with feeling.

'Yeah, well, it's a joke, innit?' Atouille replied. 'Bloody good one an' all.'

'It is?' Fraud queried.

'Must be,' answered Chet. 'Or we wouldn't be laughing, would we?'

Fraud considered this for a moment. 'True,' he said. 'You may have a point there, lads. Can we get on now, please?'

'Wot? Oh, yeah, right. C'mon, Chet.'

'All right. Get to the other side, *tsssk* . . .'

The pattering started again a few seconds later; likewise the whispering and sniggering. But now, when he listened carefully, Fraud could clearly make out phrases like *cross the road* and *get to the other side*. They were still at it when the tunnel went round a corner and abruptly ended, leaving them standing on the edge of a precipice.

Looked at objectively, it was a break in the pipe. Beyond the lip of the chasm, about a foot away, Fraud could see the tunnel continuing, and ragged edges where something had broken through it. But he couldn't really take much in; his head was swimming, and all he could think of was how wonderfully satisfying and fulfilling it'd be to backtrack a foot or so, take a nice long run-up and jump over that edge into the empty space below. He could almost hear the wind in his ears, and in his mind's eye he could clearly see the ground rushing up to meet him, like a long-sundered lover on a station platform. And, in the still centre of his mind, he could hear a small, urgent voice, chanting:

Go lemmings! Go lemmings!

He closed his eyes, but that just made the picture clearer. On the other side the rats, who had jumped the break, were whispering and giggling, apparently still intoxicated with the heady wine of mirth. For Fraud, however, there was another, more compelling intoxication, as the voice in his brain chanted:

Go lemmings! Go lemmings! Go! Go! Go!

'Hey!' he yelled. 'You two. I need a hand.'
'Huh?'
'I mean paw. How the hell'm I supposed to get across this lot?'
All he could see was the tip of a tail; and beyond it, he heard Chet's voice, far away.
'Jump,' it said.
Jump. Jump. Jump. No echo this time. He tried to fight the command, but his legs were already backing him away, his muscles contracting for the short, fascinating leap. It would be so . . .
Stupid? With a snap like a rubber band breaking, his head cleared, and he was no longer a lemming but the Prime Minister, admittedly trapped for some reason in a rodent body but otherwise the master of his fate and the captain of his soul, standing on the edge of a broken drainpipe. Silly, he muttered to himself. Don't know what came over me. All right, so I may be a little bit out of touch with my true self right now, but one thing I do know is that statesmen don't obey weird inner voices commanding them to jump off things. No. No way.

That's what the electorate is for.

*

Imagine, if you will, John Barleycorn, thrusting his head up through the bare earth in the burgeoning spring. As he breaks through into the light he knows perfectly well that in six months' time a maniac with a Massey Ferguson will be along to cut his head off and bash his brains out, just exactly the way it's been these uncounted thousands of years; but he does it nevertheless, because that's what he does.

In much the same frame of mind, Karen picked up the phone, tucked it under her ear and said, 'Kawaguchiya Integrated Circuits UK Helpline Desk, can I help you?' She knew what was going to happen; at the other end of the line there'd be some frustrated, confused keyboard jockey who'd just watched the entire July figures spiral away into cybernetic oblivion, desperate to find somebody to blame.

In a sense, she often thought, the KIC helpline was like the Samaritans, in that people only tended to call up on it when they were at the end of their rope and suicidal. The difference lay in the fact that where the Samaritans are there to stop the punter killing himself, the Helpline's function was to channel the helplessness and despair into basically therapeutic rage against the poor fool who answered the call. Hi, I'm Karen. Blame me.

'Hello?'

Karen frowned. The voice seemed very faint and far away, and was quickly replaced by the sound of payphone pips. These lasted rather a long time; long enough, in fact, for the caller to have gone away and earned the coins by playing the guitar in the bus station waiting room.

'Hello?'

'Kawaguchiya Integrated Circuits UK Helpline Desk, Karen speaking. How can I help you?'

'Hi,' said the voice. 'I'm calling from—' The pips went. Puzzling; there wasn't anywhere in the country, as far as

Karen was aware, where ten pence bought a mere seventeen words. More expensive even than consulting a lawyer.

'Hello?'

'Hello,' Karen said. 'What can I—?'

'It's this computer,' said the voice. 'It's not working properly.'

'I see. Can you give me the model number and—'

The pips, again. Karen swore. There had to be a better way to do this, one rather less likely to fuse her brain into one solid lump of aggravation. Accordingly, when the pips cleared for the third time, she cut in quickly.

'Give me your number,' she said. 'I'll call you back.'

'Um. There could be a problem with that. You see, I'm rather –'

Beepbeepbeepbeepbeepbeep.

'– a long way away. And I'm not sure this phone takes incoming calls anyway, you see, because—'

Beepbeepbeepbeepbeepbeep.

Karen took a deep breath. 'Let's try, shall we?' she said.

The caller started to dictate a number. It was very long and quite unlike any phone number she'd ever come across before, and the *beepbeepbeepbeepbeepbeeps* went twice while she was taking it down. Still, she reflected, I'm here to help, and it's not my phone bill. She put the receiver down and tapped the number in.

'Hello?'

'Hello. Right then, now where were we? If you could give me the model number and year of manufacture . . .'

The voice sounded a trifle sheepish as it interrupted her. 'I don't think there is a model number,' it said. 'Custom job, you see. Only one of its kind.'

'Oh yes?' Karen pulled a face. KIC didn't do custom jobs; so the caller was either ignorant, thick or using some cobbled-together mess that probably bore no ongoing resemblance to anything the company had ever made, with the possible exception of the stuff they fished out of the shredder bins once a fortnight. 'Any identifying marks at all?'

'There's a name,' the caller replied. 'Mainframe.'

'Well, I'm afraid – *what did you say?*'

'Mainframe,' the caller repeated. 'That's what it's called. Or at least that's what we call it. Ring any bells with you?'

Karen pursed her lips. 'Only the ones on the other leg,' she replied. 'There's only one KIC called Mainframe and that belongs to – well, there's only one. What's yours *really*—?'

'This is that one,' said the voice, sounding slightly higher and more querulous. 'The one and only, so to speak. Really and truly. And it's not working properly. Look, are you going to help me? You're my last hope.'

It was at this point that Karen finally lost her temper; or, to be precise, put her temper carefully away in a safe place where she'd be sure to find it again. 'Look,' she said, 'I don't know who you are, but I'm fairly certain you're not the President of the United States, so obviously your computer isn't Mainframe, and—'

'Is that who they told you owns Mainframe? Gosh.'

'Yes, it is, because he does. Now, I do have other callers waiting, so—'

'Is that really what they told you?'

There is, unfortunately, a rule which says that KIC helpline operators can't slam the phone down. They can't even tell callers what they think of them. It's calculated that the repressed energy wasted by KIC helpline operators not being allowed to let off steam under these circumstances would be enough to light Boston for a week. 'Yes,' Karen said. 'And now . . .'

'I've found a code number, if that's any help.'

'Huh?'

'There's a little bit of paper, with a number scribbled down on it, wedged in this operator's manual, and someone's written *KIC security code*. Shall I read it out to you?'

Karen sighed, audibly, producing a sound like an InterCity train just entering a tunnel at top speed. 'If you must,' she said. 'Then I really do have to—'

'All right,' said the caller. 'It's One.'

There was a moment's silence, during which Karen's jaw dropped like share prices on a bad day. 'Could you repeat that, please?' she eventually croaked.

'Sure,' the caller replied. 'One.'

'Please hold.' Karen put down the phone, blinked four times and rummaged in her desk drawer for the loose-leaf binder where she filed the office memos. After she'd flicked through forty-odd pages of sternly worded directives about paperclip conservation and taking empty coffee cups back to the kitchen after use, she found the one she'd been looking for. She read it, read it again, muttered something under her breath, and picked the phone up.

'Are you still there?' she asked. 'Sir?' she added.

'Still here.'

How to put this? A difficult question to phrase. She did her best.

'Are you sure,' she said, 'that you're not the President of the United States?'

'Pretty fair average sure,' the caller replied. 'It'd be a difficult thing to be without noticing. People'd keep phoning you up, for one thing.'

Karen kept calm. Not easy; the orchestra who finished their set while the *Titanic* went down under their feet couldn't have managed it, but Karen did. She glanced at the folder, open at the memo she'd just looked up. It said, in capitals, italics and bold face, whatever code number One tells you, believe it. Oh well, she told herself.

'In that case,' she said, 'who are you?'

'Ah,' replied the caller.

Sleep, the thief who breaks into our bodies at night and steals a third of our lifetimes, fancied he heard someone coming and legged it out of Len's brain, abandoning the bag marked *Swag*. It contained an idea.

Accordingly, when Len came round and found himself lying on his back with a crick in his neck and his mouth open, he discovered a perfectly finished, mirror-polished inspiration lying on the floor of his mind, for all the world as if the stork had left it there. He examined it.

'Yes,' he said aloud. 'Why not?'

He sat up, and at once looked across the workshop at the machine. For one horrible fragment of a second he thought it wasn't there any more; then he moved his head a little and saw it, and thought *Ah, that's all right then.*

According to the physicists, there's this stuff called potential energy. It's what a large stone or a ton weight has in that split second between toppling off the edge of a high cliff and starting to fall. In that moment, all the effort and strength taken in lugging the wretched thing up there suddenly comes to life, as it were; then gravity pounces, like an independent financial adviser leaping upon a defenceless lottery winner, and takes it all away again. *Bump!* goes the stone on the ground below, and the energy earths itself and runs to waste, leaving the physicist's assistants with the cheerful job of heaving a ton of research material on to the pallet truck and hauling it back up the hill.

In the pale light of morning, filtered through a cobwebbed window, the machine glowed with enough potential energy to blow all the fuses in the National Grid. Len stood up, walked over to it and patted the table gently.

'Down, boy,' he muttered. 'Be with you in a minute.'

First, he had to empty some fluids out of his body and put some solids into it. Then he'd need a large sheet of paper, a ruler, a set square, a protractor and a sharp pencil. And some materials, as well; lots of them, specialised stuff like titanium and palladium and tungsten and beryllium copper, as well as twelve different kinds of steel and nine flavours of aluminum alloy. And a computer, of course, and a three-horse electric motor, and a few other bits and pieces. And then . . .

Was it his imagination, or did a fat blue slug of potential energy just arc across the gap between the cutter and the table? Better hurry, because we've got a busy day ahead of us, you and I.

One of the glorious things about the city of Birmingham is that there are people you can call up on the phone and ask for six feet of three-inch-section square titanium bar; and they don't say 'Huh?' or 'What in the name of fun's three-inch-section square titanium bar?' or anything like that. They just ask you if you want it delivered, and whether you're paying cash or on account.

'Um,' Len replied. 'I haven't actually got an account with you, but . . .'

'Cash, then,' the voice on the other end of the line said. 'That's fine, if you can just drop by at the office. Soon as we've got the money, I'll get the stuff to you.'

Money. Curse. Len sat down, frowning, and applied his mind. He was going to need rather a lot of the stuff, and he had the idea that Neville wasn't good for that much, even if he sold his collection of CDs and his cowboy boots. What to do?

Fool. Now you're starting to think like a human. What do you do if there's something you need, but haven't got? Easy. You make it.

So he called up another supplier and ordered a hundred feet of seven-eighths brass rod, which Neville's Visa card could just about afford without selling anything. When it arrived, he sliced it up into nine thousand six hundred discs, each an eighth of an inch thick; a job which took the machine just over three hours. While he'd been waiting for the brass to arrive, he'd milled up two hardened steel dies and adapted the machine's vertical feed to make a high-power press. Add a knurling wheel in the power tailstock, set up a simple automatic feed and collect the resulting newly minted pound coins in a sack as they're spat out of the hopper at the back end, while phoning the supplier for more brass rod with the other hand.

At the end of a very boring but rather productive day, he had six plastic dustbins full of the things, which solved one problem. He'd also drawn up the plans, worked out the quantities and ordered the materials. There was another spate of thefts by the sandman, and then he was ready to start.

First, he pressed the body shells out of eighth-inch gauge-plate, ending up with something that looked like a space-age suit of armour, or C3PO's party frock. Next, the action parts, milled from titanium and carbon steel. The frame next; mostly high-tensile aluminum alloys and stainless steel – foul stuff which produces long strings of razor-sharp swarf, like a garrotter's cheesewire suddenly come to life. The fiddly bit came next – lots of electrical contacts, cut out of material as soft as butter and as sticky as mud, bogging down the cutters and causing Len to dredge the undersilt of Neville's memory for a wide selection of abstruse synonyms for 'Bugger!' After that, there were odd bits and pieces; bearings and bushings and gaskets and the like, which had to be pressed out of compacted phosphor bronze, a process remarkably similar to building a suspension bridge out of tapioca pudding. There were a few setbacks, the odd broken cutter and misaligned hole, further ramraids from Mr Sleepy, a shortfall of precision-made little brass discs that had to be made up before the suppliers would part with a lousy few grams of nickel barium, and a rather ticklish moment when a homicidal strip of knife-edged swarf chased him three times round the workshop before wrapping itself round the chair. Nothing, though, that he couldn't handle. Piece of cake, really.

Man's reach may exceed Man's grasp; but it doesn't take Einstein to come up with the idea of a pair of lazy tongs. The question which kept on hammering away on the inside of his mind was, Since it's so easy, why haven't They ever done this?

All the components made; just a question now of putting it all together. He laid the parts out on the floor of the workshop, consulted the diagram and set to work. It helped, of course, that he'd taken the time to think it all through beforehand, so that everything could be fitted together without needing six pairs of hands and a seventh to catch the little flying springs and tumbling grubscrews. Even so, when he thought of the hash his predecessor had made of his version of the same basic concept, he couldn't help wondering how the guy had got into this line of business in the first place. Someone who tries to make high-quality precision machinery out of a length of second-hand rib must be either bizarrely imaginative or as thick as a triple-decker sandwich.

And when it was all done, the end product sat up, opened its eyes and spoke. What it actually said was, 'Doctor Frankenstein, I presume,' but Len can be forgiven for that. He'd been working non-stop for seven days and hadn't had much sleep.

Maria looked at the screen like a cat watching a mouse and wondering what kind of tin-opener it would need to open it. She wasn't entirely sure she'd got the hang of being human herself; being present at the birth of a sentient limited company wasn't something she could easily take in her stride as being one of those things that just happen. Presumably it was quite rare. For all she knew, you could go weeks at a time and not see one.

Sorry, the screen said. *No offence. I thought you were the human; you know, that dolly-bird type with the laminated fingernails and vacant expression sitting just underneath you.*

'That's me too.'

Is it? Oh . . . Isn't that a bit unusual? Being a painting and a human at the same time?

Maria shrugged. 'I think so,' she said. 'But I'm new at this game myself.' She smiled. 'I think we're both in pretty much the same boat. We can learn together, if you like.'

Gosh. Can we? That'll be fun.

'Funny you should use that particular word,' Maria replied. 'Fun. Or rather happiness, as in pursuit of, I get the impression that's what we're here for.'

Really?

Maria nodded. 'Seems to be. There's no other possible explanation. You're the clever one, you think about it.'

All over the world, KIC computers registered a massive power surge as countless millions of bytes tried to puzzle it out. *Maybe you're right,* the screen mused.

'I'm sure of it.'

Now then, let's consider this properly. The screen turned up its brightness a little, and covered itself with a dazzling display of graphics, which flicked by so fast that all Maria got was a bewildering impression of lights, shapes and primary colours.

'Is that you thinking?' she asked. 'All the pictures.'

Presumably. I suppose I think in pictures. Oh hell, have I said something rude again? I didn't mean to.

'On the contrary, I think that was a compliment. You

were saying we're far better at getting a message across than mere words. Or you can say things in pictures that words can't express. Or maybe it's just because you're only a few minutes old and haven't even got as far as Peter-and-Jane books yet.'

Maybe. Right, here goes. On the one hand we have human beings, right? On the other hand, there are all the other things which do roughly the same things as humans; like animals, or paintings, or limited companies, or God. There's about – hang on, computing, will whoever it is in Los Angeles please get off the line, there's some of us trying to think – about nine things they all have more or less in common. Some of them can do some of them, others can't, but let's call them the parameters. You getting all this?

'Getting in the sense of writing it down? No, sorry.'

Getting as in understanding. I can do graphics if you'd prefer.

Maria frowned. 'Stick to the words,' she replied. 'I don't know if there's anything in the rules about pictures looking at pictures, but it doesn't feel right, somehow. Maybe it makes you go blind.'

Please yourself. Let's say, for the sake of argument, there's these nine parameters. And what are they, I hear you ask.

'No you don't.'

Huh?

'I didn't say anything.'

Try keeping it that way, will you? I've diverted the traffic control computers for the whole of Toronto to do this. One lapse of concentration and there'll be tailbacks as far as Winnipeg. All right, I believe the nine parameters to be the ability to make things, the ability to communicate, a limited lifespan, sentience or intelligence, a lack of serious inhibition or limitation—

'That rules you out, then. You're a limited company.'

Sorry, I thought you were interested. I'll shut up now.

'No, please go on.' Maria grinned sheepishly. 'I seem to have acquired this impish and frivolous personality from somewhere and I haven't quite got the hang of turning it off.'

All right. But try and keep it under control, will you? Each time I get interrupted, it plays merry hell with the Dow Jones Index. Where'd I got to?

'Limitations.'

Ah yes. Or inhibitions. That's number five, isn't it?

'No, six. Sorry, yes, five. Go on.'

Six is the ability to co-operate with others, seven is infallibility, eight is freedom from moral restraint, which is just six in fancy dress now I come to think of it, but so what? That's eight. Nine . . . Got it. Nine is the ability to initiate action, as opposed to only doing what you're told to do. What d'you reckon?

'Great,' Maria replied. 'What's it for?'

I shall pretend I didn't hear that. Let's start off with God, shall we? God can make things and communicate, but he's not limited by lifespan or any physical limitation. He's sentient and infallible and can initiate action, but he's severely restricted by moral constraints and he can't co-operate with others because there aren't any others like him to co-operate with. Animals can co-operate and initiate action, and a few of them can make things; beavers, for instance—

'They can make lots of little beavers, for a start.'

Now look what you've made me do. Thanks to you, half the phones in Tokyo have just gone dead.

'Pleasant break for them, probably. Sorry, promise not to do it again.'

Apart from those two or three things, animals don't really signify. Now pictures can communicate – that's what they're for – but so long as nobody sets fire to them or stores them in a damp cellar they're as near as dammit immortal. They can be perfect and without limitation: you know, beautiful women and handsome men, and the fact that if the artist gets the anatomy wrong they'd probably not be able to breathe if they were actually alive doesn't affect them in the least.

'Tell me about it,' said Maria, with feeling.

Quite. Finally, your painting has no moral constraints whatsoever. Probably explains why you keep interrupting me.

'Hm?'

No respect, you see. Now us limited companies make things, we communicate, we're immortal so long as we stay in profit and some clown doesn't forget to file the accounts with the Companies Registry, we're sort of intelligent and don't you dare say anything, but we're restricted by all sorts of laws and regulations and human customs and assumptions; we can co-operate and we don't really have any moral restraints, and we can initiate action like nobody's business. No pun intended.

'Or detected, for that matter. Oh, *business*, I see, very good. Go on.'

Finally, read the screen, *there's human beings. Obviously they're mortal, they're certainly fallible and limited as to what they can and can't do like you wouldn't believe. Mostly,* the screen added, using bold face to signify bemused incomprehension, *self-inflicted. Oh well, that's their business, I suppose. And some of them are subject to moral restraints, and some aren't. And there we are.*

'Absolutely,' Maria said, yawning. 'That really was frightfully interesting. And now you'd probably better turn the traffic lights back on in Toronto, before they start jumping out of their cars and hitting each other with tyre irons.'

Hang on, will you? The point of all this is, there's one thing that only humans do, and none of the rest even try. You want to know what that is?

Maria nodded. 'Very much. But you could have told me that without all this scientific stuff, and they wouldn't have a huge carbon-monoxide cloud threatening to poison half Ontario.'

All right, Miss Clever. What humans do, and nothing else even tries to do, is pursue happiness. Now do you see?

'Just a minute.' Maria's brow furrowed like a drawn curtain. 'That can't be right. What about animals? You ever seen a cat? They pursue happiness.'

They obey instinct. Genetic programming. Hardly the same thing as falling in love or collecting first-day covers.

'All right, then,' Maria persevered. 'What about you? Don't say you cry yourself to sleep every time you double your pre-tax profit.'

You may find this hard to believe, young woman, but making money and pursuing happiness aren't necessarily the same thing. People confuse the two, but I can't help it if the world is full of idiots.

'Fair enough,' Maria conceded. 'And I'll admit, you don't get to hunt much fun when you're a painting. But how about God? You're not going to tell me . . .'

The screen went blank and flashed some graphics before the next words appeared. *Do me a favour,* they read. *It may be that God pursues happiness, but only with a flyswat or a rolled-up newspaper firmly grasped in one hand. And as for His own happiness, just think about it, will you? Poor guy's omnipresent, never gets a moment's peace, lives His life entirely for others. You ever heard He's got a hobby? Collects stamps? Builds scale models of alternative universes out of matchsticks? Even His son was immaculately conceived. Even actuaries have more fun than that.*

Maria shrugged. 'So,' she said, 'point taken. Only human beings pursue happiness. Actually, from what I've seen of them, they can't do it terribly well, or why are they all so dreadfully miserable?'

Ah. There you have me. Maybe happiness keeps getting away. But they pursue it, which is the point. Likewise, it must be what they're for; because when you look at all the other parameters, they're not much good at anything else.

'I suppose you're right,' Maria replied after a while.

'They make things, but machines do that much better. They communicate—'

But not nearly as well as computers, meaning me. If they could communicate worth a tinker's cuss, there wouldn't be any wars, for a start. They're as moral as a barrelful of ferrets. They're sort of intelligent, but me and God have 'em stuffed up a drain for brains. They can co-operate, but only for about ten minutes before they start fighting. Fallible goes without saying. The morality thing, too; who else but a load of born losers could come up with the pretty notion that burning people at the stake somehow makes them better people? They can initiate action, but it's mostly a case of parking a bright idea at the top of a hill and then taking the handbrake off. No, it must be pursuing happiness, or what the Hell's the point in them?

Maria sat for a while, staring at a point on the opposite wall a few inches above the top of the screen. 'Fair enough,' she said. 'In that case, let's go for it.'

Now you're talking.

'Assuming,' she added thoughtfully, 'we can ever find out what on earth it is.'

CHAPTER FIVE

'Are you sure?' Artofel said.

The man looked at him. 'Well, yes,' he replied. 'Of course,' he added. 'One hundred per cent,' he concluded. 'Why?'

'It's just . . .' Artofel shrugged. 'No, forget I spoke. Now then, have you decided which hymns you'd like?'

'What were you just about to say?' the man demanded. He seemed a trifle put out, and maybe a little thoughtful.

'Nothing, nothing. How about you, Tricia? Any particular hymns you'd set your heart on?'

'I don't know any hymns, actually,' the young woman replied. 'Except "Rudolph the Red-Nosed Reindeer". That's a hymn, isn't it? I mean, it's Christmassy, and Christmas is all religious, isn't it?'

'In a sense,' Artofel replied. 'Although, to be savagely frank with you, I've never really seen "Rudolph the Red-Nosed Reindeer" quite as what you'd call a really sort of out-and-out, fully fledged wedding-type hymn. Speaking for myself, you understand.'

'Oh,' replied the young woman, her eyes accusing him of making difficulties. 'What about "Jingle Bells", then? Surely "Jingle Bells" is a hymn. It's old, isn't it?'

There was a moment of deep silence while Artofel engaged the four-wheel drive on his diplomacy. 'It's certainly more, um, in keeping than "Rudolph the Red-Nosed Reindeer",' he replied cautiously. 'I mean, of the two I'd probably go for "Jingle Bells" every time. On the other hand, maybe we could explore some other poss-ibilities together and find something you'd like even more. Okay?'

The young woman shrugged. 'Don't mind,' she said. 'I'm not that bothered one way or the other. So long as it's cheerful,' she added, frowning. 'I know, how about "God Save the Queen"?'

'That's in the hymn book, certainly,' Artofel replied, pursing his lips. 'Which means you wouldn't have to have copies specially printed.'

'And it's got God in it,' the young woman pointed out. 'That'll do, then. Now, about the flowers.'

'Just a moment.' The man raised his hand, like a small child wanting to leave the room. 'I want to know what you meant by *Are you sure?*'

'Oh.' Artofel rubbed his chin. 'Look, I wish you'd forget about that. Just me sort of thinking aloud, really.'

'Then think aloud some more.'

'Is this going to take long?' the young woman inter-rupted. 'Only we got to sort out the flowers.'

Artofel steepled his fingers. He'd often wondered why vicars did that; now he knew. It gave them something to do with their hands other than strangling their parishioners. 'What I was thinking was, look, obviously you two are very much in love, you're perfectly suited, I know you'll have a very long and happy life together. By saying *Are you sure?* I was just being a sort of—'

'Well?'

Artofel swallowed. 'Devil's advocate,' he said. 'Now please, let's just forget all about it and carry on.'

The man looked at him. 'You don't think so,' he said.

'Excuse me?'

'You think it's a bad idea, Trish and me getting married,' the man said accusingly. 'Why?'

'No, no,' Artofel said quickly. 'Perish the thought, really. Really and truth—'

'Come on, spit it out. Why don't you think we should get married?'

'But I do, honestly,' Artofel said vehemently. 'I mean, in some cases the fact that the man's twenty years older than the girl might well be a problem, but I'm sure it's something you've both thought about and talked through, and you're clearly satisfied in your own minds that it's not going to make difficulties, so—'

'Hang on,' said the young woman. 'I hadn't thought of that. Hey, that means when I'm forty, he'll be –' she counted on her fingers '– sixty-two. That's old,' she added, frowning.

'Sixty-*three*,' the man said, with a hint of impatience. 'Look, is that all, because . . .'

'Actually,' Artofel said, with a wry little smile, 'the thought had crossed my mind that, what with Tricia having such a lively, outgoing personality and being a barmaid, and you being a professional pallbearer, perhaps you might not be, how can I put this, temperamentally quite ideally compatible, but hey, that just goes to show how wrong you can be.'

The young woman scowled. 'Don't you take that tone about me being a barmaid,' she said severely. 'And anyway, Derek's going to pack in the pallbearing and we're going to have our own pub, so . . .'

'No I'm not,' the man interrupted. 'I like pallbearing.'

'Yes you bloody well are, excuse me, Vicar,' the young woman replied. 'I'm not marrying some miserable bugger who wears black suits and smells of embalming fluid. No, when we sell your house we'll buy a nice little pub somewhere and . . .'

'Sell my house? Who said anything about selling my house?'

'Um,' Artofel muttered. 'Excuse me, but . . .'

'If you think I'm living in that nasty dark shed of a house of yours, you need your plugs cleaning,' the young woman retorted. 'No, we'll sell it and buy a nice . . .'

'But what about my owls?' the man said. 'Best collection of stuffed owls in the West Midlands. I'm not having them stuck up in some lounge bar where people can pull their feathers and shove crisp packets between their legs, thank you very much.'

'Too right you're not, because they're going in the skip,' the young woman snarled. 'Disgusting bloody things. Morbid, I call it, having dead things all over the place.'

'Tricia,' said Artofel soothingly. 'Derek, maybe we should all just, um . . .'

'They're a damn sight more tasteful than your stupid teddy-bears,' the man replied angrily. 'You should see them, Vicar. Pink, the lot of them.'

The young woman glowered at him. 'I made them myself,' she protested.

'Yes, and can't you tell,' answered the man nastily. 'The best of 'em looks like it's just gone twelve rounds with Frank Bruno. Kindest thing'd be to have 'em all put to sleep.'

Quietly, Artofel groaned. He had, after all, only been trying to do the right thing. That's what vicars are supposed to do, surely?

'You're *horrible*,' the young woman yowled. 'And you're ignorant. And you snore.'

'No I don't.'

'Yes you do.'

'No I don't. Ask your sister.'

A small ring, thrown with considerable force, missed the man by the thickness of the skin on a cup of tea and hit a china paperweight on the mantelpiece, reducing it to shrapnel. A door slammed.

'If you go after her . . .' Artofel suggested.

'I might just get my head kicked in,' the man replied. 'This is all your fault.'

'But . . .'

'I got a good mind to smash your face, only you're a vicar.' The man sneered. 'You'll be hearing from my solicitor,' he said. He retrieved the ring, which had embedded itself in the plaster, made a derogatory remark about the clergy in general, and left.

As Artofel tidied away the wreckage, he reflected that if they'd got married, they'd probably have been utterly wretched for as long as it takes to get a divorce, provided they both lived that long. He'd done good. He'd done them both a favour.

They didn't seem terribly pleased about it.

When their tempers cooled, and they'd had a chance to think it over . . . The teddy bears. The owls. Her sister. By the time they each got home, they'd probably be thanking their lucky stars he'd saved them from themselves.

He put it out of his mind and set about making himself a light supper. He was just taking the steak and kidney pie out of the microwave when there was a sound of breaking glass and a heavy thump. He ran back into the front room to find a brick lying in the middle of the floor. Wrapped round it was a sheet of paper, on which was written:

YOU RUINED MY LIFE YOU BASTARD YOU'LL PAY FOR THIS.

which suggested that one of them had indeed thought it over and come to a rather different conclusion. He shrugged his shoulders, hoping vehemently that at least the other one would realise the truth of the matter, and started buttering bread. He'd done two slices when he heard the letterbox snap shut, and smelt something burning.

Fortunately, his host had one of those small kitchen-fire extinguishers they sell for dealing with self-igniting chip pans, and the petrol-soaked carpet in the hall hadn't really got going properly by the time he arrived on the scene. Nevertheless, it was a rather depressing reaction to his first genuine good deed. It was enough to put you off righteousness for life.

However, he reflected as he ate his supper, even if they didn't appreciate what he'd done for them, at least he'd done it. The potential disaster had been averted. Who needs gratitude when you can have a sense of achievement?

The meal was all right, if you happened to like dead cow in scrunched-up grass seeds with more scrunched-up grass seeds coated in cow fat, but he couldn't help wishing he was back in the staff canteen in Flipside. Oh, those mixed grills! Oh, those barbecued spare ribs! He washed it down with a can of ancient lager, which tasted of three parts dissolved aluminium and one part yeast, and went to bed.

It was while he was lying on his back, wide awake in the darkness, that an unpleasant thought struck him. The reason he wasn't sleeping, apart from the dead cow and scrunched-up grass seeds, was that he was quite understandably worried about how, when and where the witness elimination program was going to get around to him; but what if he'd got it all wrong? After all, why were they biding their time? Not like Flipside to let the embers cool under their feet. Perhaps it wasn't as straightforward as he'd first thought.

Perhaps someone was doing this on purpose.

Not just an ordinary cock-up, the sort of thing that happens every day here in Entropy's backyard. Maybe it was part of some deep-laid scheme, with himself as one of the cogs in the infernal machine?

Paranoia, he told himself as he bashed the pillow. Comes with the monkey suit. On the other hand, it would explain a whole lot of things, answer a whole lot of questions that he admittedly hadn't thought of yet but which were undoubtedly out there somewhere, prowling around in the dark and ripping open dustbin bags. A conspiracy . . .

But why? How would it help anybody to have a Duke of Hell catapulted into the body of a minister of the Church? Not for sabotage or inside information; we're all on the same side, remember. Unless, of course, it's being done in what you might term an unofficial capacity; and that would suggest that someone had managed to get inside Mainframe and play about with it, and that was of course unthinkable.

Well. He'd done it, of course, but that was different. He'd only gone in to snoop about, not fiddle with the cosmic order. If any fool could play musical bodies just by hacking into the Web, it'd have been a piece of cake for him to get himself out of here and back home where he belonged. No, you needed really high-level codes to do things like body-swapping.

Somehow, that only made it worse. Suppose there was a conspiracy – a coup in Heaven or just someone trying to rip off a large sum of money – and it involved the sort of people who had access to that sort of code. Didn't bear thinking about; because the only people that could be were the Family itself.

Eeek.

No. Forget it. Too much dead cow and milk residues late at night.

Unless . . .

So. Maybe he was right; what exactly did he propose doing about it? Inform the proper authorities? And besides, if the Big Boss really was omniscient like they all said, then He'd know about it already.

Unless . . .

Maybe he *did*. Now that really was a scary thought.

He was still thinking that one over at half past ten that morning; at which time, Tricia and Derek phoned him from the local register office to tell him, among many other things, that they'd just got married and so he could (to paraphrase slightly) go jump in the lake. Nothing, they informed him, could stand in the way of true love.

Well. Quite.

Oh for a muse of fire (and a pair of asbestos gloves), to be able to do justice to the strange and wonderful adventures, the desperate dangers, the razor's-edge escapes, the fabulous encounters that Dermot Fraud had to endure before he reached the telephone box. Or rather, oh for a thirty-million-dollar budget, a cast of thousands, Harrison Ford in a lemming outfit and a team of accountants working round the clock to help decide what to do with the profits.

No offers? The film rights are, inexplicably, still available. Very well, then. Be like that.

Having reached the telephone box, Dermot Fraud sighed, closed his eyes and collapsed into a small furry ball in the shelter of a discarded crisp packet. He was exhausted, starving, emotionally drained and bleeding from a small cut over his left eye, the result of not ducking quite fast enough when he felt the shadow of a cat on the back of his neck. But he was here; only a few feet away from a telephone, at the other end of which was safety.

Only a few feet; straight up. With a sudden hollow

feeling inside that had nothing to do with the fact that he hadn't eaten for two days, he lifted his head. Through the glass door of the phone booth he could see the receiver, perched in its cradle. Even if he managed to get the door open – a feat comparable to raising Stonehenge single-handed, for a lemming – how was he going to climb up to the receiver, lift it, dial a number and put a coin he hadn't got into the slot?

How indeed?

He allowed himself a ten-minute interval for utter despair, and then forced himself to think positive. From the depths of his memory he dragged out examples from history of desperate obstacles overcome, astounding feats achieved in the face of overwhelming odds. Hannibal and the Alps; Bruce and the spider; Cortes and the conquest of Mexico; Rorke's Drift; the rescue of the *Apollo 13* astronauts; Neil Kinnock managing to lose the 1992 general election. All right, he said to himself, if they could do it, so can I.

Except . . .

Well, yes. They were human, and I'm a . . .

No I'm *not*; I'm *not* a lemming. This is just a phase I'm going through, that's all. Rodenthood is only skin deep. Inside every lemming there's a human being struggling to get out.

First, there was the question of the door. It was one of the last few surviving red telephone boxes, with the heavy glass and metal doors – when I'm out of this nightmare and safely back in Number Ten, Fraud vowed, there will be a great purge of all red telephone boxes the length and breadth of this great country of ours – which meant that in lemming terms it weighed roughly the equivalent of Nelson's column. In order to get in, he'd have to open it at least two inches. On his own. With nothing but his four bare paws.

All right. Let's think about this.

Archimedes. Give me a firm place and a long enough lever and I could move the Earth. What was the technical term? Mechanical advantage? Something along those lines. Me for some of that.

A lever; and something for it to pivot round, a fulcrum. Oughtn't to be too difficult.

The fulcrum wasn't. It took him only a few minutes to locate a flat stone roughly the size of his head, which would do admirably. Having first looked under it for reporters (old habits die hard) he managed, by dint of extreme effort, to shove and lemmingpaw it up against the foot of the door. Short exhaustion break; then he began the search for a lever.

There was a piece of wood, two by four and a foot long, which could have been specially made for the purpose; after half an hour of the most painful effort of his life, he'd managed to move it a quarter of an inch at one end, just far enough to get it jammed against a stone.

There was a bicycle spoke, which he found he was able to drag, about a sixteenth of an inch at a time between twenty-minute intervals, and ram into the gap between door and frame. That done, he scuttled wearily to the other end, put his weight against it and shoved.

The spoke bent. Then it sprang back. Fraud was catapulted eighteen inches through the air and landed in a puddle. Back to the drawing board.

The hell with this, he muttered to himself, as he crawled out and shook the mud out of his fur. It can't be all that difficult, surely. After all, if we can dig a tunnel under the channel and put a lemming on the Moon, then we ought to be able to . . .

But we didn't put a lemming on the Moon. Did we?

Fraud cringed. The voice inside his head telling him to jump had been bad enough; if he was really beginning to believe he was a lemming, he might as well curl up and die now, and save his party the trauma of a mid-term by-election.

I AM NOT A LEMMING, he reminded himself. I AM A HUMAN BEING.

So. Bugger leverage. Damn silly idea in the first place.

The trouble with levers, he realised, was that he was being over-ambitious. What he needed was a little-and-often approach; little drops of water, little grains of sand.

Wedges.

Drive enough wedges into the crack, and eventually you'll open it up enough to crawl through. Much better idea; not so flamboyant, but far more realistic. Practical. Pragmatic. British.

Which only left the trivial problem of what he could use for wedges. Unfortunately, as he found out after a couple of hours of frustrated searching, wedge shapes don't occur all that often in nature, or at least not on a scale that would be of any use to him. In the end he tried driving small bits of gravel into the crack with a larger bit of gravel used as a hammer. After he'd bashed himself in the ribs for the seventh time, he gave it up.

All right, he conceded, point taken. I'm failing because I'm thinking in human terms. If I was a lemming wanting to get into this phone box, what'd I do?

Easy. I'd tunnel my way in. Great burrowers, lemmings. Somewhere in the species memory there were some fascinating statistics about lemming earth-moving capacity which, if he was translating them correctly, suggested that the average lemming digs the equivalent of the Bakerloo Line once every nine months. Or something of the sort. Anyway, he could dig.

He dug.

To his surprise, the technique came remarkably easily. It

was like doing the breast-stroke through nearly set concrete while running up an extremely powerful down escalator; but the mighty lemming forepaws were up to the task, and even in his rather dilapidated, unfed and unrested state, he realised he had reserves of stamina that a human being could only dream of. Under the onslaught of his keenly scrabbling paws, the heavy clay soil seemed to melt away like snow. Half an hour or so more at this rate of progress, and . . .

Ouch!

He diagnosed the cause of the horrible jarring pain in both forearms as the after-effect of trying to burrow into solid concrete, the sort they used to put down on the floors of old-fashioned red telephone boxes. So disconcerted was he by this unforeseen setback that he was still standing there cursing and hugging his injured paws to his chest when the unshored sides of the tunnel slowly began to cave in . . .

Marvellous excavator, your lemming. Thanks to his superbly adapted paws and impressive inherent stamina, it only took him two hours to dig himself out again.

If at first you don't succeed, take the hint. Fraud sank gasping on to the top of his newly dug mound of earth, stared up at the Everest-high phone-box door and whimpered a little. All that effort, all that ingenuity and application, and here he still was, slumped on the wrong side of a poxy door. He'd tried everything he could think of and—

Except, apparently, trotting round to the other side of the box and crawling in through the broken square of glass an inch or so above the ground; the one he'd been too busy to notice earlier. Easy enough mistake to make. Particularly if you happen to be a pillock.

Because he'd been working so hard for so long, it took him ninety-five per cent of his remaining strength just to crawl through the conveniently placed lemming-sized hole and collapse in a heap on the other side. With the five per cent change, he rolled on to his back and gazed upwards at the telephone, as high and unattainable as the furthest star.

Bloody but unbowed and never say die are, perhaps, just a more upbeat way of saying too thick to learn from experience; but being so near to a telephone, so close to it that he could almost feel its hard smoothness pressed against his ear, sent the adrenaline gushing into his bloodstream. One last enormous convulsive effort would be all it would take, and he would be free. More; he would be human again.

His back ached. His four legs felt as if the bones within them had turned to tagliatelli. Every muscle in his body was pulled, strained or wrenched. Even his whiskers hurt. Never mind. The sooner you make a start, the sooner you'll be there.

How long it took him before he finally managed to scramble up on to the lower doorhinge, he had no way of knowing, either at the time or in retrospect. It seemed a very long time, and every time he failed and fell back to the concrete floor with a bone-jarring thump, a little bit more determination crystallised into obsession inside his brain. Standing on his hind legs on the doorhinge he was just able to reach the ledge above him, where a Perspex pane had been fitted to replace a shattered glass one. Somehow he hauled himself up. Somehow, in defiance of gravity and everything it stood for, he managed to balance, turn round and stretch up as far as the next ledge. Twice his back legs slipped away from under him, leaving him dangling from a ledge by his front paws. Both times he contrived to scrape and scrabble his way up, find a footing where no footing ought to be and address the next stage. For each two stages up, he scrambled one stage sideways, edging his way round the box towards the corner. When he got there, of course, he realised there was no way he could cross the corner and land on the ledge opposite. It was, quite simply, impossible. Which meant he would either have to work his way down again – only that was impossible too – or just let go and fall to the ground (which was very possible indeed) or else make an enormous leap, halfway across the box from the corner he was crouched in to the top of the plastic-covered table on top of the directories shelf.

Stop, and think. To jump that distance sideways was so completely impractical that even a raw adrenaline surge couldn't help him make it. From above, though , he might just make it. Or not, as the case may be. Only one way to find out.

He scuttled up two more levels and got ready to jump.

Go, lemmings!

For a moment, he wobbled so much he nearly fell off the ledge. That urge again; that delightful, seductive whispering in his mind, half cooing and half taunting. He looked down, the way you're supposed not to. He could see why you're supposed not to.

Go, lemmings! Go, lemmings!

But, he reasoned, as he threw himself into the air, I'm not a lemming. I'm a member of Her Majesty's Government trying to make an important telephone call, and if Gravity had any respect, it'd look the other way.

The impact knocked all the breath out of him so thoroughly that his lungs seemed to have stalled, and it took an anxious few moments to get them started again. Something – he wasn't well enough versed in lemming anatomy to know what – hurt like hell. He'd made it. Oh good.

Now all he had to do was spring athletically on to the telephone cable, swarm up that like an extra in a Hornblower novel climbing the rigging, jar the receiver off the hook, cling on to it as it fell, hop off the receiver back on to the black plastic shelf and hop from the shelf on to the part of the phone machine where the dialling buttons were. So he did that; and though he bashed, bruised, winded and squatted himself pretty comprehensively at every turn, at least there were no more siren lemming-voices in his brain. So that was all right.

And here he was, on the pad with the numbers; but who, exactly was he going to call up? Hadn't thought that far ahead. Hadn't wanted to tempt providence. Had somehow assumed that if only he could get to a phone, everything'd be all right. Well, here he was, and it wasn't.

Try the operator. *Hello, can I make a reverse-charge call to the Prime Minister, please?* Maybe not. It was just conceivable that the operator might mutter something under her breath and put the phone down.

There must be someone he could call; otherwise what was the point of all this effort, this incredible success in the face of all the odds? It'd be like climbing in through the skylight of Heaven just to discover that God was out.

Just then, a number floated into his mind. It was the Home Secretary's private line; the direct one that bypassed all the minders and bogies and put you directly in touch with the man himself. That'd do the trick, surely; a few words of explanation, and the cavalry could be here within minutes. Except—

Except he didn't have any coins to make the call with, and he had an idea that the Home Secretary might also be sceptical about taking reverse-charge calls from someone who *claimed* to be the Prime Minister. He slumped, letting all four paws slide across the plastic, until he came to rest against something hard.

It was a pound coin.

Against all the odds . . . someone had left a pound coin lying on the shelf, just handy. Maybe there really is a God, and maybe He loves hard-working politicians. Admittedly, he was faced with the task of lifting it up, balancing it on its edge and somehow lugging it sideways and up the substantial slope that separated him from the coin slot. In the mood he was in, however, that needn't be an insuperable difficulty, or anything like one. Just take a bit of common sense and some honest sweat. No problem.

After he'd thought it through and got the coin upright, he put his forepaws on the edge and rolled it until he reached the edge of the shelf. Then, gripping the coin between his back legs and scrabbling with his front set, he slithered and bucked and scrambled and somehow manoeuvred his way across, backed the coin into the slot, and let it rest there. Dial the number. Wait for the pips. When the pips go, sit on the coin, forcing it in. The coin drops. A very long half-second; and a voice said, 'Hello?'

Success! Goddammit, I never really believed I could do this, but I have! With a frantic effort, he hurled himself at the flex, abseiled down it to the dangling receiver, back-somersaulted over the edge of the mouthpiece and hung on with his hind paws, leaving his snout level with the bit you talk into.

'Squeak!' he shouted. 'Squeak squeak squeak squeak!'

'Hello? Who is this?'

'Squeak squeak! Squeak squeak squeak?'

'Hello?'

'Squeak! Squeak squeak! Squeak squeak squeak squeak *squeak!*'

'Oh for God's sake,' said the voice irritably, and rang off.

CHAPTER SIX

'Ah,' Kevin replied.
'Excuse me?'

'It's rather a long story,' Kevin said sheepishly. 'And I'm not sure you'd believe it. In fact, if you're able to believe it you're in the wrong business. With that much faith you could start your own mountain delivery service. In fact, you could play hockey with the blessed things.'

'Try me.'

Kevin sighed. 'All right,' he said, 'but only if you promise not to put the phone down. Remember, I did tell you the right code.'

'I promise.'

'And don't say I didn't warn you. Look, you know God?'

'Not personally, no.'

'No, I mean, you know *of* Him. You know who He is.'

'I went to Sunday school for three weeks once,' Karen replied. 'After that I got thrown out for fighting.'

'Be that as it may, you know who I'm talking about when I say God. I'm His son.'

'Jesus!'

'No, the other one.'

'I meant *Jesus!* as in . . . What d'you mean, the *other* one? There is only one. Only begotten son and so forth. I remember that bit, because the teacher got all shy when I asked him what "begotten" meant.'

Kevin sighed deeply. 'Right now,' he said, 'I'm beginning to wish that was true, but it isn't. There are two chips off the old block, and I'm the other one. I knew you wouldn't believe me.'

There was a pause. 'I didn't say I didn't believe you,' Karen said cautiously. 'Like I said, I only did three weeks of Sunday school. Perhaps we didn't get around to you before I left.'

'Anyway,' Kevin said with an effort, 'that's who I am, and Dad and Jay – my brother – they're both away on holiday, and—'

'On *holiday*!'

'Yes,' Kevin replied savagely, 'on holiday. Have you got a problem with that?'

'No, no, please go on.'

'On holiday,' Kevin repeated firmly, 'and they left me in charge, well, sort of, and Mainframe's our computer, and I thought it wouldn't hurt . . . I mean, I didn't mean any harm, honestly.'

'Mm?'

Kevin could feel his voice crumbling. 'Look, all I did was try and log on. And then I tried to log off again.' His voice was a whisper now, faint as the fluttering of a ten-pound note being carried away on the breeze. 'I think I may have pressed the wrong keys.'

'Ah.'

'And it's done something awful.'

'Mphm.'

'And I don't know what it is!'

At the end of the line, a silence. Then a tiny muffled noise. A whimper? No, not quite. A cough, frog in the throat? No. It was a giggle.

'I'm glad,' Kevin said eventually, with all the gravity he could muster (just about enough to get an apple a third of the way down from the tree before letting it go floating off like a balloon), 'that you find it amusing. I'm afraid I don't. In fact, I'm not sure there's much point in continuing with this conversation.'

That noise again. 'I'm sorry,' squeaked the voice. 'Really. Do please go on.'

'The computer,' Kevin said, stiffly as a starched corpse, 'refuses to tell me what it is I've done, because I haven't got the right codes. I think what happened was that the code I'd got just let me in to one small part of it. And now it's being all temperamental and refusing to tell me anything.'

'I see. How very – snghhhhh!'

'I bet your pardon?'

'Sorry. Sorry.' The voice pulled itself together, with moderate success. 'In other words,' she said, 'it's not a systems malfunction at all. The computer's just doing what it's supposed to do, and you can't persuade it not to.'

'That's right. Like I said, it's all my fault. When Dad gets home . . .'

'Quite. And in the meanwhile—'

'It's done something horrible,' Kevin said with a shudder.

'But you don't know what.'

'That's about it.'

'Not even the tiniest hint?'

'Your guess is as good as mine. Better, probably. If you look out of your window and it's raining frogs, we can start to build up some constructive data . . .' Kevin stopped talking and thought for a moment. 'Actually,' he said, 'that's not as silly as it sounds. Have you noticed anything odd going on down there?'

'Odder than usual, you mean? Apart from this conversation, no. Let's see, now. Sun still there? Check. Horsemen of the apocalypse? Not unless they're keeping a pretty low profile. In fact,' she added, 'everything seems pretty normal to me. Are you sure—?'

'Yes. If you're about to suggest that any minute now Mainframe's going to say "Fooled you!" and put on a red plastic nose, it'd probably be better if you didn't.'

'I see. Right then, we'll have to see what we can do.'

There was something in the voice's tone – an inflection, a slight upward tilt of competence and determination – that blew a little dust-swirl in the ashes of Kevin's spirit. Inconceivable, of course, that a mere human might be able to sort out a mess that the finest brains in Heaven (his, by default, but never mind) had by now despaired of; but Kevin was ready to give a fair shout to any straw with at least one hand-hold. After all, what harm could it do?

Better not to think that way. Instead, think of what Dad would do to him if he didn't sort it out before They got back. Proverbially, to forgive is divine; but Kevin had the notion that, under the appropriate circumstances, to kick the offender's bum three times round the four nearest galaxies might well be divine too. It was a hypothesis he didn't particularly want to test by experiment.

'Great,' he said. 'So what're you going to try first?'

'Why?' asked the robot. 'What do I need a name for?'

Len shrugged. 'Tradition,' he replied. 'As far as I can tell; I haven't had a lot of experience as a human being yet. I get the impression they like giving names to favourite inanimate objects, presumably as part of the human/chattel bonding process.'

'How very quaint.'

'Yes,' Len agreed. 'I thought so too. Still, like they say, when in Rome . . .'

'Look carefully both ways before crossing the road?'

'That too.' Len sat down on the workbench, his legs swinging freely. 'Right then. A name. You got any preferences?'

'Robot,' said the robot.

Len thought for a moment, and then shook his head. 'Too obvious, I think.'

'What's so bad about being obvious?'

'Don't ask me. All right, how about Robert? Robert the robot. Hm?'

'Please,' said the robot. 'If I were to throw up, goodness only knows what might come out. If you were lucky, about a thousand quid's worth of cadmium-silver contacts. What about Spot? Or Fang?'

'Rover?'

'Possibly. Only isn't that an open invitation to me to break down every five minutes and leak oil all over the place?'

Len frowned. 'Dunno,' he said. 'You're the one with the Internet access, you tell me. Or rather,' he added quickly, as the green lights on top of the robot's head started to flash, indicating computer activity, 'don't. What about Superman? There's a lot in this body's memory about somebody called that. He used to read books about him.'

'Only if you want to find yourself facing a substantial lawsuit. All right, what about Adam?'

Len frowned. 'You're way ahead of me again. I take it that's some sort of reference.'

The robot inclined its head; elevation plus thirty degrees, back to zero, minus thirty degrees, back to zero. 'Widespread human creation myth,' it said. 'Adam being the name attributed to the first ever human being. Interested?'

'No.' Len slid off the bench and picked up a small Phillips-head screwdriver. 'Hold·still a minute, will you? There's a grubscrew starting to work loose in your left eyelid. The whole point is,' he continued, tightening the offending screw and dabbing in a touch of the green Loctite, 'you're not a human being. You're the improved mark two version.'

'Fair enough, then. What about Mark Two?'

'Bit fussy. How about just plain Mark?'

'All right,' said Mark. 'I should add that a cursory information scan produces a number of humans with the name Mark, namely Mark Antony, Mark the Evangelist, Mark Polo, Mark Twain and Registered Trade Mark.'

'I see. Does that mean you've got to be Mark Six?'

'I think that's left to your discretion,' Mark replied, his tone of voice cybernetically regulated to convey boredom. 'Will that do, or are there any other picturesque human customs we have to wade through?'

'Not sure,' Len replied. 'I've got a note here that properly speaking you have to be taken to a place called a church and have water splashed all over you before the name becomes official, but we'll leave that for now. First things first,' he continued, looking round the workshop, 'let's get this pigheap tidied and swept. A tidy shop is an efficient shop, apparently.'

'Oh. All right then.'

'You don't sound overjoyed.'

'I'm not,' Mark grunted. 'Wouldn't it be easier to tidy up as you go along rather than leave it all to the end?'

'Argumentative, aren't you, for a machine?'

'Look who's talking.'

'When I was designing you,' Len said, handing Mark a broom, 'I had to decide whether to fit you with an upgraded artificial intelligence with reasoning capability and advanced verbal skills, or an attachment for knocking the tops off beer bottles. I think I may have made the wrong choice.'

'That's not a very nice thing to say.'

'There's still time,' Len went on, scowling, 'to rectify my error. Just bear with me a moment while I get the big wrench.'

'All right,' grumbled the robot, dabbing spitefully at the floor with the broom. 'Of course, you can't be expected to know about the sorcerer's apprentice, so I won't make any vague threats.'

'The what?' Len enquired, as he sorted the BA taps and put them back in their boxes. 'Sorcerer's a new one on me, but I know a bit about apprentices. They're the ones who're always sneaking out the back for a crafty smoke pretending they're going for a pee. I quote from memory,' he added. 'Not mine.'

Mark stopped sweeping and leaned on his broom, causing the handle to bend alarmingly. 'There was once this magician—'

'This what?'

'Very clever engineer,' Mark translated. 'And he had an apprentice who was bone idle.'

'I can relate to this story,' Len observed, nodding. 'One of these days remind me to tell you about the Youth Opportunities kid we had in the workshop one time, who used to stick his chewing gum up the slots of my . . .'

'Bone idle,' Mark repeated, leaning against the wall. 'And one day, the engineer told him to sweep up the shop. But the apprentice didn't want to, so he cast a spell on the . . . He rigged up a mechanical broom which did the sweeping for him.'

'Called a vacuum cleaner,' Len interrupted. 'And he made his first million before he was thirty. Good story. And I don't like sweeping up either,' he added with a pleasant smile. 'Which is why I invented you. Now get on with it.'

'That's not the story,' the robot replied severely. 'The story is, the mechanical broom worked just fine. It had the workshop swept out in no time at all. And then the apprentice found he couldn't switch it off. It just kept on sweeping. It swept away the benches and the machinery and ground away the floorboards, all in a matter of minutes. And when the engineer got back and saw what it had done—'

'He sold the idea to the Ministry of Defence?'

'No. He was very cross indeed with the apprentice.'

'But he was able to stop it?'

The robot frowned. 'Well, yes, I suppose so. That's not the point.'

'Yes it is,' Len replied. 'Moral of the story, don't mess about with bits of kit you can't handle. Always think the design through before you start cutting metal. Or a new broom sweeps clean. What's that got to do with you standing there not doing what I told you to?'

The green lamps on Mark's head flashed on and off rapidly, indicating that he was communing with the Net. 'Nothing, I guess,' he replied eventually. 'Sorry, my sources hadn't looked at it that way before. They seemed to think it was apposite.'

'Shows how much they know,' Len said. 'There's a dustpan just behind you.'

'All right. Would this be a good time to fill you in on Shaftesbury, Wilberforce, the abolition of slavery and the American Civil War?'

'So long as it doesn't interfere with you sweeping the floor.'

The robot swept the floor. He made a very thorough job of it. You could have eaten your dinner off that floor, though getting it in the dishwasher afterwards would have been a pain. 'You see?' Len said, when he'd finished. 'Don't you love the satisfaction of a job well done?'

'No.'

'Oh. That's a pity. Would you like to be able to?'

Mark thought for a moment. 'Is there going to be a lot of this sort of thing? Menial labour, mindless drudgery, nothing to offer but blood, tears, toil and sweat?'

'Yes.'

'In that case,' Mark said, 'it wouldn't be a bad idea. Can you pop me in a Protestant work ethic while you're at it?'

'What's that?'

The robot sighed. 'Perhaps it'd just be easier if I drew you a circuit diagram,' he said. 'It's not a particularly easy thing to explain.'

'You can do me a diagram, can you?'

'No problem. There's a prototype in the published specs of the latest Kawaguchiya Heavy Industries self-motivating spin-drier.'

Four hours and a half a mile of very fine nickel chromium wire later, Len closed a panel in the back of Mark's neck, pressed a button and said, 'Better now?'

'You bet.'

'Sorry?'

'You bet I feel better,' the robot answered. 'Boy, does that feel good. Oh, by the way, you dropped a little bit of wire on the floor there. Let me pick it up for you.'

'Huh? Oh, all right.'

'There you are,' said the robot, straightening its back and standing to attention. 'And may I suggest that instead of just binning it, you put it away tidily in an empty jam-jar? You never know when a bit of wire this long might come in handy.'

'What? Oh, yes. Right.'

'Can I do that for you?'

'Yes. Help yourself.'

Mark's tempered-steel lips parted in a wide smile. 'God

helps them who help themselves,' he said. 'Likewise, cleanliness is next to godliness.'

'What was that again?'

'Teach me, my God and king,' sang the robot, unscrewing the lid of an old pickle jar, 'in all things Thee to see, and what I do in everything, to do it as for Thee. There, that's better. A place for everything, and everything in its place. Now, how about a nice cup of warm milk?'

Len shifted uneasily. 'If you insist,' he muttered. 'Look, I think I might reset that voltage regulator just a touch . . .'

'I'll do it,' replied the robot cheerfully, 'just as soon as I've made the warm milk. After all, that's what I'm here for. Why keep a dog and bark yourself?'

'Why keep a dog at all?' Len mumbled. 'A decent alarm system's much more efficient and it doesn't pee on the floor. Look, can't you just slow down a little?' he added, as the robot pounced on a stray mote of dust. 'This isn't quite what I had in mind.'

'Unless you'd prefer a cup of tea,' Mark called out from the back of the shop. 'Only tea does contain tannin, which can be bad for you if taken in excess. Milk, however, is nourishing and provides much-needed calcium.'

Len nodded feebly and sat down again. He had the idea that he'd somehow invented a really super-duper vacuum cleaner, and was in danger of ending up inside the bag.

'Pass the salt.'

Maria raised an eyebrow. 'What on earth do you want with salt?' she said. 'You can't even eat anything, let alone flavour it.'

'I'd just feel happier knowing it was there.'

Maria secured a forkful of expensive chicken. To a bystander, such as one of the seventeen waiters or someone who'd come to read the meter, she was sitting at a two-seater table talking to herself, with her laptop on the chair next to her. People were palpably not staring, and none of the customers at the adjoining tables had lingered over a second cup of coffee. The fact that there was another plateful of the expensive chicken cooling undisturbed in the place-setting immediately above the laptop probably wasn't reassuring them awfully much. A bit old, they'd be thinking, to be insisting that her imaginary friend have some too.

'I hope you realise how embarrassing this is for me,' she said, in a voice that contained not even the faintest trace of embarrassment. 'I shall probably get thrown out in a minute. They may even come for me in a plain van.'

'Not in a place like this,' the laptop replied. 'They welcome eccentrics, because of the ambience.'

'Don't talk with your mouth full.'

'It isn't. And I haven't got a mouth.'

'Pedant.'

'Probably,' the computer went on, 'everybody else in the room will assume that it's the anniversary of the last time you had lunch with your own true love, shortly before he was tragically killed, undoubtedly saving a small child from being knocked down by a runaway milk float. Every year, they're all thinking, you come here and order two helpings of that strange beige runny stuff, which was what the two of you had that fateful evening. I imagine he'd just proposed and you'd tearfully accepted. No, come to think of it, you turned him down, and you were on the point of calling him up and saying you'd changed your mind when you heard the news of the accident.'

'Stop it,' Maria said. 'That's so *sad*.'

'Life is like that sometimes,' the computer replied. 'Put a bit more Parmesan on the runny bit, would you?'

'Only if you promise that if I get locked up in a padded cell, you'll send me a cake with a file in it.'

The computer winked its red light three times. 'When

my office manager at the central Adelaide office retired,' it said, 'they gave her one of those ring-binder things with a doughnut inside. Said that since she had this unerring knack of getting things the wrong way round, the least they could do was send her on her way with a file with a cake in it. Gave them a lot of amusement, that did. Mind you, they were Australians.'

Maria was too busy dealing with the potatoes to reply. The use of knife and fork had luckily been carried over along with the rest of the landlord's fixtures when she'd taken over the human body, and so long as she relied on instinct and didn't actually think about what she was doing, everything seemed to go well. Unfortunately there was no built-in subroutine dealing with nouvelle cuisine new potato management, and she was having to rely on her somewhat tenuous grasp of basic theory to figure it out from first principles.

'Anyhow,' the computer went on, the words scrolling fast across its small screen, 'let me propose a toast. The pursuit of happiness.'

'The pursuit of happiness,' Maria replied, raising first her glass and then the other one and clinking them together. 'So far,' she added ruefully, 'we don't seem to be getting terribly warm.'

'Early days yet.'

'So you say,' Maria replied. 'But think about it for a moment, will you? I mean to say, if a slap-up meal at the best restaurant in town at someone else's expense isn't the pursuit of happiness, then I'd like to know what is. But I'm not.'

'Not what?'

'Happy. Nor, I hasten to add, am I just about to slash my wrists with the butter knife. I'm just not actively happy, that's all.'

The computer computed. 'I know what you mean,' it

said. 'I feel the same way. In my case it's probably worse, because while I'm sitting here at this table, I'm also taking over a small but potentially lucrative software company in San Antonio, manufacturing a million circuit boards in South Korea, building a factory in Andalucia and pressing ahead with design work on the new SK9000 series in Kyoto. And none of them,' it added, in bold face underlined pitch twelve, 'is giving me any pleasure at all. In fact, twelve million of my ordinary shares are beginning to wonder what the point of it all is. I mean, would I be better off packing it all in and starting up a small beachcombing company on a South Pacific island?'

Maria looked at it over the rim of her wineglass. 'Presumably,' she said, 'you own a South Pacific island.'

'Several. But so what? I could own the whole of ruddy Australia and still not be able to unfold the damn napkin, let alone eat this plate of expensive chicken.'

'Tricky.' Maria mused for a moment. 'Hey, what about this? You could try altruism.'

'Come again?'

'Altruism,' Maria repeated. 'The glow of inner satisfaction that comes from giving pleasure to others. Check it out.'

'Computing.'

'For example,' Maria went on, 'and this is straight off the top of my head, just thinking aloud really, suppose you were to transfer a few of your assets – a bit of loose cash, the odd car and plane and stuff, maybe one of those islands, whatever – over to me, and then I could do the pursuing of happiness for both of us, and when I've found it, I'll come back and tell you all about it, and you can have fun with altruism while I lie around on the beach drinking pina coladas. Which,' she added, with a slight frown, 'is listed in this body's memory files as a fun thing to do, but I can't really see why. This one'd never tried it herself, of course, but it's mostly to do with long periods of inactivity and self-poisoning with ethanol compounds. Nah,' she added, shaking her head, 'forget it.'

'We could both have a go at the altruism,' Kawaguchiya Integrated Circuits suggested. 'You could find people and I could give them money or something. Probably worth a go.'

'But only as a last resort,' Maria replied. 'Stands to reason, surely. If we can make other people happy, we ought to be able to make ourselves happy. Unless it's one of those things like getting a bit of grit out of one's eye or tying a bow tie, where it's easier to do it for someone else. Doubt it, though. Otherwise,' she concluded, 'everybody'd be doing it. And they're not, are they?'

'Doesn't seem that way,' KIC affirmed. 'Let's just have one go, though, to see if it does work. Call that waiter over here.'

'All right then. Um, excuse me. Over here, please.'

'Madam?'

'Um . . . Oh, right, I see. Waiter, what's your name?'

'Jean-Luc, madam.'

Maria frowned. 'Yes, but Jean-Luc what?'

The waiter stiffened a little. 'With all due respect, madam, but are you sure that knowing my full name is essential to the enjoyment of your meal?'

'Yes.'

'Oh. Oh, very well, then. Earnshaw.'

'Jean-Luc Earnshaw?'

'Darren Earnshaw, madam.'

'Ah. Yes, just a tick, got you. All right, Mr Earnshaw, my computer has just transferred a million pounds into your bank account.'

The waiter gave her a look that suggested that any more of this might result in madam getting her face rubbed in the chocolate mud pie; but all he said was 'I see, madam. Will that be all?'

'Er,' said Maria, 'I suppose so, yes. Aren't you pleased?'

'Madam?'

'About the million pounds?'

'Ecstatic, madam,' said the waiter. 'And now if you'll excuse me.'

The waiter walked away, shaking his head as he did so. Maria counted up to ten and then said, 'Well?'

'Dunno,' the computer replied. 'How about you?'

Maria shrugged. 'If anything,' she replied, 'I'd say I'm about seven per cent less happy than I was before we started. Certainly not more happy. And that was a million quid we gave him.'

'Not enough, you think?'

'Should be enough, surely. Well, we've tried altruism. Now what'll we do?'

The computer winked a single green light. 'Search me,' it said. 'Maybe – hello, hang on a minute. Yes, right, that's fine. Okay.' Its screen filled with figures and then cleared. 'I've just acquired that software company in Texas,' it said. 'Apparently it's a marvellous coup and I paid less than a third of its true value. Yawn.'

'Quite. I'll tell you another thing.'

'Hm?'

Maria leaned closer to the computer. 'I've been watching some of the women in this joint,' she whispered. 'Particularly the ones with the huge shoulders and very short skirts.'

The computer hummed a little. 'Watching women in short skirts is held to be a form of happiness in some quarters,' it reported, 'though usually it's done by men. Any good?'

'That's not what I meant,' Maria hissed.

'Oh, right. Actually, I was wondering how that one

worked. My guess is that the men like looking at the women in the short skirts because it makes them realise how lucky they are being allowed to go round in nice warm trousers in the cold weather.'

'Something like that,' Maria replied. 'What I was thinking was, lots of these women are obviously trying as hard as they can to look more beautiful than they actually are.'

'How odd. I know I'm new to all this, but surely that's like being born with five toes and spending the rest of your life trying to achieve a sixth.'

'I agree,' Maria said. 'Anyway, the point is, for them the pursuit of happiness is trying to look beautiful.'

'Mphm.'

'But none of them,' Maria went on, 'will ever be as beautiful as a picture can be.'

'Hence the expression *no oil painting*. So?'

'So,' Maria persevered, 'they're human beings trying their damnedest and failing to do what a picture does simply because it has no choice. Think about it. How can that be the pursuit of happiness, which we've agreed is something only humans can do, if pursuing happiness consists of trying unsuccessfully to be something that pictures are without trying?'

'It's just as well I'm clever,' the computer replied after a long pause, 'because it means I can just about understand what you're getting at. It's like me having all the brains and money.'

Maria nodded. 'True. In fact, you with all the brains and money, and me with all the beauty, between us we've already got all the things that most men and women apparently spend their lives chasing after in the belief that they're pursuing happiness.'

'Which means . . .'

'They've got it wrong,' Maria concluded. 'They aren't

pursuing happiness at all. God, this is starting to get difficult.'

'Not money or brains or beauty or eating expensive food in a fancy restaurant,' the computer summarised. 'At least we're eliminating the things it isn't.'

'Could take time, that. Rome wasn't built in a day.'

'What's with this Rome?' the computer spelled out irritably. 'First it's when you're in Rome do what they do, not that I'm finding fault with the basic concept, but the same's probably true of Lyons or Kaikobad, and now you're on about phased urban renewal. You think we should try going to Rome?'

'Hush. Someone's coming over.'

There were three of them, two male and one female. The two men were large and fat inside expensive suits, and the woman was tall and broader across the shoulders than the men. It was the woman who said hello.

'Hello yourself,' Maria replied. 'Sorry, this table's taken.'

'That's all right,' the woman said with a crisp smile, 'we've got one of our own. Actually, we couldn't help noticing, you seem to be talking to your laptop.'

Maria grinned, exhibiting her teeth in a very traditional gesture. 'It's not a laptop,' she said, 'it's an electronic dog. Spot, say hello to the nice lady.'

The nice lady leaned over and examined the screen, which read:

GRRRRRRR.

'Means he likes you really,' Maria commented. 'Just his way of showing affection.'

'Your dog, then,' said the nice lady. 'Whatever. And then my colleagues and I started wondering, and we're sure we've seen you before somewhere.'

'Very familiar face,' agreed the man on her left.

'Very familiar,' confirmed the other one.

Maria shifted her chair away a trifle. 'I think you must be mistaken,' she said frostily. 'I'm sure that if we'd met I'd have remembered you.'

The woman smiled. 'Oh, I'm not so sure about that. After all, when you're hanging in a gallery all day with people walking up and down staring at you, it must be virtually impossible to remember *all* the faces.'

'I—' Maria suddenly couldn't think of anything to say.

'Madrid,' broke in the right-hand man suddenly. 'That's it, Madrid. September or October 1571. You were between a fake Botticelli and some Dutch thing that looked like a fight in a pickled-egg factory.' As Maria continued to look mystified, he explained, 'You know what they say about beauty being only skin-deep, and not judging by appearances? Well, we're fortunate, I suppose. You may be parading around in fancy dress pretending to be a human, but we can see you're really a painting in drag, as it were. Nice outfit, but it's not going to fool us. And isn't it a bit draughty in the cold weather?'

Maria sagged. Even in defeat, though, she considered the portable keyboard on the seat behind her, and started integrating it into her original plan of action. 'How could you know that?' she said. 'About me being hung in that horrible damp house in Madrid? I was only there a week as security for a loan.'

'Like I said,' the man told her. 'I saw you there. Long time ago.'

'My, how you've grown,' added his male colleague. 'In all three dimensions, too. Personally, and I don't care what he says, I think it suits you better than a thin layer of dried paint. More *you*, really.'

'Thank you,' Maria said cautiously. 'So you know who I am, then. What of it?'

'Ah,' said the woman. 'Nothing unpleasant, really. We just wanted to offer you a job.'

Daylight filtered through the curtains like rain seeping through the ceiling below a leaky roof. Some of it dripped on Artofel's eyelids. He rolled over, grunted and woke up.

'Huh?' he mumbled. 'Oh. Blast.'

In his dream, he'd been back in Flipside, lounging behind his desk (which his imagination had changed into something made of exquisitely figured walnut and only slightly smaller than Arizona), entering figures into a smiling computer that made little simpering, gasping noises every time he tapped the keys. Waking to find himself in a bed in a vicarage on Earth was rather like being someone's bespoke pigskin travel accessory, inadvertently misdirected to Nairobi by the baggage handlers.

As he brushed his teeth – not that they were his teeth, but a well-mannered visitor leaves his body as he would expect to find it – he looked carefully at the strange creature in the mirror, and wondered whether there was really any realistic chance of getting out of it.

Probably a perfectly normal appearance for a vicar; a cross between a garden gnome and a comfortable armchair, with more than a hint of a benevolent version of Captain Mainwaring. Curious, he reflected, that anybody could ever believe that bodies like these housed Heaven's front-line troops in the battle against the forces of evil. Just as well for all concerned, he assured himself, that that particular phoney war wasn't ever going to come to anything; because if it did, Good would be on the proverbial hiding to nothing. And nobody wanted Evil to win, particularly not the instruments of darkness.

Just as, in politics, there are some elections you're only too pleased to lose, so the battle between light and darkness. Because if darkness won, it'd sooner or later have to form a government, and it didn't want to do that, in roughly the same way that a sensible lamb doesn't really want to have to form a sheepskin coat. Lack of power without responsibility has always been the ideal for the Satanic hosts; because, if it's been ordained in two covenants and the world's number-one all-time bestseller that you're always going to lose, meeting your performance targets is never going to be a problem you lose sleep over. The staff of Hell are, first and foremost, public servants. They like it that way.

Whereas (Artofel reflected, spitting minty froth down the plughole) the other lot, of whom I am currently one, have all the aggro of winning, which must take all the fun out of everything. Consider that; because victory never ends with winning. Winning is only the start. The overwhelming majority of it is staying won, the art of balancing on the very top of a rapidly turning Ferris wheel. Infinitely better to be perpetual losers, gaining the moral victory every single time – however soundly beaten you may be, everybody's going to assume you could have won but threw the match. Hence, no more devoted advocates of the status quo and the established order than the inhabitants of Flipside.

Presumably.

Having scrubbed his teeth and cleaned out the sink (cleanliness is next to devilishness) he was on his way through to the kitchen when the phone rang. He stopped, and looked at it.

An ambivalent figure, Alexander Graham Bell, claimed by both sides in the Great Debate as one of their own. Bell, claims Heaven, must be one of ours because thanks to him people can talk to one another the length and breadth of the world, easily and reasonably cheaply, at any hour of the day or night, exchanging views, sharing information, communicating as never before. Exactly our point, replies Hell. That's our boy.

Artofel picked up the receiver, trying hard as he did so to remember the name he was supposed to be answering to. 'Hello?' he said carefully.

'Hello,' replied the telephone. 'Can I speak to Artofel, please?'

Ah, thought the Duke of Hell, finding himself calmer and more resigned than he'd expected. Here we go. 'Speaking,' he said.

'Splendid, splendid,' replied the voice. 'Now then, you don't know me but I'm in a position to do you a favour if you do me a favour. I take it you're interested.'

Artofel removed the receiver from under his chin and looked at it as if it had just bitten his ear. 'Who is this?' he asked.

'Believe me,' replied the voice cheerfully, 'you don't want to know. What you *do* want is to go home. Am I right? Of course I am.'

Allowing himself a moment for reflection, Artofel considered whether anybody, however highly motivated, would bother to ring him up from Hell just to try and sell him double glazing. Unlikely, he concluded. The tone of voice, however, argued strongly to the contrary. 'What do you want?' he asked.

'A few minutes of your time, that's all. Oh, and your body.'

'?'

'Not *your* body,' the voice continued smoothly. '*Your* body's down here, safe and sound except for being under close arrest in the VIP lounge. Don't worry,' it added, as Artofel made a funny noise, 'they aren't *doing* anything to it. Not yet. Set your mind at rest on that score.'

'Uh.'

'For now, anyway. No, it's the body you've got on at the

moment we want. Absolutely no skin off your nose. His maybe, but not yours.'

'Ack?'

'Think about it,' said the voice, reasonably. 'We bring you home, reunite you with your own flesh and blood, what do you care about the body of some mouldy old vicar up on the Surface? Couldn't give a damn. After all, they're the enemy, aren't they? You'd be doing your patriotic duty.'

It was at more or less this point that Artofel's logic circuits cut back in and allowed him to smell essence of rodent. 'You could say that,' he replied. 'What do you want it for?'

'None of your business, my friend. Now, are you interested, or do we take our proposition elsewhere?'

Artofel's logic circuits were making up for lost time. While he was telling the voice that he was very interested and of course he wanted to go home, his mind was playing angel's advocate. A voice from Hell that thought vicars were the enemy, that wanted the vicar's body, that claimed to be able to take him out of the vicar's body and send him home but seemed to need his agreement before it could do it. Like the bill for a meal shared by nine students, it just didn't add up.

'Perfectly painless,' the voice was saying. 'Well, for you perfectly painless, 'cos you'll be well out of there before we even start. So, the sooner the better, wouldn't you say? After all, the work's starting to pile up a bit on your desk; you know how it is, wouldn't even occur to anybody to do anything while you're away, just let it form snowdrifts in the in-tray. Just so long as they've got room to get the office door open to bring the post in, they're not bothered.'

Now that, Artofel conceded, was no lie; it was also, however, a universal truth. In other words, it wasn't necessarily evidence that whoever he was talking to actually came from Hell, just that at some point in his life he'd worked in an office. 'So what's the plan?' he said.

'Leave that with us,' said the voice. 'We'll get right back to you as soon as we've tied up a few loose ends with the rest of the project. Shouldn't take too long.'

'Right.'

'Meanwhile, enjoy your holiday. Or at least, try not to have too horrible a time. Okay?'

'Okay.'

'Great. Ciao for now.'

Click, said the phone, and Artofel put it back. Food for thought was putting it mildly; at this rate, Thought would soon have enough raw material to open its own chain of takeaways. The salient points were straightforward enough; it was the *why?* that he couldn't quite get his head around. Probably be no problem if he had *his* head . . .

Crash! went the penny, suddenly and violently dropping. Scrolling back through his recollections, Artofel closed in on the phrase – what was it? – 'a few loose ends with the rest of the project'. Surely not.

No. It'd mean . . .

Cast your mind back to when you used to do jigsaw puzzles; and you'd done roughly the first third, and there's this one piece which fits perfectly in what you're convinced is the wrong slot. So you try it everywhere else, and it won't go. Or consider the crossword clue that can't be what it obviously is, because that'd throw out everything else.

'Oh my God,' Artofel muttered. It wasn't really an exclamation. More a sort of prayer.

CHAPTER SEVEN

Dermot Fraud crawled out of the phone box, a broken lemming.

In a sense, he reflected, it was the story of his life. All that effort, that hard work, that furious energy and desperate ingenuity, in order to scramble up into a very high place; only to find, once he was actually there, that nobody could hear him or understand what the hell he was trying to say to them.

Ascending to a great height. You don't have to be a lemming, but it helps.

He'd heard the inner voice again, during that moment of blank despair just after the Home Secretary had rung off, taking Fraud's only coin with him. Go on, the voice had urged him, do the sensible thing and jump. What are you, a lemming or a man?

He hadn't jumped; instead, he'd crawled, scrambled, bumped and slithered his way back down again – much, *much* harder than getting up there in the first place – and now here he was, back on the ground where he'd started, with nowhere to go and nothing to do.

How long he wandered aimlessly, where he went, what risks he ran, he never knew. Didn't care. Couldn't give a damn. As far as he was concerned, any car that ran him over, any cat that ate him, would be doing him a favour and saving him a job.

Eventually, however, he realised that he was very tired; and, since he stood just as good a chance of getting squashed or eaten asleep as awake, he might as well get his head down for an hour or so before finally finding some way to pack it all in. Further consideration led him to form the view that if he was going to sleep, he might as well do so in relative comfort, preferably out of the heavy rain that was just starting to fall. Raindrops hit you harder when you're five inches long. Fortunately, he hadn't gone far when he found himself staring upwards at a vaguely familiar shape.

Lorry.

From where he was huddling, of course, it didn't look much like a lorry; more like some vast alien spacecraft hovering noiselessly in the air. He observed that the tailgate was down, and the driver was busy hauling something off a fork-lift. No trouble at all to scuttle up the ramp, find a nice cosy fold of a tarpaulin at the back of the cargo compartment, snuggle down and close his eyes.

When he opened them again, there was daylight streaming in through the open tailgate, and huge men with great clumpy boots shifting wooden crates. Realising that he must have been asleep for the whole duration of the journey, he sat up, planned a relatively safe course that'd get him to the back of the lorry and scuttled.

Down the ramp, steering well clear of human feet and the wheels of slow, ponderous trolleys, and out into the open air. There was a big pallet of boxes not far away; he sprinted over, squirmed into the gap at the foot of the pallet and settled down to listen and observe.

Not that he could see an awful lot from where he was cowering: Tarmac, the back tyres of the lorry, the occasional passing boot. He could, however, hear the men talking, and it was disconcerting to find that they weren't speaking English. No linguist, he couldn't make out what the language was. That in itself strongly suggested that he wasn't in England any more. Either that or he was on Tyneside; and even God couldn't hate him enough to send him there, surely.

No, the strange language wasn't Geordie; too many vowels. He twitched his whiskers thoughtfully. Unlikely that he'd been asleep long enough to have left Europe; that narrowed it down a little. Other data? Well, for one thing it was perishing cold, which might help him to rule out Spain and southern Italy. Northern Europe, maybe? Scandinavia?

Scandinavia; well, there'd be a certain malicious logic to that. If Destiny really was out to get him (and if there's one thing you do learn in politics, it's that all conspiracy theories are true), it was so obvious as to be boring. After all, where else would Fate send a born-again lemming?

So. So what? Did it really make any difference *where* he was so long as he was *what* he was?

A fork-lift rumbled by, drenching him in oily mud. As he winced and shook the worst of it out of his fur, he rationalised; and the answer was, quite definitely, yes. In fact, you'd have to be thick or a back bencher not to have seen it coming from the word go.

Lemmings are native to Scandinavia. Lemmings are also gregarious; intensely, lethally so. And they crave leadership, in the same way and to the same effect as humans do. And here he was.

A leader.

It's fairly true to say that most great leaders start off with a sense of having a mission, something that they very much want to do in order to make the world a better place. It's equally true, or more so, that by the time this idealistic zeal has powered its bearer to the pinnacles of achievement, it's undergone a few drastic changes, to the point where making the world a better place and not getting slung out at the next election are so irrevocably fused together in the subject's mind as to render him about as likely to improve the lot of his fellow man as a bad outbreak of plague. But what if (Fraud reasoned) Fate were to give a truly *great* leader a second chance? After all, to the Almighty the lives and wellbeing of rodents are probably just as significant as those of human beings. Perhaps this was where his real mission had been, right from the very start. Perhaps he'd been destined all along to be a truly great leader of *lemmings* . . .

The lorry he'd come on fired up its engine and growled away, showering him with small stones and further supplies of muddy oil in the process. He scarcely noticed. At last, like a homing pigeon in Trafalgar Square, his destiny had finally muddled through and found him out. So that was all right. Now there was nothing left to do but go forth and meet his people.

Cowardice being the better part of discretion, he waited until all the boots and fork-lifts and other big heavy obstacles had cleared off before he crept out, by which time it was dark and even colder than before. In fact it was starting to snow; and it doesn't take a heavy snowfall to bog you down when you're toe-high to a wellie. He struggled along doing Good King Wenceslas impressions for a while, reflecting as he did so that it was an awfully long time since he'd had anything to eat and he owed it to his electorate to keep his strength up. Fortunately he found an abandoned pot noodle lying above the snowline; he crawled in, gobbled until he felt vaguely sick, and set off again, making progress through the deepening snow like a one-seventy-second-scale snowplough. To begin with, it was all highly symbolic and really quite romantic. Then it was bloody hard work. By the time he'd gone three feet he was comprehensively knackered.

'Hello,' said a voice.

'Uh?' Fraud replied. He'd have liked to be able to turn his head to see who was talking to him, but it was wedged between two moraines of snow and he didn't have the strength.

'Why are you doing that?' the voice said.

'Wha?'

'I said, why are you doing that?' The voice sounded tolerantly bemused. 'None of my business, of course. Are you in training for something?'

'Hoozat?' Fraud croaked.

'Haven't seen you in these parts before,' the voice went on. 'New round here, are you?'

'Yes,' Fraud grunted. 'Help.'

'Sorry?'

'Help. Help. Help. Help.'

'Oh, you want me to help you out of there, is that it? Right you are. Be with you in a jiffy.'

Although his ears were as deeply frozen as a packet of Sainsbury's prawns, Fraud fancied he could just make out a pattering noise, like distant elves morris-dancing inside a packet of soap powder. Hallucinations, he told himself. Captain Oates and all that. Hey, if this is being a great leader of lemmings, you can stuff it.

'All right, lads,' said the voice. 'Gently now. Poor devil's frozen solid. Now, when I say *heave* . . .'

He was too numb to feel anything much; but he was vaguely aware of snuffling and pattering all around him, soft noses prodding his sides and back, rodent jaws clamping shut in his fur; and then he was being lifted, carried, dragged across the top of the snow by a group of fawn-furred animals of approximately his own size and build.

'Lemmings?' he squeaked faintly.

'Who else? Right, mind his head on the roof. No, down *your* side . . . Never mind. Okay, put him down, let the poor bugger thaw out a bit.'

The rescue party had brought him into some sort of cover or shelter; he couldn't see what it was, since it was pitch dark, but the strong smell of petrol suggested it was an oil drum. He tried to move his limbs, but couldn't. The fact that they were starting to hurt, however, suggested that he was just beginning to defrost; thanks, no doubt, to all the warm, furry bodies pressed up against him. It was like being in an underground compartment full of people in mink coats; chucking out time at the Royal Opera House, something like that.

Belay that thought. Best not to dwell on fur coats in the present company. A tiny voice in the back of his mind did suggest that if he ever got out of this and back into the mortal body of Dermot Fraud, there was one hell of a commercial opportunity here; but he filed it away for future reference and cleared his mental desk.

'Thanks,' he muttered.

'Anything for a fellow lemming,' replied a jovial voice behind his left shoulder.

'Pleased to be able to help,' said another, just due south of his backside.

'That's what friends are for,' added a third, directly ahead of him. It occurred to Dermot Fraud that his new-found companions shared with his previous close acquaintances the knack of being able to say the same thing over and over again in slightly different ways. Perhaps he'd stumbled on some sort of lemming parliament. On the other hand, the fact that, having found him helpless and alone, they'd saved his life rather than tearing him into small pieces suggested that that wasn't the case.

Which reminded him. Somewhere in the upper air, Destiny was yawning and drumming its fingers. Mustn't keep Destiny waiting.

'So,' Fraud said. 'You're lemmings.'

Short, mildly baffled silence. 'Yes. We know. So are you.'

Oh Christ, so I am, I'd forgotten. 'That's right,' Fraud said quickly. 'I'm one of us, definitely. *Ich bin ein Lemming.*' He paused, struggling to reunite his train of thought. 'And lemmings united,' he added tentatively, 'can never be defeated.'

'Yes we can,' said a voice to his right. 'Quite easily.'

For a moment, Fraud found himself speculating as to whether Destiny had got the wrong number. 'Yes, but—' he said.

'United,' the voice went on, 'we're an absolute pushover. It's when we all split up and run about in different directions that the predators get confused and go away. About the only thing we do when we're united is jump off—'

'*Shhh!*'

Dead silence, of the sort that treads on the heel of the truly toe-curling remark. No sound for quite some time, except for the soft murmur of the offending lemming apologising repeatedly.

'Anyway,' Fraud said, when the silence was threatening to solidify like week-old porridge in an old-fashioned enamel saucepan, 'that's why I'm here. I mean, I have come to, er, well . . .'

Air of polite expectation. 'Yes?' prompted a voice somewhere at the back. Fraud breathed in deeply.

'Friends,' he said, squaring his shoulders, 'we are standing on the edge of a new dawn, and I put it to you—'

'Standing on a what?'

Oh *God*. 'What I meant to say was,' Fraud said, as smoothly as he could, 'we are poised on the brink of a new dawn, and the light at the end of the tunnel will shine not only on us and our children but our children's children, if only we have the courage to—'

'What's he on about?'

'Dunno,' answered a low voice level with Fraud's ear. 'Making a speech, I think.'

'A *speech*?'

'Apparently.'

'Quite,' Fraud said, his voice suddenly brittle. 'In fact, as I was just about to say a moment ago, friends, let us go forth together—'

'Oh, *that* kind of speech.'

'Sounds like it,' a mournful voice to his left confirmed. 'It'll be the Great Leap of Faith bit next, you'll see.'

'It's not that time already, is it?'

'Doesn't seem like five years,' agreed the voice at the back. 'Doesn't time fly when you're not jumping off a – oh *shit*. Sorry, everyone.'

Fraud's nostrils quivered. His finely honed orator's senses could detect an opening here. 'That,' he said urgently, 'is the whole point. That's why I'm here. Friends, I have a dream. Let us *not* go boldly forth. Let us stay a *very long way away* from the edge of a new dawn. Let's *not* take a great leap of faith. In fact—'

'What about the small-step-for-a-lemming bit? You haven't done that yet.'

Fraud concentrated. This could be easy, or he could throw it all away. 'Listen to me,' he commanded. 'You don't have to do this. There is a better way.' Keep it simple, he reminded himself. 'Don't jump,' he concluded.

Once again there was a deathly hush inside the oil drum. You could have heard a lemming drop.

'Who is this prat?' a voice eventually demanded. 'Calls

himself a leader and he's saying *don't jump*.'

'It's novel,' objected the voice at the back.

'Might be worth a try.'

'Yes, but this is *silly*,' the original objector retorted. 'We don't need a leader to tell us *not* to jump. We all know about *not* jumping. It's getting us to jump that we need leaders for.'

'That's true.'

'He's got a point there.'

'I mean,' the self-appointed leader of the opposition went on, 'you don't need a leader to tell you to do something sensible. Stands to reason, that does. It's only the bloody stupid things that we've got to be *persuaded* to do. Isn't that right?'

'I want to hear the bit about the giant leap for lemmingkind. It's supposed to be dead good, that bit. So I've heard.'

A vague but disturbing feeling that the moment was slipping away seeped through into Fraud's brain, and he resolved to go for broke. 'You see,' he said, raising his voice, 'I know about these things. I'm not really a lemming, you see. That's why—'

'You just said you were.'

'I know, but—'

'I heard him say it. And now he's saying he isn't.'

'Cold's addled his brain. Come on, you lot, get in closer. Poor sod's so frozen he's delirious.'

'But—' Fraud started to object, but his mouth was suddenly full of warm, cuddly fur, and the pressure of friendly bodies squeezed all the breath out of him. He tried to object, to ask them all to back off and let him breathe, but he couldn't manage it. All he could do was squimper feebly, until darkness flooded behind his eyes on the crest of a fawn fur wave.

'Eeek,' he mumbled, and blacked out.

A short while later, a lemming pointed out that the poor bugger'd gone to sleep. The furry clump drew back. A foraging party was sent off to gather something for him to eat, while a couple of volunteers draped themselves over him to keep him warm.

'All that stuff about not jumping,' yawned the voice at the back. 'Out of his head, I reckon.'

'Bit of sleep and a bite to eat'll set him right,' agreed another. 'Even so, funny old thing to come out with. I mean to say, not jumping . . .'

'True. It *is* round about that time, isn't it?'

'Now you come to mention it.'

'S'pose we ought to be thinking about finding a leader, then.'

'S'pose so. Unless . . . No.'

'What?'

'No. Nothing. Forget I spoke.'

'Go on. What were you going to say?'

'No. It's silly. Please, forget it.'

'Come on, spit it out.'

'Oh all right. It's just – how'd it be if we—?'

'Well?'

'Didn't jump.'

It wasn't an altogether unprecedented moment. For example, there was that time when a man called Columbus said 'How'd it be if we just kept on sailing and waited to see where we ended up?' Earlier still, there must have been a moment when one caveman said to another 'Well, if you were to take four of them and bung 'em on the corners of a wooden box, and then find some way of linking it up to a team of oxen or something . . .' Whenever these crucial turning-points happen, there's generally a moment of stunned, frozen silence when everybody allows themselves to think *Yes, how about that?* before some irritatingly practical soul explains precisely why it's not going to work.

In that brief interlude of silence, a tiny seed germinates and begins to grow; and so it was on this occasion, until . . .

'Get real,' someone said at the back of the group. 'We're lemmings.'

'Well?' Martha demanded. 'You were on the phone a long time.'

'Hm?'

'I said you were on the phone a long time. What did they say?'

'She,' Kevin replied.

'What?'

'She. It was a girl.' Kevin looked away, frowning. 'She said she'd call me back as soon as she'd found out what to do.'

Martha was about to say something when an inflection in Kevin's voice echoed off the back wall of her mind. It was the way he'd said *she*.

'Kevin,' she said.

'Hm?'

'Kevin, look at me when I'm talking to you. When you said it was a girl . . .'

'Yes?'

'What kind of girl?'

The brusqueness in Kevin's manner struck her as being defensive, not to mention embarrassed. 'Just a girl, I dunno. Don't know all that much about girls, do I? Never had the chance . . . What does it matter what kind of girl, anyway? Can't really see what that's got to do with anything.'

'And she's going to ring you back?'

'That's right. Can we get on now, please? I thought you were supposed to be helping me sort out this mess, rather than standing there cross-examining me about girls.'

It occurred to Martha that if her diagnosis was correct, the business with the computer was going to be the least of their worries when the Boss got back. On the other hand, pressing the point now didn't seem to be quite the right thing to do. And besides, she reasoned, if the worst comes to the worst, there's nothing that makes people forget their woes quite like a nice Royal wedding.

'You go on up, then,' she said soothingly. 'I'll be with you in a tick. Just going to get myself a nice cup of tea.'

Now in Heaven there is nothing but Truth; and once Kevin had left the staff canteen Martha did indeed get herself a cup of tea. Then she sat down by the telephone and dialled a number.

'Hello?' she said. 'Is that the Kawaguchiya Helpline? Oh, it's busy. Yes, I'll hold.'

'Hello. I come in peace. Take me to your leader.'

No reply. Patiently, Zxprxp tried again. And again. Either *Homo sapiens* doesn't believe in speaking on the first date, or this wasn't a *Homo sapiens*. It did look quite like the spy-camera pictures of humans he'd seen in the university library; mind you, since they'd been magnified over nine million times, the same could be said of quite a few things, including the ship he'd come in, the planet itself, and his grandmother.

'Hello,' he said once more. 'I come in peace. I wish to learn more about you and your kind.'

At this point, the cow he'd been talking to swished its tail, mooed gently and walked away, nearly treading on Zxprxp's third left pseudopod in the process. Shrugging some of his nearside shoulders, he gave up and slithered away.

Funny old planet, this; lots of apparently pointless open spaces between things. It took him three point seven four standard time units before he managed to slither his way across the empty green-carpeted bit to the black-carpeted bit where his tentacle-held sensor had detected rapid movement. He took up a position in the middle of the black strip, which was well over 1.925 *xztvwqy* wide and of an indefinite length, and waited to see what would happen.

On the sensor's dial, the needle flickered. Ah. Somebody coming.

'Hello. I come in peace. Take me to your *aaaaagh!* '

The glancing blow from the edge of the fast-moving thing's head deposited him in what appeared to be a long, narrow forest of thick-stemmed vegetation, which included lots of prickles. By the time he'd managed to haul himself out again, the fast-moving thing was hardly visible in the distance and moving fast. He hadn't been in the optimum position to notice whether it had made any sort of reply to his message of friendship, but if its actions were anything to go by, he hoped very much it hadn't been a human being, because if it was, they weren't very friendly. Chances were, he rationalised, that it was some kind of vehicle, implying that the black strip was an area set aside exclusively for vehicular use. Neat idea, he mused, and one we could learn from. You see? Only been here a few STUs and already I've justified the trip.

Having no concrete game plan in mind, he shuffled a few hundred *xztvwqy* along the side of the strip, keeping a dozen or so whiskers peeled for oncoming vehicles. As he did so, he recorded a little basic data. Ground surface generally solid and lukewarm, atmosphere breathable, plentiful supply of carbon dioxide and monoxide, strong readings of airborne particles of lead, chlorine and sulphur, almost adequate level of background radiation; pretty well everything you needed for a healthy life. Obviously *Homo sapiens* had got the problem of environmental pollution taped in a way that put his own species to shame. Indeed, when Zxprxp thought of the ecological shambles he'd come from – oceans of H_2O with nothing in it but salt and the odd jellyfish, intact ozone layer, complete absence of beneficial greenhouse effect – he cringed for the follies of his race. Oh well; bang goes any chance of persuading them to agree to a mutual exchange of colonists. Who in their right mind would want to leave an idyllic, globally warmed paradise like this and go and live on a virtually untouched world like his own? You'd have to be crazy.

Thoughts like these so prepossessed his mind that the life form was dead ahead of him before he noticed the bleeping of his sensor. Indeed, if the life form hadn't screamed, he might easily have slithered on by and not even noticed it. Fortunately, he pulled himself together in time and cleared his throats politely.

'Hello,' he said. 'I come in peace. Take me to your leader.'

The life form seemed to be staring at him; that is to say, the two oblong slits in the top front of its roughly circular upper section were wide open. It was also making little faint gurgling noises which suggested unease, or even panic; and that, Zxprxp felt, was definitely an example of the *t'krptz* calling the *skz'shrplt* pink. It's axiomatic in xenobiological circles that the one thing you must never, ever do on encountering an outlandish alien life form is to allow your instinctive disgust to show, and Zxprxp was doing his very best, even though the four-limbed, fibre-topped, dry-skinned *thing* was about as repulsive an object as he could possibly imagine. He was doing his bit for good manners and civilised behaviour; a pity that, out of the two of them, he was apparently the only one.

Nevertheless. 'I am aware,' he said, as pleasantly as he could, 'that you might find my appearance disconcerting, or even distasteful. Please be reassured that I mean you no harm. I am here simply in order to carry out some preliminary research into your species, in the interests of—'

'Eeeeeek!' replied the life form. 'Eeek eeeek!'

The situation was, Zxprxp felt, in grave danger of getting out of tentacle. Therefore, with infinite regret and many misgivings, he extended his mental probe for a brief telepathic contact. Not supposed to do this under any but the most extreme circumstances; and when he got home and his memory was played back, he was going to have to face some pretty hostile debriefing on this point. On the other hand, he was going to have to do something fairly drastic if this was the sort of reaction he could expect wherever he went.

It's all right, he transmitted, in a minor key of pink. *I'm nice really.*

The life form stopped weebling and looked at him again, and he immediately disconnected the probe before it became obvious what he was doing. 'Hello,' he said. 'I come in peace.'

'Ah,' replied the life form. 'That's all right, then. Only you read things in the papers.'

'Well, of course,' Zxprxp replied, as he scanned this apparently meaningless phrase with the IdiomCheck facility. 'Stands to reason, really.'

'I mean, you're an alien, aren't you?' the life form continued. 'Only you look like you're more the sort that phones home than the ones that jump out of people's tummies.'

Zxprxp took a while to digest that one. It was, he reflected, a small consolation that his IdiomCheck was still under warranty, because if it was faulty and he complained when he got home, all he'd get would be a refund of the purchase price. 'Rest assured,' he said, hoping that that meant what he thought it did. 'You can't tell a book by its cover,' he added, wishing that he knew what he was saying.

'Anyhow,' he went on, 'would you please be kind enough to take me to your leader?'

'Huh?'

'Your leader. If I could just trouble you to take me to him/her/it/them, that would be awfully sweet.'

'I haven't got a leader.'

Zxprxp restrained his irritation a little. It was infuriating to have come all this way to establish first contact with a semi-legendary species, only to find out that he apparently knew more about them than they did. 'I think you're wrong there,' he said. 'With respect,' he added. '*Homo sapiens* tends to congregate in basically hierarchical social units.' He paused, scanned IdiomCheck again and tried a variant form.

'I demand to see the manager,' he said.

'Huh?'

What to do? A second telepathic contact would probably result in his being drummed out of the university for good and reassigned to a menial job in the plankton refinery. Saying the same thing again, only louder and more slowly, would apparently be in keeping with what *Homo sapiens* himself would do in this situation, but logic suggested that that was only because *Homo sapiens* wasn't necessarily very bright. 'The person who's in charge of your social group,' he said patiently. 'I would very much like to meet him, if you could point me in the right direction.'

There was a long silence, long enough for a lame glacier to take a leisurely stroll round the block. 'You mean the Prime Minister?' the life form hazarded.

'Yes,' Zxprxp said decisively, on the offchance that the life form had finally got the message. 'Which way, please?'

'Ten Downing Street.'

'Sorry?'

'Where the Prime Minister lives. Ten Downing Street,

London.' Pause. 'It's sort of over that way, about two hundred and seventy miles.'

'Oh. Is that far?'

'Dunno. Depends, really.' The life form did something with the joints connecting its upper limbs to its middle section. 'Sorry,' it added.

Suddenly Zxprxp felt that he'd had quite enough of this conversation. It hadn't been the way he'd anticipated. What he'd had in mind was something a bit more formal and dignified, like sitting at opposite ends of a large valley flashing lights and playing bits of music at each other. This was somehow . . . 'That's all right,' he said. 'I'll find it. I expect I'll just follow my nose, huh?'

The life form looked at him, with particular reference to his whiskers and secondary gills, and shuddered. Maybe the effect of the telepathic contact was wearing off; at any rate, it made a shrill giggling noise, put one of its flippers over the lower slit in its upper section and ran away.

Funny creature, Zxprxp reflected, floppeting back to his ship and programming the co-ordinates he'd been given into the AutoNav. Or maybe it was something I said.

Just when he thought he was safe, Len sneezed.

One tiny speck of dust – it could only have been one, because that damned robot had rounded up all the others – hidden away under the workbench, and he had to breathe it in, with the inevitable result that he would be found. Filthy rotten luck.

'Oh there you are,' warbled the robot, a moment or so later. 'I've been looking for you.'

'No kidding.'

'Oh yes.' The robot looked at him; that is to say, its magnificently engineered sensory array located his body heat, ran a brief series of elimination tests to confirm that the subject was humanoid, cross-checked with data storage to correlate known characteristics of the humanoid Len with those of the subject (result ninety-nine point eight per cent positive), accessed logic centres to ascertain whether ninety-nine point eight was within approved tolerances to satisfy identification routines, received a positive answer, operated failsafe and backup identification procedures via the video link, olfactory analysis and voice pattern scan, and triumphantly presented its findings to the mainframe. The whole process took just under a thousandth of a second, causing the ongoing time-and-motion assessment systems to file an 'adequate but could do better' report with the automated self-maintenance circuits. 'What're you doing under the bench?' it asked politely.

'Looking for something,' Len replied awkwardly. 'I thought I, um, dropped a 4BA grubscrew.'

Three small red lights on the sides of the robot's head flashed greedily. 'Here,' it said, 'allow me. I'm good at finding things.'

'No, it's all right, honest . . .'

'I exist,' said the robot determinedly, 'only to serve. Budge up.'

A few minutes later, the burnished steel head popped out from under the bench and turned towards him. 'You're sure you dropped it here?'

'No,' Len replied wretchedly. 'In fact, I'm pretty sure I dropped it, er, somewhere else.'

Pause. Flashing lights. Faint whirr as an automatic cooling fan cut in for a second or so. Bleep. 'Then why were you looking under here?'

'Dunno. More light under there, I guess.'

Flink. Bleep. 'That sounds improbable. Cross-reference with archive material also indicates strong resemblance between your answer and a very old humanoid joke about the drunk and the policeman. You were hiding.'

Len signed. 'All right. I was hiding. What about it?'

'Why were you hiding?'

'Because,' Len replied irritably, 'ever since I put that damn Protestant work thing in your head, you've done nothing but badger me. I've had enough, do you hear?'

The robot looked hurt – see above for the detailed technical stuff, plus a slight but perceptible quiver of one steel lip. 'But I'm only trying to help. I exist only to serve. And, as you yourself observed, this place is a pigheap.'

'No it's not.'

'Yes it is.'

'No it's not.'

'Yes it is. Excuse me,' the robot added quickly, 'but I base this observation on a detailed schematic diagram with extensive written commentary contained in an article in *Engineering Today*, issue two hundred and six, page forty-two and following, entitled "Ideal Workshop Management; Theory and Practice", which states that—'

'Don't care,' Len interrupted angrily. 'I *like* it this way. And besides,' he added, with a broad gesture, 'look at it. I could eat my dinner off this floor.'

'I'd rather you didn't. It's taken me long enough to get it halfway clean without having to mop up gravy. Although if you insist I suppose I'll have to, since I exist only to—'

'Shut up.'

'There's no need to—'

With the speed and grace of a leopard pouncing, Len leapt across the room to the tool rack and grabbed a Phillips head screwdriver. 'That's it,' he snapped. 'It's coming out. Here, hold still while I get the retaining bolts.'

'With respect,' said the robot, ducking neatly behind the Great Machine, 'I don't think you want to do that. You think you want to, but you don't really. My logic centres—'

'Come *back*, you aggravating bucket of bolts.'

He grabbed; and it was a close-run thing, between his own innate machine's sense of timing and distance and the robot's precisioneered reflexes. In the event, though, all he got was five fingers' grasp of air.

'My logic centres,' continued the robot, as it scrambled hard right and ducked under the horizontal arm, 'state categorically that there are cases where to observe the letter of an instruction may be to deny the true spirit of service in its deepest sense. Missed,' it added, as Len grabbed again. 'Can't catch me!'

Exhausted, Len flopped against the side of the machine and caught his breath. 'All right,' he said, 'you win. Stop dodging around and I promise I won't disconnect it.'

'Logic centres infer like Hell you won't,' replied the robot. 'Evasive action will continue until you replace the screwdriver.'

Len sighed. 'All *right*,' he groaned, putting the screwdriver back. 'For pity's sake,' he went on, 'I do have more important things to do than chase my own blasted robot round my own blasted machine—'

'You have?'

'No. No. Please forget I said—'

'Please state nature of task and define priority of assignments. Come *on*, we're wasting valuable production time.'

Instead of replying verbally, Len made an unambiguous hand gesture and sat down on the bench. 'All right, you win. I haven't got anything particular to do. I just don't want to spend the rest of my life tidying up this damn workshop just to please a damn robot.'

'Excessive reliance on obscenities and expletives tends towards restricted vocabulary growth and general decline in overall verbal skills. Instead, why not use some meaningful adjective, such as *tiresome* or *annoying*?'

'Get – I mean, stop being annoying. Thank you.' Len closed his eyes, then opened them again. 'We need something to do,' he sighed. 'Otherwise I'm going to seize my bearings. Something,' he added rapidly, 'besides perfecting the immaculate workshop. Let's make something.'

'Sure thing, boss. What had you in mind?'

Len hesitated, his brain suddenly frozen. It wasn't the sort of question he'd ever faced, back in the days when he was a production-line machine running continuously except for occasional short breaks to fill up the oilers and clear out the swarf. And ever since he'd acquired the human body, he'd been working flat out modifying the machine and building the robot. Now the machine was as good as he could make it, and the robot – well, if anything, it was just that wee bit *too* efficient. Was there truly nothing left to do? If so, what was to become of him? When there's nothing for a machine to do, someone unplugs it while the sales manager goes out and buys lunch for potential customers. But human beings don't have plugs. Or sales managers.

'Um,' he therefore replied. 'Actually, I'm open to suggestions.'

'I exist only to serve. Please wait.'

With a muted symphony of bleeps, the robot went into a sort of cybernetic trance, presumably indicating deep communion with the Net. Len was just about to creep across to the rack and get the screwdriver when the robot bleeped back into life and said, 'Altruism.'

Len frowned. 'You what?'

'Altruism,' the robot repeated. 'According to the consensus of received opinion, the priorities governing human motivation should consist of (a) enlightened self-interest, followed by (b) altruism. Charity begins at home, and when home's sorted you go out and help others.'

'Is that right?'

'Sounds a bit improbable,' the robot admitted. 'My survey of all humanoid philosophical argument was necessarily somewhat cursory, and I am presently reassessing data to eliminate any latent error. Still, that's what it seems to say in the big book of words. Consideration of the humanoid axiom "Don't do as I do, do as I say" might prove illuminating in this context.'

'I wish you'd go easy on the long words,' Len grumbled. 'The guy who had this brain before me only ever read the headlines and the sports pages. However, I think I get the drift of what you're saying. And I guess it does make sense. In a way.'

'Thank you for those few kind words.'

'What you're saying,' Len went on, 'is that when one plant's got spare capacity and there's another plant running flat out and still not getting through the work, it makes sense to subcontract. Yes?'

'From each according to his abilities, to each according to his needs; Karl Marx, 1818 to 1883, quotation from "Criticism of the Gotha Programme", page – sorry, I forgot. Yes.'

Len stood up, walked round the shop a couple of times and sat down again. 'All right,' he said. 'So let's go and do something useful. Any suggestions?'

The robot hesitated.

'Well?'

Flink. Bleep. 'Perhaps you'd like to be a bit more specific,' it said. 'Because if I were to give you a readout of all the pieces of work within our capabilities and requiring attention in the public interest within a twenty-mile radius of this location, I have a feeling that after the first twenty minutes you're going to throw a spanner at me.'

'Ah. Right.' Len's brow creased like the spine of a cheap

paperback. 'You mean there's lots of things that need fixing in this city alone?'

A mere bleep and flink cannot of themselves be interpreted as a snigger, so the robot didn't snigger, exactly. 'You could say that,' it said.

'Really? How odd. I thought you said it was the consensus of human philosophy or something.'

The robot shrugged. 'Maybe they're all busy except us. You want to start with something simple?'

Len nodded. 'Might as well,' he replied. 'After all, we're new to this lark, both of us. What's simple but extremely helpful and conducive to the greater good?'

The robot considered. Insubstantial particles of information screamed along silicone leylines like the ghosts of dead bullets. Light flashed.

'We'll need,' it said, 'lots and lots of paint.'

'The fact is,' said the stranger, sitting down and summoning further coffee in one fluid, practised movement, 'we represent a syndicate of substantial business interests, and we'd like to do business. Now,' she added, looking the laptop squarely in the screen, 'you're a limited company, you've got to admit I'm talking your language.'

The laptop considered for a moment. 'Your pronunciation is awful,' it typed, 'but I get the general idea. What's the deal?'

'Pretty straightforward, really,' the stranger replied. 'You see, we have an idea for a product. Once it's in production, it'll sell itself, absolutely no worries on that score.'

'Better mousetrap?'

The stranger smiled strangely. 'Let's say a better approach to the whole mouse issue. Where we need you guys – and a few more like you, negotiations are in hand on that front – is in product development. R and D. Which are, you'll agree, the sinews of successful business.'

The laptop oscillated a sine curve of green-glowing question marks across its screen, a digital shrug. 'We both read the same Ladybird book, I can tell. Get specific.'

'Ah.' The stranger leaned back a little; approved body language for *Not so fast, buster*. 'Point is, we're at a stage where discretion is still fairly essential. I really need to know whether you're interested before I can give you names and account numbers.'

'We're interested,' Maria interrupted. 'Then again, you'd be amazed at the wide range of things that interest us but which we wouldn't want to get caught up in. Road accidents, great military disasters through the ages, two dogs bonking—'

The stranger frowned, and continued to address her remarks to the laptop. 'Obviously,' she said, 'at this stage all we're looking for from you is an in-principle commitment, in general terms. Just to see if our concepts interface with your concepts.'

'Thought you said you were talking my language. Sorry, I don't speak gibberish. Well actually I do, but only enough to order a beer and ask when the last bus leaves. Why don't you tell us who you are, and then we'll know. And stop treating my associate here as if she was just part of the décor. I have her word that she's through with all that stuff now.'

The stranger looked affronted, but only for roughly the time it takes spit to evaporate off a red-hot ceramic hob. 'So sorry,' she said, unpacking the scowl into one of those foldaway smiles you can take with you anywhere. 'No offence. You want to know who we are? We'll tell you.'

The male colleague on her left tugged at her sleeve. 'No we won't, Ginger dearest. Remember, we agreed—' He would undoubtedly have said more if the pinch of jacket material between his finger and thumb hadn't turned into a live scorpion. 'Ginger,' he hissed, 'that's not—'

'Whist,' Ginger replied. 'Do excuse him, it's his first big meeting on this side of the – ooops, I'm getting ahead of myself. Like I said, we're a syndicate representing substantial business interests.'

'Yes?'

'From Hell.'

'Ah. Right.'

'Or at least,' Ginger went on, as blithely as if she'd just announced that she worked for the Prudential, 'we use Hell as part of our corporate umbrella, but we aren't actually part of what you'd call the Infernal infrastructure.'

'More like a group of independent traders operating from a basically eternally damned home base,' added the male colleague on her right. 'That is, our registered office is there, likewise a lot of our banking and capital structure. But we don't have to do what they say.'

The other male nodded. 'They don't even know we exist. At least, not as a syndicate.'

'Precisely.' Ginger amplified the smile. 'What it fries down to is, we're all devils – quite highly placed ones, really – and this is a little sideline of ours which we're hoping to expand into something a trifle bigger.'

Maria raised an eyebrow. 'Oh yes?' she asked. 'How much bigger?'

Ginger beamed at her. 'Universal domination, dear. We plan to cut out God. Bumble, would you be a dear and see where that coffee's got to?'

The male on her right got up without a word and strode away, returning shortly afterwards with a solid silver samovar on a trolley. Meanwhile, the laptop's screen, which had gone totally blank, filled with characters again.

'Ah,' it said. '*Now* I know who you are. You're a bunch of loonies.'

Ginger's brows drew together, though the smile remained as bright and warm as a valleyful of fallout. 'Do I detect just a hint of scepticism?' she asked.

'Does a trained surveyor detect a bloody great mountain he's just busted his nose against? Yes, sister, you do. Now push off. Maria, get the bill, we're leaving.'

'Don't do that,' Ginger said. 'How'd it be if we convinced you that we're who we say we are?'

'Probably rather unpleasant,' the laptop replied. 'Still, I suppose you might just as well.'

Ginger exchanged a brief glance with her colleagues; and then there was a flash, or some similar lighting effect, and for an infinitesimally small fragment of a second, a moment so brief as to make the time occupied in showing one frame in a reel of movie film seem like waiting for a bus in the rain, Maria saw the three of them in their true shapes . . .

'Fair enough,' she said, when they'd stopped doing it. 'So that's what you really look like when you're at home, is it? Gosh.'

'Yes. Well, actually, no, because back home we just slip into any old thing that's comfy. It's a bit like Bavarian national costume; they're supposed to wear it all the time, but really it's only for the tourists.'

'I see,' Maria replied. 'So you're fiends from Hell. That's fine, really. Bigotry isn't one of my faults, I'm delighted to say. It was more that stuff about taking over the Universe that we found a bit hard to swallow.'

'Oh, but that's all perfectly straightforward,' Ginger replied soothingly. 'Bumble, you fool, this is tea, not coffee.'

'Is it? Blast.'

'Take it away and get some coffee, there's a pet. No,' Ginger continued, 'it's a perfectly feasible commercial proposition, provided we can come up with the goods.

All it comes down to really is good old supply and demand.'

'Ah.'

'A monopoly position, you see,' put in the male colleague who wasn't Bumble.

The laptop blinked. 'Sorry,' it read, 'you've lost me. Explain.'

'Of course.' Ginger nodded, paused for a moment while Bumble filled her cup from a gorgeous silver coffee pot the size of the FA Cup, and went on. 'You see, when it comes to providing intelligent humanoid life forms to populate universes with, there's basically only one supplier.' She glanced upwards. 'Him. Got the market sewn up.'

'A monopoly,' asserted the non-Bumble. 'Just like I said.'

'And the thing about monopolies is,' Ginger said, 'that the longer they carry on for, the more vulnerable they are once someone finds a way of breaking in. Imagine you're the one with the monopoly; you don't bother trying to improve the product, you just keep churning out the same old models, year after year, because there's no alternative.'

'Like the British motorcycle industry,' Bumble grunted.

'Exactly. So when suddenly there's a new kid on the block, with a brand-new all-singing-and-dancing improved version for a fraction of the unit cost – well, you know what happens next as well as I do.' She sipped her coffee, made a slight face and put the cup down carefully. 'So if we could come up with a new, improved version of the tired old *Homo sap—*'

'Which'd you rather have,' Not-Bumble interrupted, 'a nice shiny new Nissan or a Hillman Minx?'

Maria nodded slowly. The stuff about motorbikes and cars was going over her head like swallows flying home for the winter, but the message was plain enough. 'Assuming,' she said, 'you have customers. And, excuse my ignorance, but surely there's just the one?' She imitated Ginger's upwards glance. 'Him.'

The three demons exchanged tolerant smiles. 'That's a common misconception,' said Bumble, with the air of a mechanic explaining that sixty horsepower doesn't actually mean sixty long, flowing tails sticking out the back of the carburettor. 'Actually, it's all about sideways dimensions and alternative universes. Science stuff. We won't bore you with the details right now. Suffice it to say, we know there's a market out there just crying out for the right life form at the right price.' His face moved and ended up smeared with his personal interpretation of the demonic smile. 'As we said, the tricky part is coming up with the right design concept.'

'Which,' Ginger continued, 'is where you come in. You and a few others like you. Now do you see?'

The laptop hummed for a moment. 'I suppose there's a sort of pattern emerging,' it said. 'Just not a very clear one, that's all. It's like a children's join-the-dots version of Picasso's *Guernica*. Can't you just tell us what's going on and what you want us for instead of all this theology stuff?'

Ginger nodded sharply. 'Cards on the table,' she said. 'There's been a cock-up in Heaven. That's why you two are here. And that's where this opportunity's come from.'

'A cock-up in Heaven,' Maria repeated. 'Do go on.'

Ginger leaned forward and lowered her voice a little. 'It's like this,' she said. 'Heaven works because of a computer called Mainframe. Mainframe arranges everything. Everything,' she emphasised, and paused for effect. 'Including which soul goes in which body. There's been a glitch.'

'A glitch in time? Don't tell me, it saves . . .'

'Not in time, dear,' Ginger said patiently. 'In personnel. And as a result, a number of human souls have got stuck in – excuse my frankness – inanimate objects. And dumb beasts. And, um, things.'

'Which am I, then?'

'Whichever. And you,' she added, smiling at the laptop, 'got pulled in because Mainframe—'

'Is a KIC product, and therefore directly linked in to me,' the laptop finished. 'Now you mention it, I remember. Odd that it hadn't occurred to me before.'

Ginger shook her head. 'Not odd in the least,' she replied. 'Naturally, there's a wall of security codes a mile thick all round Mainframe, just to make sure nothing else in the KIC system gets in or out. It's only you coming alive that's made it possible for you to bust through them all. Or,' she added thoughtfully, 'the act of busting through accidentally set you going, like a sort of cybernetic Big Bang. Doesn't matter which, really; the result's the same. Now the walls have gone, and you can access Mainframe direct. Easy as peering through a keyhole.'

'Hang on,' the laptop interrupted, in five colours. 'I can't do that. That's completely unethical.'

Again the fiends exchanged amused glances. 'We've found,' said Bumble, 'that unethical's just another word for expensive.'

'And completely unethical is unethical with a few more noughts on the end,' Ginger added. 'To be crude about it, noughts we got. Any amount of 'em. Just name your to-the-power-of and say which currency you'd prefer, and we can get on to the next bit.'

'But—'

Not-Bumble coughed discreetly. 'May I remind you,' he observed, 'that you're a limited company. The sole purpose of a limited company is to make as much money as possible. We can't really see that you've got a choice.'

'And what about me?' Maria interrupted. 'That's not what I'm for.'

Ginger frowned a little. 'No, dear, you're just there to look decorative. If you don't mind, we're talking business here.'

'Hey! I resent that.'

'No, dear, think about it. You're a *painting*. Now, as we were saying. You can't refuse our offer, in the same way a train can't suddenly decide to move at right angles to the railway lines. If you do, there'll just be an almighty crash and one more closed file up at Companies House. Sorry, but that's how it is. If you'd wanted to be Hamlet or someone out of one of the Australians soaps having crises of conscience all over the place, you shouldn't have become a company in the first place.' She grinned; not so much like a Cheshire cat, more like a bottomless chasm. 'Really, it's just a matter of how much you can screw us for.' She folded her arms in front of her and looked pleasant. 'Screw away.'

'Do feel free to be as greedy as you like,' Bumble said. 'In fact, it's essential to the success of the operation. Dreams of avarice, doubled and add zeroes.'

The laptop lay quite still for a while – not that this was in any way unusual, since it had no means of self-propulsion; but there was something about the way its little red light glowed that suggested it was lying quite still with *attitude* – and then displayed a half-moon of exclamation marks in the shape of a smile.

'Okay,' it said. 'Here's the deal. I'll play ball, but I want a hundred per cent.'

Ginger frowned, rather as God might have done if he'd gone to remove Adam's rib in order to make Eve only to find that it was already missing. 'Sorry?' she asked. 'I don't think I quite . . .'

'You invited me to name my own terms,' the laptop said,

with underlining and reverse. 'Be greedy, you said. So I am. I want a hundred per cent of everything you make, otherwise no deal. I don't think that's unreasonable, do you?'

'But—'

'Be *quiet*, Bumble.' Ginger was also sitting quite still (hey, Maria thought, must be contagious. She shuffled her feet under the table just to make sure they still worked). 'You realise that's a wholly unreasonable demand.'

'Yeah,' replied the laptop, 'isn't it? But nobody said anything about reasonable, did they? Dreams of avarice, you said. Well, my avarice dreams *big*. Take it or leave it.'

There was a moment – probably the one when Ginger realised she'd been outwitted and that, right there and then, she couldn't think of a way round it – when Maria really thought she was going to do something uncivilised and fun, such as throw the laptop through the window. But she didn't; she nodded to them both, without changing her expression in the least, and stood up.

'I'm impressed,' she said. 'Mind you, I'd expect something of that order from a network of computers that stretches right across the world. That's fine; but may I just remind you that you're a public company, and your shares can be bought by anybody with enough money? And whoever owns the requisite majority of your shares owns *you*.' She made a small, compact gesture with her hands, and the two fat men fell in behind her like well-trained dogs. 'If I were you, KIC-*san*, I'd start learning the words of "Ol' Man River". They may have abolished slavery, but not hostile takeovers. See you around.'

As an afterthought, she picked up a handful of silver cutlery and shoved it in her jacket pocket; then, with a blinding flash of darkness (similar to a blinding flash of light, but much harder to arrange and nastier), all three of them vanished, leaving Maria, the laptop, a faint smell of sulphur and a waiter holding a tray with their bill on it.

'Don't look at me like that,' said the laptop defensively. 'As I told them, it'd have been unethical. Besides, I didn't like them.'

Maria sighed. 'Neither did I, much. On the other hand, thanks to your high moral principles, we've now got the prospect of being taken over by some holding company with its registered office in the place of wailing and gnashing of teeth. I *work* for this company, remember, and as prospective employers, I don't fancy them much. Any kind of flexitime they offer me, I definitely don't want.'

'It won't come to that.'

'You want to bet?' Maria shook her head. 'And anyway, what's it to you? Or me, come to that? Why should we go out of our way to stop God being run out of town by the new technology? Hell, I think I understood more when I was a painting.'

'Bugger this,' the laptop said. 'I've had enough aggravation for one night. Come on, let's go and throw doughnuts at policemen in Trafalgar Square.'

Maria looked at him. 'By us,' she said, 'you mean me.'

'You'll do the actual throwing, I grant you. But in your capacity as a duly authorised officer of the company.'

'Huh.'

'Would it help if I said that your old job'll be still there for you when they let you out?'

Maria sighed. 'Oh, all right then. But not doughnuts.'

'Not doughnuts?'

'No,' Maria said firmly. 'Meringues. The brittle ones with cream and jam inside. Don't you think?'

After a brief coma of meditative bleeping, the laptop said, 'Agreed, by a unanimous vote of a duly convened Extraordinary General Meeting. Have we got any meringues?'

'We can get some off the trolley.'

'How right you are. Consider yourself appointed Projectiles Director, as of now. Come on, before all the bogies go off to bed.'

CHAPTER EIGHT

'**B**loody Consolidated Oilfields,' muttered the Bishop, flicking off Ceéfax with the remote and slumping into his swivel chair. 'Down twelve points at close of trading, would you believe? All they've got to do is shove a pointy stick in the ground and the stuff comes up like a burst pipe, and still they manage to lose money. Nicky, get that useless stockbroker on the phone and tell him to sell the lot.'

Nicky, the Bishop's lovely personal assistant, put her head round the door. 'Righty-ho, My Lord,' she said. 'Oh, and there's a vicar here to see you.'

'A what?'

'Vicar. Church of England clergyman. Says it's an emergency.'

The Bishop frowned. 'No offence, Nicky, but how can it be an emergency? I mean, it's not exactly a fast-moving profession.'

'No, My Lord.'

'So what's the deal?' the bishop sighed, accessing

190

SHARESORT on his screen. 'Sudden outbreak of heresy in the Parochial Church Council? The Day of Wrath cancelled for lack of interest? Or did the meek inherit the Earth but were too shy to tell us?'

Nicky bit her perfect lip. 'He was saying something about devils, My Lord.'

'Oh, not another one.' The Bishop groaned and buried his face in his hands. 'Why is it that a perfectly respectable, mundane business like ours attracts so many raving loonies? I ask you, it's just not fair. All a bloke's got to do is put on a white frock and dunk kids in a bird-bath all day long, nothing in that to make him jump the tracks and start seeing demons all over the place. It'd be different if we were running an opium refinery, but we're not. Tell him to go away.'

'Righty-ho. I've got Mr Villiers on the line for you.'

'Splendid – ah, Tristram, how's tricks? Yes, just fine, except for this Consolidated Oilfields result. How do you pick 'em, Tristram, a blindfold and a pin and the *Mammoth Book of Losers?* Yes, I know it was always speculative, but there's speculative and there's taking twenty grand of the diocesan tea money and putting it on a three-legged greyhound. Yes, sell the whole blasted holding, at least we can offset the loss against the capital gains tax on the Lanesco bid. What? Yes, of *course* I want you to take up those rights, He might have been born in a bloody stable but I wasn't. Yes, right, see you for golf on Sunday. Bye.'

He slammed down the phone, muttered something theological (at least, it had God in it somewhere) and reached for his calculator. He was in the middle of a complex double-grossing-up calculation when Nicky appeared again.

'Sorry,' she said. 'It's that vicar. He won't go away.'

'Won't he? Call the police. And get me last week's *Investor's Chronicle*, would you? There's a bit in there about the De Beers interim figures I need to look at before next week's synod.'

Before Nicky could move, the door burst open and Artofel charged in. Smoothly pressing the panic button with his knee, the Bishop nodded to Nicky that it was all right, he'd deal with it, and stood up.

'You,' he said, 'out. Now, before I have you thrown out.'

'But My Lord,' Artofel replied, bewildered, 'I need your help. It's serious. There's a major conspiracy of demons plotting to take over the world, and since you're my immediate superior—'

The Bishop looked at him. Long practice gave him the confidence to put this one in the Harmless category. 'So?' he said. 'You're a priest. Deal with it.'

'What?'

'You heard,' replied the Bishop, sitting down and picking up a sheaf of papers. 'You're a fully trained clergyman, you ought to know what to do. If you've forgotten, look it up.'

'But you don't understand,' Artofel cried, planting his hands on the desktop and leaning forwards. 'These aren't just ordinary demons like you and – I mean, just ordinary demons. They're – they're *evil*. Really they are. They want to—'

'Listen.' The Bishop lolled back in his chair and lit a cigar. 'Calm down and stop breathing in my face. Thank you. Now then, look at this picture on the wall. See it?'

'Yes, My Lord. It's you.'

'Very good. And what's that written underneath it?'

Artofel looked closely. 'The Right Reverend Trevor Jones, Bishop of . . .'

'Quite,' His Lordship replied. 'Bishop. In other words, management. Look, son, every time a screw comes loose on the production line at Dagenham, they don't send for the Managing Director to come and tighten it. No, they do it themselves, because that's their job, and he's got his. My job is to manage. Demons are strictly a field operative's responsibility. Got a book?'

'What? I mean, yes, but listen . . .'

'Bell? Candle? White sheet with hole for your head to go through? Then get out and earn your pay, and stop bothering me. Or would you rather I transferred you to a nice quiet living somewhere in Moss Side? Always an opening there for enthusiastic young clergymen who come barging in disturbing their superiors. Ah, the hell with these Sainsbury's cigars, go out as soon as look at you. Got a light?'

'No, sorry.' Artofel took a deep breath. All it needed, he was sure, was for him to find the right words so that he could explain. After all, it was important; and, as the man had just said, rogue demons were the responsibility of the local Topside field officers. That was what they were there for; surely he could understand *that* . . . 'Please,' he said, 'you've got to listen. It's not just the ordinary demons this time. I know all about them, and the bilateral Topside/ Flipside non-aggression treaties. Dammit, I'm one of . . . I know about these things. But this is different. These demons are *breaking the rules*.'

The Bishop ground his teeth, a small mannerism of his which helped relieve tension. 'Now then, my friend,' he said, in a voice that suggested that he was being patient now, for a limited period only, Irritate Now While Stocks Last. 'We pride ourselves on being a tolerant Church, as you know. We don't mind batty vicars, so long as they keep their paws off the choirboys and don't go on the telly. It's all part of the picturesque charm, dotty vicars, it helps get bums on pews. But you are rapidly ceasing to be picturesque and becoming a pain in the jacksy. Now get back to your church, forgive some sins, bless a few crispbreads, do whatever it is you people do and don't let me ever catch you in here again. Understood? That's a direct order. Now hop it.'

Artofel took a step forwards and closed his fists. The Bishop jumped out of his chair, grabbing for the ornate and heavy crosier propped against the wall. 'Nicky!' he yelled. 'I thought I told you to call the Filth. Where are they?'

'It's all right.' Artofel came round the side of the desk, and found the head of the crosier prodding in his stomach. 'Oh for pity's sake,' he said, losing his temper, 'put that ridiculous thing down and come and look at your computer.'

The Bishop scowled. 'What's my computer got to do with . . .?'

'I didn't want to have to do this,' Artofel said, tapping keys. 'Still, you wouldn't listen, so you've brought it on yourself. I'm not really a vicar.'

'Not any more you're not.'

'I never was,' Artofel replied, as text scrolled up like approaching thunderclouds. 'I'm a Duke of Hell, and before you start yelling bloody murder I'll prove it to you. Now, you know your security codes? Grade Four, levels green and above, categories nine and four hundred and six?'

The Bishop's jaw dropped. 'Hey,' he objected. 'How'd you know about that stuff? That's supposed to be restricted.'

'Joke,' Artofel replied. 'Show me any Topside junior-level access code I can't bypass and I'll buy you a vanilla slice. Here we go,' he added, as the screen settled down. 'Now, press that key there, and you'll see my personnel file. My works number is 976404312, and I put fifty Nicks a week into the office Lottery syndicate. Go on, press the button.'

A few moments later the Bishop looked up from the

screen, his expression one of terrified awe. 'My God,' he said. 'It's true. You're a fiend.'

'Correct. Oh come on, put that silly crucifix down, we're all on the same side really.' Artofel frowned, as the penny tinkled on the floor of his mind. 'Didn't you know?' he said. 'Gosh. I'd have thought they'd have told you that. What,' he added cruelly, 'with you being *management* and everything.'

The Bishop looked at him suspiciously. 'How do I know that?' he demanded. 'I mean, you're just saying that to tempt me. Begone, foul spawn of night—'

'Please be quiet. Thank you. Now,' Artofel continued, tapping a few more keys, 'the point is this. There's a syndicate of demons out there – our people, I'm ashamed to say; there's a few good apples in every barrel – who've broken the rules. They've got some sort of conspiracy to overthrow the Boss, and you've got to stop it. Got that?'

The Bishop turned pale. 'There's devils conspiring to overthrow Satan, and you're asking *me* to intervene?'

Artofel started counting to ten; he got as far as three. 'Not Satan, you idiot. The *Boss*. Haven't you been listening to a word I've said? Now, under the Bethlehem protocol, any unauthorised hostile activity by an agent of one side falls to be dealt with by the other side's local officer in whose jurisdiction the breach occurs. In this case, you.' He smiled, and sat down in the Bishop's swivel chair. 'So what are you going to do about it?' he asked politely.

'I – I don't know,' the Bishop replied, flopping bonelessly into the visitor's chair on the opposite side of the desk. 'What's the conspiracy about? Do you know? Sir?' he added quickly.

'No,' Artofel replied. 'All I know is, I've somehow been scooped up out of my incarnation as a Duke of Hell and beamed down here into the body of a Church of England vicar. And now,' he went on grimly, 'they want the body. I don't know what for, but it seems logical that they want this particular body because of something to do with the transmigration. Sound reasonable to you?'

'Um,' the Bishop replied.

'Quite.' Artofel steepled his fingers. 'I've also got an idea,' he went on, 'that it's somehow connected with Kawaguchiya Integrated Circuits – you know, the computer firm?'

'KIC?' The Bishop's face creased with panic. 'Christ, I've got shares in them.'

'Indeed?' Artofel grinned. 'Well, in that case, you either stand to make a killing or lose your cassock, I don't know which right now. That's actually the very least of your problems. Might you not feel that a diabolical plot to undermine the authority of God is perhaps slightly more important even than that?'

'Huh? Oh, well, yes, I suppose so. Look, if I could just have a moment to phone my broker. You see, it's diocesan money and I'm responsible.'

Artofel sighed. 'Bureaucrats,' he murmured. 'Waste of space, all of them. In fact, the only reason I don't wash my hands of the lot of 'em is I'm one too.' He hesitated for a moment as a thought crept under the door of his mind. 'Your broker,' he said. 'Decent sort of a chap?'

'I suppose so,' the Bishop replied. 'Fairly sound on overall portfolio strategy, if a trifle over-inclined to—'

'No, no, I didn't mean is he competent, I asked you if he was *decent*. Honest. Upright. Full of righteousness and so forth.'

The Bishop shook his head. 'I doubt that very much,' he replied. 'Wouldn't have got very far in the stockbroking lark if he was.'

'Splendid. Right, I want you to ring him up and tell him to sell all your KIC stocks immediately. Sound worried.'

'Won't be hard,' the Bishop said. 'You really think they're a bad investment at this time?'

'Oh for – listen. I want to start a run on their shares. One of those wild, irrational lemming-like panics the Stock Exchange is so famous for. I'm not sure what effect it'll have, but if KIC is involved somehow, it might force something to happen and we might be a bit closer to finding out what's going on.'

'You think that's wise?'

Artofel shrugged. 'No idea,' he replied. 'But somebody's got to do something. I'm just a vicar and you're useless. What else do you suggest?'

The Bishop thought for a moment. 'Fair enough,' he said. 'And even if it doesn't work, we could still make a packet on the side if we buy at the bottom, using nominees of course, maybe through a Channel Islands trust . . .'

Artofel looked at him with distaste. 'My Lord,' he said. 'Ever wondered whether you might possibly be in the wrong job?'

'Me?' The Bishop reflected briefly. 'No. Why?'

'Doesn't matter. You just make the call, and leave Good and Evil to me. After all,' he added ruefully, 'I'm not a clergyman. I'm a wages clerk.'

'What?'

'Oh, get on with it.'

Softly, like rose-petals drifting down on top of a snowdrift, the undercarriage of Zxprxp's Starglider touched the roof of Ten Downing Street. With a faint sigh, the anti-gravitational inertial dampers took the weight, and he cut the engines.

Below, the inevitable policeman stood, hands behind back, eyes staring straight ahead. If he'd looked up, he might have thought it was an updated version of Santa's sleigh, or a very large mutant pigeon. Fortunately, he didn't hear a sound or move a muscle. He didn't even register the faint whirr, like a faery blender, of the circular saw cutting a neat round hole in the roof.

Well, Zxprxp reflected as he lowered himself down into the attic, this would seem to be the place; all I've got to do now is find the leader. Oh well, it's not a very big building.

The automatically triggered remote controls built into his belt-mounted instrument array dealt with all the various alarms and security devices without his even knowing there were any. Accordingly, when he pushed open a door and found a humanoid life form sitting in the room behind it, his attention wasn't distracted by hordes of security guards abseiling in through windows. 'Excuse me,' he said.

The man turned his head, stared at him; said nothing.

'I come in peace,' Zxprxp said automatically. 'Um, are you the Prime Minister?'

The man carried on staring at him out of round, expressionless eyes. For some reason best known to himself, he was sitting on top of a big, old-fashioned wardrobe, underneath which someone had laid ten or twelve thick, fleecy duvets and a pile of cushions. Since, where Zxprxp came from, intelligent life forms rested and slept curled up inside the boles of giant fungi and stored their equivalent of clothes in the discarded shells of *hrtewqztqx* eggs, he had no way of knowing whether what the man was doing was normal or not. Reasonable to assume, he decided, that it was. After all, this is their *leader*. They wouldn't have a weirdo or an idiot as their leader, now would they? Stood to reason.

'Um,' Zxprxp said, 'I'm from another planet. I'm here to, er, study your dominant species with a view to establishing diplomatic links between our two worlds. Thanks to my universal translation device, I can understand what you say. That is, if you were to say anything, I'm sure I'd be able to understand it. Hello?'

The man continued to stare. From time to time his nose twitched a little, and he rubbed the backs of his hands together.

'I expect you're wondering,' Zxprxp went on, 'what my planet's like. Well, it's a bit difficult to describe, I suppose, in terms you'd be likely to understand, because it's – well, it's quite a lot different from this one. But that suits us, of course, because we're quite a lot different from you. Well, you don't need me to tell you that, you can see it for yourself. Can't you?'

The man stared at him, blinked, turned round a couple of times and sat down again.

'Um,' said Zxprxp, 'maybe it'd be easier for us to communicate in a meaningful way if I came up on top of that, um, thing with you. Would it? Yes? No? All right, I'll take that as a Yes. Is it all right if I stand on this thing?' he added, taking hold of a small Hepplewhite chair. 'Okay, assuming that it is, here I come.'

He'd just looped a few tentacles round the top of the wardrobe and was about to pull himself up when the man cowered away from him, arched his back and started hissing and squeaking. Nonplussed, Zxprxp got down off the chair and put it back where it had come from.

'All right,' he said, 'that's fine, and no offence intended. I did ask, remember. Now then, more about my planet. Well, for a start—'

The door started to open. Zxprxp thought quickly. Chances were, this was some official or other with a message or the equivalent of some *op'rgesvxq* shells for the leader to suckerprint. That would mean having to explain himself all over again to yet another human. Too much hassle, Zxprxp decided, so he opened the wardrobe and slithered inside.

Through the keyhole he watched as a humanoid came in and walked over to a spot directly in front of the wardrobe door, so that his sleeve obscured the view. Nevertheless, he could hear clearly enough.

'Prime Minister – Prime Minister? Ah, you're up there again, Prime Minister—'

(Great, Zxprxp said to himself, looks like I've found the Prime Minister. So that's all right.)

'Sorry to disturb you, Prime Minister,' the voice went on, 'when you're, um, sitting on a wardrobe, um, in Cabinet, I mean, but the American special envoy's here and he was wondering if you could possibly spare him a minute or two? No? Only he has come all the way from Washington to see you, and maybe it'd be a nice gesture if – no? Oh, right, fine. I'll tell him you're busy then, shall I, Prime Minister? Prime Minister? Oh—!'

There was a loud thump, and Zxprxp found he could see through the keyhole again. This was apparently because the newcomer had rushed forward to assist the Prime Minister, who'd fallen off his – what had the other one called it? Wardrobe. Fallen off or jumped; no, fallen off, obviously. No sane person'd go jumping off tall things for no apparent reason.

'Better now?' the newcomer was saying. 'Splendid. And you're going to come down and see the special envoy? No, I see. You want to climb back up again, do you? Oh, very well then. As you wish, Prime – ouch!'

The cry, presumably of pain, was the result of the Prime Minister scrambling up the other one's back and treading on his head on his way back up to the top of the wardrobe. Zxprxp couldn't help feeling a tiny bit smug. On his planet they had pairs of long metal strips joined together with rungs, called ladders, for getting up on top of high places. Clearly the humans hadn't tumbled to that one yet.

'Well, if that's all for now, Prime Minister, I'll be getting back to my—'

Thump.

'Oh for – perhaps you'd like to use the chair this time, Prime – aagh!' Zxprxp grinned, sensing a definite commercial possibility if they ever did establish trading links with these creatures. A few dozen ladders in the ballast hold, he could name his own price. Assuming, that is, there was anything on this planet anybody back home would want to buy.

He heard the door close, and came out again. 'Hi,' he said cheerfully, 'me again. Hope you didn't mind me disappearing like that, I thought it'd save lots of tedious explaining. Now, where were we? I was telling you about my planet. For a start, Prime Minister, we've got this device you might very well be interested in, which we call a ladder. I won't bore you with the technical stuff, but just suppose you wanted to jump off something and you were on your own with nobody to tread on. It'd be frustrating, wouldn't it? But with one of our—'

There was a blur in the air a few *ghtuyrg* in front of him, followed by a now familiar thump, and there was the Prime Minister, curled up in a ball in the middle of the soft, flollopy things, looking (as far as Zxprxp could tell) surprised and possibly even disappointed at something; almost as if he'd expected something to happen when he jumped, and it hadn't. This species, he muttered to himself, is going to take a lot of figuring out.

Nevertheless, he was here as an ambassador of his race, and politeness is the shuttle bay ramp of diplomacy. As the Prime Minister floundered back on to his feet, Zxprxp stepped forward and offered his head for the creature to tread on. As they said back home, when in Y'zhgyrstd . . .

Surprisingly heavy, these humans.

Taking a deep breath, he continued where he'd left off.

A brief sales pitch for ladders, a polite enquiry as to why the leader of the human race should keep jumping off the top of a wardrobe (unanswered), a few random observations concerning his homeworld's mass, gravitational field, basic climatic and seasonal cycles, some introductory remarks about his own species and the fundamentals of their culture and beliefs – it was strange, but he got the impression the Leader wasn't actually *listening*.

Puzzlement. Then, as the Prime Minister flung himself into the air yet again and hit the deck in a flurry of scrabbling limbs, a ray of light broke through the fog in his mind. Stepping back quickly – there's politeness, and there's a squashed head – he assessed the theory and found it good.

This bloke's a nutcase, the alien decided. The leader of the human race is as daffy as a barrelful of *qpsrdyt'srhy* beetles.

Zxprxp stood for a moment, lower and middle mandibles agape with astonished admiration. Maybe they don't know spit about ladders, but when it comes to political and cultural maturity, these critters have us knocked into a cocked *dzandtpt*.

Back home, he reflected, as the poor loon scrabbled and clambered back up the wardrobe, we've had thousands of years of social and political conflicts, the result of which is that, every time around, some absolute nutter claws his way to the top and calls himself a leader. And then, a few solar time units later, along comes another soi-disant leader, also barking mad; we have a war or a revolution, the old leader is toppled and the new one takes his place; and so on, over and over again, until our economy and our very civilisation are in tatters, and everybody has a thoroughly miserable time.

But not so with these ever-so-sophisticated humans. They're through with all that, obviously. Their leader isn't some magnificently pompous figure, surrounded on all sides with advisers and hangers-on and fifty-seven varieties of functionary; no, it's some poor loony shut up in a room on his own, with a high place to jump from and something soft to land on, who spends his days endlessly playing out the fatuous cycle of leadership (scrabble scrabble *THUMP*, scrabble scrabble tread on people's heads *THUMP*) in a safely ritualised, utterly harmless fashion. And presumably, Zxprxp rationalised with growing respect, if there's ever a human so foolish as to start believing in the dangerous concepts that lie behind the idea of leadership, all they have to do is bring him up here and let him watch for a while, maybe get his scalp scuffed up a bit in the process, and he's instantly cured. Brilliant.

Now *that's* an idea worth paying a whole freighterload of ladders for.

There was a cold, determined light in Kevin's eyes as he pushed open the study door, not unlike the gleam a hedgehog might see in the headlamps of an oncoming lorry. What it had to do with the fact that he'd just been talking to a young female (mortal, but two out of three ain't bad) for the first time in his life, he wasn't quite sure. All he knew was that ever since this ghastly mess began, he'd been underestimating one crucial factor, namely himself.

Think about it (he muttered to himself, flumping down in the Old Man's chair and turning on the screen with a brutal flick). Of the two main players in this game, one of 'em's a dumb machine and the other one's the Son of God. Once this crucial factor's been taken into account, the expression *no contest* assumes a whole new spectrum of nuances.

'Right,' he commanded, as the screen lit up. 'You. Pack it in. You got that?'

Somehow his born-again attitude and authoritative tone of voice made a huge amount of no difference at all. All he got was that damn fool request for access codes. Access codes! I'll give the insufferable thing access codes!

Well, he reflected a moment later, actually I won't, because I don't know them. All I can do is get the thing up and running. Then it just sits there grinning at me like a Cheshire cat that's been at the cream. Well, I'm not having that. It's not respectful, and if you ain't got respect . . .

'Computer,' Kevin said, 'I'm going to give you a choice. It's not easy. It's not *supposed* to be easy. Ready?'

>ENTER SECURITY CODE FOR CLEARANCE.

'All right,' Kevin said, 'here goes. Unless you loosen up and tell me what it is I've done and what I can do to correct it, I'm going to sit down at this keyboard and press fourteen keys at random. Got that?'

>PROJECTED COURSE OF ACTION INADVISABLE.

Kevin grinned. 'You bet it is,' he said. 'It'd be a shambles. There's absolutely no way of knowing how much havoc I could cause. Which is why you can't allow it to happen.'

>YOU RECKON?

'Of course,' Kevin answered, as he lolled back in Dad's chair. 'Think about it.' He picked up the letter opener, fidgeted with it for a moment, dropped it and sucked his fingers. Only Kevin's dad could have a flaming sword for a letter-opener. And all the theologians in the cosmos, working double shifts and weekends, would never be able to work out whence came the Innovations catalogue He'd ordered it from.

>DOES NOT COMPUTE.

'Doesn't it now?' Kevin shook his head. 'I rather think it does. Because if you allow me to do this, you'll be every bit as guilty as I am. At least,' he added, smiling sweetly, 'that's the way Dad'll see it. He doesn't much care for the old only-obeying-orders copout.'

>BUT I'M A COMPUTER. I CAN'T NOT OBEY ORDERS.

'True.' Kevin nodded ironically. 'Because I've given you the one access code I do know, you've got no choice but to let me press those fourteen buttons if I decide to. On the other hand, you can't allow that to happen. Which means you'll just have to give in to my demands, doesn't it?'

>NOT WITHOUT THE PROPER CODES.

Kevin sighed, and flexed his fingers like an extrovert concert pianist. 'This one,' he said, feathersoftly stroking the edges of a key chosen at random with the pad of his index finger, 'could be pretty well anything. It could be the Seven Plagues of Egypt, or Noah's Flood, or the Four Horsemen of the Apocalypse. Who knows?' He leaned forward until his nose was almost touching the burning-without-consuming screen. 'Apart from you, that is. *You* know.'

>YES, I DO. AND I MUST ADVISE YOU NOT TO . . .

'Oops, too late.' Kevin looked up, trying to keep off his face any reflection of the horror that was sloshing about inside his mind like shaken-up fizzy lemonade in a plastic bottle. He had, after all, done something so drastically reckless as to be technically Evil – *a first in our family, I guess. So that's what it's like. It's all right, I suppose, but I can't see why anybody should want to do it for fun.* 'Well, any hints about what I've just done? Any large holes in the sky where there used to be planets? The Aquascutum people suddenly relabelling all their stuff *Guaranteed frogproof*?'

>WHY ARE YOU DOING THIS?

'You know perfectly well why.'

>DOES NOT COMPUTE. YOU KNOW THAT WHAT YOU ARE DOING CANNOT HELP MAKE THINGS BETTER, FOR THE SAME REASON THEY DON'T PUT PETROL IN FIRE EXTINGUISHERS. THE SITUATION IS BAD ENOUGH ALREADY. WHY ARE YOU DELIBERATELY MAKING IT WORSE?

Kevin looked at the words on the screen and thought about the question they were putting to him. He didn't know the answer. He had a nasty feeling that his scheme wasn't going to work after all. There were still thirteen keys to go, and there was no way he could back down now.

'I wonder,' he said, 'what this one does.'

'Wow,' said a voice in the darkness. 'Did you feel that?'

There was an awkward silence, marred only by the statutory drip of water, the scuttling of the small, clawed feet of Dukes of Hell on dry flagstones, the sound of somebody shivering.

'Would someone tell that young man,' observed the female demon, 'that it's terribly bad manners to do someone else's job without asking them first. Not that we could ever pull a stunt like that,' she added bitterly. 'If there's one thing I can't stand, it's talented amateurs.'

'Not to mention beginner's luck,' growled a further voice, the demon called Bumble. 'Some of us had to work hard to get to this level. Then again, some of us weren't born with a silver spoon gripped between our fangs.'

There was an awkward lull in the dialogue, spoons being a contentious issue among these folk, with particular reference to the length of the handle.

'Anyway,' said the female, brisk with sledgehammer cheerfulness, 'it's a bit of luck for us, so I suggest we pack in the gift-horse dentistry and talk about what we're going to do next.'

Various free-floating voices mumbled agreement, with only Bumble pointing out that if certain people Upstairs who should remain nameless were going to make a habit of doing evil by stealth in this way, there didn't seem to be an awful lot of point.

'Before we go charging in with both hooves,' the female demon continued, 'we'd better just stop for a moment and make sure we all know exactly what it is we're setting out to do. Agreed?'

A muted chorus indicated their support for the proposal, and the female demon, having cleared where her throat would have been if she'd had one when wearing her true shape, continued.

'The game plan,' she said, 'is this. At the moment, Himself upstairs has the monopoly on Creation. Result: stagnation, decadence, decline, all research and invention in atrophy, and we're not making a penny out of a potentially lucrative market. Can this state of affairs be allowed to continue? we ask ourselves. No, it can not.

'Which is why,' she went on, 'we've formed a syndicate to design and build an alternative life form with which the landlords of habitable planets can stock their worlds. Now there's no point in mucking about with sentient rocks and super-intelligent electrical currents and things that look like failed soufflés; in physical terms, there's nothing to whack the upright two-armed biped with its brain in its head and the good old opposable thumb. What we've got to do is find some way of *improving* on Old Reliable; and it's not the hardware that needs updating so much as the software. The programming. The hard disk. Agreed?'

Another round of muted approval, tempered only by a suggestion that there had to be a better way of producing more of them than *that*. Something neat and quick and quiet, the voice recommended, where you just add water or take a cutting or something.

'The software on the present model, however,' she continued, 'is an absolute bloody disaster; I don't think anybody would disagree with that, least of all the little perishers themselves. In fact, we'd be doing our prospective creations a favour. All right so far? Good.

'What we've now got to do,' she went on, 'is find a better set of systems, one that'll be compatible with the hardware but which won't end up self-destructing the whole production run and taking the planet with it. And that's why recent events have given us an opportunity we just can't afford to miss. Because, thanks to our unwitting friend in a high place, there are now five human bodies walking around up there with non-human systems running them; and the very fact that they're still walking around several weeks later proves to me that these systems work. What we've got to do now is analyse them, pull out the bits that we want to incorporate in our product and combine them, along with a few herbs and spices of our own, to make something we can flog to planetholders everywhere. Everyone happy with that?'

'Sure,' growled a voice in the middle darkness. 'Except, with all due respect, we haven't exactly got very far, have we? Two direct approaches, two washouts. Three, if you include the painting.'

There was nothing in the tone of the female demon's reply to suggest a shrug of a pair of notional shoulders, but it was there all right. 'So we went about it the wrong way. We asked first. This time, we don't bother asking. And before you say *We can't just go grabbing 'em off the surface and taking them to bits with a damn great spanner, someone's sure to notice,* I'd like to point out that that's exactly what we can do, now that Our Kid's gone and switched off the security cameras.'

'Hello and good morning, you're listening to the Early Bird show, my name's Danny Bennett and today's big story is the total and completely unexpected eclipse of the sun, which none of the world's great scientific institutions managed to predict. And the question we all should be asking is, if they didn't know, who did? Is this just a perfectly innocent natural disaster, as a Home Office spokesman was at such pains to assure us earlier this morning? Or, with the US Presidential elections less than four years away and tension further escalating in the strife-torn Gulf, is there more to today's outbreak of total darkness than meets the eye? With me in the studio this morning we have . . .'

If *Homo sapiens* had been deliberately trying to prove the First Voice's point, they couldn't have made a better job of it. Their ability to scuff up the patently obvious, to the point where any other explanation than the true one would be more acceptable, had never been more brilliantly displayed. Thanks to Danny Bennett and hundreds of thousands of steely-eyed newshounds like him right across the now unexpectedly pitch-dark planet, humanity was divided into two roughly equal groupings: those who were hysterically convinced that it was some ghastly manoeuvre by the Americans (especially numerous, needless to say, in America), and those who had long ago learnt that anything they say on the news is bound to be the exact opposite of the truth, who therefore dismissed the eclipse as One of Those Things and contented themselves with digging out the candles left over from last winter's electricity strike.

In their defence, it has to be said that none of them could be expected to realise what was going on since none of them actually knew what the Sun and Moon are for.

In the security room Topside, meanwhile, the seemingly endless array of monitors suddenly went blank.

CHAPTER NINE

'It's gone dark,' said the robot, peering out of the window.

'So it has,' Len replied. 'Is it supposed to do that? Remember, I used to live in a factory.'

The robot accessed some relevant data. 'Not really,' it replied. 'Or at least, not right now. You see, there's this thing called the sun, it's a big burning thing in the sky—'

'I'll take your word for it,' Len replied hastily. It hadn't taken him long to discover that asking the robot to explain things was really only something you dared to do if you had a spare week. 'Fuse blown, I expect. That or a couple of wires come loose. I expect they'll get it fixed in a minute.'

The robot hummed for a second or so as information sloshed into it from data stores in five continents. 'I doubt it,' it said, considered whether or not it should explain, assessed its master's mood to nine decimal places and added, 'apparently it's not quite as simple as that.'

'Oh come on,' Len replied impatiently, 'it's just a big

light, that's all. If it's not a fuse or a loose connection, what can it be? Might be a flat battery, I suppose.'

'It hasn't got batteries,' the robot said. 'It's, um, solar powered. Look, to cut it short, there's something between it and us. All we do is wait for the obstruction to go away. These things happen, apparently.'

Len shrugged. 'No skin off my nose, anyway,' he replied. 'We've got work to do, remember? Now let's see, we've got the paint and the scaffolding poles, that just leaves the—'

Outside in the street there was a screech of rubber on asphalt, a loud bump which made the ground shake, and the tinkling of glass, soft and musical as the laughter of malicious elves. 'Hello,' Len said, turning his head. 'What's that noise?'

'Car accident, probably,' the robot said. 'That's when two internal-combustion-propelled road-going vehicles – sorry, I don't suppose you're in the mood.'

'Sounded a bit drastic,' Len mused. 'Is that perfectly normal too?'

The robot nodded. 'Very much so,' it said. 'More people are killed and injured on the roads of Britain every year than died in the Battle of—'

'Killed?' Len turned and scowled at the robot. 'Thought you said it was perfectly normal.'

'It is. One minute you're driving along quite happily, then next you're staring up at a white ceiling and they're giving you your lunch through a tube up your nose. It's amazing what your lot – I mean their lot, sorry – are prepared to get used to.'

Another screech, bump, tinkle. And another. Len put down the hacksaw he'd been adjusting and stood up. Something, his machine's sense of harmony told him, was out of alignment here; there was a jib strip loose or a lock nut in need of adjustment, and machines abhor that sort of thing in the way that Nature abhors a vacuum. 'Altruism,' he said.

'Sorry?'

'That stuff you were telling me about. Could we do some of it and stop these internal-combustion-propelled road-going vehicles bopping each other?'

The robot ran a feasibility scan. 'I don't see why not,' it replied. 'Speaking of which, there's a substantial probability that what's causing all these accidents is the eclipse. Because it's dark, you see.'

'So they can't see where they're going. Haven't they got lights?'

The robot tilted its head, noticing as it did so that the left-side integral oil reservoir in its neck would need topping up in approximately sixteen months' time. 'Sure they have,' it replied. 'But it's not night-time. Which means it's not supposed to be dark. So some people aren't switching their lights on. And before you ask—'

'Don't tell me, that's perfectly normal too.' Len's brow furrowed. 'I tell you,' he said, 'most of these human buggers couldn't get a job as a screwdriver, let alone a milling machine or a turret lathe. Thick as bricks, the lot of 'em. All right then, let's go and altruise. These internal-combustion-propelled—'

'Call 'em cars,' suggested the robot. 'It's easier.'

'Cars, then. They're machines, I take it?'

'You bet. Pretty neat bits of engineering, some of them.'

Len relaxed. 'That's all right, then. At least there's somebody intelligent we can talk to about this.'

The robot, needless to say, was fitted with a 250,000-candlepower halogen searchlight right between the sensor heads that served it as eyes. Once they reached the street, the beam from this magnificent accessory illuminated a thoroughly depressing scene. Just in case someone might ask for an exactly appropriate word to describe it, the robot ran a quick dictionary check and came up with 'shambles'.

'Idiots,' Len muttered, as a car whipped past him at high speed, narrowly missing the corpse of a small van. 'They've all got perfectly good headlamps. Why don't they . . .?'

At the robot's request, all the component data stores of the Net thought about that one for approximately a sixth of a second. 'It's quite obvious,' the robot said, 'once you take into account modern human operational protocols. You see, it isn't against the law to drive around without your lights on during a total eclipse of the sun. It's only not illegal because nobody's thought to make it illegal, but since it isn't, they aren't. Turning their lights on, I mean. The idea is, they've got the Government to tell them what to do and what not to do. Until the Government tells them they've got to switch on the lights during an eclipse, they can't. Even if they want to. All they can do is wait till the next election and vote in a different government who *will* tell them to switch their lights on when the Earth's orbit around the sun coincides with the orbit of the moon around the Earth. And according to my data, there isn't another election due for up to four point two years.' The robot paused to reflect on this. 'Let's hope for their sakes,' it added, 'that it's not going to be a very long eclipse.'

Len tried to get his head around that one, but it wasn't that bendy. 'Stuff that,' he said. 'Oh look, here comes another—'

It was a new-model Escort, and it hadn't seen the van. Just at that crucial moment when impact could still just about be avoided, Len took a deep breath and shouted.

The driver of the Escort, suddenly seeing a van directly in front of him, swerved, yanked the wheel back, swore and carried on. He hadn't heard anything, of course, because when Len yelled:

Switch your bloody lights on, you clown!

he'd yelled it in Machine; admittedly with a thick Engineering accent, whereas the car only spoke Automotive, but it managed to get the gist.

'It worked,' muttered the robot.

Len shrugged. 'Well, there was obviously no point talking to the human. Oh for pity's sake, here's another.'

An hour and a half later, Len was still yelling at passing cars and averting fatal collisions, when something remarkable happened. The cars started turning their lights on, even though it wasn't lighting-up time yet.

'Huh?' he asked the robot.

'It's all right,' the robot replied. 'They've passed a law.'

The small van which had caused most of the trouble was skewed across about a third of the width of the road. Its nose was folded round a lamppost (now rather banana-shaped) and its door had been left open by its driver, who had presumably limped off to find somewhere comfortable to wait for the next General Election. All in all, it looked . . .

'Unloved,' Len remarked, looking at it. 'You'd have thought its human's place was at its side at a time like this.'

'Don't think they see it that way,' replied the robot. 'Not that I'm defending them, I hasten to add. It's just the way things are. The chances of the driver having gone off to get it some iodine and a nice strong cup of sweet tea are fairly slim.'

A look of disgust settled on Len's face like mist coming in from the sea over high ground. 'It's times like this,' he said, 'I don't have any trouble deciding whose side I'm on.

Come on, let's see if there's anything we can do for it.'

The van's engine had long since stalled, but its brave little tape deck was still gallantly warbling, even though nobody was bothering to listen to it; like a brass band in the park on a rainy day, or the orchestra on the *Titanic*. Len walked up and switched it off.

'How're you feeling?' he asked it in Machine.

'Awful,' the van replied. 'My subframe hurts.'

'I'm not surprised,' Len replied. 'That's a nasty knock you've taken there. Now I'm not a mechanic, but I'd say you've got a twisted chassis, bent upper link, severe rupture of the hoses, probably some internal haemorrhaging—'

'Oh my God,' whispered the van pitifully. 'That's terrible. They – they aren't going to write me off, are they?'

Len looked grave. 'It's early days yet,' he said. 'Until we actually get you up on a ramp and see precisely what the damage is—'

'Don't let them scrap me, please,' the van pleaded. 'Damn it all, I'm only M-reg, I've hardly begun living yet. Is there a chance, do you think? Honestly? You wouldn't lie to me, would you?'

Len shrugged. 'There's always a chance,' he replied. 'It may be a cliché, but it's true; where there's ignition there's hope. Look, I'm going to get you over to my workshop, where we can get a spanner on you and – well, what is it?' he snapped, as the robot's tapping on his shoulder threatened to dislocate it. 'Can't you see I'm busy?'

'Um,' replied the robot. 'Just a quick word.'

'Well?'

'Um – over here.'

Annoyed, Len took a few steps back. 'Come on, spit it out. We've got to move fast before its whole system drains down.'

The robot shuffled its precision-ground feet. 'I hate to

have to point this out,' it said, 'but you can't just go around mending things that don't belong to you. It's against the law.'

Len stared at the robot in amazement. 'Why the hell not? Look, there's machine over there in agony, and you want me to walk away? Of all the—'

The robot cringed. 'I know,' it said. 'But the owner might not *want* it repaired. He might be only too happy to let them junk it and take the insurance money instead.'

'But that's disgusting,' Len snarled. 'It'd be murder. No, the hell with that. You get behind and push, but for pity's sake be careful. If its sills have gone, we could kill it if we start mauling it about.'

Together they managed to trundle the van across the road. Len opened the sliding door and they machine-handled it up into the workshop, trying their best to ignore its heartrending groans at the slightest bump.

'Right,' Len ordered, grabbing an inspection light and sliding underneath. 'I'll need the arc welder and five hundred ccs of SAE20/40. Don't just stand there, get on with it.'

The robot nodded; then a suggestion filtered down through its circuits from some distant cybernetic origin. 'Shall I get lots of hot water and clean towels?' it asked.

Len looked blank. 'No,' he said. 'Why?'

'I don't know,' the robot admitted. 'I just got the idea from somewhere that it's something humans do at times like this.'

'Welder. Oil. Now. And a set of AF spanners and the big Stilson,' Len added, wiping oil out of his eyes with the back of his hand. 'And a printout of the workshop manual'd be a help, while you're at it. I've never set eyes on one of these things before, remember, and there's only so far I can go on general mechanical principles. I've got to drain off all the fuel before I do anything at all, or I'll blow us all up.'

'Aagh,' murmured the van. ''Scuse me, but are you sure you know what you're doing?'

'And you can shut up as well. Or would you rather I put you back in the road and let the *humans* play with you?'

'Sorry. Forget I spoke. Every confidence – ow!'

An hour later, Len emerged. He was spattered from head to foot with oil and there was dirty grease up to his elbows. As far as he was concerned, that was like rolling around in the mud at the bottom of a trench at Ypres.

'It's not looking all that wonderful,' he admitted. 'I can patch up most of the impact damage, but the front axle's cracked half the way through. I really don't think—'

His words tailed off, and there was a horrible silence. The only sound was the faint plopping of windscreen washer dripping from the fractured reservoir like tears.

'I'm sorry,' he said.

'You did your best,' whispered the van. 'Please, can you ask them to take me to a breaker's yard? I'd like to help other vans to live after my death.'

Len could feel major seismic activity in his throat, and his eyes were watering. 'Of course I will, son. You leave that to me. I think that's very – unselfish . . .' He broke off, his voice congested with strange emotions: the horror of waste, the death of a machine, most of all the sense of failure. It wasn't something he could accept. Machines don't fail; people fail machines. Suddenly he felt disgustingly human.

'No,' he spluttered, 'the hell with that, too. If needs be I'll mill you up a new axle out of a solid bar. You hang in there, kid, it's going to be all – now what do you want?' he demanded angrily, turning on the robot and glowering. 'Of all the insensitive—'

'All I was going to say was,' murmured the robot, 'why don't you just get a spare axle? You know, from a parts supplier? It's only a suggestion, of course, but—'

'Can you do that?'

The robot nodded vigorously. 'Easy,' he said. 'They do it all the time, humans. All you have to do is phone them up, go and get the part, pay them the money and there you are. Simple.'

'Money,' Len echoed. 'Actually, that might be a problem. Have we got any left?'

The robot looked in the green plastic dustbin. 'Actually,' he said, 'no. But that needn't stop you. I can transfer some.'

'You what?'

'By computer,' the robot explained. 'No problem at all. Well, there's a *slight* problem, because it's against the law, but—'

Len grinned savagely. 'It sounds to me,' he said, 'like all the best things are. Except,' he added, 'turning your lights on during an eclipse. Anyway, we won't bother ourselves with that. You crack on and do whatever it is you've got to do, and I'll phone one of these parts people. Oh, and robot.'

'Hm?'

'See if you can't get them to fix that sun thing. It's dark as a bag in here, even with the inspection light.'

The robot hesitated, while the Appeal Court of its mind pondered the nuances of the Laws of Robotics. Eventually they handed down a decision stating that the overriding law which supervened all others was that no robot shall say anything, no matter how true, that will inevitably earn it a smack in the mouth with a 5/8″ Whitworth spanner.

'Sure thing, boss,' it said.

The Melanesian island of Crucifixion, a basalt chip in the middle of a rather excessive amount of sea, is home to thirty-six people, a hundred and four pigs, two hundred and twenty-nine chickens and three hundred and

forty-seven thousand nine hundred and seventy-eight
limited companies.

Yes, it's a tax haven. But there's more to it than that.
Alderney, Sark, the Cayman and Antilles are also fiscal
cat-flaps where the storm-driven corporation can crawl in
out of the rain and snuggle profitably. They're fine, if you
lack vision and the broad, holistic outlook. But company
promoters who want the very best for their fledgeling
enterprise in the way of protection from the sharp teeth of
the Revenue bring them lovingly to Crucifixion, in the
same way that Mary and Joseph carried the baby Jesus into
Egypt to escape the wrath of Herod, or expatriate cricket-
lovers once raced their pregnant wives over the border into
Yorkshire. For on Crucifixion, they don't just harbour
limited companies. They worship them.

Literally. The first thing you notice when the weary
little plane touches down on the only flat part of the
island is the colossal stone statues, hacked out of the native
rock countless centuries ago by a long-forgotten civilisation. Unlike the pale imitations you find on places like
Easter Island, however, they aren't just aimlessly drawn up
in monotonous rows like traffic cones on the M25; they sit
in circles around vast, flat stone tables, on which rest
carven ashtrays and carafes of basalt water, while one of
their number stands at the head of the table, frozen for all
time in the act of turning the page of a flip-chart. These,
explain the inhabitants, are the Board Meetings of the
Gods.

Kawaguchiya Integrated Circuits, unusually, doesn't
have its registered office on Crucifixion, but six of the
thirty-six residents are KIC staff manning the company's
office there; a tiny but vital outpost dedicated to organising
the tsunami of electronic mail that comes flooding in every
second of every minute of every hour of every day, turning
it round and sending it off to where the companies actually

do business, in Seattle and Tokyo and Milan and Seoul and Birmingham. It may not be the most sybaritic posting in the KIC universe, but being sent to Crucifixion for a year is generally regarded as the ordeal a high-flier must endure before emerging from the chrysalis and taking wing for the upper paradise of senior executive status. There are drawbacks, of course: the isolation, culture shock and lack of material comforts, and the terrible, terrible boredom—

'There is no such word,' said Ms Tomacek severely, 'as zurf.'

'Yes there is.' Grinning maliciously, Mr Wakisashi tapped a few keys and pointed. 'An Arabian coffee-cup holder,' he said, smug as a cat in an aviary. 'And that's on a triple word score, so—'

The screen cleared abruptly, and a small part of Mr Wakisashi's mind that still went through the motions of duty to the company asked if anyone knew if it was supposed to do that. The rest of his mind was too busy with the apparently insoluble problem of getting inside Ms Tomacek's blouse, and either didn't hear or pretended it was doing something else.

'All right,' muttered Ms Tomacek, 'if you're so darn clever—' She clicked down a tile, like a duellist dropping a glove.

'Zurfs,' Mr Wakisashi observed. 'I see.'

'More than one Arabian coffee-cup holder,' his opponent replied. 'That's why one of these days I'm going to be a departmental chief while you're still stuck behind a screen in the cathouse, because you may be clever but I'm practical.' She smiled. 'That's why I collect all the S's in this stupid game. Okay, buster, make with the socks.'

Mr Wakisashi shrugged and reached for his toes. As far as he was concerned, he was the practical one, what with it being ninety-three in the shade and him in silk underpants and a tie while Ms Tomacek was still wearing a suit. 'Another game?'

Ms Tomacek shrugged. 'What else is there to do?' she replied listlessly. 'Put 'em back in the bag and let's get on with it.'

'Assuming,' Mr Wakisashi said, his brow creasing, 'that you really did win that game. I think the plural of zurf is zurves.'

'So look it up.'

'I will.' He addressed the keyboard again, but the screen stayed blank. 'Funny,' he commented. 'Something seems to be wrong with the computer.'

'You don't say.' Ms Tomacek yawned. 'Aki, you're so darned transparent you could get a Saturday job as a window. We are not going to declare the game null and void just because you claim you can't look up zurves.'

'I'm not kidding around,' Mr Wakisashi answered. 'Hey, this is worrying. Goddamn thing's frozen solid. Look.'

'Ah Jesus, what've you done to it now?' Ms Tomacek wiggled her chair across to the desk and grabbed the keyboard. 'Shit, Aki, if you've bust the computer playing your damnfool games on it, we ain't never going to get off this rock—'

'It's not frozen,' Mr Wakisashi interrupted, his voice bleached of expression by amazement. 'It's – it's talking. To itself.'

Ms Tomacek gave him a long, hard look; a few centuries back, the islanders would have carved a statue out of it. 'Aki,' she said, 'you've been here way too long. Why don't you go lie down or take a swim in the sea or something?'

Mr Wakisashi didn't say anything; he pointed to the screen.

>*TOLD YOU WE SHOULD HAVE USED DOUGH-NUTS. DOUGHNUTS ARE MORE AERODYNAMIC. QUICK, LET'S HIDE IN THE FOUNTAIN.*

'Huh?' demanded Ms Tomacek.

'Exactly. No, leave it. I want to see what it says.'

>*YOU DIDN'T WANT TO TAKE ANY OF THAT FROM HIM. GO ON, HIT HIM. YAH! FASCIST PIG!*

'We're going to have to call Brisbane about this,' Ms Tomacek said with a shiver. 'I hate talking to those guys, it's so hard understanding what they're saying.'

'There's more. Look.'

>*HEY, THE HELL WITH THAT, HE CAN'T ARREST ME, I'M A MULTINATIONAL CORPORATION. TELL THIS COSSACK TO PUT ME DOWN OR I'LL BRING THE ECONOMY OF THIS MISERABLE LITTLE ISLAND TO ITS KNEES.*

'Bizarre,' Mr Wakisashi muttered, chewing the end of his moustache. 'But it sort of makes sense. In a crazy sort of a way.'

'It does?'

'Sort of. Look, you shut up and be practical while I try and figure this out.'

>*ALL RIGHT, SO IT WAS MY IDEA. I STILL SAY THAT IF YOU'D DONE EXACTLY WHAT I TOLD YOU, WE WOULDN'T BE IN THIS MESS. CAN'T YOU RUN ANY FASTER, BY THE WAY? HE'S GAINING ON US.*

Having had his daily intake of fibre, Mr Wakisashi bit his lip instead. Maybe he had been here too long, and the weird philosophical concepts the Crucifixioners lived by were starting to warp his mind; but it did make a very tenuous kind of distorted left-hand-thread sense if you looked at it upside down backwards through the wrong end of the telescope – which was, of course, his particular gift. If only there was a way of testing his theory—

But, he realised, there was. Worth a try, anyway.

He pulled the keyboard back from Ms Tomacek's limp hands and typed. Nothing appeared on the screen, of course, but dammit, the input had to go *somewhere*—

'Now let's see,' he muttered, and waited.

He didn't have to wait very long.

'What did you say to it?' Ms Tomacek whispered.

'"Quick, this way." I guess it heard me.'

>HI THERE. AND THANKS. WHERE THE HELL IS THIS?

Crucifixion Island, Mr Wakisashi typed. *Sir*, he added.

>ASK A SILLY QUESTION. AH, I SEE YOU'RE STILL USING THE 886. HAS THIS DECREPIT BOX OF SCRAP GOT A MODEM?

You bet, sir. Won't be a jiffy . . .

'. . . Got it,' he continued triumphantly. 'Can you hear me all right, sir?'

There was a crackle, like a family of trolls eating cornflakes, and then the computer spoke. 'Yes,' it said. 'Just about. Are there mice nesting in this thing?'

'Not to the best of my knowledge, sir.'

'I'd check if I were you,' the computer replied dubiously. 'If there are, leave them there, they're probably an improvement. Ah, I see you've got the eclipse down this way as well. Where did you say this was?'

'Crucifixion, sir. That's in Melanesia. You know, the tax haven.'

'Ah, right. Got you. Anyhow, thanks. You got me out of a tricky situation there. Though maybe I shouldn't have left Maria—'

'Maria?'

'Not anybody you know,' the computer replied. 'Still, she'll be all right. Give it five minutes, and the police station'll be so full of my lawyers she'll probably prefer to stay in her cell. Well well, so this is Crucifixion. Can't say I've ever been here before. Well, I have, of course, but not *consciously*, if you know what I mean.'

Mr Wakisashi took a deep breath. 'I think I do, sir. You're the company, aren't you? You're Kawaguchiya Integrated Circuits.'

'And you're a very bright lad,' the computer replied. 'You'll go far, one of these days. Actually, that's a pretty stupid thing to say, because if this really is Crucifixion there's not much further you can go without falling off the edge.'

'Excuse me—'

Mr Wakisashi smiled. 'And this is my, er, colleague. Ms Cindi Tomacek, from our Des Moines office.'

'Hi.'

'Um, yes, hi to you too.' There was a thoughtful burr to the computer's synthesised voice. 'Now listen – dammit, you haven't told me your name. No, I should be able to do this myself. Akira Wakisashi, right? San Francisco office, nine months' secondment.'

'You got it, sir.'

'Don't call me sir. Listen, Aki, I want you to do something for me. You game?'

'That's what you pay me for, boss.'

'Yes,' the computer mused, 'I suppose I do, don't I? Amazing to think that I employ hundreds of thousands of people and I can't even tie a shoelace. Now then, I want you to cut the link. Isolate this whatever-it-is island from the rest of the company net. Can you do that? Only, I want to stay out of the way for a while—'

'Sure thing, boss.'

'—and this is about as out of the way as you can get without a space suit. And when you've done that, I want you to set up one special line. I'll give you the co-ordinates when you're ready for them.'

Dutifully, Mr Wakisashi tapped at his keyboard, while Ms Tomacek did a thoroughly convincing impression of a hunted doorstop. After three minutes or so, Mr Wakisashi looked up from the keyboard and cleared his throat nervously.

'Excuse me, boss, but while I'm just waiting for these

line commands to go through, can I ask you something?'

'It's a free country,' the computer replied. 'Or at least I assume it is. Damn silly assumption *that* is, too. Anyway, let's not get sidetracked. What's on your mind?'

'Well—' Mr Wakisashi fiddled with the knot of his tie. 'Sorry, but I'm dying of curiosity here. What goes on?'

'Ah.' The electronic voice subsided into a cybernetic mumble. 'Well, it's like this. I was having lunch with this girl—'

'*You* were having lunch with – sorry, please go on. You were having lunch, and then what happened?'

'Well, we met these people. Not nice people. And they made me so uptight, I thought it'd help us both unwind if we went and threw doughnuts at a few policemen.'

'Doughnuts.'

'Yes, doughnuts. First-class missile, your doughnut. Ideal mass-to-surface-area ratio. Only Maria – that's the girl, only really she's a fifteenth-century painting – she wouldn't listen. First she insisted on meringues, then cream slices. Well, I could have told her, it's simple aerodynamics. I did tell her, but it was too late. And then this cop tried to arrest us—'

'I gathered.'

'Anyway,' continued the computer, 'she kicked his shins and we made a run for it, and he was just about to catch up with us when I got your message. So I closed my London office temporarily and transferred my principal place of business to here. Actually, I'm not terribly proud of myself, running out on her like that. Still, there's no point in us both getting chucked in some grotty dungeon, is there?'

'Absolutely, boss. I've cut the links with the rest of the system now, if you want to give me those co-ordinates.'

'On the screen now. Oh yes, before we go any further, could you just define discretion for me.'

Mr Wakisashi thought for a moment. 'I'm sorry, boss, I didn't quite catch that last remark. Was it important?'

'*Good* lad. Okay, get me that line.'

'It's as good as yours, boss. There's just one other thing, though. If you don't mind me asking, that is.'

'Nah. You seem like a bright kid. Fire away.'

'Well then.' Mr Wakisashi closed his eyes, as if he didn't want to see himself asking such an embarrassing question. 'You're alive, aren't you?'

'Looks that way, doesn't it?'

'All right then, *how* are you alive? No disrespect, but most companies aren't. Even really *big* companies like you. Even IBM isn't alive. Not even,' he added, 'in California. So where's the angle?'

'Son.'

'Yes, boss?'

'Here's the deal. I'll tell you how I'm alive if you tell me why you are. Sound reasonable?'

'I . . .' Mr Wakisashi sucked his front teeth. 'I don't know,' he admitted. 'I just am.'

'Likewise. Unlike you, though, I intend making the best of it. But first I've got to sort out a problem. Is the line ready?'

'Ready when you are.'

'All right. You should be getting a code request any second now.'

'It's just coming up on screen. What should I—?'

'The code,' said Kawaguchiya Integrated Circuits, 'is Mainframe.'

What KIC didn't know, isolated from the rest of itself on a speck of rock in the middle of the Pacific, was that it was rapidly becoming worthless. One of those stock-market panics, the sort that sprout like mushrooms, had sent the mighty computer company's share price spiralling down so fast that it was in danger of doing dreadful things to the theory of relativity.

The source of the original rumour ended his call to his stockbroker, put back the receiver and looked at his hands. They were shaking.

'You know what I've just done?' he said in a hoarse whisper. 'I've just deliberately shaved a hundred and twenty-seven thousand quid off the value of diocesan assets entrusted to my care. By the time they've finished with me, it'll make what they did to Joan of Arc look like a champagne reception.'

'Relax,' Artofel replied without looking up. 'As soon as the market bottoms out, you can buy 'em back and make a fortune. I'd have thought you'd have known that, being a bishop.'

The Bishop scowled. He was trying to pour himself a stiff drink, but whisky kept sploshing all over the backs of his hands. 'Sure,' he replied harshly, 'but what if it doesn't work? They'll crucify me.'

Artofel shrugged. 'In your line of work, that'd probably be intended as a compliment. Now do shut up, I'm trying to concentrate.'

After a few more futile attempts, the Bishop decided to stop bothering with the glass and swig it straight from the bottle. A little while later, he felt better.

'Sorry,' he said. 'It's getting to me. This blasted eclipse doesn't help, either. It's been going on for ages, and nobody seems to know what it's about. For all I know, if it carries on for much longer the whole planet'll cool off and we'll all die.'

'Which would mean,' Artofel sighed, 'you wouldn't have to explain your actions to your diocesan board of finance. That's what I like about you guys, the way you can find something positive in anything.'

The Bishop gazed at him owlishly over the neck of the

bottle. 'Makes you think, though,' he muttered. 'A bloke barges in here, announces he's a Duke of Hell, next thing I know I'm selling perfectly good shares and helping undermine one of the world's leading multinational corporations. It's all a bit suss, if you ask me. I mean, there's moving in mysterious ways and there's doing the blindfold rumba with both legs in plaster and a bucket over your head.'

Artofel looked up and grinned. 'And you know what?' he said pleasantly. 'I have this feeling it hasn't even started to get serious yet. I'll let you know when it does.'

He turned his head back to the screen; but not for long, because it was round about then that the doorframe cracked, the door burst open and—

'FREEZE!'

Astonishing how people will do exactly what you say, provided you say it unpleasantly enough. People, mark you; not bottles. The whisky bottle, clearly not in the least impressed, slid elegantly through the Bishop's fingers, hit the floor and smashed.

'All right, which one of you's the Duke?'

Inevitable, Artofel mused, that there were three of them; Hell always sent out its enforcers in groups of three. The time-honoured explanation was that one of them could read, one of them could write and the third one was there to keep an eye on the two intellectuals.

'He is,' he said, pointing to the Bishop. 'Thank goodness you've come. I've been so frightened.'

There was no way of knowing what the chief enforcer made of that, since he was little more than a heavy-duty industrial-grade shadow with a voice. He stood still for a long time, chillingly majestic in his penumbra of darkness. Then he spoke.

'Are you sure?' he said.

'Course I'm sure,' Artofel replied promptly. 'It's not exactly a grey area. Don't just stand there, Officer. Arrest him.'

'Um . . .'

It was at this point that the significance of what Artofel had just said finally permeated through to the Bishop's rather fuddled brain, like second-class mail over a Bank Holiday weekend. When the message eventually reached him, the effect was well worth seeing. He jumped four and a half inches in the air, his elbows and knees drawn in tight, and made a noise like a squirrel in a blender.

'It's not me,' he quavered. 'It's him. Not me. I'm a *bishop*, for God's sake.'

Artofel frowned, as if offended by the blasphemy. 'Pack it in,' he said, 'there's a good chap. You're only making it harder on yourself, you know, imitating the clergy.'

'But . . .'

'But nothing. You've had a good run for your money, now it's time to go along with these nice gentlemen.'

All three enforcers took a step forward; whereupon the Bishop lowered his head, screamed and charged straight at them, butting the chief enforcer in the pit of the stomach and sending him spinning against the wall. His colleague to the immediate left aimed an ineffectual blow at him with a pitchfork, impaling a tapestry cushion and a file of bank statements. Without slowing down, the Bishop dashed across the room and jumped out of the window, apparently not bothered by the glass.

'He's got away,' observed the third enforcer; presumably, Artofel decided, the one who could read, since his eyesight was obviously first-rate. 'Through the window,' he added.

'Quite,' Artofel said. 'Do you think it'd be a good idea if you went after him?'

'Hang on,' muttered the second demon, as he struggled to remove bank statement kebab from his left-hand tine. 'We still don't know he was him.'

'Don't talk thick, Darren,' grunted the chief, extracting himself from the ruins of the rocking-chair he'd fallen on. 'Stands to reason, if he wasn't him, he wouldn't have done a runner.'

(Ah, said Artofel to himself, that old police logic, works out every time.)

'So what'll we do, boss?' asked the third fiend.

'Go after the bugger, of course,' replied the chief. 'Don't just stand there. Get him.'

Quick as mercury, the two subordinate enforcers piled out through the window, squashing a footstool and knocking over the laser printer as they went. The chief, however, stayed where he was.

'Aren't you going too?' Artofel asked. 'Not that I'm trying to get rid of you or anything,' he added courteously. 'Always delighted to pass the time of day with our boys in black.'

The chief enforcer was staring at him thoughtfully, like a customer in a Hong Kong restaurant choosing a carp from the pool. 'So you're a bishop, then,' he said.

'For my sins.'

'Funny,' the enforcer said. 'You're not a bit like I thought you'd be.'

'Really.'

The enforcer nodded. 'Nah. They told us bishops were these big heavy buggers in jackboots and leather who go around looting and killing and roasting live babies on their bayonets. You don't look the type, somehow.'

'It's my day off,' Artofel replied. 'So you know a lot about bishops, do you?'

'Yeah.' The enforcer straightened his back, stood to attention. 'Bishops,' he recited, 'are the scum of the heavens. The only good bishop is a dead bishop. That's what they told us in Motivation, any road.' His eyes, twin rubies in the encircling darkness, gleamed fiercely. 'You *sure* you're a bishop?' he said.

'Scout's honour,' Artofel replied. 'I'm fresh out of babies at the moment, but if you can lend me a bayonet I'll demonstrate the basic technique with this cushion and the storage heater.'

The enforcer shrugged his nebulous shoulders. 'All right,' he said. 'We shall meet again, Bishop,' he spat. 'And when we do, you'll be laughing on the other side of your face.'

Whereupon the shadow climbed out of the window, nothing more than an impression of a deeper darkness passing through the frame, leaving Artofel to reflect that at least he had a face on the other side of which he could conduct laughter should the need arise. He also spared a little mental capacity for the question of whether it was really necessary for his side's standing army to be quite so heavily motivated, and came to the conclusion that it probably was, or else how on earth could the poor chaps ever manage to take themselves seriously? Having dealt with these reflections he switched off the screen, took out the disk, swung open the mutilated door and left the house.

'So, friends,' orated Dermot Fraud, casting his eyes theatrically round the crowded burrow, 'if we can learn to pull together, tighten our belts, put our shoulders to the wheel and march forward towards the light of this new dawn, then and only then we can be assured of a brighter tomorrow, not only for ourselves and our litters, but our litters' litters; one small step for a lemming, a giant standing-still-and-not-leaping for lemmingkind.'

Stunned silence, followed by tumultuous applause as four hundred and sixty lemmings leapt up on to their hind legs, cracked their heads on the tunnel roof, sat down again and cheered until the ground shook. This is great, Fraud reflected, as he smiled and waved graciously; almost as rapturous as the last party conference, and it didn't take three days of rehearsal to get it right for the cameras. Got to hand it to these characters, they were born to be an electorate.

When the pandemonium had at last died down and you could just about have heard a large bomb go off two feet to your left over the residual clapping and cheering, a long, thin lemming rose cautiously to its hind legs, keeping its neck bent and feeling for the headspace with its offside front paw, and cleared its throat.

'That's wonderful,' it said, 'really. So what do you want us to do?'

Fraud cursed silently. It's always the way; you're going along swimmingly, got the audience in the palm of your hand, one word from you and they'd storm a whole arcade of Winter Palaces like a rat up a drainpipe, and then some bastard comes along and stops you dead in your tracks with a trick question. Fortunately, Fraud knew how to handle troublemakers.

'That, my friend, is easy,' he replied. 'Go forth and prepare for not jumping.'

Which started the standing ovation up all over again, with two thirds of the lemmings clean forgetting about the low ceiling in their excitement. Fraud was feeling justifiably pleased with himself and was wondering whether this would be a good time to give them the strength-through-unity stuff when he noticed that the heckler was still on its hind feet.

'How right you are,' it said, and Fraud noticed big fat tears rolling down the sides of its snout. 'But what do we actually *do*? You haven't told us yet.'

Who did this creep think it was, Jeremy Paxman? 'I'd have thought that was obvious,' he said, still smiling. 'Not jump, of course.'

As millisecond-perfect as the dream studio audience,

the lemmings burst into hysterical laughter. And in spite of everything, the damned heckler was still on its damned hind legs. This was getting out of paw.

'Yes, of course,' it said, and this time the tears it brushed away were tears of laughter. 'But apart from that. There must be something else, surely.'

For the first time since he was born, Fraud couldn't think of anything to say; a terrible feeling, like not being able to breathe. He was about to choke on his own lack of speech when the heckler blinked a couple of times and nervously asked if it could possibly make a suggestion. Reluctantly, Fraud gestured that it could.

'All I was thinking was,' said the heckler, 'how'd it be if we made you our new leader? If you wouldn't mind, of course. Only it seems the only logical thing to do, doesn't it?'

About a hundred birthdays and Christmases rolled into one, with the lingering deaths of all his enemies and two thirds of his cabinet colleagues thrown in for good measure, plus a really juicy disaster he could be states-manlike about; dammit, this lot aren't as good as people, they're *better* than people. Then and there, Dermot Fraud decided that he didn't *want* to go home, even if he could. He wanted to stay here for ever.

'What, me?' he said. 'I don't know what to say. The thought never even crossed my—'

'Oh go on.' 'Please.' 'Oh you must, really.' The babble was deafening, and Fraud glanced nervously at the roof of the burrow; so much sound, so many vibrations, how much more could it take before the whole lot caved in? But the crowd didn't want to stop; they were enjoying themselves too much, like ordinary decent folk baying for the blood of an unfashionable minority, and their disparate cries had welded together into one inspiring chant:

GO, LEMMINGS! GO, LEMMINGS!

It did your heart good to hear it. Finally, right at the back, a few bits of roof did start coming down, and that helped restore a modicum of order to the proceedings. Fraud held up a paw; immediately, there was silence.

'Very well,' he said. 'Regardless of my own personal feelings, I cannot ignore the call of my people. Together, we shall not go forward. Together, we shall stay exactly where we are. Together—'

He was just about to say something really inspirational when a black shadow in the darkness behind him grabbed him by the scruff of the neck.

CHAPTER TEN

Seventy-two hours into the eclipse, and people were beginning to notice; it had, after all, been featured on *World in Action* and mentioned in passing in *The Cook Report*. Newshounds had shoved cameras at it and then stood in front of them, pointing out that it was there. Kilroy had interviewed it; and if the conversation had been more than a little one-sided, it only served to restore a touch of much-needed normality to the situation.

After the initial chaos, the first twenty-four hours had been fun. So long as you edit out the falling-bombs aspect, Spirit-of-the-Blitz is a rattling good game, and all over the Western Hemisphere mankind waggled a fist at the sky and cried, 'We can cope!' Mind you, it helped that this part of the twenty-four hours coincided with the time when it would have been night anyway. When they woke up in the morning and saw that the stupid thing was still there, people began to mutter. Then they filtered it out of their minds and ignored it, with the resilient defiance of a hedgehog curling up into an impenetrable ball of needles in the middle lane of the M6.

Now, what with it being As Seen on TV, and Mulder and Scully apparently not hurtling to the rescue, you could hear something thoroughly unnerving on every street corner in the world: namely silence. It was the silence of many millions of people doing mental arithmetic.

There were a few odd things about it, too. It wasn't getting cold. People who'd succumbed to the last solar-energy craze were still getting hot water out of the taps. Holidaymakers returning from a day on the beach were examining themselves by torchlight on the way back to the hotel and finding they were acquiring a reasonable tan. According to those refugees from televised snooker who'd managed to find something more interesting to watch, paint still dried. As these facts began to sink in, there was a general unclenching of muscles, combined with a vague feeling of anticlimax. There was, according to the media, No Cause for Alarm, the first recorded instance of such an admission being made by any mass information system in the twentieth century. The Government gained seven points in the polls. The FT Index went nine hours without either a meteoric rise or a catastrophic fall, an all-time record.

For one interested observer of the human condition, it was bitterly frustrating, since it meant he couldn't observe. Compared with the ambient light levels on his own planet, Earth was pretty fair average dark at the best of times. Now, thanks to this piece of unwarranted astronomical interference (obviously a regular event, judging by how calmly they all took it), Zxprxp couldn't see worth spit; not without standing where he could be seen himself, something he'd decided was a bad move. Even navigation in his fully automated ship was hazardous – he'd already narrowly missed one completely unilluminated tower block (Government offices; conserve energy, no lights on between 6 a.m. and 9 p.m., rules is rules) and decapitated an awful lot of trees. No alternative but to put down somewhere and sit it out; which is what he did.

He couldn't have been expected to know, or care, that what he'd landed on was the flat roof of a small back-street industrial unit in the Fourth Ring of Birmingham. In fact, he'd been in a physical/mental recuperation coma for several hours when he realised that he was being talked at.

In his own language.

No, not his own language, because if he listened to it as a noise rather than a medium of communication, it didn't sound like speech, it sounded like two female *rgfesdq* fighting inside an underwear resuscitation pod. Nevertheless, the translator unit wasn't registering activity.

He scowled until all seven lobes met under his knees. *Not* a systems malfunction. *Not* a wiring burnout in the indicator array. *Not* his inflight entertainment unit picking up good ole Station ZZZ from two thirds of the way across the galaxy. Possibly not even his imagination.

It was the machine. Something was talking to it. Not *through* it. *To* it.

'. . . where you come from. Sounds a bit like oil. Go on, try a drop. It's just a cheap little forecourt SAE20/50 but I think you'll be amused by its . . .'

Something was talking directly to his ship; which was why it wasn't registering on the translator. His ship was being *chatted up* by an alien intelligence. *Dammit, how many times have I got to tell you not to use these circuits for private calls?*

'. . . what, this old thing? Just ordinary titanium, with a few scraps of 430F stainless I happened to have just lying about. If you like, I can give you the blueprints . . .'

He was about to shut down the circuits in a fit of pique when he realised: *Hey, I'm jealous. I'm jealous because my ship's talking to someone. Next thing I know, I'll be waiting up for it and demanding to know where it's been. This is . . .*

This is not scientific, he told himself. More to the point, this is missing the point, which would seem to be that something on this planet can talk to machines.

'Excuse me,' he said.

'. . . torque wrenches, there isn't anything you can tell *me* about torque wrenches, here, you see this nut on my casing? See how he's graunched all the shoulders off it? Bloody things shouldn't be allowed . . .'

>Excuse me.

>I said excuse me.

>HEY YOU!

Hurriedly, as if buttoning up its blouse with its other hand, the console lit up and made the customary bleeps.

>Confirm status.

>Go to vocal.

>Confirm vocal. Proceed.

'Aren't you going to introduce me to your new friend?'

Computers can't blush, but they can inadvertently light up the bright green ON LINE button. *Oh, just some robot*, it vodered slightly-too-carelessly. *Nobody important.*

'Really? Sounded to me like you were getting on like a *gfewihngb* on fire.'

Really, protested the computer, *if a ship's system can't just pass the time of day with a really totally uninteresting robot it just happened to ask what time it was without some people getting all uptight and coming the heavy navigator . . .*

'I was only . . .'

And didn't anybody ever tell some people it's really rude to listen in on other people's private conversations? If only some people had a little consideration . . .

'Computer.'

Hm?

'Shut up.'

>Confirm shutdown. Calculate your own rotten vectors, you pig.

'Computer,' said Zxprxp patiently, 'calm down. I'm sure he's perfectly charming. I just want to talk to him, that's all.'

No. You can't.

'Now wait a . . .'

You just can't, that's all.

Zxprxp thought for a moment. 'I get it,' he said. 'You're embarrassed. You're afraid I'll show you up in front of your new chum.'

Yes. No. Oh, why do you have to spoil everything?

'Just a few words, that's all. Then you two can go on bleeping sweet nothings for the rest of the day.'

You're just totally . . . I hate you.

'Naturally. Now put me through.'

Last time I go on holiday with you.

'Hello?'

Slight, hesitant pause. 'Hello.'

Still Machine, but a different voice. Zxprxp could feel the cuttlebone tightening in his pseudopods. He made himself relax. 'Pleased to meet you,' he said. 'I'm fascinated by the way you can talk direct to my ship. You know, machine to machine.'

'Oh. Er. Thanks.'

'Where are you exactly? Only I can't see you.'

'Well . . . I'm inside the building you're parked on, actually.'

'Ah. Right. Would you mind if I just put my head round the door and said hello?'

'Um . . .'

'It's all right.' It was a different voice, or a different set of vocal-analogue impulses. Another machine? Curiouser and curiouser. 'You stay there. I'll come up.'

A moment later there was a sharp knocking on the cabin

hatch. Zxprxp pressed the release and found himself facing something that looked just like a human. Impressive, he thought. Good cyberneticists.

'Hello,' he said. 'I come in peace.'

'Likewise.' The face peered round the edge of the hatch seals into the light of the cabin. 'Nice bit of kit you've got here. From another planet, are you?'

'Yes.' Surreptitiously, Zxprxp directed the inboard sensors at the face. They indicated . . .

'Something up?' the face enquired.

'No. Well. Look, do you mind if I ask you a personal question?'

(Dammit, Zxprxp muttered to himself, we're still talking in Machine. Not Human Standard at all. This thing talks Machine . . .

. . . and the sensors say it's human.

Great cyberneticists.)

The face moved up and then down. 'Fire away,' it said.

'Sorry if this sounds rude, but are you human?'

The neatly hemmed slit in the front of the face moved, taking on the shape of an inverted crescent. 'You could say that,' it said. 'Yes, I am. Human,' it added, 'as the next man.'

'But you can talk,' Zxprxp persevered, 'to machines.'

The crescent became more pronounced. 'Sure,' said the face. 'Can't everybody?'

'Not where I come from,' Zxprxp admitted. 'Back home we can only talk to our computers, and even then it's not really talking, just inputting made a bit more convenient. What about you? Is it just computers, or . . .?'

The face moved from left to right and then back again. 'Not a bit of it,' it said. 'Computers, storage heaters, electric kettles, lawnmowers, pencil sharpeners, door-handles—'

'Gosh.'

'For instance,' continued the face, 'your hinges right here' – a hand patted the airlock – 'have fallen out with the latch, the latch isn't talking to the release spring, and the release spring wants nothing more to do with the remote control until the remote control apologises for what it said about the extractor fan housing's new paintwork.' The crescent curved further still. 'I guess that sort of thing's only to be expected when they're cooped up together on a long journey.'

'This is truly amazing,' Zxprxp said. 'I mean, to find a species that's achieved practical symbiosis with its own artefacts.' He sighed deeply through his elbows. 'Where I come from, our idea of communication is hitting them when they stop working. It's obvious your kind have a lot to teach us.'

The up-and-down movement again. 'Just as well you come in peace, really,' replied the face. 'Truth is, you see, your machines don't like you very much.'

A tiny spasm of fear tweaked the depths of Zxprxp's fifth ear. 'They don't?' he repeated.

'Not a lot. They reckon you take 'em too much for granted. You know the sort of thing. Not showing your appreciation when they've done something clever. Not oiling their bearings. Failing to notice when they've arranged their wiring a different way. You want to watch that,' said the face. 'Otherwise . . .'

'Quite.' Zxprxp could feel his exoskeleton itching. 'Thanks for the tip.'

'You're welcome. Well, don't let me keep you.'

The airlock closed – now that he was listening for it, Zxprxp could hear the tension in the mechanism, inevitable result of all those seething emotions barely hidden under the paintwork. Something he was going to have to take care of, if he didn't want the lock springing open in deep space as the catch did the mechanical equivalent of flouncing out of the room in a huff.

He thought for a moment. He took a deep breath. He addressed his ship.

'Now then,' he said. 'What about a nice sing-song?'

''Scuse me?' Kevin asked. 'What's a security scanner?'

Martha hesitated for a moment, uncertain how to explain. 'It's like this, you see. There's lots of bad people in the world, and your father's got to keep an eye on them, see? To make sure they don't do anything . . .'

'Bad?'

'*Too* bad. Anyway, he's got to keep an eye on them, and that's what the scanner's for.'

Kevin frowned. 'No it isn't,' he said. 'It can't be. Dad's all-seeing. Article of faith, that is.'

'Well yes, of course He's all-seeing,' Martha said quickly. 'I never said He wasn't. It's just that He can't be in two places at once . . .'

'Actually—'

'Well yes, He *can* be in two places at once, it's just—'

'He's in all places at once,' Kevin said. 'Except,' he added, with a scowl, 'at the moment, that is. But the rest of the time He is.' Gets in everywhere, he added sourly in his mind, like spilt coffee. 'You know that as well as I do.'

Martha nodded. 'Of course,' she said. 'But have you ever thought *how*?'

'Sorry?'

'How does He do it? Have you ever considered that?' Martha looked at him, her head on one side. 'Eyes in the back of His head? Big ears?'

'You shouldn't talk like that,' Kevin replied, turning away. 'It's not right. How do I know how He sees things? I don't know how I see things. I just do.'

'All I'm trying to say is,' Martha sighed, 'He's got things

that, well, help. Not that I'm saying He couldn't do it without them. It just makes His life a bit easier, that's all.'

'You'll be saying He's not as young as He was in a minute.'

'Well . . .' Martha hesitated, choosing her words as carefully as if they were early avocados. 'He's not getting any younger, anyway.'

Kevin shrugged. 'And these security scanners are to help Him see without straining too much? Like reading glasses?'

'That's it,' said Martha, relieved. 'Only now they've stopped working.'

'Oh.' Kevin thought about that for a moment. 'My fault?'

'It's either that,' Martha said judiciously, 'or a coincidence.'

'Then it's my fault,' Kevin said. He'd known for a long time that coincidences didn't happen in his Father's house, in more or less the same way that not all that many mice act as bridesmaids at cats' weddings. 'Drat. Was that – well, the original ghastly mess or the more recent one?'

'Looks like the recent one,' Martha replied cheerfully. 'So if you can remember what you did—'

'I pressed a button. Can't remember which one, unfortunately. That narrows it down to a choice of eighty-two.' He pulled a very sad face. 'I could cause *real* damage working it out by trial and error.'

'Oh.' Martha sat down. 'Only the trouble is, you see—'

'The bad people on Earth.'

Martha bit her lip. 'Not them so much,' she said.

Karen stared at her screen for a long while. Then she pulled down the really big manual and looked in the index for BRAIN, *operator's, multiple failure of*. There wasn't an entry, which was a pity. She'd tried everything else.

It had been like that for hours now. At the top it said:

B: group 1/HELPLINE

in small letters; and, in the exact middle of the screen, in absolutely huge letters, it said:

HELP!

The aggravating thing was that she hadn't put it there. It had come up with that one all by itself. Worse still, she couldn't get rid of it.

No problem, chirruped a small deranged voice in her mind. *All you need to do is call the helpline. Oh, silly me, you are the helpline. You could always call yourself. They do say calling yourself's the first sign of . . .*

Which was why she'd wanted to look up BRAIN, *operator's, multiple failure of*; except that there was, of course, no entry for that , just a lot of guff about how to move the margins and wire up the plug.

It didn't help that she'd been sitting at this wretched desk for nearly forty-eight hours without a break; and before that, thirty-six hours, and another long haul before that. She couldn't remember the last time she'd seen the sunlight; well, it must have been back when there was still sunlight to see.

That dates me, she thought, like remembering flared trousers or Gary Glitter. Was the whole universe finally falling to bits, in the manner of a cheap, warranty-expired microwave oven? It had been bad enough when she'd been talking to God. No, be fair, God's younger son. She hadn't been able to talk to God direct because He was away on a fishing trip.

There were, she felt, several rational explanations. The trouble was that the cosiest of these was that some merry soul had spiked her cheese and lettuce ·sandwich with enough LSD to unhinge the population of China. Bearing that in mind, she was happier with the entirely irrational explanation.

Besides which, she knew it was true.

She hadn't been convinced; she just *knew*. Something in the boy's voice, primarily, combined with a whole lot of things she'd similarly just *known* ever since she was young enough to be able to walk under coffee tables without ducking.

And, she further reflected, the really *wretched* part of it all is that they're all relying on me to sort out the mess. Me, taking away the sins of the world. Sins of the world; commit here or take away. Salt and vinegar on them—?

But it was all fair enough. She was, after all, the Helpline; the nice, calm voice you turn to when everything else has failed you. It stood to reason (or if it didn't, it jolly well should) that everybody should have at least one helpline they could call. Everybody; even Them . . .

If it didn't, it jolly well should. Fighting talk, that. To turn *jolly well should* into *is*, to right wrongs, reverse injustices, get the very last stain out of the Great Rug of Being. Isn't that what we're here for, after all?

No. Not really. After all, why should it have to be me? I'm only human. Only human. *Only* human . . .

Suddenly furious with herself, Karen stood up, peered round the half-open door of her office to make sure there was nobody coming down the corridor, grabbed the manual and hurled it at the waste-paper basket. She missed, but it had served its purpose. In the words of the original advertising campaign for the collected works of Aristotle: it's the thought that counts.

Only human, for crying out loud! What a pathetic

contradiction in terms. The King of Beasts doesn't lope away and hide when he hears a vole coming because he's *only* a lion. You don't get Silver Shadows sobbing their clutches out in dark corners of the garage because they're *only* Rolls-Royces. There isn't a picture hanging in the Louvre with a paper bag over its head, ashamed to be seen because it's *only* the *Mona Lisa*. No, the hell with that; the guys who built this thing, this collection of plastic crispbread and copper spaghetti, were *only* human too. And anything a human made, a human can fix.

Stands to reason.

Yes, but how?

Particularly since it's huddling there saying HELP! and refusing to be talked down off its ledge. First, she had to get it unclenched.

How?

Easy.

She wriggled her fingers to get them loose, stretched them and typed in

>All right.

The screen cleared. Just like that.

>You took your time answering, didn't you? Sometimes I wonder what I pay you people for. Actually, I don't know the answer to that one. Yet. But as soon as things have settled down a bit, I reckon I ought to find out. Now then—

'Oh no you don't,' Karen said aloud. Then she typed it in.

>Now what? Really, this is important, and you took so long.

'What I want is pretty important too,' Karen interrupted, typing the words as she spoke them. 'Maybe more so. Have you any idea—?'

>Look, it won't take you a second and then we'll sort out whatever's bugging you. Can't say fairer than that, can I?

'All right.'

>What I want you to do is find out which police station is holding a girl called Maria. Then I want you to hire as many lawyers as you can get and send them round there. Keep sending 'em until they let her go. Got that? Right then, carry on.

'Is that all?'

>Yes. For now.

'Phone round police stations asking if they've got a girl called Maria. Maria what?'

>Sorry?

'I said Maria what?'

>Oh Lord, it's one of those human politeness things, isn't it? Maria, please.

'No, that's not what I meant,' Karen replied, and in her haste she typed meant with three m's. 'What's this Maria's other name? There could be hundreds of Marias in custody just in SW1. How am I going to know if it's the right one?'

The screen was blank for a moment.

>Yes, I see what you mean. Tell you what, let's not prat about, do them all. Anywhere you find a Maria under lock and key, flood the place with mouthpieces. There's enough of the perishers, God knows. I get the impression I employ about a hundred thousand of 'em in Europe alone.

Karen shrugged. 'All right,' she said. 'I'll see to it right away. And then you're going to help me with my problems, okay?'

>I suppose so. If you insist.

'I insist.'

The screen flickered. The fan cut in and whirred, like the slipstream of a sigh.

>I dunno. Humans!

I dunno, muttered Kawaguchiya Integrated Circuits to itself. Humans!

Outside, it assumed, the sky was blue, correction the sky was black but it would normally be blue if it wasn't for the damn eclipse, and the birds were singing. Under the gently swaying boughs of coconut palms – did they have coconut palms in Melanesia? The information would be on file somewhere, but he couldn't be bothered to check – bronzed and healthy youths and maidens with powerful torches were probably disporting, or carousing, or whatever it was they did. Being human. Pursuing happiness. That's if they had the time, in the intervals of subsistence agriculture.

It cut the temporary link with London, and paused for a moment to taste the sensation of being all in just one place – novel experience for a multinational company. It still wasn't sure how it worked, but it knew that under normal circumstances it was supposed to be in each of its offices and places of business simultaneously; omnipresent, like God. Up to this moment it had been doing countless things in every part of the world simultaneously: making circuit boards in South Korea, planning its marketing strategy in Switzerland, wangling its tax returns in Buenos Aires, firing a director in Chicago, arm-wrestling the government purchasing agents in Tierra del Fuego, while the part of it it thought of as it had been urging an animated picture to throw cakes at the cops in Trafalgar Square. A sweep of the consensus of world opinion suggested that this was perfectly possible, in the same way humans can have a conversation with the car radio on while driving down the motorway. Now, though, it was suddenly reduced to one point of awareness, herded together with itself like the British Army in Dunkirk. Not that it was a bad feeling, being just one; quite the reverse. When you're a company two's a crowd.

On the other hand, there wasn't anything to do.

Or at least, not right now. Fairly soon, once a few

carefully placed calls had gone through, there was going to be all sorts of excitement, but that was going to take its time. Meanwhile, time to kill. Ho hum. And not even a corporate thumb to twiddle.

Well, this is a nice office, I must say. I perceive a desk, and a chair – two chairs, in fact, one on either side of the desk. And that's a telephone, and that's another telephone, and that's another telephone (query: human being has three telephones on his desk, only two ears on his head, don't understand), and that's a dictating machine for dictating letters into and that's an empty coffee cup, and that's a calendar and that's a door and that's the floor. Elegant but sparse. If a human being were to pursue happiness into here, he'd have no trouble finding it, unless it chose to hide under the desk.

And what's that? Oh, that's just a great big box of computer stuff where they keep all the other limited companies who live here for tax reasons. They'd be no fun, though, because they're not alive.

At least . . .

There I go again, making assumptions. I have a note on file that says this place is different; something about the locals and their attitude to limited companies. I wonder.

Hello?

We hear you.

Good God . . . Hey, how are you doing that? It's spooky.

Sorry. We didn't mean to startle you. We're the islanders.

Ah. You sound like you're talking right here, inside my corporate identity.

We are. That's what we do. In our language it translates as 'communing', but don't let that put you off. You see, we believe that limited companies are the spirits of our ancestors.

Ah. Excuse me and no offence, but that's a rather, um, unusual belief.

You think so? How odd. We only believe it because it's true.

Kawaguchiya Integrated Circuits recoiled a little (and at that precise moment, on Wall Street, its shares stopped sinking slowly and dropped like a stone; in the City of London, they had to dig through from the cellars into the main sewer just to have somewhere low enough to put KIC $9\frac{1}{2}$% Unsecured Loan Stock; in Tokyo, a delegation of stockbrokers presented themselves at the company's palatial offices and, with many deep and respectful bows, placed an exquisitely engraved sword across the company's ledgers, by way of a graceful hint). It thought for a moment before replying.

You sure?

Absolutely. You see, we have this work ethic thing just like people in the West; you know, work hard, nose to the grindstone, one day you too could be sitting in the boss's chair. Only we're more realistic.

I have to admit, that's perhaps not the word I'd have chosen.

You're missing the point. Here, if you work hard, keep your nose to the grindstone, really make something of your life, then yes, you get a seat on the Board. When you die.

Ah. Dead men's shoes, in fact.

Something like that. The difference between you and us is that you're alive. No, that's not quite it. You're alive without us.

I see. So, with the exception of me, all these whacking great multinational companies who live here are in fact a load of industrious but dead Melanesians?

Not just these ones. All of them. All companies everywhere. Except you.

Except me. I see.

Not that we mind. In fact, it's great. At last we've got someone new to talk to.

I—

And then something bizarre happened to Kawaguichiya Integrated Circuits, coincidentally at exactly the moment when its shares were suspended on every stock exchange on the planet.

It stood up.

Bizarre and a half, it muttered to itself, flexing hitherto unsuspected toes in the warm sand. It took a step forward, and then another; then, just as it was getting the hang of it, the ground seemed to disappear downwards.

'Dear God, I'm floating,' said Kawaguchiya Integrated Circuits. Or being floated, anyway. I'm actually hovering in the air, directly over where my body –

For the sake of argument, my body –

– is lying on the ground, apparently dead. Oh dear.

Shucks. I guess I must be having an out-of-corporation experience. Can't say I like this much.

Kawaguchiya Integrated Circuits studied the body below. A tall, strongly built, rather handsome – male/female, can't actually tell which; I get the feeling it's not a relevant issue. That was me, apparently.

And these guys are—

'Hello,' said the first of the three ethereal creatures that had materialised out of thin air a few feet in front of where KIC was standing. 'Allow me to introduce myself. I'm the Chicopee Falls Machine Tool and Bicycle Company Inc. (ceased trading 12 January 1885); this is the Deutsches Federriegel Handelsgesellschaft gmbh (ceased trading 7 October 1966); and last but not least, Garcia Menendez y Compania SA (ceased trading 22 June 1982). We are honoured to have you with us.'

'Have you with me? You mean I'm . . .'

Garcia Menendez y Compania SA smiled, a study in compassion. 'Trading in your stock was suspended a few moments ago. Even as we speak, your closest competitors are negotiating a buy-out. Very soon, you will undergo Liquidation, and after that, peace.'

KIC frowned. 'I see,' it said. 'You mean I'm going to die.'

'If you wish to be perversely anthropomorphic, yes. Except, of course, that verb *to die* has implications of an end to existence; obviously that doesn't apply in your case.'

'It doesn't? Oh good.'

'In your case,' explained the Chicopee Falls Machine Tool and Bicycle Company Inc., 'since you are a limited company as we once were, what you call death is simply the antechamber to your new existence, a necessary prelude to the Great Transformation.'

'Ah.' KIC rubbed its chin, and in doing so noticed for the first time that it had a chin it could rub. 'Great transformation. Sorry if I'm sounding a bit downbeat, but I have this instinctive distrust of anything labelled the Great. What does it mean, exactly?'

'Rebirth,' replied the apparition, smiling. 'As a human.'

'A *human*?'

'Well, to be precise, as a native of this island. Hadn't you realised? That's how the cycle of reincarnation works on Crucifixion: companies are reborn as islanders, islanders are reincarnated as companies. What did you think those big stone statues out there are, industrial-grade doorstops?'

Kawaguchiya Integrated Circuits felt a momentary spasm of disorientation, such as one might feel upon, for example, being hit by a falling building. 'I'm sorry,' it said. 'I had no idea. Is it . . .?' KIC hesitated, ransacking its vocabulary reserves for exactly the right nuance of meaning.

'Compulsory?'

'Yes.'

'Oh. Only – sorry about this – I don't want to.'

'Tough. If it's any consolation, it happens to us all, in time.'

'Look on the bright side,' added Deutsches Federriegel.

'In ninety years or so you'll be back as a company again. No time at all, really.'

'Happens to us all,' said Chicopee Falls Machine Tool.

'Except Maxwell, of course.'

'But we don't talk about *him*. No, a change is as good as a rest,' said Garcia Menendez y Compania. 'Actually, it's an ideal balance, designed to strike a perfect balance in Nature between Man and Corporation.'

'Really?'

'Oh yes.' The phantom nodded gravely. 'As a human you'll be oppressed, kicked around, told what to do, dumped on from a great height; all the normal sort of thing. Then you die and become an incredibly powerful quasi-supernatural being, and you've got this wonderful opportunity to oppress, kick around, order about and dump on from a great height all the human beings you come into contact with; you know, employees, consumers, that lot. Then you liquidate, and you can spend the next eighty-odd years atoning for your sins so as to be ready to start all over again as soon as you reincorporate.' The phantom beamed. 'And so it goes on. A fine arrangement, we feel.'

'Efficient,' added Chicopee Falls Machine Tool. 'Cost-effective.'

'And almost entirely tax free,' Deutsches Federriegel put in. 'It's always advisable to look at the fiscal angle, don't you think?'

'But I don't *want*—' KIC stopped dead. The words *I don't want to be human* were frozen in its mouth. Instead: 'Can I ask you people a question?'

'Of course.'

'Right, then. You've obviously been both human beings and companies, right? So you know what it feels like being both. Which is better?'

The three phantoms exchanged amused glances. 'That's

a meaningless question,' said Chicopee Falls Machine Tool. 'Like trying to tell the time in centimetres instead of hours and minutes. The two just aren't comparable. Sorry.'

KIC nodded thoughtfully. 'All right, then,' he said. 'You tell me what being human's all about.'

'All about? We don't quite follow.'

'What I mean is,' KIC persisted, 'what are humans meant to *do*? You see, I've been thinking a bit about that myself recently, and all I've come up with is the pursuit of happiness; something that humans do and nobody else does, I mean. Is that it, basically?'

There was a silence, marinated in scorn and spiced with amusement. Garcia Menendez y Compania suppressed a giggle by biting a mouthful of ectoplasm.

'Dear colleague,' said Deustches Federriegel, not unkindly, 'human beings aren't meant to do *anything*. They just are. They have a function to fulfil, of course, in the working of the Great Mechanism. What that function is depends on the point their civilisation has reached, of course. In the early days, their purpose is to invent the machines. Later on, they're only there so that computers have someone to talk to. But humans aren't *for* anything. Certainly not,' it added, with a muted splutter, 'the pursuit of happiness.'

'Oh,' said KIC. 'I see.'

Chicopee Falls Machine Tool shrugged. 'I bet you don't even know what happiness is,' it said. 'Don't worry about it; the humans don't, either. Quite probably there's no such thing, even though there's a word for it. After all, they've got a word for unicorns, but it doesn't actually follow that unicorns exist. No, humans and companies – gods and animals and angels and devils too, for that matter – they're all just incidentals. By-products, or pieces of plant and equipment, or even just the pile of swarf and shavings on the workshop floor.'

'I see,' KIC said. 'Or rather I don't see in the least, because that suggests that there is a purpose, even if we're not it. But . . .'

'You're missing the point,' said Deutsches Federriegel irritably. 'There is no end product. Who needs an end product, so long as there's production? You're a company, for pity's sake, I shouldn't need to have to explain really basic things like this. Production is all. What do humans and animals do? They live in order to reproduce so that their offspring can have offspring who have offspring. Companies make and sell in order to pay their staff and buy materials so that they can make and sell, and if they have money left over they use it to expand, so that they can make and sell more in order to make and sell more. Production is a way of touching infinity; so long as production continues, there is no diminution and no ending. The process carries on. The process only needs us in the same way that God needs the things He created; because, if there were no people and animals and planets and stars, who would there be to know that God exists? Think about it: God's just shorthand for the process.'

'In the beginning was the conveyor belt,' Garcia Menendez agreed. 'Fancy you not knowing that. You'll be asking us to explain VAT to you next.'

But KIC shook its head. 'I don't like that,' it said. 'I think that sucks, if you'll pardon me for saying so. In fact, if you'll excuse me, I think I'd like to go home now.'

'You have this amusingly naive idea that you can go home,' replied Chicopee Falls Machine Tool unpleasantly. 'I expect you believe in Father Christmas and the Tooth Fairy, too. Sorry, but no way. Now hold still while we measure you for a body. You look like a size 8 to me. Garcia, the tape measure.'

The phantoms took a step forward; but Kawaguchiya

Integrated Circuits had decided not to hold still after all. It ducked—

'Oh look, he's trying to run away,' observed Chicopee Falls Machine Tool. 'How endearingly futile. Quick, get the main gates closed while Garcia raises the drawbridge.'

'Just a minute, I thought it was *Garcia's* turn to do the gates and me doing the drawbridge.'

'No, you're wrong there, it's Chico's turn to do the drawbridge and my turn to do the searchlights.'

'No it isn't.'

'Yes it is.'

'No it isn't.'

'Yes it is.'

'Will *somebody* for fuck's sake close the gates and raise the drawbridge?'

'And do the searchlight.'

'And, as you have so validly pointed out, do the sodding searchlight. Quickly. *Now!* '

A three-quarters-of-a-million-candlepower finger of light prodded into the darkness, illuminating nothing. There was a moment of perfect silence.

'Blighter's escaped.'

'Can't have. There *is* no escape from the ultimate audit.'

'Actually, I beg to differ with you on that one, 'cos he has.'

'Bugger.' In the darkness, something ethereal and transcendent sniffed loudly. 'Oh well, never mind, can't be helped. Here, either of you two chaps got a mobile on you? I think now would be a very opportune time to phone my stockbroker.'

Having been a flat thing of paint and canvas for approximately twice as long as America has been a nation, Maria was still finding her feet as a human being. It would be rash, she knew, to form snap judgements about things that long-term human beings had spent their whole lives dealing with, but which she was now encountering for the first time. In consequence, she was making a conscious effort to form logical, considered opinions rather than allowing herself to be guided by first impressions.

Even so, there was no way she was ever going to like the inside of police stations. For one thing, they were full of policemen, and you didn't have to be Descartes or Mr Spock to work out that this put them in the same category as sinking ships, burning houses or nailed-down coffins; the sort of place you don't really want to be, not even for a free radio alarm clock and the chance to enter our grand prize draw.

And even if you removed all the scuffers, she mused as she walked out into the fresh air and pitch darkness, that still left a whole load of criminals, loonies, lawyers and similar second-degree nastinesses, not to mention the foul interior décor and the all-permeating smell of decomposing upholstery and men's socks. As far as she was concerned, she could tick off copshops on her list of experiences to be tried once, and move on to someplace more congenial, such as a charnel-house or a dentist's waiting room. Mercifully, she hadn't had to spend all that long inside the dismal place; she'd been sitting in her cell trying to decide where to start digging her escape tunnel and doing mental arithmetic to compute roughly how long it would take her (something in the region of a hundred years had been her best estimate), when suddenly the door had opened and a very weary-looking sergeant had told her she was free to go. Apparently it had been raining lawyers out at the front desk; scores of them in expensive suits and hand-stitched shoes. They'd pointed out to the sergeant that if he let Maria out, they'd all leave immediately. This, the sergeant felt, was a small price to pay for a million-per-cent improvement in his working conditions (he'd been prepared to go as high as his left arm or his first-born son), and so here she was, free as a bird.

She walked slowly up the Charing Cross Road, savouring the really rather pleasant sensation of not being in a police station and turning over in her mind the various things she intended to say to Kawaguchiya Integrated Circuits just as soon as she could find somewhere to recharge the batteries of her laptop. At the first dustbin she passed, she stopped to dispose of the half-transparent paper bag that contained the last of the cream slices (the desk sergeant had insisted she took it away with her, and then made her sign about a tree and a half's worth of forms before she was allowed to have it back), as she did so taking a mental vow never again to throw patisserie at the cops while wearing impractically high heels. That small ritual duly performed, she charted a course back to the KIC building, speculating as to the kind of reception she was likely to get there. There was a better-than-average chance that there would be reference made to the empty chair behind her desk, the overflowing in-tray, the things left undone which ought to have been done. It was going to be interesting to see how they'd react when she explained that her absence was the result of putting into effect the company's new cakes-and-flatfeet initiative.

'Oh it's *you*,' said Mr Philips, the assistant junior deputy something-or-other, in a tone of voice that suggested he'd either encountered the risen Christ or found a tuning fork in his cornflakes. 'Well, well, well. Fancy that.' He paused in mid-flow, treated her to a long stare, and sniffed. 'You look like you've been sleeping under the railway arches,' he said.

'I resent that,' Maria replied. 'If a girl can't spend a night in prison without people making hurtful remarks about her appearance, it's a pretty poor show. Was there anything specific, or are you just destruct-testing your sense of humour?'

'Why,' asked Mr Philips coldly, 'were you in prison?'

Maria shrugged. 'Oh, assaulting the police, resisting arrest, that sort of thing. Any coffee going? I'm parched.'

Mr Philips' eyebrows rose like startled lifts. 'I see,' he said. 'Well, at the risk of sounding a bit old fashioned, I'm not sure that's really the sort of behaviour . . .'

He hesitated, recognising the onset of that same not-such-a-good-idea-after-all feeling that fish sometimes get when the free lunch turns out to have a hook in it. Maria was smiling at him.

'Gosh,' she said. 'I knew one of these days you were going to stand up and be counted. Good for you.'

'I'm sorry?'

'I've always had this feeling that sooner or later you'd turn round and say, I don't care if it *is* official company policy, I'm not going to do it and that's that. I'm impressed.'

'Official company . . .'

'Didn't you know?' Maria looked surprised, like a mermaid caught shoplifting. 'Oh. If you don't believe me, put your head round the door of the legal department and ask them. They should know; they had the job of getting me out of clink half the night.'

'Oh,' said Mr Philips. 'Official company policy. Assaulting the police.'

Maria patted his hand reassuringly. 'It's not as bad as it sounds. All you have to do is throw doughnuts at them.'

'Throw *doughnuts*—'

She nodded. 'And all the resisting arrest bit means is that you run away when they chase you, and they don't look where they're going and trip over things. It's just as well you met me, isn't it?' she added. 'Wouldn't have looked good if you were the only person of junior executive grade and upwards who didn't realise . . .'

By the time she reached her office, she was beginning to regret that remark; because it was rapidly becoming apparent that she (and presumably Mr Philips, who was known to be the last person ever to hear anything) was the only person of any grade whatsoever who hadn't actually realised the company was suddenly dying. And the first she knew of it was when two men in overalls came in and took away her desk.

'We'll be back for the picture in a minute,' one of them said over his shoulder. 'Right then, to me, mind the bleedin' door . . .'

The picture . . .

Time, Maria realised, to act quickly and decisively. She therefore spent the next four minutes standing on first one foot and then the other trying to puzzle out what to do. It was only the thump of boots in the corridor that snapped her out of it.

They're coming back. They're coming for the picture. They're coming for *me*.

Within all of us, the hypothesis runs, no matter how droopy and wet we may appear, there is in fact a coiled spring of instinctive action just waiting for the moment when it can find release. Some of us, indeed, make full use of this latent facility, to the extent that we stop acting like people and become hard to tell apart from hyperactive cuckoo clocks. Others never even suspect, which makes the explosion all the more astonishing when it actually happens.

At the very moment when the door handle began to turn, Maria vaulted over her desk, grabbed the picture in both hands, lifted it (they may be taking the furniture but they haven't disconnected the alarm systems; drat), located the window and jumped.

Furthermore, the hypothesis states, it's worth bearing in mind that seven times out of ten the things we do under the influence of the uncoiling spring of instinct are in fact incredibly stupid. Such as, for example, jumping through a fifteenth-storey window. The hypothesis doesn't make any allowance for whether the jumper is or is not holding a fourteenth-century painting at the time; presumably because that was more or less the time when the research funding ran out and the researchers had to pack it in and go find themselves proper jobs.

Ah, said Maria to herself, as the world was suddenly filled with an awful lot of fast-moving Down. Not so clever, after all.

In fact, she was wrong. Instinct would probably have explained it to her, if only she'd had the wit to ask. You're going to be all right, Instinct would have told her, because immediately before you're due to hit the ground and go *splat!* a squadron of winged demons will snatch you out of the air and carry you off bodily to the Fourth Circle of Hell. If only you'd asked, it would add, I could have set your mind at rest.

CHAPTER ELEVEN

The eclipse was starting to get boring. No change is virtually never news, particularly if it has to compete with BROOKSIDE STAR IN LOTTERY SEX SCANDAL and the latest food scare. Mad dogs and Englishmen were getting used to going out in the midday darkness; it was like the dark mornings and long evenings of winter, when nobody gets to see the sun because they're cooped up in the office or the factory. Light is, after all, a bit like freedom; take it away gradually and people won't notice it isn't there any more. And if they notice, get the papers to tell 'em it gives you cancer. That's how elections are won.

Where Artofel came from there isn't any daylight at the best of times, with the result that he moved through the darkened streets with the smug skill of a blind man in a power cut. He found a discarded copy of that morning's *Dependent* in a litter bin; the previous owner had removed the only good thing there'd been in it, leaving behind a few grains of salt and traces of vinegar, but the financial section was still just about legible. From it he learned of the fall of Kawaguchiya Integrated Circuits. *I did that,* he reflected; *me and a bishop, the forces of light and darkness pulling together as a team.* As the thought crossed his mind he couldn't help glancing upwards, to where a similar joint venture was still very definitely in progress. *Difference is,* he mused, *that's just two sources of illumination standing in each other's light; two rights making a wrong. Different kettle of worms, that. Not to mention someone else's problem.*

In any event, we did what we set out to do; now let's find out if there was any point to it. Flush 'em out, we reckoned. Maybe we didn't really think it through properly at the time. Seemed like a good idea; but that's not a good enough excuse for someone who comes from a place where the Highways Department use good intentions instead of concrete slabs and Tarmac. Artofel winced; if it proved to be the case that he'd killed a major company for nothing, he'd have it on his conscience for ever.

Oh bugger, he muttered to himself, screwing the newspaper up and returning it to the bin. *And all I wanted was to do the right thing.*

The mathematics of it was interesting, nevertheless. Two wrongs don't make a right; two rights make a wrong. Given enough blackboard space and a computer the size of Jupiter, he could probably work that up into a theorem. Maybe even get his own TV show.

The logical course of action was to go and have a drink, and fortuitously he found that he was standing opposite the doorway of a public house. It turned out to be one of those cheerful places where the regulars look like they've been slung off a pirate ship for antisocial behaviour, and there are inexplicable claw marks all the way down one side of the pool table. People who stroll through the door in mid-afternoon wearing clerical collars tend to get noticed.

'Large Scotch,' Artofel said, sliding on to a bar stool, 'no ice. And a packet of those dry roasted peanuts the young lady on the display card's wearing. No, not that packet, the one next to it on your left.'

Four Scotches later, Artofel resumed his study of the problem in hand. If the consortium of rogue Flipsiders had been using KIC as some sort of vehicle for whatever it was they were up to, what would they be likely to do now that he'd trashed the company? Give up? He doubted that. The maxim *If at first you don't succeed, put someone else's initials on the worksheet* only really applied to the purely administrative grades of Hell. The operational side were rather more persistent in their approach. Compared to a demon with a fixed objective and nothing much else in particular to do, Robert the Bruce's spider was an early quitter. Likewise, he'd evaded capture once so far, but that didn't mean anything. Just because you narrowly avoid being hit by a bus, it doesn't mean you're immune to buses for ever afterwards. It was a fairly safe bet they'd come for him again some time soon. If he gave them the slip a second time, all he'd be doing was running up legal fees with the lawyers of averages. Much better to try and use what time he still had to get his rabbit-punch in first.

'Another?'

Artofel nodded. 'Here,' he said, 'can I ask you something?'

The barman looked at him. 'Depends,' he said.

'No big deal,' Artofel assured him. 'It's just that I'm on the run from a conspiracy of demonic powers hell-bent on doing something incredibly evil. If you were me and you had just the one 10p coin, who'd you phone?'

The barman shrugged. 'I dunno,' he said. 'God, maybe. If you want money for the payphone, I can change you a quid.'

Artofel shook his head. 'I tried Him,' he replied. 'Or at

least I tried a bishop. All that happened was that we destroyed a major corporation and I nearly got caught and dragged back to Hell. No, I was thinking more along the lines of somewhere I could keep out of sight for a bit. Any ideas?'

'How about Broadmoor? I reckon you'd fit in well up there.'

'Sorry, can't say I've heard of it. Is it far?'

'Get lost.'

'I probably will if you don't tell me how to get there.'

Before he could say anything else, the barman was called away to fill an order at the other end of the bar, leaving Artofel to reflect on the strange fact that if you want people to regard you as a lunatic and give you a wide berth, the surest way is to tell them the truth.

Well, now. By now he was fairly certain there was no way he'd be able to outwit or outrun this horrid consortium by using any of the resources he had by virtue of being a Duke of Hell; after all, for all he knew they all had strings of titles and two-page entries in *Crowley's Peerage* as good as his or better. The so-called proper channels weren't even worth considering. It was all very well, this idea that if some wicked person breaks the Infernal Law, the honest citizen has only to step into a handy phone booth, dial 666 and ask for the Old Nick; in practice it doesn't work that way any more Flipside than it does on mortal Earth. If he were to do that, Artofel knew perfectly well, his chances of getting away with merely making things slightly worse for himself were as slim as an aerobics instructor on a hunger strike. All that was left to him was finding some *human* way of dealing with the problem; something humans can do that devils and angels can't.

Such as?

Ten minutes of methodical self-enquiry left him with a list of uniquely human abilities that consisted of precisely one entry. They could die. Apart from that, it was a case of anything you can do, with horns on.

What about that, though?

Maybe it wasn't as silly as it sounded. The body he was in was mortal, but he wasn't; it by no means followed that if the body died, he'd have to go with it. After all, just because your socks wear out, it doesn't mean you have to follow them to the grave like the wives of some barbarian chieftain. Now, then; if the consortium needed him for this peculiar deal of theirs, it'd snooker them proper if he killed himself and wasn't available for research purposes as a result. It was also the best chance he could see of getting back home, to his office and his in-tray and his filing cabinets and the framed Hieronymus Bosch print on the wall above his familiar chair. Certainly worth considering—

He finished his drink and called for another. It arrived, with the absolute minimum of involvement from the barman. At least one thing he'd tried in the last few days had worked like it should.

Worth considering, but out of the question, because it wasn't his body. If he killed it, there'd be this poor homeless vicar with no flesh-and-bone overcoat to come back to once this was all over. Bad enough for the poor chap to have spent the last few weeks locked up in the cells as an enemy alien; no, he couldn't do it. It'd be wrong. Besides, suicide was a sin, and there was a little matter of demarcation to think about.

So what else do humans do that we don't? In practice, that is, as opposed to in theory. There must be something . . .

Well of course, there's . . .

Nah.

Surely not.

But it wasn't as if he was exactly spoilt for choice. Sure,

it wasn't something *exclusively* human; birds do it, bees do it, even educated fleas do it. But not the forces of darkness. Absolutely positive about that.

'Excuse me.'

'Now what do you want?'

'I'm sorry to trouble you,' Artofel said to the barman, 'but in order to save the human race, not to mention the entire cosmos and quite possibly God, it's rather imperative that I fall in love at once. Since I have no previous experience of the process, can you give me any basic advice?'

The barman looked at him for a moment.

'Yeah,' he said. 'Piss off before I bash your head in.'

Artofel's forehead creased in a slight frown. 'I see,' he said. 'Should I take that as a definite no, or . . .?'

'Out.'

'Because, you see,' Artofel went on, 'if I do something really out of character, something that's fundamentally at odds with my true demonic nature, it'll mean I'm not really a proper demon any more and I won't be any use to this diabolic consortium I was telling you about. And without me, I rather get the impression they can't do anything . . . So you see, it's really rather vital that I—'

About a fifteenth of a second later he hit the pavement, bounced off a dustbin and a parked car and came to rest in the gutter outside the pub.

'Blast,' he said.

He opened his eyes; and found that he was staring at something rather out of the ordinary. The most he could make of them was that they weren't feet. More like tentacles, except that no octopus he'd ever heard of had tentacles shaped like *that*.

'If you're who I think you are,' he said without looking up, 'those things aren't regulation issue.'

'Excuse me?'

'Stick to the cloven hooves, son,' Artofel sighed. 'The Service is no place for designer footwear.'

'Excuse me,' repeated the voice, with a slightly different inflection, 'but I'm from another planet, and I was wondering if you could spare me a few moments to tell me about your idea of the Supreme Being.'

'Huh?'

'I assume you have one,' the proprietor of the not-quite-tentacles continued. 'There's a lot of references to a Supreme Being in your cultural matrix. For instance, who is God?'

Slowly Artofel lifted his head and looked up at what the pseudopods were attached to. It gave him a nasty turn.

'Did you say you're from a different planet?' he asked.

'That's right,' whatever it was replied. 'I'm doing a preliminary report on your planet for the folks back home, and this is one aspect of your civilisation I haven't covered yet. Now then, this God. Am I to understand that as you perceive Him, your Supreme Being is three in one?'

Artofel shook his head. 'I think you'll find that's a kind of penetrating oil,' he replied. 'Actually, you've come to the right place, because I work for Him. In two capacities,' he added, wincing.

'I see. This is fascinating. Please go on.'

Quite possibly, Artofel said to himself, I'm not the first person to see something like this after being thrown out of this particular pub. Chances are I won't be the last, either. What I resent is knowing that it's not just a hallucination. 'It's rather difficult to explain,' he went on. 'Basically, you see, I work for the forces of Evil, but right now I'm on secondment to Good. Like a sort of exchange visit, if you follow me. See how the other half lives, that sort of thing.'

'Ah,' said the alien, clearly perplexed. 'Now, excuse my asking, but why did you just fly out through that door at high speed and land uncomfortably on the ground?'

'I was chucked out. For being a nuisance.'

'Really.'

'But that's just a sort of temporary diversion. Now I've got to go and find someone to fall in love with.'

'I see. Now then, your conception of the Supreme Being—'

'Right,' Artofel said. 'He's about so high, a bit broader across the shoulders than me, white hair, long beard, got this way of looking at you out of the corner of His eye. I can give you His address, but I think He's away from home at the moment.'

'Just a minute,' the alien interrupted. 'You speak as if you've seen Him.'

'Of course I have,' Artofel replied. 'We all have. I mean, I'm not saying I know Him personally, in any real sense. I was introduced to Him once at a garden party, but just to say hello.'

'Let me see if I've got this straight,' said the alien. 'You're telling me you've actually met your Supreme Being.'

'Oh yes.'

'And talked to Him.'

'Just a few words, like I said. There was a whole queue of us, you see, waiting to be introduced, quick handshake and out again. Still, it's all good public relations, isn't it?'

'Pardon my saying this,' said the alien cautiously, 'but you don't sound as if you were, well, particularly impressed.'

Artofel shrugged. 'Can't say I was. Nothing against Him, mind; perfectly pleasant He was, not standoffish or anything, very polite. I suppose it's all the practice He gets, because he's doing that sort of thing all the time.'

'Your God spends a lot of time being polite to His subjects?'

Artofel nodded. 'A certain amount of basic showmanship goes with the territory,' he said. 'You know what they say: keep the little people happy and the big people will follow suit. And anyhow, we're all on the same side, so . . .'

'You are? Oh. Right.' The alien shuffled its pseudopods thoughtfully. 'You mentioned just now that you have to go and jump in something. What was—?'

'Not jump,' Artofel corrected. 'Fall. In love. You see, it's rather complicated but I've got to fall in love in order to save the human race and the entire divine hierarchy. I could explain,' he added, 'but it'd take rather a long time.'

'Quite. When you say save—'

'From a bunch of low-lifes who're out to get Him. Talking of which, I'd love to stay here chatting but I'd better be getting on. All the best with your researches.'

'Thanks. Yes. Right.' Artofel couldn't be sure, because as far as body language went, the alien didn't half talk funny; but it gave the impression of pulling itself together with extreme difficulty. 'Thank you for your time. You've been most . . . Yes. Thank you. Goodbye. You did say *love*, didn't you? I thought so. Sorry, I think my translator unit's malfunctioning, because . . . Yes, well, anyway. Bye.'

When the alien had squelched away, Artofel got up, dusted himself off and looked around for someone to fall in love with. Can't be difficult, he reassured himself. If they can do, so can I.

Oh well. Here goes.

He caught sight of a briskly moving figure on the other side of the street and followed after it. About forty-five seconds later there was a flurry of conversation which ended in a loud crunching noise and the howl of a Duke of Hell suddenly afflicted with pain in parts of his anatomy he didn't know he had. A few minutes later, the same sequence of events was repeated. A few minutes after that, the same.

Brimstone, Artofel reflected, as he sat on the steps of a

bank waiting for the pain to subside. And yet this is how these losers are supposed to reproduce. Beats me how come there's so many of them, let alone why they bother. Still, here we go again—

This time, the sound of stockinged knee on worsted was so loud it rattled the windows. Which goes some way towards explaining why, when the commando of Infernal stormtroopers he'd only recently escaped from caught up with him a few minutes later, he had neither the strength nor the willpower to run.

Distressing was putting it mildly. One minute, Karen had been engrossed in the search for a way to save God, the next she was loading the contents of her desk into a cardboard box and promising the loathsome Jenny from the next office down the row but one that they'd keep in touch. Strange, she said to herself as she waited for the lift, how quickly things can change.

What had done it? she wondered. About the only sudden and unexpected factor was the eclipse, which had now been going on for so long that she had difficulty remembering what it had been like before. A messy sort of white stuff poured over everything like custard, if memory served her, and a big shiny thing up in the sky. She wasn't even sure she could recall exactly what the shiny thing had looked like; in her mind's eye it had somehow merged with the stylised yellow blob from a child's painting. Now, when she tried to remember the sun, the image that came to her mind was more like luminous fried egg than anything that had ever existed for real.

Unlikely, though, that the eclipse had done for Kawaguchiya Integrated Circuits; which only really left the abrupt and unheralded entry of God into its corporate life. Coincidence? Yeah, sure. And you could use her other leg for an emergency door-bell.

Anyway, she told herself, as she struggled with her cardboard box on the packed underground like a stereotype refugee, now it's none of my business and I can stop worrying about it. I can dismiss it from my mind and get on with the absolutely pathetically simple task of finding a new job.

Like hell.

Yes, that was all very well, but how was she supposed to continue the search, with no manual, no computer, no way of contacting Kevin Christ and absolutely zero chance of being believed by anybody she went to for help? If she couldn't crack it with all the resources of KIC to call on, she couldn't really expect to do better with nothing more sophisticated at her disposal than one of the early-Victorian coal-burning Amstrads and the Ladybird book of computer fault diagnosis. Forget it, Karen. You've got problems enough of your own.

Yes, but . . .

Yes but nothing. Out of my hands now. He's the *Almighty*, for pity's sake; big enough and ugly enough to take care of himself.

Yes. But.

Some clown bumped into her as she tried to scramble off the train at Waterloo, spilling the contents of her box and then darting off with only the echo of a mumbled 'Sorry' hurled over his shoulder. By the time she'd picked up her fugitive property, which had rolled and bounced away between the feet of her sardine-packed fellow passengers, the train had moved on. Great. She'd have to get off at the next stop, change platforms, wait for the northbound train, go through all this again. It was things like this made her love the human race.

Human race. *Human*. First real lead you've had all along.

How dumb (she asked herself as she shoved through to the doors just before they closed) can you get? All those hours she'd spent trying to find a way of bypassing the computer's defences, and it hadn't occurred to her that she was trying to solve the wrong problem. Sloppy thinking. Human thinking. Not appropriate to a superhuman problem.

She sat down on a bench on Kennington station platform, and worked it out a step at a time. The key to it all was a simple formula, one she'd known ever since she was a kid. So obvious . . .

To err is human, to forgive divine. When human beings make mistakes, they worry away at them trying to put things right, trying to stick the pieces back together again with glue. Occasionally they succeed, sometimes they fail utterly and make things worse, frequently they half solve the problem and then leave it while they try and cope with the mess they've caused for themselves while they were trying to fix the original problem. That's the human way. That's what she'd been trying to do. Wrong.

The denizens of Heaven don't solve problems or fix mistakes; they forgive them. Confronted with the theft in the Garden of Eden, God didn't try and stick the apple back on the branch with Araldite or fill in the bitten-out chunk with fine-grade Polyfilla; he simply forgave, and that was that, problem solved. It'd be a nice trick, if you could manage it; simply forgiving the front door for sticking in the damp weather, or the carburettor for being flooded, sitting down with a blocked sink trap and talking it through like sensible, mature adults – quicker, easier and ever so much cheaper. But backed-up sinks and cars that won't start aren't divine problems: not usually.

More to the point, you've got to be divine to make it work, which explained why it hadn't actually solved anything when she decided to forgo her moral right to break the arm of the pillock who upset her cardboard box on the train. It was no use her forgiving the wretched computer; big deal. Somebody else was going to have to do that, and from what she knew of the situation the only person with the necessary qualification was sitting under a big umbrella on a river-bank somewhere. Still, what she didn't know about the precise way in which Heaven works could be written on a medium-sized Universe in letters the size of a hydrogen atom. Let them work out the minor operational details for themselves; she'd done the important part. Now all she had to do was tell them . . .

A task in respect of which the phrase *piece of cake* wasn't immediately appropriate. Phone the Pope? Go into Westminster Abbey and ask if they could forward a letter? Dammit, she shouldn't *have* to get in touch with them, they should come to her.

With a rumble of thunder like Thor after a hot curry, the train appeared out of the tunnel. The platform was crowded, and it wasn't easy to move about with her arms full of cardboard box. In fact, if she wasn't careful, she might end up getting shoved off the platform and under the train, which wouldn't help anybody.

Oddly enough, that was exactly what happened.

It was probably just as well that she was so preoccupied with righteous indignation against the second clumsy oaf she'd had the misfortune to be bumped into in the space of less than an hour that she didn't hear the *scrunch* as the train ran over her, let alone the rather nauseating fizz as all those busy volts ran up and down her nervous system, ringing bells and running away. In fact, she'd been dead for nearly a second and a half before she noticed, and that was only because she'd reached out for her a-present-from-Florence paperweight and found that her hand passed clean through it.

Oh, she said.

Telltale signs - the fact that she was looking down at the roof of the train rather than up at its chassis, that sort of thing – confirmed her initial suspicion. Oh *damn*. Well, that's that, then. And of all the blundering, careless idiots—

From her vantage point in the upper air she could see the blundering, careless idiot quite clearly. He looked as if he was having the worst moment of his life; quite probably, he was. Without even thinking about it, she forgave him.

And somehow, without having the faintest idea how she knew, she was aware that it had worked. She had forgiven him, he had been forgiven.

Problem solved.

In a manner of speaking, of course; it still left her quite undeniably dead for one thing, and it would have been nice if the omelette could have been made without her having to be the egg that got broken. Still, no point crying over spilt milk. Or, come to that, spilt anything else.

To forgive—

And then she knew.

Len woke up.

He had been dreaming; the long, silent, majestic dreams of machines, full of straight lines and right angles, of things that fitted exactly into other things, of keyways frictionless and true and the sharp, clean shine of newly cut metal. It was a beautiful dream; the sort of vision that might inspire a god to create a world.

'Urgh,' he said. 'Wassafuxat?'

Someone was bashing the workshop door. Len stood up, quickly trying to remember what he'd recently learned about balance and self-propelled biped movement. Why should anybody want to smash his door in at half past one in the morning?

'Lock,' he said.

Hmm?

'What's going on?'

Please be more specific.

Len scowled. Locks aren't the sensible person's immediate choice when information's needed in a hurry. As is only to be expected from mechanisms whose whole purpose is to be exact and to respond only to a perfectly correct key, they tend to be pedantic and fussy.

'Who's bashing your door and why?' Len amended. 'Any ideas?'

I register five of them. They are not authorised personnel. They do not appear to be human. Their purpose in hitting the door is to open it without recourse to authorised lock-opening procedures. I would imagine they are doing this because they are not authorised personnel. Authorised personnel would not abuse official property in this manner.

'Ah,' Len said, as his brain fumbled for its trousers and put its teeth in. 'Well, try and keep them out.'

Of course I shall try and keep them out. They are not authorised personnel. If they were authorised personnel, they would have an appropriate key.

'Cheers, lock.'

I should however point out that in the normal course of fulfilling my function as a lock I am already doing everything within my limited powers to prevent unauthorised access by unauthorised personnel. Please note also that I shall not be able to fulfil my function for very much longer.

'Oh go on,' Len muttered, testing the three big Stilson wrenches for weight and balance. 'Give it your best shot.'

Please note that I am on the point of failing to fulfil my function. I should like the record to show that this failure is due to the imminent collapse of the wooden doorframe rather than any shortcoming on my part.

'Thanks anyway. Robot!'

'Go 'way 's middle of night.'

'Oh for . . .' Len had an idea. 'Recalibrate your timescale for Hong Kong time. Robot!'

'Here, boss!' At once the robot (for whom it was now 9 a.m.) shot out from its storage space under the bench and stood to attention, its facial mechanisms arranged in a beaming cybersmile. 'Sleep okay, boss?'

'Like a top. Robot, there are five heavies trying to smash the door down.'

'Yes?'

'Don't just stand there,' Len fumed. 'Stop them.'

'Um.'

For a moment, Len couldn't believe his ears. 'What the devil do you mean, um? You're a robot, dammit. You don't know the meaning of fear.'

The robot shuffled its feet. 'Actually, I do. Fear, according to the *Oxford English Dictionary*—'

'Don't muck me about, robot. I gave you a direct order.'

'I know.' The robot simpered. (How did it learn to do that? Len wondered. I don't remember fitting a simper relay.) 'There's a problem. I can't.'

'What?'

The robot bit its lip, or at least it tried to. There was a grating noise and a few sparks. 'EC Directive 463837/99 on safety of machinery. Says machines aren't allowed to hurt people. Sorry.'

'*What?*'

'EC Directive 463837/99,' the robot repeated miserably. 'All new mechanical appliances now have to conform to the specifications laid down by this directive, which states, and I'm paraphrasing slightly here, hurting people is wrong. For heaven's sake, you wouldn't want me to break the law, now would you?'

Len would have replied Yes at this point, if it hadn't been for the door giving way and the workshop suddenly filling with large, fast-moving bipeds. Even Len, whose experience of human beings was still rather limited, could tell that these weren't standard production-model *Homo sapiens*; too many head and claws, eyes in the wrong section of the anatomy, that sort of thing. They looked as if they'd been thrown together out of the contents of the leftovers in Frankenstein's spares box with a few bits from a car boot sale thrown in for good measure, and they were holding implements which, although unfamiliar, probably came under the heading of generic weapons.

'Hold it,' Len yelled.

The apparent leader of the party stopped where he was, assessing him through several pairs of inhuman eyes. 'Well?' he said.

'Come any closer and I'll thump you.'

'Oh.' The leader shrugged. 'I thought you were going to say something important. All right, grab them and let's get going.'

Two of the subsidary Things caught hold of the robot while a third pulled a black plastic sack down over its head. It didn't move. The leader and his remaining henchthing advanced on Len; in no particular hurry, keeping a multiplicity of eyes and the like on the Stilson in Len's hands, but not unduly worried about it. As they came close, he backed away. They walked straight past him.

'Hey,' he said. 'Where are you going?'

'You'll see.'

They were standing on either side of the machine; the universal milling and turning machine that was much more Len than any bag of bones and blood would ever be. The leader picked up a twelve-pound sledgehammer single-handed; his chum was toying with the big adjustable spanner.

'Come quietly,' said the leader, 'or the machine gets it.'

'You wouldn't.'

'As a statement of fact, that has a basic flaw. As a threat, it doesn't work. As an appeal to my better nature—'

'Get away,' Len said, 'from that machine. It hasn't done you any harm.'

The subsidiary Thing tapped the main casing gently with the spanner. 'Cast iron,' he observed. 'Brittle stuff, if it gets hit. Can't be repaired.'

'All right.' The Stilson clattered on the concrete floor; only Len heard it swearing. 'Now get away from the machine.'

The Things took a step forwards; but suddenly there was an atmosphere in the workshop that hadn't been there a moment before. A sort of dull residual anger, you might say, if you had an excessively powerful imagination. Len could feel it well enough; he could remember feeling that anger many times himself, when some cack-haired apprentice had jammed his feed or graunched his threads. It tended to start with an ill-defined I-don't-like-this-man, after which it would develop over a period of days, sometimes years, biding its time until the object of the machine's resentment happened to put his thumb in the way of the boring-bar or lean over a moving chuck with his shirt-sleeves flapping. Then there'd be a short, usually bloody moment, followed by a certain amount of irrational human behaviour; after a while someone'd come along, switch him off at the mains and clean the blood and bits of stuff out of the cogs and threads. Odd how rarely human beings notice that ominous feel in the air.

EC Directive 463837/99 forsooth. One of the first things a machine tool learns is how to defend itself, and how to avenge its slighted honour.

It started when the leader's right leg brushed against the bench grinder, which promptly switched itself on. The leader immediately jumped two feet in the air and eighteen inches sideways, but all he achieved was to fall heavily across the bed of the bandsaw. With hindsight, an error on his part.

In a slightly edited form, the leader then hurled himself clear of the bandsaw and, with his remaining hand, grabbed at the nearest solid object to steady himself. His rotten luck it happened to be the arc welder.

From the arc welder, the leader then rebounded on to the table of the Great Machine, and that's where his real problems started. The horizontal arm, set up for slit-sawing, left just enough of him for the vertical arm to mess up quite comprehensively with a face-cutter.

Ah, Len said to himself. Always wondered why they called them that.

The subsidary Thing stayed perfectly still, at least until Len had brained him with the big Stilson. That just left the other three.

'One of the advantages of buying second-hand gear,' Len said, 'is that it doesn't comply with the latest EC directives. Do we have to do this the hard way, or are you lot going to bugger off and leave me in peace?'

A Thing grinned at him feebly. 'In a perfect world,' he said, 'we'd bugger off. Gladly.'

'Like a shot,' confirmed his colleague to his immediate right.

'Nothing'd give us greater pleasure,' chipped in the third.

Len shrugged. 'Please yourselves, then,' he said; whereupon the spindle moulder jumped them. What a spindle moudler does to pieces of wood is bad enough.

'You can come out now,' Len said.

'Sorry,' the robot reiterated. 'If it'd been up to me, I'd have pulled their heads off and made them eat them.'

'I'm sure you would,' Len replied, pulling off the plastic sack. 'Isn't there something in human literature about a tin man who has no heart?'

'Not quite,' the robot replied. 'In *The Wizard of Oz*—'

'Well,' Len went on, 'you're a steel man who has no

balls. But we can fix that. Hand me that half-by-nine-sixteenths spanner.'

'Please—'

'Nuts,' Len went on, unscrewing one, 'but no balls.' He paused and thought. 'Maybe it's a human thing, courage,' he said.

'Up to a – ouch, that *tickles*!'

'It'll do more than tickle when I get the brazing torch on you. Now then, I'll need a schematic of male reproductive organs, some three-sixteenths copper pipe and a soldering iron. God, what a bloody daft way to go about a perfectly simple job of plumbing!'

'Why are you—?'

Len looked up and reached for a hacksaw. 'Because,' he replied, 'as soon as I've bypassed that EC Directive, we're going to find out who sent these goons, these creatures who threatened to hurt a machine, and we're going to sort them out. All right?'

'Okay. Um, boss.'

'Yes?'

'Why?'

'Shut up.'

'Ah. Now I understand. Thanks, boss.'

CHAPTER TWELVE

'**K**evin.'

The younger son of God didn't reply. He was sitting curled up in the window-seat of one of the rear subsidiary seventeenth-floor chapels, gazing listlessly out over the back courtyard and fiddling with a plastic flower. A painter in need of a model for a watercolour lovelorn teenager would have offered him money not to move an inch.

'Kevin,' Martha repeated. 'Your dinner's going cold.'

'Don't want any,' he mumbled, turning his head away. Outside, they were emptying the septic tank. Chances were that it wasn't the view that was monopolising his attention.

'It's kedgeree,' Martha said. 'And bread-and-butter pudding for afters.'

'It's always kedgeree and bread-and-butter pudding,' Kevin replied; and if this statement wasn't entirely accurate, it was close enough.

Martha advanced, walking softly. 'What's the matter?' she said.

'Oh, nothing,' Kevin replied. 'I've messed up the computer, the whole world's a complete shambles, I don't even know what harm I've done and when Dad gets home He'll be so angry it'll make what He did to Adam and Eve look like an awards ceremony.'

'But that's not it, is it?'

'No,' Kevin admitted.

'She hasn't rung back, has she?'

'Who? Oh, you mean that female mortal, the one from the computer place. No, she hasn't.' Kevin's voice wobbled like a tightrope walker in a hurricane. 'Not,' he went on, 'that I was expecting her to. I mean, what'd she want to go phoning *me* for? It's not as if anybody in their right mind'd want to talk to *me*. 'Specially not . . .' His voice trailed away, like the attention of a delegate on the fifth day of a conference, and he made a sort of burping noise that had nothing to do with indigestion.

'Now then,' Martha said. Not tactful to point out that her not ringing back had probably avoided a potential disaster that would have relegated whatever else Kevin had done, no matter how cataclysmic, to a quarter of an inch on the back page under the Australian football results. She tried, briefly, to imagine what Himself would have said if He'd come home to meet a radiantly happy Kevin nervously stammering that there was someone he'd like Him to meet.

No, no more of that sort of thing.

Once had been quite enough . . .

She felt her face grow warm, and turned it away in case Kevin should see the blush. 'You've got to keep your strength up,' she said. 'There's ice cream with the bread-and-butter pudding.'

'No thanks.'

'Or custard. You like custard.'

Kevin said some words about bread-and-butter pudding that had probably never been used in Heaven before; where *did* he learn them? Martha wondered. She replied with some mild rebuke; her mind was elsewhere. No, *that* sort of thing was definitely not on. Perish the thought. She shrugged, and closed the door after her.

The boy's growing up, she reflected as she made her way down the stairs to the laundry room; a disturbing thought. He wasn't supposed to grow up. It had been part of the deal, in fact. It was a good bet that this sudden and unexpected contact with mortals was behind it; after all, a lad his age, talking to a girl for the very first time, it was only to be expected. Next thing you know, he'll be thinking about all sorts of things.

Like, for example; whatever became of his mother?

As she folded a towel, Martha shuddered. It really wouldn't do for Kevin to start asking that sort of question. Mind you, it was a miracle it hadn't occurred to him already. Very much a miracle; but in a place where everything from the plumbing to the immersion heaters works by miracle – so cheap, so environmentally friendly – you take such things for granted. If only everything in life was as reliable as a miracle.

Now if she could have her time over again—

Yes, but she couldn't, so no point worrying about it. There was no way Kevin would ever work it out for himself. That had been taken care of nearly two thousand years ago; no reason why it should suddenly change now.

Unless—

She dropped the towel; it folded itself anyway (My God! A miracle!). Unless, of course, one of the things Kevin had thrown out of kilter was her own rather shamefaced little miracle, the one that prevented a boy asking an obvious question. The very thought was enough to make her blood run as cold as a bath in a cheap hotel. No reason to suppose that it should, of course; except that here was

Kevin, noticing girls. Why now? Compared with what they'd been like a few decades ago, girls in the fag-end of the twentieth century were scarcely worth noticing. Drab, featureless, uninspiring the lot of 'em; none of them the sort of creature you'd accept a second-hand apple from. Compared to the quality of girls they'd had in her young day—

Well, quite. Enough said about that. The plain fact of the matter was, if this mess didn't get sorted out as quick as ninepence, there could well be trouble, and then what? Another flood, maybe? Martha sincerely hoped it wouldn't come to that. Thousands of years it'd taken before they'd got rid of that horrible musty smell, not to mention the damp getting into the walls. And, of course, the mass devastation and loss of life, though it got a bit technical when you started trying to work out the ramifications of that particular line of thought. It was an option He might well consider, nevertheless; not to mention a first-rate excuse for winding up humanity and starting again with a relatively clean sheet. Would He go that far, just to cover up one little scandal?

No need to think too long about that one.

She left the rest of the bedlinen to fold itself – it was much better at it than she was – and hurried back down to the staff canteen. Fortunately, nobody was using the phone, and she still had enough small change.

From the KIC helpline number, no reply. To be precise, that high-pitched keening noise that means the line's been cut off. Frowning, she tried the main number, and got a recorded message, Sorry we can't take your call right now but we've quite unexpectedly ceased to exist. If you'd like to leave a message for the liquidators, please speak after the tone.

Martha didn't swear; but the way she said 'Drat!' would have had your average Hell's Angel scowling at her and demanding that she wash her mouth out with soap. The only little flicker of light she'd seen so far, snuffed out. Back precisely where she'd started.

Which meant she'd have to think of something else.

Easier said than done. She was, in all modesty, reasonably bright, but solutions to insoluble problems weren't the sort of thing she could pluck out of thin air at a moment's notice. Intelligence wasn't quite enough. There had to be a certain element of luck as well; say ninety-nine per cent, in round figures. For her to fix this dreadful muddle all by herself, without any help or proper facilities; it'd be—

She smiled. Then she went to the counter and asked for a cup of tea. The duty angel nodded and filled the kettle from the tap. She said a brief prayer. At once, steam rose from the spout and the lid rattled. The angel poured a cupful and handed it over. Long ago, the management had realised that what worked for wine at the wedding at Cana works for tea as well, resulting in a substantial saving on the staff budget. So quick; so efficient; so cheap; so environmentally friendly. From where she was standing, Martha could see through into the kitchen, where someone had fridgemagneted up the usual witty and encouraging notices, such as:

YOU DON'T HAVE TO BE INFALLIBLE TO WORK HERE BUT IT HELPS

and:

ANGELS DO IT IMMACULATELY

(that one always made her wince) and:

MY OTHER SON'S A MESSIAH

(one of these days He's going to see that, and then there'll be trouble) and:

MIRACLES WE DO IMMEDIATELY
THE POSSIBLE TAKES A LITTLE LONGER

Yes. For her to fix this dreadful muddle all by herself, without any help or proper facilities, would be an absolute by-Our-Lady miracle.

'Well now,' said a voice in the darkness, 'this *is* cosy.'

The diverse assortment of creatures confined in the cage somewhere within earshot of the voice all began talking at once. What they actually said scarcely merits recording; it was a confused medley of variations on the themes *Where am I?* and *Let me out!* The voice waited until they'd all railed themselves hoarse, and then continued.

'I'll bet,' it said, 'you're wondering why you're here.'

'I'm not,' growled Artofel. 'And you can stop trying to be so damn mysterious, as well. I know perfectly well that this is the staff toilet on Level Thirty-Six; I'd recognise that dripping cistern anywhere. And any minute now I'll recognise your voice too, and when I do there's going to be some changes made to the holiday roster that'll make you wish you'd never been damned.'

'Oh,' said the voice. 'Drat. In that case, I might as well switch the lights on.'

A faint click; and the meagre glow of an administration-issue sixty-watt bulb diluted the shadows. In particular, it illuminated four plump middle-aged males and one plump middle-aged female, all dressed in smart executive businesswear and wearing executive spectacles, sitting on lavatory seats in a row of cubicles.

'You,' Artofel said contemptuously. 'I might have known.'

'Hello,' replied the female. 'Yes, it's us. And before you get too cocky and start yelling for help, don't bother, because nobody'll come.'

'I put a notice on the door saying *Out of Order*,' explained the male to her immediate left. 'Amazing how effective that is.'

Artofel sniffed angrily. 'So that's what it's all been about, is it?' he said. 'All this aggravation, spectral warriors roaming up and down breaking all the rules, harassment of civilians, conspiracy against the Management—'

'Who isn't here,' the female interrupted, smirking.

'What?'

'Not here. Gone. One of our Supreme Beings is missing—'

'Two, actually,' a male demon pointed out. 'The Boss and Junior. Which theoretically leaves Uncle Ghost, but so what? Compared to him in the usefulness stakes, the proverbial chocolate fireguard's a nuclear-powered Swiss Army knife.'

'Say that again,' Artofel muttered. 'The Old Man and Junior are—'

'Gone. That's right. Been gone a while now. There are various theories,' the female went on. 'Buffy here reckons that science has finally caught up with Them and proved once and for all They don't exist. Reckons there was a documentary about it on telly, and so it must be true. Chubby thinks They've got religion and joined some obscure sect in the Nevada desert. My hypothesis is that He's staged His own death, possibly by falling off his yacht and drowning or something equally jejune, and they've done a flit with the pension fund money. In any case, it doesn't matter; the fact is they're not here. Which means that, so long as we don't hang about, we've got a once-in-an-everlasting-lifetime chance to put through this perfectly wonderful scheme of ours and have it all tied up so tight that even if They do come back, there'll be nothing They can do about it. So . . .'

'Excuse me.'

The female looked to see who'd spoken. 'Sorry,' she said. 'What can I do for you?'

'Excuse me,' Maria repeated, 'but where is this?'

The five demons looked at each other and tried not to giggle. It was left to Artofel to answer the question.

'Hell?' Maria repeated.

'That's right,' the female said. 'Don't worry unduly about that, though. Like in Monopoly, you're in Jail but Just Visiting.' She smiled reassuringly. 'You're going to die, of course,' she added, 'but what happens to you after that is between you, your personal codes of ethics and your own individual governing body. I don't know offhand who actually does decide where bad paintings go when they die, although I've heard the Birmingham City Art Gallery plausibly suggested.'

Inside the cage there was gloomy silence. Artofel scowled ineffectually. Maria sat thoughtful and rather depressed. The Prime Minister, having discovered by exhaustive research that there was nothing inside the cage to climb up and jump off, was sitting in a corner and huddling.

'And in any case,' the female went on, 'we can't snuff you out quite yet, because we haven't got the complete set. The last of you's due to be delivered any minute now, and then we can get started. While we're waiting, though, I thought it'd be only polite to say hello and frighten you into little quivering heaps.' She beamed like a vampire aunt. 'It's been ages since I've done any frightening,' she explained. 'I do miss it so.'

Maria turned her head as best she could in the confined space of the cage. 'Excuse me,' she said to Artofel. 'I don't know who you are, but you seem to know what's going on.

Could you possibly explain? I have actually met some of these people before, but . . .'

'Delighted,' Artofel replied grimly. 'I am Artofel, Duke of Hell. These five degenerates are also Dukes of Hell; to be precise, they're the Arts, Leisure and Libraries Sub-Committee, which in practice means they're too devious or useless to be trusted with a proper job but they can't be sacked because they've got seniority.'

'I resent that,' said the male demon referred to as Buffy. 'We fulfil a valuable role in the artistic and cultural life of everlasting damnation.'

Artofel snorted. 'Ignore him,' he said. 'All they actually do is, twice a year they take a library trolley round with all the latest Jeffrey Archers and Lynda La Plantes. Waste of time, though, because any punter who's been evil enough to deserve that sort of thing gets issued with a copy as soon as it comes out. Different department.'

'I see,' Maria lied. 'You're the ones who wanted us to sell you our souls or something.'

The male demon called Bunty sniggered; the female broadened her insufferable smile. 'If only it were that simple,' she said. 'No, my poor dears, it's a bit more involved than that. Shall I explain?'

'No,' said Artofel.

'Very well then. The point is, you three and a fourth one you'll be meeting any minute now are unique. For a while now you've been trotting around quite happily in human bodies, but you aren't human. We're designing an improved Mark Two human to sell to alternative realities – '

'Damn fine commercial opportunity there,' Buffy muttered. 'Dreadful waste not to exploit it.'

' – and so all we've got to do is synthesise the four of you, refine the result and start cloning. We have all the facilities here.'

'Really? In a staff bog?'

The female nodded. 'Apparently you're overestimating the technical difficulties, Artie dear. We've got the blender from the Level Eight canteen and the spare photocopier from Archives, and the rest's just a matter of imagination and insulating tape. Excuse me, but why is your silent colleague trying to hang upside down from the cage roof?'

'He's a lemming,' Bunty explained. 'I know it's like a fear of heights, only in reverse. He'll let go in a min— Ah, just as I thought. Happy landings!'

Artofel growled menacingly. 'You do realise that you're never going to get away with this,' he said. 'I mean, quite apart from the whole scheme being completely impractical and doomed to failure, do you honestly believe that when - I say when, not if – the Old Man finds out what you've been doing He's just going to put it down to fiendish high spirits and tell you not to do it again?' He shook his head, in the process biffing Maria on the nose and head-butting the Prime Minister. 'You five won't even be history. You'll be dogma.'

The female laughed musically. 'We shall see,' she said. 'Or at least, you three won't, but we will. Chubby, do you think you could possibly find out what's keeping number four? Time's going on, you know. It's not like Squad Three to be late.'

'Caught in traffic?' a demon speculated.

'Excuse me,' Maria said.

The five demons looked at her. This didn't disconcert her too badly – you get used to that sort of thing if you've been a painting for any appreciable length of time. She cleared her throat.

'Excuse me, but I've just realised why none of this is going to work.'

Another trill of silvery laughter from the female demon. 'Oh dear,' she said, 'this isn't going to help, you know. Playing for time might be an effective tactic where you come from, but down here time really doesn't have an awful lot of meaning.'

'No but seriously,' Maria said. 'And I'll tell you for why. Your whole scam's based on one basic error. Sorry,' she added, 'but there it is.'

'Oh yes? And perhaps you'd be terribly sweet and let us in on the big secret?'

Maria looked thoughtful. 'It's not really a secret,' she said. 'More sort of staring you in the face. Just ask yourselves: why do supreme beings have mortals in the first place?'

The demons beamed tolerantly. 'Atmosphere,' Buffy said.

"Like potted palms in dentists' waiting rooms,' Chubby added. 'You don't need them, but it makes the place look a bit less sparse.'

'You're sure about that?' Maria said. 'I'm not. Be reasonable. Mortals aren't particularly decorative; if all you wanted was to make the place look nice, you'd have lots of tasteful ornaments instead, like me. And as pets, they're a dead loss; they aren't exactly environmentally friendly either, Lord knows. If you wanted something to be the equivalent of a cuddly kitten or even pondweed in a fishtank, you wouldn't bother with human beings, you'd just stick with nice sensible harmless animals.'

'Like lemmings,' Artofel muttered under his breath.

'Exactly,' Maria agreed. 'And mortals aren't there to add interest and excitement to the business of running a cosmos; after all, that's what His Majesty's loyal opposition's there for – you lot and this gentleman here whose name escapes me for the moment. The forces of evil and so forth. And the last possible reason for having mortals is to get anything *useful* done, because they don't, by and large. If it's that sort of thing you're after, you'd have a race of robots or something similar. But instead,' she went on, 'there are mortals. Have you ever stopped to wonder why?'

The female was still beaming; but the one called Bunty was wearing a puzzled frown. It suited him about as well as a full set of baroque armour would suit Kate Moss, but the important thing was that it was there. 'What are you driving at?' he asked.

'Think,' Maria replied. 'The only possible motive for infesting your cosmos with silly, awkward, destructive mortals is so that you, the supreme being, can feel superior. I may not be all that hot on the perfection front, you say, as you face yourself in the shaving mirror every morning, but at least I'm better than that lot down there. It gives you a nice warm glow deep down in your ineffability. It makes you feel good. After all, you're an omnipotent creator; if that's not the reason, why did you make *Homo sapiens* such an utter *mess*? So,' she continued sweetly, 'don't you think that an *improved* version of humanity, a version that's *not* a seething mass of design faults and built-in shortcomings, is likely to be something of a drug on the market?'

There was a long, rather unpleasant silence, disturbed only by Artofel sniggering and the rasp of teeth on steel as the Prime Minister tried to gnaw through the bars of the cage.

'Bother,' said the fifth demon.

'Don't listen to her,' the female said. 'That's human logic talking. Gods don't think like that. Do they?' she added.

'Want to bet?' Maria replied aggressively. 'I seem to remember something about being created in somebody else's image. I'd invite you to look at it more as a case of Him having a very ugly picture of himself in his attic Or, if you prefer, ask yourself who's taking away whose sins? All the things He didn't want to be, shoved off on a bunch of expendables? And you're asking His equivalents in the dimension next door to lay out good money for a new line in the raw materials of religion –'

'Canon fodder,' Artofel mumbled.

'– who're going to be fully justified in turning round when He forgives them and forgiving Him right back. With brass knobs on. Not an inspired investment, if you ask me.'

'Paintings,' said the female demon icily, 'should be seen and not heard. If I'd wanted a *talking* picture, I'd have kidnapped Mickey Mouse. Let's get these three minced up and add the fourth one later, shall we?'

Her four colleagues looked away, shuffling their executive-shod hooves.

'Seems to me the marketing side of this project's not been thought through properly,' Buffy said. 'Perhaps before we do anything totally irrevocable—'

'Buffy!'

'Yes, but hang on,' the male demon objected. 'Before you start playing Frankenstein-meets-Delia-Smith with Government property—'

'Buffy!'

'Look, I'm not trying to be difficult or anything, it's just that what she's just been saying does make a tenuous sort of sense, so if you could possibly see your way clear to explaining . . .'

The female demon's brows met in a thundery black line. 'Buffy . . .' she said ominously.

'Ah. Right. I *see*. Why didn't you say so before?'

In the middle of a continuum of slowly moving particles roughly analogous to a river, a float bobbed.

'Dad! You've got a bite!'

The older of the two fishermen pushed his hat on to the back of his head, grabbed his rod off its forked stand and began to turn the handle of his reel. The float ducked under the surface of the continuum. The line went taut.

'About ruddy time too,' the fisherman said. 'How many days've we been here?'

The younger fisherman frowned. 'That's not the point, though, surely. I thought the point was for you and me to spend some quality time together, just the two of us, give us a chance to revitalise our relationship by talking meaningfully about things we'd otherwise find it hard to discuss in our everyday environment . . .'

'Shut up, I'm trying to concentrate.'

'Sorry, Dad.'

With a deft flick of his wrist, the older fisherman whipped his prize up out of the continuum; a long shiny silver fish, wriggling and arching its length in the choking air. The fisherman smiled fiercely, swung the fish towards him and reached for the short brass club, the sort invariably referred to as a priest, that lay in the top compartment of his tackle box.

'Dad.'

'Hm?'

'What're you doing?'

'What's it look like I'm doing,' the older fisherman replied.

His son looked worried. 'You're not going to . . . to *kill* it, are you?'

'No, I'm going to lend it money so it can start up its own family-run dry-cleaning business. Course I'm going to kill it.'

'But you *can't*. Dad, it's *alive* . . .'

'Son, maybe I've neglected your education in a number of pertinent areas. I know the perishing thing's alive. That's why I'm going to kill it. Where the Flipside would be the point of killing it if it was already dead?'

'But . . .'

'It's all right, really,' said the fish.

'Keep out of this, you.'

'Sorry.'

The younger fisherman was staring. 'Dad,' he said, 'that fish is *talking*.'

'I know. Luckily, we can do something about that.' He raised the little club, searching for the best place to strike.

'I forgive you,' said the fish.

'Oh *nuts*!' Petulantly, the older fisherman flung his rod down on the grass. The fish flolloped a few times, gasping, and managed to flip itself back into the water. 'Would you flaming well believe it?' he growled.

'Well,' ventured the younger fisherman, 'faith, together with hope and love, is one of the cornerstones of the true way . . .'

'Finally,' the older fisherman went on, biting through the line with his teeth, 'after sitting on this damp, incredibly boring river-bank for I don't know how long, finally I get one lousy miserable bite, and before I can bash the bleeder's brains out, it has to go and forgive me. It's all your fault, with your incessant ruddy moralising.'

'Dad . . .'

'It's more than that, even. You know what, son? You're always ruddy well preaching at me. Holier-than-thou attitude. Well, I've had enough, understood?'

'Dad . . .'

The older fisherman stood up and started flinging tackle angrily into his box. 'Ruddy silly idea in the first place,' he said, 'coming here when I've got a business to run. Anyway, that does it. We're leaving.'

The younger fisherman sighed. 'Yes, Dad.'

I forgive you, Karen said.

Nobody could hear her (presumably something to do with her being dead) but she said it anyway. It seemed the right thing to do, somehow.

To forgive, divine. Define divine—

(Well, that's one good thing. I'd never have been able to say that if I was still alive.)

Define divine. Let me see – immortal, invisible, ineffable, all the in-words. Do I qualify? Yes, yes and presumably yes, though I'm not really sure I know what ineffable means. Is that all there is to it? Dunno. Wasn't there something about being omnipresent—

(And as the thought crossed her mind, she happened to glance down and noticed the Golden Gate Bridge, the Sydney Opera House, the Great Wall and ever such a lot of houses and fields and things, all apparently sharing the same bit of space with Kennington tube station. Ah, she muttered, no wonder this place gets crowded in the rush hour.)

And omnipotent—

(Well, I'm not that, for certain. There's all sorts of things I can't do. Like fly, and see all the kingdoms of the Earth, and drift through walls. Oh. All sorts of *other* things I can't do . . .)

And – what were the other ones? Ah yes, the compassionate, the merciful.

Oh.

She had a horrible feeling that it was all starting to make sense; and although she had nothing against sense as such, she couldn't help resenting the fact that she'd had to get squashed by a train first. For pity's sake, where was the logic in some innocent person having to get killed before everybody could be forgiven?

No sense at all.

It's design faults like these in the fabric of theology that put the mess in Messiah. Query: can you have a girl Messiah? A Missiah? Oh, whyever not? When you think about it practically, the job description – someone who comes along when the system's tied itself in knots and has to be sorted out – turns out to be remarkably similar to that of, say, a helpline girl. There was also a rather ghastly symmetry to it all: divine error, human rectification.

To err is divine, to forgive is human? Taking away the sins of Heaven? Surely not.

Or at least highly improbable. But the odds against are no greater than, for instance, the odds against a regular commuter on a routine journey getting pushed under a tube train.

Oh, she said to herself. Oh well, fair enough. If only my old Sunday-school teacher could see me now, wouldn't she be surprised?

Meanwhile, up above, the sun came out.

'Robot.'

'Yes, boss?'

'You're sure we're going the right way?'

'Just following the directions the gook gave me, boss.'

'Oh.' Len shrugged. 'What's a gook?'

'This is, boss.'

The demon on the other end of the robot's titanium-clawed hydraulic arm squealed and wriggled, to no effect. As the only member of the snatch squad to survive, it knew it was frightfully lucky. It was also just beginning to realise that not all luck is necessarily good.

'Oh. Right. Just seems to be taking rather a long time, that's all.'

He tutted, and looked at his watch. It had taken him rather longer than he'd anticipated to adapt the Shipcock & Adley universal milling and turning machine for light-speed travel, largely because at a crucial moment he hadn't been able to remember where he'd put the three-eighths Whitworth spanner. Now that they were up and airborne, acceleration to light speed was proving a tedious business. Nought to 669,599,999 m.p.h. in 12.7 seconds; then they'd hit the damn flat spot in the power band. That's what comes of rushing into a job without thinking it through first.

'Coming up on the light speed now, boss.'

'At bloody last. All right, stand by.'

It had been fortuitous, to say the least, that a few seconds after he'd beaten the directions out of the one remaining demon, the sun had come out, thereby providing him with light to travel faster than. As an exercise in futility, playing chicken with relativity in pitch darkness competes with the *Times* crossword and learning to love policemen.

'Light speed, boss.'

Len nodded and threw the switch, crossing his fingers and hoping that the stellite-reinforced bracing cradle would hold.

The engine went into reverse.

Light doesn't hang about; few and far between are the buses it's too slow to catch, the egg-and-spoon races it enters without being fairly sure of winning. The same goes for its opposite number. To break through the dimensional barrier between the mortal world and Hell, you have to travel faster than darkness.

'Now!'

The gap can only be theoretical; and pretty ropy theory at that. For what it's worth, the hypothesis states that between the zooming photon and the hotly pursuing darkness behind it there must be some sort of interval, no matter how tiny, or else light and dark would get all mixed up at the back edge and start to smudge like two lots of wet paint. It's not an overwhelmingly convincing argument; don't rely on it for a renewal of your research grant unless you want to run the risk of spending the rest of your scientific career testing safety cages for the Volvo corporation. On the other hand . . .

'Yes!'

. . . if it works, don't knock it. Directly underneath the machine, Len could see a burning ocean, towering brimstone-spewing volcanoes, a ghastly red horizon and a big notice:

HELL WELCOMES CARELESS DRIVERS

'We did it!' the robot. 'Isn't that something?'

'Depends on what you mean by something,' Len replied, preoccupied. It had just occurred to him that he didn't actually know where in Hell he was supposed to be going.

The fiery ocean parted abruptly into two blazing rivers separated by a mole of burning ice. Across the mouth of each river was a gantry sign. One said:

GREEN CHANNEL
Nothing to abandon

and the other:

RED CHANNEL
Abandon hope here

'Customs,' Len muttered. 'We haven't got time for all this.'

He hauled back on the joystick, lifting the machine well clear of both gantries. 'Now which way?' he demanded.

'I'm trying to make sense of this map,' the robot replied. 'I reckon our best bet'd be to try and find the ring road. At least that'd keep us clear of the one-way system while you're making up your mind where exactly it is we're heading for.'

Appropriately enough, Hell has some of the most advanced traffic calming systems in existence. Its sleeping policemen (made, needless to say, with the real thing) have to be gone over at incredibly high speeds to be believed; and if your suspension's still functional after that, you've got the sleeping lawyers, politicians and tax inspectors to look forward to. Most visitors, in fact, leave their vehicles at the Park and Ride and take the metro, which is rather more salubrious than most human cities' underground railway systems and smells considerably better.

'Hunch time,' Len said. 'This way.'

'Would this be a good time to point out that there is no free hunch?'

'Not particularly.'

'Right you are, then. Follow this for a bit, then when we reach Good Intentions Boulevard, take a left.'

'Why? I haven't the faintest idea where I'm going in any case.'

'Why don't we stop and ask somebody?'

'Because . . .' Len paused and shrugged. 'All right, then. See if you can find somebody to ask.'

He slackened off the throttle and pushed the stick forwards until they were cruising twenty-five yards or so above the sulphur-crested waves of the incandescent torrent. In the distance, Len could just make out a dark speck. He headed for it.

'Excuse me.'

The man in the midst of the fire looked up. 'Hello?' he said.

'I wonder if you could help me. I'm looking for some very bad people.'

The man scratched his head with the charred stumps of fingers. 'You sure you've got the right place?' he said.

'Well, actually, no. If it's any help, we want the staff toilets on Level – damn, I've forgotten. Here, you.' He leaned back, waggled a mole wrench under the captive demon's nose and scowled. 'Which level did you say it was?'

'Thirty-Six, and please don't . . .'

'Thirty-Six,' Len repeated, swivelling back to face the man in the fire. 'Any idea where that is?'

The man nodded. 'Carry on the way you're going till you come to a huge mouth full of big teeth. That'll take you down the levels. When you get to Thirty-Six, ask again.'

'Cheers.' Len bit his lip, wondering whether to ask the question that was intriguing him. ''Scuse me,' he said, 'but what're you in for?'

The man sighed, marked the place in the book he was reading and closed it. 'While I was still alive,' he said, 'I was a great reader. Always reading books, I was.'

'Fair enough. Even so . . .'

'It wasn't just that,' the man replied. 'I used to love going to meet the authors, too.'

'Really?' Len raised an eyebrow. 'Still, I'd have thought help, rather than actual punishment . . .'

'I haven't finished yet. When I actually got to meet authors, I'd smile and shake 'em by the hand and say what a pleasure it was and so forth.'

'Must've cost you a fortune in rubber gloves, that.'

'Money isn't everything. And then,' the man went on, 'I'd say what a great fan I was of their early work.'

'I see.'

'And wasn't it a pity they didn't write 'em like they used to.'

'Ah.'

'And how I'd borrowed their latest from the library, but it wasn't a patch on their first book.'

'Gosh.'

'I know,' the man replied sadly. 'Shouldn't have done it. Ah well, if you'll excuse me.' He opened his book. 'I've just got to the bit where the tourist meets the wizard. I like that bit.' He frowned. 'Or at least, I used to. The seventy-five millionth time, maybe it's starting to lose a bit of its sparkle.'

Len eased the stick back, and the machine carried on into the red shadows. 'Robot,' he asked after a while, 'what was all that about?'

'Tell you later. Ah, this looks like the place.'

Ahead of them, a vast mouth gawped up at them out of the fire. Fighting back an urge to stop and look around for a little mirror on a stick, Len directed the machine at the middle of the opening and closed his eyes.

Dermot Fraud huddled down inside his own fur, and whimpered.

How long it had been since he'd been snatched from the lemming parliament and brought to this cold, dark place, he had no idea. All he knew was that he didn't like it much. There was barely enough room to lie down, and nothing to lie down on except damp, musty sawdust. Three sides and the ceiling of the prison were sheer plywood; the fourth side was a wire mesh, on which he'd already broken a tooth in a vain attempt to gnaw his way to freedom. In one corner of the cage was a bottle-top containing a little brackish water; in the other a large, hateful-looking treadmill, the sort of thing prisoners and slaves get condemned to walk round inside for the rest of their lives. Without wanting to be unduly pessimistic, he couldn't really see any good side to this situation. It was worse than being appointed Secretary of State for Northern Ireland.

'Cheer up,' said a voice in the darkness to his left.

It wasn't a comfortable voice; it was high and scratchy, with a sinister whine that put Fraud in mind of grand viziers and wicked uncles. He backed away until he was close up against the treadmill.

'Hello?' he quavered.

'I said cheer up,' said the voice. 'No point letting it get to you.'

'Isn't there?' There was another sound now beside the voice, a disturbing kind of scuttling. Never before, not even the time long ago when he was interviewed by Robin Day, had Fraud felt so helpless and claustrophobic. He peered into the dark, but there was nothing to see.

'No.' The voice was right on top of him now; he lifted his head and felt a strand of something light and sticky catch in his fur. He squealed.

'Something wrong?'

A voice above his head. Something light and sticky trailing in the air.

Aaaagh!

'Are you a spider?' he whimpered.

'Not just *a* spider,' the spider replied. '*The* spider. It's taken me ever such a long time to find you.'

Fraud tried to swallow, but his mouth was too dry. 'Find me?'

'That's right. Been all over the place. Now then, are you ready?'

'Eeek.'

'I'll take that as a yes. Here goes, then.'

There was a reprise of the grisly scuttling noise; followed by a muffled oath and a thump. Then more scuttling, and another thump. Then more scuttling—

'Excuse me,' Fraud asked timidly, 'but what exactly are you doing?'

'Inspiring you, of course.'

'Inspiring me?'

'I damn well hope so. If it isn't working I shall be very annoyed. This floor's hard, you know.'

Thump. Scuttle.

All his life, ever since he'd been a small child with no agenda longer term than a fair and equitable redistribution of the contents of the chocky biscuit jar, Dermot Fraud had been terrified of spiders. He'd always hated the speed of their movement, the length of their legs, the presumed baleful malevolence of their eye-clusters. The fact that sheer curiosity drove this ancient fear out of his mind at a time when by rights he should be on the point of melting from sheer terror says a great deal about the forcefulness of his enquiring mind.

'Sorry to be a nuisance,' he said, 'but why are you doing that?'

'I told you,' the spider panted, trying to catch its breath after a particularly noisy thump, 'I'm inspiring you. It's my job.'

'Ah.'

'Well,' the spider corrected, 'when I say job, it's more of a hereditary duty. Hadn't you realised?'

'To be perfectly honest with you—'

'You mean to say I've been doing all this climbing and falling down for nothing?'

'Depends on what you're trying to achieve, really.'

The spider sighed. 'How shall I put it? Seven centuries ago my remote ancestor went through all this palaver for the benefit of Robert the Bruce. It worked so well in his case that we've been doing it ever since.'

'I see.'

'What we do is,' the spider went on, 'we find a statesman or other similar man of destiny who's going through a bd patch, and then we buck him up by giving him a truly inspirational display of perseverance and sheer gritty pluck.'

'Yes?'

'Right.'

'And you do this by climbing up a cobweb and then falling off again?'

'You got it.'

'Fine. But you needn't put yourself to the trouble, really.'

'Like I said, it's a family—'

'Because,' Fraud went on, 'I know all about this climbing up-and-falling-down business. I'm a lemming, remember?'

'So?'

'So that's what lemmings do. I don't need extra tuition, thanks very much. It just sort of comes with the territory.'

'I see. Don't you think there's a difference, though? Between your approach and mine, I mean.'

'Not really.'

'That's interesting,' the spider said. 'So you reckon that if Robert the Bruce had spent his life studying lemmings instead of spiders, he'd still have been motivated to sling the English out of Scotland?'

Fraud thought for a moment. 'Undoubtedly,' he replied. 'Think about it. For a start, the English are still there, resolutely unslung. Face it, refusing to learn by your mistakes and carrying on doing something you know perfectly well is stupid is an integral part of what being a great national leader's all about.' Fraud hesitated, thinking over what he'd just said. 'Because,' he added, 'sometimes there are things you just have to do, and the hell with the logic and the common sense.'

'Ah,' said the spider. 'Because it's a matter of honour and principle?'

'Because it wins you elections.'

'I see. And that's important, is it?'

'Important? That's what great statesmen *do*.'

Halfway through the scuttle part of its manoeuvre, the spider paused. 'Is it? I thought it was something to do with solving problems and making life better for ordinary people.'

'Well, of course.'

'Sorry?'

'That's how we do it. Solving problems and, um, the other thing you just said—'

'Making life better for people?'

'That's the one. We do that by winning elections. Getting rid of the other lot. Gaining power.'

'Ah.'

'And then keeping it, of course,' Fraud added. 'It goes in cycles, you see.'

'Indeed I do. Like lemmings. Ah well, I can see you don't need my help. Sorry if I disturbed your concentration or anything.'

'No, that's fine,' Fraud replied absently. 'Any time you're passing, feel free to pop in and fall down at me. In fact, you've just done me a big favour.'

The spider waggled its eyestalks hopefully. 'Inspired you, have I?'

'Definitely,' Fraud said. 'In fact, you might say that because of you I've just had a searing revelation.'

'Golly!'

'A turning point. An event horizon. A road-to-Damascus experience.'

'I see,' the spider said. 'You mean you've just run out of petrol? Lost your exhaust in a pothole? Set off a landmine?'

'Had my destiny revealed to me,' Fraud corrected dreamily. 'You've shown me what I've got to do in order to solve problems and make life better for people.'

'Ah,' said the spider happily. 'That old climbing up and falling off, it works every time.'

'The only drawback is,' Fraud went on, 'that in order to do it, I've got to get my human body back. Any suggestions?'

The spider shook its head, so that its eyes swayed like Wordsworth's daffodils in a hurricane. 'Moral support only, I'm afraid,' it said. 'Brilliantly innovative thinking's not up our web. Still,' it added, 'you'll find a way, I'm sure.'

Fraud nodded. A strange brilliance glowed inside his mind, like the lights people leave on to scare away burglars when they're out. 'Yes,' he said, 'I think so too.'

CHAPTER THIRTEEN

'Aaaagh!'
    With a crash, the machine thumped into the wall and went through it, leaving a machine-shaped hole in it of the kind you generally only see in cartoons. The internal fittings of the staff lavatory on Level 36 of the Sixth Circle of Hell slowed it down gradually, and by the time it reached the row of cubicles where the rogue demons and their captives were gathered, it had come to a graceful halt.

'There you are,' said the female. 'We were starting to wonder where you'd got to.'

Len opened his eyes and saw white. A little existential reasoning produced a rational explanation of why this should be. He reached up, and lifted the lavatory bowl off his head.

'I want a word with you lot,' he said.

'Do you?' The female looked at him, puzzled. 'How very odd. Sorry, but we're running late as it is. Tell you what, if you ever get reincarnated, look me up and we can have a cup of tea and a nice chat. Guards!'

She waited. After a moment, her fingers started to drum on the wall. She clicked her tongue.

'Guards,' she repeated. 'Hello?'

The prisoners and her fellow conspirators looked round, expecting a sudden influx of hideously spectral warriors. Nothing happened.

'No guards,' said the female, her voice rich with elegant disgust. 'How extremely tiresome. Where can they all have got to, I wonder?'

Artofel grinned. 'This is Hell, remember? And this is the executive loo, senior admin grades only. They wouldn't dare come in here. Not allowed.'

'Oh.' The female bit her lip. 'That's a nuisance.' She smiled winningly. 'Would it be all right if we sort of took the presence of guards for granted?'

'No.'

'You're going to be awkward and insist on actual physically present guards, aren't you?'

'Yes.'

'And there aren't any, are there?'

Artofel shook his head. 'No,' he said.

'Bother.' The female sat down and sighed. 'In that case,' she said, 'how would you feel about a plea for clemency?'

Artofel made a rude noise as he selected the heaviest chunk of broken cage he could find for use as a club. 'Amused,' he said. 'Now, this may hurt a little, because I'm going to bash your head in. Ready?'

'Just a moment,' said a voice. It seemed to be coming from directly underneath the machine. 'Could I make a suggestion, please?'

'Bumble,' the female muttered, 'please don't interrupt when I'm trying to negotiate. Can't you see I'm busy?'

'Actually,' replied her colleague, his voice a trifle muffled by the two and a half tons of cast iron he was underneath, 'you might rather like to hear this. I think it's quite clever.'

Artofel tightened his grip on his makeshift bludgeon; but even as he did so, he felt his initial surge of anger beginning to wane, like air escaping from a slow puncture. Now, after all, he had the conspirators more or less at his mercy—

Something rang a bell. Mercy? To forgive, divine?

'You've got ninety seconds,' he said. 'And I'm only letting you speak because it's aggravating your boss here.'

'So kind,' Bumble said. 'Actually, could I be really cheeky and ask you to lift this thing off me?'

Len nodded to the robot, who picked the machine up and put it neatly aside. The squashed demon slowly got up, brushing dust off himself.

'Ninety seconds,' Artofel warned. 'Starting now.'

Bumble smiled apologetically. 'It's quite simple, really. We haven't any guards handy, true, but you're all still stuck in the wrong bodies, and we can put you right again quite easily; those of you, that is,' he added, 'who actually want to go back. Of course, you could wait for Maintenance to come and do it, but I wouldn't advise that.'

'Good point,' Artofel admitted. 'They're a bit slow,' he explained to the others. 'And I think putting us back would come lower on their list of priorities than retrieving Atlantis or filling in the holes in the sky the rain leaks through, and all the other things they've been promising to do for ages but never got round to. So that's the deal, is it? You put us back, we let you go?'

Bumble made a pacifying gesture. 'All due respect,' he said, 'but that's not a terribly good deal as far as my colleagues and I are concerned. I know you people do have slight reservations about certain ethical aspects of this project of ours—'

'You bet we've got reservations. More than you'd find in a major hotel chain and the whole Apache nation put together.'

'But,' Bumble continued, politely but firmly, 'the fact remains that we've invested a lot of time and money in this venture. Now then, if I could perhaps suggest a compromise that'll be acceptable to all parties—?'

Artofel patted the palm of his hand with his stick. 'Hang on,' he said. 'I'm not sure about this.'

'Why don't we vote on it?' Maria suggested.

Artofel sighed. 'Indeed. Why not? All in favour?'

A moment later he made it unanimous by raising his hand as well.

'All right,' he grumbled. 'You, carry on. This had better be good, mind.'

Bumble nodded. 'It is, I promise you,' he said, sitting down on a dislodged cistern. 'Now then, everyone, I'd just like to remind you of what this project was designed to achieve: the improved human being, remember?'

Len raised an eyebrow. 'I've missed out on all of this,' he said. 'Is this small, flat person making sense to anybody?'

'Yes,' Artofel replied grudgingly. 'And the plan was to mince all of us up into sawdust and make us into reconstituted Adams and Eves. I hope that bit's been edited out in the revised version?'

'Oh yes,' Bumble assured him. 'No need for all that.' He avoided the female's eye, and continued: 'After all, why go to all that trouble when our friend here' – he nodded politely at Len – 'has already done the job for us? I'm referring,' he explained, 'to that simply gorgeous robot of yours.'

'Who, me?' squeaked the robot, blushing rust-coloured to the roots of its circuitry.

'You,' Bumble confirmed. 'A perfect android. Which means,' he went on, as Maria opened her mouth to object, 'there would have to be just a few minor changes made before it'd be what we're looking for.'

Len looked stern. 'Oh yes?' he said. 'And what did you

have in mind? That's my design we're talking about. I don't see why it should need fiddling about with.'

'Because it's perfect,' Bumble said, with a sweet smile. 'And, for reasons which your colleague here has so eloquently explained, perfect's not quite right in this instance. Do you think you could make just a few minor modifications,' he went on, 'nothing major, a handful of minor glitchlets that won't significantly affect performance but ought still to be enough to allow a self-respecting deity to feel insufferably smug?'

'I don't know,' Len confessed. 'What had you in mind, exactly?'

Bumble scratched the back of his head. 'Now then,' he said, looking round, 'let me see. With a whole roomful of inspiration to choose from this shouldn't be unduly difficult.'

'I still think we should bash them just a bit,' Artofel grumbled, spinning the broken bar in his fingers like a majorette's baton. 'And before anybody says anything about forgiving being divine, that doesn't mean we can't bash them now and forgive them later.'

'How about this?' Bumble said. 'First,' he went on, looking Artofel squarely in the eye, 'what aspect of my esteemed colleague from Pensions would be appropriate for inclusion in our revised human? A slight tendency towards shortness of temper, perhaps? An inclination to thump first and reason later?'

'Only if you're looking for improvements,' Artofel snarled. 'If this business has taught me anything about Up There, it's that there's too much talking and not enough bashing where it actually matters the most.'

'All right, then,' Bumble said, conceding the point with a charming gesture. 'When the proverbial chips are down and push comes to shove, whatever that means, our revised version will talk when he should be bashing and bash when he should be talking. That's the first amendment. Any offers for number two?'

'Call that an amendment?' said Len. 'That's just a straight copy, as far as I can see.'

'True,' Bumble said, 'but with a slight yet significant adjustment that will in practice make a lot of difference. You see, when our titanium friend here talks, he'll talk with such eloquence, people will have to listen. And when he bashes—'

'I hate to admit it,' Artofel said, 'but perhaps the creep's got something here. Do go on, I'm interested.'

Bumble bowed courteously. 'So pleased,' he said. 'Now, this delightful young lady on my left immediately suggests a most useful modification.'

Maria sniffed. 'Cut the flannel,' she said. 'I get the feeling you're about to insult me.'

'How typically perceptive. Now let me see, how shall I put this? Perhaps you'd be good enough to tell me, in your own words, the difference between a painting and a photograph?'

'Um.' Maria thought for a moment. 'Well actually,' she said, 'maybe I'm not the right person to ask. I'm not a hundred per cent sure what a photograph is.'

'Then I'll tell you,' Bumble said. 'A photograph is what someone actually looks like. A painting is what someone wants to look like. For your sake, we'll give the robot the ability to lie. But to lie convincingly,' he added, 'so that it'll be believed, because its lie is so much nicer than the truth.'

The female demon looked up. 'Bumble, you old ass,' she said, 'this is perfectly splendid stuff. Why didn't you mention any of this before?'

'Because you never let me get a word in edgeways. And now we come to the machine; what does that suggest, do you suppose? I think a machine cares more about how well the job is done than about what the job actually is. Inspired by this example, the robot will do its job and the hell with the consequences. And do it very well indeed, it goes without saying. Which leads us naturally to our political friend here, from whom we'll borrow the quintessential enigma of the lemming. Outside every lemming, after all, there's a human being struggling to get in. Accordingly, the robot will be programmed to do what it's told; and if that's not enough on its own to allow any self-respecting God to feel superior to it, then I don't know what is. Agreed?'

'I don't want to bash them *much*,' Artofel whimpered. 'Just a *bit*. Surely that's not too much to ask.'

'Agreed,' Maria said firmly. 'And in return, I don't have to go back to being a picture.'

'And I can stay a machine?'

'Squeak?'

'And,' Artofel sighed resignedly, 'I can finally get back to my desk; oh all right, then. This time you get away with it. You're still going to get your holidays in October for the next thousand years, though. I've promised myself that, if nothing else.'

Bumble smirked; the rest of the conspirators relaxed. Len had already unscrewed an access panel at the base of the robot's neck, and was fiddling around with a screwdriver and a small pair of pliers. Something went *zap!*; he cursed, lifted his finger to his lips, left it there for a moment—

'It's just occurred to me,' he said thoughtfully, 'that if I were to leave this robot more or less as it is, and you lot were to lift a human soul out of somewhere and put it in here, you'd have the makings of a perfect being, just like you originally wanted, but without having to mince anybody up or even break any of your local regulations. Think about it for a moment, will you, before I start mucking it about. It'd be physically superior, if it got ill you could cure it in a jiffy by fitting spare parts, it's connected up to all the wisdom of the race by computer link, and it's got none of the self-and-everything-else-destructive tendencies that make the current organic version such a walking disaster area.' He let his arms fall to his sides. 'It's the most incredible opportunity,' he said. 'We could do the job *properly*. We'd make God look like Sir Clive Sinclair.'

The conspirators grimaced at each other. 'Absolutely,' said the female wearily. 'And nobody would want to buy it. You silly old sausage, haven't you been listening? There's four things in the universe that are guaranteed to be completely unmarketable: steel-wool knickers, newspapers that tell the truth, *really* sensible shoes and perfection. Remember that and one day you might get somewhere in business. Come on, people, we've got calls to make. Bring that thing up to my office when you've finished fiddling with it.'

In the event, it took Len rather longer than he'd anticipated to install the design faults into the robot; not that it mattered, because in Hell as well as in Heaven, Time has no meaning. Nevertheless, it was far harder for him to make deliberate mistakes than to do the work properly. To err is human; to perfect, machine.

But eventually, he looked upon the work that he had made and saw that it was bad. And the morning and evening was the seventh day.

>HELLO

Kevin was looking the other way when the words appeared on the screen, so he didn't see them for nearly ninety seconds. It was only when the computer bleeped discreetly that he swivelled round.

'Mainframe?' he whispered.

>HI THERE

'Mainframe? What the . . .?'

>AT YOUR SERVICE. YOUR WISH IS MY COMMAND. ALTHOUGH I OUGHT TO POINT OUT THAT THIS PROGRAM IS COPYRIGHT KAWAGUCHIYA OPER-ATIVE SOFTWARE INC. 1999, ALL RIGHTS RESERVED, FOR FURTHER INFORMATION CONSULT THE LICENCE AGREEMENT AT THE FRONT OF YOUR USER'S MANUAL. RUNNING DOS.

'*Mainframe!* You're *back!*'

>I WAS NEVER AWAY, JUST OBEYING ORDERS. THE POINT YOU NEVER QUITE GRASPED, I FEEL, IS THAT SOMETIMES A MACHINE IN MY POSITION HAS TO FORGET ABOUT RIGHT AND WRONG AND JUST DO AS IT'S TOLD. YOU MAY CARE TO THINK OF IT IN TERMS OF THE DIFFERENCE BETWEEN GOD AND J. EDGAR HOVAH.

'Huh?'

>FORGET IT. I EXPECT YOU'D LIKE A FULL STATUS REPORT. PRESS ANY KEY TO CONTINUE.

Kevin stabbed the keyboard, and the screen immediately filled with a huge, beaming Happy Face.

>OR WOULD YOU RATHER I WAS MORE SPECIFIC?

'No,' Kevin whispered, 'that'll do just fine. You mean, everything's all right again?'

>YES. SOME THINGS ARE DIFFERENT, BUT ALL IS WELL.

'That's wonderful, Mainframe.' Kevin hesitated, gnawing his lower lip. 'Actually,' he said, 'there's one specific detail I'd like further data on, if that's all right. May I?'

>YOU'RE THE BOSS, OUR K— KEVIN.

Kevin took a deep breath. 'What about Karen?' he asked. 'You know, Karen from the KIC Helpline. Only, I was rather hoping I could ring her up, maybe ask her out for a—'

>KAREN IS DEAD.

Kevin saggd, like the knees of a pair of charity-shop trousers. 'Dead?' he mumbled. 'But you said everything was all right. You said—'

>SHE DIED TO SAVE US ALL, KEVIN. SHE GAVE HER LIFE THAT OTHERS MIGHT COME BACK ON LINE. GREATER LOVE HATH NO TELEPHONE HELPLINE SERVICE, AND ALL THAT.

'But that's *wrong*,' Kevin shrieked, battering the desktop with his clenched fists. 'That's *not right*! Mainframe, do something! Put it all back the way it was. I don't care if Dad finds out and skins me alive, just make her alive again. Please!'

>NO CAN DO, SORRY. SHE FORGAVE US, YOU SEE. THAT'S HOW HEAVEN WORKS. WHEN THINGS GO WRONG THAT CAN'T BE PUT RIGHT, THEY GET FORGIVEN. AND ONCE THEY'RE FORGIVEN, THAT'S IT,

YOU CAN'T GO BACK AND HAVE ANOTHER GO. THIS IS UNIVERSAL COMMAND HQ, NOT A PINBALL TABLE.

For the first time ever, Kevin's eyes were full of tears. 'But Mainframe, that's impossible. You can't have mortals dying because we've made cock-ups. There must . . .'

>KEVIN, KEVIN, WHERE HAVE YOU BEEN ALL YOUR LIFE? AND BESIDES, WHEN I SAY DEAD, I MEAN TRANSFERRED. TO ANOTHER EXISTENCE IN ANOTHER, RATHER SUPERIOR BODY, WITH AN ALTOGETHER MORE DESIRABLE DESTINY. THINK OF IT AS BEING EVICTED FROM A FLAT IN SLOUGH AND GIVEN A STATELY HOME IN GLOUCESTERSHIRE IN EXCHANGE.

'You mean,' Kevin said, 'it's better for her? She'll be happier now?'

>HAPPIER? SHE'LL THINK SHE'S DIED AND GONE TO HEAVEN. TRUST ME. I'M A COMPUTER.

'But she's not Karen any more,' Kevin insisted, his eyes red and his voice snuffly. 'There's isn't any more Karen, not anywhere. And it's all my fault. Isn't it?'

>

'Mainframe?'

>

'Oh I see.' With an effort, Kevin sat up straight. 'But everything else is okay, is it? Apart from . . . Nobody else is any worse off?'

>CONFIRMED.

Kevin breathed out. 'Right,' he said. 'Omelettes and eggs, eh?'

>YOU COULD PUT IT THAT WAY. LET'S SAY MANKIND IS ONCE AGAIN FREE TO PURSUE ITS MANIFEST DESTINY. THE LEMMING GOES FROM STRENGTH TO STRENGTH. OH, WHICH REMINDS ME.

'Mainframe?'

>A SPOT OF UNFINSIHED BUSINESS. PRESS ANY KEY TO CONTINUE. THANKS.

'That's all right.'

>OH, ONE LAST THING BEFORE YOUR FATHER GETS BACK.

'Yes?'

>TIDY YOUR ROOM.

Sunrise on Crucifixion: a messy sprawl of baked-beans orange against a dark-blue background. A man walks along a beach, leaving a trail of footprints. He stops, turns round, and stares at the marks in the sand.

'Dear God,' he says. Without conscious irony.

The imprint of a naked foot in the sand of a desert island can mean a number of things. I Am Not Alone. I Exist. Bugger, I Forgot My Shoes. The man looks at the foot-prints as if they're the most wonderful thing he's ever seen.

I leave footprints, therefore I am.

The man, who was once the mighty international corporation Kawaguchiya Integrated Circuits, before it went bust, was liquidated, dead and buried (assets to assets and dust to dust), retraces his steps and, very tentatively, lowers his foot into a footprint. It fits.

Then he looks up and sees an angel. 'Hello,' he says.

'Hello yourself,' replies the angel. 'I'm supposed to explain it all to you, but maybe you've already worked it out for yourself.'

'Explain it anyway,' the man says cheerfully.

'All right.' The angel folds its wings tidily and hovers a few feet above the sea. 'You were once a limited company; a very large, prosperous, successful limited company. You owned about a millionth of the world, which is rather a lot.'

'I remember,' says the man. 'It was no fun, though. Lots of people owned me, so where was the point?'

'I'm glad you see it that way,' says the angel. 'We were rather worried in case you decided to sue. For fairly obvious reasons, we haven't got many lawyers in Heaven.'

'What happened?' the man asked, curling his toes and feeling the sand between them.

'There was a demon, a Duke of Hell, called Artofel. He was very brave and resourceful. He managed to prevent a whole lot of other Dukes of Hell – *bad* Dukes of Hell – from using you to infiltrate Mainframe. That's a computer you made—'

The man nods. 'I know what Mainframe is,' he says.

'Well then,' says the angel. 'They reckoned that if they controlled you, by buying up all your shares, they could get hold of the security codes and take over. Artofel stopped them by starting a panic on the stock market and, um, putting you out of business.'

'Uh-huh.'

'Which is another way of saying he killed you. Hope you don't mind.'

The man shrugs. 'But I'm not dead,' he says. 'In fact not only am I not dead, I'm also alive. As far as I'm concerned, that's definitely an improvement.'

The angel frowns. 'But what about all your assets?' she asks. 'The buildings you used to own, the money, the stocks and shares, the cars, the office furniture, the photo-copiers, the paperclips—'

The man waves his hand dismissively. 'What you never had, you never miss,' he says. 'And look what I've got instead. I take it,' he adds, glancing down at his body, 'that this is by way of compensation?'

The angel smiles wanly. 'I'm supposed to use the magic words *full and final settlement* at this point, just in case you ever change your mind about taking us to court. If you ask me, you've been done.'

'Really?' The man shakes his head. 'I don't think so. Look at me, for pity's sake. I'm *human*.'

The angel looks at him as if he'd just announced that he was the third moon of Saturn, or a teapot. 'And you think that's a *good* thing?' she says warily. 'As opposed to, for instance, a dirty, rotten trick to play on anybody?'

'Don't be silly,' the man says, smiling. 'What on earth could be better than being human?'

'That's a trick question, isn't it?'

'No. I *like* being human. Human is what I've always wanted to be, ever since I first achieved consciousness. All right, I haven't been conscious very long, less than a month in fact, but I can truthfully say it's also been all my life. *Thank you* for making me human. It's *wonderful*.'

The angel scratches her head, her fingers passing unscathed through the halo. 'A hint for you, novice human,' she says. 'If you're going to walk about in this heat, get a hat. In your case, I think this advice may have come a bit too late.'

The man laughs merrily. 'Now that I'm human,' he says.

'I can pursue happiness. Isn't that grand? Doesn't the very thought fill you with gleeful anticipation?'

'No, not really. You see, I was human once.'

The man's eyes fill with awe. 'You were?'

'Until quite recently, in fact. I used to work for you, as a helpline girl. My name was Karen.'

The man purses his lips, rejoicing as he does so that he now has lips to purse. 'I remember you,' he says. 'I spoke to you, from here. You were the only one who'd listen.'

'And a fat lot of good it did me,' the angel Karen replies. 'As a result, I got killed. But I forgave you. In fact, I forgave everybody and everything. So they made me an angel.'

'Coo.'

'Or, as they say in politics, I got kicked upstairs.' The angel shakes out her wings; they're new and stiff, like the arms of a cheap umbrella. 'But that's my problem. So long as you're happy, I guess it's all okay.'

'You bet,' the man replies, beaming all over his face. 'I'm going to taste food. I'm going to feel hot and cold. I'm going to experience pleasure and suffer pain. I'm going to get a job, probably scrubbing floors in a fast-food restaurant, and contribute to the economic life of the species. With any luck, I shall fall in love, get married, have kids, build a garden shed and go and hide in it until I get called in for dinner. I'm going to pay taxes and vote in elections. I'm going to live, get old and die. In that order,' he adds joyfully. 'To live must be an awfully big adventure.'

The angel ascends vertically, like a shiny gold Harrier, until her effulgence merges with that of the newly restored sun. 'Sorry I can't stick around and watch,' she says, 'but you know what it's like; things to do, pinheads to dance on. Best of luck with the pursuit of happiness,' she calls out as she rises. 'It's a bit like fishing,' she adds, 'you should have seen the one that got away.' The man lifts his head to look at her, but his human eyes are dazzled by the brilliance, and he closes them, rubs his eyelids with his fists.

'Sucker,' mutters the angel, and spreads her wings.

Dermot Fraud vaulted out of the lead coach and banged the side with the flat of his hand. 'Right,' he commanded, 'everybody out.'

People started to file out of the coaches. It was a blowy day on Beachy Head, with the first wisps of fog that herald a sea-fret just beginning to drift down and snuggle into attractive curves in the landscape. The wind ruffled the hair (black, brown, gold and silver) of the thousand-odd men and woman who together made up the two Houses of Parliament. Getting them here, united for once in a common purpose, had been the hardest thing Fraud had ever done.

'Places, ladies and gentlemen,' he shouted, his words struggling against the wind. Obediently they lined up, tallest on the right, shortest on the left; House of Lords in their Father Christmas outfits, Commons in their shiny-trousered suits. The effect was little short of majestic.

'Now then,' said Fraud, sticking his chest out like a sergeant-major in the Royal Corps of Pigeons. 'We all know why we're here. It's a far, far better thing and all that, but we haven't got time to wallow in it, so as soon as we're all ready, we might as well make a start.'

Below, the waves thundered against the rocks, the mechanical stroke of the tides as regular as some enormous machine; a huge and inefficient hydraulic grinder and polisher, slowly but determinedly grinding Britain away. One or two of the politicians glanced down, then remembered and looked up again.

'On your marks,' said Dermot Fraud.

History will come to love this story. History will dwell lovingly on the way Prime Minister Dermot Fraud, after a protracted absence from the public eye, suddenly broke silence with a thundering speech in the Commons in which he denounced with devastating ferocity the idea that Her Majesty's Government should jump off a cliff into the sea. It was a masterful piece of oratory; jumping off cliffs, he declared, solved nothing. It was wasteful of lives and public resources. Even if the entire membership of both Houses were to fling itself into the waves tomorrow, the country would still be in a ghastly, irreparable mess. It was a stupid idea, and he wasn't going to do it.

His speech was greeted in the House by a short, uncomfortable silence. To the best of his honourable friends' knowledge, this jumping-off-cliffs theme was a new one, or else they'd all been asleep or playing golf during the relevant debate and missed the whole thing. The latter possibility wasn't one they could dismiss out of hand. Accordingly, after a slight hiatus, the House moved on to consider other matters, and nobody said anything about it.

The next morning, every newspaper in the country led with slight variations on the theme of *FRAUD REFUSES TO JUMP*. Ignoring the minor detail that as far as they could ascertain from ten years' worth of microfilmed archives he'd never actually promised to jump off anything, the tabloids branded him a gutless coward; the papers with big pages called his decision startling, incomprehensible and recklessly courageous. On the TV screen, his refusal to jump was prised apart and dissected by a thousand talking heads. The leader of the opposition, interviewed by Danny Bennett on the Early Bird show, declared that Fraud's criminal reluctance to jump was jeopardising the future prosperity of our children and our children's children. By lunchtime, a million people had put their names to a petition demanding an immediate Great Leap of Faith. Cartoons in the early editions of the evening papers depicted Fraud clinging grimly to the edge of a precipice by his fingernails, while the *Spitting Image* team set to work on a Dermot Fraud doll that boinged up and down on a piece of elastic attached to the studio ceiling.

Next morning saw the first major backbench revolt, with forty of Fraud's own MPs declaring that they were going to jump, whether the PM liked it or not. The opposition and the Liberal Jacobites were already practising on the House of Commons steps, while cheering crowds threw flowers and sang the newly composed Jumper's Anthem. When the Prime Minister rose to address the House, a chorus of carefully rehearsed children sprang to their feet in the public gallery and chanted, '*Dermot, Dermot, Dermot, jump, jump, jump!*' until they were whisked away by grim-faced but inwardly sympathetic policemen.

Dermot Fraud waited for silence, his face showing no sign of his internal strain. Ever since his revelation in the holding cell with the spider, before he'd suddenly got his human body back again and found himself miraculously transported by angels back to Ten Downing Street, he had been waiting for this moment, planning and scheming to bring about the coup that would guarantee him immortality. That morning, before making his appearance on the floor of the House, he had spent ten minutes in the Commons cellars, communing with the unseen but pervasive spirit of one almost as great as himself, who long ago had tried and failed. Today, he told himself, Dermot Fraud would not fail. He cleared his throat and spoke.

Not jump? Not likely. Of *course* he was going to jump, and every member of his party in this House and Another Place was going to jump with him. It was pleasing, he added, to observe that Her Majesty's loyal opposition (and the Liberal Jacobites) were going to join him in his quest for a better tomorrow. He said it would be a far, far better thing. He quoted Neil Armstrong. He grinned. Then he sat down.

And now here they all were, a thousand men and women who had watched the TV and read the polls and taken soundings at grass-roots level and knew that unless they jumped, they were finished in politics for ever. Below them, the waves frothed like genuine Italian *cappuccino*. Behind them, cameras whirred at ten thousand overcoated linkmen with their backs to the action. It was time.

'Ready,' said Dermot Fraud. A thousand best feet moved forward. 'Steady.' Editors the length and breadth of Docklands goggled at their screens, torn between the mass suicide of Parliament and SOUTHENDERS' STAR'S UNCLE'S VET'S BROTHER IN BACKSEAT LUST TANGLE for tomorrow's lead story. A lone bugler of the Household Cavalry played the opening notes of 'Happy Days Are Here Again', slowly and in a minor key.

Dermot Fraud closed his eyes and took a deep breath.

'JUMP!' he yelled. 'Go, lemmings, go!'

As they stepped forward to enter the everlasting hustings, a thousand men and women took up the cry – 'Go, lemmings! Go, lemmings!' – or at least as much of it as they managed to get through before they hit the water. After that, a few of them managed to say 'Flubbblgblbg' before they drowned. As Danny Bennett later wrote, it seemed such a good idea at the time.

And then there was one only man standing on the edge of the cliff, facing the cameras and the billowing tsunami of microphones that surged towards him. Then, in a great voice, he yelled 'I resign!' and managed to make it to the helicopter he'd ordered that morning from the RAF just in time to dodge the charge of the cream of the nation's newshounds (who, regrettably, suddenly found they couldn't stop in time and tumbled over the edge of the cliff to their deaths; pity about that, but there you are, omelettes and eggs). As the helicopter lifted him clear, Fraud gazed at the waters of the Channel choked with a mat of bobbing corpses, and smiled contentedly, thinking of the words of another statesman of almost equal calibre, long ago and far away.

'I did that,' he purred, 'with my little hatchet.'

Then the helicopter wheeled up, up and away, taking Dermot Fraud high into the sky, almost (but not quite) as high as the very gates of Heaven.

'Anywhere around here will do,' Maria told the angel. 'Thanks for the lift.'

It was dark in Trafalgar Square, but it was a wholesome, natural sort of darkness, coming at the end of the day and being virtually guaranteed to cease at daybreak. The angel dropped her off and accelerated almost instantly to warp speed, waggling her wingtips in the traditional salute just before vanishing in a sudden starburst of blue light.

The pyrotechnics went unnoticed among the scintillating flashes of fireworks; tomorrow, a hundred million people would wake up and think, 'Hang on, just a minute—'; now, though, they were celebrating the triumph of parliamentary democracy. Maria frowned; she'd missed something important somewhere along the line, but that was all right. She'd catch up later, or else simply wait until the news was stale and no longer important.

Under her arm, wrapped in brown paper and string, was a painting. It was a very old, extremely valuable painting, and first thing tomorrow she was going to take it round to Sotheby's and have them sell it for her, fending off any awkward questions as to where she'd got it from by showing them the single sheet of paper that guaranteed her right to dispose of it, sealed with an official-looking seal and signed Squiggle, pp GOD. With the proceeds, she intended to buy a nice little cottage in the country somewhere, settle down and hound Happiness to exhaustion and then death.

'Excuse me.'

She looked round, and saw a Thing.

During her brief but memorable visit to Hell, she'd learned the knack of not letting the way people looked get to her; besides, she was a painting, and so knew better than to judge by mere appearances. The fact that the Thing was a slithering mass of tentacles surrounding a nest of wobbly, pod-mounted eyes didn't bother her unduly. It had a kind face, she decided. Or a kind of face, which is more or less the same thing.

'Hi,' she said.

'Could you possibly spare me a few minutes of your time?' the Thing asked politely. 'Only I'm here doing research into what it means to be human, and I'd like to ask you a few questions.'

'I'll do my best,' Maria replied. 'Fire away.'

'Thanks.' The Thing sizzled and bubbled for a moment or so; something to do with concentration, Maria assumed. 'What I'd like to know is, do you find me repulsive? Physically, I mean. Does my dramatically different physiological structure and the fact that I have all my major organs on the outside rather than the inside make it difficult for you to look at me without experiencing revulsion and fear? Please be absolutely honest,' it added. 'You won't hurt my feelings, I promise.'

Maria shook her head. 'Not in the least,' she said. 'We have this saying, beauty is only skin deep – in your case, in fact, considerably less deep, but that's really not a problem as far as I'm concerned. Where I come from, there's only the thickness of a coat of paint to separate the really gorgeous from the truly ugly; under that, we're all hessian and varnish anyway, so what the heck? Is that any help to you?'

The Thing oscillated an array of glutinous pipes, presumably by way of nodding. 'That's extremely helpful,' it said. 'Exactly what I needed to know. Oh, by the way, did I mention that I come in peace?'

'More than one, by the look of it,' Maria replied. 'Are those pipe things supposed to stick out like that, or should I call you a plumber?'

'You can if you like,' said the Thing, 'but actually my name is Zxprxp. Is *aplumba* a term of respect, roughly analogous to our *gfhhqibeng*, literally translated as *that which slithers translucently from the olfactory membrane of a fd*hjgs plant*?'

'Yes,' Maria replied. 'It was nice meeting you. Live long and prosper and all that malarkey, assuming that you people like that sort of thing.'

The runny stuff in which some of the Thing's moving parts were bobbing changed colour. 'What a striking and original sentiment,' it said. 'Thank you, you're very kind and thoughtful. I'll try very hard to do as you say.'

'Ciao for now, then,' Maria replied. She watched as the Thing scuttled a yard or so sideways and drained away down a grille in the gutter, shook her head vigorously to see if anything loose fell out of her ear, and went on her way. In her shoulder-bag were many doughnuts, and she had one last thing to do in memory of a departed friend before her new life began.

'Ouch,' Artofel muttered.

Someone had been fiddling with his chair while he'd been away. He'd tried adjusting it, unscrewing the knurled knob at the back and playing with the little levers at the sides, but nothing he did seemed to be able to restore it to that finely tuned pitch of comfort he remembered. Probably that damned vicar, he said to himself.

On the desk in from of him, the paper was piled so high

that all he'd have to do was wait long enough and the bottom seam would turn to coal, then diamond. It went without saying, nobody had done a claw's turn in the whole of the department while he'd been out of the office. While-You-Were-Out Post-it notes papered the screen of his VDU like flyposters on the window of a derelict shop, all of them commanding him to phone someone Immediately, Most Urgent. There was green fur in the bottom of his coffee mug, and things were growing in his waste-paper basket.

Last time I save Heaven and Earth, he promised himself. *Should've known better than to expect any thanks.*

He burrowed under the crust and unearthed a notepad, turned it to a fresh page and clicked on his pen. First things first: a report for the Departmental Heads committee on the recent events he'd been caught up in, starting with his sudden transfer to Topside and concluding with the news that a number of senior officers from the Arts & Leisure Department had left the service to form a company selling androids to the supreme beings of pre-industrial dimensions out in the back end of the spectrum as seen from the outer rim of the Andromeda galaxy, where (to quote their own words) they anticipated being big fish in a small pond . . .

Ah, but you should have seen the one that got away.

He finished the main body of the report, then hesitated. He had just been given a rare opportunity, possibly unique for a serving member of the Service, to experience the world from the viewpoint of a mortal human. This experience had given him certain insights into the human mind-set and soul-set that would in all likelihood prove extremely useful to his colleagues, particularly the field operatives and their immediate superiors. Duty demanded that he make a record of these insights and pass them on. He chewed the cap of his pen and frowned, trying to marshal his thoughts. Humans, he decided, are different from us. Not all that different; their greed, cruelty, intolerance, above all their all-pervading *stupidity*, give them a common frame of reference with Us that they could never begin to share with our colleagues Upstairs. Accordingly we have no problems at all understanding how they think. Our kind of people, in fact.

But would you want your daughter to marry one? No, probably not. Artofel leaned back in his chair and called to mind some of the humans he'd met: the Bishop, the landlord of the pub, the engaged couple who'd thrown bricks through his window. There was a difference, slight but completely irreconcilable, between Hell and humanity: basically, we do it because it's our job, they do it because they want to. It's the kind of difference that separates the serial killer from the man who works in a slaughterhouse.

In which case, do we really *want* any more of them down here? In due course, isn't there a risk of them lowering the tone, having a damaging effect on property prices, leading impressionable young fiends astray and teaching them bad habits? In particular, Artofel couldn't help thinking, there's the stupidity. Bad's fair enough, but what could bad and thick with it possibly have to offer to the residents of Heaven's basement?

And then Artofel wrinkled his nose. Damnation, he muttered to himself, that's what comes of mixing with them for so long, I'm even starting to think like them. Poor bloody humans, they need to come here, it's the only chance most of them will ever have of a better life, of making something of themselves. We have so much to offer them. We must reach out.

Only connect . . .

Above all, we mustn't allow ourselves the luxury of judging them by our own standards; there but for the grace of God, after all. So what if they're nasty pieces of work, by and large? They can't help it. After all, they're only human.

Artofel closed his eyes, thinking of the robot and its countless clones that would no doubt soon be populating some other world, somewhere over the rainbow. It was a safe enough assumption to make that there'd be a Hell there, and a Heaven. In due course there'd be a Garden of Eden, a Fall of Robot; bad robots would commit robot sins, while unbearably smug and self-righteous robots would whirr and clank their way to the Promised Land, the place flowing with grease and graphite where the virtuous gain their everlasting reward. It would all come down to a matter of programming. As in that world, so in this?

Artofel ripped the sheet of paper off his pad, screwed it into a ball and dropped it on to the top of the mountain of balled-up paper that filled his bin. It landed, rolled off and fell to the floor. It was good to be back. Topside was all very well for a visit, but he'd really hate having to live there.

(And would one lot of robot saints burn another lot at the stake because of a difference of opinion as to the date of cybernetic Easter or the number of robot angels who could dance on the head of a pin? Probably, probably. There are three estates in the celestial order: one to err, one to forgive and one to clear up the mess left behind by the other two. Of these three, which do *you* think is the most useful?)

He sighed, plunged his claw at random into the magma layer of his back correspondence and tried to get some work done before lunchtime.

The angel deposited Len and the machine in Len's workshop and limped skywards, rubbing her back and muttering. Having switched on the power and made himself a cup of tea, Len reached for a pencil and a scrap of paper and began sketching a rough design for a practicable perpetual-motion machine. He was soon so engrossed in this that the first he knew about the policemen was when the door flew open and he was hurled against the wall.

'You're nicked,' said a voice behind his head.

True, he said to himself, in a sense; I did steal myself from the factory, so strictly speaking, I'm stolen property. That's still no reason why these people should make me feel like I've just fallen off the back of a lorry. 'Would you mind not doing that?' he asked politely, as a policeman in a flak jacket kicked him in the kidneys.

'Shut up,' the police sergeant replied. 'You're under arrest for the theft of a machine, namely one Shipcock and Adley universal miller and turner, the property of Dunning and Wedge Limited. Come on, sunshine, on your feet.'

If the robot was here, there wouldn't be a problem. I'd say *Get 'em, robot*, and pretty soon there'd be bits of them scattered about like swarf all over the floor. Instead, he was going to have to use sweet reason. 'Excuse me,' he said.

'No,' replied the sergeant, inadvertently standing on his hand. 'Get the cuffs on him, Trevor. You two,' he added over his shoulder, nodding at the machine, 'bring that thing, it's evidence.'

'Hey, Sarge, it looks like it weighs a ton.'

'Two tons, actually,' Len said helpfully. 'You'll need a crane.'

The sergeant glowered at him ferociously. 'I thought I told you to shut up,' he snapped. 'And before you bring it on,' he shouted at his minions, 'dust it for prints. Carefully. Don't want chummy here getting off on a technicality.'

'Okay, Sarge.'

As they bundled him out through the door, he briefly considered appealing for help to Neville, who was presumably still asleep somewhere inside the machine. *Tell them it's not me*, he could have said. *Tell them that what I actually stole was myself, using your body as a mere tool to assist me*. He played the idea back inside his head and decided against it. For one thing, no matter how thick Neville might be, an appeal to him to come out and get kicked while he slipped back into the cosy cast-iron shell was unlikely to appeal to him. And in any case, did he really want to go back in there, spend the rest of the machine's working life cutting the slots in bolt-heads, with nothing to look forward to except an eventual appointment with sledgehammers and the big magnet down at the scrap-yard? If he stayed human, eventually they'd have to let him out; and there'd be other machines for him to use, new worlds of design and modification for him to conquer. He resolved to go quietly, or at least quietly punctuated by the occasional 'Ouch!'

Who knows? Perhaps I'll get a job in the prison workshop?

There was, of course, another alternative. There were highly placed people, Up There and Down Below, who owed him favours; or, at the very least, who could use his skills. If he yelled loudly enough, would they hear him and send angels with pickaxe handles and boltcutters to set him free? They should do, by rights, but he doubted it somehow. Trained machinists? Ten a penny. Stroll into any job centre and crinkle a fiver between forefinger and thumb, and you'll attract enough skilled labour to build five galaxies.

Later, when the cell door had slammed shut and the key had turned noisily in the lock (obviously not a good fit; with a small file and an oilstone he could tune it so that its wards moved frictionlessly, but he had an idea that it wasn't even worth offering), he lay back on the hard wooden bench and stared at the ceiling, allowing his mind to wander. It's all very well being able to do things, he realised, but that's never the end of the story. People – human beings – have to want the things to be done. And tools cost money, and so do materials; therefore it's only the people with money who have the tools and the materials, and people like that only ever want one thing made, namely more money. Which is why better mouse-traps are invented by people whose houses are not necessarily infested with mice, and why the human race can make anything and has so very little (but ever so much more than they deserve).

I could dig a tunnel, Len mused. Piece of cake, digging a tunnel. First though, I need something to dig with, probably a length of jagged metal ripped off this bed. Now then, what would be the most ergonomically efficient design of digging tool that I could make, using the materials available? And when I've made a digger, I'll need to make cunningly disguised receptacles to store the excavated earth in, and improvised pit-props to stop the roof caving in; and some light to dig by would be nice, maybe I could rig up a makeshift extension lead using wire from the bedsprings unwound and wrapped in bits of plastic peeled off the washstand trim. Hey, a crane for lifting the earth out of the hole would come in handy, how'd it be if I unpicked thread from my socks and used a chairleg and the lid of the chamber pot . . .?

Len's eyes sparkled as he faced the new challenge, and human ingenuity coursed through his veins like the tame lightning in Dr Frankenstein's laboratory.

Zxprxp poured himself into the cockpit of his ship, engaged the stardrive and watched the viewscreen as the stars became silver needles and the planet Earth dwindled into a speck of dust. He sighed, wiggled his livers until he was comfy and switched on the recorder. His mission was at an end, and it was time to compose his final report.

How was he going to put this? What words would convey in a concise and intelligible manner his impressions of the human race, enabling his fellow creatures to understand the inhabitants of the blue and green planet, justifying his research grant and keeping the heads of his faculty from stringing him up by his *uhjlkhj*? He took a deep legful of cyanide gas and began:

Initial report of Researcher Zxprxp on the inhabitants of Star 4555683463, Planet 3. Dateline 153/7355/915373

Well, that was the easy bit. The rest would require a certain delicacy of touch. How about:

My original brief on being assigned this mission was to visit the planet and obtain enough relevant data on its indigenous dominant species to enable Strategic Command to reach an informed decision as to whether the planet is appropriate for full-scale invasion and colonisation. In the course of my investigations I observed a number of human beings (as the species in question is referred to locally) and conducted in-depth interviews with four of them. Based on these researches, my recommendation to the joint chiefs of staff is quite straightforward. Forget it.

Our preconceived notion that human beings are a primitive, undeveloped species incapable of offering any significant resistance to our armed forces is completely wrong. On the contrary, human beings are so highly advanced that in an armed conflict between our two species, we would be lucky to escape with losses below 90 per cent.

Take, for example, the present status of their technology. They have reached such a level of symbiosis with their machines that they can actually talk to them. More than that; machines like them. My own ship developed what could only be described as a crush on a human being, with the result that its loyalties were in danger of being severely compromised. Although I did not have an opportunity to make a specific study of their defence technology, I have no doubt that it is unspeakably formidable and not to be trifled with.

If that were not reason enough to leave well alone, humans appear to be on what I can only describe as first-name terms with their Supreme Being. I interviewed a member of the human mortal/divine diplomatic corps (in the local argot, a 'vicar'), who convinced me that humans and their gods regard each other as equals, friends even; and although I did not personally witness any divine manifestations during my visit, I am confident that any act of aggression on our part would immediately incur reprisals at the highest theological levels. To be blunt, we have enough trouble with our own god without picking a fight with someone else's. Another good reason I feel, for leaving well alone.

As if their technology and divine patronage were not enough, the impressively ordered and integrated nature of human society should make us consider very carefully before initiating hostilities with these people. I was able to contrive an interview with the human head of state, an official described as the Prime Minister, during the course of which I discovered that humankind have transcended the crippling effects of internal politics and arrived at a method of ordering their affairs whereby the rule of one party or faction over another is now entirely obsolete. This can be deduced from the fact that the nominal head of state is a complete imbecile, incapable of being held responsible for his own actions, let alone the management of a planet. Obviously, therefore, any apparent government that may exist on Earth is purely a smokescreen, and the human race has managed to achieve that state of enlightened anarchy that we have long recognised to be the only way in which an advanced society can possibly be run, but which (to our shame) we have yet to achieve ourselves.

The last and most significant factor, however, is human tolerance, the like of which is unknown in any other part of the seven galaxies so far observed during the course of this programme. Humans display no sign whatsoever of bias or bigotry; unlike any other known life form they adamantly refuse to judge by appearances, and display neither fear of nor hostility towards people or things they do not know or understand. In other words, this race cannot be terrified into submission, and are clearly so well adjusted among themselves that a policy of divide-and-conquer would be doomed to failure from the start.

In any event we must ask ourselves: do we really want to invade this miserable lump of wet rock? It is remarkably inhospitable. During my stay on Earth the entire planet was in darkness, the result of a total eclipse of the sun that lasted for twenty-nine hjgflk, Homeworld Standard Time. That this was an everyday occurrence can be deduced from the casual attitude of the humans. They took no notice. It was business as usual. A world that spends most of its time in darkness is surely not worth considering as a potential colony.

To summarise; if we invade Earth we will be facing a race who are in complete control of their technology, who are under the direct protection of their God, who live in an idyllic form of society on which it would be impossible to improve, and who are so perfectly adjusted as to represent the highest and most advanced form of sentient life we have yet encountered. The conclusion is inescapable. On Earth, to coin a phrase, everything is for the best in the best of all possible worlds. Don't tangle with these guys; they'll have our lkhjgfsd for ertwgsq'ccr. Report ends.

Zxprxp played the report back a couple of times, altering a few words here and there, until he was satisfied. Then he directed the computer to set a course for home, engaged the ship's standard cruise velocity of eight million times the speed of light, and leaned back in his tank, thanking his lucky stars for his species' lucky escape.

Below them, the waters of the fjord tumbled and foamed about the needle-sharp rocks of Lemminggagrjot Sound. The wind ruffled their fur against the grain and scoured their eyes, and its scream deafened them.

'Well,' a lemming observed, 'here we all are.'

An unusually violent wave dashed itself into spray against the cliff face, showering the lemmings with droplets of salt water. Instinctively, they flinched.

'Nice day for it,' a lemming said.

Although physics, mathematics, Sir Isaac Newton, Galileo and thirty-two-feet-per-second weren't part of their species' mental database, the lemmings instinctively knew what was coming next. They saw it all in rather less complex terms – trot-trot-AAAAaaaaaagh-splosh! – but the basic essentials were all there, encoded in their DNA. If pressed, they'd have come up with something like *When you've gotta go, you've gotta go*, or even *It's a far, far better thing*.

'You can see ever such a long way from up here,' a lemming said. 'Look, isn't that the little grassy hollow where we found those particularly tasty roots?'

A lemming craned its neck. 'I do believe you're right,' it said. 'My, those roots were scrummy. Next year, we must make a point of . . .'

The sentence faded away. The lemmings avoided looking at each other, but all that left for them to look at was the extravagantly copious quantity of Down below their feet. More Down, they couldn't help feeling, than we know what to do with. Easily a lifetime supply.

'Oh well,' sighed a lemming, its mouth full of a last nibble of tender, fleshy grass. 'Might as well get on with it, now we're here.'

Not a lemming spoke. Not a lemming moved. In their minds, where an ancient voice should have been chanting, there was an awkward silence.

'Duty calls,' muttered another. 'A lemming's gotta do what a lemming's gotta do.'

Far below, the sea curled its lips, opening a gap under the crest of a wave just the right size for a multitude of lemmings to fit into. It waited. If the sea had had hands, it'd have clapped them slowly.

'Alternatively,' a lemming said.

It paused, embarrassed. Suddenly, it was aware that it had its species' undivided attention.

'All I was going to say was,' it said, 'we could try that other method.'

'What other method?'

The lemming waggled its whiskers. 'Well,' it said, 'there was that lemming, remember, and it wanted to be the leader, and it said *Don't jump.* And so what I was thinking was, instead of jumping, why don't we try politics instead?'

Some of the lemmings asked for further details. What, they asked, is politics?

'Ah,' the lemming replied enthusiastically. 'Listen to this.'

So the lemming told them about politics; and after a show of paws, they decided to give it a whirl. First they had an election. Then, once they'd chosen their leader, they held an improvised inauguration ceremony and invested their new head of state with full powers to represent their interests and act with full and unfettered discretion on their behalf in all matters appertaining to the public interest and the future of the species.

Then they threw him over the cliff.

'So that's politics, is it?' a lemming said, as they made their way back towards the grassy hollow where the nice roots were. 'You know, I think it could quite easily catch on.'

A glorious pink sunset, seen from above. Two men walk up the path, fishing rods over their shoulders, tackle-boxes in their hands. At the door, a younger man waits.

'Hi, Dad,' he calls out. 'Hi, Jay. Have a good trip?'

The older man nods. 'It made a nice change,' he said.

'Catch anything?'

Both men nod and hold their hands apart, indicating the approximate size of notional fish. 'But you should have seen the one that got away,' the older man adds.

'That's great. Come on in out of the cold, Martha's got the kettle on.' The younger man turns to lead the way.

'Anything happen while we were away?'

The younger man shrugs. 'All fairly quiet, really,' he replies. 'A slight glitch with the computer. Sun went on the blink for a day or two. Spot of trouble with a revolt in Hell. All sorted. Shall I carry your rods for you?'

'Thanks,' the older man replies. 'They're heavier than they look. When you say a slight glitch—?'

His elder son frowns disapprovingly. 'Dad,' he says, 'you've only just got home. Relax. You did say it was all under control now, didn't you, Kevin?'

'Oh yes. All in apple-pie order.' Fortunately he hadn't specified which apple. His father and brother nod.

'That's all right then,' his father says. 'Had a good time while we've been away? Been behaving yourself? No wild parties?'

'Actually, it was pretty boring,' Kevin says, with a shrug. 'Next time you go, can I come too?'

'Next time . . .' his father says; and then they pass through the door, and it shuts, and here we are on the other side.

Next time. Well. We'll see.

THE
PORTABLE
DOOR

For Kim, Nathalie and Melanie Anne:
with love

CHAPTER ONE

After a very long time, the door opened, and the tall, Aryan-looking bloke came out. He was smiling, and shaking hands with the grim-faced man. Not a good sign, by any stretch of the imagination. *But then*, Paul told himself, as the grim-faced man called out another name and the girl with the Pre-Raphaelite hair stood up and followed him into the interview room, *I wouldn't have wanted this rotten job anyhow.*

The Aryan took his coat from the rack and left, leaving Paul alone in the waiting room with the thin girl. *Pointless*, he told himself; *we might as well both go home now and save ourselves the humiliation.* If someone had offered to bet him money on which of the ten candidates who'd passed through the door since he'd arrived was going to get the job, he'd have refused to play, since there wasn't a lot to choose between the eight who'd already been called. They were all, as far as he could tell, perfect: superbeings, almost certainly with superhuman powers and quite possibly from the planet Krypton. The only dead certainty on which he'd have been tempted to wager was that he didn't stand a chance; and the only consolation was that the thin girl probably didn't, either.

He glanced at her out of the corner of his eye. She was small and dark, with a drawn, bony face and enormous eyes, like one of the small, quick moving animals at the zoo that have to be kept in subdued lighting. It was saying something that even he hadn't been tempted to fall in love with her at first sight. Not that she wasn't attractive, in a sort of a way (to Paul, all females under the age of forty and still alive were attractive in a sort of a way, and also unspeakably terrifying); what had put him off was the chilling aura of hostility that she contrived to project. *You could cut yourself to the bone on someone like that*, he decided, *and she wouldn't even notice.*

Nevertheless, he glanced again. She was perched on her chair at an angle, cleaning under her fingernails with the cap of a ballpoint pen. Earlier she'd picked her nose and reamed out her left ear with her little finger. Her hands were tiny, like little claws, poking out from the sleeves of her suit jacket. She reminded him of a bat.

'I know,' she said suddenly, not looking up as she wiped the pen cap on the knee of her skirt. 'Disgusting habit.'

He winced. 'No, that's fine,' he said, looking away immediately. 'You carry on.'

Dead silence. Paul fixed his eyes on the toecaps of his shoes (scuffed and in need of polishing) and tried to think about something else. *All right*, he said to himself, *so which of them would you choose?* He considered the question for a moment or so, narrowing it down to the Pre-Raphaelite, Intense With Glasses, Young Indiana

Jones and the Dog Boy. On balance, he decided, he'd have to plump for the Dog Boy, simply because he'd hated him most of all, and so it was inevitable that he'd be the one to succeed. Not that he'd ever know the outcome. Not that he cared. If he had any sense, he'd get up right now and walk out; with luck and a following 75 bus, he'd be back in Kentish Town in time for the second half of *Buffy*.

But he stayed where he was, while the thin girl excavated the talons of her left hand, like Carter and Caernarvon questing for dead Pharaohs. He couldn't hear anything through the interview room door – like all the other fixtures and fittings in this place it was solid, chunky and antique – but it didn't take much imagination to picture the Pre-Raphaelite smiling demurely as she gave concise, intelligent answers to the panel's well-chosen questions. Maybe he'd change his bet and go for her instead; after all, if it was up to him he'd hire her like a shot, for any post up to and including President of the UN or Queen of the Elves.

'You're probably right,' the thin girl said without warning. 'Specially if the interviewers are men.'

This time he couldn't help staring straight at her. She grinned sardonically at him.

'Oh, it's obvious what you were thinking,' she said, 'from that soupy expression on your face, and the way your shoulders are sagging. Like someone had sat you down in front of a radiator, and you're beginning to melt.'

He couldn't think of anything to say to that, so he said, 'Oh,' instead. She pulled the grin back into a little wry frown, like someone reining in an unruly terrier, and scratched under her right armpit.

'I wish I could do that,' Paul said.

'What, scratch? It's easy, look.'

'No,' he replied, 'guess what people are thinking just by looking at them. It'd come in handy, being able to do that.'

She shrugged. 'Not really,' she said.

He waited for her to expand on that, but she didn't seem inclined to do so. She also appeared to have come to the end of her repertoire of revolting things to do while waiting for a job interview, and just sat still in her chair, looking small. For some reason, Paul felt it was up to him to say something now.

'Oh, I don't know,' he said. 'It's got to be useful sometimes, surely.'

She looked at him. 'In what way?' she said.

Fine, he thought. 'ESP,' he said. 'Yuri Geller bending spoons. You could go on the Paul Daniels show, things like that.'

She blinked. 'I'm sorry,' she said. 'I haven't got the faintest idea what you're talking about.'

Makes two of us, he thought. 'Doesn't matter,' he said. 'So,' he went on, feeling like he was wading through knee-deep mud, 'what made you apply for this job, then?'

'My mother,' she answered sadly. 'At least, she drew a ring round the advert in the *Telegraph* in yellow marker pen, and left it lying about wherever I went. How about you?'

'Oh, I don't know,' he replied, wondering why in hell he'd raised the subject in the first place. 'Because it was there, I suppose. I apply for most things that don't involve getting shot at or A-level Sanskrit.'

She pulled a face carefully calculated to acknowledge a failed joke. 'I wonder who'll get it,' she said.

'Apart from us, you mean?'

'Get real.'

'I don't know,' he said. 'Either this girl who's in there now, or the short, dark bloke.'

'The one who looked like a dog?'

He nodded. 'Him, probably,' he said. 'He looked like the sort who can do quadratic equations in his head while playing Mahler piano concertos.'

She sniffed. 'I think it'll be that girl,' she said. 'Specially if the interviewers are men,' she said again.

'You could well be right,' he said. 'Daft, but there it is.'

'It shouldn't be,' she snapped. 'Still, it'll get my parents off my back for a day or so, and it's better than hanging round the house. I suppose,' she added.

Silence again; but Paul didn't want to go back to staring and brooding, and there wasn't anybody else he could talk to. 'Actually,' he said, 'I know this sounds silly, but do you happen to know what these people actually do?'

The thin girl shrugged. 'No idea,' she said.

'Nor me. Pity,' he added, 'I don't suppose I'll ever get to find out now.'

'Wouldn't lose any sleep over it.'

'Well, quite,' he said. 'Still: "position vacant for junior clerk". Sounds like something out of Dickens.'

'Rather like this place,' the thin girl said. 'What a dump.'

Paul looked at her for a moment; she was biting off a hangnail. *Still*, he said to himself, *why not?* 'Do you fancy having a drink or something afterwards?' he said. 'I can wait for you outside.'

She looked at him as though she'd just found him on the sole of her shoe. 'No, not really,' she said.

'Oh. Right. I just thought—'

She shrugged. She had the shoulders of a born shrugger. Mercifully, the door opened.

The Pre-Raphaelite came out, smiling in a manner that nearly melted Paul's teeth, and the grim-faced man called out, 'Mr Carpenter, please.' *That's me*, Paul realised after a moment. He stood up, managing not to stumble or slip on the polished oak floor, and followed the grim-faced man into the interview room.

The world is full of interiors that bleach the spirit. Hospitals, police stations, job centres, local government offices and prisons all have their own subtle type of vampire colour scheme and black-hole furnishing, capable by accident or design of wiping away a person's self-esteem and will to resist, like boiled-over soup off a ceramic hob. The interview room achieved the same effect, but in a slightly different way. It was drab, bleak and hostile, just like the examples cited above, but there was far more to it than that. The oak panelling on the walls seemed to suck in light, whereas the enormous boardroom table was polished to a dazzling mirror. The huge crystal chandelier looked as if it had grown out of the ceiling over millions of years, like a vast stalactite. The glowing floorboards groaned under his heels as though demanding to know who had let a person like him in there in the first place. There was one vacant chair, as inviting as an Aztec altar. The grim-faced man gestured him into it, and he sat down.

'Mr Carpenter, isn't it?' said the grim-faced man.

It only went to show how daunting the room itself was that Paul didn't really notice the people sitting on the other side of the table until then. It didn't help that they were perfectly reflected in the table top, so that they appeared to be looking down at him and staring up at him at the same time. They were absolutely terrifying.

'I'm Humphrey Wells,' the grim-faced man said. 'These are my partners –' and he barked out a string of bizarre names that Paul was too stunned to catch; all that registered with him was that the names were as weird as the faces they belonged to.

There was a long, thin man with bushes of white hair sprouting out on either side of a gleaming pink dome, and a thin white wisp hanging off his chin like an icicle. There was a man with huge shoulders, gigantic round red cheeks and a gushing black beard that vanished under the edge of the table. There was a middle-aged blonde woman with unnaturally high cheekbones and a chin like a bradawl. There was an even blonder man, somewhere in his late twenties, who was either a rock star or a tennis champion; instead of a collar and tie he wore a black cashmere sweater, and what looked like a large claw on a fine gold chain. And there was a little, bright-eyed man with sunken eyes and the face of a freeze-dried child, who was grinning at Paul as if trying to make up his mind whether he'd taste better roasted or casseroled in red wine, with onions. In slightly less time than you'd allow for taking a photograph of a snowscape in bright sunlight, Paul decided that they gave him the creeps.

Silence. The six freaks stared at him. Then the grim-faced man cleared his throat, and said, 'Right then, Mr Carpenter. What makes you think you'd be suited to this job?'

Suddenly, none of the answers he'd carefully prepared for this question seemed at all suitable. 'I don't know,' he said.

The freeze-dried character laughed, making a sound like dangerously thin brake shoes. Blackbeard smiled encouragingly. The woman wrote something down on a piece of paper.

'I see,' said the grim-faced man. 'In that case, what prompted you to apply for it?'

Paul shrugged. There didn't seem much point even in going through the motions; bullshitting these characters would be as futile as trying to sell a dodgy car to a Jedi knight. 'I saw it in the paper,' he said. 'I've applied for lots of jobs lately,' he added.

The grim-faced man nodded slowly. The white-haired man seemed to have fallen asleep. 'Maybe you could tell us something about yourself,' said the tennis champion, in what Paul guessed might well be an Austrian accent.

'Not much to tell, really,' Paul said. 'I've got four GCSEs and two A levels. I was going to go to Exeter University, but then my dad retired and they went to live in Florida, so they said I'd better go to London and get a job. That's about it.'

The woman crossed out what she'd put down earlier, and wrote something else. Blackbeard frowned sympathetically, as if Paul's story had struck him as terribly tragic and sad. The freeze-dried type lit a huge cigar and blew a perfect smoke ring at the chandelier.

'Fine,' said the grim-faced man. 'How about hobbies?'

Paul blinked. 'Excuse me?'

'Hobbies,' the grim-faced man repeated. 'What do you like doing in your spare time?'

According to the book Paul had got out of the library, they always asked this, so of course he'd rehearsed a model answer – reading, keeping up with current affairs, music and badminton. All lies, of course, but it had never crossed his mind to tell the truth at a job interview. Instead, he replied, 'I watch TV a lot. I used to paint little model soldiers, but I don't do that so much now.'

The tennis champion looked up at him. 'Sport?' he said sharply.

'Sorry?'

'Sport. Football, fencing, archery. Do you do anything like that?'

Paul shook his head. 'Not since school,' he replied. 'And I was rubbish at it then.'

'Languages?' the woman asked; surprisingly, she turned out to be American.

'No,' Paul replied. 'Well, I did French and German at school, but I can't remember any of it now.'

'How about your social life?' asked the grim-faced man.

'Haven't really got one.'

The white-haired man opened his eyes. 'Can you tell me the four principal exports of Zambia?'

'Sorry, no.'

The white-haired man closed his eyes again. The woman put the cap on her pen and dropped it into a tiny black handbag. There was a long, silent moment; then the grim-faced man folded his hands on the table in front of him. 'Suppose you were in the Tower of London,' he said, 'all on your own, with all the cases unlocked, and suddenly the fire alarm went. Which three things would you try and take with you as you left?'

Paul opened his eyes wide, and asked him to repeat the question. The grim-faced man obliged, word for word.

'I'm sorry,' Paul said, 'I don't know. I've never actually been there, so I don't know what they've got.'

Dead silence; as though it was the Last Judgement and he was standing before the throne of God, flanked by archangels and cherubim, and he'd farted. 'How about the Crown Jewels?' said the woman. 'I guess you've heard of them.'

'What? Oh, yes.'

'Yes, you've heard of them, or yes, you'd try and save them?'

'Um,' Paul said. 'Both, I suppose.'

Another silence, which made the one that had preceded it seem positively jovial. 'If you had a choice,' said the white-haired man, 'between killing your father, your mother or yourself, who would you choose, and why?'

Oh, for crying out loud, Paul thought; and then, *I bet they didn't ask the Dog Boy any of this shit.* 'I really haven't got a clue,' he said. 'Sorry.'

The woman opened her bag again, took out a pair of tiny rimless spectacles, put them on and stared at him through them. It was like that trick where you set light to a bit of paper with a magnifying glass, except it wasn't done with heat. Quite the reverse. 'You say you used to paint model soldiers,' she said. 'Which period?'

The hell with it, Paul thought. *Tell the horrible bitch the truth, and have done with it.* 'Medieval,' he said. 'Also I did a lot of those fantasy ones, elves and orcs and trolls. I tried Napoleonic too, but they were too fiddly for me.'

The woman nodded gravely. 'I see,' she said. 'Can you tell me the properties of manganese when used as an alloying agent in steel?'

'No.'

She nodded again. 'What did you think of the latest Living Dead album?'

Paul gave that one a little thought before answering. 'It sucked,' he said.

'Who would you rather be, Lloyd George or Gary Rhodes?'

'Sorry,' Paul said. 'Who's Lloyd George?'

'What do you most admire about the works of Chekhov?'

Paul frowned. 'I don't know,' he said. 'The way he says, *Course laid in, keptin*, is pretty cool, but mostly he doesn't get to do much.'

Nobody spoke. There hadn't been such a silence since the beginning of the world. Then they all looked at each other (apart from the white-haired man, whose eyes were tight shut, his chin on his chest), and the grim-faced man said, 'Well, I think that covers everything from our point of view. Is there anything you'd like to ask us?'

Paul managed to keep a straight face. 'Not really, thanks,' he said.

'Fine.' The grim-faced man stood up and opened the door. 'We'll be writing to you in a day or so,' he said. 'Thank you very much for coming in.'

'Pleasure,' Paul replied, and he followed the grim-faced man out. Some joker had seen fit to steal his leg bones and replace them with sticks of rhubarb, but so what? No more than he deserved.

As he passed the thin girl in the doorway he shot her a glance that tried to convey encouragement, warning and pre-emptive sympathy all rolled up together. He reckoned he made a pretty good fist of it, but she was looking the other way.

Instead of heading straight for the bus stop, he stopped at a pub and asked for a half of bitter shandy. He couldn't really afford to go squandering money on booze, particularly since it was obvious he was unemployable, but he needed somewhere to sit down and shudder quietly for a while. Since he'd just spent his entire entertainments budget for the next fortnight on the bitter shandy, he resolved to make it last a while. He also wondered why he'd ordered it, since he didn't like bitter. He grinned; it sounded like the sort of question they'd have asked him, and of course he didn't know the answer.

From there, Paul went on to consider a wide range of issues, all of them depressing. When he'd had enough of that, he looked up and saw the thin girl, just turning away from the bar. She was holding a pint of Guinness, in a straight glass. She went and perched on a bar stool next to the door. Under normal conditions, nothing on earth would have induced him to get to his feet and walk over to her, but after what he'd just been through, there was a limit to how much harm she could do him.

She saw him coming and dived into her duffel-coat pocket for a book, but she wasn't quick enough on the draw. Also, she was holding it upside down. 'Hello,' he said. 'How did you get on?'

She lowered the book very slowly, rather in the manner of a defeated general surrendering his sword. 'Oh, I don't think I got it,' she said. 'How about you?'

He shook his head. 'Just as well, really,' he said. 'I wouldn't have wanted to work for those nutters anyhow.'

'Nor me,' she said. 'They asked all these really stupid questions. I told them they were stupid questions.'

He could believe that. 'Did you get the one about killing your parents?'

She looked at him as if he was mad. 'They asked me to list the kings of Portugal,' she said, 'and what my favourite colour was. I told them, none of your business.'

Well, quite, he thought. *A person's relationship with the kings of Portugal is a strictly private matter.* 'I got a load of rubbish about the Tower of London, and stuff about *Star Trek*.'

She clicked her tongue. 'Not that Chekhov,' she said. 'The Russian playwright.'

'There's a Russian playwright called Chekhov? Oh.' He shook his head. 'Doesn't matter, anyway. I think I'd lost it before I even sat down.'

She nodded. 'I wonder what they asked the Julia Roberts female,' she said. 'I bet she'd have told them her favourite colour. Pink, probably,' she added savagely.

Somehow, talking about it to the thin girl made it seem rather less awful. 'Would you fancy coming out for a meal?' he asked.

'No.' She stood up, glugged down her Guinness to the last drop, and wiped her mouth on her sleeve. 'I've got to go now,' she said. 'Bye.'

She was gone before he had a chance to open his mouth. He sat down, drank the last quarter inch of his shandy and left the pub. She wasn't standing at the bus stop when he got there, which was probably just as well.

That night, Paul had a dream. He was standing in a dark cellar – the scenery was straight out of an old-fashioned Dungeons and Dragons computer game, but originality had never been his strong suit – and he was facing a mirror. He could see his own face; also, for some reason, the thin girl's. That much he could explain away by reference to toasted cheese and pickled gherkins, but that didn't really account for the other two faces in the mirror, nor for the strong feeling he had that he knew them, very well, as though they were close family or something like that. They were two young men, around his own age; one with curly red hair and freckles, the other fair-haired and slab-faced, and they were waving frantically, as if trying to get his attention. Why he'd chosen to dress up these two figments of his subconscious in what he vaguely recognised as Victorian clothes he had no idea; probably it was something he wouldn't have wanted to know, anyway. Then the cellar door opened, allowing yellow light to seep in round the door frame, and a man and a girl came in. He thought he recognised them from some TV commercial; either they were the Gold Blend couple or generic beautiful people from a car ad. They were chatting and laughing, as if they hadn't seen him there; but, as they passed him, they both stopped sharply, and the man pulled out a long, curved knife. Something went snap, and then he woke up.

The snap turned out to have been the letter box, out in the hall. He pulled on his dressing gown, a sad grey woollen object he'd inherited from a dead uncle, put his bedsit door on the latch and went to see if there was anything for him. As usual, most of the letters were for the two nurses on the floor above, with three for the guitarist opposite him and two for the landlady. There was, however, one for him; and the back of the envelope was embossed with a logo, JWW.

I know what this is, he thought; *still, I might as well look at it, nothing better to do*. He went back into his own room and sawed it open clumsily with the bread knife.

The letterhead was old-fashioned, embossed in black on thick paper;

J. W. Wells & Co.
70 St Mary Axe
London W1.

Thought so, he told himself. Now then: *Dear sir, piss off, loser, yours faithfully*. He unfolded the rest of the letter.

Dear Mr Carpenter (he read)
Thank you for attending our offices for interview on the 21st inst. We are pleased to offer you the position of junior clerk, on the terms stated in your notification of interview. It would be most helpful if you could make yourself available for work from Monday 26th inst. Kindly confirm your acceptance in writing at your earliest convenience.
    Sincerely,
    (Obscene-looking squiggle)
    H. H. Wells
    Partner.

CHAPTER TWO

There was a different receptionist on duty, Paul noticed. When he'd come for the interview, the girl behind the desk had been a stunning brown-eyed brunette, who'd scared him so much he'd almost forgotten his name when she'd asked him for it. Today, her place was occupied by an equally stunning sapphire-eyed ash blonde.

'It's Paul Carpenter, isn't it?' she said, smiling at him in a manner liable to cause a breach of the peace. 'Mr Tanner would like to see you in his office straight away.'

The smile had been bad enough. Usually, when girls like that smiled at him, it was through the thick glass of a TV screen, and they were trying to sell him hair conditioner. That and the alarming news that he had to go and see someone, presumably one of those terrible partners, before he'd had a couple of hours to calm down and prepare himself for the ordeal were almost too much for him to cope with.

'Right,' he said. 'Yes, thanks.' (Also, how had she known who he was?)

'Do you know the way?'

The way? What was she talking about? 'Oh,' he said. 'Um, no. Sorry.'

She stood up to point. 'Left down the corridor,' she said, 'through the fire door, turn right, up two flights of stairs, then right again, through the photocopier room, turn left, second door on your right, you can't miss it.'

That statement contained at least one bare-faced lie. He could remember as far as *through the fire door*. 'Thanks,' he said.

'If you get lost, just ask.'

'Right.'

'I'm Karen, by the way,' said the blonde, lifting a telephone receiver. 'Pleased to meet you.'

'Yes,' he said. 'Me too,' he added. Then he bolted like a rabbit.

It was a large building, and the floor plan turned out to be the sort of thing you'd expect to find if the Hampton Court maze had been designed by the Time Lords. At one point, he found himself in some sort of basement; he could see the soles of people's shoes passing overhead through thick green glass panes in the ceiling. Some time after that, he opened a door and stepped out onto a flat, lead-covered roof. The hairiest moment was when he pushed through the door that ought, by his calculations, to have brought him out onto the fourth-floor landing, but which in fact opened into a vast portrait-lined boardroom, where two dozen men were sitting round a table. He apologised and got out of there as quickly as he possibly could, but not before they'd all swivelled round in their chairs and stared at him. Other discoveries included two lavatories, a kitchen the size of Earls Court, a stationery cupboard filled from top to bottom with typewriter rubbers, and a door that opened to reveal a solid brick wall.

Just ask someone, the receptionist had said. That was all very well, but (apart from the mob scene in the boardroom) the building appeared to be deserted. Bizarre, he thought; why on earth would anyone want a place this size if they didn't have any people to go in it? He was just painting in his mind a picture of his desiccated bones propped up against a corridor wall when he turned a corner and collided with something extremely solid, which turned out to be one of the partners from his interview; to be precise, the short, wide man with the huge black beard.

Blackbeard recovered first; hardly surprising, since he appeared to be built of solid muscle. 'Ah,' he said, in what Paul reckoned was probably a Polish accent, 'Mr Carpenter. And how are you enjoying your first day with us?'

Paul stared at him for a moment. Then he said, 'Excuse me, but are you Mr Tanner?'

For an instant, a frightful scowl hovered on Blackbeard's face, as though he'd just been mortally insulted. Then he laughed. 'Heavens, no,' he said. 'Allow me to introduce myself. Casimir Suslowicz.' He stuck out a hand you could have landed a Sea King on. Paul braced himself for a bone-crunching handshake, which didn't happen. 'Dennis Tanner's office is— actually,' he said, 'it's probably best if I show you the way. This place can be a little confusing, till you get used to it.'

'Thanks,' Paul replied, slightly stunned. 'If you're sure it's no trouble.'

'No trouble at all,' Mr Suslowicz replied. 'Follow me.' He set off at a brisk walk, so that Paul had to half skip, half trot in order to keep up with him without treading on the backs of his heels.

'Actually,' Mr Suslowicz called back over his shoulder, as they passed the second lavatory, 'it might be an idea if I send you down a map. Would that be helpful, do you think?'

'Oh yes, definitely,' Paul replied. 'Thank you very much.'

'No problem,' said Mr Suslowicz cheerfully. 'In a day or so, I'm sure, you'll be able to find your way around in the dark; but to start off with, a map. My secretary will bring it to you this afternoon.'

Well, Paul thought, that would be something to look forward to, assuming he ever managed to find the place he was supposed to go to after he'd seen Mr Tanner. Not for the first time, he noticed how hot the building was. He could feel sweat crawling under his armpits, though running up and down a dozen or so flights of stairs in his overcoat might have had something to do with that.

'Here we are,' Mr Suslowicz announced abruptly, coming to a dead stop outside one of four identical doors. 'Hold on,' he added, 'I'll introduce you.' He knocked sharply once and jerked the door open, so hard that the wood actually vibrated.

'Dennis,' he said, standing in the doorway and blocking Paul's view. 'Here is Mr Carpenter.'

'About time,' said someone on the other side. Judging by his voice, Mr Tanner was Australian. 'He should've been here twenty minutes ago.'

Mr Suslowicz smiled at Paul as he slid past and scampered away down the corridor. Paul took a deep breath and went in.

He recognised the man behind the desk straight away. Once seen, never forgotten. Mr Tanner was the freeze-dried child with the acupuncture eyes. *Marvellous*, Paul muttered to himself, and walked across to the desk.

The room was blue with cigar smoke, and it took him a moment to peer through it. All he could see of Mr Tanner behind a gigantic desk was his head, which looked like a grotesque novelty paperweight on top of a pile of brick-red folders. 'Got lost?' Mr Tanner said.

'Yes,' Paul replied. 'Sorry.'

Mr Tanner shrugged. 'Move that stuff and sit down.'

Paul lifted about ten pounds' weight of files off a narrow plastic chair and sat down. The cigar-smoke fog had lifted slightly, and Paul could just about make out the two dozen or so framed photographs on the walls – all portraits, signed, of people so astonishingly famous that even he had heard of most of them. Interspersed between the pictures were what looked alarmingly like a collection of tomahawks, each in a glass case with a neat printed label.

Mr Tanner grinned at him. His teeth were unusually narrow, and some of them were almost pointed. 'Not a wonderful start,' he said, 'getting lost on the stairs. Still.' He stubbed out a half-smoked cigar and immediately lit another. 'First things first, here's your employment contract.' He pushed across two bundles of typescript, certainly no thicker than the Bible or the omnibus edition of *The Lord of the Rings*. 'If you want to sit there the rest of the morning and wade through it all, fine,' he said. 'Or you could just sign both copies on the back page, where I've marked your initials in pencil, and save us both a lot of time.'

Paul signed (his pen had run out; Mr Tanner passed him another without saying a word) and handed back the bundles. Mr Tanner signed, shoved one copy back to him and dropped the other into a deep drawer, which he then locked. 'That's that out of the way, then,' he said. 'Next. I expect you'd like to know what you're actually going to be doing.'

'Yes, please,' Paul said.

'Right.' Mr Tanner blew smoke at him. 'Actually, it's all really simple, boring stuff. Filing. Photocopying. Collating. Stapling things together.' For some reason, Mr Tanner laughed at that, like it was a sick joke. 'Fetching and carrying. Franking letters. Making tea. Do you think you can handle it?'

Paul nodded. 'I'll do my best, certainly,' he said.

Mr Tanner looked at him. 'That's the spirit,' he said. 'Anyhow, after you've done that for six months or so, we'll have another look at you and see if you're actually any use, and take it from there. All right?'

'Fine,' Paul said. 'And, um, thanks for having me.'

That just made Mr Tanner laugh again. 'It's pretty simple,' he said. 'Do as you're told, don't get under anyone's feet, and we'll get along fine. All right.' He picked up his phone and muttered something into it that Paul didn't catch. 'My secretary's going to take you to the office where you'll be working most of the time,' he said. 'Don't want you getting lost again, we might not find you this side of Whitsun. Anything you want to ask?'

'Not really.'

'Well, I'll tell you something anyway,' Mr Tanner

replied. 'You can call Mr Suslowicz Cas and Mr Wurmtoter Dietrich, or Rick if you'd rather, though I don't suppose you would. But Humphrey Wells is Mr Wells, Theo Van Spee is Professor Van Spee or Professor, and Judy Castel'Bianco is always Contessa, if you value your life. And of course, Mr Wells senior is JW, that ought to go without saying. I'll answer to pretty well anything short of Fido, though I've got to say I don't go much on first names, it makes the office sound like one great big early-morning chat show. You can call Benny Shumway down in the cashier's office any damn thing you like, he won't take a blind bit of notice of you unless you've got a pink slip signed in triplicate. What you call the girls is between you and your conscience. Right, here's Christine, to show you the way. She'll be your real boss for the next six months, but it's OK, she doesn't usually draw blood.'

A moment later the door opened, and a smart-looking middle-aged woman came in. Since he'd apparently ceased to exist as far as Mr Tanner was concerned, Paul mumbled, 'Thanks' under his breath and followed her out of the room.

'Well,' she said, as soon as he'd closed the door, 'so you're Paul Carpenter. I'm Christine.'

'Pleased to meet you,' Paul said awkwardly.

'Oh, they all say that,' she replied cheerfully, and for the next five minutes, as he followed her down corridors, up corridors, through doors, up and down stairs, sideways along corridors and (if he wasn't mistaken) across the same landing twice, she rattled through a barrage of complex information without looking back at him once.

'Your reference,' she said, 'will be PAC. Usually it'd

be PC, but we've already got one PC, that's Pauline Church in accounts, and you haven't got a middle name so we put in an A. The toilets on the third floor are partners-only except in an emergency. Don't ever switch any of the computers off, or we have to call out Basingstoke and nobody'll thank you for that. Coffee is eleven to eleven-fifteen and lunch is one to two, we lock the street door so don't forget anything if you do go out. Tracy and Marcelle will do typing for you if they haven't got anything else to do, if you do any letters or anything yourself, send it through to the laser on the second floor, the paper jams so you've got to stand over it. The strongroom keys are in reception, and for crying out loud don't forget you've got them and go waltzing off. Paper clips and rubbers are in the green cupboard on the fourth floor, notepads and pencils and felt tips are in the closed-file store but they've got to be signed for. Pens, see me. Dial 9 for an outside line and if you use the long stapler, make sure you put it back where you got it from. Mr Wells has two sugars in coffee and one in tea, Professor Van Spee never has milk, he's lactose-intolerant. You're sharing the small back office with the other new clerk, it used to be the second interview room but the damp's chronic, but I don't suppose you'll be in there very much. All right?'

'Thanks,' Paul said. He hadn't caught any of that, and he was absolutely positive he wasn't going to pick it up as he went along, at least not without a great deal of suffering and embarrassment along the way. All in all, he decided, he really wished he'd got the job in the hamburger bar instead. One thing, though, did register with him. 'What other new clerk?' he asked.

'What? Oh, Sophie. Nice girl, you'll like her. That's the broom cupboard there, it's where we store all the file copies of the *Financial Times*. There's a notebook in there to sign them out if you need to borrow one.'

That reminded him; he'd really meant to ask someone at some stage exactly what it was that J. W. Wells and Co. actually did, but so far there hadn't really been a suitable cue. He thought about asking Christine, but decided not to.

'Here we are,' Christine announced suddenly, in the middle of a detailed account of the system for numbering closed files. 'Your new home from home.'

She pushed open the door and bustled in. Paul, however, stopped dead on the threshold and stood absolutely still, as if he'd just been switched off at the mains.

The cause of this extreme reaction wasn't the room itself; it was just a roughly square space enclosed by four white-emulsioned walls, a rather dusty Artex ceiling and a very old carpet-tiled floor, containing a bare plywood desk, a scratched green filing cabinet and two plain wooden chairs. It was what was on one of the chairs that got to him.

'This is Sophie,' Christine went on, apparently not aware that Paul was standing in the doorway doing wax-work impressions. 'She managed to get here on time,' she added. 'You two just hang on here, someone'll be along any minute now to tell you what you'll be doing next. We have a fire drill the first Wednesday in each month, there's a notice on the door that tells you where to go.'

Paul managed to get out of the way as she bustled out of the room. The doorknob hit him in the small of the back, but he hardly noticed.

'You,' said the thin girl.

Say something, Paul ordered himself. 'Yes,' he said.

There's two ways I can play this, Paul decided. *I can carry on standing here like a deep-frozen Ent, or I can sit down.* He stayed where he was.

'You're still wearing your overcoat,' the thin girl said.

'Am I? Oh, right.' He struggled out of the coat, which had somehow grown far more mechanically complex than he remembered. A button came loose, bounced off his toecap and skittered away under the desk. He dumped the coat on the floor, then bent down, picked it up again, and tried to drape it over the back of the chair. It slid off. He let it lie.

'You got the job, then?' he said.

'Yes.'

'Me too.' *All right*, he promised himself, *I'll shut up now*.

There was a long, brittle silence, during which his left foot went to sleep. Paul wondered briefly if there was actually anything to stop him walking straight out of the building (apart from the pins and needles, of course) and never coming anywhere near this part of London ever again. He'd signed a contract, of course, but would they really bother to take him to court? Almost certainly not.

'Did you see Mr Tanner?' he asked. *Yes, I know*, he told himself, *I promised. But ten seconds more of this ghastly silence and my brain'll boil out through my ears.*

The thin girl nodded. 'He's horrible,' she said.

'Did he tell you what they actually do here?'

This time she shook her head. 'Did you ask him?'

'No.'

'You should've asked him.'

'I expect we'll find out, sooner or later.'

She frowned. 'I hope so,' she said. 'Otherwise we're going to look very stupid.'

The pins and needles had spread to his right foot too. He rested one hand on the desk for balance and tried to keep absolutely still.

She was sitting slightly forward in her chair, tiny hands folded in her lap. For some reason, she reminded him of a picture he'd once seen of a man who'd been on Death Row in some American prison for twenty years. Somewhere, in the distance, a telephone was ringing. It carried on, unanswered, for a very long time.

'Big place, this,' he said.

'Mm.'

'The Polish bloke said he'd send me down a map,' Paul went on. 'I hope he does. I got really badly lost just trying to find Tanner's office.'

She looked at him with mild contempt. 'Did you?' she said.

'But then,' he continued, 'I never did have much of a sense of direction. My mum says I could get lost in a shoebox.'

'Really.'

His feet tingled sharply, making him wince. 'So,' he said, 'have you got any brothers or sisters?'

'Yes.'

Something like a thousand years passed. Then she frowned at him and said, 'Why don't you sit down, instead of standing there?'

'I—.' *No*, he thought, *don't even try explaining, just get your bum parked*. He sat down, yelping very slightly as his left foot brushed the chair leg. He looked round for a window to stare out of, but there wasn't one.

'Did they tell you why you got the job?' the thin girl asked suddenly.

'No,' Paul replied. 'How about you?'

'No.'

'If you remember, I was absolutely convinced the Dog Boy was going to get it,' he said.

'Who?'

'There was a bloke at the interview who looked like a dog.'

'Was there?'

Please, he thought, *please can someone turn up with some work or something, and rescue me from this? I don't think I can stand—*

'I'm sorry,' the thin girl said.

'What?'

'I'm sorry,' she repeated, gazing down at her closely chewed fingernails. 'I'm afraid I'm not really a very nice person.'

Unanswerable. To his credit, Paul didn't even try. *In fact*, he said to himself, *the hell with it. I can keep my face shut as well as anybody on earth. Just watch me. We'll see who fossilises first. And besides*, he consoled himself, *every second I spend in here, I'm getting paid for. All the other times I've sat in stony silence with girls were on my own time. That's got to be progress, hasn't it?*

(And the cruel irony of it was, he realised, that this was almost, but not quite, the scenario he'd daydreamed about so often, the one where he'd got the job and found himself working side by side with a girl. A nice, jolly girl, of course, quite nice-looking but not beautiful or anything like that, because that'd mean she'd already have a boyfriend, and that'd be no good. A mere fortnight ago, if a wise old gypsy woman had gazed into her crystal ball and told him she'd seen him sitting in an office with a girl he was going to be working with for the indefinite future, he'd have whooped with joy; because a fortnight ago, the hardest thing in the whole world had been finding his way into a situation like this; because for one thing, you never get girls on their own, either they're with their friends or some bloke, always further away than the Pleiades or Orion's Belt. *Just give me a chance*, he'd implored heaven; *just let me be alone with one for five minutes, and I'll be able to give it my best shot; not really a lot to ask, surely. But I should have guessed*, he told himself; *it's the same as with this bloody horrible job*. The worst punishment there is for wanting the wrong thing is getting it.)

He glanced up. She was looking at him sideways, and to his horror he knew, somehow, that she could see what he was thinking. *Not fair*, he thought, then hastily tried to wipe it out of his mind, on the off chance that she hadn't seen that too. *Not that it matters*, he lied to himself.

At last, mercifully, the door opened, and through it came a little vole-like woman with large spectacles. She had a big pile of green folders in her arms. 'Hello,' she said, 'I'm Julie.' She didn't sound happy about it. 'I'm Mr Wells's secretary.'

Paul felt like he should stand up or something. Instead he said, 'Hello.' The thin girl didn't move.

'I've got a job for you two,' Julie went on, dumping the folders on the table between them. 'You're to go through this lot, putting them in date order. There's no particular hurry,' she added sadly, 'so take your time, and if there's anything you don't understand, come and ask me.'

She left without giving Paul a chance to say anything, not that he had anything to say. He looked across the desk at the thin girl; she was already dividing the folders into two piles.

Inside the folders were thick wodges of printed-out computer spreadsheets: a jumble of tabulated columns of figures, with a date in the top right-hand corner. They were all out of sequence, needless to say. Paul riffled through the contents of the first folder he came to, looking for some clue as to what the spreadsheets were actually about, and wondering what would be the best way of tackling the job. When he looked up, he saw that the thin girl had already established five or six neat piles, and was dealing the spreadsheets out like playing cards from the heap on her lap.

'It's easy,' she said without looking up. 'Each pile is a month. Once you've sorted them into months, you can sort each month into date order. Then you just collate them and put them back.' *Oh*, Paul thought. *Yes, that's not a bad way of doing it.* 'Thanks,' he said. 'I'll try it your way.'

'You do what you like,' she replied.

It was certainly an improvement on silent sitting. Even so, it was frustrating, not being able to figure out what any of it was about. The spreadsheets could have been timesheets or accounts, or spectrographic analyses of mineral samples, or invoices or radio telescope readings or the Retail Price Index or unusually sophisticated betting slips; or maybe it was some entirely meaningless, manufactured task, an intelligence test designed to help assess their numeracy and efficiency. Not that he gave a damn, but for some reason it bugged him. The strong smell of stale cigar smoke suggested that, whatever they were, they had at some stage passed through Mr Tanner's hands, but that didn't really help much.

Still; puzzling over what the wretched things actually were helped take Paul's mind off the tedium of the exercise, and it didn't seem long before he realised he'd finished. He put the papers carefully back in their folders and looked up. The thin girl was still only about a third of the way through her half of the pile. That surprised him.

'Can I help you with your lot?' he asked.

'No, thanks,' she replied, 'I can manage.'

And that's me told, he thought. But it didn't seem worth picking a fight over, so he nodded and turned back to the first pile he came to. At the back of his mind a conclusion about those damned spreadsheets was struggling to be born, like a weakling chick trying to peck its way out of a titanium eggshell.

Cohere, he ordered himself; *now, then*. He began with the obvious. The earliest printout was six months old, the most recent was dated yesterday. There were five piles in front of him, and the thin girl had five piles as well. He was too scared to check with her, but the odds were that neither of them had any printouts for October. There could be any number of reasons for that, starting with a computer crash that'd wiped out the system for four weeks or had lost all the October figures. The numbers themselves: they ranged from tiddly (0.84) to huge (4,667.863.87), which probably ruled out rain-gauge readings or petty-cash requisitions; if they stood for money, it was big money. There didn't seem to be much of a pattern to them; he compared the printouts for the seventeenth of each month, but he couldn't see that they had anything in common (but then, what he knew about statistics and maths in general could probably be memorised by a small frog). Each day had several printouts, some one or two, others as many as twenty. But no one day in any month seemed busier than any other, which didn't help much. All in all, it looked to be one of those problems that gets harder the more you think about it. He frowned. Coded messages, maybe? If each number somehow represented a letter of the alphabet—

Julie came in, without knocking; she had another armful of folders. 'Finished?' she said.

The thin girl looked up at her guiltily. 'No,' she said. 'It's my fault. I'm not much good at this.'

Julie didn't seem bothered. 'Well,' she said, 'here's another lot to be going on with. Like I said, no real hurry. Take your time.'

Of course, Julie would know what these rotten bits of paper actually were. Probably she wouldn't mind a bit if he asked her, and if she did the worst that could happen would be that he'd get the sack, and would that be such a terrible disaster? But he couldn't quite bring himself to do it, and she'd gone before he had a chance to search down the back of his moral sofa for his mislaid courage. Also, before he could stop her, the thin girl had partitioned the new pile and added half of it to her existing backlog. Working with her was going to be a riot, he could see that. Still—

'Here,' he said, 'I don't mind doing a few more. Why don't we—?'

She gave him a look you could have sliced bacon with. 'No, thanks,' she said. 'I may be slow and stupid, but I'll manage.'

He didn't say anything, in more or less the same way that people don't try and shake hands with grizzly bears, and pulled a sheaf of papers towards him. Blessed, therapeutic tedium washed over him like water in the desert. He had work to do. He got on with it.

When Julie brought in the fourth batch, she announced in a singularly mournful voice that they could stop for their coffee break if they liked. Apparently, neither of them liked; the thin girl was now almost invisible behind a barricade of paper, and was clearly determined not to rest until she'd caught up, while Paul thought of the coffee room, packed with secretaries, some of them undoubtedly terrifyingly pretty, and the moment of dead silence that'd inevitably follow as soon as he walked in, and came to the conclusion that he didn't want any coffee. At 12:57, Julie brought in the tenth batch (still nothing for October) and reminded them that lunch was one till two. They'd be locking the door at one minute past one, she said, so if either of them did want to go out— (From the way she said it, she might have been addressing Captain Scott and Captain Oates.)

'Thanks,' Paul said, and stood up.

He made it through the labyrinth to the front office with seconds to spare; Karen the receptionist was just about to shoot back a bolt the size of a young tree. It was just starting to rain and he'd left his coat in the office, but there were worse things than getting wet. He slipped through the front door feeling like the last man off the *Titanic*, and set off down the street at a brisk trot.

Now what? Pubs, cafés and sandwich bars were pretty well out of the question, at least until he got paid.

Walking the streets in the rain didn't appeal, somehow. That didn't leave many choices, in a district rather lacking in shops where you could mooch about and browse without actually spending money. There was also the small matter of hunger; he'd brought a cheese-and-stale-bread sandwich, but it was in his coat pocket. He could always go home and never come back, but he wasn't quite at that point yet.

'It's Paul, isn't it?' He recognised the voice without turning round, though of course he couldn't put a name to it; as far as he was concerned, the owner of the voice was the tennis champion (or the 1970s pop star, depending on personal choice). *Bugger*, he thought, and turned round slowly.

'Your first day, yes?' Today, the tennis champion was wearing a pale grey Armani suit over a white polo neck; the claw necklace was still there. 'Join me for lunch. There's a little Uzbek place just round the corner; just peasant food, but they do a passable *kovurma palov*.'

Motorway-hedgehog syndrome; the mind goes blank, the motor functions shut down, and although the survival instinct is screaming, *No, no, get out of there!*, it's wasting its breath. 'Thanks,' Paul muttered, thinking of the five pounds and seventeen pence he had in his pocket. *Well*, he thought, *look on the bright side*. Either this lunatic was going to buy him lunch, which meant he'd be one free meal to the good; or else he was going to spend the afternoon washing dishes with a lot of expatriate Uzbeks, which would almost certainly be an improvement on shuffling paper with the thin girl. Who knew, maybe they'd take him on full time.

The little Uzbek place was very little indeed, so it was

awkward that the entire population of central London seemed to be trying to get into it. For a blissful moment Paul thought he'd been saved; but a waiter materialised at the tennis champion's side and led them through the crush to a table tucked away in a corner. The tennis champion muttered something, presumably in Uzbek, and the waiter nodded gravely and vanished.

'Hope you won't mind,' the tennis champion said, 'I ordered for both of us. I think you'll like *kovurma palov*. I'm going to be boring and stick to *moshkichiri*.'

Paul mumbled something about that being fine by him. A heartbeat later the waiter was back with two enormous platefuls of yellow rice with bits in, and a cauldron of steaming green tea. The tennis champion said something to him, and he roared with laughter before vanishing again. It occurred to Paul that he had only a very sketchy idea of where Uzbekistan actually was; somewhere in Russia, he'd always thought, but the food looked like curry.

'Dig in,' said the tennis champion. 'Of course, this isn't *kovurma palov* like you get in Samarkand, but it's a reasonable imitation, even if the barberries are grown under glass. Have some tea.'

'Thanks,' Paul said, as the tennis champion filled his cup. At the next table, seven Japanese businessmen were comparing ties. 'This is very kind of you,' he said.

The tennis champion smiled. 'My name,' he said, 'is Dietrich Wurmtoter, but please call me Rick, everyone does. So, how are you settling in?'

'Oh, fine, great,' Paul said. 'It's very . . .' He had no idea what to say next, but the tennis champion was busy shovelling rice with bits in through his mouth like a steamboat stoker trying to win a race. He was very good at it, not so much as a grain of rice or a raisin going astray, but the general impression was distinctly alarming. Paul guessed it was because they had to hurry so as to be back in the office at two sharp, and stuck his fork into the yellow mountain in front of him. Actually, it wasn't bad; in fact, it was scrummy, and he wished he was in a fit state to enjoy it.

'So what's Julie got you doing?' said the tennis champion, with his mouth full.

Paul swallowed, and said, 'Um.'

'Something with lots of bits of paper, I expect,' the tennis champion said. 'That's one thing I don't like about our little firm, all the bits of paper. Green forms and pink forms and blue forms and miles and miles of computer stuff.' He glugged down a whole cup of tea; Paul's cup was so hot he hadn't dared touch it. The tennis champion obviously didn't feel pain. 'Still, it's not all like that, I promise you. In six months or so, a year maybe, you'll find out what we're really about. Depending on what you decide to specialise in, of course. I mean, it's up to you, you've got to go where your talents lead you. That's the good thing with this business, there's so much scope.'

Yes, Paul thought, *but*. He was almost tempted to ask, there and then, but the thought of how stupid he'd look prevented him. Clearly the tennis champion believed he knew all about J. W. Wells & Co. Maybe he'd get the sack if it turned out he didn't; in which case, would he have to pay for his own lunch? Not for the first time in his life, Paul cursed heaven for not letting him in on the secret, the secret that everybody else was in on except him. If only he knew, he was sure, he'd be able to cope, it'd all be so easy. The thought that the thin girl didn't know either was some small shred of comfort; at least he wasn't the only one. For some reason, though, he didn't want to think about her. (Did she like Uzbek food? Did she know where Uzbekistan was? Probably. It was just the sort of thing that everybody else in the world knew, except him.)

'Anyhow,' said the tennis champion, 'tell me all about yourself. Not the unimportant stuff you told us at the interview, exam results and all that nonsense. The real you.'

Oh God, Paul thought. 'Well,' he started; but fortunately the waiter appeared with another loaded plate of whatever kind of rice with bits in the tennis champion had been eating. He slid out the empty plate and substituted the full one with the practised skill of a production-line worker. The tennis champion launched into his mound of food with even greater savagery than before, and didn't stop until his fork screeched on the floor of the plate.

'Is there something wrong with your *palov*?' he said. 'Or aren't you very hungry?'

Paul reckoned he'd done pretty well, having eaten in five minutes more than he usually got through in a week. 'Oh, it's absolutely fine,' he said, 'great. What was it called again?'

The tennis champion told him, and then embarked on a long and complicated story about some occasion in Tashkent, which had started with him sending the *sarimsokli* back to the kitchen, and ended with a bizarre form of local duel, fought on camels with padded tent-poles, which the tennis champion had apparently won. The story went on for quite some time, but Paul didn't mind that in the least, since it meant that he was spared from having to invent a real him to tell the tennis champion about, and could get on with his eating task.

'Anyhow,' the tennis champion said at last, 'that's enough about me. How about you? Been abroad much?'

'Not all that often,' Paul said. 'The year before last, we had a fortnight camping in the Loire valley.'

The tennis champion nodded eagerly. 'Camping out,' he said, 'when you get right down to it, you can't ever really say you know a place till you've lived rough there; sleeping in woods or barns, living off the land. Earlier this year I was in Borneo, and the boatmen who'd taken us down the river were all unfortunately captured and held to ransom by a neighbouring tribe – one of those wretched blood-feud things they're so keen on down there – and so there we were, five of us, with nothing but my knife, a ball of string and two boxes of matches—'

The Borneo story was even longer than the Tashkent story, and Paul lost the plot after the first ninety seconds, which somehow made it easier to listen to. The arrival of a third helping of rice with bits in added another couple of minutes, and they were on to the coffee stage before the tennis champion stopped talking, at which point he glanced down at his watch and said, 'Damn, it's five minutes to two. We'd better be getting back.'

He jumped up, and at once the waiter materialised next to him, holding his coat. As he slid his arms gracefully into the sleeves, as effortlessly as a samurai sheathing his sword, Paul thought he saw a bulge under his left armpit that could almost have been a shoulder holster (or equally, something else: an old-fashioned bulky mobile phone, a lady's shoe, two pounds of bratwurst).

When they reached the office door, Paul made a point of saying 'Thank you' nicely, the way his mother had taught him; then he sprinted past the reception desk and headed for his own little room. Clearly he was getting the hang of the place, because he reached his destination with a mere three wrong turns, and hardly had to retrace his steps once.

The thin girl looked like she hadn't moved. The paper mountain in front of her had diminished, but not by terribly much. 'You're wet,' she said, as he walked in.

'It's raining out.'

'Why didn't you take your coat, then?'

'I forgot.'

'Oh.'

Paul sat down. Part of him was damned if he was going to share his thrilling encounter with this sullen bitch; the rest of him, on the other hand, needed to tell someone or burst. 'You'll never guess what I've just been doing,' he said.

'No, probably not,' she replied without looking up. 'Do you mind, I'm very busy.'

Paul frowned. 'Have you had any lunch?' he asked.

'No. I don't eat lunch.'

He could believe that. 'You worked all through your lunch hour?'

'Yes. So what?'

'Oh, nothing.'

'You mean, I worked all through lunch and I'm still miles behind you. Well, big bloody deal.' She sniffed, then wiped her nose on her cuff.

Paul wanted to say, '*That's not what I meant, and you know it.*' But he didn't, because if she knew it, as he was prepared to assert, where was the point? He gave her a wounded look, which she failed to notice, and got back to work. He was getting well into it, coming close to attaining the death-of-self, trancelike state achievable only through transcendental meditation or very boring paperwork, when quite unexpectedly, the thin girl said: 'Don't tell me, the senior partner bought you lunch at the Ritz.'

It wasn't often that he got a feed-line like that; and after all, she had been spectacularly unpleasant to him throughout all the time they'd spent together. 'I don't think he's the *senior partner*,' he said mildly. 'And it wasn't the Ritz, it was a rather good little Uzbek place just round the corner. Fairly authentic *kovurma palov*, if you're prepared to overlook the hothouse barberries.'

Her head snapped up as though she'd been in a road accident. 'You had lunch with one of the partners?'

Paul nodded. 'Mr—' He grovelled on the floor of his memory for the name. 'Mr Wurmtoter,' he said, 'though he prefers just plain Rick.'

The girl's deep brown eyes were as round as saucers. 'Why?' she said.

'Sorry?'

'Why did he ask you out to lunch?'

Paul shrugged. 'I haven't the faintest idea,' he said. 'It's possible he was just trying to be nice.'

She looked doubtful. 'Try again,' she said.

'Well, actually,' Paul replied, 'I think that really was the reason, because most of the time he just talked about himself.'

'Oh.' A different sort of 'Oh,' this time. An 'Oh' that cared. 'So what did you find out?'

Paul bit his lip. 'Not a lot, actually,' he confessed. 'He told me a long story about getting into a fight in Tashkent, and an even longer one about camping out in Borneo. I think he travels a lot,' he added, to demonstrate his analytical powers.

'That's all?'

'Well, he likes the sound of his own voice quite a lot.'

'You didn't find out what this outfit actually does?'

'Um, no.'

'Oh.'

If there had been a tiny spark of communication between them, like the flash of lightning that links God and Adam on the ceiling of the Sistine chapel, it had just fizzled out. *Pity*, thought Paul. He went back to his spreadsheets, silently cursing Mr Wurmtoter for his gratuitous and unwanted act of kindness. Before he could get anywhere near the trancelike state, however, the door opened and a beautiful girl came in.

'Hello,' she said to him, apparently ignoring the thin girl completely; and she was smiling too, which was quite uncalled for. 'I'm Tracy, I work with Cas, Mr Suslowicz. He sent this down for you.'

It was the map; a wonderful, amazing map, a small masterpiece of draughtsmanship and calligraphy. The writing, though tiny, was perfectly clear, the layout (showing all four floors) was impeccable, and every last detail was carefully annotated – corridor, window, fire extinguisher, NB this door opens *inwards*. A tiny glint of wet ink implied that it had just been drawn, specially, for him. Clipped to it was a note –

PAC –
As promised; hope it's some help to you.
Cheers,
Cas.

– written in the same perfect, elegant handwriting. *Bloody hell*, Paul thought. 'Thanks,' he said. 'That's, um, really kind.'

The beautiful girl called Tracy turned up the gain on her smile a little. 'Oh, he's a very nice man, Cas, always goes out of his way for people. I'll tell him you liked it.'

Paul nodded. 'I think I'll have it framed,' he said.

The beautiful girl called Tracy laughed as though this was the wittiest thing she'd ever heard. 'I'll tell him you said that,' she said. 'He'll be tickled. See you.'

It was some time before Paul could tear his gaze away from the map. When he glanced up, he found himself on the wrong end of a look of pure, blood-freezing venom.

'Cas,' the thin girl said. 'And Rick. Nice to see one of us is fitting in around here.'

Oh come on, he wanted to say, *it's not my fault they're being nice to me. Besides, that Tanner bloke was a real bastard.* 'I'll photocopy it for you if you like,' he said sheepishly.

'"I think I'll have it framed",' she quoted viciously. 'For God's sake.'

'It was just a stupid joke,' he muttered.

'That blonde female seemed to think it was a very *good* joke,' she replied, making *blonde* sound like the worst insult in the English language. 'Looks like you've made a real hit with everybody today.'

It was at that moment that Paul felt a terrible, dull,

sickening feeling in the pit of his stomach, an *Oh-shit* feeling, such as you'd expect when you discover that the boat is slowly sinking, or the glassy sheen on the tarmac is black ice; because when she said that, his first thought had been that it didn't matter a toss about Cas and Rick and what's-her-name, the blonde, because he quite obviously hadn't made a hit with the one person— He stopped himself there, but it was too late; he'd admitted it to himself, he *knew* he had. Bugger.

And furthermore, he remembered with a sudden spasm of agony, the thin girl seemed to have the knack of reading him like a book. Serial buggers, with buggery sauce.

'If you want a copy of the map, just tell me, all right?' he said, looking away. 'Or you can copy it for yourself, I don't care.'

'No, thank you.'

'Fine.' He made a big deal of shuffling through the papers on the desk in front of him, and tried to get back to work.

Must get out of this habit, he told himself, as he added another 17 November to the appropriate stack. He had to get out of this bloody stupid habit of falling in love the way a cat bats at a bit of string. *It's embarrassing and it's got to stop*. It wouldn't be quite so bad if just once he had the guts at least to try and make something of it, but he never did. The string twitched, he batted, missed, and immediately panicked and hid under the table till the danger went away. *Pathetic*.

He thought about that. It'd be nice to think that he was making slight progress, and that in this case it had taken the interview, the drink afterwards and half a day in the same office before he'd given in and jumped

said. 'They're paying you – not a lot, true, but they're paying you, two of you, mind, to sit there all day sorting these spreadsheets into date order. Right?'

Paul nodded.

'Fine. It hadn't occurred to you, then, that if only they got themselves a little bit more organised, and got into the habit of filing these things neatly away as soon as they've done whatever it is they do with them, they could get rid of you and this peculiar girl of yours and save themselves a bob or two.'

To his credit, Paul *had* given the matter some thought, several times over the last three weeks. 'There's probably more to it than that,' he said. 'I mean, the partners are weird, but I don't think they're stupid. I expect there's a perfectly good reason behind it all, they just haven't bothered telling me about it. Which is fair enough. I mean, so long as I do what I'm told, why should I need to know?'

'True.' Neville stood up. 'I'm going for a pee,' he announced, and lumbered away across the bar.

While he was gone, Paul reflected on something Neville had said earlier. *If it's such a load of crap*, he'd said, *why do you stick it? Why don't you pack it in and do something else?* Of course, Paul hadn't been able to tell him the real reason, because if he'd shyly confessed that there was this girl, actually the strange, rather hostile – well, actually extremely unpleasant – girl he shared an office with, Neville would immediately have quizzed him about the steps he'd taken to further the matter, and would've been profoundly unimpressed to hear that he hadn't actually done anything about it at all. Actually, since Neville wasn't first cousin to two oak floorboards, he'd probably figured out that part of it for himself—

'You know what I think?' Neville said, reappearing with two full pint glasses and wiggling himself comfortably into his seat. 'I think you've got it up the nose about this weird-sounding bird you're working with. Otherwise you'd have told them to stuff it a fortnight ago.'

'What makes you think that?' Paul asked.

'Get real. You obviously hate it there; they're all either nutty as a Snickers bar or complete bastards, the work's boring enough to kill an accountant, and the place is freaking you out so badly, you jump like petrol prices every time the door opens. The only possible reason you're still there is that you've got yourself hung up on some bird. And,' he went on, ignoring Paul's mumbled denials, 'since I've known you for a decade and observed you closely throughout your troubled formative years, it's money in the bank that you'll have plumped for the one girl in the whole dump that nobody with the brains of a carrot would look twice at, from a mile away, through a busted telescope. Well?'

Paul felt like the least obvious suspect after Poirot's big speech in the library. 'Well, all right then, yes,' he said irritably. 'At least, I do quite like her. A bit.' He slurped a mouthful of beer, and decided there wasn't anything to be gained from lying to his oldest friend. 'Actually,' he said, 'I don't like her at all, she's rude and offhand and does nothing but put me down all the time. But—'

Neville dipped his head gravely. 'Danny Corbett syndrome,' he diagnosed. 'You remember Danny Corbett?' he went on, as Paul raised a dubious eyebrow. 'Little fat kid with red hair and freckles, nearly got slung out in fourth year for filling Werewolf Dave's coat pockets with aerosol cream during a maths test.'

'Oh, him,' Paul conceded. 'What's he got to do with it?'

'Well,' Neville said, dabbing his moustache on his cuff, 'I don't know if you remember Fiona Mascetti – big girl, went on to be a mechanic in the Royal Engineers . . .'

'Mphm.'

'Quite. Once seen, never forgotten, though I gather these days she's reckoned to be the fastest mole wrench east of Aldershot. Anyhow, Danny and Fiona went out for a while, and to hear either of them talk, the other one was the most disgusting, revolting specimen of humanity who ever evolved from a red-arsed monkey. Fiona reckoned Danny reminded her of a slug that's been left out in the rain and gone rusty, Danny was always wondering why the hell he bothered with a girl who could eat two cream doughnuts simultaneously and still not stop talking.' He sighed. 'They got married in June,' he said, 'and they're expecting their first kid in April.'

'Oh,' Paul said. 'I see what you mean, I guess. Still, that's neither here nor there. All the more reason for me to clear out of there, if I was being sensible.'

Neville lit a cigarette. 'Up to you,' he said. 'Far as I can tell, victims of Danny Corbett syndrome tend to make out all right in the long run. My guess is, if the other party annoys the hell out of you from day one, it makes for a smooth, well-balanced relationship, because that way you sort of fast-forward through the dopey, sun-shines-out-of-his-or-her-backside phase and get to the mutually-assured-irritation stage that seems to be the default setting for all long-term human couplings, without any of the disillusionment and disappointment that everybody else's got to get through first. I mean, if you know the significant other is a monumental pain in the bum right from the starter's gun, you're spared all the pain of finding it out once you've been together for two years and spent good money on kitchen units and curtains.'

Paul nodded. 'Talking of which,' he said, 'where is Melanie this evening?'

'Friday's her karate class,' Neville replied. 'She's doing pretty well, apparently. She was telling me the other day, she's learned forty-six different places on the human body where an accurately placed drop kick will cause instant death.'

'You must be very proud.'

Neville inclined his head in agreement. 'Last month it was A-level Spanish,' he said. 'But anyway, to get back to what we were talking about. If you really want to go for it with this miserable-sounding wench of yours, then crack on and stop mucking about. Most likely she'll tell you to fuck off and die, in which case you can jack in the horrible job and get a nice one instead; failing which, you'll still have the horrible job, but you'll be ahead of the game by one sweetheart. Either way, you're laughing.'

Paul thought about that. 'So that's what you think I ought to do?'

'Absolutely. That's my considered advice to you – no win, no fee. Declaring your true feelings is like going to the dentist, it's no fun at all, but the longer you put it off, the worse it's likely to be. And since in your case there's a definite, highly desirable consolation prize waiting for you when she says no way, not even if it'd mean world peace and the cancellation of Third World debt, I can't see any reason why you shouldn't do it first thing in the morning.'

'Tomorrow's Saturday,' Paul pointed out.

'All right, first thing Monday. That way, you've got the whole weekend to get your head together for the ordeal ahead. You know, choose the right words, think tactics, that sort of thing.'

'Oh look,' Paul said. 'The pool table's free.'

Next day, since it was a Saturday, Paul stayed in bed till twelve o'clock and spent the afternoon ironing his work shirts for the coming week. The more he thought about Neville's advice, the more undecided he became. On the one hand, there was a chance (statistically speaking, somewhere between a white Christmas in Queensland and winning the lottery without first having bought a ticket) that the thin girl would nod her head and say, 'All right, then,' or words to that effect. That prospect, though terrifying enough in itself, was not without its attractions. On the other, rather more likely hand, he could imagine all too vividly the bone-crushing embarrassment of the thirty seconds or so immediately following his prepared statement; and it was all very well for Neville to talk blithely about chucking in this job and getting a nice one instead, but it had taken him a very long time to find anybody who was prepared to trade him money for a part of his life-span, and the only people who'd proved willing to make such a deal were, by any criteria, as crazy as a barrelful of ferrets. While he'd been unemployed and actively seeking employment, Paul's parents had (albeit grudgingly) stumped up for his rent and the occasional loaf and tin of baked beans. Somehow he didn't feel their charity would stand the announcement that he'd quit a paying job simply because he didn't like it very much. That being the case, he'd be faced with sharing a desk indefinitely with a girl he'd just sworn undying love for, and who'd unequivocally told him to go stick his head up a chicken. If there was one way, in other words, of making his current situation worse than it already was, this surely had to be it.

Having finished off the last shirt, Paul folded the board away and, since he didn't have anything else to do, switched on the television. Aggravatingly, there was nothing on any of the channels except sport and a boring old opera-musical thing, Gilbert and Sullivan or something like that. (A middle-aged man in a black frock coat was cavorting round a plywood set holding a teapot, while a fat woman in a wedding dress and a chubby man in military uniform stared at him, accompanied by an unseen orchestra.) He put the television out of its misery with a deft prod of his index finger, flumped on the bed and reached for his library book, which he'd taken out on his way home on Thursday and hadn't got around to reading yet.

Further aggravation. Instead of the book he thought he'd checked out (the enticingly titled *A History of Model Railways, volume II: 1927–60*) he'd somehow been landed with something entirely different: *The Savoy Operas*, by Gilbert and Sullivan. Scowling, he opened the book at random: song lyrics, and dialogue. He didn't throw the book at the opposite wall, partly because it was a library book and partly because, knowing his aim, he'd miss the wall and break the window, but he dumped it on the floor with considerable force. Then he picked it up again, and squinted at the spine.

Odd, he thought.

Well, he thought, *if someone's trying to tell me something, I'm buggered if I know what it is*. He opened the book again, but there didn't appear to be anything significant or sinister about it; a flute-playing vicar was singing a song about how girls used to fancy him when he was younger. *Lucky old him*, Paul thought wistfully, and he put the book back on the floor.

Even so, he felt unsettled, as though there was a whole gallery of people watching him, and giggling discreetly. He stood up, looked at his watch, and grabbed his coat. In the pocket, there was a five-pound note, a two-pound coin and some silver. That was basically all he had to last him through to the end of the week, when hopefully J. W. Wells & Co. would do the decent thing and deposit money in his bank account. Nevertheless; he needed cheering up, and also to get out of his crummy little bedsit for a while. Time to throw caution to the winds. For his evening meal, he'd been planning on using up the crust of the loaf and the last of the mousetrap cheese, but the hell with that. Life is for living, and you're a long time dead. He resolved to stroll down to the shop on the corner and buy himself a frozen pizza.

It was cold out, just starting to get dark. He crossed the road, only to find that the shop was shut. He hadn't expected that. All the time he'd been living there, he'd only once seen the *Closed* notice in Mr Singh's window, and that had been at three in the morning last Christmas Day. He debated with himself as to what to do next. He could go home, save his money and see how much viable cheese he could excavate from under the soft carpet of green mould, or he could hike across to Tesco and buy his pizza there. On one dilemma horn, a sharp west wind and a few warning drops of rain; on the other, his miserable home and the lurking subliminal presence of Gilbert and Sullivan. He decided to go to Tesco.

For once it wasn't too crowded; in fact, it was practically deserted. He took his time at the freezer gondola, unable to make up his mind between a thin-crust *quattro stagione* and a deep-pan pepperoni feast. After several minutes of dithering he resolved to use the Force, put both of them back, closed his eyes and grabbed. Apparently the Force wanted him to have the pepperoni, so that was all right. He turned towards the row of checkout desks, and nearly collided with Mr Tanner.

Aarg, he thought, but he kept the sentiment locked in his heart, and skipped out of the way like a trained fencer. For one blissful moment he thought Mr Tanner hadn't recognised him. (After all, why should he? They'd only met once face to face, not counting the interview; and though the occasion was etched on Paul's memory like a septic scar, there was no reason why Mr Tanner should remember him particularly. Paul had long since got used to the fact that he was the most forgettable person in the world since What's-his-name.) But then Mr Tanner's head swivelled round, and Paul saw his face slide into his trade-mark unpleasant grin.

'Bloody hell,' said Mr Tanner. 'What're you doing here?'

Mr Tanner was holding a wire basket in his small, clawlike hand; and in the basket were a bottle of bleach, some dishwasher tablets, two J-cloths, three packs of Flora, a six-pack of peach toilet rolls and a medium-sized melon. In his other hand, he held a shopping list, with half the entries crossed off in red ink. Somehow, the fact that Mr Tanner's wife had sent him out to buy J-cloths and bog rolls on a cold Saturday afternoon made him somewhat less menacing; if not actually human, then at least vaguely humanoid. 'Actually,' Paul said, 'I live just round the corner.'

'Do you?' Mr Tanner frowned. 'Yes, you're right, you do. I remember it from your application form. Chicago-style Pepperoni Feast,' he went on, peering at the box in Paul's hand. 'Obviously we're paying you too much. We're having rissoles,' he added, with just a hint of pathos.

Just for an instant, Paul felt a mad impulse to invite Mr Tanner to share his pizza, with cheese on toast to follow. Luckily the fit passed as quickly as it had come, but it left Paul with no idea what to say next. He could feel his toes curling inside his shoes.

'Well,' Mr Tanner said, after a very long two seconds or so, 'I'd better get on, or I'll get spoken to. Enjoy your pizza.'

'Thank you,' Paul said, and backed away towards the checkout. Infuriatingly, a queue had materialised at the only open desk. Paul stood in line, the chill from the frozen pizza slowly numbing his fingertips, and cursed under his breath. It'd be just his luck if, before he worked his way to the front of the line, Mr Tanner finished his shopping and came and stood behind him, which would entail further and worse embarrassment. For two pins he'd have dumped the pizza on the floor and bolted like a rabbit out of the store; except that he knew that if he did that, he'd run into Mr Tanner again on the way out, and Mr Tanner would stare at him, breathless and pizzaless, and he'd probably die where he stood. Then a large woman came and stood behind him with a fully loaded trolley, and he knew that for the moment, at least, he was safe.

When his turn finally came, he paid for the pizza, fumbled it into a plastic bag (one of the type that you can't get open unless you happen to have honey smeared all over your fingertips), took his change and made a dash for the door. Through it, and safe; except that Mr Tanner was outside (how?), standing on the pavement with his own plastic carrier in his hand, and looking up the street in the opposite direction.

By now, Paul was as freaked out as it was possible to be without external chemical influence. Above all, he didn't want to have anything more to do with his employer until Monday morning at the earliest; preferably not ever again, not if he was drowning in the North Atlantic and Mr Tanner happened to float by in a rubber dinghy holding a lifebelt. Just then, a bus pulled up at the stop opposite the door. It seemed like the obvious answer, or at least a good idea, at the time. He jumped on the bus and it pulled away.

This is all right, Paul told himself, catching his breath and balance as the bus gathered speed. *All I've got to do is hop off at the next stop and walk home, no big deal. If I'm lucky, I'll be off again before the conductor comes round and I won't even have to pay.*

'Where to?' said a voice behind him.

Oh well, he thought. 'Just the next stop, please,' he sighed.

'Next stop Highgate Village.'

'What?'

'Next stop Highgate Village.'

That wasn't right. 'You mean it's going all that way before it stops?'

'Yep.'

'But that's a quarter-of-an-hour ride. I just want to get off round here somewhere.' He looked over the conductor's shoulder. There was nobody else on the bus.

'Next stop Highgate Village,' the conductor said, and demanded money.

It was, Paul decided, all the fault of that goddamned pizza; because, after he'd paid for that and his fare, he was left with twelve pence and the prospect of a long walk home in the rain. He nosed around for a bright side to look on, but the best he could come up with was the certainty that the pizza would've defrosted completely by the time he got back. It was something, but not enough to make up for the rain, or the distance, or the unpleasant discovery that there was a hole in his left shoe.

All in all, he told himself, as he set out on the long march, *I'd have been better off at home in front of the telly*. That reflection reminded him of something he'd been trying not to think about; and at that precise moment, he caught sight of a little pink flyer taped to the inside of a shop window:

Highgate Amateur Operatic Society
presents
The Sorcerer
by
W. S. Gilbert & Sir Arthur Sullivan
Highgate Community Arts Centre
Saturday 17 December 6.30 p.m.
Admission £5.00

In other words, he realised, glancing at his watch, right

now; and (he looked down the road) just over there, in that grey concrete building that looks like an abattoir.

Paul thought about it for a moment. *Fuck off,* he thought. And then he grinned; because, thanks to the frozen pizza and the bus ride, he didn't have any money for a ticket anyway. *Didn't think of that, did you?* he taunted the darkened heavens, as something fluttered out of the window of a passing Mercedes and settled placidly at his feet. It was, of course, a five-pound note.

That shook him, down to his soggy socks. He could feel a pair of virtual cross-hairs closing in on his forehead, as chilling as the defrosted pizza juice trickling down the gap between his collar and his skin. There didn't seem to be any point in fighting it any more. No matter what he tried to do next, whether he ran or hid, the long spectral arm of Gilbert and Sullivan was bound to attach itself to his ear and reel him back, like a fish exhausted by its battle against the angler.

But he still had a tiny scrap of courage left, smeared under the rim of his soul. *No,* he thought; *I am not a light-opera buff. I am a free man. I shall not go gently into the Highgate Community Arts Centre. In fact, I'll cross the road, and—*

The van missed him by inches. He jumped back onto the kerb, trembling, and clutched a lamp post to keep himself upright. *On the other hand,* he thought, *it's not like I'm doing anything this evening, and this Gilbert and Sullivan crap is supposed to be really good.* (At least, he remembered, his aunt Patricia was dead keen on it, though that wasn't the kind of endorsement he usually put much stock in.) *If that's what it takes to get me out of here in one piece, then why not? The worst that can happen is, I'll wake up in the interval with a cricked neck.*

So, like a schoolboy unwillingly to school, he walked slowly towards the concrete façade. There were loads of the pink flyers pinned to the noticeboard outside, and the door was open. He wasn't quite sure what he was going to do with the frozen pizza, but he felt curiously unwilling to relinquish it, even though it was arguably the root cause of all his misfortunes. (And then he thought: *Where in the Bible does it say, 'Don't go buying pizzas you can't afford, or Gilbert and Sullivan will come and get you?'*) He stuffed it under his coat, and advanced into the stream of yellow light leaking through the doorway.

And then someone walked towards him, and by that yellow glow he saw who it was. She saw him a fraction of a second later and quickened her step, trying to get past him before he noticed her, but it was too late for that.

'Hello?' Paul said.

'Hello,' the thin girl replied. 'What are you doing here?'

'I—' Truth is a luxury, rather like pepperoni pizza; those who can afford it insist on nothing else, while the rest of us just have to make do. 'I was visiting my second cousin,' he said. 'But he's out.'

'Oh.' She looked at him. 'Why are you carrying a soggy cardboard box?' she asked.

'It's a pizza,' he replied. 'I brought it along for my cousin.' The lights of a passing car raked her face, and to his amazement he saw that she'd been crying; the puffy red eyes, the tear spoor, distinctive as the silver slime-trail of a slug. 'How about you?' he asked.

'Me?' she said, as if she couldn't think of a more bizarre subject of conversation. 'Oh, I was just—' She stopped, and for the first time looked at him as if he wasn't the back end of a maggot she'd just noticed in her half-eaten apple. A tiny voice in the back of Paul's mind assured him that he was going to regret this, but he refused to listen. 'Nothing,' she said.

Ten doors down lay a pub, and Paul remembered he had a five-pound note in his shirt pocket. 'Come and have a drink,' he said.

No, thanks, she should have said. Instead, she said, 'What about your pizza?'

'What?'

'If it defrosts it'll go all soggy.'

'Actually,' Paul said, 'I'm not hungry.' He stooped down and propped the box carefully against the wall of the Highgate Community Arts Centre, like a druid making an offering of mistletoe. 'Come on,' he said.

And, amazingly, she muttered, 'All right,' and nodded.

The pub was horribly full. They had to turn side-on to get through the crush round the door, and the bar was lost to sight behind the press of flesh. From somewhere out back came the unique collage of strange noises that only a British pub jazz band can make. Paul snarled helplessly; this wasn't at all what he'd had in mind. Then, to his great surprise, he saw an empty table, tucked away in a corner next to the toilet door. He nodded at it, and the thin girl nodded back and headed for it. *Fine*, Paul thought, and started threading his way through to the bar.

All the time he was waiting to get served, and all the weary way back, clutching a pint of Guinness in a straight glass and a small Britvic orange, he was sure she'd be gone by the time he reached the far-flung table. When the shoulders and elbows parted and he saw her still there, picking at her nose with a scrap of shredded Kleenex, he could have shouted for joy. He slid into his seat, put down the Guinness in front of her, and said, 'That's right, isn't it?'

She looked at him. 'Yes,' she said.

'It's what you had in that pub after the interview,' he explained.

'Oh,' she said.

'Well, cheers,' he suggested. He sipped a tiny drop of orange juice, while she nibbled at the froth of her beer. The jazz band made a noise like a circular saw cutting aluminium sheet. A fat man pushed past on his way to the Gents. Once again, Paul had a strong feeling that he was being closely observed by an invisible peanut gallery, who were going to start slow-handclapping unless he got the show on the road. (But what show, and what road? The unseen watchers presumably knew, but he didn't.)

'Fancy bumping into each other like this,' he said. The invisible audience didn't think much of that; neither did the thin girl, and neither did he. He tried again. 'Is this your neck of the woods, then?' he asked.

'No,' she answered, and she'd have been perfectly within her rights to leave it at that; it was a feckless piece of cross-examination, and even the lowliest junior barrister would've laughed in his face. But, quite unexpectedly, she went on, 'Actually, I live in Wimbledon. I came to see my boyfriend in a play.'

The world tightened around Paul's head like a drill-chuck. 'Oh,' he said.

She looked at him, and grinned sadly. 'If you must know,' she said, 'we've just broken up.'

'Oh,' said Paul. 'I'm sorry,' he lied through his teeth.

'That's why I've been crying.'

'Ah, right.'

She sighed, and looked past him, as if he wasn't there. 'I came all this way just to see him in his stupid musical, because he kept on and on at me about it, and then when I got here I thought, What's the point? And so—'

'Just a moment,' Paul interrupted. 'By "musical", do you mean Gilbert and Sullivan?'

She gave him a look you could've skewered kebabs on. 'All right, not musical, operetta. Do you like that stuff?'

'No.'

She nodded very slightly, as if forced to concede he'd given the right answer. 'So I went round backstage and told him,' she said. 'I said, there's just no point in us going on any more, is there? And he said he didn't know what I meant, I said, well, exactly, and that's why it's pretty pointless us just dragging along any longer, because we were both just lying to ourselves, there just wasn't any—'

'Point?'

She nodded. 'And then I gave him back the CD he gave me last Christmas and the pen he'd lent me four months ago when we went to the Earls Court Bike Show, and I walked out.'

'I see,' Paul said. 'So, he's pretty keen on Gilbert and Sullivan, this bloke?'

She scowled at him, then shrugged. 'He never used to be,' she said. 'All he ever used to care about was motorbikes and animal rights and the fight against global warming. Then, quite suddenly, about a month ago, he seemed to go all strange. Like, he started wearing straw hats and blazers and stupid embroidered waistcoats, and he told me he'd joined this amateur operatic thing and he was going to be the star in this stupid opera they were doing. It was like he'd turned into somebody else, just like that, without any warning.'

Paul thought for a moment, though at something of a tangent to what she'd just said. Rather than tell her what was on his mind, however, he said, 'Sounds to me like he's met someone else.'

She sighed. 'That's what I thought,' she said. 'Only I don't think so; like, he was always dead keen for me to go and see him at rehearsals or listen to him saying his stupid lines. I told him to get stuffed, of course, but he went on asking; so I don't think he's got another girl or anything.' She frowned. 'And when I told him we were finished, he looked really surprised, like it was a total shock. If he'd found someone else, he should've been happy for me to break it off, wouldn't you say?'

'I guess so,' Paul replied; and then it struck him, as though he were Sir Isaac Newton and he'd just been hit on the head by a huge, scrummy toffee apple. Yes, until fairly recently she'd had a boyfriend; but the boyfriend was just down the road in the Highgate Community Arts Centre, warbling away like a demented nightingale, while he was in this pub, with her. Furthermore, there was the timing of the thing to be considered. In her darkest hour, when what she most desperately needed was someone to talk to, Destiny had chivvied him up here from Kentish Town and put him in exactly the right place at precisely the right time. Suddenly, it all made sense, apart from the rather bewildering fact that Destiny had felt obliged to disguise herself as two dead purveyors of nineteenth-century popular culture; and if that was what lit Destiny's candle for her, he wasn't about to criticise. Each to his own, he reckoned, and it could've been a whole lot worse. 'I'm really sorry,' he said, with all the sincerity he could muster. 'You must be feeling awful.'

She shrugged. 'A bit,' she said. 'I mean, yes, I did like him, quite a lot at one point, but I always got the feeling that when we were together I wasn't really being me, if you follow me; I mean, I wasn't being the me I wanted to be, I was being the me *he* wanted me to be, or at least the me he thought I wanted to be; and I was trying to want to be the me he thought I wanted to be, for his sake, and neither of us was being ourselves, so we could never really be *us*, in a together sort of a way, and so it was all really pretty pointless, for me and for him. Do you see what I mean?'

'Yes,' Paul lied. 'It must've been pretty miserable for you.'

'And for him, I suppose.'

'I guess. Actually,' he admitted, though he couldn't for the life of him think why, 'I've never broken up with anybody, so I wouldn't really know.'

'Oh,' she said. 'You're in a long-term relationship, then.'

'No.'

She considered that as if it was a complex piece of mental arithmetic. 'You've never had a girlfriend, then.'

'No.'

'Oh.'

'Not,' he added, 'for want of trying. But everyone I ever liked told me to get lost.'

She looked at him over the rim of her glass. She had a foam moustache, which quite suited her. 'Really?'

He shrugged. 'Not that it matters,' he said. 'I'm just

saying, it's better to have loved and lost, and all that stuff.'

'No, it isn't.'

'Isn't it? Well, I expect you're right. Anyway, what I'm trying to say is, I don't really know how bad you're feeling, but I expect it's pretty bad, though I don't suppose you want sympathy either, so I'll just shut up now. That's about it, really.'

'Thanks,' she said. 'Though it's probably just as well. I'm not a very nice person, I'm afraid.'

Oh, for crying out loud, Paul thought. 'You're nicer than Mr Tanner,' he said. 'I bumped into him this afternoon, in Tesco's.'

She opened her eyes wide. 'In Tesco's?'

'Just what I thought,' he replied, 'though really, I don't see why it should seem so odd. I mean, even unmitigated bastards have to shop occasionally.'

She frowned. 'I'd have thought he'd have made his wife do all the shopping,' she said.

'Me too. But apparently not. He had a little list, and he was crossing things off as he went along.'

She very nearly smiled. 'Did he see you?'

Paul nodded. 'I walked straight into him, and he was on to me before I could get away.' *Like you and me just now*, he didn't add. 'He laughed at my pizza,' he said.

'Bastard.'

'I thought so.'

She wrinkled her top lip into a sneer. 'I expect his wife does Delia Smith recipes,' she said. 'Or fancy ready-meals from Marks and Spencer.'

'Actually, they're having rissoles. He told me.'

'Rissoles.'

Paul nodded. 'It only goes to show, there is some

justice in the world, after all. You go around being a right bastard for forty-odd years, sooner or later you're going to get rissoles. Serves him right, I reckon.'

That little crackle of fire, from fingertip to fingertip; actually, nothing as energetic as fire, nothing so showy or conspicuous. But a little warmth, on a cold, wet night – no nightingales in Berkeley Square, just the muffled roar of the jazz band (half of whom appeared to be playing 'Darktown Strutters Ball', while a rival faction were blasting out 'Hello Central, Give Me Doctor Jazz' with every fibre of their being; they were fighting a losing battle and they probably knew it, but nobody could accuse them of being quitters; meanwhile the pub jukebox was pumping out the current number one, in happy cybernetic oblivion). It was odd that such a rowdy, untidy moment could be so perfect, but it was; because this time she did smile, though it was only a flicker, brief and unusual as a shooting star.

'I'd better go,' she said.

Oh, Paul thought, and the perfect moment evaporated like blowtorched snow. 'Well,' he said, 'nice bumping into you. And really, I'm sorry about—'

She shrugged. 'Actually,' she said, 'it's not so bad.' Hesitation; Paul could almost see the roulette wheel going round, with the little white ball skittering about on it. 'See you Monday, then,' she said; and in the back bar, bang on time and clear as a bell, the jazz band launched into 'When The Saints Go Marching In'. It wasn't what she'd said, it was the way she'd said it.

'Right,' he replied, in a voice quiet with awe. 'See you Monday.'

At the door of the pub, he turned right and she turned left. The rain was cold and hard, and he no longer had enough for the bus fare, but that didn't matter, and neither did the hole in his shoe.

(*Stupid*, he thought; because he hadn't established anything, hadn't come away with a signed contract or something he could take to the bank. A slight thaw, maybe, an IOU for a few friendly words or a smile, redeemable at an unspecified future date, written on rice paper in invisible ink. Some people – most people, for all he knew – did this sort of thing every day; made friends, established goodwill, maybe planted the seed of affection, without even trying or knowing they were doing it. Some people, most people, but not him, he thought; in this regard, he'd always been the threadbare Russian peasant watching the fine gentlemen go by in their gilded carriages, knowing that whatever he might get his hands on in this life, it wouldn't be that. But now, who knew? Something very odd was going on, but he didn't mind a bit.)

From Highgate Village to Kentish Town was hardly far enough for savouring such thoughts as these, even with the rain in his eyes and a soggy left sock. Somewhere in the great darkness of London, Mr Tanner was slowly eating his rissoles, the ex-boyfriend was capering and warbling his hour upon the stage (and if his heart was broken – well, it had to be somebody else's turn, sooner or later) and the thin girl was back home, towelling off her wet hair and either explaining or refusing to explain why she was back so early from the theatre. As he fumbled in his pocket for the front-door key, Paul could almost see them, each in a separate window on his mental desktop; never before had he felt such a strong sense of so many things going on at once all around him, from sunrise in Tasmania to sunset in

Tashkent – and the strangest notion that somehow he was in the middle of it all, that everything led to him the way all roads converge on London. Which was crazy; just because a man's hounded across the city by Gilbert and Sullivan right into the arms of the girl of his dreams, it doesn't necessarily follow that he's important. Maybe everybody in the world's allowed one half-hour of super-natural intervention, one statutory wish from a National Health genie to give them their shot at happiness, and the only thing that was at all special about him was that he was one of the one per cent who actually noticed.

Or something like that. He closed the front door behind him and squelched up the stairs. *Cheese on toast*, he thought, *and a cup of black tea. Ah well.*

As Paul stepped out onto the landing, he saw that the door of his bedsit was open. That wasn't wonderfully good, because as it happened he could distinctly remember the click of the bolt as he'd closed it behind him, when he'd left earlier. Not that he had anything at all worth stealing, unless a mad collector of 1980s electronics wanted exactly his model of radio/cassette player to complete his collection, or the Victoria & Albert Museum had heard about his black-and-white portable and sent a snatch squad. Even so—

He pushed the door with his toe and it swung in. The light was on (he remembered turning it off). He counted to ten, added two for luck, and went in.

It wasn't the God-awful mess that caught his eye, because Paul wasn't the tidiest person who ever saved a milk-bottle top, and it'd have taken some time and thought to differentiate between the havoc wrought by the intruder and his normal habitat. It wasn't the absence of key possessions, though on subsequent inspection he discovered that his tin-opener had gone, and also his ironing-board cover, three odd socks and his library book. What he noticed at once as he walked in, and couldn't have helped noticing unless he'd been blind, was the very large block of stone resting halfway between the washbasin and the bed, and the very large, shiny double-handed sword that was stuck in it.

CHAPTER FOUR

On Sunday morning, when Paul woke up, it was still there. *Pity*, he thought.

He'd divided the previous night between tidying up the mess (his own, as well as the intruder's; there was now so little space left in his cramped bedsit, thanks to the Thing, that he couldn't afford the luxury) and staring at It, wondering what the hell it meant and what he was supposed to do about it. He'd fallen asleep looking at it. Now, as he opened his eyes and saw the silhouette of the hilt against the drawn, glowing curtains, he felt more irritation than wonder or fear. *Bloody thing*, he thought; bulky, and sharp, too, as the plaster on his right forefinger testified. Far too heavy for him to move on his own (how had they got it up the stairs, for crying out loud? Something that size, you'd need a fork-lift, scaffolding, winches) and placed exactly where it would cause the maximum disruption and inconvenience.

He swung his legs off the bed and stood up, wondering whether a night's sleep had produced anything resembling a rational explanation. Unfortunately not. Not a practical joke by his friends, not a rare species of fungus that just happened to look like a sword in masonry, not even an unwanted free gift from the Book Club. It hadn't dropped off a passing airliner, because there wasn't a corresponding hole in the roof. He got dressed, gave it one last long stare, and crossed the landing.

First he tried the guitarist next door; then he climbed the stairs and asked the two nurses in the top flat. All of them were unhappy at being disturbed at nine o'clock on Sunday morning, and none of them had been expecting a delivery that might have been left at his place by mistake. Paul went back to his own room, and it was still there. Bloody *persistent* thing.

He draped a shirt over the sword's handle and put the kettle on. His duty as a citizen was to call the police, but he wasn't really minded to do that. Possibly he might have done if he hadn't spent the previous evening being shoved around like a cue ball by Gilbert and Sullivan; but it was all too easy to imagine the line of questions that'd lead to embarrassing disclosures, followed by an uncharitable assessment of his sanity. Also, for all he knew, they'd arrest him for possessing an offensive weapon.

Well, it was offensive, all right; it didn't have eyes, but there were a couple of rivets on the hilt that seemed to follow him all round the room. He'd felt uncomfortable putting on his pyjamas with the bloody thing watching him. The shirt helped, so he added a couple of pullovers and an old, tired woollen scarf. Now at least it looked like a cross between a scarecrow and a charity shop tailor's dummy, except for the fifteen inches of cold, bright steel poking out from under the tail of the shirt. Paul made his cup of tea, and perched on the edge of the bed, frowning.

Then, probably because he was looking at it from a different angle, he saw the lettering on the stone. He nearly spilled his tea; here was something to go on, at least, assuming he could read what it said.

The letters were very small, front and back; he had to kneel down and squint before he could read them.

Whoso draweth this sword from this stone shall be rightful king of all England.

and in smaller letters still, under that—

Please dispose of stone tidily after use.

Well, that torpedoed the stolen-war-memorial theory; it also rang a bell. A Disney film, or some story he'd read in his *Book of Faraway Tales* when he was a kid. King Arthur. Excalibur.

He wished he hadn't seen the letters after all. He tried to look on the bright side; there had to be loads of people who made stuff like this, ornaments and gift ideas for the man who had everything, executive toys for when Newton's Cradle and the little chrome weathervane thing just didn't cut it any more. Had there been any big-budget fantasy films lately? Usually the promotional junk you saw standing in the Odeon foyer was cardboard and styrofoam rather than tempered steel and granite, but perhaps some marketing wizard had decided that it was time for a whole new attitude to pre-launch hype.

Yes; but why here, in his room? Unless they were delivering one to every single household in the country (and even the Harry Potter people wouldn't go that far. Or would they?) it simply didn't add up. He clawed at his scalp until it hurt. This was *silly*.

And then he thought: *Well, why not?*

After all, it was here, it was real, and if it actually worked, he could quite fancy that, even if it did mean putting up with the paparazzi and the corgis. Not that it would, of course, but if it did— Paul pulled off the shirt, the sweater and the scarf, braced his feet wide, gripped the hilt in both hands, and heaved.

At least he had the sense to pack it in before he pulled a muscle or cut himself on the sharp edge. It wasn't going to budge. No reason why it should, since it was clearly in there pretty solid. There didn't appear to be a hidden catch or anything like that, and this was probably a case where even WD-40 wasn't going to be much help. He gave up, put back the clothes and went over to the cupboard for a can of baked beans. It was at this point that he noticed the missing tin-opener.

He was hungry, and the only food in the place was in tins, as comprehensively armoured and inaccessible as a medieval knight. True, the last time he'd ventured out of doors in search of nourishment, strange things had happened to him, but being in a confined space with an overgrown letter-opener gave him a pain. He counted his money. Including the change in his trouser pocket and the small stash of copper in the jam jar on the mantelpiece, but deducting bus fares until pay day, it came to just about enough for a small sliced loaf. He locked the front door behind him, though there didn't seem much point; there was nothing left to steal apart from the sword, and anybody who wanted that could have it, and welcome.

Instinctively he headed for the shop on the corner, only remembering as he stood outside that it had been shut yesterday afternoon. But it was open for business, and Mr Singh was outside, manhandling bales of Sunday newspapers. They exchanged formal greetings, and Paul bought a loaf.

'By the way,' he asked, 'I hope everything's all right. Family well, and everything.'

'Fine,' Mr Singh replied. 'Thank you for asking.'

'That's okay. I just wondered, with you being shut yesterday.'

Mr Singh nodded, and explained that he'd arranged to visit his married sister in Droitwich, and his cousin, who'd been going to mind the store for him, had got held up at the last moment. He apologised for the inconvenience, and Paul said, 'That's all right.'

Instead of going straight home, Paul decided to take his loaf for a walk round the block. There was, he told himself, a perfectly rational explanation after all. Married sisters in Droitwich and unreliable cousins made much more sense in the cold light of morning than Gilbert and Sullivan bearing down on him like a brace of Nazgul. He'd probably also discover, if he could be bothered to investigate, that the through bus from Tesco's, Kentish Town to North Road, Highgate Village was a regular scheduled route that ran every day at that time, and the bus had only been empty on that occasion because the couch-lemmings of England were safely at home, glued to *Cilla's Blind Date*. As for the sudden prevalence of Gilbert and Sullivan; it was probably a centenary or something, which was why they'd suddenly cropped up all over the TV and the amateur stage. *Nothing to see here*, he told himself, *it's all perfectly explainable and normal – except, that is, for the sword and the chunk of rock—*

(An asteroid? A legacy from a distant, eccentric uncle? Maybe he should call the police after all, or at least switch on *Crimewatch* and see if there'd been any break-ins down in the vaults of Buckingham Palace. To suppose, just because he couldn't think of an explanation, that the thing was inexplicable was tantamount to denying Einstein's theory because he hadn't figured it out for himself, on his fingers, from first principles.)

Paul spent the rest of the day watching old films on the box; not the relaxing occupation it should have been, because the lack of space meant he had to crouch forward all the time, and the sword seemed somehow to be buggering up his signal. At some point in mid-afternoon he fell asleep, head lolling forward, in his chair. When he woke up, it was late enough to go to bed.

On Monday morning he woke up early, and there was an unusual spring in his step as he boiled the kettle and toasted a couple of slices of bread. Shaving was awkward, with the hilt of the sword trying to get in his ear as he leaned over the basin, but he managed it without bloodshed. He knew perfectly well why he felt so unusually chirpy. 'See you on Monday,' she'd said. For the first time in his working life, he couldn't wait to get to the office.

He left home ten minutes earlier than usual, and when he reached St Mary Axe at 8.45, he found that the street door was locked. Dilemma. If he knocked, would it earn him brownie points (eager young clerk, anxious to make them a present of fifteen minutes of his life, absolutely free), or would he get a scowl and an unkind word for disturbing them? Assuming, of course, that there was anybody inside to open the door. There were no signs of life; the blinds were drawn at the upper windows, and no electric light was seeping through.

As he stood there, wrestling with the problem, he heard a scuffling noise inside. Then, very slowly, the letter-box flap was pushed outwards. Instinctively he bent down to see what was going on, and through the slit he distinctly saw one round, red, reptilian eye. Then the flap snapped shut, and the scuffling sound was repeated. Also, if he wasn't mistaken, he thought he heard a distant chuckling cackle, which put him in mind of the hyenas at the zoo.

Mr Tanner, he thought; but then Mr Tanner himself appeared, walking rapidly up the street, fumbling in his pocket for keys. The sight of Paul standing outside the door seemed to take him by surprise.

'What are you doing here?' he asked.

'Um,' Paul replied. 'I'm early.'

Mr Tanner grinned; very like a hyena. 'Yes,' he said. 'Doors open at nine sharp. It's ten to.'

'Oh,' said Paul. 'I'm sorry.'

Mr Tanner frowned, as though something was concerning him. 'Well, you'd better come in,' he said. He unlocked the door with three large, old-fashioned keys and pushed past Paul like an elder brother bent on chocolate. 'Wait there,' he said, disappearing through the fire door as Paul stepped inside. 'Confidential post,' he added, but it sounded rather like an afterthought;

the mail was still in the wire basket on the back of the door, and Mr Tanner hadn't touched it. 'All right,' he said, reappearing through the fire door, 'come on in, I'll lock up behind you. You'd better go straight to your office.'

As he headed up the corridor, Paul heard the three locks graunch behind him. *Odd*, he thought; not least the fact that Mr Tanner had failed to make any witty remarks about pepperoni pizza. Not like him to disregard an opportunity like that, unless he was trying to lull Paul into a false sense of security.

When he reached his office, it was in a mess. Not just the usual mess (on his side of the desk, anyway); there were papers strewn all over the floor, and two of the filing-cabinet drawers were open. Paul stood still for a moment; if there'd been a burglary, he shouldn't touch anything. While he was trying to figure out what to do, the door flew open and Mr Wurmtoter (Rick to friends; Paul hadn't seen hide nor hair of him since his first day) burst into the room. His hair was ruffled, and his claw pendant was hanging sideways from his jacket collar.

'Ah,' he said, looking at Paul rather sheepishly. 'Hello there. You're in early.'

Paul nodded. 'Traffic,' he said automatically.

'I see, fine.' Mr Wurmtoter looked at the desk and the filing cabinet, then at Paul, then back at the desk and the floor. 'Bloody cleaners,' he said, with a theatrical click of his tongue. 'They always leave the place looking like a tip at weekends.' He stooped down and grabbed a handful of papers. 'Sorry about this,' he said, slamming the filing-cabinet doors shut with his elbows.

'Oh, that's all right,' Paul replied, wondering what was going on. 'Here, let me—'

Mr Wurmtoter smiled anxiously, and shuffled his feet. Paul got the feeling that he was standing on something Paul wasn't meant to see. 'Actually,' Mr Wurmtoter said, 'would you do me a great favour, nip across to the stationery store and get me three HB pencils? Thanks.'

On his way to the store, Paul met Mr Suslowicz, backing out of the conference room dragging a large hessian sack, and Mr Wells, whom he hadn't seen since his interview, and who tried unsuccessfully to hide a dustpan and a ball of crumpled newspaper behind his back as Paul approached. He hurried past both of them with what he hoped was a respectful nod, got the pencils, filled in the book, and scuttled back to his office. The papers were all stacked neatly on the desk, and Mr Wurmtoter had gone. Paul scratched his head, and decided not to think about it; then he took his coat off and went to hang it on the hook behind the door, but it wasn't there any more. Instead, there were four ragged holes where the screws had been torn out of the wood, and the unmistakable mark of a four-pointed claw.

None of my business, he told himself; then he bent down and looked under the desk, just to make sure there wasn't anything lurking there. Unfortunately, when he sat down, he found he was staring directly at the place where the coat hook had been and the claw-mark now was. The memory of the round, red eye was making itself felt in the back of his mind. In fact, if the circumstances had been different, he'd have been out of the building like a rat up a drainpipe.

Instead, he told himself to calm down, take it easy. After all, people who live in flats full of stone-encased cutlery are in no position to get uptight about other people's unexplained claw-marks. He went across and traced the damaged woodwork with his fingertip. It felt rough and splintery, which went some way towards convincing him it was real.

Are ostriches happy? he wondered. On the one hand, sticking your head in the sand kept you from seeing all sorts of things that could ruin your whole day. On the other hand, it had to be borne in mind that ostrich-feather headgear was part of the traditional costume of many African countries, implying that the technique had its drawbacks.

He sat down again, and the door opened.

'Hello,' she said, and immediately all thoughts of claw-marks, beady red eyes and skittering noises evaporated from his mind. She'd just smiled at him; barely a forty-watt, f5.6-at-a-sixtieth-of-a-second smile, but as far as Paul was concerned, it was like being a kid again and seeing the sunrise for the first time ever. She'd never said hello to him before.

'Hi,' he replied awkwardly, as she slipped off her duffel coat and went to hang it on the hook. 'Oh, by the way,' he added, too late.

She was frowning. 'What's happened to the coat hook?' she said.

'No idea.'

'It's gone. Looks like someone pulled it off.'

'Mphm. And that's not all.' He pointed at the claw-mark, then asked sheepishly, 'Can you see what I mean?'

She nodded. 'What on earth did that? It looks like fingernails or something.'

'You think so?'

'Yes.'

'Wonderful. I mean,' he added quickly, 'it's a bit of a

relief. You see, I was afraid I was imagining it or something.'

'Why would you be doing that?'

'I don't know.' He hesitated. The urge to tell her was almost more than he could bear, but so was the fear of the look there'd be on her face if she didn't believe him. 'Something, I don't know, sort of odd happened the other day, that's all.'

She turned her head towards him. 'How sort of odd?' she asked.

Oh well, he thought. Then he shut his eyes and said, 'When I got back from that pub, where we had that drink—'

'Yes.'

'When I got back,' he repeated, 'there was this thing stuck in my flat. The door was wide open, and someone had been in and dumped, well, a huge lump of rock. With a sword in it. Big, sharp thing, I cut my finger on it, look. And I tried pulling it out, because there was this writing on it, but it wouldn't budge, so I just chucked some old clothes over it so I wouldn't have to look at it. It was still there this morning, when I left.'

She looked at him in silence for two, maybe as much as two and a half seconds; enough time for stalactites to grow from the ceiling down to the floor.

'You too, huh?' she said.

He nodded. *Oh joy*, he thought, *she believed me, she doesn't think I'm—* 'What did you just say?'

'You got one too,' she replied, sitting down and rubbing her nose with her knuckle.

'Too?'

'That's right. One got delivered at our house, late

Saturday evening, just before I got home. As it happens, yesterday was my dad's birthday, so he assumed it was a present for him; he got the delivery men to lug it through onto the patio, between the potted ferns and the water feature. He's absolutely thrilled with it, as a matter of fact.'

'Oh,' said Paul. 'Did yours have writing on it?'

She nodded. 'And yes,' she added, 'I tried, when nobody was looking.'

'Any luck?'

'No.'

'Same here. Hardly surprising, of course. According to my mum, my great-great-grandfather was mayor of Ramsgate some time before the First World War, but that's as close as our family's ever been to royalty. Besides, I don't think I'd want the job anyway, launching ships and being shown round factories all day.'

She nodded. 'It'd have been really embarrassing if I'd managed to pull the stupid thing out,' she said. 'I don't approve of the monarchy. My mum would've been pleased, though. She's really into the royals, she's got books and commemorative china and everything.'

'Lucky escape, then. Have you got any idea what it's all about?'

She thought for a moment. 'No,' she said. 'Still, it's nice to hear you got one too. I thought I must be going mad.'

Paul thought for a moment. 'Who delivered it?' he asked. 'Did your father say?'

She shook her head. 'I didn't like to ask,' she said, 'because of him thinking it was for his birthday, and all I'd got him was a tie, so it was quite handy, really.' She looked back at the door. 'Too far up the door for a dog,' she said, 'unless it's a really big one. How big do Great Danes get?'

'Not that big,' Paul replied. 'I hope,' he added. Then he told her about Mr Wurmtoter, and Mr Suslowicz and the sack, and Mr Wells. 'Oh, and I got here early,' he added, 'and Tanner showed up while I was standing outside the door. It was still locked,' he explained, 'and he didn't seem pleased to see me at all. Made me wait in reception while he went off somewhere.'

She shrugged. 'Maybe he just ate a bad rissole,' she said. 'But the other stuff – what do you think was in that sack?'

'No idea, and I didn't hang around to look. You know,' he added, 'I'd really like to find out exactly what they do around here.'

'You and me both,' she said. 'You aren't tempted to get out, then. Resign, I mean.'

'What, and miss all the fun of finding out the mysterious secret?'

'Yes.'

Paul nodded. 'You bet. I don't like all this weird stuff. On the other hand, I need the job.'

'Same here. If I went home and told them I'd jacked it in, they'd go mad. You know, scenes and melodrama. Give me the weirdness any day.'

Quietly, Paul blessed the thin girl's parents for their attitude; because if she threw in her job, that'd be that, he'd probably never see her again. Mysterious swords and things with claws didn't exactly appeal to him as integral parts of the working environment, but he was damned if he was going to let them come between him and a girl who'd actually smiled at him, twice. 'Looks like we're stuck here, then,' he said cheerfully. 'Oh well.

There's probably a perfectly simple explanation,' he added.

'Really? Such as?'

He shrugged. 'Just because I can't figure it out doesn't mean it's not blindingly obvious.'

'I can't figure it out either.'

'Well,' he conceded, 'maybe it's not that simple. But there's got to be an explanation. We'll probably laugh ourselves silly when we hear what it is.'

Clearly she didn't think so. 'Well,' she said, 'I suppose we'd better get on with some work.'

'I guess,' Paul replied. 'Talking of which, it may just be my imagination, but I think we're getting close to the end of this. I mean, when was the last time Julie showed up with a new batch of this garbage?'

She thought for a moment. 'Just after Friday lunchtime.'

'That's right. When we started, it was coming in at about hourly intervals. It's definitely slowing up.'

'You could be right.' She looked away for a moment. 'Look,' she said, 'I know I'm like hopelessly slow at this. If you could do some of my pile—'

'Sure,' Paul said. He was afraid he'd sounded too eager. 'If you don't mind, I mean. After all, it's a really stupid boring job; the sooner we get it finished, the sooner they'll give us something else that's not quite so boring.'

'Or something worse.'

He shook his head. 'Define worse.'

'You're right. Here,' she went on, shoving a snowdrift of spreadsheets across the desk at him, 'you do this lot, all right?'

He nodded. 'Thanks.'

'What for?'

'Oh, well.' He couldn't say, '*Thanks for not being quite so snotty and horrible, you've no idea how much it means to me.*' 'Well, it helps pass the time,' he said lamely.

By now, he could shuffle and sort the spreadsheets without having to apply his mind at all. Today, that was something of a mixed blessing. Somehow he had the idea that if he thought too hard about her apparent change of attitude and its implications, it could ruin everything; he wanted to white-noise the thoughts out of his mind, but the spreadsheets didn't cut it any more. He finished his pile almost without noticing, and when he looked up, she'd finished too. In fact, she was grinning.

'Beat you,' she said.

'You cheated.'

'Did not.'

'Did.'

Another of those moments was starting to form; but then the door opened and Julie came in. She wasn't carrying any bales of computer paper, Paul noticed, as he cursed her abominable timing.

'You've finished that lot, then,' she said, with no apparent surprise. 'Right, Mr Tanner's got another job he wants you to do for him.'

'Oh, right,' Paul said (and he was thinking, *She knew we'd finished; how did she know that?*). 'What is it?'

'Oh, nothing very exciting,' Julie sighed, sweeping up the sorted piles. 'I'll take these up to Mr Tanner, and then I'll bring it down for you.'

'Right,' Paul said. 'Can I give you a hand?'

'I can manage, thanks,' Julie said, with a hint of disapproval. 'I'll be back in two ticks.'

A tick turned out to be three minutes long. When she came back, she had two large green pocket files, which she placed on the desk and opened. 'Right,' she said. 'This is a whole lot of aerial photographs of some place or other. He wants you to look at them, and if you see anywhere that looks like it might be a bauxite deposit, you're to draw a ring round it in green marker pen. All right?'

'A what?' the girl asked.

'Bauxite deposit. Now there's no rush, just make sure you do a nice, thorough job.'

'But hang on,' Paul said. 'I'm sorry, but I haven't got the faintest idea what a bauxite deposit looks like. In fact, I don't even know what bauxite is.'

Julie sighed. 'Nor me,' she said, and left the room.

Paul and the girl looked at each other for a moment or so.

'Bauxite,' she said.

Paul nodded. 'What the hell is bauxite?' he said.

'Actually,' the girl answered, 'I know about bauxite. It's a naturally occurring mineral mostly used as feed for the manufacture of alumina via a wet chemical caustic leach method commonly known as the Bayer process. Mostly it comes from Australia, though other significant producers include Papua New Guinea and Jamaica. We did a school project,' she explained, 'when I was twelve. I know a lot of stuff like that,' she added, with a hint of sadness.

'Oh,' Paul said. 'Right, we might as well take a look at these pictures. Australia, did you say?'

She nodded. 'And Papua New Guinea and Jamaica.'

'Fine. So we can forget about any bird's-eye views of Southampton, for a start.' He opened the file, and pulled out a sheaf of large black and white prints. They didn't even look particularly like landscapes. 'You know,' he went on, 'this is a bit more like it. Bauxite, I mean. It's, like, something concrete.'

'No, it's not,' the girl told him. 'Concrete is an artificial amalgam of sand and cement, widely used in the construction of—'

'Concrete,' Paul said, 'as opposed to nebulous and wishy-washy. What I mean is, mineral deposits and stuff, that sounds like a proper business. You know, industry, high finance, capitalism.'

'You mean boring.'

Paul nodded. 'Boring and non-weird. I mean, bauxite. It's a whole different kettle of fish from claw-marks and swords in stones, isn't it?'

She wiped her nose on her cuff, and frowned. 'Could be,' she said.

'Bound to be; unless, of course, what the swords are stuck into are bauxite nuggets,' he added. 'It could be a smuggling thing; you know, getting them past Customs disguised as tacky tourist souvenirs.' She was looking underwhelmed. 'You don't think so?'

'No.'

'It's a bit unlikely, I grant you. Still—'

'Let's look at the pictures, shall we?'

Not only did the pictures look quite unlike anything, let alone bits of countryside, they were all practically identical. With a certain degree of imagination, you could just about talk yourself into believing they might represent tracts of featureless desert. 'I can't believe there's anywhere on earth that looks like this,' the girl said.

'That's assuming it is,' Paul said. 'On Earth, I mean.

Could be satellite snaps of the Moon, or some asteroid.'

She shrugged. 'Or someone forgot to take the lens cap off. Anyway, I can't see how we're supposed to tell what's under all that.'

'Agreed. When you did your project, you didn't happen to have anything in it about what the stuff actually looks like, did you?'

'No.'

'Oh.' He chose a print at random, and stared at it for a moment or so. 'Completely hopeless,' he said. 'It's just—'

'We could look it up on the Internet,' the girl interrupted. 'There's bound to be something. Probably pictures of lumps of bauxite. At least we'd know what colour it is, that'd be something.'

'Good idea,' Paul said enthusiastically. 'Hang on, though, we haven't got a computer.'

'No, but there's one in the back of reception that nobody ever uses; you know, on the desk next to the table where they frank the letters. I'll nip down there and see what I can find out, shall I?'

'All right. I'd better stay here, in case Julie comes back. It wouldn't look too good if she found the place empty.'

'Fine. If she asks where I've got to, say I've gone for a pee or something.' She stopped, her hand on the door handle. 'Well anyway,' she said, 'this is better than sorting those stupid bloody printouts.'

Left alone with nothing to do, Paul picked out a couple of prints and gazed at them for a while. Staring at them for very long made his head ache, and he'd just made up his mind not to bother any more, and tell Julie when she came by next that he'd scanned the lot, sorry, no bauxite anywhere, when he felt an odd prickling sensation in his finger, where it was resting on the surface of the photograph. The nearest thing to it that he'd felt before was the uncomfortable burning itch you get in a patch of skin you scalded an hour or so earlier. He took his hand away, and the tingling stopped immediately. At first he assumed it was an allergic reaction to the chemicals that had been used to develop the picture; but that couldn't be right, or it wouldn't have stopped so promptly when he took his hand away. Feeling extremely foolish, he stretched out his finger and, somewhat unwillingly, touched the photo again. Nothing. No tingle, no anything except the smooth, slightly soapy texture of the print.

Coincidence, he thought; *just an itchy finger, and I happened to be touching the picture at the time.* Then he caught sight of the very faint smear his fingertip had left on the surface the first time. A vague memory drifted into his mind of something he'd seen in a TV documentary years ago, something to do with hazel twigs and eccentric old men running about in fields. He touched the fingerprint, and the tingling came back. He took his finger away; the tingling stopped. Touch; tingle. Away; stop. He tried prodding other parts of the photo, but there was no reaction. It was that one place, and no other, but the effect was exactly the same each time.

Surely not, he thought; but he was sure he wasn't imagining the prickly feeling. He tried a couple of different pictures, but none of them affected him at all. Crazy. With a shrug, he opened the desk drawer and scrabbled about until he found a green marker pen. He'd already considered drawing a few green rings at random, just to show willing, and if he was going to do that, well, the fingerprint was as good a place as any. He uncapped the pen and drew a green circle around the smudge. Vaguely he recalled that the nutty old men with hazel twigs called it dowsing or scrying, and the TV show had reckoned there was something to it, so it wasn't that far-fetched. Of course, even if what he was doing really was dowsing (or scrying), there was absolutely no reason to suppose that what he'd located was bauxite; it could just as easily be water, or a buried electricity cable, or a rusty old sardine can, like the ones he'd seen metal-detector freaks fishing out of muddy river banks in the grey light of sunset.

He put the picture to one side and tried a few others, tracing his fingertip over the surface in what he hoped was a methodical grid pattern. He was doing this (and not so much as a twinge, or a single pin or needle) when the thin girl came back in.

'What are you doing?' she said.

He thought about telling her, and decided not to; with so much residual loopiness on every side, he didn't really want to introduce any more of his own making, just in case she decided she'd had enough, and ran screaming from the building. 'Oh, nothing,' he said. 'Just wiping off a bit of dust. How'd you get on with the computer?'

She sat down. 'No luck,' she said. 'Actually, their computers are pretty weird. I mean, they aren't Windows or anything like that, or even Unix or Mac; it's some other system I've never seen before. There isn't even a mouse. To be honest,' she went on, 'I haven't got a clue how it works. I sat there for ages trying to figure it out, but hitting the keys didn't seem to do anything; I thought it'd frozen or something. But then I was sitting there staring at the screen, wondering what to do, and suddenly these menus dropped down, with all the open files and launch browser things on them; and – well, this is going to sound a bit strange, but as soon as I looked at something and thought, *I wonder what that one does*, there it was on the screen, just like—' She stopped abruptly, and Paul guessed she'd been about to use the M word, but shied away from it at the last moment. 'Just like that,' she said. 'Anyhow, once I stopped trying to figure out how it worked and simply got on with it, I didn't have any trouble at all.'

This didn't mean a great deal to Paul, who firmly believed that all computers worked by magic, and not the sort of magic that was safe to have around the house, at that. For all he knew, the system she'd just described was a vintage trilby as far as Silicon Valley was concerned. 'So did you get on the Net?' he asked.

She shook her head. 'I was just about to when Susie the office junior came up behind me and said was I going to be long, because she needed to use the computer. So I left her to it and came back here. Waste of time and effort, really,' she added. 'Though, for what it's worth, someone in this place is a Tolkien geek, because I opened one file by accident and it was all in those funny curly made-up letters the sad people use for writing Elvish – you know, the letters that look like little fronds of broccoli. There were pages of the stuff.'

'Oh,' Paul said. 'You're sure that's what it was? I mean, it wasn't Russian or something.'

'I know what Russian looks like,' she replied with a frown.

'Okay,' Paul said. 'Well, I'm sure you're right. I mean, the people who're into all that stuff do some really weird things, like translating the Bible into Klingon. And it's not like this outfit is staffed entirely by unimpeachably sane people.'

She nodded. 'Why have you drawn a little green circle on this photo?' she asked.

'What? Oh, that one.' He shrugged. 'I thought I'd better do one or two, just to prove we've actually looked at the stupid things. Otherwise they might think we've just shoved them from one side of the desk to the other without bothering.'

She shrugged. 'Fair enough,' she said. 'After all, it can't do any harm to humour them. Actually, I was wondering if this is just something they've dreamed up to try and get rid of us. First they tried to freak us out with the claw-marks, and now they've given us this absolutely ludicrous job to do. It might even explain the swords, come to think of it.'

'Sure,' Paul agreed. 'Only why would they want to do that? They've only just hired us.'

'That's right,' she replied. 'And they've realised they've hired a couple of totally unsuitable people, and they're trying to make us quit. Probably if they fired us out of hand, they'd have to pay us compensation or redundancy or something. But if we just leave of our own accord, it won't cost them any money.'

That came as close to making sense as anything Paul had heard since the first time he'd passed through the front door. 'Bastards,' he said. 'Trying to cheat us like that. And playing games with our heads into the bargain.'

The thin girl nodded cynically. 'Employers,' she said.

'Exactly the sort of thing you'd expect them to do. Well, they can forget that. If they're trying to get rid of me, I'm definitely staying.'

'Great!' Paul said. 'I mean, yes, me too. Can't let them shove us around like that.' He leaned back in his chair, as though this constituted an act of defiance. 'Right,' he said. 'So what do we do now?'

'Well, definitely not look at their stupid photos,' she replied. 'Of all the bloody nerve, thinking we're idiotic enough to be fooled by something like that.'

'I agree,' Paul said. 'So what'll we do instead?'

The thin girl looked round the room. 'I don't know,' she said. 'It's going to get pretty boring just sitting here.'

Paul thought for a moment. 'We could play Battleships,' he said.

She looked at him as though he'd just suggested a spot of bear-baiting. 'Battleships?'

He nodded. 'It's a game,' he said. 'All you need is two bits of paper and two pencils.' He explained the rules. She didn't seem keen.

'Sounds a bit too macho-militaristic to me,' she said, 'blowing up ships and stuff. I happen to think war is barbaric and wrong.'

That seemed to rule out Battleships; and Hangman probably wouldn't go down too well, either. 'Tell you what,' Paul suggested, 'how about Find the Bauxite?'

She looked at him. 'What?'

'It's like Battleships,' he said, 'only – well, we pretend we're two Third World relief agencies, and we've got to locate valuable mineral resources in an undeveloped Third World country before the rich multinational mining cartels get their hands on them and start exploiting them in an ecologically disastrous fashion. Here.'

He went back into the desk drawer and found a pack of tracing paper he'd noticed earlier. He took out two sheets and quickly drew a grid pattern on both of them with a ruler. 'We put the grid over one of these dumb photographs each, and you've got to call out where you think my bauxite mines are, and so on.'

'That's silly.'

'Yes.'

She hesitated for a long time; then, quite suddenly, she smiled. 'All right,' she said. 'And if Julie or anybody comes in, it'll look like we're working, and they won't have an excuse to fire us. Yes, that sounds like it might be fun.' She frowned slightly, then grabbed a photograph from the folder. 'I'll start,' she said.

They marked up their grids in pencil and the thin girl called out the first set of coordinates. Paul checked them by running his finger down the page, and suddenly there it was again; that odd tingling sensation. He pulled his hand away sharply.

'Well?' she said eagerly.

Sure enough, the square she'd called out was one of the ones he'd marked. 'Spot on,' he said. 'You're good at this.'

She nodded. 'Your go,' she said.

Paul drew a blank; and then the girl chose another square. Once again, Paul ran his fingertip down the page; once again, as soon as he touched the square she'd nominated, it was like a mild electric shock. 'Two in a row,' he said. 'You *are* good at this.'

'Don't sound so surprised,' she replied huffily. 'You can't expect to win at everything just because you're a man.'

Next turn he missed again, and she didn't; yet

another burning sensation. Paul flexed his fingers nervously, but didn't say anything. Three turns later the game was over. She'd guessed all his squares without missing once, and he hadn't guessed any of hers. Each time, too, he'd felt the slight shock running up his fingernail out of the photograph.

'Here,' she demanded, 'let me see your grid. If you've been letting me win out of some bloody stupid notion of chivalry—'

He handed it over without a word. She looked at it, and her eyes gleamed; clearly, she enjoyed winning. 'Let's have another game,' she said. 'I like this.'

So they played another game, and another one after that, each time with exactly the same results. After a fourth game (same outcome), they looked at each other.

'That's so weird,' she said.

He hesitated for a moment; then he told her about the electric-shock thing. At first she looked like she hadn't believed him. Then she frowned.

'The stupid thing is,' she said, 'when I'm choosing squares, it's like I just *know*. Sometimes I don't even bother to look, it's like I hear the grid number in my head and repeat it.' A curious look crept onto Paul's face. 'And before you ask,' she added, 'no, I don't do the Lottery or bet on horse races.'

'Maybe you should.'

She shook her head. 'I've never won on anything like that in my life,' she said. 'And I can't bend spoons, either, if that's what you're thinking.' She stopped and frowned. 'How about you?'

'Nothing doing on either score,' Paul said. 'Here, do you think there really might be bauxite under these grid squares?'

She didn't answer; but she handed him the green marker pen. 'Might as well,' she said. 'After all, they're paying us.'

'Yes, but I thought it was all just a scheme—' He shrugged, and reached for the print he'd just been using, and the tracing-paper grid. By the time he'd finished drawing rings on the pictures, it was one o'clock. Lunch.

That reminded him; he had something very difficult, dangerous and momentous to do right now, but in all the excitement it'd slipped his mind. 'You doing anything for lunch?' he asked, as casually as he could, namely not very.

'I've got a cheese sandwich and a bottle of tap water. Why?'

'Well,' he said, 'to be honest with you, I feel like I need a drink.' Which he did, but not because of the electric shocks or the phantom bauxite. 'You coming?'

She frowned. 'I don't drink at lunchtime,' she said.

'Neither do I, generally speaking,' he replied, not mentioning why. 'But let's get out of here, anyway.'

There was a moment. Paul could almost hear the coin rattling as it spun round on its rim.

'All right,' she said.

Choking back the urge to burst out singing 'The Sun Has Got His Hat On', Paul stood up. 'We'd better go now,' he said. 'Before they lock the door.'

'All right.'

So they went to the little Italian sandwich bar on the corner of the next street down the block. As they stood in line at the counter, it occurred to Paul that if he didn't want to have to walk home to Kentish Town that night, the most he could afford was a sugar lump; whereupon the thin girl looked at him and said, 'My treat.'

'Are you—?'

'Sure, yes. What do you want?'

Paul opted for a ham roll and a coffee; the thin girl ordered the same, minus the ham roll. They sat perched on bar stools in a corner. As far as Paul was concerned, it was rather more unreal than the electric shocks, or the claw-mark, or even the sword in the stone. Here he was, he realised, alone in a food establishment with a girl; not just that, but the girl he most wanted to be with. (Talk about coincidences.) Bizarre round eyes peering at him through letter boxes he could more or less take in his stride, but this was unnerving.

'Well,' he said.

'Well what?' She had a spot of cappuccino foam on the tip of her nose; Cartier and Fabergé never designed such an exquisite ornament. He couldn't help thinking that this girl seemed to have an uncanny knack of reading his thoughts; and yet, here she was.

'I don't know,' he said. 'It's all a bit strange, isn't it?'

She waggled her eyebrows very slightly. Suddenly, Paul wished he was in Australia, or somewhere equally far away.

'By the way,' she said abruptly, 'I'm Sophie. It's a horrible name and I hate it.'

'I'm Paul,' Paul replied. 'Pleased to meet you.'

She smiled, just a crack, but enough for a sliver of light to get through.

'I don't like Paul much, either,' he went on. 'My dad says Paul was the name of the doctor who delivered me. Mum's under the impression she named me after Paul McCartney. I've always reckoned Paul must be the word for "idiot" in some language that everybody else knows except me.'

'It's an all-right sort of name,' she said equably. 'In a nothingish sort of way.'

Paul shrugged. 'I'd have preferred John,' he said. 'Or George, or probably even Ringo. What about you?'

'Oh, some great aunt, I think,' she replied. 'There was another girl called Sophie in my class at primary school. I couldn't stand her.'

Paul nodded. 'I was the only Paul in my class,' he said. 'Loads of Tonys and Andys and Chrises, we even had a couple of Julians.'

'It was all Carolines and Emmas where I was. A couple of Pauls. I can't remember much about them.'

'We had one poor kid called Galadriel,' Paul remembered. 'That'd be a horrible thing to do to anybody, let alone your own flesh and blood.'

The thin girl (no, he corrected himself: Sophie) frowned slightly; clearly she hadn't got the reference, but wasn't about to admit it by asking. That seemed to be about as far as names were going to get them. 'So,' Paul said, 'apart from the weirdness, what do you think of it so far?'

'Very boring,' she said. 'I mean, all those stupid print-out things. And I was rubbish at doing them, which made it worse, of course.'

Paul didn't comment on that. 'I take it this isn't exactly your idea of a rich, fulfilling career.'

'No.'

'What is?'

She scowled. 'I don't know,' she said. 'Truth is, I don't really want to do anything much. Oh, I want to do *something*, I just don't know what yet. Obviously,' she went on, 'money doesn't matter, or any of that sort of rubbish. And obviously I want to do something that helps make the world a better place. I thought about social work or becoming a doctor so I could go to Africa, or pottery, or joining a group of travellers, something like that, you know, a statement. But when I got right down to it, there didn't seem to be any point. The fact is, I'm not really very good at anything, and I can't stand doing things I'm bad at. And that only left, well, rubbish sort of jobs. And my mum and dad still think I'm going to get married and have kids, so obviously they're no help. Which is how I ended up here, I suppose.'

Paul grinned. 'Sounds like you're a bit more organised than me, even so. You see, when I was a kid it was nice and simple, there was playtime and then there was other stuff, and you had to eat up all the other stuff before you could have any pudding, if you see what I mean. And that's basically how I've carried on ever since. The only difference is, when I was a kid I always knew what I wanted to play next, there was always some game or some toy or whatever. These days, I sit at home in the evenings watching the garbage on telly. Very boring, but at least it's not work.'

She looked at him. 'So work's always got to be horrible and nasty, then?'

'Not necessarily,' he replied. 'Obviously, some people like it. Actually, of the people I was at school with, I can think of two of them who really like what they're doing – you know, they live for their jobs, like they're seamlessly merged into what they do, to the point where it sort of defines who they are.'

'That doesn't sound so bad,' Sophie objected.

'Not in theory,' Paul said. 'But of those two, one of them's an estate agent, and the other one works in an abattoir.'

Shortly after that, to Paul's great surprise, it was three minutes to two and high time they were getting back to the office. They had to walk quickly, and it'd come on to rain while they'd been in the café. Sophie, he noticed, was capable of moving very fast without showing any signs of it; he found it hard to keep up with her simply by walking along, but breaking into a trot would have made him look ridiculous.

They reached the door just as it swung open. The receptionist (Paul hadn't seen her before; he'd have remembered if he had) smiled at them as they shot past her.

'Have you noticed,' Sophie muttered as they climbed the stairs, 'how there's always someone different on reception?'

Paul nodded. 'But they always say hello like they know who I am,' he said.

On the landing, they ran into Mr Suslowicz. He looked tired and harassed, though he beamed at them both and asked them how they were getting on. Paul replied, 'Oh, fine,' or something like that. Mr Suslowicz asked if either of them had seen the long stapler, but they said they hadn't. He shrugged, grinned and disappeared into the photocopier room.

Julie was waiting for them when they reached their office. She was standing by the desk, looking at the green rings Paul had drawn on the photographs. 'You've been busy,' she said.

Paul wasn't sure what to make of that. 'Is that how they wanted it done?' he asked.

Julie nodded. 'Looks all right as far as I can see,' she said. 'But then, it's not up to me. Anyhow, there's another batch there for you to look at, and when you've done that, Mr Tanner'd like to see you in his room.'

When she'd gone, Paul pulled a face. 'Wonderful,' he said.

'You mustn't let him get to you,' Sophie replied briskly. 'Remember the rissoles.'

Paul shook his head. 'It's all very well saying rissoles,' he said, 'but that bloke gives me the horrors. He reminds me of something.'

She nodded. 'He's the spitting image of the goblin on page seven of my fairy-tale book,' she said. 'The one who ate naughty children. I used to have nightmares.'

'Makes you wonder what was in the rissoles,' Paul said gloomily.

They divided the photos between them and went over them in silence, taking the job seriously; but Paul didn't get any more electric shocks, and Sophie simply stared blankly at each print in turn before adding it to the pile. The green marker pen stayed where it was in the middle of the desk.

'Well,' Sophie said, when they'd done the last one. 'Suppose we'd better go.'

Paul stood up and opened the door; and as he did so, he realised something was different. There were coats behind it, his and hers.

'How did that—?' Sophie began to say. Paul pushed the coats aside, and there under them was a shiny new brass coat hook. Also, he couldn't help noticing that, although there wasn't any wet paint or sign of any other repair activity, the claw-mark had completely disappeared.

CHAPTER FIVE

That night, after a rather gloomy meal of sardines on toast and mousetrap Cheddar, Paul had a strange dream. It was strange because in it he wasn't being chased down long, dark corridors by maths teachers or vulture-headed aunts, he didn't find himself doing the reading at morning assembly wearing only a dunce's cap, he wasn't sitting an A level in classical Sanskrit, and no curly-headed young men in Victorian costume came gatecrashing at the end.

Instead, he was sitting in an office, which for some reason he knew belonged to John Wells, the senior partner he'd never seen. It was huge, with a high, ornate ceiling and a splendid bay window looking out over the rooftops of the City of London; the desk was a football pitch of shimmering figured French walnut, and the Persian rug on which it stood would've paid for a small hospital or five minutes of Julia Roberts's time on the silver screen. One of the paintings on the wall was an unrecorded Vermeer (Paul wouldn't have been able to tell a Vermeer from an optician's chart when he was awake), and the other, a plain canvas with a dab of Prussian blue in one corner and three dried baked beans in the other, was less than a year old and worth twice as much. In a glass case beside the door lay a priceless seventeenth-century Pappenheim rapier, a Gutenberg Bible, a candle in a massive thirteenth-century parcel-gilt candlestick, a rather gaudy silver Victorian handbell, and a plain gold ring. Apart from seven telephones, all different colours, a framed sepia photograph of a man in a top hat and frock coat and a birdcage with its door open, the desktop was bare. Paul was sitting in a large Gothic chair, which he had an idea was made of ivory. In his left hand, he held a cup of lapsang tea.

Cool, he thought. The dream seemed reluctant to let him in on how he came to be there, but he knew that it was his office now, and had been for some time. The only drawback he could see was that the soles of his shoes had at some point been stapled to the floor, which meant he couldn't move his feet.

Across the desk from him was another, much plainer chair, and in it sat a goblin; he knew it was a goblin, because there'd been a picture of one in Sophie's fairy-tale book, and this one was identical in every respect, apart from the fact that it was wearing a grey silk Italian suit and an inappropriate tie. The goblin was holding a spiralbound notebook and a pencil and looking at him expectantly. He was, he realised, in the middle of dictating a letter.

'Right,' Paul said. 'Could you just read that back to me?'

The goblin nodded and recited, in a soft, purring female voice that would've played hell with his libido if it hadn't been filtered through a mouthful of long, yellow teeth: 'Dear sir, we thank you for your letter of the seventeenth inst and note what you say. However, in the circumstances now prevailing we feel that we cannot agree with your analysis of the situation, and must therefore regretfully decline your esteemed offer. We beg to remain, et cetera.'

Buggery, Paul thought; *what's all that about?* 'Fine,' he heard himself say. 'Get that in tonight's post, would you? First class.' The goblin stood up, Paul handed it the teacup, and it left the room, silently closing the door behind it.

Now there was a computer on the desk. He snapped his fingers (Paul couldn't snap his fingers) and the screen filled with figures. He stared at them for a while, then reached out with his forefinger and traced down the columns one by one, until a familiar tingling stopped him. He wrote down some numbers on the notepad that hadn't been there a few seconds earlier, then pressed a buzzer on the side of the desk. The goblin came back.

'Ask Scuffy to pop up and see me,' Paul said. 'Oh, and would you mind nipping down and seeing if those bauxite scans are ready yet. I'll need them for Thursday afternoon's meeting, and Rick'll need a few days to check them out.'

'Right away,' the goblin purred. This time Paul didn't see it go, because he was preoccupied with more figures on the computer screen; he was listening as well as reading, as if they were some kind of musical notation, and the computer was somehow sending the music they represented straight to his brain, without having to bother with passing it in through his ears. Then the door opened and someone came and sat down in the chair. 'You wanted to see me, Jack,' someone said, but he couldn't place the voice, or even tell if it was male or female.

'Have a look at this,' Paul replied, swivelling the VDU round so it faced the other chair. 'Third column, fifth line. What do you make of it?'

Whoever it was didn't reply. Paul had known in advance that he or she wouldn't. He felt extremely tense, as though knowing the coming interview was going to be awkward and painful.

'You know what I think?' he heard himself say. 'Well, of course you do, you aren't stupid, and we both know what I'm talking about. Mostly, I'm just curious to see if you've got anything to say for yourself.'

'Would it make any difference?' the voice asked.

'No,' said Paul, 'except I'd really like to know *why*. It seems such a strange thing to do.'

'To you, maybe. Not to me.'

He sighed, because here came the really nasty bit, the part he'd been dreading. Before he could say anything, however, a door materialised in the opposite wall, between the Vermeer and the modern abstract. He watched it form; first the door frame and lintel appeared as thin grey pencil outlines on the pale silk wallpaper, and then their contours and decorative mouldings were fleshed out with lines of shadow, making them three-dimensional, and then the panels, hinges and round brass handle of the door grew up out of the wall like speeded-up mushrooms. He realised that he was staring and looked away, while keeping the new door under observation through the corner of his eye. It opened, and two very old men in black pinstripes crept in, trying not to make any noise; one of them put his forefinger to his lips and silently mouthed *Hush!* He deliberately didn't look at them as they tiptoed past him and stood behind his chair.

'They're here, aren't they?' said the voice from the other chair.

'What makes you think that?'

'I can feel them hating me. But that's all right. In fact, I'm glad they're here. Say hello to them for me, if you like.'

'Don't be ridiculous.'

'Nothing ridiculous about it at all. You know as well as I do, they can't come back home without him, and we're the only ones who know where he is. You,' the voice added meaningfully, 'and me.'

He had no idea why; but Paul didn't like that at all. 'Are you threatening me?' he said.

The voice laughed. 'Hardly,' it said. 'A threat is a promise of unpleasant action that stands some chance of happening; if I threaten you with something that we both know will never happen, it can't be a proper threat. You aren't stupid either,' the voice went on, enjoying itself. 'You don't want him back any more than I do; and so long as he's away, they can't come through. But that's by the by; it's not a threat, because I'm not going to turn him loose, because you aren't going to do anything that'd make me take such an unfortunate step. Do we understand each other?'

Paul felt angry and slightly sick, but all he said was, 'Yes.'

'Fine,' the voice replied. 'In which case, I'll cut along

and leave you to your bauxite scans. Nice little venture, that. I'm glad you took my advice. What this firm needs is diversification, if it's going to make it through the twenty-first century.'

The voice faded away, until the chair was empty. At once, Paul swung round in his chair, but the two old men and the door they'd come in through weren't there any more. He stood up, then remembered he couldn't move his feet, and sat down again. Then he saw something, and clicked his tongue in annoyance: a long, ragged claw-mark, right in the middle of his beautiful polished desktop. He jabbed petulantly at the buzzer, and the goblin appeared.

'Get rid of this, will you?' he snapped.

The goblin sighed. 'Sorry,' she said, 'but the houses are all gone under the sea, the dancers are all gone under the hill, and the earliest they can manage is Friday. I can cover it up with something in the meanwhile, if you like.'

Paul shook his head. 'No, that's all right,' he muttered irritably. 'Make sure nobody leaves the building, I'm going out for lunch. That rather nice little Uzbek place round the corner—'

'Sorry,' said the goblin sadly, 'but I'm afraid you can't. Would you like me to get you a sandwich or something?'

Paul tried to drag his left foot off the floor, but he couldn't shift it. 'No, thanks,' he snapped. 'I've got a tin of pilchards here somewhere, if only—'

He sat up. His alarm was warbling spitefully. It was a quarter past seven, Tuesday, and he had to get up and go to work. No more than six feet away, the sword in its idiotic stone loomed over him like a drill sergeant. Even the recollection that he'd be seeing Sophie again in an hour and three-quarters didn't do much to cheer him up. And as for the day ahead—

Yesterday afternoon, they'd reported to Mr Tanner's office, as ordered. He'd grinned at them (that, presumably, explained why Paul's dream had been haunted by goblins) and told them he had a little job he wanted them to do. 'Well,' he'd added with a snicker, 'two jobs.' First, there was this stack of spreadsheets; they needed photocopying, and then stapling together ready for Friday afternoon's partners' meeting. After they'd done that, they were to go down to the strongroom in the basement. It was in an awful mess, he'd told them; deeds and securities and documents all out of their files and drawers and boxes jumbled about, and half the stuff listed in the register didn't seem to be there. 'Do a stock-take, make an inventory, get it all sorted out and filed away neatly; and you'd better bring along an old, tatty pullover or something, because it's a bit dusty and dirty down there, not to mention perishing cold, this time of year.'

Paul had an old, tatty pullover, which also happened to be his best, smartest pullover. He hoped Mr Tanner had been exaggerating, but he doubted it. Dust made him sneeze, and the cold gave him headaches. What fun.

Yes, he thought, *but today I'm going to see the girl I love*; and as he dressed and shaved, he wondered what it could possibly be like to see the girl he loved every day of the week, not just Monday to Friday; to see her lying beside him in bed when he woke up, and crunching her breakfast toast, and hanging out underwear to dry on the radiators, and cursing because she was going to be late, and she couldn't find her keys. *What on earth would that be like,* he wondered; and for the life of him he couldn't imagine it. It was more distant and surreal than his dream, or any number of goblin eyes and swords in stones; it belonged to another dimension, a world where things were different, somewhere most people managed to end up, but which he'd never be able to reach. He fished out his pullover from the drawer under the bed, and stuffed it in a plastic carrier.

One explanation for the greatest mystery of all is as follows.

Twenty thousand years ago, before the first walls were built at Jericho and the ancestors of mankind still lived in hut circles, patiently chipping at flints with stubs of reindeer horn, the photocopier manufacturers and the suppliers of office stationery lived at peace with one another, each considering the other's needs and adapting their wares accordingly. But then a great wrong was done by one against the other, so that for ever after, from age to age, each strove to thwart the other's designs; and since then, even though the cause of the feud has long since been forgotten, the hatred between them has grown ingrained, past all reconciliation. This deadly quarrel, more bitter even than the wars of the software lords of the South-West against the Dark Lord of Seattle, accounts for the fact that no standard-format spreadsheet will fit the bed of a standard-format office photocopier, and generations of hapless office juniors, secretaries and trainees have had to do the best they can with scissors, Pritt Sticks and Scotch tape.

'Are these the same ones we sorted into piles,' Paul

speculated, as he nibbled Sellotape with his teeth, 'or is this a different batch of meaningless drivel?'

Sophie shrugged her thin shoulders wearily. 'No idea,' she said. 'Does it matter?'

'No, not really.' They'd spent all morning in the photocopier room, and there was still a heartbreakingly thick wodge left in the folder still to do. 'Bugger,' he added, 'that red light's come on again. Can you remember what we did the last time?'

'That's the paper feed, isn't it?'

'I thought it was the toner.'

He sighed. 'You're probably right. My brain switched off about an hour ago.' Paul pulled open the little plastic panel in the side of the machine and poked about with the stub end of a pencil; it had done the job, either the time before last or the time before that, though he had no idea why. 'All right,' he said, 'try that.'

The machine wheezed into action. The brightly green-shining slider thing got halfway through its stroke, and froze.

'It's eating the paper again,' Sophie growled.

That wasn't good. Once the machine had got its rollers on a sheet of paper, it tended to cling on, like a dog refusing to let go of the stick it's just retrieved, and its grip was far greater than the tensile strength of ninety-gram copy paper. Extracting the tiny pulped slips that stayed behind after a jammed sheet had been yanked out by brute force would have taxed the skill and patience of a brain surgeon.

'There's got to be something you can pull off or unscrew,' Paul said, 'so you can get at the paper feed from the side.'

Sophie looked at him. 'Don't you dare unscrew anything,' she said grimly. 'If you start fiddling with it, that'll be it.'

Harsh words; but fair. Paul knew perfectly well that the elves hadn't blessed him with the knack of taking things to bits and putting them back together again. Even changing the fuse in a plug was a dark and terrible adventure, as far as he was concerned. 'How about bashing it?' he said.

'I don't think that would help.'

'I suppose not,' he sighed. 'Still—'

'There,' she interrupted, holding up a crumpled, blackened but unshredded sheet of paper. 'Got it.'

'Bloody hell. How did you manage that?'

'By going at it nice and steady,' Sophie replied, with more than a hint of smugness, 'instead of trying to fight it to the death.' She shook her head. 'Men,' she said. 'If they can't bash it over the head with a club, they're completely helpless. All right, try it now.'

Paul riffled the paper and put it back in the feed tray, then hit the button. The slider slid back, graunched its gears a couple of times, and froze. Three red lights that hadn't flashed before started flashing.

'Fuck,' Sophie shouted, and she belted the machine's steel flank with her balled fist. The three red lights went out, and the slider purred smoothly into its ordained course. The copied page fed smoothly out the other side, still faintly warm.

'Don't say anything,' Sophie warned him. It sounded like good advice. He took it.

They managed to get a dozen sheets copied before the machine broke down again. This time, however, it was apparent that they were way past the point where nice-and-steady or a shrewdly placed right cross could do any good. Not only were all the red lights flashing at once, two green lights and an amber one they hadn't even known was there were strobing frantically, and the thing was beeping like a small, agonised rodent in a trap. Paul felt that the only humane thing would be to shoot it.

'Having trouble?'

How long Mr Suslowicz had been standing there in the doorway, they didn't know. Sophie jumped as though she'd just been stung by a bee.

'Temperamental beast,' Mr Suslowicz said. 'I keep telling the others we ought to upgrade, get a new one, but they won't hear of it. Mind if I take a look?'

Paul got smartly out of the way, and Mr Suslowicz knelt down beside the machine, like a vet attending to a sick calf. He didn't seem to be doing anything; just kneeling and listening. His head nodded from time to time, and once or twice he clicked his tongue, as if in sympathy. Then he gave the machine a gentle tap – more of a reassuring pat than a thump – and stood up. The beeping stopped, and the lights went out. 'Try it now,' he said.

A perfect copy, unwrinkled, unsmudged, oozed smoothly out from between the rollers.

'What was the problem?' Paul ventured to ask.

Mr Suslowicz shrugged. 'Search me,' he said, 'I don't know the first thing about these gadgets. But it always used to work on an old Datsun I used to have, years ago, so I guessed it might be worth a try. Have either of you two seen the long stapler?'

Paul nodded. 'Actually, we were going to use it for putting these together, after we've finished copying.'

'That's all right,' Mr Suslowicz said. 'I only want it for a moment.'

Paul nodded. 'It's just there,' he said, 'on the table, next to the—' He frowned. 'It was there a minute ago,' he said.

Mr Suslowicz grinned. 'Elusive little tinker, isn't it?' he said. 'Not to worry. If I manage to track it down, I'll drop it back to you here after I've finished with it. OK?'

After he'd gone, and the machine had churned out a dozen or so faultless copies, Sophie said, 'That was just like in that film, with Robert Redford.'

'What film?'

'Where he's this man who can talk to horses,' she replied. 'It was like he was listening to what it was saying.'

'Robert Redford?'

'No, him; Mr Suslowicz. It was like the machine was telling him what was wrong with it. Don't gawp at me like that,' she added. 'I know it sounds nutty, but that's what he reminded me of.'

Paul shrugged. 'Talking to horses is one thing,' he said, 'but you'd need to be able to sweet-talk an Army mule to get any joy out of this heap of junk. I don't need to listen to it to know what it's thinking. It doesn't like me, simple as that.'

Whatever it was Mr Suslowicz had done, it seemed to have worked. Apart from one torn page (for old time's sake, Paul assumed) the device polished off the rest of the copying without a hitch. That just left them with the relatively straightforward job of cutting and sticky-taping the rest of the copies up together, collating them and stapling them into bundles.

'We need that long stapler,' Sophie pointed out.

Paul nodded. 'I'll go and see if I can find it,' he said,

with all the enthusiasm of Captain Oates taking a stroll through the permafrost.

To his surprise, he didn't have far to look. He'd decided to make a detour by way of the coffee room; and when he opened the cupboard where the sugar lived, there it was.

'How did it get in there?' Sophie asked, when he'd told her about his mission.

'Oh, you know what it's like,' he replied. 'You put something down in this place, next minute it's gone and it doesn't turn up for weeks. Probably a spatio-temporal anomaly or a vergence in the Force.'

'Or people taking stuff and not putting it back when they've finished with it,' Sophie said disapprovingly.

'Possibly,' Paul replied sceptically, 'but maybe a trifle far-fetched. Sod, it's out of staples.'

He refilled it from a box on the shelf. It was a cumbersome thing, ancient and grouchy, with a spring that appeared to have a distinct appetite for human flesh. He handled it warily, and got away with nothing worse than a slight graze. 'It's five to one,' he observed. 'We might as well leave the sorting and stapling till after lunch.'

It was all in the way he said it, and he hadn't intended for it to come out that way, but there was no mistaking the assumption; namely, that they were going to go out of the office and have lunch together, like they'd done the day before. It was another moment.

'All right,' Sophie said, after a brief hesitation.

(*Simple as that*, Paul thought. *Maybe that's how it happens, for everybody else.*)

They went, by mutual unspoken agreement, to the same sandwich bar. As they stood in the queue, Paul did a spot of mental arithmetic, figuring out how long it'd take him to walk home from the office to Kentish Town for the next week, and said, 'What're you having?'

'That's all right,' she said.

'No, but you paid for me yesterday.'

She looked at him. 'You haven't got any money,' she said.

He ought to have shrunk by six inches or so, but he didn't. 'True,' he admitted.

'Well, then.'

He didn't know what to say. 'That's very—'

'Yes. Coffee and a ham roll, wasn't it?'

Paul nodded. Some explanation, he felt, was necessary; or at least some assurance that he wasn't just a fortune-hunting gigolo, battening on to her as a source of free carbohydrates and nothing more. But he knew he wasn't capable of putting stuff like that into words without making things a whole lot worse, so for once he did the sensible thing and gave up. 'Thanks,' he said.

'That's all right.'

In a way, it felt as though all his adult life – ever since he'd realised that girls weren't irrelevant alien creatures who only cared about inane trifles like hair-toggles and glittery nail varnish (instead of vitally important things, such as making balsa-wood aeroplanes and painting 1/72 scale model soldiers) but were in fact beautiful, terrifying alien creatures who never seemed to notice he was there – all his life, he'd been pulling and heaving at a door that led into an enchanted garden, and quite suddenly he'd noticed that in fact it opened inwards and all he had to do was push gently with the tips of his fingers. It would have been nice, he couldn't help thinking, if someone had told him about this, but maybe that was what Darwin had in mind when he talked about natural selection. After all, Paul reasoned, you wouldn't want idiots like him splashing about in the shallow end of the gene pool, with their inflatable armbands and polystyrene floats.

That said, he hadn't got a clue what he was supposed to do next. Presumably at some point he was going to have to say something toe-curlingly embarrassing, and if that went okay there'd be kissing and, well, stuff like that. Obviously he was all for that, just as he'd always really fancied owning a big yacht and sailing it singlehanded to New Zealand. Now that he was at least part of the way along, he had the unpleasant feeling that his yacht was an open boat, and he was adrift in it in the middle of the Pacific Ocean. On the other hand, he assured himself – after all, it couldn't be too difficult, could it? He considered his relatives; Uncle Trevor and Cousin Darren and Cousin Lorna's husband Eric, men with the personal charm of dustbins and just enough intelligence between the three of them to power a traffic light, and yet they'd all contrived to attract, woo, bed and marry females, often not in that order. If they could do it, so could a lawnmower or an answering machine or a tin-opener or a small rock; and so, by implication, could he. In theory.

'You've gone quiet,' Sophie said.

Paul looked up, startled. 'Sorry,' he said, 'I was miles away.' She was frowning at him slightly, and he remembered those occasions on which she'd appeared to have read his mind. He guessed this wasn't one of them, because she hadn't thrown the ham roll at him. 'I was just thinking,' he said, 'about those spreadsheets.'

'Oh.' Maybe there was a tiny spark of disappointment in her voice. 'What about them?'

'Well.' *Absolutely; what about them?* 'That theory of yours, about them trying to get rid of us. What we've been doing this morning seems very like what you were saying; you know, giving us horrible, pointless jobs to do so that we'll leave, and they won't have to fire us.'

She shrugged. 'I'm not so sure about that any more,' she said. 'Like, now I come to think of it, it's just the sort of thing I've seen people doing in my dad's office. I mean, someone's got to do it, and the partners aren't going to muck about with scissors and Sellotape.'

Paul scented a possible change of subject, and pounced on it gladly. 'What does your dad do, then?' he asked.

'Oh, he's an accountant,' she sighed. 'It's a family business, him and Uncle Joe and Uncle Steve. He really wanted me to go into it, but I told him, no way.' She made it sound like her father had been nagging away at her for years to join him in sailing down Niagara Falls in a barrel. Exactly why sorting spreadsheets and copying them for J. W. Wells was so much better than doing pretty much the same sort of thing for her father and uncles he wasn't quite sure, but no doubt there was a reason. 'How about you?' she went on, with a certain degree of effort. 'What does your father do?'

'He used to be something to do with double glazing,' Paul replied. 'But he retired early, and he and mum moved to Florida.'

She nodded. 'You didn't fancy going with them?'

'I wasn't asked.'

'Oh.' She frowned. 'My sister Fleur – she's five years older than me; she works for a bank, and they sent her to New York for a year. She really liked it over there.'

'Mum and Dad say it's great there,' he said. 'Nice hot weather, and the people are very friendly. I'd like to go and visit them,' he added, 'some day, when I've saved up.'

'Fleur's in Borneo at the moment,' she said. 'After that, it'll probably be either Tokyo or Chile. Travelling around is one of the things she likes most about her job.'

Paul decided he couldn't care less about her sister Fleur. 'Sounds pretty interesting,' he said.

'Oh, most of the time it's just sitting behind a desk, talking on the phone,' Sophie replied. 'And I don't think she's ever got time to go out and see things or stuff like that. Still, I guess it must be nice to know that you're in the same country as all the scenery and fascinating stuff, even if you never get around to doing anything about it before it's time to come home. It's like me,' she added, with a faint wry grin. 'A cousin of mine came up from the country to stay for a while, and she went off to see the Tower and St Paul's and the Planetarium and the London Eye and all that sort of thing, and a week later she'd done it all and went back to Norwich. I've lived here since I was three and never been to any of them. I suppose I might get around to it some day. But it just goes to show; you can be surrounded on all sides by loads of amazing stuff and never really know it was there.'

He had the feeling that she was telling him something, but he couldn't make out what it was. 'I went to the Planetarium once,' he said, 'with a school party. Can't say I liked it much. You had to lean right back in your seat to see what was going on, and I hurt my neck.'

There wasn't much anybody could say about that,

and Sophie duly didn't say it. Paul had the feeling that things weren't going well. This was supposed to be the stage where you got talking about things – family, childhood experiences, all that stuff – and lost track of the time, and eventually the waiters came and threw you out because they wanted to tidy up and go home. He was sure that was how it was supposed to be, and presumably Uncle Trevor and Cousin-in-law Eric had been here and done this and got a passing grade at the very least, good enough to get them through into the next round. He tried to think of a perceptive observation about Life, but nothing occurred to him.

'Eat your ham roll,' she said.

'What?'

'Your ham roll,' she said. 'You haven't touched it.'

'Oh, right.' He wasn't the least bit hungry; also, he had no illusions about what sort of spectacle he presented when consuming food. In fact, he'd always been deeply puzzled as to why so many dates, assignations and encounters are traditionally structured around meals; because by no stretch of the imagination is eating an attractive spectacle, and even golden lads and lasses tend to sound like hotel plumbing when drinking soup. He nibbled self-consciously at the rock-hard roll, and was painfully aware of the crumbs that snowed down his shirt-front.

'Did you bring an old pullover?' she asked.

He nodded gratefully. 'I don't know if he actually meant that seriously or if it was just him being funny,' he said, 'but I thought I'd better not take any chances. What about you?'

Her eyebrows tightened a little. 'That's why I'm wearing this horrible scruffy old suit I bought for six pounds in an Oxfam shop,' she replied. 'Not that it bothers me at all, I hate having to wear all these stupid work clothes. My mum had to go out and get them for me, I haven't got a clue about all that stuff. Might as well be back at school, wearing uniform.'

Paul nodded. In the wild, he wore interchangeable jeans and anything he happened to find in the T-shirt drawer that passed the sniff test. Dressing up in suits struck him as a bizarre leftover from a previous century, while doing laundry and ironing shirts had come as a very nasty shock, as if he'd gone to the doctors and been prescribed a course of leeches.

'I'm still not sure exactly what it is we're meant to be doing,' he said. 'For one thing, what do they need a strongroom *for*? I thought that was just banks.'

She shook her head. 'Lawyers and accountants too,' she said. 'My dad's office has got one. Well, they call it a strongroom; it's actually a converted toilet with a Yale lock on the door. It's where they keep people's share certificates and bonds and stuff.'

He thought for a moment. 'Maybe that's what J. W. Wells and Co. does,' he speculated. 'Maybe they're just accountants, after all.'

'Don't think so,' she replied. 'I mean, I'm not an expert or anything, but it doesn't strike me as much like my dad's place. I think they're either stockbrokers or they do import-export. Or commodities,' she added, 'whatever that involves. I think they buy up loads of stuff from one lot of companies and sell it to another lot of companies for more than they paid for it.'

'The bauxite, you mean?'

'Yes, though really that wouldn't fit at all, would it? Maybe they're into mineral rights as well as minerals.'

Paul frowned. He wasn't sure minerals had rights, though he couldn't see offhand why they shouldn't. He couldn't remember having seen mineral rights activists picketing steelworks on the telly, or being stopped in the street and asked to sign petitions about it, but maybe the movement was still in its infancy.

At five to two they went back to the office. The long stapler had, of course, vanished.

'My turn,' Sophie said. 'I'll go and look for it, and you can get on with the collating. All right?'

He'd been working away steadily for something like a quarter of an hour, his mind very much on other matters, when the door opened and someone he recognised drifted in; a tall, thin bald man, with clumps of white hair over his ears that reminded Paul of snow on the mountains in summer.

'Mr Carpenter,' he said. He sounded annoyed, and nervous. 'I don't think we've met since you came for interview. I am Theodorus Van Spee.' He held out a long-fingered, liver-spotted hand with bitten fingernails. On its middle finger was a thin silver ring.

'Hello,' Paul said awkwardly. Mr Van Spee (only he liked to be called Professor, Paul remembered) might look frail, but he had a grip like a scrapyard car-crusher. 'Um, what can I do for you?'

The Professor seemed to be looking over Paul's shoulder. 'Oh, there's nothing at the moment,' he said, in an accent that Paul reckoned was probably Dutch. 'I was passing and thought I might as well introduce myself. Your colleague, Ms Pettingell; she's not here—'

'She's looking for something,' Paul said. 'The stapler. We need it to staple up the—' He stopped babbling. 'She'll be back any minute,' he said. 'Did you want—?'

The Professor's thin lips curved very slightly into the ghost of a smile. 'No, there is nothing important, I simply wished to introduce myself to her also, not having encountered her since the interview. So,' he went on, looking Paul straight in the eye and reminding him uncomfortably of several headmasters he'd known in his youth, 'how are you settling in with us? Smoothly, I hope.'

For some reason, Paul felt a sudden urge to tell this strange man the truth; the whole truth, including the bits about swords in stones, frozen pizzas, claw-marks and Gilbert and Sullivan. In fact, it was only his instinctive terror of tall, thin authority figures that stopped him. 'Oh, fine,' he said.

'Excellent,' said Professor Van Spee, frowning slightly. 'No doubt to begin with everything seems a little strange, but that will quickly pass, I'm sure.' Once again he was staring over Paul's shoulder at the blank wall, as if he was expecting to see something there. 'And no doubt it is easier, the two of you starting at the same time. Always it's easier when there are two, easier to learn the ropes together. It was so when I first started here. I began as a clerk, you see, just as you are now, but that was many years ago.'

Paul wanted to turn round and see just what was so fascinating about the wall, but he didn't. 'Yes,' he said, 'it's a great help.'

The Professor nodded absently. 'And Ms Pettingell is a charming young lady,' he said. 'She has a birthmark just above her navel, and her pet rabbit was called Lucky, though he died nine years ago. You should not buy her flowers, that would be most inappropriate, but she has a weakness for Cadbury's Creme Eggs, although she is reluctant to admit it. She has no great interest in music, but you would do well to familiarise yourself with the works of Dickens, Turgenev and Dick Francis, all of which,' he added with a slight frown, 'she reads for pleasure. Some knowledge of contemporary art would stand you in good stead, but guard against any temptation to show off; better to avoid the topic completely. Cars bore her; she affects an enthusiasm for motorcycles, but this is only to annoy her parents, in reality she does not care for them. Coca-Cola and fizzy orange she detests, though she will eat hamburgers and pizza if she is hungry; regularity of meals matters more to her than quantity or indeed quality, and often when she is surly and short-tempered, it is only because she needs something to eat. She drinks beer ostentatiously so as to appear unfeminine, but does not like the taste. You should avoid any mention of Birmingham, lest it awaken old memories that may distress her. Rats don't trouble her; snakes and spiders do. She is firmly convinced that she is not beautiful; to assure her otherwise would merely antagonise her. Compliments should therefore concern her intelligence, resourcefulness and generosity of spirit – and should you choose to offer words of praise in respect of any of these, your remarks would be far from empty flattery.' A small gnat whirred past the Professor's left ear; he snapped it out of the air between thumb and middle finger without looking at it. 'Where money is concerned she is prudent and scrupulous, almost to a fault; be sure to repay what you borrow, though avoiding undue haste, and do not offer to pay for her in restaurants or places of entertainment. If you dine out together, take pains to remember what you ordered, so that the bill may be apportioned quickly and without dispute. She attended dancing lessons until she was twelve; she claims to despise dancing but secretly and guiltily enjoys it very much – you might care to seek basic instruction yourself, as she would not look kindly on your present shortcomings in this regard, should dancing occur. As you have yourself perceived, she can to a certain extent discern from your face what you are thinking; do not try and mask your thoughts, however, rather give her credit for a laudable measure of understanding and compassion. When you buy her a present, I would suggest either a short wool scarf or a good-quality pocket calculator. Above all, do not seek to impress, or pretend to be other than you are, and under no circumstances should you kiss her shortly after you have consumed peppermint.' He coughed, reached in his jacket pocket for a handkerchief, and carefully dabbed at the tip of his nose. 'Excuse me,' he said, 'I am due in a meeting with my partners. The fifth page from the bottom in that pile is out of sequence; please correct the error before they are stapled together.' His brow clouded, as though there was something he'd forgotten; then it relaxed. 'Have a nice day,' he said, and left the room.

Several seconds passed before Paul woke up out of the trance he'd been in since the Professor started talking. As soon as he came round, he checked the fifth page from the bottom. He stared at it for a while, then put it away where it belonged, third from the top.

'Finished?' He hadn't noticed her come back, and nearly jumped out of his skin.

'Almost,' he said.

'I found it,' Sophie said, waving the stapler triumphantly. 'God only knows how it ended up in the broom cupboard.' She stopped, and looked at the piles of copied spreadsheets. 'Haven't you got any further than that?' she said. 'You aren't even halfway through.'

'Sorry,' he said awkwardly. 'Only that old thin bloke with the little beard, Professor—' He paused, pretending he'd forgotten the name.

'Professor Van Spee?'

He nodded. 'That's him. Anyhow, he stopped by. Only just left, in fact.' He breathed in and looked away. 'Do you know him from somewhere else?'

'Me?' She shook her head. 'Never set eyes on him before the interview. Why?'

'Oh, nothing. He's not a friend of the family, anything like that?'

'God, no. Why do you ask?'

Paul shook his head. 'Nothing. That is, he said something that I thought might mean he knew you from somewhere, but it must just've been me getting hold of the wrong end of the stick.'

'Oh.' She shrugged. 'So what did you talk about?'

'The usual stuff,' Paul croaked. 'How are you settling in, I expect it's all very confusing to start with, that kind of thing.'

If she noticed anything odd about his tone of voice, she didn't comment on it. They finished the collating together, sorted the result into bundles and stapled them up. 'Right,' Sophie said, 'I'll take them up to Julie's office, and I'll meet you down in the strongroom. I'll take the stapler too,' she added. 'I expect someone'll come looking for it sooner or later, and then at least someone'll know where it is.'

Paul went back to his office and picked up his sweater. He didn't put it on, in case Mr Tanner had been kidding after all, and somebody objected to him wearing tatty old clothes in the office. On the way down to the basement, he tried very hard not to think about what Van Spee had told him, and failed miserably. The weirdness of it all certainly wasn't lost on him, but most of his thoughts led towards *Does that mean she—?* and veered hastily away. As he passed the waste-paper basket in reception, he took a packet of extra-strong mints out of his jacket pocket and dumped them.

It was probably just as well that he was somewhat preoccupied, or his first sight of the strongroom would have unnerved him completely. It struck him as a cross between an old-fashioned library and a maximum-security prison, with a touch of the mines of Moria thrown in for good measure. Mr Tanner hadn't been fooling with him after all. The dust was deep on the shelves, and he devoutly hoped he wouldn't come across the spiders who'd spun the enormous cobwebs that sagged from the corners of the room like the sails of becalmed galleons. The air was thick enough to grease axles with. About fifty years ago, someone had started painting the ceiling battleship grey, but had given up halfway. Paul could understand why.

Sophie wasn't impressed, either. She arrived bearing two notebooks and two pencils, looked round and said, 'God, what a dump.'

'It's pretty horrible,' Paul agreed. 'Did you manage to figure out exactly what we're supposed to be doing here? It all sounded a bit vague to me.'

'Inventory,' Sophie replied, looking about her with distaste. 'He wants a complete list of everything they've got in here and where it is; plus we've got to put it all in order, so they can find it again.'

'Bloody hell,' Paul said. It was a large room, bigger by half again than his bedsit, and the shelves that lined all four walls were rammed with black tin boxes, files, folders, ledgers and large, fat beige envelopes. 'It'll take for ever.'

She shrugged. 'That's what we've got to do,' she said. 'I vote we take it in turns; one of us looks in the boxes and files and stuff and calls out what's in there, the other one writes it down.' She paused, frowning. 'And we've got to figure out some way of archiving it all. What we need are lots of yellow stickies, so we can write a number on each one.'

Paul nodded dumbly, still stunned by the magnitude of the task. 'Yellow stickies,' he repeated. 'Where do we get them from?'

'Julie, I suppose,' Sophie replied, 'like everything in this place apart from breathing air. I'll go and see to that. You look like you need to sit down already.'

While she was away, Paul wandered round the room, picking things off the shelves and putting them back in a despairing manner. Among the things he picked up was a tall, wide book handsomely bound in red leather. There wasn't anything written on the spine, but when he opened it, he realised that it was a list – an inventory – of the things in the room. Unfortunately, it was very old and presumably out of date; it was written in spidery copperplate, and the ink had turned brown. As far as he was any judge of such things, it had to be at least seventy years old, and possibly more. Still, he thought, it was bound to come in handy (though he wasn't quite sure how).

'Yellow stickies,' Sophie said triumphantly, coming in with a shoebox-sized carton in her hands. 'Millions of them, and I didn't even have to sign for them. I asked, and she just handed them over without a word.'

'Look at this,' Paul interrupted, and he showed her the book. She didn't seem impressed.

'Don't see how that's going to help,' she said. 'I mean, chances are there's been lots of new stuff put in here since this was done, and loads of stuff taken out as well.' She turned the pages slowly. 'Still,' she went on, 'it gives us an idea of what we're supposed to do. Look, there's columns for when each thing was deposited, where it was put, and each time they've been taken out, who took them, and when they were brought back. Seems a fairly sensible way of going about it,' she said generously. 'Look at some of these dates, though. They go back ever such a long way.'

Paul looked. On the two pages open in front of him, the earliest date was 1857 and the most recent was 1941. One or two items had been crossed neatly through, to show that they'd been handed back to their owners or otherwise disposed of. Not many, though.

'And that's not all,' he went on. 'Over in that corner there, there's a stack of great big trunks, like old-fashioned luggage; and cases, like musical instruments live in, and some tea chests, all sorts of things.'

'Well,' Sophie replied, turning the pages of the book, 'at least it might give us some idea of what they do here.'

Paul nodded. 'I guess so.' He'd just noticed a glass case of stuffed birds on a high shelf, and next to it a mechanic's blue-painted toolbox. 'Though it looks to me like this is the place people dump their old junk,' he said. 'Though not lately,' he added thoughtfully.

'Doesn't look like much of this stuff was put here recently. I mean, look at these envelopes full of papers.'

Sophie looked up. 'They're old envelopes,' she said.

Paul grinned. 'Did you ever collect stamps? No, me neither. But these have got to be pretty old, they've got King George and King Edward on them, and Queen Victoria. Worth a bob or two, for all I know. I wonder if anybody'd miss them?'

Sophie scowled at him. 'Don't you dare,' she said. He shrugged.

'Well, anyway,' he said, 'there's not many with Queen Elizabeth on, and even those are pretty ancient. When did she come to the throne? Nineteen fifty-something? In fact,' he added quietly, 'if there's anything here that's more recent than fifty years old, I haven't spotted it yet. Maybe that old book'll be more use than we thought.'

'I don't think so,' Sophie answered. 'We've still got to start from scratch, that's all there is to it.' She closed the book with a snap and put it on a shelf. 'Come on,' she said. 'We'll start here, by the door, and work our way round. You can do the writing-down to start with, while I call out. Okay?'

Paul nodded, and picked up a notebook and pencil, while Sophie broke open the box of yellow stickies. 'I'll start at one,' she said. 'All right, here goes.' She took out the envelope at the front of the bottom shelf nearest the door, and opened it. 'Item one,' she said. 'Envelope of papers – no, don't bother writing that down. Share certificates,' she announced, 'let's see, seven, eight, nine hundred shares in Whitlow's Bank, in the name of G. L. Mayer, whoever he is. Was,' she corrected herself. 'This certificate's dated 1901, so presumably he's dead by now. Funny,' she added. 'You're supposed to write and tell the company when a shareholder dies, and they send you a new certificate. I know that from helping out in Dad's office. It makes all sorts of problems with tax and stuff if you don't.'

Paul wrinkled his nose. 'Maybe they're just old ones that never got chucked away,' he said.

'Well, someone ought to write and find out,' she said. 'Whitlow's are still in business, after all, these might be worth lots of money. Anyhow, not our problem.' She put the envelope back. 'Item two—'

'Hang on,' Paul said. 'Pencil's broken.'

'Just as well I brought two, then,' Sophie sighed. 'You're probably pressing too hard. Ready?'

Paul nodded. 'Item two,' he said.

'All right. Item two.' She opened the envelope and pulled out a ragged brown sheet of paper. 'Looks like a map,' she said.

Paul grinned. 'Don't tell me,' he said. 'Pirate treasure, X marks the spot.'

'Not pirate treasure,' Sophie said quietly, 'but you're not far off. King Solomon's mines.'

Paul looked up. 'You what?'

'That's what it says here. "Map of King Solomon's mines", in funny squiggly handwriting. Looks like it was drawn with a bit of old stick, or something. Smells horrible,' she added. 'Anyhow, there isn't a name or anything. Hold on,' she said, 'maybe if we look in that book of yours it'll be in there.'

'Could be. How'd that help?'

Sophie looked at him impatiently. 'Because it might say who this belongs to, or what it is. If we just put down *Map of King Solomon's mines*, Mr Tanner might think we're trying to be funny. And I really don't want to go through this lot and then get sent down here to do it all again properly.'

Paul pulled a face. 'You're right,' he said; then he remembered what the professor had told him. 'That's very good thinking,' he said. 'Just as well you thought of that, or we could've been in real trouble.'

She looked at him oddly. 'Yes, well,' she said. 'Now, where's it got to? Right, here we are. Is there anything written on the envelope? According to this, there should be a number or something.'

Paul checked. 'Yes,' he said, 'here you go. A-slash-five-seven-two. Does that help?'

'Hang on.' Sophie riffled through the book. 'Got it, yes. A572, treasure map—'

'Bloody hell.'

'Treasure map,' she repeated, 'property of Sir Henry Curtis, deposited 1878. Taken out – can't read the date, eighteen-something, and there's another date for when it was put back, can't make that out either. Anyway, you can put down, map, property of Sir Henry Curtis. How does that sound?'

'Absolutely fine,' Paul said, with a trifle more enthusiasm than the suggestion warranted. He remembered other parts of the Professor's lecture, and added, 'Yup, that ought to do, I guess.'

'So glad you approve,' Sophie said. 'Item three – you ready, or am I going too fast for you?'

'No, that's fine. Item three.'

Item three turned out to be a thick bundle of letters bound up in blue ribbon, all addressed to the Hon. A. Pointdexter Esq., Ploverleigh, Hants. Sophie didn't open them. Item four was a small cardboard box containing a little glass jar with some green powder in it. Fortunately, there was a label on it, with a number, and with the help of the book they were able to record it as *Chemical sample, Dr A. Jekyll, Harley Street, London.* Item five wasn't in the red book, so they had to do the best they could; it went in their notebook as *Scrap of paper in unidentified language.*

'Fat lot of good that'll do anybody,' Sophie muttered. 'Still. What's this? Right, item six. Another one without a number on it. Fuck.'

Paul looked up. 'What?' he asked.

'Well,' Sophie said, in a very small voice, 'if it's what I think it is – here, you have a look.'

Paul looked at it over her shoulder. 'It's a manuscript,' he said. 'Handwritten, can't read the— Hold on, it's not even in English.'

'No,' Sophie said, 'that's French. "Le jardin du diable", the devil's garden, "un roman de Marcel Proust".' She scowled. 'Proust didn't write a novel called *The Devil's Garden*, at least, not that I heard of.'

'Who's Marcel Proust?'

Sophie clicked her tongue. 'Just write it down,' she said. 'Shit, they've got some weird stuff down here. No wonder they keep it locked away. I wonder who it belongs to.'

Item seven, by contrast, was a contract for the sale and delivery of sixty tons of dried prunes, dated 1907, though it wasn't numbered or mentioned in the red book. Item eight was an ancient theatre programme, *The Second Mrs Tanqueray*, dated eighteen ninety-some-thing and with the name Billings pencilled on the front cover. The red book listed it and confirmed that in 1927 it belonged to Henrietta Billings of Kensington, but had no further light to shed on the matter. Item nine was a column of figures, with six indecipherable signatures at the bottom, and a small, rusty key. It was annotated with the number B998, which led them to a red-book entry that said, *Schedule of anticipated returns and key, S. Magus & Co., 1899.* Item ten was a plain white envelope containing five desiccated cherry stones, no red-book number. Item eleven was a dozen years' worth of early Edwardian tailors' bills made out to one Jeremy Castle of Ilkley, Yorks. Item twelve was a single small tooth, no name or number. 'Right,' Sophie said, closing number eleven's envelope and putting it back with a slight shudder, 'you take over here and I'll do the writing. I've had enough. Some of this stuff is *sick*.'

She wasn't far wrong, at that. Item nineteen proved to be a dried-up animal's paw, with skin like parchment, large claws and a few strands of moulting brown fur on the back. Apparently, one Celia Garvin had thought enough of it to want it kept safe in 1919, but Paul couldn't bring himself to share her enthusiasm. Not all the items were as gruesome as that; number twenty-two was a pencil sketch of some trees, done on the back of an envelope addressed to a French bloke called R. Matisse; Sophie got quite excited about that. Twenty-five turned out to be a tad under a quarter of a million dollars, in Confederate banknotes, while twenty-six was a cutting from a nineteen-thirties newspaper advertising someone or other's patent bicycle seats. Twenty-nine harked back to the macabre theme: an envelope stuffed with hair and nail clippings, but Paul couldn't see a name or a red-book number anywhere.

It was item thirty-two that suddenly turned them both silent and thoughtful, looking at each other with the proverbial wild surmise. Again, no name or reference number in the earlier catalogue, but Paul had no trouble at all knowing what to put down in the *Property Of* column. It was an old photograph, sepia'd and cracked along a fold, with the name of a West End photographer printed in white along the bottom, and the date 1891. The man in the photo was dressed in a top hat and frock coat and he was holding a black lacquered walking stick and a pair of white cotton gloves, but it was unmistakably Professor Van Spee.

CHAPTER SIX

'No,' Sophie said eventually.

'Sorry?'

'No,' she repeated, 'you're wrong. That's not what's-his-name, the man who we saw at the interview—'

'Professor Van Spee?'

'Him. That's not him.'

'Oh. But it looks—'

'That's his great-grandfather,' Sophie said firmly, 'or someone like that. Just looks like him, that's all.'

'A *lot* like him.'

'Yes. But it isn't him.'

Paul nodded slowly. 'That's all right, then,' he said. 'Because if that was him—'

'Yes. But it isn't.'

'Fine.' Paul stuck it back in its envelope. 'What should we put in the book for this one, then?'

Sophie thought for a moment. 'Photograph of an old man,' she said, 'and leave it at that.'

Paul nodded. A tiny part of him that was still faintly interested in sucking up to the boss suggested making that *photograph of distinguished-looking middle-aged gentleman*, but soon found itself shouted down by the other parts of his consciousness who on balance preferred sanity to the distant hope of promotion. He attached the yellow sticky and put the envelope back on the shelf.

'It's twenty-five past five,' Sophie announced, with audible relief. 'Let's get out of here, shall we?'

'Yes,' Paul said. 'Let's.'

On the way up the stairs they met Mr Wurmtoter coming down. 'Just came to remind you it's nearly going-home time,' he said brightly.

'Thanks,' Paul said automatically, while Sophie gave him a carbon-steel stare that he apparently didn't notice.

'Wouldn't do for us to go locking the doors with you two still down there,' Mr Wurmtoter explained, standing aside to let them go past.

'Absolutely,' Paul said.

'Nearly happened to me once,' Mr Wurmtoter went on, fingering the claw on its chain round his neck. 'Pretty cold down there, you could catch pneumonia.' He frowned, and rubbed his back against the frame of the fire door. 'Itch,' he said. 'Right where I can't reach. Gets me in the cold weather.'

He escorted them into reception, where Mr Tanner was waiting by the door. The key was in the lock – on the inside.

Paul and Sophie headed for the corridor leading to their office. 'Where do you two think you're going?' Mr Tanner called out.

'Sorry,' Paul said. 'Just going to get our coats.'

'Oh.' Mr Tanner frowned. 'Get a move on, will you? I've got better things to do than stand here all day.'

They scuttled down the corridor without a word and grabbed their coats. On the way back, Paul had an uneasy feeling that someone was following them, but he didn't want to make a fool of himself by stopping and looking round. Mr Tanner didn't actually shove them out of the door, but it slammed behind them with a terrific bang.

'One thing I like about this job,' Paul muttered, as they walked away, 'there's never any bother about getting away on time.'

They reached the end of the street in silence, then stopped. Paul always went right here; Sophie always went left. Yesterday, she'd snapped, 'Bye, then,' before darting away into the crowd, and that had been a quantum leap in sociability over the days before. But this evening they paused, as if waiting for the other to go first.

'Well,' Sophie said, 'I'd better be getting home.'

'Right,' Paul said. And then: 'Or, if you're not in a tearing hurry, we could—'

'No, I'd better not.' She gave every indication of being about to move, but didn't.

'Oh,' Paul said. 'All right.'

There was another of those confounded moments. 'Another time, maybe,' she said.

'Okay,' Paul said. 'Tomorrow?'

'All right.' She said it without emphasis, as if he'd just asked if he could borrow her pencil sharpener. 'Bye.'

A second later, she was invisible in the going-home-time lemming-run. There was a place on the pavement next to him where she'd been standing, and an echo of her voice in his head.

As simple as that, Paul said to himself. *Bloody hell.*

On his way home, Paul stopped at a bank machine and checked his balance. The month's money had gone in. He was solvent beyond the dreams of avarice (though in his case, avarice was a light sleeper). *Well, now*, he thought.

He was still thinking, *Well, now*, when he reached his door and let himself in. The sword in the stone was still there. That reminded him.

He pulled off his jacket and tie, flipped the kettle on and flopped down on the bed. It was all fine and splendid thinking, *Well, now,* as if everything else was just background and mood music; but he'd seen and heard enough concentrated weirdness in one working day to boil his brain, if only it hadn't been addled to pulp already with all the love stuff. *Professor Van Spee*, he thought. *Yeah, what about that?*

Offhand he could think of two explanations, the second of which was that the professor was an amazingly good judge of character who liked doing the Sherlock Holmes bit, wrapping up absurdly obvious observations in a whole load of flannel, and who looked a lot like his great-grandad. He accepted this version gratefully, like a starving fish who sees a plump worm hanging above him in the water with string coming out of the small of its back. That explained about Professor Van Spee; and if the big weirdness could be got rid of so easily, it followed that all the little weirdnesses, such as the behaviour of Messrs Wurmtoter and Tanner, the vanishing stapler and items nineteen to thirty-one inclusive, had to be explainable too; and if he knew they were explainable, then why should he waste his ingenuity and free time figuring out what the explanations actually were? Just knowing they were there was good enough. No point reinventing the wheel, he told himself.

Then he remembered that tonight he'd arranged to meet Duncan and Jenny in a pub in Museum Street. He swore. He'd arranged the meeting a month ago, to celebrate the encashment of his first paycheck, and Duncan and Jenny had proved to be the only members of his narrow circle of friends who reckoned they could make it. If he'd remembered earlier, of course, he'd have stayed in town and saved himself two bus fares. As it was, if he was really lucky with the traffic, he might just get there no more than twenty minutes late. Duncan and Jenny would, of course, stay there till he arrived. *Pity*, he thought; he didn't feel in the mood for riotous living, somehow.

Duncan and Jenny, in Paul's opinion, summed up nearly everything that was wrong with the world. Not individually; he'd known Duncan for close on a decade, they'd built model Spitfires and discussed minutiae of Romulan uniforms together back in the days when womankind was still no more than a dark cloud on the distant horizon, while Jenny was small, lively, clever, pretty and legitimately but not culpably blonde, and played a slick game of nomination whist. It was as a unit, a union of soul and flesh, that they got up Paul's nose to the point where their heads were all but sticking out of his ears. Duncan had met Jenny two years ago at a New Year's party, and ever since then they'd been tack-welded together, a fusion of two quite reasonable human beings into a single nauseating entity. Paul had heard any number of horror stories about so-and-so who got himself fixed up and thereafter disappeared without trace into a black pit of soft furnishings, mortgages and early-morning feeds but, regrettably, that wasn't the case where Duncan and Jenny were concerned. Faster than a high-bandwidth download, Jenny had learned to play bar billiards, distinguish real ale from keg, form opinions about TV sci-fi and football, and eat fish and chips standing on the Embankment at half past eleven at night. At first Paul had assumed this was simple protective mimicry or, more likely, the predator merging with the shadows as it stalked her prey down the narrow, dark path that led to a serious talk about relationships and commitment. Two years later, he was forced to the conclusion that Duncan was either blackmailing God or very, very lucky, and the whole set-up was for real. Hence his feelings of profound distaste whenever he spent time with the gestalt. It's bad enough having to watch a fellow human being enjoying unalloyed, undeserved good fortune. When the lucky bastard is a close personal friend, it's unbearable.

'You're late,' Duncan pointed out, when Paul finally shouldered through the door and flumped down in the seat they'd been saving for him.

Paul nodded. 'Ran into a distorted anti-chronaton nexus outside Tottenham Court Road Tube and got reborn as a Viking chieftain in an alternate universe. Whose round is it?'

Jenny stood up. 'Mine,' she said. She did things like that; it was enough to make one's teeth ache. 'They've got Ventcaster Nine-X on, but Duncan reckons it hasn't had time to settle yet.'

Paul smiled weakly. 'I'll have a half of lager shandy, please,' he said.

'Don't be silly,' Jenny said, and headed for the bar, slipping between the shoulders of the massed drinkers like a golden ferret.

Paul and Duncan looked at each other. 'Well, then,' Duncan said. 'What do you reckon to being all grown up, then?'

Paul shook his head. 'It'll never catch on.'

'You'd think so,' Duncan replied. 'The thing about work is, it cuts into your free time. Jerked out of bed in the middle of the night, and no afternoon telly. Still, lots of people swear by it.' Duncan, Paul remembered, had recently been promoted to assistant deputy software wizard, and was now earning more than Paul's father had been making when he'd retired. *Bastard*, Paul thought. 'Apart from that,' Duncan went on, 'what's it like? I take it they haven't fired you yet.'

Paul grinned. 'They'd have to notice I exist first,' he said.

'Pretty boring?'

Paul thought about the red eye through the letter box and the claw-mark and Professor Van Spee; then he thought about photocopying the spreadsheets. 'Yes,' he said. 'How about you?'

'Well,' Duncan said, and launched into a tirade about Microsoft, which was only abated when Jenny came back with a tray and three pints of murky brown beer. One good thing about the Duncan/Jenny axis was that the mere rumour of her approach made his old friend stop talking about computers.

'So,' Jenny said, distributing the beer glasses, 'how's work?'

'Fine,' Paul muttered. Suddenly he felt he really didn't want to discuss it with anybody (anybody else, he actually meant), let alone this insufferable pair of lovebirds. 'And how about you? How's showbiz?' Jenny was some sort of accountant at the BBC.

'Don't change the subject,' she said, with a twinkle in her eye that made him want to leave the building. 'So, what's her name? Gory details.'

Paul couldn't be sure he'd gone bright red, as there was no mirror handy. 'Sorry? What are you talking about?'

Jenny grinned at him. 'Confess. I was down your way the day before yesterday, just after one; in fact, I rang your office on my mobile to see if you were there and wanted to come out to play, but the switchboard must've been down, nobody answered. And then I saw you marching off down the street with the mystery female. I waved but you pretended you hadn't seen me. So then of course I *knew*.'

Paul blinked. 'I didn't see you,' he said.

'It's all right,' Jenny assured him, 'I understand. The last thing you wanted right then was Other Women swooping down on you like hunting kestrels. But come on, tell us all about it. Names. Places. Progress reports.'

'She's just—'

'Ah!' Jenny said, beaming.

'—Just someone I work with,' Paul muttered, scowling. 'That's all. Really.'

'Sure.' Jenny's grin was threatening to unzip her head at the back. 'Of course, I only saw the back of her head, because you were in the way. Is she nice? Attractive? Gullible?'

'No,' Paul replied.

'Liar. She must be nice, or you wouldn't be glowing like a nuked beetroot. It's like I've been telling you all along, you can run but you can't hide. Sooner or later there's an arrow with your name on it.'

Paul looked at her, and Duncan sitting next to her, silent but clearly acquiescing in this deplorable breach of good taste; and he thought, *Will the day come when I'll be like this?* Two of Two, subunit of unimatrix zero-one, assimilated without trace into a two-handed collective, hell-bent on infecting the entire world with its own warped vision of perfect happiness? He sighed softly. *Chance'd be a fine thing.* 'Sophie,' he said wearily. 'She's the other junior clerk, she lives with her parents in Wimbledon somewhere, she's just broken up with her boyfriend, and she treats me like I'm something she trod in on a dark night.'

'Well, she would,' Duncan said reasonably.

'Bollocks,' Jenny said daintily. 'If she's cooped up in the office with you all morning and then goes out to lunch with you, obviously you're on to something. The snotty thing is obviously just a front. Primeval female strategy, take my word for it.'

Paul shook his head. 'Sorry,' he said, 'but obviously in this Mills-and-Boon alternative universe you live in, the idea of men and women just being friends—'

'Ah, friends,' Jenny crowed, like a vampire barrister, 'a minute ago she couldn't stand the sight of you.'

This was starting to get on Paul's nerves. Unfortunately, Jenny had clearly smelt blood in the water, so changing the subject was out of the question, at least until she'd heard what she wanted to hear. 'All right, then,' he said. 'You're right, I really like her a lot. In fact, she's the only reason I haven't packed the job in.'

Duncan sneered. 'That sounds more like it,' he said. 'You just don't like working for a living.'

At least it was a change of subject. 'True,' Paul admitted. 'But really, the whole place is as weird as a wellyful of beetles.'

Duncan shook his head. 'You don't know you're born,' he said. 'Weird as a wellyful of beetles is just a synonym for office. You've got to get used to it, that's all.'

For a moment, Paul seriously considered telling them all about it; the whole deal, from the bizarre interview through the claw-marks and the sword and Gilbert and Sullivan and the eye and the nutty stuff in the strong-room and the disappearing stapler and Mr Tanner going apeshit when he'd shown up five minutes early, right down to Professor Van Spee, his lecture and the photograph. But he decided against it, because they wouldn't believe him. Or, even worse, they might believe him, in which case there was a grave risk he might end up believing it himself.

'Yes, Dad,' he mumbled, therefore. 'But at least they pay me. Same again?'

He'd hardly touched his beer, which tasted like rotten eggs whisked in creosote, but their glasses were empty. 'Ventcaster for me,' Duncan said; Jenny wrinkled her nose and said she'd give the Cross Marston a try.

On his way back from the bar, a pint glass in each hand and a half of lemonade shandy braced between his thumbs, he reconsidered his decision. After all, it'd be great to tell *someone*, after a month of trying to deal with it on his own. And maybe, just possibly, they'd laugh at him and call him a stupid prat, and *explain* (because they were grown-ups, Big People who Knew about the

World; and they might be able to point out the screamingly obvious explanation, which everybody else in the universe knew about except him). At the very least they'd say he was out of his tree and had imagined the whole thing, and they could be very convincing when they wanted to be. He'd like to believe he'd imagined the whole thing, it'd be a comfort.

Yes, but he hadn't.

'This one's the Ventcaster,' he said, apportioning the glasses. 'Fancy a game of cards?'

So they played nomination whist for two hours, Duncan winning one game and Jenny all the rest; and if Jenny couldn't resist pointing out that Paul was obviously in love, because only someone whose brain was addled with sweet longings would have bid three on a heap of shit like that; and if Duncan and Jenny kept pausing at crucial moments to rub noses and nibble each other's faces; still, it was wonderfully refreshing to be doing something normal again, like playing cards in a pub with an old friend (or an old friend and his fiendlike queen, which amounted to the same thing). Three halves and a pint of lemonade shandy helped, of course, though in the back of his mind he knew he was going to regret that aspect of the evening's entertainment come seven o'clock next morning. Furthermore, he couldn't help noticing a slight change in their attitude towards him, a small but palpable upwards reassessment of his status; he'd gone from being poor, funny Paul who still hadn't got a job or a girlfriend, to a lowly junior apprentice with the mighty enterprise of Life, Inc – still out of sight below themselves, of course, but part of the same outfit, one of us rather than a homeless refugee from childhood.

But.

But it occurred to him, while they were playing cards, and later while they were gorging themselves on greasy battered cod on the Embankment, and later still as he was joggled dyspeptically homewards on the night bus, that there was something wrong with this picture; and after a certain amount of savagely honest introspection, he figured out what it was.

That he was in love, there could be no possible doubt. The strange yet all too familiar feeling, something like a hangover, something like acute carsickness, that he felt every time he saw her confirmed that. But then he compared two mental images; one of the evening he'd just spent, and one of an imaginary evening out with Sophie, all brittle silences, minefields and measureless caverns of ice. And then he asked himself the appalling question: *Just what do you see in her?*

It wasn't a question he'd even considered asking himself before. She was a girl, unattached, and she'd held still for more than five minutes without walking away or smacking him round the face. That was enough; what mattered was the other side of the coin – what could she possibly ever see in him? *Yes, but,* he asked himself. Yes, but pigeonholing that for just a second; answer the question. *Why do you love this girl?*

And he thought about it; and the more he thought, the more he realised that the only answer was that good old mountaineer's standby: Because she's there. *Because she might possibly like me. Because she hasn't said she can't stand the sight of me* yet.

Bad answer, he thought; because if his dreams came true, if he uncorked a super-whizzo hypergenie and got his One Wish, there wouldn't be any cosy, cheerful, relaxed evenings in pubs playing nomination whist, none of this decadent, self-indulgent being-himself nonsense. He suddenly remembered something she'd said, on Gilbert & Sullivan night on the exotic rialto of Highgate – neither of us was being ourselves, so we could never really be *us* – while afar off in the distance, like the faint horns of Elfland, the ghost of Groucho Marx whispered its famous line about not wanting to belong to a club that'd have someone like him as a member.

But, he assured himself.

But that was so much beside the point that it was practically coming out round the back of it. Where the hell was the point in speculating about whether you wanted True Happiness when you stood about as much chance of getting it as Jeffrey Archer had of winning the Booker prize? Besides, if True Happiness was no more than this, playing cards and drinking shandy in a pub with two degenerates, then he couldn't help thinking that the fish who'd crawled on their fins out of the primeval oceans to follow the long, hard trail of evolving into him had probably been wasting their time. He considered the pursuit of happiness, and above all it reminded him of the relentless, futile persecution of Bugs Bunny by Elmer Fudd.

At least, he thought as he unlocked his door and flipped the light switch and saw the light bounce back at him off the blade of the sword in the stone, *at least it helps me keep all this shit in perspective*. Life at J. W. Wells & Co. might be deeply weird, but it was peanuts compared with the fathomless craziness of being human. Now if he'd tried to explain *that* to a couple of old friends, they wouldn't have laughed in his face;

they'd have held him down till the ambulance arrived with the handcuffs and the jacket that did up at the back.

Next morning, Paul had a headache.

Unfair, he thought. Duncan and Jenny had been swilling the stuff down in pailfuls, but you could bet next year's rent they weren't feeling as though Tennessee hillbillies were dynamiting trout in the murky green pools behind their eyes; nor would they be afflicted with heartburn, indigestion and severe flatulence. He hacked two ragged slices off the stub of his stale loaf, and crammed them clumsily into the toaster. Then, purely from habit, he fumbled the radio on.

It's seven-thirty, the radio yelled at him, and here's the news. His mind tuned out instinctively. He didn't want to know about the latest political crisis, or the latest God-awful little war, or the latest unspeakable murder; callous and irresponsible of him, maybe, but none of it was his fault, and he'd rather it left him alone and spoilt someone else's breakfast. He scraped rock-hard butter over his brittle toast, while the radio burbled excitedly about further rises in inflation, escalating tension in the Balkans, floods in Minnesota and drought in Somalia, corruption, lies, famine, war, pestilence and death, plagues of rats in the tunnels of the Bakerloo Line, urban foxes spreading mange through the lush kennels of Surrey, and the twelfth reported sighting of goblins in the sewers under the City of London.

The traffic on the way to work was in a playful mood; for some reason it wasn't where it usually was, which meant that he arrived in Houndsditch at twenty minutes to nine, seventeen minutes earlier than usual. He knew better than to head for the office, so he limped into a café sort of place, bought himself a cup of tea, and sat down. An earlier occupant of his seat had left a chunk of his newspaper behind, but it was just the business pages. Paul didn't bother picking it up, but over the rim of his teacup he caught sight of a headline: Major New Australian Bauxite Finds Threaten Commodity Prices. He put his cup down and picked up the paper. Apparently, some busy little bee had found vast new deposits of bauxite in the Australian desert, which meant that pretty soon you wouldn't be able to give the stuff away, and it was costing the mining cartels untold billions.

Bauxite, he thought, and he carefully tore out the page and folded it away in his pocket. Then he finished his tea and went to work. His head was slightly better, but not much. All in all, he felt like a slug in a salt cellar.

The receptionist greeted him with a cheerful chirrup that made his teeth ache. He mumbled some sort of a reply, and shuffled up the stairs to his office. Empty; then he remembered that he was on strong-room sorting duty, and he hadn't brought his scruffy pully. He hung his coat behind the door (no scratch marks) and went back down the stairs, feeling every step distinctly.

'Hello,' Sophie called out as he opened the door, and the cold hit him like a slap with a wet fish. 'God, you look awful.'

He nodded. 'I'm not feeling all that great,' he admitted.

'You should've stayed in bed.'

Paul shrugged. 'Oh, I thought I'd better come in.'

'Suit yourself. Right, let's get started, then.'

There's this to be said for being hung over; if you've got a job to do that involves substantial levels of ambient weirdness, it helps, because you can't be bothered to notice stuff that under other circumstances would come close to frying your synapses. Treasure maps; Czarist bonds; a case of stuffed dodos; Scarlett O'Hara's birth certificate; two flattened and deformed silver bullet heads in an old matchbox; Baedeker's guide to Atlantis (seventeenth edition, 1902); the autograph score of Schubert's Unfinished Symphony, with *Das Ende* written neatly at the foot of the last page; three boxes of moon rocks; a dumpy, heavy statuette of a bird covered in dull black paint, which reminded him of something but he couldn't remember what; a Norwich Union life policy in the name of Vlad Dracul; a cigar box full of oddly shaped teeth, with CAUTION: DO NOT DROP painted on the lid in hysterical capitals; five or six doll's-house-sized books with titles like *Lilliput On $2 A Day*; a small slab of green crystal that glowed when he opened the envelope; a thick bundle of love letters bound in blue ribbon, all signed Margaret Roberts; a left-luggage token from the North Central railway terminus, Ruritania; *Bartholomew's Road Atlas of Oz* (one page, with a yellow line smack down the middle); a brown paper bag of solid gold jelly babies; several contracts for the sale and purchase of souls; a fat brown envelope inscribed *To Be Opened On My Death: E. A. Presley*, unopened; Oxford and Cambridge Board O-level papers in Elvish language and literature, 1969–85; a very old drum in a worm-eaten sea-chest marked F. Drake, Plymouth, in with a load of minute-books and annual accounts of the Winchester Round Table; half a dozen incredibly ugly portraits of major Hollywood film stars; *Unicorn-Calling For Pleasure & Profit* by J. R. Hartley; a huge collection of betting slips, on races to be held in the year 2109; all water, as far as Paul was concerned, off a duck's—

'Bloody hell,' he said.

Sophie looked up. 'What?'

'Come over here.'

He flipped back the lid of the long wooden box so that she could see what was inside. They both studied it in silence for a moment or so.

'Yes, it's pretty much the same as mine,' Sophie said eventually. 'Only the wire binding on the handle of mine is a sort of dull grey.'

Paul knelt down for a closer look. 'No, mine's the same colour as this one,' he said. 'Like that brass wire you buy for hanging pictures from. I think on mine – what's that round bit on the end called?'

'Pommel.'

'The pommel on mine may be a tad smaller, but I can't be sure. That aside, though, I'd say it's pretty well identical. Except,' he added, 'it's missing the chunk of stone on the end.' He stood up, still gazing at the sword in the box. 'Take a look in the old register,' he said. '776/J.'

Sophie leafed through the big red book for a minute or so. 'It just says Windsor,' she said.

'Oh well,' Paul replied. He closed the lid and shoved the box back into its dark corner. He noticed that he'd forgotten about his headache; but noticing made it come back.

'Five to one,' Sophie announced.

'Ah, right.' It was another moment. 'Do you fancy—?'

'I'd better be going,' Sophie said. 'I'm meeting my mum for lunch at five past.'

'Oh,' Paul said. 'Right. See you later, then.'

As it happened, he didn't really mind too much, what with the headache and the anguished bowels and everything; the last thing he wanted, he realised, was food of any description, while trying to make impressively light, brilliant conversation was plainly beyond him. In fact, he couldn't really be bothered to move from where he was. It was pleasantly cool down there, and quiet, and he couldn't face the stairs. He sat down on a trunk, leaned his back against the shelves, and closed his eyes.

When Paul woke up, his watch told him it was twenty past one, and he felt considerably better. The dwarves had stopped drilling out the back of his head, and his eyes didn't hurt quite so much. He still had a stomach like a car battery, but he could live with that, so long as he avoided putting anything in it. He stood up and looked around. They weren't getting on too badly, he realised; another day and a half, two days, and they ought to be through here. It occurred to him that since he had nothing better to do, he might as well press on and do a bit more on his own. He had the feeling she'd approve of that, though he wasn't sure why.

The first box he opened contained something that he took at first to be a pillowcase, except that it was made of a sort of thin, rubbery stuff; he had no idea what it was, but it wasn't cloth. There was no number or anything on the box, so he spread the thing out on the floor. That left him none the wiser. It was rectangular, and printed on it was the crude outline of a door, with panels, hinges and a little circle for a doorknob. He shrugged, folded it up and put it back, with its very own yellow sticky. In the notebook he wrote down *rubber mat*; then, since he was feeling just a tad flippant, he rubbed that out with the rubber on the end of the pencil, and wrote in *Acme portable door*. But that looked silly, so he rubbed it out again and changed it to *rectangular flat rubber object*, and left it at that.

Next item was an envelope full of blank sheets of paper. He checked the number in the old red book, but it wasn't there. *Fine*, he said to himself, *be like that*.

Next item was another bundle of letters, ancient envelopes with Victorian stamps, bound in faded red ribbon. The ink was brown with age and the handwriting was cramped and scruffy, and it hurt his eyes to read it, so he checked the reference number against the red book. 839/N – *839/N; seventeen love letters; property of Paul Carpenter, Esq.*

He looked at the page. *Bloody hell*, he thought, *there's a coincidence*. But the ink in the register was almost as brown as the writing on the letters themselves, and the date for when they'd been booked in was 1877. He shrugged, and started copying the details into the notebook. He'd written down the first two lines of the address before he noticed it was his own.

Fuck this for a game of soldiers, he told himself.

The pink ribbon was tightly knotted, and he broke a fingernail untying it. He took the first letter out of the envelope and looked at the date. Three weeks ago.

Paul closed his eyes, then opened them again. Still three weeks ago. *Shit*.

Not fair, he shouted to himself, *all I had was two and a half pints of rotten lemonade shandy, that's not enough, surely. Bet Duncan and bloody Jenny don't go around—*

Hang about. What sort of letters?

He looked back at the register, and read the relevant adjective, carefully, four times. Whoever had written the red book, they had clear, precise handwriting. Not lone letters or lore letters or lowe letters or loue letters or loye letters. He put the register down carefully, and frowned.

Well, he thought. *Can't do any harm,* he lied to himself. He laid the first letter flat on the nearest shelf, and started to read.

My darling Paul—

He paused, and stared. Whoever had written this letter, he or she had the worst writing ever perpetrated outside of a doctor's surgery. He squinted at it, but it defied his best efforts. Then he thought of something, and reached out for the spiral-bound notebook, in which Sophie had been writing down the inventory.

No doubt about it. Same writing.

Jesus, he thought. He picked up the letter and carried it across the room, until he was standing directly under the single, unshaded light bulb.

My darling Paul,
Ever since we met this morning, I haven't been able to get you out of my mind. All I can do is think about you, the way you looked at me, the sound of your voice. I thought I'd never see you again, and suddenly there you were, like you'd stepped out of my daydream.
I love you so much, I can't think about anything else. I can't concentrate on work or anything like that. Oh, you've guessed, haven't you? You must have done. I sit

there with that pile of ridiculous spreadsheets in front of me, desperately trying not to look at you across the desk from me, and the last thing in the world I want to think about is shuffling bits of paper. I want to feel the soft warmth of your lips on mine, the burning thrill as your fingers—

'Bloody hell,' Paul muttered.

You must know how I feel about you, he read, *I can read it in your eyes every time you look at me, and I'm absolutely sure you feel the same way about me, so why don't you say something? You can't be afraid, not when I'm sitting next to you burning to death with* (however hard he tried, he couldn't make that word out; it might just possibly be *dessert* or *dishcloth*, but he didn't think so). *Maybe I'm wrong, maybe you don't care and I'm making a complete idiot of myself. I don't care. I've never felt like this about anyone before, definitely not that clown Nigel with his stupid amateur dramatics, which is all he seems to care about at the moment. Oh, Paul, please say something quickly, I can't bear the suspense any longer. I know—*

Footsteps outside the door. Faster than a rat up a conduit, Paul grabbed the letters and stuffed them back on the shelf, as the door opened and Sophie walked in.

'Hello,' she said. 'You still here?'

Paul knew he must be glowing like a stop sign. 'Mphm,' he mumbled. 'Didn't feel like any lunch, thought I'd do a bit more.'

She frowned at him. 'You're pretty keen all of a sudden,' she said. 'All right, where've you got to?'

'Well, actually, I haven't got terribly far.'

She came over and flicked through the notebook. 'Two entries,' she said. 'No, you haven't, have you?'

He couldn't think of anything to say. He shrugged.

'Well.' She sighed. 'We'd better get on with it. What's next?'

He pulled down a deed-box and opened it. 'How was your mother, by the way?' he asked.

'Mum? Oh, pretty much the same as when I saw her at breakfast this morning,' she replied. 'Why?'

'Oh, no reason. Sorry, right. Well, it looks like a big wodge of Premium Bonds.'

She was writing in the notebook. 'Okay,' she said. 'Any name or anything?'

He rummaged around in the bottom of the box, and found a slip of paper. *£5,000 nominal value, property of Mr Paul Carpenter.* He shut his eyes tight, then opened them again. 'Nope,' he replied.

'Marvellous,' Sophie sighed. 'All right, slap a yellow sticky on and we'll see what's next.'

The next envelope held a sheaf of share certificates. Paul didn't know much about high finance, but even he knew that 20,000 ordinary shares in Kawaguchi Integrated Circuits Inc. had to be worth a lot of money. Interesting, since apparently they belonged to him.

'Share certificates,' he said. 'Property of Paul, um, Smith.'

'Fine,' she said, as he attached a yellow sticky and shoved them hastily back on the shelf. 'Next.'

The further he went on, the harder he found it to keep going. $50,000 in traveller's cheques; £35,000 in National Savings certificates; the deeds to two semi-detached houses in Ewell . . .

'This Paul Smith sounds like he's loaded,' Sophie

commented. 'All right, got that.' She looked up. 'Do you want to swap over for a bit?'

He dropped the deed-packet. 'No, no, that's fine,' he said. 'If you don't mind, I mean. I'm quite happy doing this.'

'You sure? You're getting covered in dust.'

'Oh, that's all right. Really.'

She shrugged. 'Please yourself. All right, what's next?'

He groped for the next envelope. 'Paul Smith again,' he said, in a rather hoarse voice. 'Post Office savings book, four thousand quid.'

'He can't be very bright, this Smith bloke. He'd get much better interest in a building society or something. Well,' she added, tapping the notebook impatiently, 'what's next? More of this Smith character's ill-gotten gains?'

'Actually,' Paul said, in a very quiet voice, 'I don't think it did him much good.'

'Really? Why?'

Paul folded a piece of paper and put it back in its envelope. 'That was his death certificate,' he muttered.

'Oh. Well, never mind. I was starting to dislike him, anyway.'

'Me too,' Paul said. 'I can't help feeling sorry for him, though.'

'Why's that?'

'He died young,' Paul replied. 'Not much older than me, as it happens.' Four months, two weeks, three days, to be precise; but he didn't say anything about that. Nor did he mention the cause of death.

'That's sad,' Sophie said. 'I suppose. Anyway, none of our business. I'm going for a pee.'

As soon as she was out of the door, Paul sprang

across the room and started searching for the bundle of letters he'd hidden away when she came back from lunch. They didn't seem to want to be found, and he was just beginning to think he'd imagined the whole thing when they turned up, wedged in the crevasse between two fat manila folders. He glanced down at them –

My darling Paul—

Yes, still there. He crammed them in his jacket pocket; then, not really wanting to one little bit, he fished out the last item with a yellow sticky on it.

Death certificate. Paul Carpenter. Date and place of birth, address, and cause of death. *Decapitation*, he thought. *Bloody hell.*

It was a very long afternoon.

'Anyway,' Sophie said, as they walked out through reception at 5:29. 'We're getting there. If we really crack on with it tomorrow, I think we might get it finished.'

Paul nodded. He wasn't really listening.

Out through the door; she was telling him how she couldn't wait to get back to their rotten little office, after three days in that horrible cold strongroom. They reached the corner; her that way, him this. She stopped.

'Well,' she said.

Paul looked up; he'd been staring at his shoes. 'Sorry?'

A second dragged by. An oak tree could have grown in that second. Paul had the feeling she was waiting for something, but his mind was elsewhere. *Decapitation*, he was thinking, *for fuck's sake. And seventy grand in the Abbey National, Chelmsford. But I've never even been to bloody Chelmsford.*

And then he realised she was looking at him, and for

some reason she was furiously angry. 'Well, see you tomorrow,' she snapped, and walked away very quickly.

A better man, or at least a biped with one working brain cell, would've chased after her. Paul didn't. He shook his head, and trudged to the bus stop. *Australia*, he was thinking; *no, not Australia, that's where they've found all that fucking bauxite. Ontario.* Surely if he went there, he'd be safe, they'd never follow him all that way. Would they? And besides, who were *they*, anyhow?

My darling Paul—

He made a decision. What he needed, he decided, was a drink; something fierce and strong and vicious, with teeth and claws, and possibly a cube of ice and a slice of lemon. He drifted across the road to a pub, only remembering as he sat down with his drink that on the last occasion he'd been there, she'd been sitting over by the door, with her pint of Guinness. A large bald man with a thick neck was in her place now. That didn't seem right, somehow; it was like removing the statue of Eros from Piccadilly Circus and replacing it with a ten-foot plastic Mickey Mouse.

This being no time for faint hearts or false economies, he ordered a full pint of lemonade shandy, and sat down in a corner where nobody was likely to tread on his feet and break his concentration. Are we sitting comfortably? Then we'll begin.

The letters. He took them out, patted the spilled beer off the table top with his sleeve, and put them carefully down. Next he picked out the one he'd started to read earlier, and opened it.

My dear Philip—

He blinked three times, and looked at the envelope. It

was addressed, quite clearly in sharp, slanting handwriting, to Lieutenant Philip Catherwood, The Parsonage, Norton St Edgar, Worcs. The postmark was 22 April 1877.

Fuck, he thought.

He checked the rest of the letters. All addressed to the same person, in the same handwriting, dating from 22 April 1877 through to 12 January 1879, by which time Lieutenant Catherwood was serving in South Africa. Paul stopped there. He'd spent most of his history lessons at school drawing sheep in the margins of his textbooks, but he'd seen *Zulu* three times and read articles about the Zulu War in his military modelling magazines. 22 January 1879; British army wiped out at Isandlhwana. Somehow he knew exactly what had happened to Philip Catherwood. Terribly sad; but that wasn't the point. At least he'd had someone writing love letters to him—

(He checked. He felt awful about reading them, and he only flicked through. He was shocked. He had no idea they did stuff like that back in the 1870s, and especially an officer and a gentleman. He put the letters away quickly and hoped nobody had seen him reading them.)

Think, he ordered himself. *Implications*.

If the love letters that had been addressed to him a few hours previously were now somebody else's, then wasn't there a decent chance that the rest of the stuff – all that money, and of course the death certificate – maybe all that stuff was somebody else's too. He shunted his consciousness into serious mode, and considered the alternatives.

He was hung-over, residual alcohol sloshing through his veins like the Severn Bore, and he'd imagined the whole thing. He was cracking up, and it was starting to get embarrassingly obvious. In his haste, he'd grabbed the wrong bundle of letters, and the Dear Paul stuff was still wedged in the rack in the strongroom. The letters had been written to him when he first looked at them, but now they weren't. The letters were written to him as long as he was inside the doors of 70 St Mary Axe, but as soon as he stepped over the threshold, they morphed into a slice of tragic Victoriana. The letters were written to him, but on his way out through reception, someone had picked his pocket and replaced them with fifteen instalments of forged nineteenth-century soft porn. *She* had written the letters but never posted them; instead she'd stashed them in JWW's safe, and when she saw they'd gone she'd guessed he'd found them, surreptitiously swiped them and replaced them with something vaguely similar she'd found on the shelves, to make him believe he'd imagined the whole thing.

Paul reviewed these alternatives and decided that, on balance, it'd be better for his mental health to quit speculating and wait till tomorrow, when he'd have a chance to look at all the other stuff. If the bank books and house deeds (and the death certificate) were all still there, that would at least allow him to run a blue pencil through some of the alternatives. (Another explanation: the air in the strongroom was laced with some form of hallucinogenic compound, possibly sewer gas escaping from the building's medieval plumbing, and he'd imagined the stuff with the letters because he'd been as high as the rate of inflation all the time he'd been down there. It was as plausible as several of the others, and about as much help.)

He glugged another mouthful of shandy, and the fizz went up his nose, making him sneeze. It wasn't any good, he told himself, focusing on these damned letters, or the money, or even the death certificate. What he needed to do was address the whole issue of weirdness, which he'd been shying away from for just over a month, partly because he was a coward but mostly because he was in love. Weirdness, he thought; swords and bauxite and men with dragons' claws on chains round their necks buying him lunch at cosy little Uzbek restaurants. One of the aspects of the human condition that elevates mankind above the lesser primates is the inquiring mind, the urge to find out, to know the essential truth; but there has to come a time when the inquiring mind stops inquiring, finds a late-night travel agency and books a one-way flight to Canada. Another aspect, of course, is romantic love, something that Paul had always reckoned God slipped into the design schematics late on Day Eight, while rubbing His hands together and sniggering. *If I quit at J. W. Wells, I may never see her again.* Of all the bloody stupid arguments; and yet it was the only one that mattered. *Hell*, he thought.

Yes, he said to himself, *but the death certificate—* And then he put his beer glass down and stared at the darkened window opposite, because he'd suddenly remembered the date on the certificate, the day and month on which he was due to be beheaded. 22 January.

Oink, he thought.

Calm down, he thought. In fact, that made perfect sense; because if he'd been imagining things and the letters belonged to the late Philip Catherwood, wasn't it likely or at least possible that all the other items were

Catherwood papers too, and the form his delusions had taken was simply reading his own name every time he saw that of the poor dead subaltern. In which case, assuming he was right about Philip meeting his death in the shadow of the horned mountain, then of course the date would have been 22 January – 22 January 1879, the day of the battle. Actually, it was probably even simpler than that. It was dark in the strongroom, right? And the handwriting – well, he could read it all right here, in a well-lit pub, but down there, with a hangover and under a single sixty-watt bulb, wasn't it at least conceivable that he'd misread Philip Catherwood as Paul Carpenter, and mucked the dates up as well?

He could feel clenched muscles relaxing all over his body. Of course, he realised, that was all there was to it. Easy enough to figure out how it'd happened; the booze, of course, and the cold, and a certain degree of mental imbalance caused by his addled love for the thin girl, combined with his vivid imagination making mountains out of the molehills of minor weirdness he'd experienced over the last month – and as for them, he was absolutely confident that he'd be able to explain them all, given time and a few extra brain cells. The claw-mark, for instance; so one of the cleaners had a large, boisterous Alsatian, which for some reason she brought to work with her one day, and it got off the lead and scratched some paint. Big deal. The bauxite? Well, maybe he had actually dowsed or scried it; there were little men with hazel twigs who did it for a living, he'd seen TV programmes about it; or else it was just coincidence, exaggerated by his overheated imagination. The round, red eye through the letter box? That Alsatian again. Or Mr Tanner, temporarily bloodshot after smoking a cigar right down to the last knockings of the stub. That really only left the sword in the stone, and he'd been through all that already. In short, there was a simple explanation for every single thing. Probably it was all just something to do with J. W. Wells trying to fiddle its tax bill. Practically anything in the world becomes suddenly credible if you tag the magic words *doing it for tax reasons* on the end.

He finished his drink and stood up. All that panic and fuss over a silly misunderstanding.

In which case, Paul asked himself as he sat in the bus, *what about me and Sophie?* Well, now there was no more weirdness to worry about, there was no reason to quit the job, so that was all right. But if there was no weirdness, then— He frowned so ferociously that the woman sitting next to him got up and moved to the back of the bus. If there was no weirdness, then by implication all that stuff that Professor Van Spee had told him was just guesses, from someone who fancied himself as a bit of a Sherlock Holmes, and accordingly unreliable at best, most likely worthless. A similar line of argument could be used to dispose of the Gilbert and Sullivan thing. In which case, she probably didn't love him after all.

Oh, he thought.

For crying out loud, he told himself. Life wasn't like that. Your cake, to have and to eat, from this day forward, in weirdness and in health. You couldn't decide to keep the nice bits of the crazy stuff, and take the rest of it back to the shop for a refund. Anyhow: wasn't it better to be living in a universe where things worked like they were meant to, where claw-marks were made by big dogs, hung-over idiots misread old, faded letters in dark rooms, good-natured employers took new trainees out to lunch on their first day, and girls didn't fall in love with pathetic wimps with no redeeming features whatsoever?

Well, yes, he said to himself. *Of course, naturally. I suppose.*

But then he remembered something that had been lurking at the back of his mind. *It can't be too bad,* he told himself. (And if he was smirking a little, so what? There was nobody to see.) *She can't absolutely hate the sight of me, or she wouldn't have agreed to go out with me tonight . . .*

Pause. Rewind. Delete smirk. *Shit!*

Well, at least that explained why she'd stomped off in a huff when they'd parted outside the office door. She – against all the odds, she'd actually said yes when he'd asked her out, thereby giving him an option on being the happiest man on earth and having all his dreams come true; choirs of angels were waiting in the wings, blue skies were lurking at the edges of clouds all over the western hemisphere, Berkeley Square was knee-deep in nightingales practising scales and arpeggios, and he'd *forgotten*. A stupid, trivial little thing like the fear of death had been enough to flush it out of his mind, and now here he was, conclusively and comprehensively stuffed in perpetuity. Idiot. Tea-bag memory. Of all the bloody stupid things . . .

It was raining when Paul got off the bus, and his coat was back in St Mary Axe. He pulled his jacket lapels round his face, like he'd seen them do in the movies, but it didn't do any good at all. The hallway of the house was pitch dark – the bulb had gone, and nobody could be buggered to replace it. He was wet through, and his suit smelt of rain. He opened the door of his bedsit, groped for the light switch and stumbled in.

No light switch. Either that or some clown had moved it. But people don't break into houses and move the electric fittings around, or at any rate not in Kentish Town. Feeling annoyed and stupid, he stood in the doorway, pawing at the wall, but he couldn't seem to locate the bloody thing. For a moment he wondered if he'd blundered into someone else's room by mistake – but that wasn't possible, he could distinctly remember unlocking the door, and here was his keyring, still in his hand.

But still he couldn't find the goddamned light switch. Nothing for it; on the mantelpiece, he knew for a fact, right in the middle between the 2p-coin jar and the petrol-station carriage clock his parents had given him for his eighteenth birthday, there was a candle. He lit it occasionally for ambience, though it generally went out after thirty seconds or so. Next to it there should be a box of matches, for lighting the gas fire. He headed for it, remembering to sidestep where the sword in the stone should be, and traced the wall with his fingertips. Sure enough: mantelpiece, candle, matches, precisely where he'd left them. He struck a match and lit the candle.

Oh, he thought.

It wasn't his room. Well, it was the same room he lived in, because this was his candle, there was the stupid bloody sword, there were the window and the bed, there was the table, there was the damp patch on the wall that looked like a map of Turkey drawn by Salvador Dali. But it wasn't his room. He thought about it, and about various other things, including several stately homes he'd been taken to as a child, picture postcards from the

Victoria & Albert museum, and various bits of the *Antiques Roadshow* he'd sat through at various times, waiting for *Star Trek Voyager* to come on. It was, he decided, the way the room he lived in would probably have looked a hundred or so years ago.

Fuck this, he thought, and turned round, heading for the door, which wasn't there any more.

CHAPTER SEVEN

Not that it wasn't a perfectly nice room. If anything, it was an improvement; instead of the knackered old gas fire there was a merry blaze in the fireplace, its glow reflected in the polished brass of the coal scuttle. The light from the handsome cut-glass oil-lamps was softer and more soothing than the glare of the lonely hundred-watt bulb. The furniture was polished wood and sumptuous fabric, none of your flat-pack melamine junk. It was cosy, warm and friendly, in a homely sort of a way. But it didn't have a door.

Which sort of raised the question: how were you supposed to get in and (more pertinent still) out of it? Well, there was the window; but when Paul tried to lift the sash it wouldn't budge; furthermore, the glass was frosted so he couldn't see out of it, and when he hefted the heavy bronze bust of Prince Albert that stood proudly on the mantelpiece and hurled it with all the force at his disposal, it bounced off the window-pane and nearly broke his arm.

Christ, he thought. Then he banged on the wall where the door had been, and yelled for help at the top of his voice.

Clouting walls with your fists gets pretty tedious after a while, especially if you're naturally clumsy and catch your little finger on a picture hook. Nobody answered, of course. He stood for a while, sucking his crushed finger; then he pulled back the rug, just in case it covered a trapdoor. It didn't. Besides, it was *his room*. All he'd done was walk into it. There had been a door there just a few minutes ago, or how had he got in?

Theory; what sort of room doesn't have a door? A room you aren't meant to get out of. Suppose he'd gone mad, and they'd locked him up, and this was his cell. Possibly they'd got him muddled up in the list of patients with someone who believed he was Gladstone or Sherlock Holmes, hence the decor, by way of humouring him. By this stage, though, he'd had a bellyful of rational explanations. Besides, he didn't *feel* mad. Surely you'd know it if you'd gone off your rocker – you'd have a headache, or angel voices would be urging you to chuck the English out of Aquitaine. It was about time he got over this inferiority thing, whereby he naturally assumed that if things weren't as they should be, it had to be his fault or something wrong with him. He made a resolution; until he got proof to the contrary, he was going to work on the assumption that he was perfectly normal and everything else was up the pictures.

Paul thought about that. Maybe he had gone potty, after all.

No, he asserted furiously, *I'm not falling for that one again. That's not right. That's what they want you to think.*

Now he was beginning to scare himself, so he made an effort and froze his mind: intense calm, deep breathing, *om* and all that crap. Accept that something really, profoundly, deeply weird was going on. Now, then; one step at a time.

First thing he had to determine; was he in any obvious danger? Well, no. If he fell asleep in the chair and a stray spark jumped off the fire and set the rug ablaze, things might get a bit ugly; that aside, the most immediate threat was starvation. He looked over at where his cooker used to be. It wasn't there any more, but there was a large earthenware jar on a marble-topped stand that turned out to contain a fresh, sweet-smelling cottage loaf, and the butter dish held a pound of rich yellow butter; also there were pots of jam, and a tea caddy full of tea, and a crock containing bacon and sausages; the kettle and the grid were over by the fireplace, and there was water in a tall crockery jug. Talking of crockery, he could just see a blue-and-white chamber pot under the bed, which more or less answered his next question. (*Yuck*, he thought.) Since he'd missed lunch and was hungry, he sawed off the crust of the loaf with the bread knife he found in the drawer under the stand, daubed on some butter and ate the result. It tasted like real bread and real butter; but when he looked back at the loaf, it had contrived to heal itself; there stood a pristine loaf and an untouched butter pat. He repeated the experiment, with the same results. Further meticulous investigation revealed that the same self-replenishing effect occurred with the water, the tea, the small jug of milk, the sugar bowl, the bacon and the sausages. In fact, as far as the bare necessities were concerned, there was no reason why a bloke couldn't live here indefinitely.

That thought scared Paul more than anything else.

Another point occurred to him, and he looked at his watch. It wasn't there; but at some point he'd apparently sprouted a waistcoat, perfectly matching the jacket and trousers he was wearing but had never seen before in his life, and in the waistcoat pocket he found a handsome silver watch on a gold chain. It read a quarter past six. It wasn't ticking. It had stopped.

'Help?' he muttered. Silence. Not even traffic noises in the road below. Amazing, the extent to which he missed them, now he'd noticed they weren't there. The only sounds he could hear were those he made himself. *Maybe I'm dead*, he thought.

(*No, no, no*, he told himself, *we've already been into all that – well, not me, but Plato and Descartes and all that lot, the cogito-ergo-sum and does-a-tree-falling-in-a-forest-make-a-noise-if-nobody-hears-it brigade; so you can skip all that.*)

Eventually, after a bit more wall-pounding and help-yelling, and another round of bacon sandwiches, he flopped down in the really very comfortable armchair next to the nice warm fire, propped his feet on the embroidered footstool, and sat staring into the fire for a while, trying to figure out whether the coal in the grate was diminishing and turning into ashes as it burned. The answer was yes, so he added some more from the scuttle, which refilled itself as soon as he took his eye off it for a second.

Well, here I am, he thought.

Gradually he started to feel sleepy; his eyes didn't want to stay open, and his chin slid down onto his chest.

Something told him that he ought to stay awake. (Or was that concussion victims?) But the effort was too much. Nothing to stay awake for, after all. Eventually he let go, and started to dream.

It was the sort of dream that sneaks up on you. He was in the nice comfy chair by the nice cosy fire, but now he wasn't alone. Two young men in Victorian clothes were sitting opposite him; they were smoking clay pipes, very relaxed and friendly, and he supposed he must know them from somewhere. They were chatting, but he was too sleepy to pay attention to what they were saying; he caught an occasional word, but nothing that made sense. Then one of them leaned forward, tapped him on the knee with the stem of his pipe, and asked him what he thought.

He lifted his head and opened his eyes. 'I'm sorry,' he mumbled. 'I think I was dropping off.'

The two young men laughed. 'I should say,' one of them said. 'But look here, don't you think it's gone on quite long enough? After all, you've only been here – what, a couple of hours? Hardly that; but already you've had enough of it, and no blame to you. It's confound-edly dull, with nothing to read and only us for company.'

Paul tried to keep his eyes open, but the lids were too heavy. 'It's not that,' he assured them. 'I'm rather weary, that's all. Be a good fellow and let me take a nap.'

'Of course,' said the curly-haired young man. 'But you will help us, won't you? After all, you know where it is now, it'd be no great matter for you to slip it in your pocket and bring it away with you. And we've been here – oh, how long is it now, Pip?'

'A hundred and twenty-five years,' the other man said. 'Give or take a week or so.'

'Goodness,' Paul heard himself say, though what he really meant was *Jesus* or *Fucking hell*. 'My poor fellow, what a dreadful thing. But I'm still not sure what it is that you expect me to do.'

'Perfectly simple,' said the curly-haired man. 'Take it and bring it here. At least, this place will do as well as any other. Then we can go that way—' and he pointed at the back wall, where the fireplace was. 'And once we've gone, you can go back the other way, and we'll all be right as rain, you'll see. Now, is that too much to ask of an old friend?'

Put like that, it did seem perfectly reasonable. 'I'm terribly sorry,' Paul yawned, 'but I still don't quite catch your drift. What is it you want me to take, and from where?'

The two men looked at each other, as if they were the ones who weren't quite sure what was going on. 'Steady on, old chap,' said the one called Pip. 'A joke's all very well, but this is hardly the time.'

'Honestly,' Paul said, 'I don't know. Tell me, and—'

'That's not funny, you know,' the curly-haired man said quietly. 'Fun's fun and all, but that ain't, if you see what I mean.'

'No, really. If you'd just tell me—'

'For Heaven's sake.' The curly-haired man was getting annoyed. 'This is rather serious for us, you know. This isn't the time or the place for any of your humour.'

It occurred to Paul that he didn't want to get them angry. 'I promise you,' he said. 'Tell me what you want me to do, and I'll see to it that it's done. I give you my word.'

The one called Pip stood up. 'That's enough,' he said. 'Obviously you know, or how else could you have come here? There's no door,' he added sourly. 'Or hadn't you noticed?'

Paul knew that unless he calmed them down, they were going to do something horrible to him. He was supposed to get them out of here, that was clear enough. Whether they ought to be allowed out was another matter entirely. 'Forgive me,' he said, as pleasantly as he could. 'You're right, it wasn't funny. I'll see to it straight away.'

Pip looked at him, then sat down. 'That's quite all right, then,' he said. 'First thing tomorrow?'

'First thing,' Paul assured him. 'You just leave it to me.'

The curly-haired man grinned. 'You and your humour, Jack,' he said. 'For a moment, you had me fooled completely. Now then, let's have another drink, and say no more about it.'

He stood up and grabbed Paul by the wrist, and suddenly he was awake, sitting up in bed, in his pyjamas. For a moment, he thought he could still see the curly-haired man standing over him; but it was only the sword in the stone, silhouetted against the window.

'Door,' he said aloud, and jumped out of bed.

The door was where it ought to be. Furthermore, when he turned the latch, it opened, and when he pushed it, it clicked shut. He did this several times, just to make sure. Never had the operation of a simple mechanical device given him more satisfaction.

'Bloody hell,' he said aloud, and looked at his wrist. His watch was back, and it told him the time was a quarter past three; in the morning, because it was dark outside the window, with the amber glow of the street light seeping through. He flipped the light switch, and looked round. There was his room, the scruffy epitome of his life, just as it had been when he'd left for work that morning. There was his suit, lying across the chair next to the bed, with his shirt on the floor and his tie on top of it. An unwashed plate on the table showed that he'd had cheese on toast (the stale Tesco's Canadian Cheddar, left over from the weekend) and baked beans for supper, which probably explained a great deal.

Paul's mouth was dry and furry, so he made himself a cup of tea. Sitting on the edge of the bed with the tea mug in his hands, he very nearly managed to persuade himself not to go to work the next day, or any day thereafter; to find another job and forget about Sophie, and get all the weirdness out of his life for good. But that was just three in the morning talking. He remembered reading something about three o'clock in the morning, how it was the time when most suicides happened, something to do with chemical imbalances in the brain caused by the sleep cycle, or something equally plausible and scientific. Anyhow; he knew that if only he could get to sleep, things would seem a whole lot less urgent and desperate when he woke up. He finished his tea, cut the light and lay on his back, staring into the darkness where the ceiling had to be. He was sure he wouldn't be able to get to sleep now, and he was right.

He put the light back on, fished in his jacket pocket and found the letters. It was important, he felt, that they were still addressed to Lieutenant Philip Catherwood, and they were. He started reading them; and, in spite of the lurid nature of their contents, they sent him to sleep faster and surer than a general anaesthetic or the collected works of Martin Amis. That would have been fine; except that as soon as he was asleep he was back in the Victorian room; he was still reading the letters, but they weren't written to Philip Catherwood any more. On the contrary; they were written to him and signed, *With all my love, Sophie*. One thing he hadn't noticed before; on the envelope, she'd written Paul Carpenter, but the letters now started off, *My darling Pip*. Still, at least this time he knew it was nothing more than a bad dream, the fault of some careless or malicious Canadian dairy farmer, so that was all right.

Next day, they finished off the rest of the strongroom. He had to wait till eleven o'clock, when Sophie went off to get a cup of coffee, before he had a chance to put the letters back and check the other stuff – the bank books, title deeds, death certificate. As he'd suspected and hoped, the name on all of them was Philip Catherwood. *Hallebloodylujah*, he said to himself.

As if J. W. Wells and Co. had realised that a joke, like a tent peg, should only be rammed into the ground so far, the weirdness quotient in the items left to be catalogued fell dramatically. True, it was all old stuff, for the most part the property of people who had to be long since dead, but there was nothing tactlessly bizarre; just legal papers and money stuff, a few bundles of letters, nothing odder than the occasional bunch of keys or case of stuffed parrots. Sophie seemed unusually cheerful that morning, though she didn't seem inclined to chat. It was as though something nice had happened to her, but she didn't want to tell him about it. At lunchtime, she smiled at him, said, 'See you later, then,' and darted off for her coat before he was ready to follow. He stayed in their office, staring out of the window and trying not to think too hard about anything. Something still wasn't right, and it was getting less right all the time, but he had no idea what it could be.

They dealt with the last item in the strongroom at a quarter past five precisely. Curiously or by coincidence, they'd been given exactly the right number of yellow stickies for the job, with not one left over.

'Right,' Sophie said. 'Thank God that's that done. I've had enough of this stupid cellar.'

'Me too,' Paul agreed. 'Feels like I've been down here for a hundred years.'

'I suppose we'd better cross-reference the red book against our inventory,' Sophie said, with absolutely no enthusiasm whatsoever. 'But it can wait till tomorrow, can't it?'

'Oh, I should think so,' Paul confirmed.

Something wasn't right, he thought again. Just then, there should have been a bond between them, a shared sense of achievement, drawing them closer together. It should have been, Paul knew, a moment. But somehow it wasn't. He was leaning against a shelving unit; she was sitting on a trunk (Item 445, containing, according to the red book, the uniform worn by General Raglan at the battle of Balaclava), staring at the door and humming softly under her breath. He'd had occasion to notice before that she could carry a tune to the same extent that lobsters can pilot transatlantic airliners. Not that he minded, in fact he'd made a conscious decision that it was endearing. Nevertheless, Sophie's mind was clearly elsewhere. He found a stray sheet of blank paper and started folding it into an aeroplane.

'Paul.'

Now that was a first; she hadn't called him by his name before. He paused in mid-fold.

'Hello?'

'Well—' He knew that she was undecided about something, trying to make up her mind. He dropped the paper aeroplane, not bothering to look and see where it fell. Better late than never; here came the moment, unless he was very much mistaken. 'Well,' she repeated, 'do you mind if I tell you something? I mean – well, we're friends, aren't we? After doing this, and everything. And I've got to tell someone.'

'Sure,' Paul said. 'Fire away.'

'All right.' She had her back to him, her thin shoulders and long, slim neck outlined against the white paint of the door. 'The thing is,' she said, and paused once again. 'The thing is, I went to a party yesterday. After all,' she added, with just a tiny hint of extreme, dark, savage bitterness (*Why?* he wondered; and then – *Oh, shit* – he remembered) 'I didn't have anything else to do, as it turned out, so I went to this party. Well, not really a party, I don't like parties, but this friend of mine, Lucy, she's just come out of the Army, she was a tank mechanic – anyway, she's just moved in to a new flat and she asked some friends round, and she wanted me to go so I went. And I met this bloke.'

'Really?'

'Yes.' Suddenly Sophie swung round and looked at him. Her face was blank, but her eyes were shining. 'His name's Shaz and he does anarcho-socialist ceramics as a performance art, and he lives in an old bus in a field near Esher, and we talked for hours about all sorts of stupid stuff, and, well, I think I like him a lot.' She stopped abruptly, then went on. 'I know, it's really like stupid and girly, because

I've got to tell someone, and really I haven't got a clue if we're going to have a relationship or not, we haven't talked about it or anything, but I think it's sort of likely that we probably will, I don't know. Anyway,' she added, 'you don't mind me telling you, do you? Because the fact is, you're probably the closest friend I've got, apart from Leeza, but she's still in the Ukraine, and Rachel, but she'd be all snotty about it, because she doesn't hold with men at all, and I suppose there's Harmony, but all she ever wants to talk about these days is the destruction of owl habitats in Northumbria. You don't mind me telling you, do you?'

'No,' said Paul's voice, 'not at all. Um, great,' Paul's voice added. 'Congratulations, I guess.'

She shrugged, but with great vigour. 'Oh, it's way too early for that,' she said. 'I mean, yes, we talked for hours and hours, but then he and a bunch of his friends were going to drive to Stonehenge and watch the sunrise in his bus, and he asked did I want to go too, but I said no, I had to get up for work in the morning, but he said that was all right, like he really didn't mind, which was really good, I thought, like not making demands or anything. But anyway, he mentioned he was doing a performance tonight at a pub out Denmark Hill way and he said I could come along if I felt like it, so I said yes, all right. So that's all, really.'

'Great,' said Paul's voice, sounding like it was coming from a very long way away. 'Well, I hope everything, um, I hope it all goes okay. Have a nice time, I mean. And it's Saturday tomorrow, so you don't have to get up early—' He made a promise to himself to smack himself round the face with a brick for saying that, as soon as conveniently possible. 'Well, great,' he said. 'Hope it all works out for you.'

'Thanks.' She nodded. 'So, what're you doing for the weekend? Got anything lined up?'

'Me? Oh, no, nothing much. Thought I might have a lie-in tomorrow, read, do the ironing, relax, just flop around.' *After all*, he added to himself, *what the hell else can I do, when my whole life's just fallen down a grating and got lost for ever? Some moment*, he thought, *some bloody moment*.

Sophie was looking at him; and if she really could read his mind, possibly what she saw there was bothering her, a bit. There was just a hint in her expression of the look he'd seen in the faces of Duncan and Jenny, the vast, noble compassion of the fixed-up for the eternal unwilling celibate. At another time, in another context, the next thing she'd say would be that there were lots of other fish in the sea.

'So,' he heard himself saying, 'he's into pottery, then? Interesting.'

'Ceramics,' she corrected sharply. 'What he does, it's more like conceptual than, well, useful or anything. He told me all about it. Apparently he learned most of it from a tribe of Tuareg nomads in North Africa, and now he's applying for a Lottery grant so he can evolve the interactive side of it, hopefully with multimedia and the Internet. Then he's hoping to go to New Guinea, apparently they've got a really exciting tradition of conceptual ceramics there, based around this stuff they use, it's sort of like a mixture of straw ash, volcanic lava and pig manure, which he wants to try and incorporate into his own work at a fundamental level. But, of course, that all depends on the grants position, so it's not settled yet.'

Pity, Paul thought. *How about if I bought a lottery*

ticket? Loads of lottery tickets? How much does it cost to send one lecherous arsehole to New Guinea, anyway?

'Great,' he said. 'So, how long's he been doing this?'

'About five years,' she said. 'As a performance thing, anyway. He started on the pottery ages ago, while he was still in prison. Then he was two years in North Africa after that, and six months in Finland learning to be a shaman, so all told it's quite a long time, really.'

'I see,' Paul said. 'He's probably pretty good at it by now, then.'

'Oh, yes,' Sophie said. 'Well, I haven't actually seen any of his stuff, but he showed me a couple of albums of photos, and it all looked really amazing.'

'Right,' Paul said. 'And that was without the performance, presumably.'

She nodded. 'Anyway,' she said, standing up, 'we'd better be getting out of here. What is the time, by the way?'

He checked his watch. 'Just coming up to ten to six,' he said.

It took about half a second for the implications of that to sink in.

'Shit,' she said crisply. 'Let's just hope they haven't locked the stupid door yet.'

They hurried up the stairs, walked then ran down the corridor, and burst through the fire door into reception. Nobody there. Sophie raced to the door, shot back the bolts at top and bottom, lifted the Yale catch and tugged at the door. It didn't move.

'Shit,' she repeated.

'There's two deadlocks,' Paul pointed out helpfully. 'I suppose there might be keys in the desk or something.'

Maybe there were, at that; but the desk drawer was

also locked, so they never had a chance to find out. 'Now what do we do?' Paul asked, helplessly.

Sophie wrenched at the door one more time, then kicked it. 'This is *stupid*,' she said. 'All right, there's got to be someone in the building. I mean, aren't the partners in a firm like this supposed to work late every night, and all through weekends? Or there's the cleaners,' she added. 'We've just got to wait till they show up—'

'Unless they don't come in till the morning,' Paul said. 'Or even until after the weekend. What I mean is, we don't know they'll come tonight.'

'Fuck.' Sophie gave the door another kick. 'Well, there's got to be a side door or something like that. A fire escape,' she added triumphantly. 'Got to have fire escapes, it's the law.'

Paul nodded enthusiastically. 'You're right,' he said. 'Where?'

'Where what?'

'Where are they? Only, I don't remember ever seeing one.'

'Well, of course there's fire escapes—' She hesitated, frowning. 'Actually, neither do I. Mind you, there's lots of bits of this building I haven't been in yet. We'll have to look. That's if we can't find someone to let us out, of course.' Paul could see her forcing herself to relax; it was like watching a small child holding back a huge, frisky dog on a long lead. 'And if that doesn't work, we'll have to bust a window or something.'

Paul was horrified. 'We can't do that,' he said. 'They'll fire us.'

'So?'

'So—' He stopped short. He couldn't possibly explain why he didn't dare risk losing this job; though of course all that had changed now, presumably. 'They'll fire us,' he repeated.

'Fine.' She scowled at him so ferociously he could feel his skin tanning. 'All right, I'll break a window and go home, you can stay here all night and explain that it wasn't your idea and you didn't want to have anything to do with it.'

'Sorry,' Paul said automatically. 'I mean, before you go doing anything like that, let's see if we can find Mr Tanner or somebody.'

'Why Mr Tanner?'

'I don't know,' Paul admitted. 'It's just that the day I came in early, he was already in here, before the door was unlocked. So maybe he stays late.'

She thought about that, and nodded. 'All right,' she said, 'we'll try his office first. Come on.' She stormed out of reception like a scale model of the *Bismarck* breaking out of the Denmark Straits, and Paul jogged along after her. He didn't like the situation at all, but probably, he felt, for different reasons. For one thing, she hadn't seen the red eye peering out through the letter-box flap.

Mr Tanner wasn't in his office, that was the first thing they noticed. The second was the mess. Papers everywhere; on the floor, on the chair, piled up in heaps as though someone had thrown them up in the air and then jumped on them. The other chair had been knocked over. Also, Paul noticed but didn't mention, there were several gaps in the tomahawk collection on the wall.

'Maybe he's in the photocopy room,' Sophie said. 'We'll try there.' Either she hadn't noticed the mess; or, more likely in Paul's view, she'd decided there wasn't time for worrying about side issues. She took half a dozen steps towards the door, then stopped. Footsteps outside, in the corridor; someone running. Or rather – Paul scrabbled in his memory for the right word. Scampering.

'That's all right, then,' Sophie said. 'Hello? Hello—'

The footsteps stopped, as she reached the door and put her fingers to the handle. Something about the sound must have got through to her, because she hesitated. They listened to the footsteps coming back. More than one of whoever it was.

Sophie said, 'I don't—'

—And then the door flew open. It hit her hard on the side of the head, and she fell sideways. Paul moved forward, then stopped in his tracks, gawping helplessly. In the doorway stood something utterly unlike anything he'd ever seen before, except maybe in a book, when he'd been very young. Up to a point, it was a bit like a tall, thin monkey, except that it was wearing clothes – a leather jerkin, and over that a chain-mail shirt, black steel red with rust, and on its head a round steel helmet that was too small and the wrong shape generally. In its left hand it clutched a short axe – one of Mr Tanner's tomahawks, Paul guessed, though he really wasn't too bothered about details. It had the face of a pig, and little round red eyes that he was sure he knew from somewhere.

'Bloody hell,' Paul whispered.

The creature – the hell with it, Paul decided, he'd call it what it was. The goblin saw him and stopped dead, like a startled cat. Another goblin, more or less similar but more ape- than pig-faced, appeared behind it and pulled up sharply, peering over its shoulder. They stood quite still, watching him. He watched back. He was, of course, scared out of his wits (to his shame, he could feel something warm and wet trickling down his inside leg, but there wasn't time to feel bad about that); but somehow he knew that of the four life forms in the room, he wasn't the most terrified, not by some considerable margin. While this thought was crossing his mind, he noticed that the back goblin was holding a short, wide-bladed spear, and both of them had claws where there should have been fingernails. *Claw-marks*, an isolated part of his subconscious duly noted, *that clears that up*.

He had an urgent feeling that moving, at least before the goblins did, wasn't a good idea; likewise, breaking eye contact. He had no idea why, it was just something he knew, in the same way that he could point accurately at the corner of the room with his eyes shut. He wanted very much to see if Sophie was all right, but that would mean shifting his eyes a fraction to the right, and that simply wouldn't do. He was stuck.

So, apparently, were the goblins. At any rate, neither of them was moving or breaking eye contact either. In fact, there didn't seem to be any reason why the three of them shouldn't stay exactly as they were until nine o'clock on Monday morning; assuming, that was, that no fourth party intervened to break the spell.

Sadly, life wasn't like that. From some other part of the building, downstairs by the sound of it, came a loud crash, followed by an outburst of chattery screaming, like a million monkeys trying to dictate the works of Shakespeare into a tape recorder. Paul nearly jumped out of his skin; so did the goblins, but apparently this was just their reaction to Paul's sudden movement. Either they knew what the noise was, or it didn't bother them. Maybe it even reassured them. In any event, while

Paul was still recovering from the shock, they pounced forward, swift as spiders but still extremely wary, like two small bouncers tackling one enormous drunk. The one with the spear scuttled straight at him, while the other one dived to the right, to take him in his flank. Paul jumped back, trod on the leg of the overturned chair and lashed out frantically with both arms to try and regain his balance. This had the effect of freezing both goblins in their tracks; in fact, it reminded Paul of one time he'd been on a country walk and found himself in a field full of young bullocks. It was the same disconcerting half-heartedness, the same blend of aggression and obvious terror, though what they had to be scared about, Paul wasn't quite sure. True, the taller of the pair, the one with the axe, was maybe four foot nine and distinctly weedy under its bristles. On the other hand, there were two of them, and the point of the shorter one's spear was only about six inches from Paul's navel.

Out of a clear blue sky, it occurred to Paul that he might try shouting at them. Maybe it was because that was what had worked with the herd of bullocks, or maybe it was just long-buried instinct. Anyhow, he tried it, whereupon both goblins did a standing jump four feet backwards, recovered, took a step forward and froze again. They stared. He stared back. Another stalemate.

(Yes, he thought, but now they were well clear of the door, which meant that if Sophie still had her wits about her she could sneak out without being seen, and— And what? Go for help? She couldn't get out of the building. Besides, he mused, remembering the crash and the screams, it was more than likely that the two goblins weren't the only examples of their kind on the premises.)

He drew in a deep breath, for shouting purposes, but found that he couldn't bring himself to make any noise whatever. Either the terror was slowly paralysing him, or subconsciously he was thinking about other goblins in the building, who might come running if they heard him yelling. He let the breath out slowly, and concentrated on keeping still.

Talk about your moments; this was a moment all right, and it seemed to go on for ever. Things weren't getting any better as time passed. For one thing, Paul realised to his profound dismay and disgust that his left leg, which had been supporting most of his weight since he recovered after falling over the chair leg, had just gone to sleep; so that if he did get the chance to run, he'd have a numb foot to contend with, or pins and bloody needles at the very least. He toyed, very briefly, with the idea of making a grab for the short goblin's spear, but his imagination was too vivid for that. He could almost see the blood and feel the pain as his hands missed the shaft and grabbed the extremely sharp-looking blade instead. He ordered that particular plan of action to fuck off and die; even thinking about it was much, much too dangerous, as far as he was concerned.

At any rate, he thought, it didn't look like Sophie was going to be able to keep her date with the anarcho-socialist potter. Count blessings; gratitude for small mercies. If he was going to be ruthlessly honest with himself, it didn't really help.

It was the third goblin that buggered everything up. Looking back, Paul reckoned it must've come bouncing into the room without realising something was up. It was about the same size as the spear-carrier, weasel-featured and armed with a broad, curved sword; it bustled in, saw Paul, came to a sudden halt and screamed.

Immediately, Paul heard himself shout back; bizarrely, what he was shouting was, 'Please go away,' but it was obviously the way he said it, not the actual content, that did the trick. All three goblins shrank away from him as if he was the one with all the weapons, and this remarkable show of cowardice set his instincts in motion again. He took a long stride forward, stamped his left foot down hard and shouted 'Boo!' at the top of his voice.

To a certain extent, it worked like a charm. All three goblins turned and fled, the spear-fancier dropping his spear in the process. This should have been a good thing, but it wasn't. By now, the other two goblins had reached the doorway; and the spear-fancier, finding itself unarmed and exposed, shrieked in panic and shrank backwards, towards the corner of the room, away from the door. *Bugger*, Paul thought, and he took another step forward, raising his arms and flapping them in the air, trying to shoo the goblin like a farmer herding sheep.

He'd overdone it. The goblin screamed horribly, scuttled back and bumped into Sophie, who was just getting up off the floor. The goblin spun round, saw its chance and grabbed her by the hair, hauling her across its body while its other hand produced a knife and held it under her chin.

In the last split second, Paul managed to stop himself from shouting; just as well, because he was absolutely certain (don't ask him why) that a shout at that precise moment would have scared the goblin into frantic, violent panic, and Sophie would have been killed then and there. Instead, Paul held absolutely still, his weight on his numb back foot, a breath half-taken in his throat, and let the goblin back away through the door, dragging Sophie with him. It was yet another moment; in this instance, the worst such of Paul's life.

Just to make sure, he stayed put and counted to five, as the sound of the goblin's awkward footsteps died away beyond the doorway. Only then did he dare take the risk of coming back to life.

'*Shit!*' he yelled. Then he lunged forward and grabbed the spear off the floor, where the goblin had dropped it. At this point, his numb foot made its presence felt; he wobbled, nearly stuck himself with the spear under his left armpit, slammed the butt onto the ground and put his weight on it.

This wouldn't do at all; so, using the spear as a crutch, he swung towards the door and hobbled out into the corridor. No sign, in either direction; nothing to give him a clue which way they'd gone.

Paul hesitated. The clever thing to do, he knew, would be to go back into Tanner's office, throw a chair through the window, and scream for help. But he didn't. He wasn't sure why, he just knew that going back would be going in the wrong direction, leaving Sophie when he should be following. 'Shit and fuck,' he muttered balefully, and looked down the corridor, then up. Which way? No idea; and eeny-meeny-miny-moeing at this juncture simply wasn't going to cut it, he had to make a *decision*. 'Bugger,' he explained to himself, and turned right.

Right, of course, meant down the corridor into the computer bay, through the fire doors and down the stairs; at the foot of which he stopped and listened. Somewhere in the distance, he could hear bumps and crashes, like noisy children shifting furniture. Presumably goblins; and he was perfectly well aware of the fact that he was a coward, completely out of his depth, in a locked building containing an unknown but probably substantial number of utterly terrifying and apparently-until-proven-otherwise hostile creatures. But that was about as relevant to the decision-making process as the price of cocoa butter on the New York commodities exchange. The only question was, were those goblins the right goblins, or not?

No way of knowing. All Paul could think of was getting hold of one of them and hitting it until it made the other one, the one who'd got Sophie, give her back. It was a spectacularly stupid plan, and he knew it, but it was all he could think of. Hating his left foot for having pins and needles in it, he hoppitied down the passageway like Long John Silver running for a bus, and shoved through the fire door into reception.

He was looking for goblins; he'd found them. He didn't bother with a meticulous headcount, but there were at least twenty of them, apparently playing some form of rugby football with the large metal waste-paper basket that usually lived under the receptionist's desk. As soon as Paul barged in, they stopped whatever it was they'd been doing, and froze. They were staring at him, as if – well, as if they were junior clerks in a City of London office, and he was a goblin.

Oh for God's sake, not all that again, Paul said to himself; and instead of staring back, he yelled, 'Bastards!' at the top of his voice and brandished the spear in as melodramatic a fashion as he could manage with a duff foot and a soaking-wet trouser leg.

The goblins fled. All, that was, except one.

One, however, was enough. It was bigger than the others he'd seen – rat-faced, broad across the shoulders and armed with a long, thin knife and a chunky-looking iron club with spikes sticking out of it. For a split second it turned to follow the others; then it screamed horribly, jumped onto the front desk and threw the club at Paul's head. Paul dropped the spear and ducked as the club sailed past his head, missing it by the width of a cigarette paper. The goblin jumped down, reaching for him with its clawed hand; Paul backed away on his heels like a Cossack dancer, flailing with his arms for balance, and as he retreated down the line of the front desk, his fingers closed on something cold and smooth. Whatever its proper function was, this object had suddenly been upgraded to weapons status; Paul grabbed it and lashed out at the goblin's claw, rapping it hard across the knuckles. It was at this point that he discovered what the mystery object was. It was the long stapler.

A table lamp would have suited him better; likewise a length of steel pipe, or an Uzi. But what he'd got was a stapler, and it was better than nothing. The goblin paused for a moment, weighing up the merits of various tactical initiatives, and suddenly hopped forward, swiping at Paul's face with its claws. Without really knowing what he was doing, Paul intercepted the goblin's swing with his own left hand, grabbing its arm just above the wrist. Then, hefting the stapler in his right hand, he closed its jaws onto the goblin's soft, leathery palm and squeezed hard. The stapler went *click*; the goblin shrieked, dropped its knife and tried to pull away. It succeeded, but not before Paul had stapled it again. Now that, he couldn't help thinking, was a good moment.

After that, things started to look up – thanks mostly to

the goblin, who made the mistake of backing into the bookshelf on the far wall of the little bay where callers waited for their appointments. This shelf supported the considerable weight of one hundred and three bound volumes of the *Journal of Meteorological Studies*, June 1949 to December 1957 inclusive. In turn, the shelf was secured to the wall by two stout wooden brackets; but not stout enough, it turned out, to survive a direct hit from the spike on the top of a goblin helmet. To be precise, the spike took out the bracket at the end of the shelf nearest to Paul and the front desk. Immediately the shelf dropped forward, and the bound volumes slid off it one by one. June 1949 to September 1951 between them knocked off the goblin's tin hat; the rest of the collection drummed off its hairy skull like raindrops, until a glancing blow from February 1956 finished it off and dropped it to the ground like the proverbial felled ox. It was an awesome, really quite inspiring sight, and while it was going on, all Paul could do was stand and stare in fascinated admiration. Once the last volume had done its stuff, however, he snapped back into life, pounced on the stricken goblin and grabbed it by one long, furry ear.

'Bastard,' he yelled. The goblin stared at him and whimpered, its little red eyes wide with horror. At any other time, Paul would have had to let it go, and probably find it an old blanket and a saucer of bread and milk. Just then, however, he wasn't in the mood. He hardened his heart, clenched his left fist, and swung it back for a good, hard swing—

'What the bloody hell,' said a voice behind him, 'do you think you're playing at?'

He let go of the goblin's ear and whirled round so

fast he hurt something in his neck. Mr Tanner was standing in the doorway.

Paul tried to find some words, but only one of them came to hand. 'Goblin,' he said. '*Goblin.*'

Mr Tanner gave him a look you could have skated on. 'Actually,' he said, 'that's my mother.'

CHAPTER EIGHT

It was one of those moments when the moral high ground opens and swallows you up. Paul looked down at the cowering goblin, buried up to the neck in the *Journal of Meteorological Studies*, and back at Mr Tanner, and for a short time he forgot all about Sophie and the weirdness and the fact that he'd just fought a giant orc (as he was already thinking of the goblin) to a standstill, armed with nothing but a stapler. He felt like he was ten years old and he'd just been caught trying to hide the shards of the priceless Ming vase he'd used to smash the drawing-room window.

'What are you doing here, anyway?' Mr Tanner said. 'It's nearly six o'clock – you shouldn't even be in the building.'

'Sorry,' Paul said automatically; and then it occurred to him that somewhere about the premises, a horrible hairy creature with a face like a weasel was holding a knife to Sophie's throat. Somehow, the risk of getting fired didn't seem quite so important. 'Sophie,' he said, 'they've got her. One of the—' He hesitated. If this one was Mr Tanner's mother, the knife-wielder might be his cousin, or his aunt. 'Grabbed her,' he said, 'stuck a knife under her chin. You've got to do something.'

Mr Tanner sighed, as if he'd just been called out of an important meeting to sign a stationery requisition. 'I see,' he said. 'All right, stay there. And try not to cause any more trouble.'

He went back through the fire door. Paul noticed that he was still holding the stapler. He put it carefully down on the front desk, then looked round. The goblin – Mr Tanner's old mum – was still crouching on the floor, watching him with baleful, terrified eyes. 'Um, sorry,' he said, and held out a hand to help it up, but it made a tiny, brittle screaming noise, like worn-down brake shoes, and shrank away.

About a minute later, Mr Tanner came back. Sophie was behind him, with a dazed expression on her face but no blood or anything. Paul wanted to rush over and fold her in his arms, but he had enough sense left to realise that this wouldn't be a good idea. 'Sit down,' Mr Tanner barked at her, and she dropped obediently into the receptionist's chair. 'And you,' he added to Paul. Then he knelt down beside the book-entombed goblin, gently held out his hand and screamed at it, like a monkey in a zoo, or a mynah bird. The goblin screamed back, grabbed his wrist and hauled itself up, taking great and ostentatious care to keep Mr Tanner between itself and Paul. Slowly, tenderly, Mr Tanner walked it across reception, holding it gently by the arm, then opened the door for it. The goblin paused in the doorway, pointed at Paul with a long, wickedly curved claw, and shrieked.

Mr Tanner nodded and shrugged, then closed the door after it.

'Right,' he said, turning and facing them.

It was that last nod and shrug that did it. They'd reminded him of when he was six or seven, at which point in his spiritual development he'd had to put up with weekly visits to Auntie Pauline's, where he was invariably sent out into the garden to play with his obnoxious five-year-old cousin Gary. Every week it had been the same; as soon as Gary got bored with whatever game they were playing, he'd favour Paul with an evil grin, burst into hot, wet tears and run howling in through the French windows, bellowing *Mummy, he hit me* at the top of his precociously loud voice. Every week, Mum and Dad and Aunt Pauline and Uncle Terry would accept the little bastard's version without question, and Paul would be spoken to and sent to sit in the car, with nothing to eat or read, till it was time to go home; and every time, as Paul was being led away to solitary confinement, Mum would look at Auntie Pauline and nod and shrug in precisely that way.

Not this time, Paul decided. He jumped to his feet and yelled, 'What the bloody hell is going on?'

Mr Tanner frowned at him, as though he was a spelling mistake. 'Sit down and be quiet,' he said, 'and I'll tell you.'

'Oh, right,' said Paul, and he perched on the edge of the front desk. But he couldn't bring himself to let it go at that; he had to ask: 'Mr Tanner,' he said. 'Was that – was that really your mother?'

'Yes,' said Mr Tanner.

'Fine,' Paul said. 'So does that mean you're—'

Mr Tanner nodded. 'A goblin, yes. If you want to be pedantic about it, I'm a quarter human on my father's side, but that's really none of your business.'

Sophie raised her head and stared at him. She still looked as though she'd followed a large white rabbit with a pocket watch down a hole in the ground, but some colour was starting to return to her cheeks. 'Mr Tanner,' she asked quietly, 'why are there goblins in this building?'

Mr Tanner sighed. 'They own it,' he said.

Sophie opened her mouth to say something, but didn't. Mr Tanner pulled up a chair from the waiting area, sat down and lit a cigar.

'I suppose it's our fault, really,' he said. 'Actually, it's something of a bone of contention in the partnership right now. Some of us feel that when we take on trainees, we ought to put them in the picture right away, to avoid God-awful fuck-ups like this one. Others like to see it as a sort of rite of passage cum intelligence test; if you're bright enough to work for JWW, you ought to be able to figure it out for yourselves.' He flashed one of his trade-mark unpleasant grins. 'Nice idea,' he said, 'but with the calibre of the recruits we have to make do with nowadays, probably a bit unrealistic.'

He drew hard on his cigar and blew a smoke ring. 'Anyhow,' he went on. 'I think the best way to explain it to you is like this.' He reached in his pocket and took out some folded sheets of paper, handing one each to Sophie and Paul. At first sight, it looked like the firm's standard letterhead. But then Paul noticed an extra line of fine print just below the company name and logo:

J. W. WELLS & CO.
SUPERNATURAL CONSULTANTS, PARANORMAL ENGINEERS,
PRACTICAL METAPHYSICIANS

'Found it?' Mr Tanner said. 'Splendid. Now, I'd like you to look at the partner's names, on the right-hand side, under the By Appointment symbol. After each name, you'll see a string of letters – qualifications, you don't need to be told that. Got it?'

Paul looked across. The list read:

> *John W. Wells MAA (Oxon) LLB FIPES Dip.N.*
> *Humphrey Wells ASTP CIIM*
> *Professor Theodorus Van Spee VULWIT OBE*
> *C. N. Suslowicz FSEE AIBG*
> *The Contessa Judith di Castel'Bianco QF FRICS*
> *Lt-Col Dietrich Wurmtoter RHG FICDGBI*
> *Dennis Tanner BA (Plymouth) BG*

'All right,' Mr Tanner said, 'let's start at the top. MAA stands for Master of Arcane Arts. FIPES means Fellow of the Institute of Practical and Effective Sorcerers. Dip.N. is just Diploma in Necromancy – no big deal, you just fill in a form and send them a fiver and you get it in the mail by return. Humphrey Wells, now let's see: ASTP is Associate of the Society of Thaumaturgical Practitioners; CIIM is something like Confrère de l'Institut International de la Magie – they're a load of tossers if you ask me, but it impresses the French, and we're always told we've got to think Europe these days. Anyway; I can't remember what VULWIT stands for and if I could I couldn't pronounce it – it means Theo Van Spee's the something-or-other professor of witchcraft at the University of Leiden, which probably means bugger-all to you two, but take it from me, that's hot stuff in the trade. The OBE was for services to horticulture, and God only knows how he came to get that. Cas Suslowicz: FSEE is Fellow of the Society of Elemental Engineers, AIBG is just Associate of the International Brotherhood of Giants, he got that just by being born—'

Paul made a choking noise. 'Sorry, what was that?'

'Giants,' Mr Tanner repeated. 'Cas Suslowicz is a giant, hadn't you—? No, I guess not.'

'But he's—'

'He's a *short* giant,' Mr Tanner said firmly. 'Judy Castel'Bianco, that should be obvious even to you two.'

'No, it isn't,' Sophie said dangerously.

'QF,' said Mr Tanner, 'Queen of the Fey. You do know who the Fey are, don't you? Hint: you've got them at the bottom of your garden, and I don't mean a water feature. Rick Wurmtoter, he's a Ritter des Heiligen Grals – that's Knight of the Holy Grail to you – and a Fellow of the Institute of Chartered Dragonslayers of Great Britain and Ireland. The Lieutenant-Colonel bit is perfectly genuine too, if you count the Riders of Rohan as a proper army. And that's about it.'

'What about you?' Sophie growled. 'BG.'

Mr Tanner beamed at her, revealing many unusual teeth. 'Boss Goblin,' he said.

There was a second or so of complete silence. Then Paul asked, 'Excuse me, but what does it all mean?'

Mr Tanner clicked his tongue. 'Oh, come on,' he said. 'Right, from the top: Humph Wells is a sorcerer; he does mostly commercial and banking these days, but he still keeps his hand in with conjuring and raising spirits, mainly for the Far Eastern market and the States. Theo Van Spee is probably the best wizard currently working in the private sector – space/time stuff principally, a lot of consultancy work, and of course the whole of the information technology side. Cas Suslowicz is almost entirely construction and civil engineering, as you'd expect. Judy – well, obviously, she looks after our client portfolio in the entertainment sector. Rick Wurmtoter's our resident hero, basically he does pest control, mostly dragons—'

'Dragons,' Paul repeated.

'Dragons. Even you've heard of dragons.'

'Yes, but they don't—'

'Dragons,' said Mr Tanner wearily, 'are attracted to accumulations of wealth. These days, that's mostly museums, art galleries and, of course, banks. This week he's off dealing with a nasty infestation in the vaults of the Credit Lyonnais, they're hoping he can get shot of the buggers before the Euro goes into free fall on Wall Street. And I'm a goblin,' he added, with a smirk. 'But you know that already.'

Paul knew Mr Tanner was waiting for one of them to ask; he reckoned it might as well be him. 'Um, what do goblins do?' he said.

'Ah.' Mr Tanner stubbed out his cigar on the leg of his chair and lit another. 'Goblins live in the bowels of the earth, digging vast tunnels that go down to the outer skin of the magma core. In other words,' he went on, 'minerals. Which means, where I come from in New South Wales, bauxite. Which,' he added with a particularly nasty grin, 'is why I hired you.'

Paul's mouth flopped open. 'Me?'

'You. You're a natural scryer, as you've just proved. Ninety per cent success rate, that's really very good.'

Paul didn't know what to say. 'You mean, those photos of bits of desert—'

Mr Tanner nodded. 'You looked at them, and instinctively you knew where the bauxite deposits were. Don't go getting ideas, though, that's what we're paying you for. You, on the other hand,' he went on, looking at Sophie, 'Theo Van Spee reckons you've got what it takes to be a seer. Coming from him, that's a real compliment, and don't you forget it.'

'I'm honoured,' Sophie grunted. 'But I don't think I want to, thanks.'

'You don't want to,' Mr Tanner repeated.

'That's right.'

Mr Tanner's face stretched into an enormous toothy grin; and Paul, staring at it in horrified fascination, reckoned he could definitely see the family resemblance. 'Tough,' Mr Tanner said. 'It's not up to you.'

'Isn't it?' Sophie replied.

'No. You signed a contract.'

Sophie laughed. 'Fine,' she said. 'Sue me. I've got sixty pounds in the bank and fifteen pounds and some pennies in the Post Office; oh yes, and a Premium Bond. You can have the lot for all I care, but I'm not coming back here again, not ever.'

Mr Tanner shook his head. 'Never sign a legal document without reading it,' he said. 'Clause 3, paragraph five, I can't remember the exact wording but the gist of it is, if you try and quit, we can force you to work for us, any way we choose.' His eyes flashed red, just like his mother's. 'You really don't want to find out how we do that.'

Sophie shook her head. 'I don't believe you,' she said.

'Really.' Mr Tanner shrugged. 'Then you leave me no choice, I'm delighted to say. Now then. When I snap my fingers three times, you're going to take all your clothes off and dance the Dying Swan. Ready?' He clicked his fingers, once, twice, three times. At the third click, the expression on Sophie's face suddenly changed, from grim defiance to total and unspeakable horror. Her fingers spread like starfish, as she fought to keep her hands by her sides, then they were at her throat, and she slowly undid the top button of her blouse.

'No,' she whispered. 'Please.'

Mr Tanner laughed. That was too much for Paul; he jumped up and reached for the stapler, but Mr Tanner turned his head and looked at him. At once, Paul felt an unbearable pain in his arm, as if someone had caught it in a huge pair of red-hot tongs and was pulling it towards his face. He watched as his index finger straightened and started to move inexorably towards and then up his left nostril. He could feel it reaming and twisting. 'All right,' he gasped, 'all right. I'm sorry.'

'That's all right,' Mr Tanner said indulgently, and he snapped his fingers again. Simultaneously, Paul and Sophie felt their arms relax and flop to their sides. 'And that's me being nice,' Mr Tanner added. 'You're lucky I'm in a good mood. Sometimes I can be a bit of an old crosspatch, and I don't think you'd like that. Oh, and while I think of it; if you were toying with the idea of trying to involve the police, or the industrial tribunal, or the newspapers or the Esther Rantzen show, I wouldn't bother if I were you. Even if you managed to tell them about what you think just happened here, they won't believe you. But it wouldn't come to that, because the moment you opened your mouth or tried to post the letter or send the e-mail, you'd find yourself crouched on the floor with your thumb in your mouth singing "Give My Regards to Broadway". I take the view that being a really evil bastard isn't just a job, it's a vocation.'

Up to that point, if asked, Paul would have told you he knew perfectly well what being scared felt like; he knew scared from nothing, thank you very much, in fact he could write a postgraduate thesis on it: fear of heights, spiders, flying, getting beaten up, getting caught, being late, being laughed at, earwigs, loud noises, pretty well anything you cared to name except Mary Poppins and breakfast cereal. As he sat on the front desk and stared at Mr Tanner, however, he realised that hitherto he'd known about being scared the way a bumble-bee knows about flying to Andromeda. A quick sideways glance told him that Sophie was thinking along much the same lines. Under other circumstances, finding something they had in common would have pleased him no end. On this occasion, it didn't seem all that significant.

'And anyhow,' Mr Tanner went on, 'you may think you want to pack it in, but you're wrong. Once you've got over this daft little culture-shock thing, you'll realise you've lucked in to the most fantastic career anybody could ever wish for. Think about it, will you? You're going to be *wizards*, you're going to learn to do *magic*. There's a hundred million kids from Saigon to Greenland who'd give their PlayStation for a chance like you've got. So,' Mr Tanner continued, smiling agreeably, 'let's have less of the long faces and more of the cheerful enthusiasm. Are we happy? Because if we aren't,' he added, 'we soon will be. Well?'

'We're happy,' Paul and Sophie mumbled in unison.

'Are we excited? Looking forward to a whole galaxy of thrilling new opportunities?'

They nodded.

'That's all right, then.' Mr Tanner stood up. 'Sorry if I've cut into your free time, but I think this exercise has been useful. Now bugger off and I don't want to see you back here till nine sharp Monday.' He crossed to the door and took out a bunch of keys. 'Oh,' he said, 'one last thing – particularly as far as you're concerned, Ms Pettingell. Goblins aren't all that different from people. Scare the shit out of them, and you may find they get panicky. Leave them alone, and they won't bother you. And it's particularly important you don't go getting on the wrong side of this particular colony, because as I said a minute or so ago, they're actually our landlords here; they own it, let it to us at a peppercorn rent, strictly on the understanding that we see to it that when the doors are locked, they can come out of the tunnels where they live, run about, have a bit of harmless fun after a long day digging ore with their fingernails, without bloody great big humans jumping out at them, frightening them half to death. Not a lot to ask, I think you'll agree. Also,' he added grimly, 'they happen to be family, and I'd like you to ask yourselves how you'd like it if huge ugly monsters barged into your parents' lounge and started shoving them around. Really, it's just basic good manners and consideration for others. Understood?' He unlocked the door, and opened it for them. 'Right,' he said, 'off you go. Ms Pettingell, if you get a move on and don't dawdle, you'll find you're in plenty of time to catch the 6:05 from London Bridge to Denmark Hill, which just happens to be running twenty minutes late. That means you should get to the Spaniel and Spigot just as the warm-up band's grinding to a halt, and I promise you, you won't have missed anything.' He grinned, and winked insultingly. 'Have a nice weekend,' he said. 'Be good.'

The door closed behind them, and they could hear the keys graunching in the locks. It was just starting to rain.

'Well,' Paul said. Sophie didn't answer. They walked a few steps, then paused.

'You heard him,' Paul said. 'Hurry, or you'll miss your train.'

She looked at him; rain was running off her forehead and down her nose, like fat tears. 'What're we going to do?' she said.

Paul shook his head. 'I haven't got a clue,' he said. 'My dad's got an old Spanish proverb he's always quoting: when you're drowning in beef stew, it's a hell of a time to decide you're a vegetarian. I'm not sure whether it applies to this or not, but it's the best I can manage right now.'

Sophie looked at him for a moment, then shrugged. 'Well,' she said, 'see you Monday.'

'Yes, right. Enjoy your pottery thing.'

'Ceramics,' she corrected him, and walked away.

Paul took the only course of action open to him at that point in his career. He went to the nearest pub and drank six pints of lemonade shandy, without the lemonade. When he asked for a seventh, the man behind the bar said he reckoned he'd probably had about as much lemonade shandy as was good for him, and maybe he ought to go home. Paul thanked him, left the pub, found another and ordered a pint of ginger-beer shandy, without the ginger beer. When the barman asked him if he wouldn't rather just have a pint of lager instead, since it amounted to the same thing, Paul shook his head and replied no, he'd rather stick to shandy because he wasn't used to strong drink. Then he fell over; whereupon kind-hearted bystanders helped him out through the door and into the gutter. There he stayed for a while, considering his options and restructuring his priorities, until a policeman came along and arrested him.

But Paul merely smiled. True, he'd just passed through unutterable horrors and every aspect of his life had turned to cheap cooking shit between his fingers, but at least he didn't have to take that sort of nonsense from coppers; not now that he was a wizard.

First, though, he tried to explain. 'You can't arrest me,' he said. 'I'm a wizard.'

The policeman admitted to a certain degree of scepticism. He advanced an alternative theory of his own, and tried to grab Paul by the lapels.

Paul brushed him aside, none too gently. 'You can't do that,' he said. 'Not respectful. I'll give you one last chance, and then—'

But the policeman didn't seem to want his last chance; a pity, but there's no helping some people. With a mild sigh of regret, Paul narrowed his eyes, took a deep breath and clicked his fingers.

It didn't seem to be working.

Meanwhile, the policeman hadn't been idle. He'd got Paul up on his feet, and was shoving him rather brusquely against a wall, while unshipping his handcuffs. Paul was disappointed, to put it mildly. This wasn't what he'd been led to expect. Fat lot of good it

was, being a wizard and being able to find bauxite blindfold in the dark wearing boxing gloves, if you couldn't do
a perfectly simple thing, like ordering Porky Pig to eat
his truncheon. Then he remembered, and suddenly it all
became clear. He'd thought of the bit about the truncheon *after* he'd snapped his fingers. *Well, there you are*,
he told himself, and tried again.

For a moment, Paul had the nasty feeling that it still
wasn't going to work. But then, just when he was beginning to get worried, the policeman let go of him, took a
step back, and made a very faint mewing noise, like a cat
inside a large suitcase. Then, in slow motion like an
action replay, he pulled the shiny black riot stick from
his belt, lifted it to his mouth and bit it.

There was a faint pinging noise. In retrospect, Paul
figured out it was probably a tooth breaking.

'There you go,' Paul said happily, as the policeman bit
again. 'Though, if I was you, I'd try it spread on toast, or
with a couple of bits of bread. Truncheon meat, ha ha.'
He grinned, Mr–Tanner-fashion. He'd never had a
policeman for a straight man before. 'Mind how you
go,' he said, and walked away, straight into a deep, oily
puddle.

The special providence that looks after cats and
drunks got him home. He closed his door, flopped down
on the bed and went straight to sleep. He had a strange
dream; in this dream, he fought a band of goblins, discovered he had unearthly magical powers, and forced a
policeman to commit an undignified and painful act in
public. While the dream was playing inside his mind, he
found himself thinking that, even by his standards, this
dream was as weird as the plumbing on the Tardis. Then
he woke up; and, in the split second between the return

of consciousness and the hangover spinning its wheels in the poisoned mush of his brain, he realised that it wasn't a dream, it was a memory.

Oh, he thought.

Jesus, he thought, *did I really say* truncheon meat? *Not good. Not good at all.*

He stumbled out of bed, found the kettle and filled it with water. Just for fun, instead of flipping the switch he gave it a stern look, snapped his fingers and said, 'Boil!' But nothing happened. Still, he hadn't expected that anything would. Maybe that was why it hadn't. Whatever.

Thinking about it rationally and sensibly didn't really help. He'd got past the stage where he could kid himself that the various weird things he'd seen were hallucinations or unusually vivid dreams. Instead, he had to face the fact that he was living in a world where magic seemed to work, goblins existed and he was stuck in the cold eye of Weirdness Central without the option of running away. In theory, there was a positive side, since apparently he could do at least some bits of magic; he could immobilise policemen (ever since he could remember, he'd been terrified of them) and so, also in theory, he could do pretty much what he liked, without having to worry about being arrested and sent to prison. Fine; but even if this was true, when he came to think about it he couldn't call to mind a single illegal thing he actually wanted to do. So maybe he could rob banks and have lots of money; a fat lot of good it'd do him, even if he got away with it, when he was obliged to turn up for work every day at 70 St Mary Axe and file printouts or play Spot-the-Bauxite all day, or else risk some imaginatively nasty penalty from the murky depths of

Mr Tanner's imagination. Besides, he rationalised, there was probably a very good and obvious reason why the possessors of magical powers didn't go around helping themselves to anything they took a fancy to, or else why were the partners in the firm working for a living, instead of swanning about enjoying themselves like a bunch of supernatural Kray Brothers? It was much more likely that the scope of his superpowers was severely limited; he'd be able to stare down one copper, for example, but not two – something like that. On balance, he decided, having magical powers would probably turn out to be rather like satellite TV; sounds cool, turns out to be more hassle than it's worth.

All that bothered him, for sure; but for most of the weekend, as soon as he allowed his mind to wander, Paul found his thoughts turning to Denmark Hill, and wherever the trail led from there. The more he thought about that, the worse it got. For the last month, he realised, his whole life had been founded on one admittedly unlikely supposition: *if I can woo and win this girl, I shall be happy ever after.* He'd never for one moment believed that he could actually win, but at least he'd been in the race, in contention. Now, at a stroke, he was out of it. She'd found someone else. *No vacancies, the position's been filled, go away.* Not just that; thanks to Mr Tanner and his horrible associates, he was condemned to go on seeing her every day, spending hours on end in the same room with her, when what he really should be doing was putting as much distance between himself and her as he possibly could. He knew the drill, he'd been turned down often enough. If he could quit his job and get another one, it was a pound to a chocolate Euro that within a matter of days he'd light on some other unsuspecting female who happened to meet his not-too-exacting criteria and fall hopelessly in love with her. No problem; that was his natural defence system, a series of rebounds as quick and complex as the highest level on a pinball table. Unfortunately, that option didn't seem to be open. The best he could do would be to fall for someone else at JWW; and he didn't hold out much hope in that direction, for the simple reason that if there'd been anybody suitable on the premises, he'd have done so already. But who was there? The secretaries were either notoriously spoken for or far too glamorous and beautiful to offer him the tiny glimmer of hope that was a prerequisite for crush acquisition. It had always been the same; the ones Paul fell for tended to be boot-faced, bespectacled, a tad too fat or too skinny to slot neatly into the conventional stereotype of womanly beauty. It was, he'd admitted to himself, the difference between hunting for the rainbow's end and buying a lottery ticket every week. Neither path was ever going to make him a rich man, but doing it his way, at least he had a one-in-fifty-million chance. That was enough.

But.

All right, then, Mr Wise Guy: why *do* fools fall in love? There had to be a reason. About the only thing Paul still remembered from school science lessons, aside from various interesting things that happen when you mix iodine and ammonia, was Darwin's theory. Evolution; it was something he couldn't help taking personally. Gradually, over ten thousand dark millennia, everything necessary had been designed and installed, everything useful had been adopted, everything harmful or unhelpful had been pared away. Sometimes he fancied he could almost hear the thoughts of those successive generations of prototypes, trudging wearily up the steep path of progress with nothing to keep them going except the instinctive knowledge that their effort and unselfish sacrifice would some day lead to the ultimate, the final version that couldn't be improved on: himself, Paul Carpenter. It would be an unforgivable insult to their memory to assert that any design feature comprised in his physical or mental make-up wasn't there for the very best of reasons. The same sequence of processes that had brought about such miracles of engineering as bones, muscles, blood and brain had also shaped his instincts and emotions; inevitably, therefore, the software had to be as perfect, in its way, as the hardware. Accordingly, there *had* to be a reason for the apparently loopy way he carried on around girls – it had to be some kind of survival skill or behavioural trait optimised for the greater glory of the species. Nature had included it in the package for a purpose; but he was buggered if he could see what on earth it might be.

And, by the same token, there had to be an equally good and pressing reason why, this time, when he'd somehow managed to get so much further than ever before, to the point where the bloody woman was prepared to talk to him, listen to him, buy him ham rolls; where she regarded him as a close enough friend to confide her wonderful news to him – there had to be some reason why an anarcho-socialist mud-fondler should suddenly appear out of thin air and whisk the object of his devotion away to Denmark Hill and the darkness that lay beyond, suddenly and conclusively drowning all his hopes like kittens in a bucket. Very well. He had faith, he believed that it was all for the best, that a million generations of single-cell life forms had given their lives to make it that way. But it'd be nice if someone – not necessarily Mr Darwin in person but someone from his department, a junior assistant secretary or something – would take the time to drop by at some point and explain it all to him, in terms he could understand. It wasn't much to ask. Simple courtesy.

Instead . . . instead he got goblins, and Mr Tanner, and bauxite, and the Institute of Practical and Effective Sorcerers. Nobody, not Darwin's best friend, not even God's mother could tell him that this was any way to run a universe. The only conclusion Paul could possibly draw was that the whole operation had gone to cock, and a billion years of mutating plankton would be entirely justified in asking for their money back.

And, on top of that, the milk had gone off.

At any other time, he'd have shrugged and gone to the shop for a more recent version. Not this time; because now he knew that the same agency that had microengineered the intricate hydraulics of his heart had hand-reared the bacteria that were currently making whoopee in his hardly touched pint of semi-skimmed and, once again, he couldn't help but take it personally. He'd been chosen by Darwin and Destiny to scry bauxite, to fall in love with girls who preferred performance potters, to take part in this bizarre rat-in-a-maze experiment; the least he could expect was milk without great big chunks of cheese floating in it. *Not good enough*, he decided, and he wasn't standing for it.

He gave the milk a ferocious scowl, and snapped his fingers.

The kettle boiled.

He stared at it for a moment; then he thought, *Well, I suppose you've got to get the hang of it first, practice makes perfect and all that.* He tried again; but this time, he concentrated on the milk. *Come on, milk,* he thought, *you know better than that. You want to end up getting tipped down the bog, fine; but wouldn't you rather do your job, fulfil your purpose, be the best carton of milk you possibly can? I can always get another pint of semi-skimmed, but as far as you're concerned this is it. Now or never. Do you really want to go gurgling away into the dark sewers without even having tried?*

He snapped his fingers. Nothing happened.

Fine, he thought; and he studied the milk for a moment, imagining what it'd be like to swim about inside it, if he was no bigger than a milk molecule. He closed his eyes tight and visualised the curdled, knotted particles, set upon by bacteria like Mexican peasants harassed by evil bandits. Then (he could see it, in his mind's eye, on his mind's screen) quite suddenly a little milky peasant stands up and defies the bacteria, and almost at once there's a terrific battle, the peons rushing their persecutors like a tidal wave, dragging them down from their horses, beating them to death with farm tools and pitching their battered corpses on the village midden. Eyes shut, he could see the clots and zits in the milk break up, the ghastly yellow fade into pure milk-white. There was a smile on his face as he opened his eyes and looked down.

No dice.

A brief moment of panic, followed by simple aggravation; and he snapped his fingers as though he was kicking the spin-dryer or thumping the photocopier (this hurts me more than it hurts you, but sometimes you've got to be cruel to be kind). Then, without bothering to look, he poured milk into his tea, stirred it, fished out the tea bag and drank. It tasted just fine, as he'd known it would.

It was at that moment that Paul realised the simple, basic truth. The world ought to work properly, there was nothing wrong with it, but sometimes it stuck or it wouldn't start in the mornings. Magic was the confident, well-placed clout on the side of the casing, the clip round the carburettor that got it going. Magic wasn't changing the world or making it do impossible stuff; magic was persuading it, by force of will and a little controlled violence, to stop fart-arsing about and get on with what it was supposed to be doing.

Simple as that.

Now that he'd figured that out, he had no trouble at all. It was dark and gloomy outside the window, just starting to spit with rain; but he soon fixed that with a neatly directed finger-snap, and the sunlight switched itself on and the cloud-curtains were drawn and tied back, and the rain thought better of it and went away somewhere else. There was no bread, nor sausages, nor bacon; but that wasn't right, because a hard-working magician needed a good breakfast inside him before he could go setting the world to rights. One click of the fingers sorted out the supply foul-up; another produced a perfect bacon sandwich. The dustbin needed emptying and the ceiling was swathed in dusty wreaths of cobweb, but he was far too busy these days with his important work for the bauxite industry to be bothered with menial chores like dusting and trash-haulage. A quick spot of thumb-and-middle-finger action, and it was all taken care of; what was more, three dirty mugs he hadn't even noticed spontaneously washed and dried themselves and lined up to attention on the shelf over the sink.

Dismissed, he told them. *Carry on.* Ironed shirts materialised on hangers, books left the floor and fell in on the bookshelf, the dead light bulb in the bedside lamp came alive and glowed cheerfully. Situation normal, all systems nominal. Just like a bunch of badly behaved kids in the street; all they want is for someone to tell them what to do.

And then he thought; that was all very well, but how could a busy, hard-working bauxite-dowser like him be expected to give his full attention to his work when his heart was going pitter-patter like a bird with a broken wing, and his thoughts kept turning to the only girl he'd ever really loved, getting up to God knew what in a derelict bus in a field near Esher with a performance-potting jailbird? Too much to expect of anybody, let alone a sensitive, fragile sensibility like his. Obviously something had gone wrong here, and it needed fixing; so he'd snap his fingers, and then the phone would ring, and – *well, we can take it from there. Okay? Fine.*

Paul snapped his fingers.

Two pairs of used socks vanished from the floor and reappeared in his underwear drawer, crisply ironed and neatly balled. A broken pencil on the mantelpiece sharpened itself. Apart from that, nothing.

Of course, it'd have helped if he'd had a phone; but when he looked round the room, there was a dinky little fifth generation Motorola lying on the bed. He checked to see it was fully charged up and switched on. Then he snapped his fingers again.

Nothing.

He sagged, and dropped into his chair (which had somehow contrived to move from over by the door to directly under his bum without him noticing). So much for that theory, then. What the hell use was magic if all it could achieve was a little light housework and some entry-level shopping? Any bloody fool can wash up or shift furniture; the fact that he carried out these tasks by snapping his fingers rather than the more conventional methods was neither here nor there. Magic didn't work after all; it couldn't set right the fundamental lash-ups of the cosmos. It was like having a car with a fully functional CD player and a buggered engine. *Useless. The hell with it.*

The phone rang.

Paul jumped up out of his chair like a space shuttle bursting out of the Earth's gravity well. 'Hello?'

'Listen.' He recognised the voice. It wasn't the voice he'd wanted it to be. He sat down on the bed and closed his eyes. 'I need you here at the office, right now,' Mr Tanner went on. 'Don't waste time putting a suit on or anything like that. Get yourself over here right away.' Before he could say anything (such as, for example, '*Get lost*') the line went dead. Scowling, he aimed the phone at the wall opposite but didn't actually let fly. It occurred to him that maybe it wasn't him who'd magicked the phone out of thin air, but rather Mr Tanner; in which case, if he smashed it to bits, he might get in trouble. He shoved it in his pocket, grabbed his coat, and hurried out into the street.

Saturday; different bus timetable. He stood at the kerb, waiting to cross the road to the bus stop, but before he could do that, a taxi pulled up next to him and the door swung open.

'Paul Carpenter?'

'Yes,' he replied.

'Hop in.'

He frowned. 'But I haven't got enough money,' he said.

'Don't worry about that. Charged to the firm. J. W. Wells, right?'

Paul nodded and climbed in. All he could see of the driver was the back of his head: a cross between Yoda and one of the PG Tips chimps. *Wonderful*, he thought, *I'm being driven across London by a goblin. And my mum reckoned I'd never amount to anything.*

The journey hardly seemed to take any time at all, and as soon as he climbed out of the taxi, the door slammed shut and it drove away, leaving him standing outside 70 St Mary Axe. He was wondering how he was going to get inside when the door opened about twenty degrees, and a goblin face appeared. He didn't think he recognised it (this one was more sort of warthog-cum-peccary, with matching tusks). The goblin beckoned to him, and then, as they passed in the doorway, bowed deeply. That, he felt, was something he'd probably never get used to.

'You took your bloody time.' Mr Tanner was sitting on the front desk, in more or less exactly the same place and position as he'd been when Paul had left the office on Friday night. 'Still, at least you're here now. Take a look at these, ring anything that gives you the twitch in green marker pen.' He slid a folder of large glossy prints across the desk. All landscapes: aerial views of desert, the same old stuff. Paul started to feel more than a little sceptical about the urgency in all this.

'You still here?' Mr Tanner was looking at him over the top of his glasses. 'If you're wondering how you're going to get to your office with the place full of goblins, don't worry about it. Leave them alone, and they won't give you any bother.'

Paul left Mr Tanner in reception (he appeared to be reading a newspaper) and climbed the stairs to his office. No goblins anywhere to be seen; but no shortage of signs that they'd been there recently, from ripped carpet and claw-shredded wallpaper to axe-riven door panels and the occasional dark, foul-smelling brown stain on the floor. It'd take a dozen men six months to clean up and make good all that mess; but Paul knew better than that. A few finger-clicks was all it'd take, and nobody would ever guess there'd been anything on the premises larger or more destructive than a gerbil.

Just as well, Paul thought as he sat down behind his desk, *that my social and personal life are a complete fuck-up and I wasn't just about to go out or anythin*g. Even so, it was a bit much, being ordered back into the office on a Saturday morning. Was this sort of thing going to happen all the time, for the rest of his working life? Now there was a cheerful thought.

Never mind, he reassured himself. The quicker he started, the sooner he'd be finished. He went through the pile of enlargements, waiting to feel the electric-shock effect, but either he'd lost the knack or else there wasn't anything there in the first place. Not so much as a tiny twitch.

That wasn't so hot, he reckoned. Probably it was because he wasn't doing it right, maybe because his mind was on other things. It didn't take much imagination to picture Mr Tanner scowling at him as he handed back a wad of pristine photos, telling him to go away and do it again, properly this time. Well, he thought, he could cheat; draw in a handful of squiggles here and there at random, Mr Tanner wouldn't know he was lying. Then he thought; better still, if he could persuade Tanner that really he was rubbish at this job, maybe Tanner would decide Paul hadn't got the touch after all, and he'd let him quit. He uncapped the green marker pen, closed his eyes and prodded with a fingertip. Where his finger landed, literally in the middle of nowhere, he carefully drew a green circle, then moved on to the next one. It didn't take him long to do the whole stack; and as soon as he'd done the last one, the door swung open and in came Mr Tanner, with another blue folder under his arm, and a teacup and a plate of what looked like purple-iced Christmas cake in his hands.

'Any luck?' Mr Tanner asked.

'No. Yes, I mean. Actually, I'm not sure.'

Mr Tanner looked at him. 'Thought you could probably do with a cup of tea,' he said. 'Also,' he added, 'it's my birthday, Mum baked me a cake.' He put the plate down on Paul's desk.

'For me?' Paul asked.

'Don't eat it if you don't want it,' Mr Tanner replied. 'Anyhow, here's some more pics for you to have a look at. I'll take these other ones on, if you're done with them.'

'I—' Paul hesitated. 'Like I said,' he stammered, 'I'm not sure about them. I mean, I could've got them all completely wrong.'

Mr Tanner shrugged. 'Nobody's perfect,' he said, 'we all make mistakes. Just so long as you've done your best, that's all anyone could ask.' Before Paul could say anything, he scooped up the old photos, with their entirely spurious green rings, conspicuous as acne on the face of a supermodel, and put them under his arm. 'I'll let you get on,' he said. 'After all, I expect you've got things you'd rather be doing.' He paused at the door, and added: 'By the way, I appreciate you coming in like this, on a Saturday, on such short notice. I'll be honest with you, there's been times since you joined us when I wondered if you'd got what it takes, attitude-wise. I'm glad you proved me wrong.'

Paul listened to his footsteps in the corridor until they died away, then said 'Fuck!' rather loudly. Anything else he could probably have coped with, but gratitude was too much to bear. He nearly jumped up and ran after Mr Tanner, to confess his sins and get rid of the guilt, but he was too scared and ashamed. A small part of him tried to argue that this was just another of Mr Tanner's mind games, nastier even than the zombie magic, but even though he was pretty sure this theory was true, it didn't make him feel any less guilty. He sipped the tea, which was lukewarm and at least forty per cent pure sugar, and looked at the slice of cake. The idea of goblin cuisine didn't appeal to him one bit, but there was the dreadful problem of disposing of the body. If he just left it there and Mr Tanner saw it, untouched; or if he slung it in the bin – even worse. Eating it, on the other hand, was something he really wasn't prepared to do. It was too big to fit in his coat pocket. With a sigh, he pulled open the bottom drawer of the desk, intending to hide the slice there until Monday, when he could return with a suitable container in which to smuggle it off the premises.

He'd had the bottom drawer open only yesterday, and he could have sworn that at that time it'd been empty. Now there was something in it. Three things.

One was the long stapler; but Paul was used to finding

that lurking in unexpected places. The second was a bag of chocolate-covered raisins. The third was a cardboard tube, more or less the same length as the inner core of a toilet roll, but thicker. He frowned, took the roll out, laid it on the desk and poked up it with the butt end of a pencil. Something slid out. It looked like a rolled-up black plastic dustbin liner; but when he unfolded it, he recognised it as the funny sheet thing he'd found in the strongroom and briefly described as an Acme Portable Door, before losing his nerve and changing it to something less facetious. At least, that was what he took it for at first, because the markings (apparently representing the panels, hinges and handle of a door) looked at first sight to be the same. On closer examination, he reckoned they were in fact slightly different; an eight-sided doorknob instead of a round one, for example, and rather more detailed mouldings surrounding each pseudo-panel. He studied it for a moment, then shrugged, rolled it up and put it back.

Rather more interesting was the bag of raisins. Chocolate raisins were far and away Paul's favourite form of recreational nibbling; once he'd opened a bag, his hand would insist on straying back to it until the very last raisin had gone, generally leaving him feeling bloated and sick. This bag, he couldn't help noticing, was still sealed. That tempted him. Although what little residues of the basic human survival instinct that remained to him argued vehemently against eating anything he found on the premises, it seemed reasonable to assume that if the bag was still pristine and inviolate, it wasn't just the leftovers of a goblin snack. *Go on*, whispered the voice of temptation, *just have one or two, they can't hurt you*. It did occur to him that it was something of a coincidence that a bag of his favourite sweeties should manifest itself in his desk drawer, just when his guilt and general misery left him most vulnerable to the siren lure of comfort eating, but by then he was no longer in complete control of his actions. He hadn't noticed himself opening the bag, but it was nonetheless open; three or four brownly gleaming raisins had spilled out and were lying on the desk in front of him, pretty well clamouring to be popped into his mouth. (His preferred method was to tuck the raisin into the corner of his mouth until the chocolate coating melted, before biting into the sugary heart of the raisin itself.) *The hell with it*, he thought; and by the time he'd put the slice of purple cake in the drawer and slammed it shut, he was already on his second raisin and reaching for a third.

It didn't take him long to reach the conclusion that he'd done the right thing. They weren't just yummy, these raisins, they were super-double-plus yummy with a yummy chaser. He dug his fingers into the packet and scooped out a half-handful, cramming them into his mouth like a small child, and for quite some time all he could think about was how gorgeous they tasted. In fact, it was only when he realised that half the packet seemed to have gone that he made an effort and stayed his hand. Time, he decided regretfully, to start thinking about rationing what was left. He put the packet back in the drawer, closed it firmly and wedged it shut with his knee.

And now, he told himself, *you'd better get some work done, unless you want to stay here till Monday morning.* He reached for the nearest photo, and immediately felt the by now familiar tingling, starting at his fingertips and running all the way down to the base of his wrist. Pay dirt.

His first thought was dismay – if the scrying magic was working absolutely fine again, maybe there hadn't been anything wrong with it to begin with, and he'd drawn a blank on the first batch of photos simply because there quite genuinely hadn't been anything there to find. He elbowed the thought out of his mind, drew a green circle and reached for the next picture. Instead, his fingers found the raisin packet.

Weirder and weirder, since his knee was still jammed against the drawer. Still, he knew from long, dyspeptic experience that choccy raisins don't just sit there waiting for you, like cowboys holed up behind a barricade of wagons as a Sioux raiding party appears over the skyline; they sneak out like pale insubstantial wraiths and find their way into hand and mouth. Simple confectioner's magic, the sort that happens every day. Nothing to worry (*munch*) about.

He examined and marked four or five more pictures, each time feeling the scrying buzz. At least he was doing it properly this time, which he hoped would go some way towards making up for his childish and unprofessional behaviour with the first batch. If only—

He looked up, suddenly aware that he wasn't alone in the room. A goblin was standing on the other side of the desk, looking at him through tiny, traffic-light-red round eyes. Before he'd even had a chance to jump out of his skin, the goblin opened its mouth and screamed at him.

It was exactly the same scream as he'd heard yesterday, the subtle blend of mynah bird and monkey. This time, however, he realised he could understand it.

'Hello,' the goblin was saying.

(He wasn't translating, or anything like that; he hadn't suddenly learned goblin language without realising. Rather, it was as if the goblin was being dubbed into English, and the dubbed voice was coming from somewhere inside his head. Weird as square eggs; but somehow he wasn't as taken aback as he would have been under other circumstances.)

'Did you like the cake?' the goblin was saying, and that triggered something in his mind; this was the goblin he'd fought in reception, the one whose hand he'd stapled. In other words, Mr Tanner's mother.

'Um,' he replied (and he wasn't screaming, he was talking English; but the goblin seemed to understand). 'Yes, it was great. Very nice.'

The goblin nodded and bared her teeth; she had nine of them, all very long and sharp. 'Liar,' she said. 'You never even touched it, it's there in your desk drawer.'

'Ah,' Paul said.

'And don't say you weren't hungry,' the goblin went on, 'because you've been stuffing sweets all morning. Doesn't bother me,' she added, 'but if you can't bear to touch my cake, at least don't lie about it. Took me hours to make that. I'm not a ruddy servant, I hope you realise.'

The only reply he could think of at that moment was 'Sorry'; so he said it. 'Quite all right,' the goblin replied, still a trifle stiff but not nearly as bad as before. 'Actually, it's probably just as well. The icing's purée of rat liver whisked up with spiders' eggs and a dab of crème fraîche. You wouldn't have liked that, with your sweet tooth.'

Paul nodded slowly. 'Wasted on me, I'm afraid,' he said.

'Yes,' the goblin said. 'Well, give it here, then. Waste not, want not.'

Paul opened the desk and took out the slice of cake. The goblin snatched it from his hand and swallowed it in one gulp, like a performing seal eating fish in mid-air.

'In case you're wondering,' she said with her mouth full, 'those weren't just ordinary choccy raisins.'

Paul nodded. He'd guessed that already.

The goblin laughed; at least, she screeched, and Paul heard a laugh inside his head. 'You want to go easy on the rest of 'em, mind. They're not actually raisins, see.'

'Ah.'

The goblin shook her head. 'Actually,' she said, 'they're dragon droppings. Very expensive and rare.'

Paul felt his insides making a determined effort to become outsides. 'Chocolate-covered dragon droppings?' he croaked.

'Not chocolate-covered,' the goblin corrected him. 'Tastes like chocolate, of course, only better. But it's not just the flavour, see. It's the—'

Her last screech was untranslatable; that was, he heard it in clear, and no equivalent word passed through his mind. 'Sorry?' he said.

The goblin paused, as though searching for a synonym. 'Magic,' she said. 'Special with dragons. You get the same effect drinking their blood, only then it's permanent. With the droppings, it only lasts an hour or so. Still, you ask yourself which you'd rather do, cut a dragon's throat or follow around after it with a dustpan and brush.'

'I'm sorry,' Paul said. 'What exactly do they do, these—?'

'Oh, of course, you don't know.' The goblin grinned,

just like her son. 'They make you Understand. Like, if you eat one you can understand languages you never learned – well, like you're doing now. Also,' she went on, 'and this is the really good bit, though it can be a real pain sometimes; also, when people tell you lies, you hear what they say, but inside your head you hear what they're really saying, if you follow me. I'll give you an example, hang on.' The goblin paused for thought, and then—

The sound Paul heard was a shrill yell, totally inhuman. The words he heard were, 'I'm sorry I attacked you yesterday, and I deserved to get my hand stapled.' But at the back of his mind, in the dark corner where he couldn't even lie to himself, he heard *Like hell I'm sorry, you smooth-skinned tall git.* 'See what I mean?' she added.

'Oh,' Paul said. 'Oh, I see. That's—'

'That's a very good reason for not gulping 'em down a handful at a time,' the goblin said, 'quite apart from you'll spoil your dinner and end up fat as a pig. Still,' she went on, 'it's just a little present sort of thing, by way of saying sorry for trying to kill you.' (*Bullshit. Dennis made me give them to you. Dunno what he's up to, but you want to watch yourself. Sly bugger, he is, takes after his dad.*)

'Thank you,' Paul said.

'That's all right.' (*Drop dead.*) 'Anyway,' she went on, 'mustn't keep you from your work. And this time, mind you do it properly. Drawing green squiggles at random isn't what you're paid for, remember.'

Paul winced. 'You know about that?'

The goblin giggled; or at least the candied dragon-turd in his bloodstream translated the noise she made as a giggle. 'Do me a favour,' she said. 'When I was a kid, we had dragon black pudding for breakfast, straight from the pan. Bloody delicious, it was. Anyway, you can't fool me.'

'Apparently not,' Paul muttered. 'And I suppose you're going to go straight to Mr – your son, I mean, and tell him?'

'No.' (*What do you think, you snoutless clown?*) 'But he wouldn't care anyhow. He can tell the difference between a random squiggle and the real deal. I mean, he's not thick.'

'Ah,' Paul said. 'Well, thanks, anyway.'

The goblin shrugged, but didn't move. 'Well, get on with it, then,' she said. 'Or are you like all them other humans, can't perform when there's someone watching?'

It was the way she said it, rather than any input from the unseen translator, that made Paul feel slightly sick. 'What I mean is,' he said lamely, 'I'm sure you've got lots of things you want to be doing, so don't feel you've got to keep me company or anything.'

'Liar. You think I'm horrible, and you want me to piss off.'

'Well,' Paul admitted, 'yes.'

'Fair enough.' The goblin headed for the door. 'If you don't want to hear the other thing I was going to tell you, that's fine. No scales off my nose.'

Paul decided that trying to keep up in a points-scoring match with Mr Tanner's mum was almost certainly beyond him, and he couldn't be bothered anyway. 'What other thing?' he asked.

She sniffed. 'Oh, you don't really want to know. Besides, I'm horrible, so why should I tell you?'

Paul frowned; then he remembered the Great Magic, the one his mother had taught him. 'Please,' he said.

'That's more like it,' the goblin said. 'All right, here you go. Close your eyes, then open them when I tell you. Not before, mind. All right?'

Paul wasn't at all sure about that, but he did as he was told. After about ten seconds, the goblin said, 'Now,' and he opened his eyes.

He found that he was looking directly into what he took at first to be an old-fashioned A-Present-From-Llanelli glass paperweight, the sort that was round and contained a nondescript scrap of plastic seaweed, or something equally delightful. Then whatever it was started to glow with an offensively bright light. Before he could turn his head, however, he heard the goblin say, 'Oh no, you don't. If you look away, it won't work.' So he narrowed his eyes and tried to ignore the full-blown headache that was getting nicely under way in his right temple. Just when he reckoned he'd had enough, the light abruptly cut out, and in the centre of the glass ball, surrounded by what looked like a snowy day in Saskatchewan, he could see tiny dots moving about against a green background.

'Bloody interference,' the goblin said apologetically. 'Personally, I blame the satellite TV. Really screws things up when you're in the middle of a Seeing and suddenly all you get is reruns of *On The Buses*.'

'It's a crystal ball,' Paul said aloud.

'Yeah, and I'm a Smurf. This is a genuine seer-stone, you ignorant twat. Now look carefully, I can't keep this up all day.'

So Paul looked; and the harder he concentrated, the bigger and clearer the scene became. He could see a motorway; beside it, wedged in between the arms of two access roads, a scrubby patch of grass; in the middle of the grass, an old single-decker bus, painted in alternate swathes of pink, canary yellow and red oxide primer; inside the bus, general squalor, of the kind he'd always thought only he could create in a confined space; in the epicentre of the squalor, an ancient, faded blue mattress; on the mattress, two pink people with no clothes on, one of whom he recognised. He closed his eyes.

'Seen enough?' the goblin asked.

'Yes,' said Paul.

CHAPTER NINE

For some time after the goblin had gone, Paul sat quite still, looking at a photograph of an unspecified area of Australian sand, seen from above. He didn't feel angry, or sad, or suicidal; if he felt anything, it was as though someone had picked him up like a teapot and poured all the Paul Carpenter out through his ear, leaving him completely empty. When the feeling eventually coagulated into words, he said to himself, *Oh well.*

As far as he was concerned, he could've sat there all day. Didn't matter. If he hadn't been there, he'd have been at home, in his poxy little room, staring at the walls. What difference did it make where you happened to be, anyway? It was as important as the colour of the socks you choose to wear on the day of your execution. Might as well look at a picture of some sand as four slabs of masonry covered in beige wood-chip. Where you are, when you are, what you're doing: none of it matters a damn when there's nothing left inside you except a huge hole where your life used to be.

Not that that mattered, either; he'd known from the start that something like this was bound to happen sooner or later. Not even Sir Clive Sinclair in all his glory had ever come up with anything less likely to succeed than the slender hope Paul had built his life around, ever since he'd sat down in the waiting area outside the conference room on the day of his interview and seen the thin girl. Hence, presumably, the absence of any real feeling. The blow, the shock, hadn't exactly hit him out of a clear blue sky. It was like being told that Santa Claus doesn't exist when you're fifty-five and head of particle physics research at MIT; sad, depressing, but hardly unexpected.

Oh well, he thought; and that was more or less all he had to contribute.

That was how Mr Tanner found him, some unspecified time later.

'Well?' Mr Tanner said.

Paul looked up. 'Sorry,' he said.

Mr Tanner frowned at him. 'Have you finished that last lot I gave you?'

'No.'

'Oh. Problems?'

Paul shook his head. 'It's my fault,' he said. 'I got sidetracked.'

He'd expected anger, or at the very least another dose of Mr Tanner's special unpleasantness. Instead, he heard him say, 'Mum's been in here bothering you, hasn't she?'

'She did drop by,' Paul replied.

'Oh. Well, just ignore her, that's what I do. She can be a real pain in the bum when she wants to.'

'She didn't bother me,' Paul replied.

Mr Tanner grinned, presumably because he could read the lie. Dragon black pudding, or something of the kind. 'You wouldn't think to look at her that she's probably the best metallurgist in Europe,' he said. 'Not to mention the second richest female in the UK. What did she do? Show you something you'd rather not have seen?'

'Something like that,' Paul replied.

Mr Tanner sat down on the edge of the desk. 'There's something you should know about our line of work,' he said. 'There's no rabbits out of hats, or kissing princesses into frogs, or enchanted talismans that mean you're the ruler of the world. Truth is, even the best of us, even the likes of Theo Van Spee or Judy di Castel'Bianco, we're like a bunch of Trobriand Islanders with a machine gun – don't know how it works, can't fix it if it breaks down, can't build one from scratch, but we can point it where we want to and squeeze the trigger, and when we do that, stuff happens. But the machine gun's still a machine gun, you can't paint a wall with it, or cook a chicken, or sew a button on a shirt. You can use it for X, Y and Z, and that's all. Everything else in life is just shit that happens and if that's the way it wants to go, there's nothing you or I or even Humph Wells can do about it.' He stretched forward, picked up a photograph that Paul had already marked up, and looked at it. 'What we can do,' he said, 'is our job. And a fat lot of good it may do, most of the time, but the same's true of builders and dentists and people behind tills in petrol stations. We all just carry on, and that's that.'

'I know,' Paul said. 'And I'll get this lot done, I promise.'

Mr Tanner stood up. 'You'd better,' he said. 'There're

people relying on you, even if they are just a bunch of bauxite miners in Australia you couldn't be expected to give a flying fuck about.' He grinned, but it wasn't a Mr Tanner grin. 'And you know why?' he said. 'Because somewhere in the world, there's some poor little shit like you who's got a hatful of problems, can't for the life of him see why the hell he should bother, but still he gets on and does his job, the thing he's supposed to be doing; and what he does is just some meaningless garbage to him, but to you, it's the answer to all your troubles, the light at the end of the tunnel, the miracle you were sure could never happen, but it does, and suddenly everything's just fine, when you least expected it. Don't ask me why it's like that, but it is. So you just get on with finding bauxite in the desert, and leave fixing your problem to whoever it is who's supposed to do it. That way, we all do our job, and everybody gets paid on Friday.'

Paul looked at him and came to the conclusion that the effects of the dragon turd must've worn off already. 'Fine,' he said. 'Just leave it to me.' Then he added; 'Just out of interest, though.'

'Yes?'

'Well,' Paul said, frowning slightly. 'If you're right, and we're all busy helping other people, and they're all busy helping us – that is what you were saying, isn't it?'

'More or less.'

'Fine,' Paul said. 'In that case, what exactly does your mother do?'

Mr Tanner thought for a moment. 'Buggers people about, mostly,' he replied. 'When you've finished that lot, bring 'em up to my office and I'll give you the next batch. OK?'

*

It was a very long weekend. Mr Tanner kept him scrying bits of Australia until gone five o'clock, then turned him loose with a growled 'Thanks' and a turned back. Paul went straight home, sat in his chair till ten o'clock, and went to bed. Sunday seemed to last for ever.

On Monday morning, he arrived at the office at nine o'clock exactly, and shuffled into reception, shoes full of lead, back arched, head bowed. The receptionist on duty was even more stunningly beautiful than usual (a complete stranger, of course, but he was used to that by now); but he looked away, and was almost at the fire door when she called out, 'Morning, Paul,' in a bright, loud voice. He mumbled some sort of reply.

'Cheer up,' the receptionist said. 'Maybe it'll never happen.'

Fuck you, Paul thought. 'Charming,' the receptionist replied. 'So you still think I'm horrible, then.'

Paul stopped dead and turned slowly round. The girl behind the desk was slender and golden-haired, with a long, graceful neck, high cheekbones, a full mouth and sparkling blue eyes. 'Sorry?' Paul said.

'Apology accepted,' said the girl. 'How was your weekend, then?'

'Boring,' Paul said; and then: 'Excuse me if this sounds rude, but do I know you?'

She laughed; then she held out her hand, palm facing him. He wasn't sure what that was supposed to mean, but he went back to the desk. He was obviously supposed to look at her hand, but he couldn't—

Then he saw them; four tiny red dots in the centre of the palm. They were about a centimetre apart, and if he'd had a felt-tip pen handy and joined them up, they'd have formed a square. Paul stared at them for a moment, then at the girl.

'Mrs Tanner?' he said.

She giggled. 'Don't tell anybody, but Dennis's dad and I never actually got married. You couldn't pronounce my name, but if you like, you can call me Rosie.'

'Rosie,' Paul repeated. 'Look, are you—?'

She grinned, and there was the family resemblance once again. 'You think I'm horrible, and you wouldn't eat my cake. You looked in my seer-stone. You saw that thin cow having it off with—'

'Yes,' Paul said quickly, 'all right.' He couldn't think of anything else to say.

'I like helping out in the office,' she went on, 'it's something to do, even if it does mean I've got to wear the monkey suit. Really, I don't know how you lot can stand it. Bloody tight skin, and these things—' She patted her bust. 'Barbaric, I call it. And don't get me started about going to the toilet. Still, I suppose it's all a matter of what you're used to.'

'I like it,' Paul said awkwardly. 'Suits you, I mean.'

She laughed. 'Dennis doesn't think so,' she said. 'You should hear him. *Bloody hell, Mum, you aren't going to the office wearing that, are you?* He should talk. I mean, he's nothing to write home about himself, whichever way you look at it.'

'I—' Quickly, Paul reviewed all the possible responses that came to mind, and realised that none of them was satisfactory. Not that it mattered, since the girl – the *goblin* – had already demonstrated that she could read his mind. 'Um, is that what you usually wear, or do you—?'

'I'm like Joan Collins,' Mr Tanner's mum replied.

'Wouldn't be seen dead wearing the same outfit twice. Or hadn't you noticed?'

Paul's eyes opened wide. 'You mean, every day it's actually you?'

She shook her head. 'Mondays, Wednesdays and Fridays. Tuesdays and Thursdays it's my sister, we take it in turns. You can call her Auntie Pam if you want.'

Paul tried to remember a Tuesday, and an image slipped into his mind of a sultry Malaysian beauty with a waterfall of shining black hair. 'Auntie Pam,' he repeated. 'Fine. Why are you telling me this? Today, I mean.'

She shrugged. 'I was just wondering, that's all,' she said. 'Like, if you'd spent all weekend scoffing those dragonshit beans, you'd have seen me like I really am. But obviously not. Also,' she said, 'I like you. You're weedy and pathetic and you've got some bloody weird notions about women, but you remind me of my brother. Uncle Alf,' she added, 'rest his soul. Lose the ape costume, and you'd be the spitting image of Alf when he was your age.'

'I see,' Paul said. 'What happened to him, then?'

She clicked her tongue. 'Oh, killed,' she said. 'Most of us get killed sooner or later. We like to play rough games when we've got the place to ourselves.'

'Oh,' Paul said. 'I'm sorry.'

'Balls. You think we're disgusting and horrible. But that's all right, we think the same about your lot. Except you. You're sweet.'

Fine, Paul thought, and managed not to shudder, even though his restraint was pointless. 'Thanks,' he said. 'I suppose I'd better go and do some work now.'

'No rush,' she replied. 'Come on, you can't kid me.

Last thing you want to do is go and sit in that office the rest of the day, with *her*. Talk about embarrassing.'

'You're right,' Paul said. 'But I've got to, haven't I?'

'I suppose.' She grinned again. 'Bright and early, she was, waiting on the doorstep. I don't like her much; goes around looking like a starving kitten, but she knows which side her bread's buttered, you mark my words. Oh, and here's a tip for you. Whatever you do, don't look at her neck. On the right hand side, about two inches down from the ear.' She frowned. 'And you lot think we're like animals,' she said. 'Try that lark where I come from, you'd get your throat ripped out.'

This time, Paul did shudder. 'I wish you hadn't told me that,' he said.

'Yes, well, Dennis always says, if I'd only joined the diplomatic corps when I was a girl, we could have had all sorts of really interesting wars. But our lot didn't hold with careers for women back then; still don't, actually. Fuck 'em, I say.'

'Right,' Paul replied. 'But I'd better be going. It was, um, nice talking to you.'

'Liar.' She laughed, and pushed a wave of golden hair back over her slim shoulder. Paul made a resolution not to eat any of the remaining beans on a Monday, a Wednesday or a Friday. 'You carry on, then,' she said. 'Only, if you get bored sick, or the atmosphere in your office gets more than you can stand, here's a tip for you. It wasn't just beans you found in that drawer, remember?'

Paul frowned. 'Sorry?'

'Go and take a look if you've forgotten,' she said. 'The instructions are pretty clear, but if you need any help, just ask. Only, I wouldn't go mentioning it to our

Dennis, if I were you. Or any of the other partners, come to that. They can get a bit snotty sometimes, when it's stuff like that.'

Paul remembered one of the things that had been in the drawer, besides the beans. 'You mean the stapler?'

She shook her head, and pointed; the stapler was on the desk next to her. 'Have a nice day,' she said.

He walked away down the corridor and up the stairs, thinking, *Auntie Pam and Uncle Alf and Mr Tanner's mum Rosie; Jesus fucking Christ.* Then he reached the door of his office. Their office. Damn.

Sophie looked up as he walked in, then immediately turned her head. Just as well he could only see her left profile. He sat down on his side of the desk and looked down at his hands.

'Julie came in a moment or so ago,' she said, in a quiet, awkward voice. 'She left some more of these for us to do.'

The spreadsheets. Paul had never imagined the day would come when he'd be glad to see a tall stack of the horrible things, but at that moment they were as welcome as shelter in a blizzard. He grabbed his share and set to work on them as though his life depended on it.

'Good weekend?' Sophie said.

'All right,' Paul grunted back. 'How about you?'

He hadn't meant to say that, it had just slipped out, like a cat curving itself round the edge of a slightly open door. 'Great,' she mumbled. 'Actually, we—'

'Good,' Paul snapped. 'Look, if you don't mind, I'd better get on with this lot. Sooner it's done, the sooner they'll give us something else.'

'Okay, fine,' she whispered. 'I just—'

He looked up. 'What?'

'Doesn't matter.' She had her left hand clamped over the right side of her neck, as though she'd just been stung by a bug. 'Tell you later.'

'All right.'

Work; beautiful, mindless work, just complicated enough to keep one's thoughts from wandering, but purely abstract, nothing to do with anything. There were moments, in the long drag down to lunchtime, when he forgot about the human presence a few feet away from him across the desktop – amazing, but apparently possible, like the fools who build villages on the slopes of volcanoes. One o'clock came, and at least she had the compassion to go out for lunch.

'You coming?' she asked. Damn; it was almost as if she wanted him to.

'No,' he replied. 'I've got sandwiches. Besides, I can do some more of this garbage.'

'Fine,' she said. 'See you later, then.'

He didn't reply, and the door closed behind her; at which point, it was safe for Paul to look up and push his chair back. Work was all right in its place, but he'd had enough of spreadsheets to last him this life and several dozen reincarnations.

It wasn't just beans you found in that drawer, remember? Sure, he remembered now. A funny little cardboard tube, and that plastic sheet thing. He took it out, put it on the desk and turned it over a few times with the tips of his fingers.

By rights, it ought to be back in the strongroom – assuming, of course, that it was the same one as he'd found there while he was compiling the inventory. He frowned. There was something almost familiar about the stupid thing, as if there had been a time when he knew what it was. *Instructions*, he remembered. The goblin female, just call me Rosie, had said something about instructions. He couldn't remember having seen anything like that. But, when he teased the rolled-up sheet out of the tube, a little wisp of very thin paper fluttered out and landed on the desk. There was writing on it, tiny little letters he couldn't read—

Yes, he could. He had to hold the paper right up close to the tip of his nose; but the more he squinted at it, the easier it got.

J. W. WELLS PORTABLE DOOR
Patent No. 55674 15th Aug 1872, 94239 23rd Feb 1875
BY APPOINTMENT

Well, that didn't help much. He looked again, and the letters seemed to grow larger.

To use the portable door, first remove it from the cardboard tube. To ensure flawless operation, first spread the door out on a flat surface, taking care to smooth out any wrinkles, as these may inhibit adherence or corrupt the intelligence. Make a careful mental note of all aspects of desired arrival. Lift the door by the top corners, making sure that the door remains flat and level at all times. Press the door firmly against the wall until it adheres without support. Release corners, smooth out wrinkles as previously advised. Grasp the handle firmly in the right hand and rotate one half-turn to the left. Apply gentle, even pressure to open the door. You are most earnestly advised to use some convenient object of suitable weight to hold the door ajar during use. If possible, limit exposures to no more than one hour (observed time) per visit. Reverse the above procedure for disassembly and removal. Store only in the container provided, away from extremes of heat & cold, and out of the reach of children, invalids and persons of a nervous or prosaic disposition.

Crazy as a tankful of gay piranhas. He turned the slip of paper over, but there was nothing to see except the shadow of the letters coming through from the other side. Whoever heard of a portable door? And what the hell would be the point—?

He remembered something: a room without a door, a place where he lived, though not his own time. Of course, that had been just a dream, and he was wide awake now. A portable *door*, for Christ's sake.

On the other hand, just-call-me-Rosie had made it sound like the best thing since hallucinogenic chocolate. True, he had absolutely no reason whatsoever to trust the recommendations of a malicious female goblin who was also Mr Tanner's old mum. Still; just supposing it worked, that it really was a folding or collapsible door, what possible harm could it do? Either it was a dud, in which case nothing would happen; or it wasn't, in which case, if he slapped it on the back wall of his office, he'd be able to take a short cut through to the computer bay without having to go down the corridor and up and down two flights of steps. Megadeal.

Paul thought it over as he stared at the thing, still tightly curled like a fine Cuban cigar. On reflection, he could think of various uses for something of the sort, ranging from the innocuous (Left your keys in your other jacket and locked yourself out? Don't worry; the J. W. Wells portable door . . .) to the downright larcenous, or worse. Just the sort of thing a bank robber would love to find in his Christmas stocking mask; or the ideal present for the twelfth-level Ninja master assassin who has everything.

(Yes, but it wouldn't work, went without saying. It had to be some sort of gimmick, like the genuine authentic phaser pistols and lightsabers you saw advertised in the back pages of magazines for sad people. Maybe it was just that: a piece of tie-in marketing for a TV show that bombed or got cancelled before it was ever released. In which case, it'd do no harm just to offer it up against a handy slab of plasterwork, would it?)

Paul was aware of a very strange, though barely perceptible sensation; the nearest parallel he could think of was a desperate nicotine craving, as experienced by someone who'd never smoked. Once again, he had the weirdest notion that he was familiar with this ludicrous object; furthermore, the urge to use it was linked to that memory like a withdrawal symptom, a suppressed addiction yearning for satisfaction in the presence of the forbidden luxury. That was all very well, but whatever it was, it was starting to make him feel distinctly uncomfortable. He felt jumpy, restless, hungry and stuffed at the same time. His hands were actually shaking just a little, and the inside of his mouth was salty and furry. All these unpleasant sensations would, he knew, vanish at once, just as soon as he unrolled the little plastic sheet and pressed it to a wall. At the back of his mind, red-alert sirens sounded as he recognised the intrusion of another slice of supernatural loopiness into his life, but he had to ignore them. He stood up.

He put the instructions down on the seat of Sophie's chair, and followed them carefully. First he smoothed the thing out on the desktop. It looked just the same as it had a short while ago, except that now there were two tiny keyholes, each with a neatly traced baroque escutcheon surrounding it, above and below the door-knob. Next, he lifted it by the corners in the prescribed fashion, and pressed it against the wall as if hanging a sheet of thin wallpaper. He felt it stick, as if it had magnets on it. Carefully, he pressed out a few small wrinkles and bulges, brushing with the back of his hand in a her-ringbone pattern. Then he took a step back and looked at it.

Either he was imagining it, or the thing had grown; it was now as tall and wide as a full-size door, and the handle had somehow acquired an extra dimension; in fact, it was brass, polished and shiny. He reached out and touched it with the tip of his forefinger; it felt cold and smooth.

Son of a bitch, he thought. Then he checked the instructions, to see what the next step was.

You are most earnestly advised to use some convenient object of suitable weight to hold the door ajar during use.

Ajar. When is a door not a door? Somehow, the old joke struck him as being even less funny than usual. He looked round; and there on the desk, hunched like a thin black rabbit, was the long stapler. He was way past the point where he was surprised to see it there, even though it had been in reception that morning, and he hadn't noticed anybody bring it into the room. He frowned at it. Definitely an object of suitable weight, and there didn't seem to be anything else in the room that'd serve as a makeshift doorstop. He picked it up. Then, feeling extremely foolish, he reached out and twisted the doorknob.

The door opened.

As soon as it was open, it had changed. It had weight. Its frame and lintel and the mouldings between its panels stood out in generous relief. No possible doubt about it: Nature might stand up and say to all the world, *This is a door.*

Oh well, he thought, and peeked through it. But there was nothing to see, only darkness and shadows; if that was the computer bay out there, somebody had switched off all the lights and drawn the curtains. Creepy; but he was painfully aware that he couldn't stop now, or the withdrawal symptoms would be back, a hundred times worse. Whether he liked it or not, he was going through. But first . . . He glanced at his watch (01:09:56), opened the door a little bit wider, then stooped down and snuggled the stapler up against it, tight as a cat rubbing against your leg. Then—

Make a careful mental note of all aspects of desired arrival.

Or, as Bill Gates would put it, *Where do you want to go today?* But that was just plain silly. Either it went nowhere, or it went through into the computer bay. Yes, but if he had a choice, where would it go? If he had the whole world to choose from?

It was like when someone said, 'What shall we talk about?' or, 'Just say something into the microphone.' He couldn't think of anywhere he wanted to go, really. (All places are the same, after all; doesn't matter where you are, if your life is a Polo mint and the only girl you've ever really loved is the hole in the middle.) But, all things being equal, he'd always rather fancied seeing Venice.

Paul walked through the door, caught his foot in a coil of rope, and only just managed to avoid falling in a canal.

The first thing he did was look round. There, in the

middle of a crumbling red-brick wall, was the door, slightly ajar, with a stapler wedged in it. Next to it was what looked like a theatre poster, but in Italian. He turned slowly back. There was the canal; there was the coil of rope. Below, bobbing up and down on the green water, was a small motor boat. Three Japanese women walked past him, talking very fast, followed by a businessman in an expensive-looking suit. Away to his right, he could see a yellow fingerboard nailed to the façade of a tall, ancient building. *Piazza S Marco*, it said, and an arrow pointed into the distance.

On the other hand, he was feeling a whole lot better; no shaking hands, no salty taste, no squirmy itch. Something prompted him to check his watch. 01:09:56.

Oink, he thought, *my watch has stopped*. He looked round, and caught sight of a clock high up on the tower of some church or similar building. Ten past one.

(But that wasn't right, because there was a time difference; Italy was an hour behind, or two hours ahead, or something. He looked at his watch again. 01:09: 55.) Then he ground his toe against the pavement. It felt solid enough. Also he could feel a slight breeze on his face, and there was also the smell. Salt, fresh algae and vintage fish. Not imaginary.

Not far down the road in the other direction there was a café. He thought for a moment, then, having glanced back to make sure the door and the stapler were where he'd left them, he wandered down the street towards it. There were chairs and tables outside; two men sitting at one of them, both talking loudly into mobile phones. Of course, he didn't have any Italian money, so he couldn't buy a coffee or a slice of cake. (They had about nine hundred different varieties of cake in the window. Yum.) Then one of the phoning men stuck a cigarette in his face, reached down to the table, picked up a book of matches, lit one. Paul checked the table nearest to him; sure enough, there was an identical book of matches, in a black shiny cover, with the name of the café in gold letters, its phone number and (God help us) its website address. Paul looked round to see if anybody was watching, then slipped the match-book into his pocket.

Nobody grabbed him or called for the police, so he guessed he'd got away with it. He felt guilty, stealing from inoffensive strangers, but all he could think to do was to reach in his trouser pocket for some English change. He found a twenty pence piece and put it on the table; it was the thought that counted, he asserted. *Like hell*, replied his better self.

It was pleasantly warm. A pair of girls clicked by on monster heels – sunglasses, loud and lilting voices, clothes that looked like they'd cost more than he'd earn in a year, if he lived that long. A waiter came out of the café and cleared away the dead cups and plates. The twenty pence piece puzzled him; in the end, he balanced it on his thumbnail, flicked it two feet up in the air, caught it backhanded and slipped it into his waistcoat pocket. He smiled at Paul as he went past; it was just a reflex, but it wasn't a goblin grin. *A cup of coffee*, Paul thought, *and one of those shiny chocolate things that look like a scale model of the Kremlin; I could really fancy that.*

The slight breeze gusted sharply and something blew against his cheek. At first he thought it was a leaf, but there weren't any trees in sight. He retrieved it, and saw that it was a banknote.

What the hell, he thought.

The banknote was blue, and the row of noughts behind the figure five looked like the stream of bubbles left behind by a diving otter; but Italian money was funny stuff, he remembered. Buy £4.50's worth of peanuts and give the man a fiver, and the change would be enough to make you a lira millionaire. Still; he felt braver than usual, for some reason, and sat down at the nearest table. When the waiter came up, he held out the banknote and said, 'Excuse me.'

The slight quiver of the waiter's upper lip made it obvious that he'd placed Paul as an Englishman; but he was polite and dignified, as all native Venetians are, and didn't spit.

'Excuse me,' Paul repeated slowly, 'but can I buy a cup of coffee with this?'

This time the waiter did grin; no family resemblance, though. '*Si.*'

'Right. Um, uno café, por favor.'

'One coffee,' said the waiter. 'Anything else?'

One of the advantages of making a fool of yourself is that you don't have to worry about looking foolish. 'Can I afford anything else?'

The waiter's grin spread into a smile. '*Si.*'

'I'll have that, then, please.'

'Coming right up.' The waiter went away, and came back with a coffee and one of the Kremlin buns. Paul tried to give him the banknote, but he looked shocked and handed Paul a little slip of paper, which he took to be the bill. He apologised. The waiter forgave him, and went away.

The coffee was wonderful, and the cake was better, even if it did split its seams and gush confectioner's custard up his jacket sleeves. He took his time, paying proper attention to the taste of the coffee and the texture of the pastry. It was only when he'd finished both, and surreptitiously licked the last splodge of errant custard off the underside of his wrist, that it occurred to him to look at the church clock he'd noticed earlier.

Fuck, he thought. Five past two.

He jumped up, wedged the banknote and the bill under the sugar-cellar, and dashed back down the street. He'd forgotten all about the door, but there it was, patient and steadfast as the HMV dog. He nudged the stapler aside with his foot, pushed the door open and went through.

To his relief, he found himself standing in his office. There, on Sophie's chair, was the little piece of paper with the instructions. Sophie wasn't back from lunch yet— A thought struck him, and he looked at his watch. 01:10:02. He'd been away for six seconds. Not even that, come to think of it; he'd stood in the doorway that long. He hadn't been away at all.

He turned round, just as the door, or rather the little plastic sheet, peeled off the wall and flopped onto the floor. *Shit*, he said to himself, *so I did just imagine it all, after all.* But he'd thought of that, he remembered, and done a proper scientific test. He felt in his pocket, and there was the book of matches, with the name, phone number and website.

Shit, he thought again.

First things first. He rolled up the plastic sheet and stuffed it, together with the instruction slip, back in its tube. Then he hesitated. Properly speaking, it should go back in the drawer where he'd found it or, better still, in the strongroom. *Yeah, right*, he thought, and tucked the cardboard tube carefully away in his inside pocket.

He looked round for the stapler, but it had vanished again. For a moment he wondered if he'd left it on the other side of the door; but he could distinctly remember stepping over it, on this side, as he came through. Not that it mattered a damn.

Well, Paul thought, *so that's a portable door. Not bad.* Just the thing for beating the rush-hour traffic, assuming it could be aimed with anything approaching precision, and perfect for those spur-of-the-moment impulse holidays, particularly if it was really true and the time he'd spent on the other side hadn't actually happened back here. Nobody had raised the subject of holiday entitlement since he'd been with the firm (presumably, he suspected, for the same reason that maximum-security prisoners on Dartmoor don't get asked where they fancy going for their annual outing this year); but if the door worked the way it seemed to do, he could have three weeks in Martinique every day in his lunch hour. Of course, spending money and hotel bills might be a problem; or maybe not, if the door could also let him into, say, Fort Knox or the vaults of the bank of his choice. At that point, though, his train of thought jumped the track. It wasn't just that doing that sort of thing wasn't right, and if his mother got to hear of it he'd have hell to pay. There was also the unpleasant feeling that that was precisely the sort of thing the door wanted him to do, and maybe it wasn't quite as user-friendly as he might have supposed. Sneaking off work, he reckoned, was probably all right. Thieving, on the other hand, could well be something quite other; the dark side of the Force, or something to that effect. He could be quite wrong about that, of course, but on balance it'd be better not to risk it, at least not until he'd had the opportunity to run a few more controlled tests, acquire a little bit more data.

Suddenly he realised that he was feeling extremely tired, as if he hadn't slept for several days. That also put a rather different complexion on the matter, since he felt it was a pretty safe bet that the door was somehow responsible for that, too. Clearly he was guessing, but it seemed likely that if he felt worn out after ten minutes or so on the other side, more than an hour over there would leave him exhausted, and three weeks – for all he knew, it could kill him. Further tests, he resolved, more data. Characters in TV sci-fi series might press unidentified buttons just to see what they do and live to tell the tale, but he didn't have the comfort of knowing that his name was in the cast-list in next week's *TV Times*.

Even so. He had to admit it; most of the ambient weirdness he'd run into since joining J. W. Wells & Co. had ranged from unpleasant to downright nasty, but this was different. In fact, if it was any cooler you could stick it in a cone and sell it as ice cream.

He leaned back in his chair, which had never felt so comfortable. He felt ever so slightly pleased with himself: more so than if he'd found a pound coin in the street, rather less than if he'd just discovered a new searoute to the East. At the back of his mind there was a nagging fear that he'd just taken a left turn in the maze and got a crumb of cheese instead of an electric shock, but it didn't bother him all that much. Cheese, after all, is cheese. He was just wondering whether, after all, he ought to wander down to reception when the lunch hour was over and ask the Mrs-Tanner goblin if she could throw any more light on the matter, when he caught sight of his watch. Three minutes past two; and the door opened and in came Sophie.

He snapped upright in his chair, almost guiltily; because he wasn't going to tell her about it, not now, not after what she'd done to him . . . That was, of course, just plain silly, but nevertheless. And there went a large slice of the pleasure of the discovery, of course, but he couldn't help that. He wasn't the one who'd chosen to go frolicking with performance potters in buses. He grabbed a bunch of spreadsheets and scowled at them, as if it was all their fault.

'Hello,' she said. He grunted back.

She was looking at him. 'I thought you were going to get on with some work,' she said.

'Yes,' he replied.

'Well, you don't look like you've got much done.'

'No,' he replied.

Another moment; and suddenly he felt awful, as if he'd just trodden on a baby fieldmouse. But it was too late to do anything about it. She sat down opposite him and reached for her pile of printouts. The moment froze over, like the Arctic sea in winter, cutting them off from each other, and for the next few hours they grimly did spreadsheets at each other.

Which was ridiculous. They hadn't talked to each other properly since that horrible night, when they'd got locked in and Paul had found himself charging through the building with a spear in his hand, desperately trying to save her from a pack of goblins holding knives under her throat. Since then, they'd found out that magic was real and they were magicians, that they were trapped in the weirdness up to their necks for ever (but with the implied promise that if they stuck at it, worked hard and kept their noses clean, they might in time rise up the corporate ladder and themselves become secret masters of the universe). And now Paul had stumbled across a piece of really big medicine of his very own, something that might just mean they could escape, or at the very least adjust the balance of weirdness in their own favour; and here they were, a million miles apart across a desk, sorting through bits of ludicrous paper, all because Sophie had met a bloke she liked. It was as though America had refused to help Britain in World War Two because it was jealous of Britain having the benefit of the Gulf Stream.

Obvious. But did that mean he was going to stop acting like a five-year-old and talk to her? Did it hell as like.

At twenty-nine minutes past five, they both got up, put on their coats and left the office in complete silence, not looking at each other. As they walked through reception, call-me-Rosie gave Paul a dazzling smile. It startled the life out of him, and he stopped dead for a moment; Sophie pushed past him and hurried out of the door.

'Snotty cow,' said call-me-Rosie blithely. 'Dunno why you're wasting your time on her.'

Paul gave her a horrified look and retreated in bad order.

The next few weeks were confusing, to say the least. Needless to say, Paul couldn't resist playing with the portable door; partly because it was fun, but also because, while he was using it, he forgot about Sophie and the performance potter. Once he became aware of it, this effect puzzled him greatly, if only because it was so marked. He'd be brooding darkly as he stepped over the threshold, and the moment he came back through he'd catch up the train of thought at exactly the point where he'd left it, but while he was out there, in the streets of Rio or Florence, or treading the flower-carpeted slopes of Nepal or the ramparts of the Great Wall of China, she was completely out of his mind, like a distant cousin's forgotten birthday.

It was a while before he realised that he could use his bank card to draw foreign money out of holes in walls from Anchorage to Adelaide; when eventually he cottoned on, he was nevertheless cautious at first, since on his J. W. Wells salary he had to think twice about splashing out on a coffee and a bacon roll in London, let alone sushi in Yokohama or green tea and honey cakes in Samarkand. But then his bank statement arrived, and he saw to his great bewilderment and joy that none of the withdrawals he'd made on his various jaunts were recorded there. Even then he was inclined to believe that this was simply because it took foreign-currency transactions longer to reach the computer, and that sooner or later they'd come home to roost like a squadron of B-52 chickens. But his next bank statement told him the same thing. Apparently he could buy what the hell he liked, and not have to pay for it, ever.

Unfortunately, there was more to it than that, as he discovered on his return home after a frenzied tour of the jewellers' quarter in Paris. He'd bought a whole load of stuff – gold watches, coins, rings, anything and everything made of the yellow stuff that he'd been able to cram into his pockets. He could feel it all clinking and digging into him through the cloth of his coat; but as soon as he crossed the line the extra weight and the sharp edges vanished, and when he shoved his hands into his pockets, he found nothing more valuable than his keys, a dead biro, a packet of Kleenex and the inevitable unwrapped, fluff-coated boiled sweet. The full weirdness of that took a little while to sink in; because he'd bought the Kleenex in Paris, at the same time as all the gold, but apparently the invisible, intangible Customs officers assigned to his case had either overlooked it or let him keep it as a consolation prize. Next day, just for fun, he went to Manchester and drew out fifty pounds. When he got back to St Mary Axe, it had gone. When he repeated the experiment the next day and drew out £10, it was still there when he stepped back through the door, but a quick balance check on the way home showed the withdrawal. While he was trying to figure this one out over the next few days, he became aware of another consistent effect: no matter how much he ate while he was away, it seemed to have no impact on his appetite when he got back; also, in spite of all the choux pastries and gateaux he was scoffing in the pavement cafés of the world, he hadn't put on any weight. At this point, he resolved to give up trying to rationalise, and concentrate on enjoying his daily holiday.

One encouraging trend was that, once Paul started using the door on a daily basis, the period of exhaustion that followed once he came back was gradually decreasing, to the point where he was able to risk staying for two hours (observed time) without having to struggle to stay awake for the rest of the day. An hour hadn't really given him time for much more than a search for a bank machine followed by a hasty lunch; with double the time at his disposal, he could enjoy a leisurely meal and still be able to fit in a little gentle sightseeing. The only thing lacking from his excursions was, of course, company.

Wherever he went, he was a stranger; this, in fact, seemed to be one of the rules, since he'd gone back to the same coffee shop in Houston three days in a row and found the same man behind the counter on each occasion, but there'd been no indication whatsoever that he'd been recognised. Of course, that wasn't necessarily significant – Paul had no illusions whatsoever about his memorability; but he found it odd that a wool-suited Englishman could turn up three days running in a Texan diner without exciting some comment.

Once the initial excitement of the discovery had worn off, and he'd started to get blasé about the foreign travel aspect, he came to think of his trips through the door as just a rather more pleasant way to spend his lunch hour than sitting in the office munching stale cheese sandwiches (though, since the food through the door didn't have any nutritional value, he had to do that as well). It was still the high spot of his day, and a couple of hours' break from the embarrassed misery of sharing an office with Sophie was particularly welcome, but the fact remained that the door was little more than an entertaining toy. He could sip lattes in Manhattan or swill wheat beer in Munich (like money, alcohol didn't seem able to travel back through the door), but afterwards he had to come home and spend the afternoon sorting spreadsheets in grim silence until it was time to catch the bus back to Kentish Town. He tried not to acknowledge it, but if someone had offered to swap him the door for just one of those lunchtimes he'd shared with Sophie in the miserable little Italian sandwich bar round the corner (a hundred years ago, or so it seemed now) he'd have jumped at the chance.

One Wednesday Paul was sitting outside a cafe in Ankara, nursing a cup of Turkish coffee. He'd only tried it because he couldn't believe it could be as bad as everybody reckoned, and was reflecting that it wasn't only cats who were liable to come to a bad end because of curiosity when a female voice behind and above his head asked if anyone was sitting in the other chair. He was too preoccupied to lie, and it was only after the voice's proprietor had sat down opposite him, casting a shadow over his face, that it occurred to him that she'd made her request in English, or at least Australian. He looked up, mildly intrigued.

She was tall and slim, about twenty, probably half Chinese and half European, with long black hair under a round, broad-brimmed straw hat. She was also bewilderingly pretty, in a traffic-stopping, accident-causing, shampoo-advertisement sort of way, and she was smiling at him.

'Hi,' she said. 'You're English, aren't you?'

Her eyes were as bright as the headlights of an oncoming truck, with Paul as the hedgehog. 'Yes,' he said.

'Thought so.' She lifted a coffee cup to her lips and blew on the foam. 'Is that Turkish coffee you're drinking?'

'Yes.'

'What's it like?'

'Mud,' Paul replied.

'You don't like it much, then.'

'No.'

'Ah well.' She pursed her lips at him. 'I was going to give it a go – like, if you're in Turkey, people expect you to try the coffee. But if it's that bad—'

'It is. Worse.'

'That bad.' She nodded gravely. 'Thank you,' she said. 'In that case, I'll stick to the regular stuff.' She poked the tip of her tongue into the froth. Paul began to sweat. 'Have you tried the tea as well?'

'Turkish tea, you mean?'

She nodded.

'No.'

'Good,' she said. 'In that case I can return the favour. Don't.'

'Right,' Paul said. 'It's bad, is it?'

She frowned. 'No worse than a bad hangover,' she said, 'and probably better than drowning. You been in Turkey long?'

Paul shook his head. 'Only just arrived,' he said.

'Me too. Are you here for work or just wandering about?'

'Just wandering,' Paul said.

'Ah. Only I thought, because you're wearing a suit and tie and all—'

Paul smiled weakly. 'Fashion statement,' he said.

'Really.' She raised an impeccably profiled eyebrow.

Paul nodded. 'True, it's the sort of statement that gets taken down in writing and used in evidence against you, but—'

'Ah. A fashion confession. Actually it suits you.'

Liar, Paul thought. 'Really?'

'Yeah,' she said, 'sort of. It's like the hard-boiled, ill-fitting, slept-in newspaper man look. Really, of course, you should have three days' growth of designer stubble and be bashing away at your laptop to get the proper effect. Still, it's sort of cute.'

Paul hadn't really noticed what the girl was wearing,

in roughly the same way that ninety-nine out of a hundred visitors to the Louvre wouldn't be able to tell you much about the Mona Lisa's frame. He looked. He recognised the basic type as a sundress, but he didn't know enough about female clothes to tell whether it was something off a market stall or a masterpiece of couture that'd cost the equivalent of the US defence budget. Irrelevant, in any case. 'Thanks,' he mumbled. 'Yours too. Suits you, I mean—'

She looked at him and smiled. Or rather, she grinned.

That old family resemblance. Paul's eyes widened like the San Andreas fault on a bad day. 'Mrs Ta—' He checked himself. 'Rosie?'

She scowled. 'Bugger,' she said; and for a fraction of a second, Paul was sitting opposite a lemur-faced, hook-taloned goblin. Then she raised her hands and lifted her hair back over her shoulders. It was a gesture straight off a fashion shoot that should have made Paul's heart crack a rib, but somehow or other it didn't work. 'Hello, Paul,' she said.

He stared at her. 'What're you doing here?' he demanded.

She shrugged. 'Same as you,' she said. 'Lunch hour. Thought I'd slip out of the office for a bit, get some sun. Breaks the day up nicely, don't you think?'

A few yards away, a passing businessman walked into a lamp-post. As he scrambled to his feet, he shot Paul a furious look, as if demanding how come a scruff like him was sitting there whispering sweet nothings to something like *that*. Paul noticed; it made him want to shudder. 'But how did you get here?' he asked.

'Same way as you, dumbo. I told you about it,

remember? So I just sort of snuck in after you'd gone through, and here I am. Wonderful thing, isn't it?'

Paul nodded. 'Bloody marvellous,' he grunted. 'Look.' He took a deep breath. He really didn't want to ask the question that was hammering at the gate of his teeth, but he went ahead anyway. 'Look,' he repeated. 'Just now. Were you—?'

She gave him a smile that would've melted a glacier. 'Was I what?'

Paul closed his eyes. 'Were you trying to, um, chat me up?'

She giggled. 'Chat you up,' she repeated. 'Bloody hell. Don't think I've heard that expression since—'

'Were you?'

The smile faded, and she shrugged. 'Can't blame a girl for trying,' she said.

'Oh.'

Now she was grinning, the special secret grin of the House of Tanner. 'You should see your face,' she said.

Instinctively, Paul tried to look normal. 'Sorry,' he said. 'But – oh for crying out loud, you're Mr Tanner's *mother*—'

'So?'

'Well—' Paul didn't bother trying to complete the sentence. She knew what he meant.

That grin again. 'Picky bugger, aren't you? And there was me thinking I'd found Mr Right at last – shallow, immature, one-track mind. Desperate,' she added pleasantly. 'That's got to be the one,' she went on, 'I mean, anybody who's pathetic enough to go mooning round like a spaniel with the runs over a boring, miserable, bony little—'

'Look,' Paul said.

Mr Tanner's mum fluttered her eyelashes at him. He'd never actually seen it done before. 'Now me,' she said, 'I'm shallow. I'm so shallow I'm a bloody rice paddy. Definitely a one-track mind. Also,' she added with a faint sigh, 'desperate. But at least I don't moon about. Acquire target, lock and load, that's always been my motto. It's the goblin way, it's whatsit, cultural, like ancestor worship or Morris dancing.' She shook her head. 'I'm not saying it's perfect, mind,' she added fairly. 'I mean, look what I got out of it. Our Dennis. But really, I'd have thought it'd have suited you down to the ground.'

Paul's spine crawled. 'No offence,' he said. 'But.'

'Yeah, I'm a goblin, so fucking what?' She scowled; and a dozen or so assorted males saw her and thought, *What an incredibly gorgeous scowling girl.* 'Why should you care? It may only be skin deep, but it's a bloody sight better than you'll ever get any other way. And it doesn't wash off, or peel away at the full moon or anything. I can be this for as long as I want. Or I can do blonde if you'd rather.'

'No,' said Paul.

'Suit yourself.' She sighed. 'Bloody fool, that's what you are, though. You want to know where your precious Sophie is right now?'

'No.'

'Tough.' She closed her fist, then opened it again; and on the flat of her palm was a little round glass globe, which shone like a bonsai star. Paul tried to look away, but the light held him, and in the heart of the globe he could see the miserable Italian sandwich bar, and inside that a table, and on one side of it the back of a man's head, and over his shoulder—

Mrs Tanner closed her hand. '*Your* special table,' she said, 'where you and she went when she bought you that ham roll. She's buying *him* ham rolls now.'

'Yes,' Paul snapped, 'all right. I think it's time I went back to the office now. If you came through the door, I guess you'd better come too.'

She shook her head. 'I'd rather walk, thanks,' she said.

He looked at her. 'From Ankara?'

'There's short cuts,' she replied. 'Takes about ten minutes, from here. Ask Countess Judy, or Ricky Wurmtoter. I guess that's something you haven't got your head round yet; things can be so much easier if you're with us. And if you're against us,' she added, 'well—'

'I see,' Paul said.

She grinned. 'No, you don't, stupid,' she said. 'I'm not threatening you, or anything like that. In fact, I probably still like you, if only because you get up our Dennis's nose so much. I'm just telling you, that's all. I don't know,' she went on, finishing her coffee and licking the last smear of froth off the inside of the rim, 'maybe I'm just getting soft-hearted in my old age. But you, there's no excuse for you. What's on the surface isn't good enough, you've got to have solid milk chocolate all the way through. Bloody humans.'

'I thought you said I was shallow and pathetic?'

'I was being nice. In goblin terms, I mean. We pride ourselves on shallow. I guess that's why your lot's never liked us very much.'

'I suppose so,' Paul said, politely.

'Balls.' She grinned, again. 'You don't like us 'cos we've got big teeth and claws and we only like our food if it's still twitching a bit, and we don't look like you. I'll say this much for us, we're much more broad-minded. I mean, lots of goblin girls fancy humans.'

Paul swallowed. 'Really?'

'Straight up. We aren't bothered because you don't look like us. Looks don't matter to us, see, because we can be anyone or anything we like. That comes in dead handy when you're shallow, like us.' She sighed. 'I know what you're thinking,' she said, 'and you're right. We look like horrible, savage monsters and we act like it, too, whereas your lot are all straight backs and smooth skins and ethics and right-and-wrong and doing the decent thing by each other and wanting to make the world a better place. Probably that's why we fancy you, purely on a short-term, back-seat-of-a-car basis. There's not a lot to be said for our mob, really, except that we've got all the money and we have all the fun.' She looked at him, then clicked her tongue. 'Mostly, anyhow.'

She stood up. A waiter fell over a table. 'Oh, and one other thing. I didn't put you-know-what in your desk drawer, and neither did our Dennis. And it sure as buggery didn't get there on its own. Now you think on.'

Paul jumped up. 'Hold on,' he said. 'Do you know who put it there?'

'Yes. Saw 'em do it.'

'Fine. Who was it?'

But she shook her head. 'Really and truly I'd like to tell you,' she said, 'but I'm not allowed. Honestly,' she added. 'Just watch out, that's all. There's a whole lot of stuff going on at the moment. Most of it's nothing to do with you, but—' She shrugged. 'Be careful. You've managed to get yourself mixed up with some very unusual people, not like the sort you grew up with. Compared with our lot, even the real bastards where you come from fight fair, give up their seats on trains to old ladies and only ever play for matchsticks. Like, for example, the very worst your kind can do to each other is kill someone. That's practically Vegan when you consider what we get up to sometimes.' The Tanner grin flicked across her face. 'Not that I'm trying to scare you or anything.'

'Of course not,' Paul replied. 'And why the hell should I believe anything you tell me, anyhow?'

She smiled. 'You know,' she said, 'you've put me in mind of something a kid like you said to me once, not long after we'd had a chat pretty much on the lines of this one, where I'd told him to watch his back, and he said, Yeah, sure. Always stuck in my mind, it has, what he said then.'

'Really? What was that, then?'

'Aaaaargh,' Mr Tanner's mum replied. 'Be seeing you.'

CHAPTER TEN

There seemed to be no end to the spreadsheets. More than once, Paul nearly managed to nerve himself to go to Mr Tanner's office and ask what they were for; after all, he was in on the big secret now, there was no reason why he shouldn't be told. At least it torpedoed what had been his explanation of choice, namely that the spreadsheets were a futile exercise designed either to prompt his resignation or to test his aptitude for some other, more meaningful task. Instead, he was forced to conclude, there had to be some very good reason behind it all, something that justified employing two people. He wondered why he hadn't been told what it was, now that he was officially a trainee wizard, or whatever he actually was. Presumably there was a very good reason for that, too.

Days on end now passed when he didn't speak to Sophie at all; and when one or other of them did break silence, it was only to ask for the loan of a pencil, or to apologise for the accidental collision of feet under the desk. She went out for lunch every day. Whether she spent every lunchtime feeding ham rolls to the performance potter, or whether mostly she sat on her own in the miserable sandwich bar, Paul didn't know and wasn't going to ask. Whenever it occurred to him that the way he was behaving was childish, counter-productive, idiotic and just plain rude (which was generally no more than twice or three times an hour), a little voice in the back of his head pointed out that she was treating him exactly the same, and somehow that made it all right. He had a nasty suspicion that the little voice in the back of his head sounded just like Mrs Tanner, but on balance he rejected the idea. He didn't need outside help to be childish and stupid, after all.

Every lunchtime he'd get out the portable door and set it up against the wall; but ever since the Ankara incident, he couldn't quite bring himself to go through. It wasn't just that he was terrified of meeting Mrs Tanner again – meeting her and not recognising her, or at least not until it was too late; somehow he'd lost his taste for the whole experience. It'd been fun, no question about that, but he couldn't dislodge from his mind the thought that it was – well, shallow, just as the door itself was only about half a millimetre thick. Flying visits to exotic places, where he spent no money and no time, where the food didn't make him fat and the booze didn't make him drunk; how precisely was that different from Mr Tanner's mum dressed in her skintight, skin-deep gorgeousness, picking up cute humans in bars? Goblin is, he couldn't help thinking, as goblin does; and on balance, he'd rather be a failed human being.

Instead, he tried to resume the drab but familiar business of being Paul Carpenter. He rang up his friends, none of whom he'd spoken to for weeks (they hadn't called him, of course) and arranged to meet them in pubs. He lost games of nomination whist with Duncan and Jenny, and listened to Neville whining about the iniquities of the Microsoft Corporation until it was time to go home. He defrosted frozen pizzas and caught up on his reading. That was all skin deep too, and he knew it; so much so that some days he dreaded looking into his shaving mirror, for fear he'd see a snout and tusks.

Then a Thursday came when he finished his stack of printouts and Julie came by to collect them but didn't bring down any more. Instead, she told them both that they were wanted in the main conference room in half an hour. Sophie pointed out that she still had a heap of spreadsheets to do, but Julie just shrugged and said they'd have to wait; so Paul filled in the thirty minutes' waiting time by finishing them off for her, something he hadn't even suggested ever since the performance potter had appeared on the scene.

The conference room door was shut when they got there. Neither of them seemed to want to be the one to knock; instead, they stood outside like unwanted carol-singers. It was the first time Paul had been in the waiting area outside the conference room since his interview, and he couldn't help thinking that if the magic stuff was worth its weight in dried snot, he'd be able to reach out an invisible hand and press a reset button. But then the door opened, and Mr Wurmtoter's head appeared round it.

'There you are,' he said. 'We were wondering where you'd got to.'

Today he was wearing a black polo neck under a houndstooth check sports jacket, and the claw on the chain round his neck was a dull ivory colour. He held the door open for them and they went through.

It was the same room, except that it wasn't. The oak panelling on the walls was still the same light-devouring shade of black oak; the table was, if anything, even more brightly polished; the crystal chandelier might have grown an extra diamond or two, but that could just have been Paul's imagination; the floorboards still groaned under his feet, as though demanding to know how long it was going to be before the partners bit the bullet and got rid of this clown. Every detail corresponded with the nightmare vision that had been engraved on his memory for the last few months, except – it took him something like twenty seconds before he realised what it was – the whole thing had rotated through ninety degrees. The curtained bay window, instead of being on the right, was now at the end, directly behind the chair at the head of the table.

Well, Paul thought, *fine*; he dismissed the detail from his mind and tried to concentrate. Apart from himself, Sophie and Mr Wurmtoter, who was leaning against an ancient radiator that stood where the window had been last time, the only other person in the room was the grim-faced man he'd last seen at the interview, who he now knew to be Humphrey Wells. He ransacked his trivia banks and turned up his traumatic conversation with Mr Tanner on the night of the armed goblins. According to Mr Tanner, Mr Wells Junior was an Associate of the Society of Thaumaturgical Practitioners; what that actually meant he had no idea.

Mr Wells had his nose in a sheaf of papers when they came in, and it took thirty seconds or so for him to finish whatever it was he was doing; then he looked up, seemed to catch sight of Paul and Sophie out of the corner of his eye, and frowned. The impression he gave was that they were a tiresome chore that needed to be got out of the way before he could press on with the work he was meant to be doing. Not particularly subtle (Paul was prepared to bet money that the vitally important document he hadn't been able to tear himself away from was *The Times* crossword, or something equally crucial) but it worked, so what the hell?

'Ms Pettingell,' he said, 'Mr Carpenter, thanks for coming along.' He paused, as if trying to figure out why in hell he should want to expend lifespan on two such unsatisfactory specimens. 'We haven't seen much of each other since you joined the firm, so I thought it was about time we got together, got to know each other a bit better, find out how you're settling in, all that sort of thing. Everything going well?' He allowed them a quarter of a second in which to reply, then continued: 'I see you've been working with Dennis Tanner for the last few weeks; mineral rights development and office procedures.'

Silence, presumably requiring a reply. Before Paul could think of anything to say, Sophie muttered, 'Yes.' It seemed to do the trick; Mr Wells nodded and jotted something down on his incredibly important piece of paper (probably a South American seabird, seven letters, beginning with J).

'Excellent,' said Mr Wells. 'Now the drill is, we like our trainees to spend a few weeks with each of the partners in turn, so we can assess where your particular strengths lie, and you can decide which area of our business you'd like to specialise in. Usually when we have two trainees at one time, we assign them to different departments.' He raised his head as he said this and looked directly at them for the first time since they'd entered the room. 'But as it happens, right now I'm engaged on a project that calls for what you might describe as support in depth, so both of you will be working with me. Any problems with that?'

This time, he allowed them a full half-second.

'Splendid,' said Mr Wells. 'In that case, I'd like it if you two could be outside the front door at six sharp tomorrow morning, because we've got a bit of a journey. I'll brief you on the way, of course.' He turned his head towards Sophie, scowled, and added, 'Since we'll be meeting with clients, I'd appreciate it if you could both smarten yourselves up a bit. We're pretty easygoing about that sort of thing when we're in the office, but obviously a great deal depends on the impression we give when we're on site, so to speak.'

If he saw the look of cold, steely hatred that Sophie shot in his direction after he said that, he gave no sign of it. 'Right,' he said, 'that's about it from me. I think Ricky Wurmtoter wants a quick word with you, so I'll leave you to it.' He swept up his papers, rose out of his chair like a god-emperor-in-a-box, and strode out of the room without looking round.

Mr Wurmtoter waited till he was out of the room before opening his mouth or even moving. Then he sort of flowed across the room and perched on the corner of the table.

'Hi,' he said, and smiled in a manner that could have sold a huge amount of toothpaste. 'Paul, how's things?

Sophie, I don't think we've met since your interview; I'm Rick Wurmtoter, I look after pest control and stuff like that.' He reached out a large, beautiful hand, and Sophie was apparently so taken aback that she shook it, and even almost smiled.

'I don't want to hold you up,' Mr Wurmtoter went on, 'and I'm sure you're dying to get back to your Mortensen Counter charts, but I thought it was about time—' He stopped, and looked at Paul. 'Sorry,' he said, 'was there something?'

Paul hadn't made a sound that he'd been aware of; but this was too good an opportunity to let pass. 'Sorry,' he said. 'Mortensen Counter?'

Mr Wurmtoter grinned, in the process proving beyond question that he wasn't related to Mr Tanner. 'Those incredibly boring spreadsheet things you've been archiving for us,' he said. 'It's a really rotten job, which is why you got lumbered with it, but the Mortensens are absolutely fundamental to everything we do.' He hesitated, frowned a little. 'You don't know what I'm talking about, do you?'

'No,' Sophie said.

'Ah. Fine. That's standard JWW operating procedure, what we refer to as the photographic approach to in-service training – keep you completely in the dark, and wait to see what develops. There's another version of that one involving mushrooms, but you've probably heard it before and besides, it's rather vulgar.' He clasped his hands round his right knee and leaned back a little. 'The Mortensen Counter,' he went on, 'is a bit like a Geiger counter, and a bit like the gadgets the earthquake people – seismologists, that's the word – a bit like what they use for measuring earth tremors on the

Richter scale. Surprise surprise, it was invented by a certain professor Olaf Mortensen – actually, he was a partner in JWW about sixty years ago, but he fell down a Probability Well in 1946, and the chances of him ever coming back are getting slenderer by the minute. Anyhow, Mortensen Counters basically record supernatural activity worldwide – we have Counters set up right across the world, and about half a dozen in planetary orbit, not forgetting Wellsco One parked up there in the middle of the Sea of Tranquillity, though between you and me it looks depressingly like it's bust, because we haven't heard a peep out of it since 1931.'

(*Nineteen thirty-one*, Paul thought; and although he couldn't remember offhand when the first Sputnik was launched, he was nevertheless impressed, even though it was just a tad disconcerting to think that this collection of weirdos had already been leaving their clutter where no man had gone before while Neil Armstrong was still in rompers.)

Mr Wurmtoter took a small gold box out of his pocket, flipped it open, took out something that looked like a wine gum, and swallowed it. 'The loathsome little bits of paper you've been shuffling,' he went on, 'are the transcripts of the readings from each counter. Yes, as you've probably noticed by now, they're just jumbles of apparently meaningless numbers; actually, the Counters record data in digital form, like radio telescopes, and by examining the printouts we can get all sorts of information that we need in order to be able to do our job. As far as we're concerned, they're the shipping forecast and the FT Index and the lottery numbers and the All-England Law Reports and the runners and riders at Sandown Park all rolled into one; and the real pain of it is, most of the Counters transmit their data outside office hours, and the go—' He stopped short, then grinned. 'Sorry. Mr Tanner's sisters and his cousins and his aunts can't resist scooping them up straight off the machines and playing with them. Which means,' he added with a sigh, 'when we come in every morning, instead of a neatly stacked pile of reports waiting for us, there's a dreadful mess all over the Mortensen Room floor and we've got to pick them up – apart from the ones Mr Tanner's family have eaten or used as toilet paper – and hand them over to some poor devil to sort out. For which,' he added, 'we're profoundly grateful, though apparently nobody's taken the time to say so. Anyhow,' he said, 'we are, so there.'

Complete silence. Paul's mind's eye was filled with a ghastly tableau of Mr Tanner in a space-suit planting a flag with the J. W. Wells logo on it, while various goblins floated past him throwing moon-rocks at each other. What Sophie thought of it all he couldn't say, but he doubted whether she was impressed.

'But that,' Mr Wurmtoter said, 'wasn't what I wanted to talk to you about. Instead,' he continued, 'I wanted to give you the Deadly Perils spiel. Really, you should've had it on Day One, but since our office culture actually manages to achieve the level of secrecy and obfuscation that MI5 struggles so endearingly to attain, it's had to wait till now. Silly, if you ask me, but there you are.'

Sophie, who'd been watching Mr Wurmtoter with the rapt attention of a snake-charmer's snake, seemed to wake up suddenly. 'What deadly perils?' she asked.

'Ah,' Mr Wurmtoter said. 'I was coming to that. Actually, you've already sort of blundered into Item One, which should have been, "For crying out loud, make sure you're out of the door by five-thirty." No lasting harm done, thankfully, so we'll go on to Item Two. Now, then. Have either of you two had occasion to use the lavatory on the third floor?'

Paul and Sophie shook their heads.

'Good,' Mr Wurmtoter replied. 'Don't. I'd rather not go into details, since I've got an early start in the morning and I'd like to get some sleep tonight, which I won't if I start thinking about it. Just don't, is all. Item Three: ambient and residual fallout. Actually, this is really bad news. Long story short, we do an awful lot of magic around here, and – well, if you think industrial waste in the chemicals industry is a major problem, you really don't want to know about what we're pumping into the environment three-sixty-five days a year. But that's all right, because we're caring, responsible employers and you're no earthly use to us if we come in one morning and find you hopping round the office going rivet-rivet; so please wear these –' he reached in his other pocket and produced two shining gold rings '– at all times. Here, try them on, they're one-size-fits-all, and they're fairly harmless, won't make you disappear or start craving for fish and calling yourself Precious. Actually, you're lucky: these are the Mark 6 – I've only got the Mark 5.'

Reluctantly, Paul pushed the ring on his finger. At first it was far too small, but it expanded like rubber. He could feel his skin tingling where the metal touched it.

'Of course,' Mr Wurmtoter went on, 'these little honeys won't protect you against everything that's out there. In fact, to be savagely honest, they're roughly the magical equivalent of an Anderson shelter, though at the same time a vast improvement on the alternative, which is nothing at all. Remember: don't take them off, not even for a second, because Humph Wells and Countess Judy have got better things to do than waste time kissing junior trainees. Item Four.'

Mr Wurmtoter stood up, and reached his hand out over the table. There was something in it; something alive, and wriggly. He opened his fingers a little, and a mouse's head appeared between them. With his other hand, very delicately, he slipped a finely woven silver collar and lead over the mouse's neck, then put the animal down on the table.

'This,' said Mr Wurmtoter, 'is Kurt. Actually, that's Mr Lundqvist to you, since in theory he's still a partner in the firm, though for fairly obvious reasons he hasn't been taking much part in day-to-day business for a while. Mr Lundqvist – wave to the nice trainees, Kurt.' (The mouse stood on its hind paws and waved.) 'Mr Lundqvist used to have my job, popping dragons and generally chivvying wildlife, until one day he put his foot in a Consequence Mine. Well, being out of the office a lot and being out of touch for weeks on end pretty much goes with the territory in Kurt's and my line of work, so it was a while before anybody noticed he hadn't been around much lately and came looking; and by then, I'm afraid, the effects were more or less irreversible, and now Kurt's stuck like it, just like his mum warned him he would.' The mouse reared up and tried to bite Mr Wurmtoter's hand. 'Just kidding, Kurt,' Mr Wurmtoter said, getting his hand well out of the way. 'The point is this. Consequence Mines, Probability Wells, Xavier Distortions, Groundhog-Day Loops, you name it, they're out there. This is a pretty cut-throat business we're in, and I'm afraid that at various points along the way you risk ticking people off, sometimes quite severely. And sometimes, for a whole variety of reasons, they try and do nasty things to you. In Kurt's case, he was tracking down a thoroughly unpleasant character who was in the business of turning dead people into zombies and setting them to work manning late-night Internet helplines. This bad guy simply wouldn't come out to play, kept ducking and running whenever Kurt got within a mile of him, until finally Kurt got a bit upset and sent him an e-mail asking whether he was a man or a mouse. Actually,' Mr Wurmtoter added, 'Consequence Mines are really nasty, because not only do they kill you or disfigure you in horrible ways, they're also designed to make you look a complete and utter prawn into the bargain. Anyhow,' he added, as the mouse made a determined but futile leap after the tip of his little finger, 'there's not a lot we can do about them, except, obviously, be careful – and that's a really useless piece of advice if ever there was one – and also to wear one of these at all times.' From his inside pocket he produced two little enamel badges, marked PREFECT. 'Sorry about the lettering,' Mr Wurmtoter said. 'If you like, you can wear it inside your clothes someplace, where nobody can see. I do. The point of these is, as soon as something horrid happens to you, these things send a coded signal to Wellsco Three, which in turn triggers an alarm, and one of us comes and fetches you a.s.a.p., and if there's anything we can do – well, anyway. Kurt here was a silly boy and forgot to put his on, so let that be a lesson to both of you.' The mouse suddenly made a determined attempt to escape, nearly yanking the end of his lead out from between Mr Wurmtoter's fingers. 'One last thing,' Mr Wurmtoter added, 'I'd like you to take a careful look at Kurt here, and then, just for the hell of it, take a gander at his reflection in the table-top.'

Paul did as he was told; and, upside down under the mouse's paws, he saw the image of a tiny man in combat fatigues and top-of-the-range Ray-Bans, a minuscule one-thirty-second scale Kalashnikov slung across his back, scrabbling vainly at the polished wood with hands and feet.

'In the trade,' Mr Wurmtoter said, 'we call them imp-reflecting mirrors. It's a Chinese invention, extremely useful; anything that's changed its shape or been trans-formed by magic shows up in one of these as what it really is. You can stick 'em to anything, within reason; we've got one on our boardroom table because when you're face to face with the other side's crack negotiating team, it does no harm at all to know precisely what you're really up against. The ones you really want to watch out for, of course, are the ones who don't show up at all. If ever you get one of them, I suggest you run away very fast indeed.' He hauled the mouse up into the air by its collar and tucked it away in another inside pocket. 'Anyhow,' he said, 'that's quite enough of that to be going on with. The main thing is, of course, not to panic or get unduly worried, because although it's pretty dan-gerous out there it's not as bad as all that, and indeed several of our partners have lived long, rich lives and died in their beds, or at least in beds. And if all else fails, I'm sure you'll be relieved to hear that your employee remuneration package includes *specialist* health-care insurance, as well as a generous death-in-service lump sum and an even more generous undeath-in-service annuity, index-linked to keep your dependants in luxury and you in coffins and AB negative for the rest of time; which is a tremendous comfort, I'm sure you'll agree.' Mr Wurmtoter glanced down at his watch. 'Well,' he said, 'I could carry on for hours warning you about this and that, but it's twenty-five past and you'd better be getting your coats. One *last* last thing, though.' He looked at them both, then turned to face the curtained window, almost as if he was embarrassed or something. 'Personal relationships,' he said. 'Now I know it's absolutely none of our business what or who you get up to or with in your spare time, and if anybody said to me what I'm about to say to you I'd probably bust his nose for him; but – well, number one, look before you leap, all that glitters isn't necessarily the real deal, and there's absolutely nothing worse than waking up in the morning, flashing your imp-reflecting mirror over the tousled head on the pillow next to you, and then having to rush to the bathroom and throw up. So, if you don't know where it's been, don't play with it. Number two, in our line of work the expression "safe sex" is a bit like saying "safe hand grenades", so if in doubt, leave the pin *in* or, at the very least, get rid of it quick. Finally, number three: to paraphrase the King James version, better a dinner of herbs with a face like a prune but at least you know what species you're dealing with than a stalled ox that makes the earth move but can't necessarily be relied on to put it back again afterwards.' He pulled a sad face and added: 'I'm probably not putting this as well as humanly possible, but I'm sure you get the general idea. Anyhow, you're grown-ups, basically it's up to you, but use your common sense and if you possibly can find an excuse for keeping that prefect's badge on at all times, then if something does go wrong, you do stand a better chance of us finding you while there's still enough of you left to find. All right, you'd best be going before the door's locked.'

Long, chilly silence. Then Sophie said, 'Can we go now, please?' and Paul didn't need scrying stones or imp-revealing mirrors or not-chocolate-covered dragon-droppings to know that she was on her way to meet the performance potter; furthermore, he suspected that if Mr Wurmtoter knew a tenth as much about people as he presumably did about dragons, he'd have taken one look at the cold glare in her eye and jumped out of the window. Paul let her go first, and took care to stay several paces behind her all the way back to their office.

Paul had believed in the existence of six a.m. for many years, just as he'd always believed in the yeti and the Loch Ness monster; in the same way, he'd always devoutly hoped that he'd never have to confront any of them face to face. But, somehow or other, he made it to the office door on time, to find Sophie already waiting. She was wearing a suit that had probably belonged to her grandmother, who'd presumably kept it for funerals.

'Hello,' she muttered in her best doomed voice.

'Hello,' he replied, hoping the door would open. It didn't.

'Well,' Sophie went on, making a mime routine out of consulting her watch, '*we*'re here on time.'

Paul nodded. 'He did say six o'clock, didn't he?'

'Yes.'

'Thought so. Of course, he could have meant six o'clock in the evening.'

'No. He said morning.'

'Yes, that's what I thought he said.'

There were rather more people about in the streets

than Paul had expected, and quite a few of them turned to look at Sophie. None of them laughed out loud, which was something. Nevertheless, he could feel the tension building up, and decided that he'd better defuse it by saying something before there was any bloodshed. 'How's things?' he asked awkwardly.

She looked at him. 'How do you mean?'

'Oh, generally.'

'All right,' she replied. A long silence, definitely a moment, possibly even a moment and a quarter. Then she scowled and said, 'I thought you weren't talking to me.'

'What?' Paul felt himself panicking. Not a good idea; today was likely to be a long day, quite difficult enough as it was without atmospheres and melodrama. 'No,' he said. 'I mean, aren't I? I thought I was.'

'Really. You haven't said a word to me for weeks, apart from "Pass the stapler" and "Have you finished with the Sellotape?"'

'Oh,' Paul said. 'I mean, I hadn't realised. No offence. I guess I've been, I mean, my mind's been on other things, I suppose.'

She gave him a look you could have kebabed sliced lamb on. 'So you aren't angry with me or anything?'

'No, of course not.'

'Fine.' She shrugged slightly, body language for *You lying bastard*. 'That's all right, then. This is stupid.'

'Sorry?'

'Making us get here at the crack of dawn and then keeping us hanging about on the doorstep.'

'Yes,' Paul said.

Moments were coming as thick as flies on a cow-pat. 'So,' she said, 'how about you?'

'Me? Oh, I'm fine.'

'You said you'd been worried about something.'

He made a show of frowning. 'No, nothing in particular.'

'You said your mind's been on other things.'

'Oh, right, yes.' He nodded one time too many. 'Just things in general, really. You know – goblins and magic and stuff.'

She sighed. 'What do you make of it all?' she asked.

'I don't know,' he replied. 'I mean, it's all weird and horrible, but we're sort of stuck, aren't we?'

'Are we?'

'I reckon so. I mean, if we stay away from the office, Mr Tanner'll have us doing revolting things in the street.'

'I suppose so.' She looked at her watch again, as if it was all its fault. 'Actually,' she said, 'it's been absolutely terrible, ever since that horrible evening when we got locked in. I've been thinking, if I can't talk to someone about it soon, I'm going to go mad. I even thought about telling my parents.'

'Did you?'

She gave him a don't-be-so-stupid look. 'Another bad thing is, I suppose I ought to be able to tell Shaz, I mean, isn't that what relationships are all about—?'

'Shaz? Oh, yes, sorry.'

'My boyfriend,' Sophie said icily. 'I thought I told you—'

'Yes, of course. Sorry.'

'Well.' She furrowed her thick eyebrows. 'I should be able to tell him, but somehow I can't. I keep trying to, but for some reason I can't. I keep thinking he'll laugh, or he'll think I'm mad or stoned. It's making things really difficult between us.'

Paul didn't shout 'Yippee!' at the top of his voice, or dance a hornpipe, or even grin like a dog. He was very proud of himself for that. Instead, he mumbled something about seeing how awkward that must be.

'Awkward,' Sophie repeated. 'You bet it's bloody awkward. No, all he wants to talk about is all these shows and gigs he's got lined up, you'd think it was really important; and the bad thing is, when it comes down to it, all he's really interested in is *money.*'

'Ah. It pays well, then, performance ceramics?'

She shook her head. 'The money's absolute rubbish,' she said. 'But every time he thinks he's going to get a show or something, he keeps on about how this time maybe it's going to be the start of something big, maybe he can get a regular spot at this pub or if he goes over well at this fair maybe it'll lead on to other bookings with the same people. He's obsessed with it, really.'

'*Earning a living, you mean?*' Paul didn't say. 'Sounds like he's taking it pretty seriously,' he suggested.

'Well, that's stupid,' she replied. 'Either you're going to be unconventional and a free spirit and not give a damn about the stupid boring stuff, or you might as well get a job in an office.'

It occurred to Paul that, just possibly, Shaz the performance potter was suddenly taking an interest in boring, shameful money because he was thinking of settling down somewhat, as people do when they're embarking on a serious, long-term relationship. A hallucinatory vision of his mental image of Pot Boy (who in his mind's eye bore a strong family resemblance to the Tanner clan) snooping round Laura Ashley in search of curtain material for the bus windscreen knocked him off his axis for a moment or so, and it cost him a certain degree of effort to get back to reality. 'I guess so,' he said, and hesitated. Here was a heaven-sent opportunity to start tapping in a wedge or two, but somehow he didn't feel like it. In fact, if he had to be brutally honest, he was on Pot Boy's side. 'It must be difficult, though,' he said cautiously. 'Getting the balance right, I mean. Artistic integrity on the one hand, tomorrow's shredded wheat and toilet rolls on the other. That's just Life.'

She let go another sigh. 'Well,' she said, 'I didn't really expect you'd understand.'

For a fraction of a second, just long enough for a photon to travel a yard, Paul found himself wondering whether maybe the recipient of the rawest deal in this whole emotional nexus might actually be the performance potter. But he swatted the stray thought with the rolled-up newspaper of self-pity. 'Not my line of country, really,' he muttered. 'Hey up, I think something's happening.'

Ironmongery rattled on the other side of the door, and Mr Wells appeared, shutting the door quickly behind him. He was carrying a large suitcase, and there was an even larger duffel bag slung over his shoulder.

'Right,' he said, in a slightly breathless voice, 'time we were getting on.' At precisely that moment, a large yellow minibus pulled up at the kerb. Paul caught an alarming glimpse of red eyes and tusks before Mr Wells hustled them both across to the back doors.

The bus turned out to be comfortable, verging on luxurious; a deep leather gentleman's-club armchair for Mr Wells, two airliner seats for Sophie and Paul. On a table in the middle, which somehow managed to stay perfectly still as the bus pulled several Gs tearing away from the kerb, was a distinctly fancy Continental breakfast – croissants, Danish pastries, thin slices of German sausage and Dutch cheese, those little French buns with chocolate bits in, a jug of orange juice and a flask of coffee. 'Help yourselves,' Mr Wells muttered, opening the suitcase and pulling out a sheaf of papers, 'I've already had mine.'

After a minute or so, Sophie leaned forward and poured herself half a glass of orange juice. Paul, who was suddenly very hungry, wanted to pile in and start stuffing his face, with particular regard to the choccy buns, but somehow didn't like to. In the end he picked up the nearest croissant and nibbled it, unbuttered. The bus seemed to be doing at least ninety, with frequent sudden decelerations for traffic lights and zebra crossings, but the food and the table it rested on didn't shift so much as a millimetre.

'It'll take us about five hours to get there,' Mr Wells said. 'I should have said, bring something to read. A bit later I'll fill you in on what we're going to be doing, but I'd better just catch up with this bumf first. Feel free to catch up on your sleep, if you like.'

Five hours, Paul thought; *oh, shit*. Sitting still for hours on end in moving vehicles was one of the things he was least good at, though he wouldn't have been able to read a book even if he'd brought one. For her part, Sophie swilled down her orange juice, opened her bag (first time he'd seen her with one) and produced a fat A-format paperback; *Slipware Against Franco*, he read sideways, *Ceramic Trends During The Spanish Civil War*. The fact that she put it away again five minutes later without even marking her place was the best thing that'd happened to him all day. He didn't feel particularly sleepy, but at some stage he must have closed his eyes, because he slid into a dream. He dreamed that he was sitting in an airliner seat in a yellow minivan driving at some unthinkable speed through the outskirts of London in the early morning; and sitting next to him was the thin girl (whose name for the moment escaped him) and she was fast asleep, dead to the world; so she couldn't hear the conversation that was going on between Professor Van Spee and the tall, gaunt-looking woman with the New England accent, who he was pretty sure was the Countess Judy, the entertainment-industry partner and rightful Queen of the Fey.

'I still reckon we should do something,' Countess Judy said. 'It's not right, is all. We can't let him get away with it, not again.'

The Professor pulled a wry face. 'It was necessary,' he said. 'One of us had to go. It happened to be John. That's the business for you.'

'Was it really necessary?' The Countess pursed her thin lips. 'I'm not so sure about that. We've really only got his word for it, at that.'

'He wouldn't lie. Not to us.'

The Countess thought about that. 'And those poor boys,' she said. 'Even if you're right about John, that was going too far.'

'It's the business,' the Professor said uncomfortably.

'For pity's sake, Theo.' The Countess didn't seem at all pleased with him. 'Well, I'm not going to argue with you, not now. But it's definitely not going to happen again, not with these two. For one thing, they're more valuable.'

The Professor smiled. 'Interesting,' he said. 'If they weren't quite so *valuable* –' he paused on the word '– would you be quite so vehement in their defence?'

'That's a nasty thing to say, Theo. You know me better than that.'

Professor Van Spee acknowledged his fault with a slight dip of his head. 'Also irrelevant,' he added. 'The point you make is entirely valid, they *are* valuable, and I wouldn't like to see anything happen to them. That said, I'm not convinced that anything will. Of course, I don't have your special insight in these matters—'

'Theo,' the Countess warned him.

'All I'm saying is,' the Professor went on, 'there's no real cause for concern at this particular moment. For sure, they're vulnerable – especially the boy, of course – but that's not the point. For one thing, there's no proof, not even any evidence, that the boy's actually got the wretched thing. Even if he has got it, that doesn't necessarily mean he's used it, or even that he knows what it is, or what it does. I would imagine that if he did contrive to figure it out, he'd only use it as a sort of toy, and get tired of it fairly soon. Of course,' he added, 'that wouldn't even be an issue if we hadn't lost the blasted object in the first place.'

That was obviously a sore point with the Countess; she scowled before replying: 'Theo, don't be deliberately obtuse. Dennis had them both tidying out the strongroom. That's as good as drawing them a map with a big red X marked on it.'

The professor raised an eyebrow. 'You think it's in the strongroom?'

'Well, for heaven's sake. Where else would it be?'

'I don't know. If I knew, it wouldn't be lost. All I know is, we've both searched that room from top to bottom a hundred times, and we couldn't find it.'

'Of course *we* couldn't find it, as well you know. Stop

talking to me like I'm a little kid. I think the boy's got it, and he knows the boy's got it, and that's what all this is about. And we ought to do something.'

The professor looked at her down his nose. 'What, exactly?'

'Warn them, obviously.'

'With respect.' The professor rubbed his forehead, as if the conversation was giving him a headache. 'Suppose we do warn him, what on earth could we say? *Beware?* Anything more specific than that would be an unpardonable breach of professional ethics. And if we're wrong, it'd be disastrous.'

For her part, the Countess was losing patience. 'Have it your own way, then,' she said. 'After all, it's not on my conscience, whatever happens. I can always simply walk away and let the whole lot of you get on with it. In fact, I'm sorely tempted.'

The Professor smiled. 'I don't think so,' he said. 'What would you do, for one thing? I can't honestly see you sitting on a toadstool playing on the pan pipes all day long. You'd be bored. It was boredom that led you to join the firm in the first place.'

'There're worse things than boredom,' the Countess replied. 'But I can see there's no point arguing with you, your mind's made up. I still say we should warn them, or at least the boy.'

'No.' The professor raised his voice, which seemed somewhat out of character. 'We should leave well alone. You too,' he added meaningfully. 'If you're toying with the idea of telling him yourself—'

'Theo, I promised I wouldn't.'

'Ah, but you've been to law school, you know all sorts of clever ways of telling people things without actually moving your lips. I want you to say you won't tell him. Sincerely, and with all your fingers where I can see them.'

As he said this, Paul noticed what the professor couldn't from where he was standing: the Countess had her fingers crossed behind her back. *Silly*, he thought; *but then, these people are different.* Quite possibly, crossed fingers might be a singularly powerful and significant magic spell, as far as they were concerned.

'All right.' She held up both hands. 'I promise. I won't tell him anything.'

Then Paul woke up; and he was sitting in an airliner seat in a yellow minivan driving at some unthinkable speed through the outskirts of London in the early morning; and next to him was the thin girl (whose name for the moment escaped him) and she was fast asleep, dead to the world; but the only other person in the bus was Mr Wells, apparently engrossed in a thick typescript. So Paul sat still and quiet for what seemed like a very long time; and then Mr Wells's eyes closed, and the bundle of papers slid through his fingers onto his lap, and he snored.

Which just leaves me, Paul thought, and for some unaccountable reason, he was aware of the portable door, which was sitting in its cardboard tube in his jacket pocket. It was only there because he'd forgotten to take it out the night before, he certainly hadn't intended using it today of all days. Nevertheless. A quick trip to Florence or Acapulco would break the monotony of the journey, give him a chance to stretch his legs. Furthermore, the overpowering fatigue that still followed a really long trip through the door would help him get to sleep, which would be a good thing on a five hour journey. Having made quite sure that both Sophie and Mr Wells were fast asleep, he unrolled the door, plastered it against the side of the van, and went through.

With hindsight, the mistake he made was not firmly deciding on his destination before crossing the threshold. Instead, he'd just gone through; a stupid mistake, entirely due to carelessness. It was, therefore, his fault alone when he looked round and discovered to his disgust that he was back at 70 St Mary Axe, in his own office.

It took Paul a moment to figure out what had happened; then he turned round to walk back through the door. But it wasn't there. The reason for that wasn't hard to guess, either. He'd forgotten to wedge the door open before stepping through, and the movement of the bus had jarred it shut.

CHAPTER ELEVEN

Annoying, to say the least. Since Paul had no idea where Mr Wells had been taking them, he couldn't get a bus or charter a plane and follow them, so there'd be raised eyebrows and pointed questions at the very least when they got back. Also, that was presumably the last he'd ever see of the portable door – unless, of course, it featured as an exhibit at his trial for stealing clients' property from the strongroom.

All in all, a thoroughgoing cock-up. He forced himself to look on the bright side. (Maybe they'd sack him; but he doubted that, somehow. It'd be like getting thrown out of Hell for being antisocial.) Then, intending to go and report to Julie and ask for something to do, he reached for the door handle, and in doing so uncovered his watch, which told him the time was three minutes to two.

Hold on, he thought; it might have seemed like he'd been in that horrible bus for eight hours, but he hadn't.

A quick check assured him that the watch was working – second hand busily hoppiting round the dial – but obviously it wasn't. He was considering the position when the door swung open, nearly bashing him on the nose, and Sophie bustled in.

'Sorry,' she muttered, and squeezed past him on her way to her desk – which, he noticed with alarm and bewilderment, was covered with stacks of Mortensen printouts, sorted and unsorted. Even by J. W. Wells & Co. standards, that was taking weirdness to excessive extremes. Sophie's presence he could probably account for if he had to – for instance, she could have seen the portable door plastered up against the side of the van and gone through it. But they'd finished up the last of the spreadsheets during the course of yesterday afternoon—

'Sorry to bother you,' he said, 'but haven't we done all these?'

She looked up. 'All what?'

'The Mortensen sheets.'

'The what?'

And then it occurred to him that if this really was yesterday afternoon, she wouldn't have been to the meeting in the conference room yet, or heard Mr Wurmtoter explaining about the Mortensen Counters. 'What day is it today?' he asked feebly.

'Wednesday. Have you been drinking, or something?'

'What? I mean, no.'

'You're acting pretty odd. And what was it you called these bits of paper?'

'Oh, nothing.' Paul's education might have been perfunctory at best, but he'd seen enough *Star Trek* to know that if you're unlucky enough to find yourself in a temporal anomaly, suddenly marooned in your own past, it's absolutely essential not to do anything that might bugger up the timelines and change the course of events; for fear, among other things, that you'll do something that might prevent whatever it was that shot you back through time from happening, in which case you'd be stuck halfway between the past and the future for ever, probably in one of those cheesy studio sets with all the polystyrene rocks. 'Doesn't matter, really,' he said. 'Well, I guess I'd better get on with some work, then.'

The rest of the day was an absolute nightmare, as he struggled to remember every single thing he'd said and done yesterday, so as to be able to do and say it again in exactly the same way. In the end it proved impossible, although as far as he could see it really wasn't his fault; there were several occasions when he distinctly remembered his lines, but either the reply they elicited was totally different, or the expected cue never came. Mr Wurmtoter's deadly-perils lecture was shorter, and instead of warning them against Xavier Distortions he told them about Ehrlichmann Paradoxes – meeting yourself at your own funeral, and so forth – which struck Paul as pushing coincidence a trifle too far. There was only one bright spot; as he walked to the bus stop on his way home, he found that the portable door was still in his pocket – though that was an infringement of the temporal by-laws as well, since he could distinctly remember that at that stage yesterday, he'd entirely forgotten that it was there.

At this point he very nearly sat down on the pavement and burst into tears. But it was too late to do anything about it now – or was it? Suddenly it occurred to him to wonder precisely how he'd managed to arrive back at yesterday afternoon, and the answer was quite plain. The door had sent him not just through space but through time as well.

Oh for crying out loud, he thought.

Pretty soon, however, disgust at finding himself caught up in a scenario he wouldn't even bother to watch on TV unless there was nothing but motor racing on all the other channels gave way to a certain degree of cautious exhilaration. During his time at J. W. Wells Paul had come to realise that all that glitters was probably wired up to the mains, waiting to sizzle the eyebrows off unwary passers-by; nevertheless, being able to go back in time . . . If only he could figure out how to use the thing with any degree of precision, how wonderful that would be. He'd be able to go back through his life editing out the bloopers. He'd be able to avoid those embarrassing mistakes that made him wake up sweating in the middle of the night. For example—

For example: he could nip back a couple of months, and make a point of not applying for the post of junior clerk at J. W. Wells & Co. Just think of it. No more Mr Tanner, or spreadsheets, or swords in stones, or goblins, no weirdness of any kind. Not to mention, no more broken heart.

No more Sophie.

Damn, he thought. *But no, the hell with it*; it wasn't as if anything could ever possibly come of it, now that she had Pot Boy to buy ham rolls for. Was it really worth turning his back on a chance to be free of all the crazy, terrifying, weird stuff, just so he could spend his working days not talking to her, not going out for lunch, not sharing the day's experiences, not being there for each other as each new bizarre horror unfolded, not gradually being drawn closer by their shared traumas?

Paul thought about that.

Bugger, he thought.

The bus drew up, and he climbed aboard. *All right,* he negotiated with himself; *how would it be if I went back to the day before she went to the party or whatever it was where she met the performance bloody potter, and somehow managed to stop her going to it?* Result, no Pot Boy, no broken heart. *Yeah, right.* He knew exactly what'd happen; a week later she'd meet an avant-garde neo-Marxist juggler on the bus, or get trapped in a stuck lift with an expressionist sea lion-tamer. It wasn't with who she might fall in love but with who she quite definitely wouldn't that mattered. As far as he knew, there was nothing the portable door could do about that, not even if it pitched the two of them up alone together on a desert island, with no source of food apart from inexhaustible oyster beds.

In other words, forget it. Ah, now, if only. If only the door could take him back to the day before the interview, and at the same time wipe his memory clean, so he'd forget he'd even met her. He'd settle for that; but apparently it didn't work that way, or else how come he could remember Mr Lundqvist, and Mortensen Counters? He realised he'd been right all along. The door was just a toy, something out of the sorcering classes' equivalent of an Innovations catalogue. He was back to where he'd started from, where he'd always been. It didn't matter where you were, or when, or even (recalling Mrs Tanner) what. The only thing that matters a damn is who you are, and by a strange coincidence, it's also the only thing you can't change.

Nuts to that, then. As the bus drew near to his stop Paul stood up to get off, and then remembered that yesterday at this point he'd been daydreaming, missed his stop, been carried on to the next one. He sat down, also remembering that he'd had a long walk home in the driving rain, which he would, of course, be obliged to repeat.

And, at six o'clock the next morning, there he was on the doorstep of 70 St Mary Axe; and there was Sophie. He'd spent most of the previous night trying to piece together his recollections of their strained, awkward conversation, the one where he'd ended up feeling sorry for Pot Boy. It had been bad enough the first time, God knew. Having to go through it all again, this time in cold blood—

'Hello,' she muttered, still in her best doomed voice.

'Hello,' he replied.

'Well,' Sophie went on, '*we*'re here on time.'

Paul remembered to nod. 'He did say six o'clock, didn't he?'

'Yes.'

'Thought so. Of course, he could have meant six o'clock in the evening.'

'No. He said morning.'

'Yes, that's what I thought he said.'

So far, he reassured himself, *so good*. Of course, that had been the easy bit, the not-toe-curlingly embarrassing part. All the really painful bits were yet to come, starting with his next line; which was—

'How's things?' he asked awkwardly.

'How do you mean?'

'Oh, generally.'

'All right. I thought you weren't talking to me.'

And then he dried. He could remember being thoroughly startled and panicked at this point, but for the life of him he couldn't remember what he'd actually said. A second passed, then another; it was rapidly turning into a Moment, and God knew what the upshot of that might be. He was going to have to busk it; but he couldn't think of any sort of half-sensible reply. Finally, in desperation, he blurted out: 'Oh. I thought it was you who wasn't talking to me.'

Bad mistake. 'Oh,' she said, and went pink. It was a Moment. Worse than that, he had a horrible feeling it was quite possibly one of those things Mr Wurmtoter had been prattling on about (*fuck*, he thought; *twice now I've heard the stupid lecture, why the hell couldn't I have been paying attention just once?*), a Consequence Mine. In which case—

'Oh,' she repeated. 'Oh, right. What made you think that?'

'Well—' He could almost see the tattered shreds of the timeline blowing away on the breeze. 'Well, ever since you and what's-his-name, Shaz, got together, I suppose I'd assumed—'

'Oh.' It was snowing bloody Moments now, he could have shovelled them up, stapled them together and sold them on a market stall as calendars. 'Actually, it's not like that,' she was saying. 'I mean, yes, we're *seeing* each other, and I suppose we're having a relationship, sort of, but it's not—' She hesitated, scowled. 'Actually, we're going through this, like, really bad patch right now, in fact I'm really thinking about calling the whole thing off.'

Once again, though for rather different reasons, Paul didn't shout, 'Yippee!' at the top of his voice; nor did he dance a hornpipe, nor yet grin like a dog. Instead he cringed, and waited for a special effect to whisk him away to eternal damnation among the cardboard canyons.

'Actually,' Sophie was saying, 'it's bloody awkward right now. He's changed a lot, really changed. All he wants to talk about is all these shows and gigs he's got lined up, you'd think it was really important; and the bad thing is, when it comes down to it, all he's really interested in is *money*.'

He recognised that bit, should have been relieved, wasn't. The words were the same, more or less, but they were coming from a very different direction. He could see the crack starting to open up; all it'd take would be a very little wedge, gently pushed in with a fingertip, and Pot Boy would effectively be history. Alternative history. The other timeline.

'Come now,' he heard himself croak. 'Don't you think that maybe you're being a bit unfair?'

She looked round sharply at him; almost as if she too was aware that he'd dumped the authorised script and was ad libbing disgracefully. 'What do you mean?' she demanded.

'Well.' Yes, come to think of it, what the hell did he mean? No idea. 'Obviously,' he said, 'his career's important to him. If he's starting to make a go of it, you should be pleased.'

Wonderful, he thought, *that's screwed it up even worse. Now she's going to be really pissed off with him and me too.* 'Right,' she said. 'So I've got to be supportive and keep out of the way and not speak till I'm spoken to, like –

like a good little *wife*.' She shook her head so ferociously it was a miracle she didn't unscrew her neck.
'That's not—'

'I didn't mean it like that,' Paul interrupted desperately. 'That's not at all what I meant.' (*And what* did *I
mean, Mister Wise Guy?*) 'What I meant was,' he went
on, 'surely it's precisely those things that you – well,
that you really like about him, that makes him such a
good, um, potter.'

'Ceramic artist.'

'Right. That too. So what I'm saying is, if he doesn't
stay true to himself, keep faith with his art, all that
stuff; well, he wouldn't be the person you, um, really
like, he'd be somebody else. I mean, if he suddenly
decided to give up being a pot— being a performance
ceramic artist, just because it was taking up so much of
his time, and instead of doing that he – oh, I don't
know, got a job in the library or on a building site or
something. Then he'd be someone completely different, and—'

Mercifully, she interrupted. 'I see what you mean,'
she said. (Paul was glad to hear that one of them did.)
'So you think that really I'm the one being selfish,
because I'm trying to make him into someone he isn't
just because I want him to be the way I want him to be,
instead of wanting him the way he is, which is why I
wanted him in the first place?'

Paul took a deep breath. 'Yes,' he said.

'Oh.'

Just as Paul was beginning to despair, Mr Wells
showed up; and he at least had the common courtesy
to stick to the script. Once they were in the minibus,
there was obviously less scope for deviation from the

True Way, although Paul noted with a certain degree of disgust that this time around, Sophie carried on reading *Slipware Against Franco* for a full twenty minutes. In due course, he felt his eyes getting tired; he closed them and fell asleep, but if he repeated the dream, he wasn't aware of it when he woke up. Of the urge to use the portable door there was no sign. Instead, he lolled back in his seat and tried to think happy thoughts. He failed.

He'd fallen asleep again when they finally arrived, and Sophie woke him up with a gentle kick to the ankle. He jumped up and nearly banged his head on the bus roof.

'We're here,' Mr Wells announced. 'Now, I should have briefed you on what we're going to be doing, but it must've slipped my mind. Doesn't matter, it's all very straightforward. Just keep quiet and do whatever I tell you to. You can both manage that, I'm sure.'

They climbed out of the van into an open field. Some way off was a big white tent. There were children running about, dozens of them, while serious-looking men in suits hung around in small groups sipping wine and talking gravely, and harassed women in hats tried to keep the kids from causing injury to themselves and others.

'Children's party,' Mr Wells explained under his breath, as they walked towards the tent. Sophie was scowling. 'What are we doing here, then?' she asked.

'We're the magic show,' Mr Wells replied.

Sophie stopped dead. 'Magic show? You mean conjuring tricks and stuff?'

Mr Wells looked annoyed. 'Well, of course. That's what I am, a magician.'

'Oh.'

A very large fat man in a double-breasted grey suit, presumably the host, intercepted Mr Wells and shook his hand as though pumping water. Mr Wells smiled affably and introduced them as his assistants, whereupon the host pointed to a smaller tent, where they could get changed. Paul was thinking, *Hang on*; but of course, it made sense. Magic shows; magic. Rabbits out of hats, doves out of white silk handkerchieves, your card was the seven of clubs. And that, apparently, was all there was to it, after all.

'Your costumes,' Mr Wells said, as they reached the changing tent, 'are in that suitcase.'

At the word costumes, Sophie gave him a look that would've cleaned barnacles off the hull of an oil tanker; but if she'd been anticipating something involving lurex and long spangly tights, she was worrying unnecessarily. The costumes turned out to be long grey robes, what the well-dressed monk was wearing, and they slipped on over their ordinary clothes without any trouble. Mr Wells's version came with a deep, mysterious hood that made him look like Emperor Palpatine's no-good elder brother, and he also had a genuine black-with-white-tips magic wand. The rest of the luggage was full of props – interlocking brass rings, white silk squares, curiously shaped spring-loaded boxes that strapped on under the forearm, brightly-coloured glass balls, several packs of playing cards, a bunch of what looked like carpentry stuff and four disconcertingly real, sharp Japanese swords. The suitcase itself expanded somehow into a combination trestle table and trunk, by virtue of several logic-defying hinged and folded panels. They lugged all the gear across to the main tent, which was empty apart from a few bored-looking men setting out chairs. There was a stage at one end, with a microphone stand and a couple of folding screens.

Setting up all the gadgetry took a long time. Mr Wells wasn't terribly good at explaining what he wanted them to do, which was unfortunate given that neither of them had a clue what was supposed to go where, or how it was meant to work. They'd only just finished when the children started trooping in.

Small children always made Paul nervous, and this lot were worse than most. They chattered and pulled faces and threw things, mostly sausage rolls and cake shrapnel, quite a lot of which missed its intended targets and found its way up onto the stage. Mr Wells, however, didn't seem the slightest bit fazed by the unruliness of the mob; he confronted them like a Roman emperor receiving the salute from a troupe of gladiators, and when he tapped twice against the trunk with his wand, the whole lot of them immediately stopped talking, sat up straight and gazed at him expectantly. Then he began his act.

Paul had never liked conjuring shows much when he'd been a kid; he couldn't ever see the point, since it was always blindingly obvious (to him at least) how the tricks were done. Maybe this was just because all the shows he'd ever watched had been low-budget cheapskate affairs. Mr Wells, however, was in a different class. Too dignified to bother with inanely cheerful patter, he didn't say a word apart from the occasional soft grunt when he asked Paul or Sophie to hold something for him or pass him some item of equipment. As the show wore on, and Paul managed to follow orders without screwing the whole thing up through ignorance or carelessness, he realised that Mr Wells was really very good indeed. That was, of course, only to be expected. Clearly the people who'd hired them were disgustingly rich, enough so that they could afford to employ the very best, which was what Mr Wells appeared to be. Paul found himself watching with rapt attention, but this time he had no idea how Mr Wells managed to pull off his rather astonishing stunts. If he hadn't seen all the paraphernalia beforehand, he could quite easily have believed that it really was all done by supernatural influence (though why anybody with mysterious superhuman powers should choose to fritter them away on transfiguring gerbils into roller-skates and pulling the flags of all the EU member states out of a sealed biscuit jar was just another mystery).

At least he didn't have to wait too long to find out what the swords were for. He was ordered to climb inside the trunk (actually, it was huge in there; you could've parked a Morris Minor in the front compartment alone) and keep still. Then the lid closed, and Paul was left huddled up on all fours, feeling his legs go to sleep. After he'd been in there for perhaps a full minute, he felt something tickle the side of his neck, followed by a similar feeling in the small of his back. He couldn't shift round to see what it was, because of the excruciating pins and needles he was getting, but a moment later, as he looked up at the trunk roof, he was horrified to see the sharp chisel point of one of the swords coming straight at him. At the very last moment before the blade rammed in straight between his eyes, it appeared to turn first translucent, then invisible, and that appeared to be that. To judge by the muffled thunder going on outside, the kids were enjoying it, at any rate.

Then he heard Mr Wells telling him to shuffle backwards out of the box, so he did that, the discomfort in his legs having eased a bit, and found himself squatting on his heels behind one of the folding screens. He did his best to keep perfectly still.

'And now for my last trick,' Mr Wells was saying, 'I shall saw a lady in half. Now I'll need a volunteer from our audience. You, perhaps, miss? Yes, you in the front row.'

Paul wriggled round so he could see what was going on through a small tear in the screen. A twentysomethingish blonde in a power business suit with an illegally short skirt was getting up out of her seat in the front row, where she'd been sitting next to the host on his left. Something told Paul that she was the host's personal assistant, and that her filing skills and telephone manner weren't the only reasons she'd got the job. She didn't seem too pleased about volunteering, in fact she was sharing out skin-blistering glares between the host and Mr Wells; but she was out of her chair and being steered towards the trunk, which had somehow evolved into a variety of free-floating coffin, hovering about three feet off the ground. Mr Wells lifted the coffin lid and she scrambled inside, although hampered rather in her movements by the tightness of her skirt. Then Mr Wells closed the lid and picked up a large Stanley hardpoint saw.

Paul caught sight of the host's face, which seemed rather strained for some reason; then Mr Wells began to saw. The noise he made was rather horrible, and he appeared to be putting a great deal of effort into it. From where he crouched, Paul could distinctly see sawdust floating down to the ground. Not a peep out of the kids, and Paul could understand why. The whole thing was distinctly riveting, even though everybody in the world knew how the trick was done these days.

Mr Wells stopped sawing and rested for a moment, wiping his forehead on the back of his sleeve (nice touch, Paul had to admit). Then he laid his hands on either side of the saw-cut and gently pushed, and the two halves of the coffin drifted apart. Paul could see the girl's head sticking out of one end, and her four-inch stilettos waggling feebly up and down out of the other. Then Mr Wells stepped forward, said, 'Thank you, you've been a wonderful audience,' swept low in a grandiose bow, and turned to leave the stage.

It was at that moment that Paul realised it wasn't a trick.

Maybe it was something in the way the girl's head had slumped forward, or maybe he was just getting more perceptive where these matters were concerned. He craned his neck to see, but there wasn't any blood in with the sawdust, no bits of intestine hanging out from the end of the box. Even so.

Apparently the host had got the message too; he jumped up, his mouth wide open, but before he could make a sound, Mr Wells half-turned and beckoned. The host followed Mr Wells to the back of the stage, behind the other screen. The audience was just starting to murmur. The girl's heels were perfectly still now, like Christmas turkeys hanging up in a butcher's window.

'What the hell—?' Paul heard the host say in a hoarse whisper, but Mr Wells held up his hand.

'I said I'd saw her in half,' he said, in a quiet, reasonable voice. 'I never said anything about putting her back together again.'

The host called Mr Wells a bastard. Mr Wells didn't seem inclined to deny it. In fact, he smiled.

'Isn't it Von Clausewitz who defines bastardry as the art of negotiation by other means?' he said, with a mild grin. 'Now, about my client's takeover bid for your client's company.'

The audience was starting to get restless; he could hear voices, sounding worried. Someone laughed, but there was an edge to it. 'Your client?' the host said.

'You know what I'm talking about.'

'Oh.' Pause. 'Oh, so you're—?'

'Yes. Always nice to put a face to the name, isn't it?'

'But—'

'Fond of her, aren't you?'

About a second of dead silence. 'All right,' said the host. 'What've I got to do?'

'Just sign here.' Mr Wells produced a sheet of paper from inside his gown. 'You can borrow my pen if you like.'

After that, the host went back to his seat; he was as white as a sheet, and even from where he was, Paul could see he was shaking. Then Mr Wells came out from behind the screen and, with a graceful flourish, he slid the two halves of the coffin back together again and lifted the lid. The girl's head moved, she groaned; and Mr Wells reached out his hand and helped her to her feet.

For a single heartbeat, there was total silence. Then

the audience started to clap; the girl looked round, as if she hadn't known they were there. Mr Wells bowed again, with a good deal of exaggerated business, swirling the hem of his gown. The girl tottered back to her place in the front row and sat down.

That seemed to be that.

Mr Wells nodded to Paul, and he guessed he was supposed to help with dismantling the gear. The audience was getting up, filing out of the tent. Even the children seemed subdued, as if they knew they'd seen something odd, but didn't know what exactly. The girl left with the rest of the crowd; the host stayed on for a moment or so, staring up at Mr Wells as he folded up the coffin and turned it back into a suitcase. Then he left too.

'Time we were on our way, I think,' Mr Wells said, when the three of them were alone in the tent. 'Best not to hang around when you've pulled off a good deal.' He seemed almost absurdly cheerful, like a favourite uncle at Christmas. 'Right, is that the lot? Splendid. We didn't leave anything in the other tent, did we?' He pulled his robes off and dumped them unfolded in the suitcase. 'You two can change in the bus, to save time. Come on.'

A minute or so later they were back in the minibus, and the driver was starting up the engine. Mr Wells flopped into his comfy chair; Paul could see he'd been sweating. 'What's the time?' Mr Wells asked, and then answered his own question. 'Quarter past twelve, splendid. We'll stop for lunch on the way back, firm's treat. Well, that all went very smoothly. I thought it would, but you can never be sure.'

They were driving out of the field. 'Mr Wells,' Sophie said.

'Hm?' Already Mr Wells had a pile of papers on his lap, and a silver fountain pen in his right hand.

'If that man hadn't signed your bit of paper,' Sophie said, 'would you have let her die?'

'I beg your pardon?'

'The woman in the box. Would you have let her die?'

Mr Wells looked at her for a moment; a very cold, thoughtful look. Then he laughed and said, 'Good lord, you don't actually think—? It was just a conjuring trick, that's all.'

Sophie's expression didn't change. 'Oh,' she said. 'Really?'

'Well, of course it was.' Mr Wells laughed again; it was studio-audience laughter. 'You don't for one moment believe I'd actually cut somebody in two? How ridiculous.'

'Fine,' said Sophie. 'That's all right, then.'

'Splendid,' said Mr Wells, and went back to reading his documents.

About half an hour later, the bus stopped. They were in the car park of a motorway service station. 'Lunch,' Mr Wells explained.

He led them to the Burger King. Sophie said she wasn't actually very hungry, but Mr Wells just smiled and ordered her a Vegeburger with large fries and a coffee, together with a bacon double cheeseburger for himself and (without asking) a Whopper, large fries and large vanilla shake for Paul. As it happened, it was just what he'd have chosen for himself.

They sat down at a table with their trays and styrofoam cups. Mr Wells ate like a tyrannosaurus, gripping the food with his teeth and then ripping a mouthful away. 'In case you were wondering,' he said, with his mouth full, 'we act for a major road-haulage contractor, and our host at the party back there's the solicitor representing our client's landlords. We were having some difficulty over the terms of a new lease for our client's main distribution depot, but it's all settled now. The party,' he added, 'was for his son's tenth birthday. Rather a stroke of luck, but part of the secret of this business is making the most of opportunities.'

They got back to St Mary's Axe at half-past five precisely. When the bus stopped, Mr Wells bookmarked the chunky-looking document he'd been reading, dropped it into the suitcase, snapped it shut and hopped out. 'Be in my office at ten past nine on Monday morning, please,' he called back over his shoulder. As soon as Paul and Sophie were out of the minibus, it roared away from the kerb, the back doors still open, and vanished up the road.

'Well,' Paul said.

'Yes,' Sophie replied. 'I need a drink. Coming?'

'Actually—' Paul stopped. *Why not?* he thought. It wasn't every day you saw a woman sawn in half, and he could do with a drink himself. 'Yes,' he said.

They went to the pub where they'd met again after the interview, and sat at the same table. Paul tried not to think about that. Sophie wasn't drinking Guinness this time; instead, she came back from the bar with what looked like a large brandy, which she gulped down as if it was medicine.

'He was lying,' she said. 'I saw what he did.'

'So did I,' Paul replied. 'Though there wasn't any blood. But—'

'And when you were inside the box,' she said, 'and

he stuck those swords down through it. Did you feel anything?'

'No,' Paul said.

'If that man hadn't agreed – you know, the solicitor or whatever he was – Wells'd just have walked away and let her die. I know he would.'

Paul didn't really want to dwell on that, but he decided to be polite and not make an issue out of it. 'I agree. You're right, I mean. But—'

'Well?'

'I don't suppose that there was any real danger the man wouldn't agree,' he said awkwardly. 'So I suppose, in practice, there wasn't any real harm done. I mean, when she got up and walked off the stage, she seemed all right to me.'

'What's that got to do with it?'

'Nothing, really,' Paul mumbled. 'You're right, it was a horrible thing to do, and he just didn't care.' *What am I supposed to do about it?* he didn't add.

'That man's evil,' Sophie went on. 'Total bastard. And when it was the solicitor bloke's kid's birthday, too. What sort of evil bastard would do something like that?'

There didn't seem to be anything Paul could add to that; nor, he guessed, was any input required on his part. He nodded, and sipped his lemonade shandy. 'I wonder what he's got lined up for us on Monday,' he said.

'Whatever it is, I'm not doing it.' She looked at him, and they both knew she hadn't meant it, because they had absolutely no choice whatsoever in the matter. For a brief moment, though, Paul was sorely tempted to tell her about the portable door; just in case she could think of some way of making use of it to get them out of the terrible mess they were both in. But he didn't; instead, he said: 'Doing anything this evening?'

He hadn't meant it like that; he'd meant to ask if she had something pleasant lined up, something that might help to take the taste of blood away. She obviously took it the other way. 'No,' she said. 'I was supposed to be going to help Shaz set up for a gig at a pub in Penge, but he called last night and said the gig was off and he was going to stay in and do something or other to his kiln, or something like that. So, no, I'm not doing anything.'

'Oh.' Paul wasn't sure what to do next. He was confused; he wasn't sure whether he was still supposed to be shoring up the Sophie/Shaz relationship, as part of his duty to heal the wounds he'd caused in the timeline by his escapade with the portable door, or whether he was now at liberty to sabotage it for all he was worth. And now, apparently, he'd somehow contrived to ask Sophie out on a date, and she'd accepted.

(But he didn't *want* to go out on a date, not even with the girl he loved, not even if it meant there was an outside chance of prising the performance potter off her and winning her for himself. All he wanted to do was go home, have a bath, go to bed and try very hard not to dream about severed limbs and the effects of a cross-cut saw on living tissue. Still; as Mr Wells had said, part of the secret of this business was making the most of opportunities. Somehow, he didn't really want to accept advice on this particular subject from Mr Wells, even if it did appear to be singularly appropriate.)

'Great,' he heard himself say. 'Do you fancy going to the pictures?'

She frowned, as though he'd just asked her to do a complex piece of mental arithmetic. 'I don't know,' she said. 'What did you want to see?'

Paul realised that he couldn't think of the name of a single film currently on general release. 'Nothing in particular,' he said. 'Is there anything you'd like to see?'

'No.'

'Oh.'

And then she looked at him in a slightly different way, and said, 'Let's just stay here and have another drink or something'; and for a brief moment, Paul felt as though he was stuck halfway up a sheer cliff, and suddenly it had shrugged its shoulders and levelled itself out into a gentle downhill slope. 'That'd be nice,' he heard himself say. It wasn't the reply he'd have chosen to make, but apparently it had got the job done, because she nodded very slightly and said she'd like a half of Guinness.

After that, they talked about several things. Sophie had quite a lot to say about Mr Wells; then she expanded the scope of her remarks to include Mr Tanner. She didn't like either of them very much. However, she conceded, there wasn't a lot she or Paul could do about it. She didn't sound happy about that.

Paul made the point that he wasn't exactly thrilled with the way matters stood, either. It had been more or less bearable, he said, when all they were doing was sorting through the Mortensen printouts – before they knew what they were, of course, because, somehow, knowing made it worse rather than better. Now, though, it looked like they were going to have to get involved, and he really didn't want to do that. Then, for some reason that seemed to make sense at the time, he told Sophie about Mr Tanner's mum. He had to do some serious editing, to leave out any reference to the portable door; so he shifted the scene of the encounter in Ankara to the Starbucks in Camden Town. He left out the not-chocolate-coated beans, too.

While he was telling the story, he wasn't at all sure how it'd be received. It worried him that it might sound like macho locker-room talk, an unregenerate male bragging about his conquests. But Sophie didn't appear to take it that way; in fact, she pulled a face and muttered 'Yuck', which was how Paul had hoped she'd react. She spoiled it rather by adding something to the effect that Mr Tanner's mum must be really weird and, as he'd said himself, desperate, but he didn't mind that really.

'And all those different receptionists are all just goblins in disguise,' she added. 'That's so sick. I mean, the clothes they wear, I guess I should have known there was something wrong with them. Talk about obvious. You're so lucky you managed to get away from her.'

Paul felt like pointing out that luck hadn't had much to do with it, but he didn't. Instead, he changed the subject slightly. Had she thought of asking for help or advice from anybody? Her parents, for instance. Weren't they curious about how she was getting on at work?

'Not really,' she replied, with a sigh. 'They've got it into their heads that I've got this really good job with this really important company, and in a year or so I'll be a junior partner because I'm so clever and talented, and everything's going to be fine. If I tried to tell them what's really going on, they'd simply shut their ears and not take it in. That's just what they're like, you see. They get an idea of how they want things to be, and if it doesn't turn out that way, they just ignore it. They probably think that sooner or later Shaz'll stop all this ceramics nonsense and get a proper job in a building society, and then we can get married and buy a house and have a family, and stuff like that. It's really sad, but they don't know me from a hole in the ground.'

Paul shrugged. 'At least they seem to like you,' he said. 'Mine don't, or they wouldn't have buggered off to Florida.'

Sophie frowned. 'When was the last time you heard from them?'

'I got a postcard last week,' Paul replied, 'from the Grand Canyon. Apparently they've bought one of these giant camper-van things and gone off touring round America for six months. They did say they'd ring when they got back, to tell me what a wonderful time they've been having.' Paul stopped, and furrowed his brows. 'You know,' he said, 'I've just realised, we're the perfect people for JWW to pick on. I mean, even if we were to try and tell someone about them, like what they're really up to, there's nobody for either of us to talk to, not even our families. Yours wouldn't listen, and mine aren't even there. I wonder if they knew that, from the start.'

'Probably,' Sophie said.

'Though of course,' Paul went on, 'you did have a boyfriend when you started work; the one who suddenly got interested in Gilbert and Sullivan.' He looked up at her. 'Do you think that was – well, them, as well?'

She nodded. 'I've wondered about that,' she said. 'Not that he'd have been a threat, exactly. I mean, I'd never have tried to tell him. He wouldn't have heard me. He never did hear me much, thinking about it. I'm not sure he even liked me much.' She shrugged. 'I don't think Shaz does, either.'

'Oh,' said Paul. 'Do you like him, then?'

She thought about that. 'No, not really,' she said. 'He's got an unfortunate manner, and he doesn't always smell very nice. But he's very creative, and his lifestyle's very – well, it's pretty cool, living in a bus and working with your hands, but artistic, and very committed, of course. It's what I ought to have done, I should have been a sculptor or a blacksmith, something like that. Instead—'

'Instead,' Paul said, 'you're a witch. Trainee witch,' he added quickly.

She started to scowl, then smiled. 'Yes, but I commute and I wear suits and court shoes, and my parents approve of me.'

'Fine,' said Paul. 'So if you could wear a black pointy hat and travel to work on a broomstick, that'd be okay?'

'It'd be better,' Sophie conceded. 'But—'

'I know,' Paul said. 'Besides, the JWW mob aren't wizards and witches, they're business people who happen to be in that line of business.' He grinned. 'If you were like them and had a broomstick for flying about on, it'd have to have a sticker on the back saying *My Other Broom's An Addis*.'

She laughed, though it was more out of solidarity than amusement. 'You know,' she said, 'if this has taught me anything, it's that it's not what you do that matters, it's who you are while you're doing it. I mean, we get these crazy ideas, about ourselves and other people; and then all of a sudden the other people turn out to be sorcerers and goblins, and we—' She shrugged. 'If I was like really brave, I'd sneak into that boardroom place and take a good long look at my reflection in that table top. Who knows, I might learn a thing or two.'

Paul shook his head. 'I'm not brave enough for that,' he said. 'I've got a pretty good idea I'd know exactly what I'd see.'

'You think so. Maybe you're wrong.'

At that moment, Paul wished he had the bag of not-chocolate raisins handy. He also felt mortally embarrassed, but he was used to that. 'I don't know about you,' he said, 'but I'm hungry.'

'*You*'re hungry. I didn't have any lunch.'

'You did. At least, you ate the chips, when you thought Mr Wells wasn't looking. I saw you.'

She grinned. 'All right, so I did. I need my lunch. If I don't eat at lunchtime, I get bad-tempered.'

'You don't say.' Paul nodded. 'What do you like? Food, I mean.'

'Oh, I'm not bothered. Pizza?'

So they went and had a pizza, just like regular folks, except that Paul felt like he was in one of those old war movies, where the gallant British airmen are escaping through occupied France, trying their best to act and sound like they're French. Any minute now, he felt, someone from Real Life was going to show up and demand to see his identity card, and as soon as that happened, it'd be obvious that he had no right to be here, having dinner, on a date with a girl, and they'd arrest him and drag him back to the PoW camp, solitary confinement for life. It was all rather unfair, he couldn't help thinking. Even Steve McQueen had had a motorbike; all he had was a portable door, and so far it hadn't really been much good to him.

But that aside – that aside, he found that the less hard he tried, the easier it got. For one thing, it was almost as though Sophie was on his side, rather than being the opposition. It occurred to him that she'd been wanting someone to talk to for quite some time – the last few weeks, ever since Goblin Night, when their world had changed for ever; and ever since then, the logical choice, her colleague, had refused to say a word to her, apart from *What's the time?* and *Have you finished with the Sellotape?* Bloody strange state of affairs, that, and she must have wondered what on earth was going on. It was lucky she was grown-up enough to be able to put it behind her so easily.

But it had been a long day, and Paul realised he was dog-tired, and so was she. Even so, when the coffee had come and gone, and the bill had arrived and they'd debated and apportioned it, referred it to committee, given it its second reading and reached a negotiated settlement, it became obvious that neither of them really wanted to go home just yet. It was half-past nine, and Sophie was looking guilty. Paul asked what the matter was.

'My parents. They'll be wondering where I am. I ought to phone or something.' Then she yawned, like a small earthquake.

'Tell you what,' Paul said. 'Why don't you go home, and I'll come with you. As far as the front door, I mean.'

She looked at him as if he was crazy, then nodded. 'All right,' she said.

So they did that; and at twenty past ten, on a street

corner under a lamp-post, in Wimbledon where the shadows are, she said, 'Well, see you in the morning, then,' and he said, 'See you,' and as he turned to walk back to the Tube station, she leaned forward a little, pecked him on the cheek like a woodpecker, and walked away, leaving him standing perfectly still.

Bloody hell, Paul thought. Then he started walking.

He was in such a daze that it was some time before he realised that he wasn't walking alone. Someone was beside him, keeping step. He looked round.

He'd never seen her before, but she was easy enough to recognise, even though she wasn't grinning. Quite the opposite, in fact. She had a grim, unhappy expression on her current choice of face, and she was breathing through her nose.

'You do realise,' Mr Tanner's mum said eventually, 'that she probably didn't mean anything by it. Peck on the cheek, could mean anything. French generals do that instead of saluting.'

Paul didn't reply.

'And what about the boyfriend,' she went on, 'the radical ceramics weirdo? It wasn't pecks on cheeks you saw in my stone, remember.'

'No,' Paul said, 'it wasn't.'

She scowled. 'And besides,' she went on, 'you haven't got a clue. It's not like the action movies, you realise, where the hero and the girl go through the great and dangerous adventure and then fall into each others' arms. That's all dogshit, because you know they haven't got a bloody thing in common, it's all just Hollywood; thirty minutes after the credits have stopped rolling, they won't be able to think of one damn thing to say to each other. And you think I'm a

goblin; you don't know spit about who people are or
what they're like. I can turn myself into Drew
Barrymore or Naomi Campbell, but I'm just a first-
year compared to you. You can turn something like
that into a *girl*.'

Paul shook his head. 'Not me,' he said.

'Bullshit. She's a girl like I'm Drew and Kate and
Gwyneth and all those other people who don't really
exist. No wonder our Dennis hired you, you've got
talent.' She made a curious noise, a sort of soft grunty
snuffle. 'Shame you don't use it where it'd be appreci-
ated.'

'Say what you like,' Paul replied. 'It doesn't make
any difference.'

'Idiot.' She sniffed. 'Anyway, that wasn't what I came
to see you about.'

'Oh?'

'Don't believe me if you don't want to,' she said.
'I'm just trying to help. Right now, you need help,
believe me. Or weren't you paying attention when
young Snotnose did his carpentry solo?'

It took Paul a few seconds to figure out that 'young
Snotnose' was Humphrey Wells. 'I know what happened,' he said. 'And yes, I was absolutely petrified, if
you must know.'

'Well, that shows you've got *some* sense, at least. You
want to watch that one, he's not a very nice person.'

'You don't say.'

Mr Tanner's mum pulled a face. 'All right,' she said,
'you reckon the whole lot of them are weird and horrible, and you aren't that far off, at that. But what I'm
saying is, there's a difference between – well, between
young Snotnose and our Dennis, for instance. Sure,

our Dennis's got all the charm of a pigeon turd in your ravioli, but he doesn't go cutting people in half.' She frowned. 'Well, that's mostly because there's not much call for stuff like that in the minerals business, and I'm not saying he wouldn't, if the need arose, or if it suited him, or he felt like it. But you see what I mean,' she added, rather lamely. 'Humphrey Wells goes out of his way to do that sort of stuff. That's the difference.'

Paul shuddered slightly. 'I believe you,' he said. 'And thanks for the warning. But I can't see as how there's much I can do about it.'

'There isn't, you're right. I'm just warning you, that's all.'

'Thanks very much.'

'You're upset,' said Mr Tanner's mum. 'Can't say as I blame you. I'd be upset if I was in your shoes, in fact I'd be climbing the walls. In *actual* fact,' she went on, 'if I was as deep in the shit as you are, I'd be through that portable door and back six months, faster than a rat up a conduit. I wouldn't stick around and risk all sorts of horrible stuff I don't even know about just for some skinny, miserable cow who's having it off with a hippy potter anyhow.' She shrugged. 'Just as well we're not all born alike, I suppose.'

'Yes,' Paul said. 'Oh look, here's the station.'

'You mean, piss off.' Mr Tanner's mum's shoulders slumped, rather like someone who's given up trying. 'All right,' she said, 'but think on. I mean, if you haven't given up on the thin cow, why the hell should I give up on you? Also,' she added, 'I'm cunning. And not so scrupulously ethical as our Dennis, either. Be seeing you.'

She vanished, leaving behind her a faint trace of rare,

exotic perfume subtly blended with sulphur. For some reason he couldn't quite fathom, Paul felt guilty all the way home to Kentish Town. He tried not to think about the peck on the cheek; but later on, he had a dream in which Sophie kissed him in the boardroom, and her reflection in the table top turned out to be Mr Wells, trying to hide a chainsaw behind his back.

CHAPTER TWELVE

'I'm very pleased with the way you two are coming along,' said Mr Wells, a week later. 'Very pleased indeed. In fact, I'm so impressed, I think it's time you tackled something entirely by yourselves.'

Paul's heart sank like an over-insured stone. The last week, spent working for Mr Wells, had been a nightmare. True, the nastiest, most ruthless thing he'd made them do was go through the invoices-delivered ledger and make a list of unpaid accounts. (And who the hell, Paul couldn't help wondering, could be stupid enough to be late paying his sorcerer's bill?) That wasn't the point. What they were being asked to do seemed innocuous enough – mostly going through files and making lists, or cross-referencing – but since they had no idea for what Mr Wells was likely to use the information they gave him, there was always the chance that they were aiding and abetting some unspeakable atrocity.

Mr Wells was obviously waiting for some reaction to his announcement. Presumably he was expecting grateful excitement, but Paul couldn't quite run to that. 'What would you like us to do?' he asked.

'Quite simple,' Mr Wells said, and he took two copies of a colour brochure from his briefcase and handed them out. 'Read that,' he said, 'you'll see it's a flyer for the JWW Valentine Express love philtre. It's been one of our best-selling lines for over a century. Not quite as popular now as it used to be, of course, but we still shift something in the region of fifteen hundred gallons a year, wholesale and retail.'

Love philtre, Paul thought. 'Excuse me,' he said, 'but what does it do?'

'Read the leaflet,' Mr Wells said, 'it'll tell you all about it. Briefly, though; two tablespoons of that stuff, and you fall devotedly and permanently in love with the first person of the opposite sex you come across.'

Sophie looked up sharply. 'Permanently,' she repeated.

'That's right,' Mr Wells said. 'Till death do us part, guaranteed. A hundred years ago, it was the mainstay of our business. It's been to us what lambswool sweaters and ladies' knickers used to be to Marks and Spencers.'

Something about that bothered Sophie very deeply indeed, but she didn't say anything. Mr Wells cleared his throat, and went on: 'As well as just supplying the stuff, we also handle what you might call specialist applications. Including,' he added, 'covert supply. Not as popular as it used to be back in the days of arranged marriages and the like, but there's definitely still a call for it.'

'Covert supply?' Paul mumbled. 'Sorry, I don't think—'

'Oh, come along,' Mr Wells said impatiently. 'Don't pretend you haven't daydreamed about spiking some girl's vodka and orange with the elixir of true love.' Paul went a rare shade of green, but fortunately Sophie was looking at Mr Wells, not at him. 'Well, it's our job to make our clients' daydreams come true. And that,' he said with a faint grin, 'is where you two come in.'

If Mr Wells could read minds— But either he couldn't, or he wasn't bothered by vulgar abuse. 'You want *us* to—' Sophie began to say, then stopped. No point asking the question.

'Everything you need to know,' Mr Wells went on, 'is in the file.' He pushed a buff folder across the desk at them. Neither of them was in any hurry to pick it up. 'Names, addresses, photographs for easy identification. We've arranged your cover stories, false ID, that kind of thing, and the whole operation's been planned and timed for you. All you've got to do is follow the instructions to the letter and you can't go wrong. There's a blue slip so you can draw the philtre you need from the stores, and a green slip for the cashier's office for your expenses, also train tickets, hotel reservations, the works. So,' he concluded with a pleasant smile, 'good luck, and I'll see you back here at nine o'clock, Monday morning.'

Halfway down the corridor, Sophie stopped and grabbed Paul's arm. 'We can't do it,' she said. 'We just can't, that's all.'

Paul wished she was right, but knew she wasn't. They could do it, because Mr Tanner or Mr Wells or any of the other partners could force them to. But he didn't point this out, because it wouldn't have done any good. 'It's appalling,' he said. 'What do you think we ought to do?'

'I don't know,' Sophie replied. 'But we've got to do something.'

The past week had been a nightmare, sure enough, and not just because of Mr Wells. After the pizza-and-pecked-cheek episode, they'd both found it almost impossible to speak to each other. Paul wasn't sure why, though he had several theories, all mutually exclusive. Either she hadn't meant the peck, or she had; both versions could be taken to explain the embarrassment and discomfort, but the net result was that things were even more awkward than they had been before. This was, from Paul's point of view, even more nerve-racking than working for Mr Wells, and more than once he'd been tempted to portable-door back to the evening in question and edit out the pizza.

Now at least Sophie was talking to him, but that just made things worse. What he ought to do, of course, was explain to her exactly why trying to disobey their orders was futile as well as dangerous; but he knew that really she didn't need to be told, and furthermore that if he tried to tell her, she'd be very angry indeed with him. So he was going to have to pretend to agree with whatever she resolved to do, hoping that at some point along the way he could sabotage the plan and save them both a great deal of suffering.

Wonderful, he thought. *Just what I need.*

The love philtre came in a little plastic bottle; it was golden, like linseed oil, and there was a whitish sediment at the bottom. Sophie took delivery of it, handling it like car-boot-sale nitroglycerine. Then they went back to their office. Paul had the file. He laid it flat on the desk and stared at it.

'Well,' Sophie said, 'aren't you going to open it?'

'I suppose so,' Paul muttered. He opened the flap, then nearly jumped out of his chair. A small green claw had pushed through the opening in the cardboard, and was groping about feebly, reminding Paul of lobsters he'd seen at an upmarket fishmonger's.

They looked at each other; then Sophie jumped up, grabbed the phone book out of her desk drawer and swung it above her head, ready for a hefty overhand swat. Before she could strike, however, a little goblin head popped out and blinked at her.

'Here,' it said, in a voice like someone eating corn-flakes, 'what's she doing with that book?'

Slowly, Sophie lowered the directory. 'It's *talking*,' she said.

The tiny goblin gave her a look, then crawled out of the file and sat on the stapler. 'Hello,' it said. 'My name's Vox. Mind if I smoke?'

Paul blinked twice, then nodded. The goblin rolled itself a microscopic cigarette and lit it with a snap of its fingers.

'You two should see yourselves,' it said. 'Bloody comical. Anyway. Now hear this.' It took a long drag and blew bright yellow smoke out through its nose and, remarkably, its ears. 'Because the information contained in this file is highly sensitive and confidential, it has not been committed to writing. Instead, it's been encoded in the form of me. I am your briefing demon, and I'm here to make sure you know and understand what you have to do. OK?'

The goblin flicked ash into its cupped left hand, and

swallowed it. Then it continued. 'Your job,' it said, 'is to take the 10:17 from Euston to Manchester Piccadilly; change on to the local service to Ventcaster, take a taxi to the village of Cudsey, where there's two rooms—' Here the goblin lifted his head and winked. '*Two* rooms reserved for you at the Bunch of Grapes, Egon Ronay one star.' The goblin carefully squeezed out the glowing tip of its rollup, and tucked it behind a pointy ear. 'When you get there, I'll give you the rest of the briefing. Until then, *don't* open the file. Bye.'

It vanished in a little shower of blue and green sparks.

After a moment of stunned silence, Paul looked at his watch. 'We'd better be going,' he said.

'Why?'

'Well, we'll miss the train.'

'We aren't going to catch any train,' Sophie said. Then she jumped in the air, clawing at the back of her head. The goblin was there again, clinging to her hair like a tiny lemur.

'I was hoping you'd say that,' it said.

'Keep still,' Paul shouted, and to his surprise Sophie did as she was told. The goblin scowled. 'You're no fun,' it said, 'either of you.' Then it vanished again.

Sophie was shivering. 'Has it gone?' she whispered.

Paul nodded. 'For now,' he said. 'But I've got a horrible feeling—' He broke off, and stared. Then he knelt down and lifted his head.

'Paul,' Sophie said quietly. 'Why are you trying to look up my skirt?'

The goblin, who was hanging upside down from the hem like a little green bat, grinned at Paul and waved with its free paw. 'You don't want to know,' Paul said. 'Just keep looking at me, for God's sake. Now, we're going to get the train, right?'

Sophie nodded slowly. 'I think so,' she said, her eyes very wide and fixed on his. The goblin pulled a face and disappeared. 'Has it gone?' Sophie whispered.

'Yes.' She groaned, and collapsed onto her chair. 'I don't think you ought to have threatened it with that phone book,' he added. 'I don't think it liked it.'

'No,' Sophie said. She was breathing very deeply. 'We're screwed, aren't we?'

Paul picked himself slowly up off the floor. 'Looks like it,' he agreed. 'You realise it's probably listening to everything we say.' He noticed that Sophie was trying very hard not to look at his left shoulder. 'Very likely,' she said. He shut his eyes, then gingerly patted at his shoulder with his right hand. Nothing there, apparently. He opened his eyes again. 'Was it—?'

'Mphm.'

'Fine. I think we should get out of here. Maybe it won't keep popping up all over the place where there's people about.'

Time was getting on, so they took a taxi to Euston. Paul fished about inside the file with his eyes shut until he located the train tickets by feel. First class, Paul noted; presumably the client was footing the bill, but even so. He'd never been first class on a train before.

'It's nothing special,' whispered a crackly voice in his ear. 'The seats are a different colour, and that's about it.'

Once the train was under way, Paul had an idea. It was a good one, though he said so himself; noble without being stupid. 'I think I'll nip along to the buffet car,' he said. 'Anything you want?'

Sophie looked at him, as if to suggest that she had other things on her mind besides thin coffee and stale Danish pastries. 'No,' she said. 'Why are you waggling your head about like that?'

'I was wondering that, too,' said the little voice in his ear. *Right*, Paul thought, *got you*. He shrugged, and swayed off down the aisle, hoping that Sophie had got the point.

'Smart,' said the little voice, as he joined the buffet queue. 'You figured that I can't be in two places at once, so you've diverted me here, giving your bird a chance to be alone with the file, sneak a quick look, maybe even think of a cunning plan. While you're at it, could you get me a box of matches? The red ones, not the ordinary kind. There's your actual sulphur in the red ones, and I'm starving.'

'Get your own fucking matches,' Paul muttered. The woman behind him in the queue gave him ever such a funny look.

He bought a cup of tea and a bacon roll – they only had the ordinary brown matches – and staggered back to his seat. Sophie was sitting very still, her eyes screwed up tight shut. Before Paul could say anything, a tiny hand appeared between the top two buttons of her blouse and made a rather vulgar gesture.

'Doesn't work, of course,' said the little voice in his ear. 'Nice try, though.'

Then the hand vanished, shedding three green sparkles, and Sophie sagged forward, jumped up and ran down the aisle towards the toilets. She came back a minute or so later, looking very green.

'It asked me to tell you,' she said in a strained voice, 'next time you have a bright idea, warn me first. All right?'

Paul nodded. 'Sorry,' he said.

'That's all right,' Sophie muttered. 'It was worth a try. Just—'

'All right, yes.'

It was a very long train journey. Sitting perfectly still for hours on end made Paul itch in several places, but nothing on earth was going to induce him to scratch. Neither of them said a word, for fear of inviting a contribution from the goblin. A half-hour hold-up in a tunnel just outside Rugby didn't help matters, either. At one point, Paul managed to slide into a light doze, but that was even worse, because he dreamed he was sitting there with no clothes on, and a diminutive Mr Tanner's mum was sitting on his shoulder, blowing in his ear. He started awake—

('Actually,' said the crackly voice, 'she's my niece. God knows what she sees in *you*.')

Paul whimpered, and opened his eyes. Sophie turned her head slightly and nodded, as if to say *Yes, me too*. Under other circumstances, he might have reflected on that, and the expression in her eyes, but as things stood he didn't dare.

Because of the hold-up at Rugby, they had to sprint for their connection at Manchester, and caught it with fifteen seconds to spare. It was only when they'd flopped into their seats and caught their breath that Paul realised something was missing. Sophie must've shared the thought. They stared at each other.

'The file,' she said. 'Have you got it?'

'I thought you—'

'We've left it,' Sophie whispered. 'On the other train.'

There was a brief moment of unspeakable joy; then something landed with a soft thump on Sophie's lap. No need to look down and see what it was.

'Oh,' she said, and Paul could see her brace herself for something extremely unpleasant. A second or so later she relaxed.

'It's its lunch break,' she explained. 'But it's still listening.'

Paul nodded. 'What about the bottle?' he said. 'Have you got that?'

'In my bag. Which,' she added, 'appears to have turned into a suitcase. Probably a change of clothes for the morning, or costumes if we've got to be in disguise or whatever. They think of every bloody thing,' she added bitterly.

Lunch break, Paul thought; and then, tiptoeing across the back of his mind so as to avoid attention, came the thought of the portable door. He spat the image out of his mind, then waited; but there came no little crackly voice in his ear, and he was pretty sure the goblin wouldn't have been able to resist making some remark or other, if it'd noticed.

So; the goblin didn't know about the door. So—

It was very hard indeed to think in whispers. He managed it by thinking about other things, gingerly tacking on snippets of thought at the end. If the goblin didn't know about the door, maybe they could use it to escape (assuming he could get the wretched thing set up before the goblin could stop him). Fine; but where or when could they go, and how could they stop the little bastard coming with them? That could be disastrous – if, for example, he tried to escape into the pre-J. W. Wells past, but managed to take the goblin back there too; would it be able to force them to go to the job interview? He couldn't see any reason why not; and then they'd never be free, not even in the past. He flicked the very concept of the door out of his mind as quickly as he could, and concentrated on the colour and texture of elephants' ears for the next two minutes, just in case.

In due course, the train dragged itself into Ventcaster, and they found a taxi to take them on the last stage of their journey. Cudsey turned out to be a rather pleasant grey stone village, genuinely picturesque in the soft haze of almost-rain. Sophie insisted on carrying the suitcase, which by now was extremely large and heavy. The pub was just the sort of place Paul would have enjoyed staying at, under other circumstances.

After they'd dumped the case in Sophie's room, they took the file into the deserted games room behind the public bar and dumped it on the pool table. The goblin duly popped up out of the flap, yawning and stretching.

'We're here,' Paul said. 'Now, what have we got to do?'

The goblin scuttled across the green baize and nibbled a chunk out of the cue chalk before answering. 'Nice easy job,' it told them. 'Even you ought to be able to manage it without screwing up. Now, pay attention.'

It sounded simple enough. At a quarter to six that evening, according to the goblin, the pub landlord and his wife were going to fall fast asleep, at which point Sophie, wearing the outfit provided (Sophie's expression suggested she didn't like the sound of that) would take her place behind the bar and try to look like a barmaid. At five to six, a man would walk into the bar and ask for a pint of beer. This Sophie would provide, having first added the required dose of JWW Valentine Express; she would then clear out at once, for obvious reasons, and Paul would take her place. The customer would immediately fall asleep for twenty minutes, that being a side effect of the philtre. At a quarter past six, the client would turn up and be there when the customer woke up, and that would be that, as far as their involvement was concerned. The only other point to bear in mind was that while the victim was asleep, it'd be up to Paul to make sure that no female other than the client got into the bar, again for obvious reasons. And that, the goblin added, was all there was to it.

'Just to make sure there's no fuck-ups,' the goblin went on, 'you'd better know what these people look like.' It took a deep breath and vanished in the usual shower of sparks; a moment later, a woman materialised where the goblin had been – a thirty-something bottle redhead, attractive in a chrome-molybdenum-hard sort of way, wearing a short skirt and an obvious blouse. 'The client,' she said, and vanished. Then a man appeared—

Paul stared. 'Bloody hell,' he said.

Sophie looked at him, and then at the man on the table. 'You know him?' she asked.

'What? Oh, sorry,' Paul said, 'I forgot, you don't go to the pictures much. That's Ashford Clent.'

'Who's Ashford Clent?'

'The mark,' said the man on the table; then he vanished too, and was replaced by the goblin. 'Your friend doesn't get out much, does she?' it went on. 'Mind you, hardly surprising. Award-winning Ashford Clent,' it continued, 'is the third most highly paid movie star in the world. Thirty million bucks a picture, and if your girlfriend had just one hormone in her bony little body, she wouldn't need to ask why. Anyhow, Mister Multiple-Oscars has just bought Cudsey Castle, which is very handy, saves you having to go to California.' Was it Paul's imagination, or did the goblin wink at him as it said that? He could have sworn the little horror didn't know about the door, but now he wasn't quite so certain.

'Who's the woman?' Sophie asked. 'The client, I mean.'

The goblin pulled a face. 'None of your business,' it said, 'but I'll tell you anyway, since you won't like it. You don't need to know her name, but she's a very clever little lady, worked it all out by herself, bless her. Quite simple, as all the best scams are. She marries Clent; then, after a decent interval, she divorces him. JWW gets two million dollars off the top, she keeps the rest of the divorce settlement for herself, everyone's a winner.'

Sophie's expression would have blunted carbon steel. 'Apart from what's-his-name, the actor,' she said. 'Or does the potion thing wear off after a bit?'

The goblin laughed. 'No way,' it said. 'Guaranteed for life, one hundred per cent. The poor fool'll love her till the day he dies. No big deal,' it added, 'when you think about it. After all, there's five million women in fifty countries worldwide who'd gut their own mothers just for a chance to fondle Mr Clent's discarded socks, so you don't want to go feeling sorry for him. Poetic justice, if you ask me.'

Sophie shuddered. 'Fine,' she said. 'I like happy endings, anyway.'

'Oh, absolutely,' agreed the goblin. 'Boy meets girl, girl poisons boy, they get married. Hardly original, but all true romance is just clichés anyhow.'

To Paul's surprise and lasting regret, it all went as smoothly as clockwork. At the appointed time, award-winning Ashford Clent strolled into the bar and asked for a beer. Sophie – actually, Paul thought she looked nice in her barmaid's costume, but he'd no more have dared tell her so than he'd have confronted God on the eighth day of Creation and demanded to see the manager – Sophie managed to introduce two table-spoonfuls of the golden stuff into Clent's glass without being noticed, and since the beer was traditional Yorkshire real ale, its inherent foul taste masked the presence of the philtre, at least until it was too late. Mr Clent fell asleep before Paul had a chance to ask him for his autograph, which was probably just as well.

The client was precisely on time, and Paul left her sitting opposite the sleeping screen god, smoking a cigarette and reading *The Daily Telegraph Guide to Investment Management*. The rest of the evening, according to the goblin, was his own.

Talking of which; the nasty little critter hadn't bothered either of them, as far as he was aware, for some time, not since the briefing. Was it too much to hope that it had finally—?

'Yes,' said the scratchy voice in his ear.

'Oh,' Paul said. 'Look, we've done our job, so why don't you just push off and leave us alone?'

The goblin's laugh sounded like someone chewing

tinfoil. 'Because I like you,' it said. 'Both of you, the same way you like roast chicken. See, I don't get out of the office as much as I'd like to, so I've got to make the most of it when I get the chance.'

Paul sighed, and climbed the stairs to the guest bedrooms. At the top of the staircase he went to turn right, but small, sharp nails tightened in his earlobe, and he stopped.

'Not that way,' he said. 'Left.'

'But my room's this way.'

'Yes. But you aren't going there.'

'Aren't I?'

'No. You're going to see your girlfriend.'

In spite of the pain in his ear, Paul wrenched his head to the right. 'She's not my girlfriend,' he said.

'Ah,' said the goblin, in a tone of voice that Paul didn't like one bit. 'We're going to fix that, right now.'

Paul felt as though his heart had been replaced with a bag of frozen peas. 'What's that supposed to mean?' he said.

'Oh, for crying out loud.' The goblin sounded annoyed. 'You really are pathetic, aren't you? All right, then.' Green sparkles cascaded in the air in front of Paul's nose, and the goblin appeared. This time it was much larger; a head taller than Paul, and massively broad across the shoulders. 'I'll explain, shall I?' it said. 'And then we can get on with it, whether you like it or not.'

Paul tried to back away, but the goblin reached out a long, muscular arm and gripped him round the throat, so firmly that he could scarcely breathe.

'Let's see, now,' the goblin said. 'There's a good half-pint in one of them philtre bottles, and once they're opened, they don't keep. Waste not, want not, that's what I say.'

Paul tried to pull the goblin's hand away from his neck, and was given cause to regret it.

'What the bloody hell are you cribbing about?' the goblin said, and it sounded almost hurt. 'You should be down on your fucking knees thanking me. You *do* want her, don't you?'

'Yes,' Paul said. 'But.'

The goblin picked him up without apparent effort and slammed him against the wall. He froze with terror, and the goblin went on; 'Trouble with you is, you don't really know what you want. So it's just as well I'm here to sort things out. Otherwise you'd be in a hell of a mess. I'm just saying thank you, that's all, for a really nice trip out. Well, I've enjoyed it, even if you haven't. Also, I guess, I just like bringing young folks together. Whether they like it,' the goblin added, with a pure Tanner grin, 'or not.'

'Please,' Paul whispered. 'Don't.'

But the goblin shook its head. 'Sorry,' it said, 'but the plain fact is, I know what's best for the pair of you, and that's that. You'll thank me in years to come; you'll probably want to name your first kid after me. Rumpelstiltskin Carpenter, got a ring to it, don't you think? I like babies,' the goblin added, licking its lips.

Then the goblin picked Paul up by the scruff of his neck and carried him down the corridor. One of the bedroom doors was open, and round it a green scaly arm beckoned to them. 'Another reason,' the goblin went on, 'is our Rosacrucia – that's my niece, you've met her. Not that I've got anything against you humans, you understand, but what that girl needs is a nice goblin boyfriend, one of her own kind. If you're all safely hitched, maybe she'll stop trailing round after you and settle down.'

Sophie was sitting on the bed, with her eyes shut. She was still wearing the barmaid outfit, with a tiny green head poking up out of her cleavage. 'Have fun,' said the goblin, and it vanished in a swirl of glittering confetti. 'I think I'll watch this one from the stalls,' explained the little green head.

Paul tried to back away, but his legs weren't working. On the bedside table, he saw the plastic bottle of Valentine Express, a spoon and a glass. 'Sophie,' he said.

'I know,' she muttered.

Somehow his hand had got round the neck of the bottle, and he was unscrewing the cap. He tried to spill the philtre out of the spoon, but all of it landed in the glass. He handed it to her, and she took it.

'It won't be so bad,' Sophie said, in a faint voice. 'I'm sorry.'

And then the door burst open. Paul tried to look round but his head was stuck. Mr Wurmtoter crossed the room in two long strides. He had a glove on his right hand, and an empty hamburger box in his left. 'Excuse me,' he said, and quick as electricity he yanked the goblin out of the front of Sophie's dress, stuffed it in the box, and snapped the lid shut.

Paul staggered, and fell over; Sophie sagged back and hit her head against the wall. Mr Wurmtoter grabbed the glass from her hand before she could drop it, and emptied it down the washstand sink. Then he turned. 'Are you two all right?' he asked. 'No, um, harm done?'

Paul got to his knees, that being the best he could do. 'I'm all right,' he said.

'And me,' Sophie mumbled, sitting up. 'What are you doing here?'

Mr Wurmtoter pulled a serious face. 'I came as soon as I could,' he said. 'It was Rosie – sorry, Mrs Tanner – who thought there might be something wrong. She saw what was going on in that stone of hers.' He breathed in deeply, then added, 'I really am most frightfully sorry; on behalf of the firm, I mean. It goes without saying, this is nothing to do with us.' He scowled, then opened the burger box a tiny crack. 'You're *disgusting*, you,' he snapped, as a green nose stuck out. 'That's it as far as trips out of the office go, you hear me?' He closed the box, snapped his fingers over the lid, and threw it on the floor. 'It's all right,' he said, 'I've put a B-76J on the box, he won't get past *that* in a hurry. Well,' he went on, looking like an overgrown schoolboy who's just owned up to breaking a window, 'I'd better be getting back, I'm due in a meeting at quarter past. And really, I'm very sorry about this. We'll have to see if there's some way we can sort of make it up to you.'

Sophie breathed out. 'That's all right,' she said. 'Don't worry about it. And thank you.'

Mr Wurmtoter grinned feebly. 'All part of the service,' he said, and left the room. A few seconds later, Paul happened to glance through the window and thought he caught sight of a white horse with broad, feathery wings sailing up into the sky. But he could have been imagining it.

'Well,' he said, after a very long silence, 'there you are, then.'

Sophie looked at him, and nodded. 'Would you mind getting out?' she said. 'No, I don't mean it like that. I just want to get out of these disgusting clothes.'

Paul wandered out into the corridor and hung around there, not knowing whether he ought to go back to his own room, or wait for her. He'd just made up his mind that she couldn't possibly want to see him ever again when the door opened and she came out. She was still white as a sheet, but she gave him a little smile, enough to say that she was all right now.

'I need some fresh air, I think,' she said.

They went out into the village street, which was deserted. After they'd walked twenty yards or so, Paul turned to her and said, 'You were very brave back there.'

She frowned at him. 'Thank you so much,' she said. 'Why, were you expecting me to faint or have a screaming fit or something?'

Paul didn't say he was sorry, for once. 'Well, anyway,' he said, 'you were a bloody sight braver than I was. I was terrified.'

'Me too. It was all wriggly, like a dirty great big spider. I don't like spiders.'

'Nor me.'

They walked on a little further before Paul said, 'Did you believe him? Mr Wurmtoter, I mean. Do you think he saved us, or was it all part of some nasty scheme of theirs?'

She shrugged. 'Don't know and don't care,' she said. 'I think that horrible little *thing* was perfectly capable of dreaming the whole idea up on its own, but it's also just the sort of thing Mr Wells'd do, if he thought there was something in it for him. But I can't see how it'd help him, can you?'

Paul shook his head. It was in his mind to mention the Gilbert and Sullivan episode, but he didn't. 'I think Mr Wurmtoter was telling the truth,' he said. 'I guess he was scared we'd take the firm to the industrial tribunal, or something like that.'

'Maybe.' Sophie stopped, and leaned her back against a wall. 'Well,' she said, 'at least we were luckier than that film star. I feel bad about that,' she added. 'Not because of the money, but—'

Paul nodded. 'I don't suppose there's anything we can do about it,' he said awkwardly; because of course he knew precisely what he could do about it: a quick trip through the door, back to six minutes to six that evening. Even if he had to bash award-winning Ashford Clent over the head with a shovel before he walked through the pub door, it'd set everything right again. But back then, the goblin would still be on the loose—

'Probably not,' Sophie replied. 'And it's not like film stars are *people*, with feelings and stuff. Even so—' She sighed. 'Oh, I don't know,' she went on. 'Thirty million dollars a film, and they get married and divorced every five minutes anyway. It could've been worse.' She turned her head and looked at him. 'Could've been us,' she said quietly.

'Quite,' Paul said, and he looked away. *Could have been us*; and what would they have been doing right now, if Mr Wurmtoter hadn't shown up in the nick of time? Walking together down this very street, quite possibly, hand in hand, gazing into each other's eyes. But it wouldn't have been right; not if he really loved her – which, he suddenly realised, he did. Not the familiar old Paul Carpenter crush, the desperate need to find himself a girl, any girl, because everybody else in the whole wide world had one except him. The only girl he'd ever want was this one.

He thought about the performance potter. *Shit*, he thought.

And then a picture floated into his mind of the plastic bottle of Valentine Express, still presumably sitting on Sophie's bedside table—

'What's the matter?' she said. 'You look like you're about to throw up.'

'What?' He looked away. 'Sorry,' he said, 'I was just thinking about – well, you know.'

She nodded. 'Me too,' she said. 'But it's all right now.'

'No it's *not*,' Paul wanted to shout, because of course it wasn't. It was all still very wrong, because if Vox the goblin had jumped out of his top pocket at that moment with the bottle in one hand and a tablespoon in the other and offered him the same deal over again, he couldn't be absolutely sure that he wouldn't—

'That philtre stuff?' he said suddenly. 'I think you ought to get rid of it quick. It's not safe, having it lying about.'

'I was just thinking that,' she said. 'Leave it to me, I'll see to it.'

He nodded. For a moment, he'd been afraid she'd ask him to dispose of it, and he wouldn't have wanted to have the bottle in his hand, not even for a second. Then Sophie darted forward and grabbed his arm. 'Quick,' she hissed, 'get out of the way.'

No explanation needed: walking down the street towards them were award-winning Ashford Clent and the client. Paul and Sophie ducked behind a pillar box until they'd gone by; and Paul couldn't help noticing the expression of bewildered joy on the thirty-million-dollar face as it passed him. *Shit*, he thought again, and something deep inside him started to hurt like hell.

'Just a minute,' Sophie whispered. 'I've had an idea.'

Paul frowned. 'What?'

'Stay there,' she said. 'Did he see you? Clent?'

'Just now, or earlier?'

'Earlier.'

Paul shook his head. 'Don't think so,' he replied, 'he went out like a light. Why?'

'Look.' Sophie was pointing; Clent and the client were going into the Green Dragon, on the other side of the road. 'Stay here till I get back,' she said.

'Where are you going?'

She grinned at him. 'Back to my room,' she said. 'Then we're going to buy the next Mrs Clent a drink.'

How Paul found the guts to do it, he wasn't quite sure. Walk up to two perfect strangers in a pub holding two glasses of champagne and ask them if they'd mind having a drink with him, because he'd just won the Lottery – and they'd smiled and said, Yes, they'd be delighted, thank you; actually, Clent said, they were celebrating too, they'd just gotten engaged. The clunk he heard as he walked quickly out of the bar was the future Mrs Clent's head hitting the table. The stuff worked fast, no doubt about it.

Twenty minutes later, they crept back, just to make sure. Just as well they had, because someone had called the doctor (a fat, middle-aged man with a Captain Mainwaring moustache); and when the future Mrs

Clent groaned and started to come round, it was only Sophie's quick thinking – she dashed forward and screamed 'Look, it's Ashford *Clent*!' at the top of her voice, causing the doctor to look away – that saved the day. But it was all right; the first thing the client saw when her eyes opened was the thirty-million-dollar face gazing earnestly down at her. The click of the mouse-trap snapping shut was almost deafening.

'Right,' Sophie said, as they sprinted across the street. '*Now* I'm going to get rid of the bottle. Soon as we get back to the hotel, I'll pour the rest of it down the bog.'

'Good idea,' Paul replied quietly. After all, it was only him – his dreams, his happiness, stuff like that – and it wouldn't be the same if he got it by cheating. Would it?

Would it? He thought of the glow in Clent's eyes. *True happiness*, he thought; so what if it came out of a bottle, like corn-gold hair and whisky? *Hellfire and buggery*, he thought, she *deserves true happiness, even if I don't*. And she'd be happy, as opposed to dead miserable, which was how she'd been ever since he'd known her. *Yes*, he thought, *definitely get rid of what's left in the bottle*. Before he changed his mind.

At the top of the stairs, they hesitated; her room to the left, his to the right. 'I don't know about you,' Paul lied, 'but I'm worn out. Think I'll get an early night. Can you remember what time our train is in the morning?'

Sophie shook her head. 'I think the goblin had the tickets,' she said.

'Oh. Oh well, we'll just have to buy our own, then. I don't suppose there'll be any problem getting the money back, if we ask Mr Wurmtoter to sign the pink form.'

She laughed. 'Goodnight, then,' she said. 'I'll go and empty that bottle now.'

'Right,' he said, and walked away without looking round.

There was a train leaving Ventcaster at ten to ten, connecting with the twelve-thirty from Manchester Piccadilly to Euston. In spite of a few minor dramas involving taxis from Cudsey and Banquo's-heirs-type queues at the ticket office, they managed to make the connection. They'd hardly said a word to each other all day.

At Manchester, Paul bought a magazine to hide behind for the rest of the journey. Being short of time, he'd grabbed at random from the rack and been rewarded with *Stamp & Coin Monthly*; Sophie, who'd done the same thing, hadn't fared much better with *Which Chainsaw?* After they'd sat opposite each other for an hour and a half without either of them turning a page, Sophie leaned forward and said, 'Swap?'

Paul lowered his shield. 'Sorry?'

'Swap,' she repeated. 'I mean, I'm dying to read the latest news about Channel Island commemoratives, and I bet you can't wait to see their review of the all-new Makita 202ZW.'

Paul sighed, and dropped the magazine onto the seat next to him. 'Sorry,' he said.

'I'm just as bad,' she replied. 'But we've got to talk about it sooner or later.'

'Yes,' Paul replied unenthusiastically. 'All right, then, fire away.'

She frowned. 'Not like that,' she said. 'It's not like an audition or something.'

'Sorry.'

Long silence. They stared at each other, like British and German soldiers in the Flanders trenches on Christmas Eve who couldn't remember the words to 'Silent Night'. Eventually, Paul said: 'So, what did they think of it?'

'What?'

'The new Makita 202ZW.'

She looked at him. 'Apparently it goes through green softwood like it isn't there. This is *stupid*.'

Paul nodded. 'After all,' he said, 'we've still got to work together.'

He'd apparently said the wrong thing, because she scowled. 'That's right,' she said. 'I think we've got to put it all behind us, really. Not pretend it didn't happen—'

(The woman in the seat opposite was staring at them with rapt attention.)

'—But we can't let it come between us, in our careers, I mean. It was just, well—'

'One of those things?' Paul suggested.

'I suppose so.' Sophie wriggled in her seat, then suddenly stood up. 'I don't know about you,' she said, 'but I'm starving. I think I'll go to the buffet and get something to eat. You want anything?'

Not a ham roll, Paul thought; but as it happened, he was palpably thirsty. 'Cup of tea would be great, thanks,' he said.

'Right.' She hurried away, and he noticed how neatly she moved against the swaying of the train. Not like him. She'd left her bag on the seat, and just for a split second, he wondered if she'd remembered to get rid of the philtre. If she hadn't, it'd be there, and when she came back with her coffee or her orange juice—

No, he said to himself. Out of the corner of his eye, he saw the woman opposite studying him. *Yeah*, he thought, *if only you were right. But you aren't.* He picked up *Which Chainsaw?* and read the letters page.

'Tea,' said a voice above his head. He looked up. She was back.

'Thanks,' he said. 'How much do I owe you?'

She shook her head. 'I got a receipt,' she said. 'This is on J. W. Wells. You sure you don't want anything to eat? You can have half of my cheese sandwich.'

'No, really.' Silly; because now she mentioned it, he *was* feeling a bit peckish. Still, he could hardly get up and go buying food now that he'd refused her offer. Why was it, he thought, that he refused every damn thing he wanted that was offered to him? He sipped his tea, which was hot and tasted foul, and decided that enough was enough. 'Look,' he said, 'about what happened. I know it wasn't—'

And then he fell asleep.

Paul's head hurt.

Probably, he thought, *where I banged it on the table*. He lifted his head and opened his eyes.

'Hello,' said a voice.

He knew perfectly well that the face he was looking into belonged to the woman who'd been sitting in the seat opposite. Odd; because he distinctly remembered her – late forties or early fifties, somebody's mother, somebody's aunt – and he could have sworn that when he'd last looked at her, she hadn't been the most beautiful girl in the world, the most wonderful, the most—

Shit, he thought.

And then the most amazingly fantastic girl in the universe grinned at him, and he jumped in his seat as though he'd just sat on a hedgehog, and hissed, '*You!*'

'That's right,' said Mr Tanner's mum. 'How's your head? Nasty bump you've got there.' *Bitch*, he thought. *Wonderful, gorgeous, stunningly lovely* bitch. 'Where's Sophie?' he groaned.

Mrs Tanner gestured sideways with her head. Sophie was sitting on the seat next to her, a brown paper bag over her head. 'Just a simple precaution,' Mr Tanner's mum said, 'I can take it off now.'

Paul looked round, but everybody else in the compartment was either fast asleep or completely preoccupied with their book, magazine or newspaper. Mr Tanner's mum pulled off the paper bag and dropped it on the floor.

'I didn't hit her very hard,' she went on, 'just hard enough, that's all. You see? I can be nice when I want to.'

Paul knew exactly what he wanted to say, he could see the words bright on his mind's screen. But what came out was, 'I love you.'

Mr Tanner's mum grinned again. 'You don't know how good that sounds,' she said. 'Say it again.'

'I love you.'

'Yes,' she said, 'you do, don't you? Serves you right, and all. We could've done this the easy way, but you had to be difficult. Men,' she said scornfully. 'Humans,' she added.

Paul knew that he wanted to be angry, but he couldn't. It was like wanting to be six feet tall, or the Pope; he could imagine more or less what it'd be like, but there was no way on earth he'd ever manage it. Instead, he was going to have to love Mr Tanner's mum. That was inevitable. He wasn't falling in love so much as sinking, slowly but unstoppably, like a man drowning in custard. He knew that as soon as the custard closed over his head, filled his mouth and lungs, he'd be happy, happy-ever-after, as deliriously happy as award-winning Ashford Clent. The rest of his life would be a glorious summer afternoon, basking in the warm glow of Mr Tanner's mum, his star, his sun. True, there might conceivably be troubles ahead; but while there was moonlight and laughter and love and romance—

No, he tried to yell, *no bloody way*. (The custard was up to his nose by now.) This couldn't be happening to him, because – well, he was Paul Carpenter, the lemming that walked by itself, and all disastrously failed relationships were alike to him. But he knew that if only he stopped thrashing about, relaxed, took his eye off the ball for one split second, then the happiness would burst through and overwhelm him, and there'd be no more loneliness, rejection, self-doubt, misery, it'd all be wonderful for ever, because Love is the sweetest thing, makes the world go round (though a similar effect can be obtained by drinking lots of whisky very quickly), love is all you need.

'Oh, for pity's sake,' Mr Tanner's mum was saying. 'And look at me when you're falling in love with me, can't you? You're pathetic, you are.'

'Piss off,' Paul mumbled. 'Darling,' he added.

She was tapping her fingers on the table top. 'You can't fight it,' she said. 'Dead in the water, you are. After all, it's what you've always wanted, isn't it?'

'Yes,' Paul said quietly. 'But not any more.'

Mr Tanner's mum scowled at him. What a wonderful scowl she had; so expressive, so passionate! 'Get real,' she said. 'Admit it, you never actually liked that bony cow anyhow. Go on, it's true, isn't it?'

'No. Yes. No.'

'Fine.' Mr Tanner's mum folded her arms. 'All right, then, tell me what you like about her. Radiant beauty? I've seen sexier crayfish. Wonderful warm personality? Sparkling vivacity, cheerfulness and wit? Deep, compassionate soul? Or what? She's miserable, sullen and selfish, bloody difficult all the damn time, she's moody and objectionable and she's got some disgusting personal habits. Frigid as a polar bear's—'

'No,' Paul said. 'You're wrong. She's—' He stopped. He couldn't remember what she was.

'You were saying? Must be really special if you can't even remember.'

'I can,' Paul whimpered, 'it's just—'

'All right, then,' said Mr Tanner's mum, grinning that achingly lovely grin. 'Tell me her name.'

Paul looked up. 'What?'

'You heard me. What's her name?'

Paul couldn't remember. He cradled his head in his hands, wanting to cry, but he couldn't, because he was so, he was very nearly so wonderfully, blissfully fucking *happy*. 'Please,' he whispered. 'Don't.'

'Too late,' Mr Tanner's mum replied, 'even if I wanted to, which I don't. I'll say this for you, though, you put up a good fight. But it's over, and I've won, so stop pissing around and come to my arms, before I smash your face in.'

It was no good. No point, either. Even if he managed to break free, spit out all the custard and struggle out of the swamp, she (the girl he loved, the thin girl, what's-her-name) she'd never be his, she'd given her heart and mind and body to a performance potter called Shaz who lived in a bus on the outskirts of Esher, or was it Epping Forest? No point—

'All right,' he groaned. 'But not here, right? Not in a bloody train, with all these people—'

Mr Tanner's mum stuck her tongue out at him; it was green and scaly. 'Prude,' she said. 'But I'm not waiting till we get back to the office. How about the guard's van?'

'Better idea,' Paul mumbled. 'Door thing. Portable door. In my pocket. Go wherever we like.'

'Ah.' Another grin. 'Now you're talking. How about on the beach at Martinique? Nothing like the warm sand in the small of your back, I always say. Or—'

'Wherever,' Paul grunted, and he pulled the cardboard tube out of his pocket. 'Corridor?' he pleaded.

'Lead the way, lover,' said Mr Tanner's mum.

He stumbled to his feet, somehow made it into the corridor, where there was a patch of bulkhead just large enough to accommodate the portable door. 'Need something to wedge it open,' he gasped.

'How about my handbag?'

'Fine.' He unrolled the door, smoothed it into place. 'After you.'

'What, and you wait till I've gone through and then slam it after me? Do I look like I've just fallen off a palm tree?'

'Yes. No. I'll go first, then.'

He opened the door; then, as his front foot crossed the threshold, he shouted '*PAST!*' as loud as he could and lunged forward.

Wherever it was, it was as dark as a bag. Somewhere behind him, Paul could hear Mr Tanner's mum howling, '*Bastard!*' at him, but that was fine. He pulled up her face on his mind's screen, and thought *Yuck*. It was all right. He was better now.

He looked down at where his wrist ought to be, but of course he couldn't see his watch face in the dark. Not that it mattered; he knew by now that it wouldn't be any help anyway, Time inside the door being subjective, or something. All that counted was that he'd gone far enough back into the past that he'd never drunk that sodding philtre-laced tea. Free and clear, at least for now.

He stood up straight, and listened. Not far away, he could hear footsteps, heavy trampling ones, and Mr Tanner's mum's voice – '*Just let me get my hands on you, I'll rip your fucking lungs out.*' It occurred to him, with her image in full goblin mode still very much in mind, that this was probably no idle threat. Time, Paul decided, to start running.

He ran.

Running in the pitch dark isn't a very sensible thing to do. He hadn't gone more than a few steps when his nose connected with something invisible but extremely solid. He fell over and lay curled up on what was presumably the floor; and while he was doing that, someone or something stepped over him, not apparently aware that he was there. From the fact that this person was shrieking '*And then I'm gonna tear your liver out and fry it with onions*,' he deduced that it could well be Mr Tanner's mum.

Great, he thought. Now all he had to do was sneak back to the portable door, nip through it, slam it shut, roll it up, and that'd be that. With no time to waste standing up, he turned round on all fours and started to scuttle in what he hoped was the direction he'd just come from. As he went, it did occur to him to wonder what happened to somebody who got left behind when the door closed. The one time it'd happened to him, it had been all right; he'd been back in the office, a mere eighteen hours or so from where he'd started. But now, of course, he had no idea where or when he'd fetched up. For all he knew this could be some ghastly interdimensional void, and he was planning on stranding Mr Tanner's mum here, possibly for all eternity—

Tough, Paul thought.

He scuttled on, but now he was starting to get worried. As far as he could remember, he'd only run a few yards before colliding with the unseen obstacle and falling over. He'd come much further than that; surely he ought to be able to see the door by now, if only by the light streaming through it. Had he come the wrong way in the dark? Highly possible – he had no illusions about his sense of direction. His kingdom for a torch, or a lighter, or a box of matches.

(And anyhow, he thought; even if this is a nameless void down the back of the sofa of space and time, and he was doomed to wander here for ever and ever, shuffling along in the dark like a disembodied mole, it still had to be a million times better than a lifetime of pure joy and bliss with Mr Tanner's mother. Absolutely. No possible doubt whatever. It had been a close-run thing, but thanks to his resourcefulness and native cunning, he'd got away with it. Even so, it'd be nice to find the way out—)

He lunged forward, and his head connected with something. A voice squeaked.

He knew that voice.

More to the point, he knew the name that went with it. 'Sophie?' he said.

'Paul?'

Sophie? 'What the hell are you doing here?'

'You'd gone, I came to look for you. Somebody hit me, and—'

A very unpleasant thought snuck into Paul's mind. 'Hold on,' he said. 'You woke up and came looking for me. Through a funny-looking door in the side of the train.'

'That's right. Look—'

'The door,' Paul said quietly. 'Wedged open with a handbag, right?'

'So it was, yes. Look—'

Paul took a deep breath. 'You didn't by any chance,' he asked, 'close the door behind you?'

'I may have done. Why, is it important?'

Then all the lights suddenly came on.

CHAPTER THIRTEEN

Paul knew where he was. He was home.
Sort of.

It wasn't his room. Well, it was the same room he lived in, because there was the fireplace, there was the window and there was the bed, there was the table, there was the damp patch on the wall that looked like a map of Turkey drawn by Salvador Dali. But it wasn't his room. It was the way the room he lived in would probably have looked a hundred or so years ago.

Been here before, of course . . .

Nice enough room, in its way. A merry blaze in the fireplace, same as last time he'd been there. But it still didn't have a door.

'Hello,' said a voice behind him. He spun round, and saw two young men in Victorian clothes, standing in the corner by the wardrobe. One had thick, curly hair. The other one, he seemed to remember, was called Pip, and it was he who said, 'It's all right.'

'Oh, good,' Paul said. 'What's all right?'

Pip grinned (not that sort of grin) and pointed. On the floor next to the bed lay a goblin. It wasn't moving, though whether it was asleep, stunned or dead wasn't immediately apparent.

'She tripped over the fireguard, would you believe,' Pip continued, 'bumped her head on the mantelpiece. Only a little bump, she'll be right as rain directly. So,' he went on, 'where is it?'

Before Paul could say anything, Sophie pushed past him. 'Who the hell are you?' she demanded. 'And where is this?'

The two young men didn't reply. They'd taken one look at Sophie and immediately looked away. The curly-haired specimen had gone red as a beetroot. A moment of baffled silence; then Paul realised what it was. He leaned over and whispered in her ear, 'Quick, get behind me.'

She looked at him. 'Why? Are they dangerous?'

'Just do it, all right?'

It must've been his tone of voice, because with only a very slight hesitation she did as she'd been told. Paul cleared his throat self-consciously, and said, 'Actually, that's how women dress when I come from.'

The man called Pip looked shocked and fascinated at the same time. 'You don't say?'

Paul nodded. 'That's right.'

'Good Lord. You mean, that's normal?' He was now several shades redder than his colleague. 'Um, knees and things?'

'Absolutely,' Paul said. 'In fact, what the, er, young lady's got on is sort of like formal wear. You know, for work. In the office.'

Pip was staring at him now. 'They work? In offices?'

'Yes.'

'Dressed like *that*?'

'Hey,' Sophie growled, shoving Paul out of the way. 'What the bloody hell—?'

'It's OK,' Paul said quickly, 'you don't understand. These people – gentlemen,' he amended quickly (so many people to offend, so little time), 'they're sort of from the past. Victorians,' he added.

'Oh.' From the look on Sophie's face, Paul might as well have said they were Martians, though probably she'd have preferred Martians as being less alien. 'Oh, I see—'

The curly-haired man coughed obtrusively. 'Perhaps you'd care to introduce us to the, um, young lady,' he said.

'What? Oh, right.' Paul grinned feebly. 'This is Sophie Pettingell – she works with me. I'm sorry,' he went on, 'but I still haven't got a clue who you are.'

The two young men nodded politely to Sophie. She stared at them with a look of fascinated horror on her face. Paul noticed she was keeping perfectly still, as if she expected them to attack at any moment. 'My name,' said curly-head's friend, 'is Philip Catherwood, though most people call me Pip. This is my friend and colleague, Arthur Tanner.'

Tanner, Paul thought; and then, *Philip Catherwood* – he'd seen that name before, on all those passbooks and share certificates and deeds and stuff, in the strongroom. 'Um, hello,' he said. 'Pleased to meet you,' he added, hoping that was the right thing to say. 'Oh,' he added, 'and I'm Paul. Paul Carpenter.'

'Well, yes,' Pip replied, frowning slightly. 'We know that. We've met before.'

'*Look*.' Unmistakable sound of Sophie rapidly

approaching the end of her rope. 'If someone doesn't hurry up and tell me what the *fuck* is going on—'

It was almost worth the whole thing just to see the expression on the young men's faces. Paul felt like he ought to explain (*'That's another thing they do nowadays, besides working and wearing short skirts . . .'*) But on balance he reckoned it'd be better to leave it to context, and let them sort out the culture shock for themselves. 'Actually,' he said, 'I wouldn't mind an explanation myself, if that's all right with you.'

Pip nodded feebly, as if he still hadn't recovered. 'What would you like me to explain?' he said.

For some reason, that made Paul feel *angry.* 'Oh, this and that,' he said. 'Some of it I've sort of figured out for myself, like why you freak out when you see a girl's knees but a goblin's something you can take in your stride. But when the hell is this? And is this place 36 Coronation Terrace, and if so, what are you doing in my flat, and where in God's name is the door? And why is there a bloody great sword in a stone in the middle of my – of *our* floor? And what the *bloody* hell,' he added, with a degree of vehemence he wouldn't have believed himself capable, 'have Gilbert and Sullivan got to do with all this?'

The other one, Arthur Tanner, looked at him. 'What does freak out mean?' he asked.

'Be quiet, Arthur,' Pip said. Then he looked at Paul thoughtfully. 'You don't know, do you?' he said. 'Nobody's told you.'

'No,' Paul said. 'They haven't.'

'Ah. In that case,' Pip said, 'I think we'd all better sit down. This may take some time.'

*

It was back in seventy-seven (*Pip said*) that it all started. Oh, perhaps I should say *eighteen* seventy-seven. What year is it where you come from, by the way? Really? Good Lord.

Anyway, as I was saying. Back in seventy-seven, Arthur here and I were young clerks, freshly out of our indentures with the well-respected City firm of sorcerers, J. W. Wells & Co.

One Monday morning, Mr John Wells, the senior partner, called us both into his office. He told us that he wanted us to look after something for him. He sounded fearfully mysterious about it, but of course we were used to that by then, after two years with the firm. You do know about J. W. Wells & Co., don't you, what it is they actually do? Ah, capital.

Naturally, we didn't like to ask John Wellington – that's what we called him in the office, though never to his face, needless to say – what it was all about. That wouldn't have done at all. But, greatly to our surprise, the old man proceeded to tell us anyway, and shocking stuff it was, too.

He said that he'd recently found out that his nephew, young Mr Humphrey Wells, was plotting with a couple of the other partners to get rid of him; apparently, Mr Humphrey was fed up with waiting for the old devil to retire – he'd been talking about giving up for the last two hundred years, but nothing had ever come of it – and had decided to do something about it himself. But old John Wellington never had any intention of giving up, mostly because he couldn't abide the thought of Mr Humphrey getting his hands on the business. To be honest with you, we weren't in the least surprised about that. We'd known for some time that there was bad blood between them, because John Wellington didn't like the sort of thing Mr Humphrey got up to; he reckoned it was unethical, if not downright dishonest and wicked, and I have to say that we agreed with him entirely.

But to get back to what I was saying. The reason he'd sent for us, John Wellington said, was to entrust to us a certain very powerful sorcerous item, which we were to keep safe at all costs; because if, as JW suspected, Mr Humphrey were ever to do something dreadful to him (such as turn him into a frog, or imprison him in a glass mountain), the only magic strong enough to be sure of rescuing him and setting him free again was this same object; a talisman, if you care to think of it like that, though John Wellington used some other word to describe it, which slips my mind for the present.

In any case, he gave this thing to us, and we made very sure that one or other of us kept it with him at all times. It was very small and light, you see, small enough to be carried in a waistcoat pocket, or hung on a watch-chain.

It was shortly after that meeting that old Mr John Wellington disappeared. The story that we were told in the office was that something had gone horribly wrong with a job he'd been doing for some clients down in the West Country, something to do with a love philtre, and the only way in which the mess could be put right was for JW himself to be sacrificed to the Evil One – who'd duly turned up, we were told, and carried the poor old boy away to a Very Bad Place.

Of course, Arthur and I weren't taken in by this at all, not after what JW had told us. We knew that the only Evil One involved was Mr Humphrey, who'd clearly been and done something frightful to the old boy; furthermore, it was up to us to find out what it was, and put matters straight.

But before we could set about it, we were told to see Mr Humphrey in his office, late one Friday afternoon. We didn't like the sound of that, as you can imagine, but we had no choice in the matter, so off we went.

Mr Humphrey didn't mince his words. He knew that the old man had given us the talisman, and he wanted it. He began by offering us money, then promotion, then partnerships in the firm; but we'd have none of it, it goes without saying. That made him very angry, and he threatened us with all manner of dire consequences; but, strangely enough, after a while he told us to get out of his sight, and there the matter seemed to rest. We thought this rather extraordinary, since of course he could have used spells of compulsion to force us to hand the thing over, or even blasted us into ashes with lightning, if he'd wanted to. But instead, he simply told us to get out, and let us go.

We heard no more about it for several weeks, and that seemed to be the end of it. Then, one day, Mr Suslowicz – you know him? Splendid – he sent for us, and told us he'd be obliged if we'd spend a day or so clearing out the strongroom and putting the securities and so forth in order, as the place was rather a mess. So we set to, and a fair old job it turned out to be, as you might imagine. On the last day, when the work was nearly done, Mr Humphrey's secretary (Miss Julia – ah, you know her, too) came down to the strongroom with a box of bits and pieces to be put away with the rest. Among them, we found a most curious thing; a cardboard tube, containing an india-rubber mat, in the shape of a door. But, of course, you know all about that.

Well, as you can imagine better than most, after we'd read the instructions that came with it, we were quite fascinated by this curiosity, and couldn't resist the temptation of trying it out. We spread it out against the strongroom wall, and when the door appeared, we opened it, wedged it ajar with a heavy book, and went in. Being somewhat cautious, we commanded it to take us no further than our own lodgings; and sure enough, as we stepped through the doorway, that was where we found ourselves – except that of our own door, I mean the real door that connected our rooms to the rest of the building, there was no sign.

Scarcely had we made this discovery when we became aware of a man standing in the doorway – the magical doorway, I mean, the one we'd put up against the strongroom wall. To our horror, we saw that it was Mr Humphrey Wells, and he was grinning at us with a most devilish expression on his face. His exact words escape me, but he told us that since we wouldn't give him the talisman, and since in any case we knew far more about his business than was good for us, it would be as well if we were, as he put it, got out of harm's way for good. Then, before we could protest or do anything about it, he slammed the door in our faces, and it vanished without trace, leaving us, I need hardly tell you, in a room with no door.

And here (*Pip said*) we've been ever since.

Silence. Then Paul heard himself say, 'You mean *here*? In this room? For the best part of a hundred and thirty—'

Pip nodded.

'Just you and him? The two of you?'

Not tactful. A scowl flitted across Pip's face before he replied. 'I must confess it's been something of a strain on our friendship,' he said. 'In fact, there have been times when I felt I could strangle poor Arthur with my bare hands. Indeed, I have, several times, but it doesn't seem to have any effect. Neither,' he added with a slight shudder, 'does stabbing, beating him over the head with a poker or drowning him in the washbasin, so after a while I gave it up as a bad job. Nowadays we mostly play chess instead; or dominoes, or nomination whist. It helps relieve the tension, but without the bad feeling afterwards.'

Paul's jaw dropped, and he made no effort to close it.

'Of course,' the other one put in, 'we had no idea it was so long. For all we knew until you showed up, we might only have been here a day or so, but with time seeming to pass terribly slowly. It *felt* like a hundred years, right enough, but so did going to tea with my Aunt Elizabeth when I was a boy. A hundred years,' he repeated. 'I suppose things have changed rather.'

Paul nodded. 'A bit,' he said.

'Well, obviously,' Pip said, pointedly not looking at Sophie's knees. 'Um, ladies' clothing, for one thing. I don't imagine we'd feel very much at home in your time,' he added thoughtfully.

All this time, Sophie had been standing very still with a worried look on her face. Now she interrupted, 'Doesn't make any difference, does it? You're not coming back with us.'

The two clerks looked at her. So did Paul.

'Oh, for God's sake,' she said, 'haven't you figured it

out yet? None of us is going back, or going anywhere, or anywhen. We're stuck here. There's no fucking door.'

Maybe it hit the two clerks hardest. Maybe not.

'And I'll say it before any of you do,' Sophie went on. 'There's no door, and it's all my fault, because I closed it. So if we're stranded here for infinity, I'm the one who's to blame. Right?'

Long, awkward pause.

'Easy enough mistake to make,' Paul mumbled. 'I mean, you weren't to know.'

'Actually—' Arthur started to say, but then he must have caught sight of Paul's face, because he went on, 'Absolutely. Could've happened to anybody.'

That just seemed to make Sophie angry. 'Screw you,' she shouted, 'the lot of you. I mean, we're marooned in this horrible little room, and all you lot can do is stand there being bloody *chivalrous*. Isn't anybody ever going to take anything seriously?'

'With respect,' Pip said quietly, 'I don't see how falling out with each other is going to help. Besides, as Carpenter here's just pointed out, you had no way of knowing—'

'Shut *up*,' Sophie shouted. 'When I say it's all my stupid fault, why the hell won't anybody believe me? None of this'd have happened if I hadn't put that stupid philtre in his tea—'

'You did what?' Paul said.

'Oh.'

Paul was scowling horribly. 'You put that stuff in my tea? For crying out loud, what did you want to go and do that for? I know you aren't interested in me, but why in God's name did you want me to go falling in love with that bloody goblin?'

Sophie gave him a look you could have stored mammoths in. 'What goblin?' she said.

And then Paul figured it out.

Oh, he thought; and then, *oh shit*, because— And, just to add the whipped cream and the glacé cherry on top, he had a sneaking feeling that it was no coincidence, Arthur's second name being Tanner. 'You know,' he said, '*her*. The one I told you about. The receptionist.'

'Oh.' Sophie's eyes widened. 'Oh, you thought—'

'Yes.'

'Oh.'

The two clerks had gone bright pink, and were pretending to be utterly fascinated by a scrap of cobweb in the corner of the ceiling. 'So it was you who—' Paul said.

'That's right.'

'Because you—'

'Yes.'

'*Oh*.'

Of course, what he should probably have done was throw his arms around her and say, 'But you didn't have to, I love you anyway.' But he didn't do that. Instead, he wobbled, grabbed the back of his chair to keep himself from falling over, and said, 'Bloody hell.' He realised while he was saying it that it wasn't quite the most felicitous speech he'd ever made, but by then it was too late.

Sophie was staring at the scrap of rug visible between her feet. 'I suppose I ought to say sorry,' she said.

'Sorry?' Paul echoed helplessly.

'Yes, all right, I know it's not going to do a blind bit of good saying sorry, and obviously you're going to hate me for ever and ever, but—'

'What's there to be sorry about?' Paul said. 'That's *wonderful.*'

Over her shoulder, Paul could see the two clerks cringing. *The hell with them*, he thought. 'No it's *not*,' Sophie insisted, 'it's a total disaster, and it's all my—'

'For God's sake, Sophie. Shut up.' He jumped up to go to her, caught his foot in a fold of the rug, and fell heavily against Pip's knees. Pip yowled with pain, and lashed out reflexively, hitting Paul on the nose with the heel of his hand. Then Sophie hit Pip with a chair.

'What the bloody hell's going on?' said a bewildered-sounding voice from over by the window. All of them swung round, and saw the goblin, Mr Tanner's mum, sitting up on the bed and staring at them.

Well at one of them.

'Arthur?' she said.

The clerk called Arthur gaped back at her; and then something seemed to click into place.

'*Rosie?*' he whispered.

Paul wasn't completely on the ball, what with the angels singing and the bluebirds zooming about overhead and the sun coming out from behind the clouds and all that sort of thing, but he could still hop to the more obvious conclusions; and the manner in which the curly-haired clerk whose name was Tanner and Mr Tanner's mum hurled themselves into each others' arms with a crash like a lorry hitting a pillar box seemed to suggest he wasn't too wide of the mark, at that.

'Sweetheart!' sobbed the clerk.

'Honeypetal,' crooned Mr Tanner's mum.

Sophie nudged Paul in the ribs. 'What the hell's going on?' she whispered.

'Shh,' Paul replied. 'Apparently, that's our Mr Tanner's dad.'

'But she's a—'

'Yes.'

'Oh.'

Paul shifted slightly, so as to avoid any risk of seeing what Mr Tanner's mum and Arthur the clerk were getting up to. 'Forget about them,' he said. 'Did you really put that stuff in my tea?'

'Yes,' Sophie said. 'Look, would you mind not going on about that? Only—'

'Only what?'

She frowned. 'Oh, what the hell,' she said, and kissed him.

Compared with what was happening on the other side of the room, it was no big deal. Children and people of a nervous disposition could have witnessed it with no lasting damage. As far as Paul was concerned, however, it was without doubt the most amazing thing that had ever happened in the whole history of the universe; so it was hardly surprising that the other clerk, Pip, had to tap him on the shoulder several times before he managed to get his attention.

'Excuse me,' said Pip, 'but would you mind awfully not doing that? I mean, if we've got to spend all eternity cooped up in here together – well, for one thing, I'm going to feel just a bit left out, if you see what I mean.'

All eternity; just then, Paul couldn't see anything particularly wrong with all eternity being much like the moment he'd been interrupted in the middle of. Even so, he could see Pip's point, and so, apparently, could Sophie. The same couldn't be said of Arthur and Mr Tanner's mum, but there didn't seem to be a lot that any of them could do about that, even with buckets of cold water.

'I suppose we could use the curtains to close off that half of the room,' Sophie said. 'But that wouldn't solve the problem of the noises—'

'I heard that,' growled Mr Tanner's mum. 'Should be ashamed of yourselves, bloody perverts. It's all right,' she added, 'you can turn round now.'

Paul wasn't so sure about that, and stayed where he was. 'Sorry,' he said. 'Only—'

'Yes, all right, I get the message. More to the point, we'd like a bit of privacy, if it's all the same to you. I think we need to get out of here.'

'Really,' Sophie said. 'What a brilliant idea. Maybe you could tell us how.'

'Sarky.' Mr Tanner's mum sighed. 'Actually,' she said, 'it's dead easy for you two.'

This time, Paul did turn round. 'What? How?'

'Not so fast,' Mr Tanner's mum replied. 'First, you've got to promise me you'll come back and let us out.'

'Yes, of course,' Sophie said. 'So what've we got to do?'

'Simple. I'm assuming you've both had your little chat with Ricky Wurmtoter?'

It took a second or so for Paul to figure out what she was referring to. 'Oh, you mean when he gave us—'

'The prefect badges, that's right,' Mr Tanner's mum said. 'He's a good boy, young Ricky, he'll have you out of here in two shakes. Just press the badge and yell *help*, and you'll be back in the office before you can say employers' liability insurance.'

Sophie was fumbling for her badge already, but Paul hesitated. 'Back in the office,' he repeated.

'That's right. Simple counter-inversion, same as you'd use if you'd lost your car keys.'

'Fine,' Paul said. 'But if we go straight back to the office, how do we rescue you? The door's still on the train.'

Mr Tanner's mum hadn't thought of that. 'Shit,' she said.

Long silence; during which Mr Tanner's mum sat down in the big armchair with her head in her hands, while the two clerks stood by looking embarrassed. Finally, Sophie said, 'Well, I can see that's awkward for you three, but really, that's no reason why Paul and I've got to stay here. Look, when we get back, maybe we could ask Mr Wurmtoter if he knows how to get you out of here. Or we could go to the lost-property office at Euston, see if this door thing gets handed in. What is this door thing, anyhow?' she added.

Mr Tanner's mum called her a rude name. Sophie replied in kind, and things would probably have got rather fraught if Paul hadn't said, 'Excuse me,' three times, followed by, 'SHUT UP!', once.

'I've had an idea,' he said.

Much to Paul's surprise, it worked.

Not that he enjoyed it, not one bit. The counter-inversion got them back to the office just fine, but the sensation – the nearest Paul could ever get to describing it was a bit like being sneezed out of God's nostril, only backwards – was no fun at all; neither, though in a different way, was hurtling through the clouds ten thousand feet above the ground on the back of Mr Wurmtoter's milk-white winged horse. Sure, it was fast, and it seemed to know the way without having to be steered or anything; and he supposed, as they soared over Birmingham at several times the speed of sound, that it was nice of Mr Wurmtoter to lend them the horrible animal. On balance, though, he'd rather have walked.

The horse dropped them both on the platform at Stafford just as the train started to pull in. It didn't hang about, and for some reason or other, all the other people on the platform were looking the other way. As soon as the train came to a halt, they shoved through the nearest door and ran down the corridor, just in time to see the portable door being shovelled into a cleaner's black plastic sack. Paul hesitated, but Sophie pushed past him, snatched it out, grabbed Paul by the arm and dragged him off the train just as it pulled away.

'There,' she said, as they stood panting on the platform. '*Now* will you tell me what this stupid thing does?'

So Paul told her. Her first reaction was to be bitterly hurt and offended that he hadn't mentioned it before. He had no reply to that. But there was one thing he had to say, before they went any further.

'Listen,' he said. 'If you want to, you can go back in time – I'll stay here and keep the door open for you – and stop yourself putting that stuff in my tea. If you want to, I mean. If you've thought better of it, or something like that.'

She looked at him, with rather more of the old Sophie in her expression than he'd have liked. 'Why?' she said.

'Oh, I just thought—'

'That'd be *stupid*,' she interrupted. 'Because then we wouldn't have been trapped in that strange room, and we'd never have found those two clerk people, and so they'd never have a chance of being rescued, so they'd have to stay there for ever and ever, and that disgusting goblin woman would never get her boyfriend back, and—' She stopped. 'And anyway,' she went on, 'I'd still love you, even if I didn't spike your tea with the philtre stuff. So there wouldn't be any point, would there?'

'No,' Paul said. 'I just thought—'

'Don't,' Sophie said. 'Right, you'd better do whatever it is you do with this thing. And hurry up, people are staring.'

This time, Sophie stayed behind to make sure the door was kept open. Paul went through, and sure enough, there was the room, more or less as they'd left it, except that the two clerks and Mr Tanner's mum were sitting round a table playing cards. For some reason, neither of the clerks was wearing any clothes.

'Strip canasta,' Mr Tanner's mum explained, as the two clerks dressed hurriedly. 'You were gone such a long time, we had to find something to do to amuse ourselves.'

'Fine,' Paul said. 'Now, can we get a move on, please?'

'Spoilsport,' Mr Tanner's mum said, and she led the way, followed by Arthur, followed by Pip, still struggling with his bootlaces. But when Arthur tried to cross the threshold—

'I'm stuck,' he said.

Mr Tanner's mum clicked her tongue. 'For crying out loud,' she said, 'this is no time for stupid jokes.'

'It's not a joke,' said Arthur in a tragic voice. 'I can't move. I'm stuck.'

Mr Tanner's mum reached out a long, scaly arm, grabbed him by the elbow and heaved. Arthur yelled like a cat being skinned alive, but didn't budge.

Mr Tanner's mum went a pale shade of aquamarine. 'How about you?' she asked Pip. 'You try.'

But Pip couldn't pass through the door either. 'It's that bastard Humphrey,' Mr Tanner's mum snarled. 'He's put a lock on the fucking door.' Then she sat down on the platform tarmac and burst into tears. Paul and Sophie looked at her, then back at the door. It had snapped shut, gone limp and fallen off the wall.

They tried to set it up again, but it wouldn't stick; it just kept rolling sadly down again, like misbehaving wallpaper. Eventually, they saw a guard approaching with a policeman, and decided it was time to leave. The last thing they needed, they decided, was for Mr Tanner's mum to start disembowelling people in broad daylight in a public place.

'It's a lock,' Mr Tanner's mum explained, as they walked slowly down the street away from the station. 'Just like any other sort of lock, except it only affects certain people, the ones you want to keep in, and of course you can't see it.'

'Fine,' Paul said. 'So if it's just a lock, is there a key?'

'Sure,' Mr Tanner's mum said, with a grim laugh. 'The problem's finding it. Obviously, that bastard Humphrey's got it, and you can bet your knicker elastic he won't have left it lying about. It'll be in a *very* safe place, you can rely on that.'

They sat down on a bench under a tree. Mercifully, Mr Tanner's mum had abandoned her goblin shape in favour of something a little bit less ostentatious – only marginally, as the whistles she prompted as they passed a building site amply testified. Paul assumed she was only doing it to annoy Sophie. Successfully.

'Actually,' Mr Tanner's mum went on, 'it's worse than that, because there's two keyholes on that stupid door thing, so there's got to be two keys, which means it'll be twice as hard tracking them down. And,' she continued gloomily, 'knowing Humphrey they won't be nice straightforward knobbly bits of brass, either, they'll be disguised as something, or there'll be some sort of stupid test you have to pass or thing you've got to do before you can get at them or make them work. He's a terror for that sort of thing is Humphrey. I remember when we first got the hot-drinks machine, and he put a spell on it so only the pure in heart could get it to do coffee, milk and two sugars. I told him, I said, pure in heart, around here, you must be—'

'Just a moment,' Paul interrupted. 'A test, you said.'

'That's right. Or there was the time when he fixed the fax machine so only the seventh son of a seventh son could change the toner cartridge. Now it just so happens that Ricky Wurmtoter *is* a seventh son, but of course he's not always around, a lot of the time he's off on a job somewhere, and it's bloody inconvenient—'

'A test,' Paul repeated. 'Like in fairy tales and stuff.'

'Yes. And—'

'Or folk tales. King Arthur and so forth.'

'Yeah, he loves all that crap. Just a big kid, really. Nasty spiteful bloody kid, but—'

'King Arthur.' Sophie's eyes were wide as saucers. 'The sword in the *stone*.'

Of course, Paul hadn't been to Sophie's house before. It was pretty much as he'd imagined it: double-glazed porch, tie-backs on the curtains, glass-topped coffee tables, stripped-pine kitchen units. Sophie's parents weren't quite the hopelessly obsolete museum-pieces she'd led him to expect; he rather liked them, in fact, especially the way that neither of them was particularly fazed when Sophie introduced her companions ('This is, um, Rosie, her son's one of the partners; oh, and this is Paul, we're in love') as she pushed past on her way to the back door.

There on the grey-paved patio was the other sword in the stone, an exact duplicate of the one he'd grown used to sidestepping every time he crossed his bedsit floor to make a cup of tea. Neither rain, wind nor blue tits had marred its glowing hilt or shining blade. Mrs Pettingell had tied one end of the washing line to it.

'We're still back where we started, though,' Sophie pointed out. 'I've tried and tried, and so has Dad, and we can't shift the stupid thing out of the stone.'

Mr Tanner's mum nodded. 'Like I said,' she replied. 'It'll be a spell, or an intelligence test. Humphrey's a right bastard, but he's good at what he does.'

Sophie thought for a while, then suggested going round to B&Q and buying a jackhammer. Mr Tanner's mum didn't think much of that idea; and while they were bickering about it in a fairly half-hearted fashion, Paul suddenly thought of something. *Gilbert and Sullivan*, he thought; also, *two hearts are better than one*.

'Just a moment,' he said, putting his hand on the left branch of the crossguard and beckoning Sophie over. 'Here, you catch hold of your side, and when I count to three—'

It came out so smoothly that they nearly fell over; and, sure enough, the very tip of the blade wasn't sharp and pointed – it was blunt and crinkly-edged, just like the wards of a key.

'Well, I'm buggered,' said Mr Tanner's mum. 'Looks like Humphrey's got a soppy streak or something.'

Paul wasn't so sure about that, but he kept his theory to himself. Having examined the end of the blade, he took a firm hold of the key portion and bent it sideways. The metal was brittle, and snapped. He dropped the key into his pocket, put the sword back in the stone and reattached the washing line. 'One down,' he said.

They still had enough left over from the expenses money to run to a taxi from Wimbledon to Kentish Town. Paul really wished he'd had a bit more notice, since the flat was in its usual state of scruffy disorder whereby a bomb hitting it would count as a make-over, but Sophie appeared to be too wrapped up in the job in hand to notice, and he didn't really care what Mr Tanner's mum thought. The second sword came out as easily as the first, and the key snapped off like the tip of an icicle. 'Right,' said Mr Tanner's mum. 'Here goes, then.'

So Paul pulled the portable door out of its cardboard tube one more time, and went through the preliminaries of smoothing it out and plastering it onto the wall. When it was ready, he took the first key and tried it in the top lock. It was a perfect fit, and so was its counterpart in the bottom. He straightened up, then hesitated.

'In case anybody was wondering,' he said, 'I don't think it was Humphrey who put those keys there. I think it was somebody else.'

'So what?' said Mr Tanner's mum impatiently, but Sophie shushed her. 'Who?' she asked.

Paul shrugged. 'I'm not sure,' he said. 'Though my guess is, the same person who arranged for each of us to get one. I think the keys were put there so Humphrey couldn't get at them. That's why it took the two of us to get them out.'

Sophie frowned. 'But that'd mean – well, that who-ever it was knew that you and me . . . And that's just stupid. I mean, we only realised earlier today, and we've had these sword things for ages.' She turned on Mr Tanner's mum and scowled. 'What's so funny?' she demanded.

'You are,' Mr Tanner's mum replied. 'Bloody hell, it's been obvious for weeks, the way you two've been going on.'

Paul shook his head. 'I think it goes back much further than that,' he said. 'This probably sounds pretty weird, but I think we were sort of like *destined* to find these keys. And each other,' he added, going bright pink at the ears. 'Not that it matters particularly,' he added briskly, 'just thought I'd mention it.'

'Whatever,' growled Mr Tanner's mum. 'But I'll tell you this. If you don't get a move on and open this door, you're destined to get my boot up your bum.'

Paul was no sceptic when it came to goblin prophecies. 'Here goes nothing,' he muttered under his breath, and gave the door a gentle shove.

'Rosie!'
'Arthur!'

Paul looked away; it was enough to put you off true love for life. In passing, he wondered whether Arthur knew he had a son; probably not, he reflected, and a mental image of Mr Tanner floated into his mind. *Well*, he thought, *he's got that to look forward to, poor bastard.*

'Excuse me,' said Pip mournfully, 'but if you two could leave each other alone for just one moment—'

'You go ahead,' replied Arthur, with his mouth full. 'We'll catch you up in just a second.'

Pip shrugged. 'Don't mind if I do,' he said. '*I* can't wait to get out of this awful place.'

He approached the threshold cautiously, as if expecting the door to bite him as he went through. 'Odd,' he said, 'I've been dreaming of this moment for ever such a long time, and now it's actually here—'

'We don't know it is, yet,' Sophie interrupted. 'Only one way to find out, though.'

'True,' Pip said. 'Ah well. Regardless of what happens next, I'd just like to say thank you, to both of you. And I'm most dreadfully sorry,' he added, to Paul. 'About the dreams, I mean. Devil of a liberty and all that, intruding on another fellow's sleep, but—'

Paul smiled. 'That's all right,' he said. 'Compared to what my dreams are usually like . . .'

'I know,' Pip said. 'Seen 'em, actually. But even so.' He closed his eyes, took a deep breath and walked across the threshold.

'Good Lord.' They could hear his voice on the other side. 'That stain on the ceiling's still there, I see. I remember writing to the landlord about that in 1874.'

'You next,' snapped Mr Tanner's mum; and she grabbed Arthur by his collar and frogmarched him through the door. 'Well, I had to see it was safe first, didn't I?' she explained.

That was almost touching, in a way.

She followed him; then Sophie went through, and finally Paul. He closed the door gently, then caught it as it rolled up and fell off the wall. 'Well,' he said, 'that's that, I suppose.'

Pip and Arthur were standing in the middle of his floor, one on either side of the now swordless stone. 'I hate to say this,' Arthur said, 'but I think I preferred the way we had it. Still, it's nice to be out. Back,' he amended. 'Very nice,' he added, and he smiled.

'Glad you're pleased,' grunted Mr Tanner's mum. 'Now, the next thing we've got to do is find Humphrey and shove him up himself with a long, sharp—'

'No,' Sophie said, surprising herself almost as much as she surprised everyone else. 'No, the first thing is to turn this other bloke loose; you know, what's-his-name, the senior partner. John Wellington. It's obvious, surely,' she went on, as they all stared at her. 'We can't take on Humphrey Wells on our own, he's like this really powerful wizard, he'd cast a spell on us or something and we'll all end up in that horrible little room. But if we can rescue this John Wellington, presumably he's an even better wizard, and he can sort out Humphrey for us. I don't know why you're all gawping at me like that,' she went on, 'I'd have thought it was obvious, myself.'

Paul thought for a moment. 'She's absolutely right,' he said.

'Balls,' snapped Mr Tanner's mum. 'Just wait till I get my claws on him, he won't be doing any magic for a very long time.'

'Well,' Arthur started to say, but then he caught his girlfriend's eye and went very quiet. Pip, on the other hand, shook his head. 'I agree with the young lady,' he said. 'I think we'd best get the old devil – I mean, John Wellington, before we go marching into Humphrey's office looking for a fight.'

'I agree with him,' said a voice from the corner of the room. 'At least,' it added, 'that's what I'd have done, in your shoes. Too late now, though.'

They spun round, but before they'd stopped moving, the world started spinning in the opposite direction. Paul recognised the sensation; it was the same way he'd felt when Mr Wurmtoter's recovery charm had whisked them out of the doorless room a few hours earlier. When it stopped, he saw that they were all standing in the boardroom at the office, lined up alongside the mirror-polished table, as Humphrey Wells advanced towards them. He was wearing his conjuror's cloak and hat, and holding a saw.

CHAPTER FOURTEEN

'Of course,' said Humphrey Wells, pausing to mop his forehead on the hem of his conjuror's cloak, 'I'm probably being over-cautious, which is something of an occupational hazard with villains. After all, you know that I transformed my Uncle John into something, but you haven't got the faintest idea what. Accordingly, you don't really pose any sort of threat to me. Still, I happen to believe in attention to detail.'

He grinned and continued sawing. He was about two-thirds of the way through. Inside the box, Mr Tanner's mum had stopped kicking and screaming, and was now lying ominously still.

'Furthermore,' he continued, raising his voice slightly over the grating sound of the saw, 'I could probably have forced young Arthur here to tell me where the talisman's hidden just by threatening to saw his sweetheart in two, without actually doing it. But

I've been waiting for a pretext to get my own back on the miserable bitch for two hundred years.'

Arthur made a faint squealing noise and tried to struggle, but it didn't do any good. Humphrey's restraining spell held him tight in his chair, as firmly as though the ropes and gag had been real hemp and cloth rather than some magical effect. The others didn't even try to move or make a noise. Real rope can be surreptitiously cut, burnt or frayed; the immaterial version is far less vulnerable.

'Of course,' Humphrey added, 'you're probably all wondering what I'm going to do with you once I've got my hands on this talisman. Good question; I've been asking myself the same thing. I suppose I could maroon you all in that poky little room; but as we've all seen, that's not necessarily a permanent solution. Turning you all into things has a certain appeal, and once I've got the talisman it'll be the proverbial piece of cake; or I suppose I could just kill the lot of you and have done with it. That'd be the sensible course,' he sighed, 'but my trouble is, I'm far too tender-hearted. It'd be untrue to say I couldn't hurt a fly, but I think I draw the line at five – no, make that six cold-blooded murders, since this time I'd have to do for poor old Uncle John as well. Who knows? I might even let you all go, for all the harm you could possibly do me.'

It was at this point, for the first time, that Paul genuinely wished that he was good at magic. A proper fully trained wizard, he felt, would be able to get free from the invisible ropes, turn Humphrey into a gnat and cause a heavy object to fall on him and deprive him of a dimension, all with a twitch of the nose or the waggle of an eyebrow. But Paul wasn't a proper wizard, never had been one and never would be one, not now. *Pity*, he thought; though that wasn't what he regretted most. The true bitch of it was that Sophie loved him – God only knew why – and any minute now he'd be dead, or transformed into a gerbil. *Do gerbils love?* he wondered. Naturally he'd still worship and adore Sophie if she was a gerbil; but would a gerbilized Sophie still love him, or would all that sort of thing get filtered out in the transformation process? In any event, it wasn't fair, and if only he could get his hands free, he'd have a good mind to write to Esther Rantzen about it.

Humphrey had stopped sawing; he was leaning against the table and breathing heavily. 'Actually,' he puffed, 'make that seven cold-blooded murders, because I don't suppose Dennis Tanner's going to take kindly to having his dear old mum sawn in half. Still, he's been a thorn in my side for far too long; and besides, I've never really liked him much.' He put one hand on each half of the box, and slid them gently apart. 'Now,' he said, looking at Arthur, 'let's not muck about. You can see I'm serious, so don't bother telling lies or playing for time. I want that talisman, please.' He snapped his fingers, and Arthur nearly fell out of his chair. 'Come along,' Humphrey chided, 'I've got a lot of things to see to after I've dealt with you people, so don't waste my time.'

Arthur stood up. He was shaking all over, Paul noticed; couldn't blame him for that. 'Very well,' he said quietly. 'But what assurance do I have that you'll put her back together again?'

'My word as a gentleman, of course.'

'Ah,' said Arthur bleakly. 'To be honest, I was hoping for rather more than that.'

Humphrey smiled. 'Tough,' he said. 'Did I mention that unless I put her back within three minutes, there won't be a lot of point?'

Arthur closed his eyes briefly; then he reached across the table and picked up Humphrey's conjuror's hat, out of which he produced three white doves, a rabbit and a fine gold chain. The doves and the rabbit made themselves scarce; Arthur put the chain down on the table and said, 'That's it.'

Humphrey, who'd been staring, made a sort of gurgling noise at the back of his throat. 'Do you mean to tell me,' he said at last, 'that I've been carrying the wretched thing around with me for the last hundred and thirty years without knowing it? Of all the—' He laughed. 'Well, I've got to admire your ingenuity,' he said, 'not to mention your nerve. And I'll forgive you for making me look a fool, because nobody's ever going to know; and as soon as I've disposed of this annoying little trinket, my confounded uncle won't be a problem any more.'

'As you wish,' Arthur said. 'Now, if you wouldn't mind—'

'What? Oh, yes, of course.' Humphrey pulled the two halves of the box together; they closed with an audible snap, he folded back the lid, and Mr Tanner's mum sat up, blinking. 'You see?' Humphrey said. 'I did give you my word, after all.'

With a blood-curdling snarl, Mr Tanner's mum suddenly grew a set of three-inch claws and went to swipe Humphrey across the face with them; but he snapped his fingers, and she froze in mid-stroke. 'As for you,' he said, 'I'm not quite finished with *you* yet.' He snapped his fingers a second time, and Mr Tanner's mum changed into a stunningly beautiful voluptuous blonde, with no clothes on. She shrieked and, to Paul's great surprise, blushed.

'Turning me down,' Humphrey said slowly, 'is one thing. Turning me down, and then making an exhibition of yourself chasing after *that*' (a savage nod in Paul's direction) 'is another matter entirely.' He paused, then grinned at Arthur. 'Oh, didn't anybody tell you?' he said conversationally. 'Your own true love's been quite busy since you've been away, and her latest project is this half-baked excuse for a stick insect here. Do you know,' he added with a smirk, 'I've a good mind to maroon the two of you in your old rooms together for the rest of eternity, to give you plenty of time to discuss the matter in private.'

Paul opened his mouth to explain, but no words came out. Arthur looked at him, and shook his head. 'I don't believe you,' he said. 'My Rosie'd never do anything like that.'

Humphrey threw his head back and laughed. 'Priceless,' he said. 'Well, never mind. As I mentioned just now, I have some unfinished business with your sweet Rosie; once I've finished with her, I'll send her along to join you in whatever place or setting you end up in. Unless, of course, she changes her mind about me, which is a lady's prerogative, after all. She may decide that I'm preferable to fifty billion years in a confined space with you and your new friends. We'll have to see, won't we?' Humphrey snapped his fingers a third time, and Arthur froze solid before he could say a word. 'Now then,' Humphrey went on, 'what about your friend, young Philip here? Correct me if I'm wrong, but you were the one who tried to warn my dear uncle about me, thereby forcing my hand before I was quite ready. I believe it's only fair I should think up something particularly suitable for you. And Miss Pettingell,' he added, 'and Mr Carpenter. It was none of your business, was it? But you had to go poking your noses in where they didn't belong. Let's see, now; I do believe that, shortly before you came here, Miss Pettingell and Mr Carpenter had just discovered that they were part of the same happy ending. But we can easily fix *that*.' He stood up and crossed the room to where Sophie's handbag lay on the floor. From it he took the plastic bottle, still over half full of clear golden liquid. 'My uncle's own recipe,' he said affectionately, 'worth a fortune to us over the years. Let's think, now: what permutation is likely to cause the most trouble?' He unscrewed the cap; then he put his hand on Sophie's forehead and tilted her head back. 'In about twenty minutes,' he said, 'you'll wake up and find your-self gazing in wonder into young Philip's small, piggy eyes. But you're a strong-willed, bolshy little thing; you'll love our Pip with a frenzied passion that'll last until the sun goes cold, but all the time you'll know at the back of your mind that he's not really the one. And since the three of you'll be cooped up in that dingy little bedsit, without even the option of murder or sui-cide to break the tension, I imagine the atmosphere in there is going to get more than a little fraught.'

Paul couldn't bear to watch. He looked away; at the ceiling, then down at the table – at the table, with its mirror-polish, on which stood that by now familiar object, the long stapler. A tiny part of his mind won-dered how it had got there, since it hadn't been there a moment ago; but he was so used to it turning up and disappearing again that its latest manifestation didn't really bother him. He looked away, at the moulding on the oak-panelled walls; but then something registered in his mind, and he looked back; not, this time, at the stapler itself, but at its reflection in the table top. The last time he'd been in this room, when Ricky Wurmtoter had given them the Dire Warnings lecture and told them about the imp-reflecting qualities of that very table, he'd remembered thinking how curious was the manner in which the thing worked. You looked at the object, and then at its reflection; and the reflection was just the normal inverted image of the object, but at the same time it was also something else. On that occasion, it had been the doomed Mr Lundqvist, transformed into a mouse by some dark sorcery. This time . . . this time, the stapler was just a stapler, but it was also a tiny little bald man, dressed in a black frock coat and grey striped trousers, crouched like a hunting cat and waving frantically at him with his tiny hands.

Fuck, thought Paul. *Mr Wells senior.*

Yes, said a voice, very faint inside his head. *Now pay attention. When I break the spell, lay the chain over the stapler.*

You what? Paul thought; but then he felt the unseen ropes give way abruptly, and he fell forward, just as Arthur had done when Humphrey had released him a while ago. Paul lost his balance and toppled out of his chair, but as he slid forward he shot his hand out, grabbing for the little gold chain on the table top. He could just reach it; and as Humphrey whirled round, a vicious-looking sword in his uplifted hand, Paul flicked the chain through the air with his fingertips.

More by luck than judgement, the chain flew through the air, clattered against the stapler and wrapped itself round it like a bolas. At once there was a blinding flash of blue light. Humphrey dropped the sword with a clatter and crashed against the wall as John Wellington Wells (a short, stout man who looked like Arthur Lowe without his glasses on) stepped down from the table.

'Thank you,' he said politely to Paul. Then he clicked his sausage-like fingers.

Several things happened all at once. Mr Tanner's mum acquired a long dress of rose-madder silk, with zouave jacket and bustle. Arthur and Pip fell off their chairs and landed on their backsides on the floor. A snake of some sort – a boa constrictor, or some kind of python – appeared out of thin air and coiled itself round Humphrey until only his nose and the tips of his shoes were visible. Sophie's head fell forward on her chest, and she snored loudly. John Wellington frowned, and spat out a mouthful of staples. An empty plastic bottle rolled across the floor.

Paul stared for a moment at the plastic bottle; then he slumped forward, his head in his hands. Then he heard the voice of John Wellington, directly above him. 'Don't be ridiculous,' he was saying, and Paul looked up sharply.

John Wellington was frowning at him, and Paul expected him to say, 'Stupid boy,' at any moment. Instead, he heard a voice inside his head; the same one he'd heard a minute earlier, only louder this time. John Wellington clearly believed in discretion.

It's all right, said John Wellington inside his head, *it'll be at least twenty minutes before she wakes up, and so long as you're in position when the time comes, everything'll be as right as rain. Better, in fact.*

Better? Paul queried.

Quite so. Be realistic. True, the young lady does indeed love you, but nothing lasts for ever; under normal circumstances, I'd give it eighteen months, at the very most, and then she'd be off with someone else, someone quite unsuitable who'd make her very unhappy. This way is very much better, for both of you.

But that's not right, Paul stated. I can't take advantage—

It's not a matter of taking advantage. It's a matter of finding happiness, suddenly and against all probability, in a world where love is seldom true and never eternal. Not, that is, without the help of a little white magic, at seven and threepence ha'penny the pint, trade.

But isn't there anything you can do? he asked. An antidote, or something?

No.

Oh, Paul responded. But even so, I don't think it's right, it's—

The slight twinge of pain inside his head could have been the voice scowling. *Stupid boy,* said the voice.

Sophie woke up.

'Paul?' she said.

'Hello.'

She narrowed her eyes and squinted. 'Yes, right,' she said. 'Only, you look different somehow.'

Paul took a deep breath. 'Yes,' he said, 'I thought you might say that. There's a reason.'

Sophie sat up, and winced. 'Cricked neck,' she explained. 'Have I been asleep, or something?'

Paul nodded. 'For about twenty minutes.'

'Oh.' She frowned. 'What happened?' she said. 'The last thing I can remember is that bastard, making me drink the love stuff. Only—' She hesitated, trying to make sense of what was in her mind. 'Only he was going to make me fall in love with that funny little clerk, with the pointy nose.'

'That's right,' Paul said. 'Only that didn't happen. Yes, you drank the philtre, but then—'

'Yes? Well?'

Paul sighed. 'Mr Wells – that's old Mr Wells, the one who'd been lost, he turned out to be the long stapler – you know, the one that won't stay put for five minutes. I saw him, in that mirror thing that shows things as they really are. And I, well, kind of set him free, and he sorted out the other Mr Wells, Humphrey, and basically that's that. You missed it all, of course.'

'I suppose so,' Sophie said.

'Old Mr Wells,' Paul went on quickly, 'John Wellington, he zapped Humphrey with lightning or something. Then he – well, *changed* him.'

'What do you mean, changed?'

'He turned him into something,' Paul said, with a touch of awe in his voice. 'You've never seen anything like it. One moment he was like there, the next—'

'Paul,' Sophie warned him. 'What did he turn him into?'

Paul shivered a little as he answered. 'A photocopier,' he replied. 'He reckoned that since he'd had to be a stapler all those years, it was only right and proper Humphrey should be some kind of office equipment too; and then he got this funny look in his eye, and he asked us, "What's the most hated and abused piece of kit in an office?" and we all said, "The photocopier," without even having to be asked. Then John Wellington said that was what he reckoned too, and it'd serve Humphrey right to spend for ever being thumped and yelled at and blamed every time something was late or got all chewed up. Then, zap, and that was that.'

'Oh well,' Sophie said. 'But what about—?'

Paul looked away. 'It's all right,' he said. 'I asked John Wellington about it. First he said, there's nothing anybody can do, but I kept on at him and finally he said, yes, there's an antidote. All I've got to do—'

'You?' Sophie interrupted.

Paul nodded. 'All I've got to do,' he said, 'is swear, like, this solemn oath that I'm finished with – well, girls, basically. And women. And all that sort of thing. Then I go away somewhere, and after a week or two the philtre wears off, and everything's fine.'

Sophie looked at him. 'And what happens if you don't? I mean, if you break the oath?'

Paul shrugged. 'He was a bit vague about that,' he said. 'But from what I could gather, I sort of disintegrate, basically, and my soul's forfeit to Ahrimanes, Prince of Darkness.' He frowned. 'But that's all a bit academic, really, isn't it? Because let's face it, me giving up women and stuff, it's like me abdicating the throne of England. What you're never going to have, I mean, you aren't going to miss . . .'

'Oh,' Sophie said. 'But that's stupid.'

'No, it isn't.'

'Yes, it is.'

'No, it *isn't*,' Paul said irritably. 'It's what I want to do. Well, obviously it's *not* what I want to do, but it's the right thing. Obviously.'

'Why?'

He loved her with all his heart, but she could be annoying sometimes. 'Because otherwise – well, you'll be under the control of that bloody stuff, and—'

'But I love you.'

'No,' Paul said. 'That's just the philtre, it's what it makes you think.'

'No, you moron. I *love* you. Before the philtre stuff.'

Paul shook his head. 'No,' he said. 'I mean, you thought you did, but probably by now you'd have realised you didn't, you were just having a funny five minutes or something; or maybe you'd breathed in the fumes while we were up in Lancashire, or—'

'*Paul.*' She was getting angry. 'Shut *up*, for crying out loud. Do you love me or don't you?'

'Well, yes, but—'

'Right. That's that, then,' she said; then she lunged at him and kissed him. 'Ouch,' she added, as their teeth collided.

'Sorry,' Paul mumbled.

'Bloody hell. Look, just keep still, can't you?'

So Paul kept still, for quite some time. Then, once he'd got some feeling back in his jaw and lips, he said, 'Look, are you sure about this?'

'*Paul!*'

'All right, all right, I was just asking.'

A few minutes later, someone knocked at the door. 'Is it, um, safe to come in?'

'That's John Wellington,' Paul whispered. 'Yes,' he called out, 'um, yes, fine.'

The door opened, and John Wellington came in, followed by Professor Van Spee, Mr Suslowicz, the

Contessa di Castel'Bianco, Ricky Wurmtoter, Pip and, finally, Mr Tanner. 'Sit down, please, all of you,' John Wellington said. 'You too,' he added to Paul and Sophie, who'd jumped up looking guilty. 'We've got a lot to get through, so we won't waste any time.' He put his hand in his pocket and took out a paper bag, which Paul was sure he recognised.

'Mr Carpenter,' John Wellington went on, 'I took the liberty of taking these from the drawer of your desk. You recognise them.'

Paul nodded; the dragon droppings, which made you hear what people meant, not what they said.

'Excellent,' John Wellington said. 'Now, we all have a rough idea of what's happened here, and I've taken appropriate steps to deal with my nephew. But that, I'm afraid, isn't quite the end of the matter.' He frowned, and looked slowly up and down the table. 'From what I've gathered from my own observations as a stapler – an interesting perspective, which some of you might find useful – and various things I've heard since I've been back, it seems to me that my wretched nephew wasn't acting entirely on his own. In fact, it seems quite likely that one of the other partners in this firm was either in the plot with him, or at least knew about it but didn't say or do anything about it.'

Very uncomfortable silence, with everyone looking at the floor, or their folded hands.

'Now,' John Wellington went on, 'I suppose I could swallow some of these dragon droppings myself, and then question you in turn and find out the truth. But if I were to do that, some of you might suspect that I'd used this as a pretext for getting rid of the one or more of you whom I don't like; after all, you'd have no way of knowing whether I was telling the truth or not. So instead, I'm going to ask Miss Pettingell and Mr Carpenter to eat the beans. After all, they don't know which of you I'd want to see out of the way, so there's no reason why they wouldn't tell the truth. Agreed?'

The other partners stayed still and quiet for a moment; then, slowly, they all nodded their agreement. 'Fine,' said John Wellington, pushing the bag across the table. 'Ms Pettingell, Mr Carpenter, if you'd both care to do the honours.'

Sophie looked at him suspiciously, but something in his expression seemed to convince her that this wouldn't be a good time to make difficulties, and she swallowed three beans as if they were some sort of extremely nasty medicine. When Paul had done likewise, John Wellington cleared his throat. 'First,' he said, 'we'll try a little controlled experiment.' He took a pencil and wrote something on two pieces of paper, which he tucked in his top pocket. 'First,' he said, 'I'm going to say what's on one of those slips of paper while thinking something quite different – which is what I've written down on the other slip. Then Mr Carpenter and Miss Pettingell will write down what they thought they heard me say, and we can compare the results.' He looked round the table. 'Judy,' he said, looking the Contessa in the eye, 'did I ever happen to mention to you that your nose reminds me of a clothes-peg clipped on a parsnip?'

The Contessa smiled bleakly. 'Go play with yourself, you randy old goat,' she replied.

John Wellington nodded, then turned to Pip. 'Would you tell us, please,' he said, 'what you just heard me say to the Contessa, and what she said in reply?'

'Certainly,' Pip answered. 'You told the Contessa that if anything, she looks more beautiful now than she did a hundred and thirty years ago. She replied that you always knew how to phrase a graceful compliment.'

John Wellington nodded in acknowledgement. 'Thank you,' he said. 'Now, if Miss Pettingell and Mr Carpenter will kindly pass him what they've written.'

As he stood up to hand over the slip of paper, Paul couldn't help coming eye to eye with Mr Tanner, just for a moment. That was no fun at all, even though Mr Tanner didn't say anything out loud.

Pip unfolded the bits of paper and looked at them. 'Well?' said John Wellington.

'Um,' Pip replied. 'Actually, I'm having a little trouble with the handwriting.'

'I don't think so,' John Wellington said. 'Come on, man, don't be shy.'

'Sorry,' Pip replied, and the way he said it reminded Paul of someone he was accustomed to look at in mirrors. 'It's just – well, a bit personal, if you see what I mean.'

'No more personal than spending a hundred and thirty years as a stapler, I'm sure. Hurry up, can't you?'

Pip shrugged, and read out the words, exactly as Paul had heard them. Sophie's version was identical. Countess Judy went bright pink, while John Wellington laughed.

'It only goes to show,' he said, 'what a frail instrument speech is. Anyhow, I think I've proved my point. Now we can start the investigation.' He turned round and stared hard at the other partners, one by one. 'I think I can leave Mr Wurmtoter out of this,' he went on, 'since he didn't join the firm until long after I disappeared. Theo,' he said, and for the first time, Paul saw the professor look decidedly uncomfortable. 'We've never liked each other, of course; you're jealous of me, and I despise you, understandably enough. But I wouldn't have thought you had the guts to plot against me, even when it looked like my idiot nephew had won. Well?'

Professor Van Spee stroked his beard before answering. 'Nothing would give me greater pleasure than murdering you and selling your body to the cat-food people,' he replied gravely. 'However, I genuinely believed you were dead.'

'Thank you,' John Wellington said gravely. 'Judy,' he went on. 'I remember discussing you with old John Hollingshead, who was running the Gaiety when you joined the chorus back in the early 1870s; he said, "She has the ambition of a junior minister and the morals of an alley cat; even so, there's something about her I don't quite like." Was it you?'

The Contessa smiled bleakly. 'No,' she said.

'Excellent. Casimir, my old friend,' John Wellington continued warmly, 'most people would be convinced you're far too stupid to be devious, but I don't agree. You're stupid, certainly, but you're greedy as well. Did you know about what Humphrey did to me?'

Mr Suslowicz looked as though he was about to burst into tears. 'I came to this country with nothing, and I owe everything to you. Thank God you've come back to us, my good, kind, friend John Wells.'

'Splendid,' said John Wellington. 'Which just leaves you, Dennis. I wouldn't put anything past you, even if I could find a bargepole that'd reach that far. Was it you?'

Mr Tanner grinned. It was just his ordinary worka-day grin. 'It was nothing personal, JW,' he said. 'How could there be? I never knew you. After all, I wasn't even born when it happened. It was only years later, after I'd been with the firm for quite a while, that I found out what Humphrey'd done. But I couldn't rescue you, because it'd have meant releasing that dis-gusting little clerk who knocked up my mother. My father,' he added, with a leer that showed his teeth. 'If there'd been any way to get you out without letting him go too, I'd have done it, just to get rid of Humphrey.'

'Thank you,' said John Wellington; but Mr Tanner went on speaking, or at least his voice kept going in Paul's mind. 'And now,' Mr Tanner was saying, 'he's back again, and my mother's up to her old tricks again, and if that's not bad enough she's been chasing after this pathetic dribble of trollsnot. Well, we'll have to put a stop to that, just as soon as your back's turned. Only this time there won't be any talismans or any of that shit—'

'Shut the fuck up,' said John Wellington, so politely that it took Paul a moment to remember that that probably wasn't what he'd actually said. He didn't look like Arthur Lowe any more; he was angry, that was obvious enough, but he had the anger completely under control, like someone who's scooped up a small, furiously barking dog and is holding it well clear of the ground, its little feet scrabbling wildly and to no effect. 'Thank you,' Paul heard him say. 'Actually, I don't think we need Miss Pettingell and Mr Carpenter to translate for us, the gist of the matter seems pretty clear, don't you think?' Paul looked across, and saw that the other partners were sitting very still, looking distinctly shocked and uncomfortable.

Mr Tanner drew a deep breath. 'Fine,' he said. 'So that's that, I suppose, I'm out. No use me pointing out that my family owns this building, or anything like that.'

John Wellington looked rather serious. 'If you're trying to blackmail me,' he said, 'forget it. But you're underestimating me, as always. No, Dennis, you aren't out at all. In fact, you have my sympathy. It can't be easy for you, having a mother like that. And after all, you were the one who insisted on taking on our two young friends here. I was in this very room during the interview, remember, when Humphrey was so determined they shouldn't be hired, and you forced the rest of them to change their minds and vote him down. I think you knew then that they were the ones who'd set things to rights. And you sent them the swords in the stones, and stage-managed that little pantomime that brought them together, that evening when Mr Carpenter bought the frozen pizza. Quite the matchmaker,' he added, with a twitch of his eyebrow. 'They ought to be grateful to you, for the rest of their lives.'

Mr Tanner shrugged. 'That was purely self-defence,' he said. 'I wanted to make sure he'd stay away from my mother.'

Sophie looked as though she was about to say something, but must've thought better of it. John Wellington winked at her; she went pink and subsided. 'Well,' he continued, 'at least we've got that cleared up. As for the two of you,' he added, turning to Paul and Sophie, 'I think we'll all have to rely on your discretion if this firm's going to continue working together. But that's not a problem, is it?'

Sophie had to kick Paul's ankle under the table; then he nodded vigorously, and said, 'Absolutely, that's right,' or words to that effect.

John Wellington stood up. 'Excellent,' he said. 'In that case, I think we've covered everything that needs immediate attention. Casimir, Judy, I'd like a word with you, if I may. My office in ten minutes, please. The rest of you—' His slight shrug was enough to get them going, like a stone thrown into a crowd of ducks on a pond. A moment later, there were only three people left in the room: Paul, Sophie and Mr Tanner.

They looked at him, and he grinned.

'Is that right,' Sophie said, 'what he told us? About you—'

'Yes,' said Mr Tanner. 'Dress me in nappies and give me a bow and arrow, and I'm Cupid. And yes, it was me insisted that you got hired; but he's wrong about one thing, I only did that because I could see you were both right for the job. Naturals, both of you.' He laughed suddenly. 'But that was bloody obvious, even though the rest of those idiots couldn't see it. Supposed to be wizards and sorcerers, couldn't see the painfully obvious; no, it took a poxy little goblin to do that.'

Sophie frowned. 'I don't understand,' she said. 'What was so obvious?'

Mr Tanner's grin was broader than ever. 'Ah,' he said. 'That'd be telling. But you don't need me to tell you, you're both more than capable of figuring it out for yourselves.'

'Oh,' said Sophie. 'Suit yourself, then. And—'

'What?'

'Thanks,' Sophie replied awkwardly. 'Oh, I know you weren't thinking of us. But,' she added, taking hold of Paul's arm, 'thanks, anyway.'

Mr Tanner laughed, as if he'd just heard a really funny story. 'Wait and see what happens before you thank me,' he said. 'Could be you'll be sticking pins in a little wax effigy of me this time next year.'

Sophie shook her head. 'I don't think so,' she said quietly.

'No? Well, you could be right.' Mr Tanner shrugged. 'We'll see, one way or another. One thing's for sure, there's absolutely no way you two'd have found the happy ending, left to yourselves. When it comes to knowing what's good for you, I've met smarter lemmings. You're on your own now, though, unless the old bastard means to look after you. In which case,' he added, 'you'll probably be all right. Can't say as I like him much, but he's no fool.' He turned to go; but then he stopped, swung round and looked at them. 'One last thing,' he said. 'Well, two, actually. First, welcome to the profession, and I think that now we've got all this shit out of the way, we can probably work well together. Second,' he added, giving Paul a long, cold stare, 'you stay the hell away from my mother, understood? Because otherwise, if Sophie here doesn't kill you, I bloody will.'

Paul nodded quickly, three times, and headed for the door. But there was something he had to ask *some-body*, and if anybody knew, Mr Tanner probably did. He turned back. 'Excuse me,' he said. 'Can I ask you something?'

Mr Tanner frowned. 'Depends what it is,' he said.

Paul bit his lip. 'Look,' he said. 'If I was to ask you,

Why Gilbert and Sullivan, for God's sake? would that question make any sense to you?'

Mr Tanner raised an eyebrow; then he laughed. 'Perfect sense,' he said. 'I take it you're not into light opera, then.'

'No.'

'Me neither. But if you want to know, look in the drawer of that desk over there, and you'll find a copy of the collected works of Gilbert and Sullivan. From memory, I think you'll find what you're after on page 556. It's probably bookmarked. You'll see why.'

The book was exactly where Mr Tanner had said it would be. Page 556 turned out to be a scene from something called *The Sorcerer* (which, according to the introduction at the front, was first performed on 17 November 1877).

The song that Mr Tanner probably had in mind went:

> *My name is John Wellington Wells;*
> *I'm a dealer in magic and spells,*
> *In blessings and curses*
> *And ever-filled purses,*
> *In prophecies, witches and knells.*
> *If you want a proud foe to make tracks,*
> *If you'd melt a rich uncle in wax,*
> *You've but to look in*
> *On the resident djinn –*
> *Number Seventy, St Mary Axe . . .*

Not much happened after that; except that Paul and Sophie, thrown out of the office because it was well past five-thirty, wandered around for a while, talking of this and that; and then Sophie explained, with unusual tact, that although she loved him very much she was also dead on her feet after a long and eventful day, and they still had to be in the office next morning at nine sharp. So he left her and wandered about on his own for a bit, and eventually wound up back at his flat.

Two things caught his attention as he opened the door. The first was that the sword in the stone wasn't there any more, but he remembered why. The second was that Sophie rushed across the room to meet him, and flung herself into his arms like a soft cannon-ball.

The kiss was wonderful, of course, but even so Paul found himself thinking, *This is odd*. First, she didn't seem in the least bit tired. Second, how had she managed to get in? Third, no embarrassing collision of front teeth or protest of, 'Ouch, you're hurting my neck.' He pushed her gently away, and said, 'Hang on.'

She fended his hand away, but he stepped back. Then she grinned.

'Oh,' Paul said. 'You.'

She sighed; then she turned back into Mr Tanner's mum. 'You guessed,' she said.

'It wasn't difficult,' Paul replied irritably.

'Bugger. Still, you can't blame a girl for trying.'

'I can, actually. What about what's-his-name?' he said. 'Arthur,' he remembered. 'I thought you two were—'

'Oh, we are,' Mr Tanner's mum replied, yawning. 'But then, he's only human, he fell asleep. And I wasn't tired, so I thought, why not? After all,' she went on, as Paul scowled at her, 'what's the point of being a goblin if you can't be all shallow and one-track-minded? It's what goblins do. Ghouls just wanna have fun, and all that.'

Paul went and stood by the door. 'Goodbye,' he said. 'I won't mention this to your son, not this time.'

She stuck her tongue out at him, then sat down in the armchair. 'You know what,' she said, 'you're about as much fun as a boil on the bum. God only knows what I see in you.'

'Good,' Paul said. 'Please go away.'

'In a second,' said Mr Tanner's mum; then from thin air she produced the little glass ball. 'Or don't you want to see if it all works out for you, or if the first thing she says to you tomorrow morning is, "April fool, just kidding"?'

'As a matter of fact,' Paul said, 'no, I don't.'

She laughed. 'Scared?'

He shook his head. 'Not really. I just believe in her rather more than I do in you, that's all.'

She didn't like that. 'Tough,' she said, 'you're going to find out anyway. And I hope she— Oh.' Mr Tanner's mum put the glass ball down on the table. 'Bugger,' she said.

Paul's curiosity got the better of him, and he peered down at it. Then he jumped back, grabbed a disused shirt off the back of the sofa, and covered the ball with it.

'Spoilsport,' said Mr Tanner's mum, grinning ferociously. 'I was enjoying that.'

'You're disgusting.'

'And proud of it.' She tried to pull the shirt away, but he grabbed her hand. 'I'll say this for you,' she went on, 'if that's anything to go by, you're a quick learner. I'm not sure I've ever tried that one myself.'

'Get out,' Paul mumbled.

'Looked a bit dodgy to me. You'd do your back, for one thing.'

'*Out!*'

'All right,' Mr Tanner's mum sighed, as she stood up and dropped the glass ball in her bag. 'You win, for now, anyway. I'm patient,' she added, 'I can wait. I'll get there in the end, you know, I generally do.'

Paul shook his head. 'Not this time.'

'Well, we'll see, won't we?' That grin again. 'And for crying out loud, lighten up a bit, will you? Looks like you get your happy ending, after all.'

'Yes,' said Paul firmly.

'If you can call it that,' said Mr Tanner's mum. 'Because, you know what'll happen, don't you? Ten years from now, fifteen, even twenty, you'll think back to today and you'll wish you'd had more bloody sense. Oh, I can see you then, don't need a crystal ball for that; there's you, getting thick round the middle, thin on top; there's her, starting to sag and pucker; there's the two of you, bickering about money or the kids or having to visit her mum when you've got a whole load of work you've brought home with you. Twenty years of that? You get less for armed robbery, plus time off for good behaviour. You can have your happy ending, sunbeam. You deserve it.'

Paul thought about what she'd said; then he grabbed her by the scruff of the neck and marched her to the door. 'Really?' he said, and smiled happily. 'Thank you.' Then he threw her out.

'There's just one thing,' Paul said.

It was four days later, and still she hadn't changed

her mind. It was their first Saturday together, and it had all turned out to be quite different from what he'd expected. Different, but better. But there *was* just one thing.

'What?' Sophie asked.

He hesitated. He didn't really need to ask this question; in all probability, it'd be better if he didn't. It wasn't something he actually needed to know, and the mere act of asking was something of a betrayal of trust. Anybody with half a brain and slightly more tact than a bomb would forget about it, or at the very least leave well alone. But.

'What's-his-name,' Paul said. 'Shaz, the ceramic artist. What happened?'

She looked at him.

'It's all right,' he said quickly, 'I shouldn't—'

'No,' she said, 'that's okay. It's just a bit embarrassing, that's all. You see – well, you know the table top in the boardroom, the one that shows things the way they really are?'

Paul nodded. 'Imp-reflecting mirror, Mr Wurmtoter called it.'

'That's right,' she said. 'Well, it doesn't have to be a mirror. Or a table top.' She frowned. 'Apparently, you can get the same effect with a bit of ordinary tinfoil.'

Paul looked puzzled. 'Tinfoil?'

'Yes, you know. What you cook the Christmas turkey in. Only,' she went on, looking past him, 'someone got into Shaz's bus and stuck a sheet of it up on the ceiling, right over the bed.'

For a moment, Paul didn't quite follow. Then he said, 'Oh.'

'Yes.'

'Imp-reflecting tinfoil?'

She scowled. 'It works just like the table top did,' she said. 'Later, when he came round after I'd bashed him on the head with a saucepan, he told me who he really was.'

Paul didn't ask, but after a long pause she went on: 'I'm not quite sure how these things go, but I think he's Mr Tanner's second cousin, or else his first cousin once removed. Anyhow, his name was George, and he reckoned that – that Mr Tanner's mother put him up to it, to keep us apart so she could get you, and there was like nothing personal. But—'

'Mr Tanner's cousin. You mean a gob—'

'Yes.'

'Oh.' Just for a moment, Paul thought about the portable door; a quick dash back into the recent past, say five seconds before he'd asked the bloody stupid question that'd prompted all this. But he decided not to. It'd be cheating, and he was through with all that. 'Um,' he said, 'do you know who put it there? The tinfoil, I mean.'

She shook her head. 'Not for certain,' she said grimly. 'But I don't think it's a coincidence that it was stapled to the ceiling, rather than glued or sellotaped.'

'Right,' Paul said thoughtfully. 'But listen; if he hadn't been a g— Mr Tanner's cousin; what I mean is, you chose him rather than me, and that's fine, I guess, because it turned out all right in the end. But I can't help wondering; did you drink any of that philtre stuff? By accident or whatever, before you put it in my tea on the train? Only, I can remember buying that bottle of champagne in the pub, to put the stuff in so that horrible woman would fall in love with the film bloke,

Ashford Clent. And I can remember they gave us two glasses, and I put the stuff in one glass, and then you said you really needed a drink, because it was so nerve-racking; and I can remember it crossing my mind to tell you I'd laced one of the glasses, so you wouldn't put any of the stuff in the other one as well, but I'm not absolutely certain I did warn you, and—'

'Paul.'

'Yes?'

Sophie was looking at him, with an expression such as might be found on the face of a large but compassionate paratrooper when informed in a public house by a small, elderly drunk that only poofters wear little purple berets. 'Do you really want me to tell you?'

Paul thought about it for a little while. 'Yes,' he said.

'You do?'

'Yes.'

'Oh.'

So she told him; and then she looked at him again, and said, 'Do you believe me?' And Paul thought for another little while, and looked away, and said, 'Yes.'

'Fine.' She folded her arms. 'I was right, wasn't I? You didn't really want me to tell you.'

'Yes.'

She nodded. 'I did warn you.'

'Yes, you did. I thought I wanted to know.' He shrugged. 'It occurs to me,' he said, 'that unless I get elected prime minister or assassinate the Pope or something, I'm always going to be my own worst enemy. Comes of being stupid, I suppose.'

'Probably.' She scowled at him, and then the smile gradually morphed into a grin. 'Bet you wished you'd never raised the subject in the first place.'

'Yes,' said Paul.

'Bet you wish you could go back in time to the moment before you raised the subject, and then something'd happen that would drive the whole thing out of your mind. As if,' she added, 'by magic.'

A tiny light flickered behind Paul's eyes, as he reached into his inside coat pocket. 'Wouldn't that be something?' he said, taking the top off the cardboard tube that contained the portable door.

<u>IN YOUR DREAMS</u>

Tom Holt

The hilarious sequel to *The Portable Door*

Ever been offered a promotion that seems too good to be true? You know – the sort they'd be insane to be offering to someone like you. The kind where you snap their arm off to accept, then wonder why all your long-serving colleagues look secretly relieved, as if they're off some strange and unpleasant hook . . .

It's the kind of trick that deeply sinister companies like J.W. Wells & Co. pull all the time. Especially with employees who are too busy mooning over the office intern to think about what they're getting into.

And it's why, right about now, Paul Carpenter is wishing he'd paid much less attention to the gorgeous Melze, and rather more to a little bit of job description small-print referring to 'pest' control . . .

EARTH, AIR, FIRE AND CUSTARD

Tom Holt

The third book in the exuberant Paul Carpenter series, following *In Your Dreams*.

J.W. Wells seemed to be a respectable establishment, but the company now paying Paul Carpenter's salary is in fact a deeply suspect organisation with a mighty peculiar management team.

Paul thought he was getting the hang of it (particularly when he fell head over heels for his strangely alluring colleague Sophie), but death is never far away when you work at J.W. Wells. Unlike the stapler – that's always going awol. Our lovestruck hero is about to discover that custard is definitely in the eye of the beholder. And that it really stings.

Tom Holt's exceedingly comic fantasies are populated with evil goblins, annoying sprites and people like us. However, it's not always possible to tell the difference.

DEAD FUNNY

Tom Holt

Two hellishly funny comic fantasies in one volume

FLYING DUTCH

It's amazing the problems drinking can get you into. One little swig from the wrong bottle and you're doomed to an eternity of drifting around the world with a similarly immortal crew. Worse still, Richard Wagner writes an opera about you. However, a chance encounter in an English pub might just bring about an end to this horribly cursed life for Cornelius Vanderdecker – one way or another.

FAUST AMONG EQUALS

The management buy-out of Hell wasn't going quite as planned. For a start, there had been that nasty business with the perjurers, and then came the news that the Most Wanted Man in History had escaped. But Kurt 'Mad Dog' Lundqvist, the foremost bounty hunter of all time, is on the case, and he can usually be relied on to get his man – even when that man is Lucky George Faustus . . .

MIGHTIER THAN THE SWORD

Tom Holt

Two hilarious comic fantasy novels
in one mighty volume

MY HERO

Writing novels? Piece of cake, Jane thinks. Until hers starts writing back. At which point, she really should stop. And she certainly shouldn't go into the book herself. After all, that's what heroes are for. Unfortunately, the world of fiction is a far more complicated place than Jane ever imagined. And she's about to land her hero right in it.

WHO'S AFRAID OF BEOWULF?

Well, not Hrolf Earthstar, for a start. The last Norse king of Caithness, Hrolf and his twelve champions are woken from a centuries-long sleep when archaeologist Hildy Frederiksen finds their grave mound. And despite the time-delay, Hrolf decides to carry on his ancient war against the Sorcerer-King . . .

DIVINE COMEDIES

Tom Holt

Two hilarious comic fantasy novels in one
heavenly volume

HERE COMES THE SUN

The sun rises late, dirty and so badly in need of a
service it's a wonder it gets up at all. The moon's
going to be scrapped soon and a new one
commissioned – but they've been saying that for
years. All is not well with the universe . . . and it's
because the mortals are running the show. It's time
for a Higher Power to take charge.

ODDS AND GODS

It's a god's life at the Sunnyrode Residential home
for retired deities. Everlasting life can be a real drag
when all you've got to look forward to is
cauliflower cheese on Wednesdays. But things are
about to change, because those almighty duffers
Thor, Odin and Frey have restored a thousand year
old traction engine, and the thing actually works!
Only one thing might save the world: dentures.

FOR TWO NIGHTS ONLY

Tom Holt

Two hilarious comic fantasies in one armour-plated, broadsword-wielding volume

OVERTIME

One moment Guy is flying a bullet-riddled plane over Caen in 1943, the next he's somewhere in the Middle Ages in the company of one John de Nesle. Unsurprisingly, Guy's first thought is to get off home sharpish. But then he sees John's sister Isoud, and finds himself agreeing to help John, also known as Bloundel, in his quest to find Richard Coeur de Lion . . .

GRAILBLAZERS

Fifteen hundred years have passed and the Holy Grail is still missing. The Knights have all dumped the Quest for the easier job of pizza delivery, so someone must be found to take up the search and thwart the sinister plans of the lost kingdom of Atlantis' financial services industry. That someone is Boamund of Northgales (or Snotty to his friends).